Praise for *The Iapetus Federation*

Williscroft takes big conceptual bites in his conclusion to his hard science-fiction saga about mankind's expansion into space. Vol. 4 of *The Starchild Saga*, *The Iapetus Federation*, features FTL ships; handy, instantaneous transportation across space; the evacuation of the Jewish state to Mars; bioengineered immortality, and more, all against a backdrop of a hundred and fifty thousand years of human history. Indeed, as the novel drew to its close, I felt that its wonders would never cease. There's a type of science fiction called "Mind-blowing" (I have a book with just that title). This novel piles mind-blowing concept upon mind-blowing concept, all of it rooted in rigorous scientific speculation and theory.

And oh, how could I forget? The author takes the current threat of radical Islam and expands it into an international Jihad, all of it stemming from the failure in Vol. 3 to kill a Jihadist stowaway on *Cassini II*. Yes, actions or the lack of them often have consequences, and Williscroft brilliantly traces the malignant spread of the Caliphate into country after country. More than anything else, it is this menace that drives humanity's exodus from Earth.

Williscroft's aim in the saga, and especially in this concluding novel, is so ambitious and inspiring, it swept me right along. When I neared the conclusion, I thought for a moment he had slipped. The ending, though, was delightfully perfect, and I hope a sign of more stories to come in this universe.

– Professor John B. Rosenman, Norfolk State University
Former Chairman of the Board, Horror Writers Association
Author of *The Inspector of the Cross Series*

To be honest, I was stunned by this science fiction thriller by Robert Williscroft. I had read with great interest and enjoyment Williscroft's *Operation Ivy Bells—A Novel of the Cold War* but I had not read the preceding books in *The Starchild Saga*. Thanks to the author's extensive Preface, and Glossary at the beginning and end of this book, I entered the storyline both quickly and painlessly.

Like other science fiction novels, this series presents technological marvels such as faster-than-light travel and cheap and fast launch systems as the vehicle for moving large numbers of people throughout the solar system and beyond. But in my estimation, this novel sits alone among the genre by using technology and space travel as an accepted (but very well described) framework upon which to hang human pathos. Williscroft's Navy experience firmly establishes his credentials for his worldview that as we venture into space, the most fearsome entities we are likely to encounter are the monsters hiding in plain sight, those malignant and unavoidable bestial souls found in our fellow man. And that is a terrifyingly believable viewpoint which is revalidated day after day in the news, and page after page, chapter after chapter in this novel. As I progressed through the story, the more the tension built in this reader: was there any way out of this predicament?

Is this a fine science fiction thriller that you will not want to put down? Absolutely. But a case could also be made for *The Iapetus Federation* being a futuristic horror story. That mix of genres is rare indeed.

– Dr. John R. Clarke
Author of *The Jason Parker Series*

The Iapetus Federation is the fourth book in the author's Starchild sci-fi series centered around an ancient race of technologically advanced beings—the Ectarians—and their journey to Earth 150,000 years ago just before their star would go nova and destroy their home planet. Make no mistake, this novel is hardcore science fiction with a cast of characters that spans 4 pages and a glossary of terms that spans 9 pages. Author Williscroft delivers a rich tapestry of characters woven through an intricate story line. There is no attempt to hide the parallels with present-day strife and conflict between Christians and Muslims, but the plot goes much deeper, ultimately asking who we, as humans, are. Vesta (Earth Mother) reappears as a major character, having been introduced in the third novel. Although this is fiction, and projects what science might reveal at some future date, Williscroft's treatment of time travel is consistent with our present knowledge, which is fitting as the author has a distinguished record of achievement having served in the US Navy as a submarine officer, served at NOAA directing deep diving operations, and is an active member of the Adventurers' Club of Los Angeles.

– Dr. Dave Edlund
USA Today Bestselling Author –
The Peter Savage Thrillers

The Iapetus Federation is more than a broad-ranging and fitting sequel to *Slingshot, The Daedalus Files,* and *The Starchild Compact.* It is an epic of international intrigue, heroic fights for survival, and the opening of the Solar System on a massive scale...and that's just for starters. This book opens the door to the galaxy and both the past and future of humans and the Ectarians.

Williscroft has done it again, packing in plenty of adventures, ideas and characters. I'm looking forward to what comes next.

– Alastair Mayer
Author of *The T-Space Series*

VOL 4 IN THE STARCHILD SAGA

THE IAPETUS FEDERATION

EXODUS FROM EARTH

Iapetus illuminated by the Sun to the left
and Saturn to the right

VOL 4 IN THE STARCHILD SAGA

THE IAPETUS FEDERATION

EXODUS FROM EARTH

By

Robert G. Williscroft

The Iapetus Federation:
Exodus from Earth

Starman Press
Email: rgw@RobertWilliscroft.com
Website: RobertWilliscroft.com

Edition 4.0 2025

Cover design by Gary McCluskey
Illustrations by Robert G. Williscroft

BISAC Subject Headings:
SCI098020 SCIENCE / Space Science / Space Exploration
FIC028130 FICTION / Science Fiction / Space Exploration
FIC027130 FICTION / Romance / Science Fiction

Library of Congress Control Number: 2015908742

ISBN-13: 978-1-968367-50-3 Paperback
ISBN-13: 978-1-968367-49-7 Hardcover
ISBN-13: 978-1-968367-11-4 Ebook
ISBN-13: 978-1-968367-51-0 Audio

DEDICATION

To the girl of my dreams…you know who you are!

TABLE OF CONTENTS

Acknowledgments

Several people contributed to the creation of this book.

Most significantly, my wonderful wife, Jill, whom I first met when I returned from a year at the South Pole conducting atmospheric research, and who finally consented to marry me nearly thirty years later, pored over each chapter with her discerning engineer's eye. She kept my timeline honest, and made sure that regular readers could understand fully the arcane details of hyper-V craft and MERT portals and propulsion.

Jill's twin college sons, Arthur and Robert, also read the manuscript, and provided their input.

Jill's tabby, Tiger, deserves mention as a less-than-perfect role model for Jake, who became more important to the story than I realized when he first appeared.

Hard science fiction author Alastair Mayer reviewed the manuscript and offered his scientific, engineering, and editorial insight.

Professor John B. Rosenman, recently retired from Norfolk State University (where he taught Science Fiction writing among other things) and former Chairman of the Board of the Horror Writers Association, reviewed the manuscript and provided several thoughtful suggestions.

Hard science fiction author and diving scientist John Clark reviewed the manuscript from his unique perspective, providing helpful suggestions.

Attorney and world-class Adventurer Marc Weitz identified a couple of problems that I had missed, to the betterment of the book.

Jessica Hastings' line edit proved she is a better editor than any AI editing program.

Others have contributed with their comments and observations, and I thank them. You know who you are.

A tip of the hat to Gary McCluskey for turning a sketch and several ideas into the uniquely appropriate cover that wraps the pages of this book.

It goes without saying that any remaining omissions, errors, and mistakes fall directly on my shoulders.

Robert G. Williscroft, PhD
Centennial, Colorado
August 2018

Foreword—if you have not read
The Starchild Compact

Author's Note: In your hands, you are holding the fourth book in the Starchild Saga. This Foreword will give you the backdrop against which the Iapetus Federation story plays, if you haven't read the third volume of this series. If you have read The Starchild Compact, there is no reason to read this Preface. If you do choose to read it, however, it will refresh your memory and set the stage for what follows.

The Ectarians were a great, spacefaring civilization, spread throughout their solar system. Their planet, Ectaris, was a teeming world, overflowing with advanced engineering, sophisticated technology, transportation marvels, inspirational art and music. They had survived 50,000 years of growth, war, disease, famine, and finally peace and prosperity.

Their sun was a stable main-sequence variable G2V star. But it was older than Sol, with a slightly greater variability. The Ectarians learned to accommodate the cyclical global climate changes brought about by this variability. Indeed, it became a significant factor in spurring the rise of their civilization. They learned, first as tribes, and later as a worldwide population, to plan for, and then to hunker down and survive the glaciations that were an inevitable part of their global climate pattern. Then, a group of Ectarian solar scientists made a disquieting discovery. The variability of their G2V sun was increasing rapidly by astronomical measure. Following several years of study, these scientists determined that their star was in the first stages of a movement off the main sequence, and that in about 400 years, the sun that had nurtured their civilization for 50,000 years of recorded history would go nova.

There was no way to shelter their worlds from the coming nova. Its destructive power would be absolute. The only solution was to leave, go elsewhere, sufficiently distant to ensure their survival.

So, the Ectarians chose to build a moving world—a gigantic starship—a self-contained Ark that would hold their entire population and keep them alive for however long it would take to cross the interstellar abyss to another suitable solar system.

They had 400 years to make it happen.

The Ark started out as a suitably-sized asteroid. When completed, it consisted of a hollowed-out core containing a mini-black hole for power, and a living layer five kilometers below the surface that was two kilometers high, supported by natural rock columns left over from the hollowing-out process. Some of the columns were themselves hollowed out to contain fifty-meter-wide shafts to the surface. As much as possible, the interior was made to appear like the surface of Ectaris, complete with vegetation and normal diurnal cycles. Another three-meter layer was hollowed out twenty-meters below the surface, also supported by natural rock columns, that contained machinery. Further partial layers were hollowed out at varying depths for storage, machines, and everything else an entire civilization would need to reestablish itself on another world.

It took them nearly 300 years to remove some 14 million cubic kilometers of rock to create the interior spaces. They used the remaining available time to outfit the interior.

Now, fast forward to a more recent time in our own solar system, but still long, long ago—about 150,000 years.

From out of interstellar space a strange craft appeared. It was large, enormous by any usual standard—planetary in size, some 1,448 kilometers in diameter. The starship's relativistic hyperdrive was powered by a mini-black hole located at its core. The drive consisted of a twenty-kilometer-high tube-like equatorial ring that contained circulating charged particles moving at nearly light-speed around the planetary-sized spherical starship. This loop acted on the fabric of the universe itself, stealing a small amount of momentum from the expanding space-time continuum, to propel the starship to nearly two-thirds light speed. It acted on every molecule within its field, making the hyper-V drive not only reactionless, but making it possible to generate an artificial gravity field.

In this solar system, the star-folk found a planet with a thriving biosphere, and uninhabited by sapient beings. The star-folk parked their spacecraft in a safe orbit around the beautiful gas giant with distinctive rings, and sent exploratory teams to the new world. The new world was teeming with plant and animal life. Its underlying DNA, while dissimilar to their own, was not entirely incompatible. They discovered that some plants were edible, although they lacked critical trace nutrients and specific protein chains. The abundant game was edible as well, but difficult to assimilate—yet, they had taken 300 years to build their ship, and over 400 subjective years to cross the gulf between the stars. They could be patient while their scientists modified the new world's biology at the molecular level. For the next several weeks star-folk biologists created large batches of a virus-like molecule that they shipped to the new world, where high-altitude, high-speed aircraft sprayed the substance over virtually every square meter of the planet.

The biologists had intended for Earth's ecosystem transformation to be fully completed before the star-folk settled planetside. When the star-folk didn't wait for the complete change, and they commenced settlement, the biologists yielded and joined the planetside migration. What they didn't know—what nobody knew—was that the incomplete transformation had developed a problem. It was something deep inside the modified DNA structure that completely escaped the biologists' notice, something that lingered, replicated itself, and began to spread throughout Earth's population, both old and new.

✳

Science had not stopped during the centuries of travel from the Ectaris system and the decades since they had arrived in the Solar System. By the time the great starship arrived at Saturn, Ectarian physicists had refined both the hyper-V drive and its black-hole power source so that they could be installed in a very much smaller craft that was capable of rapidly accelerating to speeds approaching light-speed itself. After several decades of development, the hyper-V ship took an unexpected shape—looking somewhat like the popular flying discs their children used for play.

Eventually, the Ark was nearly empty of people. Only fourteen family members remained, linked by blood and intense scientific curiosity. They intended to go home—to whatever remained of their place of origin—to see for themselves what had happened. They knew they would forever lose touch with their friends on Earth as the laws of relativity inexorably separated their timelines. Nevertheless, they hoped to maintain contact with successive generations back on Earth, so that when they returned at a far future date, the descendants of Earth's new inhabitants would be waiting for them—anticipating their arrival. Their race had already proved that it could take the long view. This was just a continuation.

These fourteen star-folk visited Earth several times in their small starship, the *Merkavah*, but never stayed for very long, indeed not long enough to assimilate the spontaneously modified DNA that was, by then, working its insidious way throughout Earth's new inhabitants.

A final stop in orbit around Earth, a final trip to the surface, a final farewell to friends and colleagues they would never see again—and the small band of starfarers, the Founders, departed for Ectaris.

✳

The Founders consisted of Eber, his parents (Shem and Persia), his grandparents (Noah and Vesta), his four brothers (Asshur, Aram, Arpachshad, and Lud), his companion (Azurad), and his brother's companions (Ishtar, Sari, Rasu'eja, and Shakbah, respectively).

When the Founders returned to this Solar System a thousand Earth years later, they discovered that the flawed DNA had destroyed the civilization they had left behind. Here and there were faint ruins, but the only sapient beings were primitive pre-stone age humans.

The Founders commenced leapfrogging forward in time by traveling outward and back a specific distance that corresponded with the forward leap in time they wished to make. From time-to-time one of the men would leave genetic material behind in the form of offspring, so that their uncontaminated DNA became a factor in Earth's growing new civilization. Around the 11th century BCE, Noah, Shem, and Persia, decide to remain behind, and so insert themselves directly into Earth's history. Each of the other men took turns staying back for a ten-year stint to stabilize their lineages.

Eventually, ten surviving Founders arrived in the mid-twenty-first century.

✳

Mid-twenty-first century Earth was divided into several major power blocks. The economic and military leaders were North America, Northern Europe, and Russia, along with Australia and New Zealand. China, with its Asian sphere of influence, formed a strong second economically and a distant second militarily. The Persian Caliphate, which controlled the entire Middle-east and northern Africa, except for Israel, presented little economic presence but was a serious military rival to the whole world. In economic and military terms, the southern half of Africa, South and Central America, and the rest of the planet, presented no threat.

Earth scientists had determined that Saturn's moon Iapetus might be an artifact. The major powers, without the participation of the Persian Caliphate, assembled an international expedition headed by Jon Stokes, hero of the first Mars expedition. The expedition was to travel to Iapetus and wring out its secrets. At the Mirs Complex, a huge double-toroidal space station located at L4 in the Moon's orbit, they built *Cassini II*, the most advanced VASIMR propelled interplanetary spaceship modern humans had ever developed. The Caliphate managed to secret a Jihadist stowaway, Saeed Esmail, aboard *Cassini II* for the express purpose of sabotaging the expedition. When he failed, Jon Stock integrated him into the crew as the only viable alternative to spacing him. Despite this humane treatment, Saeed continued to harbor plans for Jihad.

The Founders had brought the Ark to full functionality in preparation for the *Cassini II's* arrival. When the explorers arrived, they discovered the true nature of Iapetus.

The expedition members learned about the Founders and discovered that the Founder's language, which they called Founder-Speak, was a sophisticated precursor to modern Hebrew. Then they met the Founders, only to learn that they were the wife, grandsons and their wives, of the Biblical Noah. The modern Israelis turned out to be the direct descendants of the Founders themselves, and thus were held in special esteem by the Founders.

The Persian Caliph was outraged by this development and staged a focused Jihad to destroy Israel. The Founders intervened, and ultimately, the Persian Caliphate was destroyed. In the aftermath, Saeed attempted to sabotage the Founders' spacecraft, the *Merkavah*. Rasu'eja, companion to the Founder warrior Arpachshad, and a fierce warrior in her own right, severed Saeed's right hand with her short sword while stopping his sabotage. Once again Saeed was allowed to live, and eventually was set free in the warrens of ancient Dubai.

Jon Stock introduced the Founders to the American Declaration of Independence and the Constitution of the United States. They were very impressed by the documents and used them as a basis for establishing the Iapetus Federation, with the blessing of the American President, Marc Bowles. Vesta, the Founder matriarch and Noah's wife, became its first president. The Iapetus Federation was quickly recognized as an independent nation by America and most other nations on Earth. Rod Zakes, who was Mission Control for the Iapetus expedition and a member of the first Mars expedition, became its Ambassador to Earth.

The Founders worked together with the *Cassini II* crew members and Rod Zakes to establish the Starchild Institute on Iapetus. Former American President Marc Bowles became its first director. The Starchild Institute adopted an operating charter called the "Starchild Compact." Its primary charge: To develop and license Ectarian technology to the rest of the Solar System. The Starchild Institute constructed a large starship with hyper-V propulsion, the Starchild, and manned it with several Founders (Eber, Arpachshad, Rasu'eja, and Ishtar) and *Cassini II* crew members (Jon Stock, Ari Rawlston, Ginger Steele, and Elke Gratz), and eight other carefully selected specialists from Earth and the Iapetus Federation. Jon Stock was chosen to command Starchild.

The Starchild would make an initial ten-light-year round-trip shakedown cruise that would last only four subjective shipboard hours, while ten years would pass for Earth and the Federation.

Following their shakedown cruise, the Starchild planned to travel ninety-two light years to a G5-V star system in the constellation of Draco with the Hipparcos catalog designation of HIP-84062, that some astronomers thought might be transmitting coherent radio signals. They expected to remain for a year exploring the system. They would return 185 earth years after their departure, while their subjective absence would be only a year and three days, including the exploratory year at their destination. Marc and the Starchild Institute promised to keep alive the memory of the Starchild and its return, 185 years hence.

Unbeknown to anyone, Saeed Esmail reached an agreement with former Persian Caliphate General Ismail Suleiman. Suleiman had personally assassinated the Persian Caliph when it became apparent that the Caliphate would lose its conflict with the rest of the world. After the assassination, he surrendered the Caliphate forces to the United States and sued for peace. Saeed and Suleiman secretly raised a Jihadist army and quietly prepared to reestablish the Caliphate following a strict interpretation of Sharia Law developed by Islam's new prophet, Saeed Esmail. The emerging Caliphate raised a light blue banner displaying a severed fist holding a dagger, with a truncated arm just below flowing red blood.

Robert G. Williscroft, PhD
Centennial, Colorado
August 2018

Foreword to the Second Edition

This second edition contains some line edits, formatting changes, and some changes to the Glossary. I also shortened my bio and added several more books that I have written since the original publication of *The Iapetus Federation*.

Robert G. Williscroft, PhD
Centennial, Colorado
January 2022

Foreword to the Third & Fourth Editions

The third edition was published April 2024 by Fresh Ink Group as the fourth volume of *The Starchild Saga*. Unfortunately, they ceased publishing in April 2025. This fourth edition is unchanged except for listing the new publisher and adding several illustrations.

Robert G. Williscroft, PhD
Centennial, Colorado
August 2025

Cast of Characters

Main Characters
(*alphabetically by first name*)

Abdul-Hasid Naseri—Real name of Rico Delgado; Caliphate Operative on Mars

Andrey Orlov—Chairman of Mirs Corp; later, Director of Mars polar water project.

Asshur—Founder; Spearheads Israeli evacuation to Mars; later, President of New Israel, Director of Mars ground-based terraforming; (former companion of Founder Ishtar).

Azurad—Founder; Research Physician /Biologist; Discovers nature of flora and fauna on Vesta's Star, planet 3, Shakbah; (former companion of Founder Eber).

Bob York—Commanding General Camp Pendleton; later, Iapetus Federation Immigration Chief.

Chino Delgado—Cover name of Ra'id Kassab; Caliphate Operative on Mars.

Danylo "Dany" Orel—Q-carbon miner; later, Deputy Director of Iapetus Federation Security.

Delgado Brothers—Chino & Rico Delgado, aka Ra'id Kassab & Abdul-Hasid Naseri; Caliphate operatives on Mars.

Dmitri Gagarin—Director of Iapetus Federation Security; (former Russian First Officer on Cassini II).

Gregory Samuelson—Texas Adjutant General; later, Commanding General of Iapetus Federation Strike Force (IFSF).

Isidor Sokolov—Chief Operating Officer of the Mirs Complex at L4; later, Director of Mars channel burning project.

Ismail Suleiman—Commander of worldwide Caliphate forces.

Jake—Dmitri Gagarin's gray Tabby cat.

Marc Bowles—Director of the Starchild Institute; later, President of the Iapetus Federation; (former American President).

Margo Jackson—Director of Space-borne Mars terraforming project; later, Director of Starchild Institute; (former Chairman of Launch Loop International). (No relation to Stanford Jackson).

Mattias "Matti" McIntyre—Deputy Director of Lone Star Mars;
later, Director Lone Star Mars.

Mordecai Rochlin—Heads Rachel Rachaf construction crew; later,
Governing Manager, New Israel.

Noel Goddard—Builds Ayers Sky at L5; (former Space Structural
Engineer on Cassini II).

Ra'id Kassab—Real name of Rico Delgado; Caliphate Operative on
Mars.

Rico Delgado—Cover name of Ra'id Kassab; Caliphate Operative on
Mars.

Rod Zakes—Iapetus Federation Ambassador to Earth; later President
of the Iapetus Federation; later Iapetus Federation Ambassador to
the Caliphate; (former Mission Director for Cassini II).

Saeed Esmail—Caliphate Prophet of Prophets. (Former Jihadist
stowaway on Cassini II).

Sam Houston—Founder Lone Star Mars; later Governor of Texas/
Lone Star Conservancy; later, Vice President Iapetus Federation.

Stanford Jackson—American President following Marc Bowles. (No
relation to Margo Jackson).

Syed Shah Bukhari—Vice President to Stanford Jackson; later, President
of the Islamic States of America.

Vesta—Founder Matriarch.

Charlie Company

(by rank)

Stephan "Steve" Brady—Captain Minnesota National Guard—
Commands Charlie Company; later, Colonel in Iapetus Federation
Strike Force (IFSF).

Pollard "Bo" Bransom—Charlie Company First Sergeant; later, Charlie
Company Command Sergeant Major; later, Capt. IFSF.

Jerri "Jer" Smyth—Charlie Company Platoon 3 Leader; later, Sergeant—Communications; later, Capt. IFSF.

Norbert "Nor" Jacobsen—Charlie Company replacement Platoon 3
Leader; later, Sergeant IFSF.

Jennifer "Jen" Gomez—Sergeant—Charlie Company Communications under Capt. Bransom.

Secondary Characters

(alphabetically by first name)

Abba Micula—Abner Garlock's Chaplain.

Abner Garlock—Commander of Israeli holding force in Old Israel.

Alexander Regent—Director of Mars Soletta and Dipole project; (former Chief Engineer, Slingshot project).

Ali Omar Elmi—Minneapolis City Council President, from Ward 6, A direct descendant of the first Somali representative to the City Council, Abdi Warsame, also from Ward 6.

Aram—Founder; worked with Asshur to establish New Israel.

Jim Grayson—Lt. Governor Texas/Lone Star Conservancy; later, Deputy Vice President Iapetus Federation.

Brad Comex—Secretary of State Texas/Lone Star Conservancy.

Carmen Bhuta—India's Minister of Health; (former Medical Officer and Language Specialist/Botanist on *Cassini II*).

Chen Lee-Fong—Head of China's Science Directorate; (former VASIMR Engineer on *Cassini II*).

Daniel Ben-Gurion—Head of Israeli Mossad.

Eli—One of three Mossad agents who rescue Asshur in the Austrian Alps.

Henri Deville—President of France, husband of Michele deBois.

Jeremiah M. Jefferson—Elder of the Quorum of the Twelve Apostles; Tonga Mormon Leader; later, founder of Heaven.

Joe Ridden—Incoming Conservative PM of Australia.

Johan—One of three Mossad agents who rescue Asshur in the Austrian Alps.

Joseph Ephriam—Israeli immigrant to Mars via Sahara Loop with his wife (Batya) and 2 teenaged girls (Chaviva & Dalia).

Klaus Blumenfeld—Director of Mars Polar Orbital Mirror Project; (former, OTEC Power Engineer for Slingshot project).

Kristopher Lambin—Director of Starchild Institute's wormhole project.

Langsley "Lee" Oxford—American Army General, head of New Zealand's Caretaker Government on Iapetus.

Levi Bar-Lev—Runs southernmost outpost in Nanedi Valles; later, New Israel Prime Minister.

Lud—Founder; Physician/Surgeon/Biologist; Developed longevity treatment (SILP) with Shakbah (Companion to Founder Shakbah).

Lynette Williams—PM of New Zealand.

Mable Fitzwinters—First CEO of Launch Loop International (LLI), the firm that built Slingshot, the world's first space launch loop.

Menachem Dubro—Samuel Meisel's Red neighbor in New Israel.

Michele deBois—First Lady of France; (former Ph.D. Biologist/Botanist on Cassini II).

Morten Obers—Outgoing Labor PM of Australia.

Omar Elmi Dihoud—Minneapolis Mayor; father of Ali Omar Elmi.

Ori—One of three Mossad agents who rescue Asshur in the Austrian Alps.

Percival Enderly—Washington State Governor; later, Chairman of Columbia Freehold.

Reyansh Acharya—Lud's research assistant from India.

Samuel Meisel—Israeli immigrant to Mars via Mediterranean Loop with his wife (Rachel) and 4 children—2 young boys (Eldad & Ezra) & an older boy and girl (Micha & Esther).

Shakbah—Founder; Biologist; Developed longevity treatment (SILP) with Lud (Companion to Lud).

Wilfred Ames—Vice President under Marc Bowles.

Original *Starchild* Crew

(*by Rank*)

Jon Stock—Mission Commander; later, Mission Commander of *Starchild II*; (former Mission Commander of Cassini II).

Eber—First Officer; later, First Officer of *Starchild II*; (former Founder Leader).

Ginger Steele—Second Officer/Astrogator; later, Second Officer/Astrogator of *Starchild II*; (former Second Officer/Astrogator of *Cassini II*).

Ari Rawlston—Chief Engineer; later, Chief Engineer of *Starchild II*; (former Chief VASIMR Engineer of *Cassini II*).

Elke Gratz—Mission Historian/Computer engineer; later, Mission Historian/Computer engineer of *Starchild II*; (former Historian/Computer Engineer of *Cassini II*).

Ishtar—Founder; Mission Historian; later, Mission Historian of *Starchild II*; (former Companion to Founder Asshur).

Arpachshad—Founder; Engineer/Warrior/Weapons specialist; later, popular holovision action-star; (Companion to Founder Rasu'eja).

Rasu'eja—Founder; Warrior/Weapons specialist; later, popular holovision action-star; (Companion to Founder Arpachshad).

(*7 more unnamed crew members*)

VOL 4 IN THE STARCHILD SAGA

THE IAPETUS FEDERATION

EXODUS FROM EARTH

Part One

CHAPTER ONE

MARS—VALLES MARINERIS

Sam Houston stood on a flat, granite-like ledge that cantilevered out over a seven-kilometer-drop, his lanky frame dwarfed by his surroundings. Fifty kilometers across Coprates Chasma to the north, the opposite canyon wall rose in a series of layered rocky shelves, sharply outlined in the thin Martian atmosphere. Suddenly, Sam felt a slight tremor beneath his feet accompanied by a sharp shock that he sensed rather than heard. The large slab on which he stood dropped several meters and then tilted, throwing him forward into the void. To his right and left, the ledge disintegrated and commenced a downward slide. Despite gravity only 40% of Earth's, it still seemed to Sam that he was falling more slowly than he expected until he realized that he and the slabs near him were falling together, gaining speed and momentum as they plunged toward the distant canyon floor.

Following his initial panicked reaction, Sam shucked his protective boot covers and tapped his big toes to activate hypergolic nozzles in the ball of each TBH Propulsion Boot. Twenty newtons of force began to slow his fall, and he tucked his knees slightly to arc himself out and away from the tumbling boulders—not enough deceleration to stop his plunge, but maybe sufficient, for Saracen to catch him.

"*Saracen*, hark!" This was Sam's prearranged signal to control his hyper-V craft remotely. "Locate and approach my position…match my velocity with the hatch as close to me as possible…open the hatch and scoop me up!!" The detached, rational part of his mind could hear the double exclamation point. The panicked part said, "I have perhaps a hundred seconds before I crash into the canyon floor…so hurry!"

"One hundred and two-point three seconds, actually, Sam," the Resident onboard system quipped as Saracen's shadow passed over Sam's position.

The saucer-shaped craft slid in beside him, falling at the same rate as Sam. The hatch slid up, but just as *Saracen* began to glide toward him, a boulder half the size of the craft struck *Saracen's* rim, causing it to spin away, and nudged Sam back toward the cascading rockfall only a few meters behind him. He splayed his toes in shock, extinguishing his boot jets. Because of the initial braking action of his boots, Sam was falling slower than the rocks just out of his reach. If he got sucked into the fall, he would be dead for sure. Sam tucked his knees and tapped both toes, projecting himself as far out from the rockfall as possible. He calculated thirty seconds or less before he hit the ground.

"Sam…above you!"

Sam looked up to see *Saracen* settling down over him, forming a protective shield. Sam continued to jet away from the falling rocks as the Resident brought the craft between him and the rocks, hatch wide open.

"Kill the jets!" the Resident commanded and slid sideways, scooping Sam into the lock with just meters to spare before he would have splashed onto the rocky surface.

With Sam inside its acceleration field, *Saracen* instantly reversed its direction, its field acting on everything it contained—the craft, Sam, the air, each molecule and atom, everything, and came to a hover over the central canyon floor, safely removed from the still tumbling rock. Sam waited for the pressure lock to cycle and removed his helmet and gloves. Once inside, he sat before the control console, watching in fascination as it seemed most of the canyon wall was still in motion. The leading edge of the falling rock mass smashed into a vast fan of debris left over from previous falls, about a thousand meters above the floor. Millions of tons of rock continued down the flattening fan for another five minutes, slowing as the main body of the fall crashed into the top of the fan, splitting into two branches, one pressing northward toward the western face of Nectaris Montes where it petered out at the north-western extent of that small mountain range. The other, larger branch seemed to be aimed directly at Lone Star Base, located in a partially hollowed-out, two-kilometer-high rocky mound about three kilometers from the canyon's north wall. The mass of rock carried on for another ten minutes, finally coming to a halt a few tens of meters from the base entrance.

✳

Sam directed *Saracen* to hover immediately before the base entrance, at ground level, directly under neat block letters that read LONE STAR MARS. He signaled the door to open and then glided Saracen through the thirty-meter-wide opening to settle on its five extended landing pads in a chamber that easily accommodated his twenty-five-meter-wide hyper-V craft and a half-dozen rovers that were very similar to the six-wheeled lander/rover vehicles carried by *Cassini II*. While the combination lock/chamber cycled, Sam doffed the rest of his pressure suit. Unlike older vacuum suits, Sam's suit was lightweight and flexible, even in hard vacuum. It worked on a technologically advanced application of earlier high-altitude suits. An inner garment formed a flexible, skintight membrane that substituted for atmospheric pressure. A slightly less tightly-fitting outer garment retained a minimal atmospheric environment inside the suit, also providing temperature control and wear resistance. The suit was entered feet first through an airtight zipper-like opening in the back. The sealed gloves were comfortably flexible. Sam wore a close-fitting skullcap with various sensors that transmitted his physiological condition to *Saracen*. His transparent, spherical helmet attached to a sealing collar around his neck and was completely invisible from inside.

Sam exited *Saracen*, walked down the short ramp, and grinned at the two men who met him.

"Asshur…Aram…How the hell are you guys?" His Texan drawl was apparent.

The two Founder brothers gripped Sam's arms with palpable relief. Both stood some twenty centimeters shorter than Sam and were swarthy with dark, curly hair, and piercing, nearly black eyes.

"What happened out there?"

"You know that I was surveying the southern rim because of the rockfalls that happened before we got here," Sam said with a wide grin. He liked these two guys. They were into everything, and they more than carried their load. Right now, they played leading roles in the construction of the Israeli settlement up in Nanedi Valles, about thirteen hundred kilometers to the northeast.

"So…what happened?"

Sam told them how the slide started, seemingly out of nowhere. He described his antics and how Saracen rescued him in the nick of time.

"That wall has been stable for the better part of a thousand years," Asshur said.

"To come apart right under your feet—that's quite a coincidence," Aram added.

Sam got quiet and looked from brother to brother. "My friends," he said, "that was no coincidence."

EARTH—SAUDI ARABIAN DESERT

Saeed Esmail's sackcloth robe and full-length flowing beard fluttered in the early morning breeze. He stood with General Ismail Suleiman by the entryway to his sprawling tent pitched atop a low mound overlooking a dry lakebed near the center of Rub' al-Khali in the Saudi Arabian desert. The lakebed was surrounded by shifting dunes, some towering thirty meters. Saeed shivered in the ten-degree air that would reach near fifty Celsius by mid-afternoon. His gaze swept over more than a thousand tents scattered across the lakebed. Outside every tent, two swarthy men stood at relaxed attention. Above him fluttered a light-blue flag displaying a severed fist holding a dagger. A few centimeters from the wrist, a truncated arm flowed red blood.

Saeed intoned the early call to prayer over the loudspeakers surrounding the encampment. *"Allahu Akbar!… Allahu Akbar!… Allahu Akbar!… Allahu Akbar!*[1]*"* As the sound of his voice faded into the surrounding sand, Saeed raised his voice across the lakebed again: *"Ashhadu an la ilaha illa Allah*[2]*."* He repeated it, and then spoke in a slightly softer, sing-song manner: *"Ashadu anna Saeedan Rasool Allah*[3]*."* Saeed repeated the phrase and smiled as his words echoed across the encampment. These words would have been blasphemy three years earlier, but Allah had revealed Himself to Saeed in a special way during his voyage to Iapetus. He reviewed the words of his revelation from the *Qur'an* at 4:74: *Let those fight in the way of Allah who sell the life of this world for the other. Whoso fighteth in the way of Allah, be he slain or be he victorious, on him we shall bestow a vast reward.*

As Saeed finished the call to prayer, two thousand Jihadist warriors prostrated themselves on the still cold ground…as did Saeed and his general.

After prayers, Saeed and General Suleiman stood and entered the tent. General Suleiman poured two cups of very sweet mint tea.

Saeed looked at his general. "How fare our Martian Holy Warriors?" He referred to Ra'id Kassab and Abdul-Hasid Naseri, two specially trained agents who spoke Spanish with native Mexican fluency and who spoke fluent Spanglish with a distinct Texas drawl. Their papers identified them as the brothers Chino and Rico Delgado and indicated they were third-generation American citizens from Brownsville, Texas, whose parents came to the United States during the great Hispanic immigration of the late twentieth and early twenty-first centuries—a period without many accurate immigration records. They were employed as mechanical engineering technicians by the Lone Star Project and had shipped out to Mars a month earlier with the third wave of technicians and skilled workers aboard a VASIMR powered freighter that got them to Mars in about fifteen days. Their assignment was simple enough: Cause as much mayhem as possible without getting caught, and as the Mars population increased, recruit disaffected workers from both Lone Star and the Israeli settlement, Nachal Rachaf.

Suleiman sipped his sweet tea. "Sahib, your Holy Warriors report that they crumbled a high cliff whereon the Texan leader Sam Houston stood.

---

1 *God is great!*

2 *I bear witness that there is no God except Allah.*

3 *I bear witness that Saeed is the messenger of God.*

They believe he is dead but do not know for sure. It should appear as an accident. They have transportation, provisions for several months, the ability to generate oxygen from the Martian atmosphere, and are free to move over the planet's surface."

CHAPTER TWO

MIRS COMPLEX

A collective gasp rippled through the crowded Great Room of Ring Kiev as *Starchild* flashed out of existence beyond the grand expanse of transparent polymer that formed a third of the massive torus. One moment the fifty-meter wide, intensely black, saucer-shaped starship blocked the crowd's view of the vast L4 complex, and then—without warning—it vanished, allowing the slowly rotating majestic double-torus to sweep past the Moon silhouetted against an impossibly full background of stars..

Vesta reached out to touch the shoulder of her Ambassador to Earth, Rod Zakes. They were standing front and center with the other dignitaries. Vesta was dressed in a brightly colored, traditional ankle-length tunic, fastened at her tiny waist. Soft, flat-heeled boots covered her feet. Small of stature, she looked impossibly young for her sixty-nine years. Her classical face was without wrinkles, although her golden hair, piled high for this occasion, showed a few streaks of gray. Her svelte body appeared to carry virtually no excess fat. Her hazel eyes flashed flecks of green as she smiled at Rod.

Things had changed dramatically in the two years since she, with the rest of the Founders and the *Cassini II* crew, had first laid eyes on each other outside the pyramid complex on Iapetus. She smiled inwardly. Even she called the Ark by its local name, Iapetus. The Iapetus Federation was a reality, and she its first President. *What a hoot! If only Noah could see me now*, she thought, looking across the crowd. *The Old Man had done right well by himself—several wives, lots of children, and countless grandchildren. And look at them now, Israel with all it represented, and the Persian Caliphate, the best and the worst, good and evil personified.* Vesta pulled her thoughts back to her present situation. Rod had been talking.

"…so, where do we go from here?" Rod towered over the svelte matriarch, light reflecting off his balding head.

"I'm sorry, Rod. My Link translator is working fine, although mostly, I can understand English without it now. I was looking back through a thirty-two-hundred-year lens. My Noah really set things in motion, didn't he?" She turned to smile at the woman standing at her side, Azurad, her eldest grandson Eber's lovely companion, and then at her grandsons Asshur and Aram a few steps away, accompanied by their towering friend, Sam Houston, wearing his ever-present white Stetson. Somewhere in the crowd, she knew her youngest grandson Lud and his companion Shakbah were keeping a low profile, her shy ones who were more interested in their longevity research than public gatherings. With a broad smile, she turned toward an approaching Marc Bowles, the holo-vision-star-handsome American President.

He took her hand, graciously lifting her fingers to his lips. "Madam President," he intoned formally.

"Marc, you silly buzzard, give a dear friend a hug!" She stretched up against him. He responded with warmth and tenderness. "Ten years," she murmured. "It seems so long…"

Marc laughed. "Says the lady who traveled one hundred fifty thousand years to get here…"

"I wish I could convey to you properly what all this means to me." Vesta shut her eyes and leaned against Marc. "What we found when we returned from Ectaris broke my heart. As we leapfrogged forward, I kept looking for something like what we had left behind when we departed for Ectaris. I began to wish I had stayed with Noah—at least I would have been with someone I knew, someone who understood me." Vesta looked warmly at Marc. "Then we found Jon and all of you!" Vesta looked up to discover that she was surrounded by smiling faces.

A feeling of joy like she had never before experienced washed over Vesta. She was genuinely happy and at peace with herself and her world.

✳

Marc looked down at the diminutive woman leaning against him. It was impossible to think of her as nearly twenty years his senior. Vesta had stepped into the Presidency of the Iapetus Federation with virtually no governing experience but had handled it well, even with the language difficulties. Mostly, the governance was in English, so that Vesta had become quite proficient in the new language. There were times when she had called on him for assistance, and he had been glad to help, but for the most part, she had hit the ground running. Under her leadership, the Federation had prospered. It was becoming what America had been in its earlier years before the general populace discovered that it could vote itself largess from the public coffers.

To Marc, it was apparent that his political party and personal political capital were on the downslope of the political power curve. Self-sufficiency and self-reliance were increasingly unpopular with American voters. They seemed fascinated with the regal, almost aristocratic appearance of Stanford Jackson, standard-bearer of the Opposition. His shock of wavy silver hair and liberal academic stance so reminiscent of Dean Acheson from a century ago struck a sympathetic chord with the American people. They had become tired of fending for themselves and turned en masse to Jackson, who seemed to be telling them that he would make sure they got their fair share. He told them that money America had been spending on space development would be much more useful at home in the hands of the people. Other nations didn't need America's support; they could fend for themselves. The military, too, was a massive sinkhole for taxpayers' money. Think about what government could do for communities across the country, Jackson said over and over, if the military didn't hog all the cash.

The people were listening, and Marc saw where it was going. The standard-bearer for his own party, Vice President Wilfred Ames, was a good man who would have been an excellent president and carried forward where Marc had left off, but he didn't have a chance of winning, and everybody knew it.

Marc sighed inwardly and looked down again at Vesta. She and what she represented were the hope for the future of humankind. Marc squeezed her gently and turned to Rod.

"What are your immediate plans?"

"I have some business on Iapetus," Rod responded with a smile. "Then I'll return to Washington."

In the crowd behind them, a swirl of white caught Marc's attention, surging toward their little group. Michele deBois, the Cassini II biologist, radiant in a white pants suit that displayed her physical assets without making an issue of it, glided up and leaned down to kiss slightly shorter Vesta and Azurad, and then reached up to kiss Marc and Rod in turn. Then she waved and blew kisses at Asshur and Aram. "*Mes Chéries*, I want you to meet somebody," she said, gesturing to a slender man in his forties sporting a closely trimmed beard and a full head of wavy brown hair. He presented a regal manner—but with a twinkle in his brown eyes. "Please meet Henri Deville, descendent of the famous French scientist of the same name, and the future president of France…*Non?*" She stretched up and kissed him lightly.

Deville blushed faintly and lifted Vesta's fingers to his lips. "Madam President," he said in flawless, unaccented English. Then he shook hands with Marc and Rod. "Mr. President…Mr. Ambassador."

"We're among friends here," Marc said back. "I'm Marc, this is Rod, and this lovely creature is Vesta." Then he took Azurad's hand in his. "And may I introduce the companion of Eber, Founder Leader, and presently aboard *Starchild*."

"See, I told you, " Michele sparkled. "These are my friends!" Michele turned and waved to a sari-wrapped diminutive woman with her long dark hair in a semi-formal up-sweep. "Carmen! Over here, *ma Chérie!*"

Dr. Carmen Bhuta smiled warmly at the small group and joined them, accepting Michele's kiss, Deville's lips to her fingers, a warm hug from Marc and Rod, and pressing her cheek to Vesta's. "Carmen was the physician on *Cassini II*," Michele said, "along with knowing more languages than anyone I know. Now she's Minister of Health for the Indian government."

Michele put her arm around Carmen's small waist, and Marc noted that Carmen did not draw close to Michele, as did the other women in their small circle. "How are your parents?" Marc asked her.

"Doing well, thanks to you and Ari," Carmen said with a warm smile.

Marc then told Deville the story of how the Israelis rescued Carmen's Christian parents from the clutches of the Ayatollah Khomeini while *Cassini II* orbited Iapetus. While the story unfolded, two more people joined the group, tall and thin Noel Goddard accompanied by the shorter Chen Lee-Fong, both *Cassini II* VASIMR engineers. Noel greeted Vesta and Marc with traditional formality while accepting a kiss from Michele and a gentle squeeze from Carmen and introduced himself to Deville. Chen shyly repeated the same routine, blushing as Michele's lips touched his.

"I miss the others," Michele said wistfully, "Jon, Ari, Elke…" Her voice trailed off. "And Eber, Ishtar, Rasu'eja, and Arpachshad." Her eyes twinkled. "I love them, but I'll never get used to those names."

"Don't forget the other eight," Marc said softly.

"*Oui*…but I never got to know them as my friends." Michele pouted slightly, and Deville drew her to him, saying quietly, "*Ma Chérie…*"

In the silence that followed, Marc swept his gaze across the intimate group before him, and then the deep black silhouette of the *Merkavah* caught his eye as it slipped over the grand window toward the docking station at the ring hub. It was pretty clear to Marc that the flying saucers he and his boyhood friends had dreamed about, sightings going back possibly hundreds or even thousands of years, may have been actual sightings of the *Merkavah* during one of her many short visits to Earth. His gaze followed a group of white-robed Raëlians. They had exchanged their "Bon voyage *Starchild!*" banner for one that read: "Farewell, Earth Mother!"

Marc touched Vesta's shoulder and gestured at the banner. "Shall we?" he asked. Accompanied by Rod, they strolled away from the group to the spoke elevator that would take them to the *Merkavah*, awaiting her small delegation at the hub.

EARTH—SAUDI ARABIAN DESERT

As before, Saeed Esmail's sackcloth robe and full-length flowing beard fluttered in the early morning breeze. He and General Suleiman stood by the entryway to his tent in the Saudi Arabian desert. The morning was cold, and Saeed shivered slightly. He glanced at his general and spoke the solemn words of the first morning prayer into the mike connected to his Link. As his words echoed across the dry lakebed encampment, two thousand Jihadist warriors prostrated themselves on the still cold ground, joined by Saeed and his general

After prayers, Saeed and General Suleiman stood and entered the tent. General Suleiman activated the holotank. Every available channel carried the same images from the Mirs complex at L4. The *Starchild* was about to depart for her ten-year test voyage.

Saeed turned to his general and said, "Ten years, General, we have ten years to lay the groundwork for the new Caliphate."

As they watched, the *Starchild* vanished. In its place, Ring Kiev appeared silhouetted against a backdrop of Moon and stars, and then the channel returned to its regular programming. A pretty blonde in a short skirt with legs discreetly crossed smiled at an aging science fiction author who wisely kept his focus on her face.

"Did it jump into Warp Drive?" she asked.

"Not really…" He smiled indulgently as the holocam moved in for a close-up.

General Suleiman turned off the holotank. "This time," he said quietly, "we will not fail, Sahib!"

IAPETUS

Merkavah settled gently into a circular opening on the crater-strewn surface of Iapetus about halfway between the equatorial wall and the pole, an opening that marked the top of a five-kilometer-deep shaft. As the starship dropped to the bottom of the shaft, an iris-like cover sealed the surface opening. Moments later, five appendages extended from the circular craft's underside, and *Merkavah* settled to the floor while another iris sealed the shaft immediately above the impossibly black ship, and air rushed into the cylindrical chamber. Moments later, the outline of a large rectangular opening appeared along part of the chamber wall. The rectangle moved inward slightly and slid up along the cylinder, exposing a sizeable garage-door-like opening that revealed a meadow and a group of people standing outside the door. A portion of *Merkavah's* inverted dish-like top slid back, exposing a lighted interior that contrasted sharply with the profoundly black exterior. A ramp extended from the opening toward the group of people on the meadow who were crowding around the outside of the garage-like door. They cheered as Vesta walked down the ramp, Rod following closely behind.

This is supposed to be my home, Vesta thought as she smiled at the crowd. *So why doesn't it feel that way?* She felt a light touch on her shoulder.

"Grandmother," Azurad said in Founder-speak, giving Vesta a warm smile, "You are exhausted. Let me take you home for a well-deserved rest."

"Thanks, Sweetheart! But I've got work to do," Vesta said as a floater glided to a stop behind the crowd. "It looks like the Mirs Complex wants to join the Federation. I'm meeting with their delegation in a few minutes."

Vesta and Rod walked toward the waiting floater as the crowd parted before them. Curiously, a small contingent of Raëlians robed in white stood respectfully at the back of the welcoming crowd holding up a banner: "Welcome home, Earth Mother!" Vesta beamed at the crowd, waved to the Raëlians, stopping to chat briefly with several people as she passed. Then they stepped into the hovering vehicle, and the doors slid silently shut as they took seats. From inside, the walls were transparent so that their view was entirely unobstructed, and Vesta watched the crowd waving at her as they sped off. Her last impression was of the Raëlians dancing in the grass.

Azurad was right; Vesta was exhausted, but this meeting was so terribly important, especially so since Dmitri Gagarin was heading the Mirs Complex delegation, and it had been a long time since she had seen the Russian First Officer of the *Cassini II* expedition. Getting to know Dmitri was special since he—with his ever-present tabby, Jake—was so very different from people she had known in the past. Of the men, Jon Stock differed very little from the people of her own world. Ari Rawlston, Jon's Israeli friend, could have been her own flesh and blood. The aristocratic Noel Goddard was a Canadian version of Jon but more distant and aloof, and she never really got to know Chen Lee-Fong, Noel's friend. But it wasn't just seeing Dmitri after so long; it was the strategic importance of the Mirs Complex becoming part of the Federation.

Vesta was well aware of what was happening on Earth. Marc had briefed her on the likely political turn-over in America in the next few months. That changed the dynamics between Earth and the Mirs Complex. With the Americans playing a lesser role, the Russians would almost certainly try to exercise greater control over their stepchild. Mirs, although built by Russian interests, was the one genuinely international entity in the Solar System. She understood completely why Mirs wished to join the Federation. Under President Marc Bowles' leadership, America would not have tried to stand up to the Federation. With America's presence, Russia dared not. Under a Jackson presidency, America probably would lose interest, allowing Russia to exert its influence everywhere on Earth, and especially at Mirs. With Mirs an extension of the Iapetus Federation, Russia would have to back off.

The floater came to a stop in front of the government compound, a stepped pyramid indistinguishable from most of the other buildings on Iapetus. A few minutes later, Vesta and Rod settled in her office in the suite occupying the pyramid peak. Their unimpeded view showed a forest of pillars extending in all directions in a hexagonal pattern, one pillar every six kilometers. They each ordered a refreshing frosty beverage from the automatic attendant.

"The Mirs delegation will be here in a few minutes," Vesta said. "Bring me up to date on the Middle East." They spoke in English, Vesta's enunciation nearly flawless.

"American surveillance satellites produced these images," Rod answered, manipulating his Link so that a high-resolution view appeared above the low table before them. "This," he said, "is a top-down view of a dry lakebed near the center of Rub' al-Khali in the Saudi Arabian desert." He made several adjustments to his Link, and the character of the image changed. Instead of emptiness, the dry lakebed now appeared to be filled with oblong structures. "These are camouflaged tents, each housing two men, we think."

He pointed to a larger structure that appeared to be located atop a berm. "This is probably headquarters." The view pulled back to show the lakebed within the greater context of the Saudi Arabian desert. It got lost in the expanse of sand. "The Americans believe this group consists of about two thousand fighters." Several red checks appeared across the desert. "They have located six other bases, each similarly camouflaged, each housing about two thousand men. That's about fourteen thousand Jihadist warriors that nobody seems to know about."

"Who is putting this thing together?"

"The Americans don't know for sure, but they have some second-hand intel that General Ismail Suleiman may be involved."

"Do we need to be concerned?" Vesta asked.

"I don't think so," Rod responded. "No matter how you slice it, that's a backwater desert in a part of the Earth that plays no meaningful role on any level. The Americans may have to deal with them at some point in the future, but all that is a long way from us—one-and-a-half billion kilometers, more or less."

"Not so very far when Mirs officially joins the Federation," Vesta countered as the Mirs delegation presence was announced.

Rod stood up to leave, but Vesta said, "Why don't you stay, Rod?" She smiled warmly. "We both know that you are the most likely person to succeed me, and I'm not going to be here any longer than necessary."

✳

The door opened, and Dmitri Gagarin stepped into the room, grinning from ear to ear, pate glistening, arms outstretched, with Jake draped over his left shoulder. "Vesta! My dear friend!" He wrapped his big arms around the diminutive woman. Then he took her shoulders in his large hands and held her out in front of him. "You are a sight for sore eyes!" He stepped back and forced himself to assume a formal countenance. "Madam President, may I present Andrey Orlov, Mirs Chairman of the Board." He indicated a slightly overweight short man in his sixties with sparse gray hair and blue eyes. Orlov smiled and bowed from the waist over Vesta's hand. "And may I further present the Mirs Complex Chief Operating Officer, Isidor Sokolov."

Sokolov was nearly as tall as Dmitri, twelve years older at fifty-five, with a full head of short brown hair, steel-blue eyes, and he sported a well-groomed goatee. He nodded respectfully toward Vesta and murmured, "Madam President…"

Dmitri had known both these men for most of his life. They were instrumental in his gaining admission to the Peter the Great SRF Military Academy, and later the Moscow Institute of Physics and Technology. Because of them, he was the First Officer on the Cassini II mission to Iapetus. Now he was here as their intermediary to facilitate their membership application to the Iapetus Federation.

Vesta introduced Rod to both men, and Dmitri smiled warmly at his old friend. "Please sit down, all of you," Vesta said, placing herself in an overstuffed easy chair, "and take a beverage if you wish." She indicated the automatic dispenser along the wall. "I think I know why Mirs wants to be part of the Federation, but I would like to hear it from you," indicating the visitors.

Dmitri settled back to watch the exchange, sipping on what appeared to be freshly squeezed orange juice. *Fresh orange juice some one-and-a-half billion klicks from Earth*, he thought to himself as Orlov cleared his throat and prepared to speak. *How remarkable.* Jake, who had been in Dmitri's lap, got up quietly and settled into Vesta's lap, purring softly.

"Madam President, the Mirs Complex is uniquely positioned both to benefit the Federation and to receive benefit from the Federation." Orlov's English was cultured with a slight Russian guttural overtone. "We are, so to speak, the stepping stone, the waystation between Earth and Iapetus. The Federation currently has a limited number of hyper-V spacecraft, and none of those are designed for cargo. VASIMR powered cargo craft need a launching facility and all the infrastructure that implies. This is what we offer. We propose to be the gateway to the Iapetus Federation." He paused and sipped from his glass, and nodded to Sokolov.

Sokolov picked up the conversation thread, his English much like Orlov's. "The Mirs Complex is in a special position. Technically, we are a private corporation officially headquartered in Moscow, but most of our Earthside operations take place out of our London offices. We have heard rumblings out of Moscow," Sokolov leaned forward, his hands forming a teepee in front of him, "that the Russian Republic may try to wrest ownership of the Mirs Complex from the corporation—to make it state-owned." He smiled grimly. "This would be a disaster for us, one that we wish to avoid at all costs." He glanced at Orlov.

"We considered unilaterally declaring our independence," Orlov said, "but we have no way to enforce that independence— basically, no way to defend ourselves." He placed his hands palms up before him. "The Republic would think twice about attacking a Mirs Complex that is officially part of the Iapetus Federation."

Dimitri was, of course, thoroughly familiar with this argument, as the three of them had gone over it piece-by-piece for several days in preparation for this meeting. It made sense to him, even though the Russian Republic was his "home." Despite being a proud Russian, he was ready to immigrate to the Federation, even more so with the Mirs Complex part of the Federation. It seemed to him that the Moon would not be long in following.

✳

Vesta sat quietly, stroking Jake and digesting what she had heard. The subject had been openly discussed for months, and she was entirely familiar with the arguments. Yet, it still took on significance when Mirs made it official. "Rod, what is your take on how the Americans will look at this?"

"Their recognition will be immediate," Rod answered, "but we should do it while Marc still is the American President." He looked around the room. "I don't trust the new guy, Stanford Jackson. His worldview is very different. Marc tells me that things will change dramatically when Jackson moves into the White House."

Vesta agreed but chose not to respond. She hoped to retire with Azurad to a plantation near the American southeast coast on the Georgia side of the Savannah River. That would be strongly influenced by what happened after Jackson assumed the American Presidency.

"Our legislature, such as it is," Vesta said, "already voted to accept your petition." She gave them one of her famous smiles. "But then, you already knew that."

The three Russians chuckled. "You're right, of course," Orlov said. "We just wanted to meet with you face-to-face. It isn't every day that a fellow gets to meet the genuine Earth Mother."

"There are statues of you in Moscow and St. Petersburg, you know," Sokolov added.

Vesta just smiled. She had come to understand that no matter how she protested, the world chose to see her in this light.

"I need to coordinate with Marc," Rod said, "so our announcement coincides with his recognition of the Mirs Complex's new status." He turned to Sokolov. "Do you speak for the Moon as well?"

"Technically, no." He placed his empty glass on the counter. "It's a bit complicated, but Mirs Corp is a majority shareholder in Udachny, the official name of the Russian Moon mining operation. There are other operations on the Moon, although Udachny is the largest. We need to coordinate with all of them before we make the move official."

Things get so complicated sometimes, Vesta thought. "Can you keep me informed, Dmitri?" She wanted everything to go smoothly, without any serious ramifications.

Dmitri nodded and then asked casually, "Vesta, have you considered how you might handle a confrontation with any party that has the capability of damaging the Mirs Complex, the Moon facilities, or even Iapetus itself?"

Vesta looked at him sharply and then responded carefully. "Not really... *Merkavah* handled the Persian Caliphate activities..." Her voice trailed off.

"That was isolated, and they did not really know our capabilities—or lack thereof," Dmitri said. "The Federation is becoming a significant factor now—especially with Mirs and the Moon becoming a part." He looked around the room and then directly at Vesta. "I think you need someone who is experienced in these matters, someone who can advise on actions to take and not to take. You need someone who can actively direct your response to any challenges that may be forthcoming." He sat back with a sober look on his face.

"You're talking about a Secretary of War," Vesta said, "or is that Defense?"

"How about Chief of Security?" Dmitri asked with a grin.

EARTH—SAUDI ARABIAN DESERT

Saeed Ismail pressed his face to the prayer mat, trying to focus on immediate Qur'anic guidance. His underlying charge was as strong and vital as ever: *Let those fight in the way of Allah who sell the life of this world for the other. Whoso fighteth in the way of Allah, be he slain or be he victorious, on him we shall bestow a vast reward.* These holy words had carried him thus far—through a solar storm all the way to the planet Saturn and its cursed moon Iapetus, and back to Earth, where his life was spared by Allah's grace. And now he headed a mighty army of warriors, dedicated to Allah's holy Jihad to cleanse the entire planet of infidels and unbelievers.

He rose to a squatting position, reached out to switch on his holotank, and tuned to Aljazeera. "The big news for today," the swarthy newscaster said in educated Arabic, "is the annexation by the Iapetus Federation of the Mirs Complex in the Moon's orbit at the Lagrangian four location. This outrageous act of usurpation has already been recognized by the United States and its lackeys, and by the European Union, China, and even the Russian Republic." He went on to describe in detail how the annexation happened, emphasizing the inability of the Russian Republic to protect its interests at L4. He detailed the American subterfuge in facilitating the annexation without the knowledge of the residents of the Mirs Complex, or anyone else, except for the governments of its closest allies, the Canadians, the British, the Australians, and the New Zealanders—the Kiwis.

Saeed stood and stretched. *So, it is happening…which means that it is time for the Caliphate to rise like a Phoenix from the ashes of its destruction at the hands of the Founders.*

CHAPTER THREE

EARTH—ISRAEL & MARS—NACHAL RACHAF

Following the Founders' decision to make this decade their home, Asshur and Aram found themselves drawn to the country and people of Israel, struck by their fragile geopolitical situation. They had seen what the Israelis had accomplished in the Negev. They had also visited Mars several times and were intrigued by the similarity of regions on Mars to the Negev. Except for atmosphere and gravity, there was very little difference between the two. Because of Israel's location on the Mediterranean, but surrounded on all sides by hostile intent, Asshur and Aram began looking for potential Israeli settlement sites on Mars, even though they did not have much support within Israel. They found a suitable canyon section in the eastern branch of Nanedi Valles about 5.4 degrees north of the equator and 1,300 kilometers northeast of Lone Star Station. They brought several Israeli eco-engineers to the location to examine it for its potential as a settlement. It was entirely doable, the engineers told them—with enough personnel, equipment, and materials.

Asshur named it Nachal Rachaf after the deepest, narrowest canyon in the Israeli Negev. The 3.8-km-long canyon segment on

Mars meandered south to north, averaged 500 meters deep and about a kilometer wide, making it an ideal location to roof over with a transparent, light-weight, radiation-resistant polymer. It had a usable aquifer and a vast array of minerals in the soil. Asshur and Aram planned to tunnel deeply into the canyon walls for living space, using the dormant Robotic Vaporizers, the RVs, on Iapetus that had originally served to hollow out that planetoid. Asshur consulted with the Starchild Institute, getting the institute to commit to appropriate backing for Nachal Rachaf. It turned out that much of the equipment used to hollow out Iapetus was still stored in a layer below the Iapetus habitat space, patiently waiting for activation.

Asshur worked with Isidor Sokolov at the L4 Mirs Complex, Andrey Orlov at Mirs Headquarters in London, Margo Jackson, CEO of Launch Loop International (LLI) in Seattle, and Sam Houston with the Lone Star Company in Texas, to set up the Mars Consortium. The Consortium raised funds for Nachal Rachaf for labor costs and to procure the necessary heavy equipment and the polymer sheeting that would cover Nachal Rachaf and seal its ends. The Consortium also underwrote Sam Houston's Lone Star operation in Valles Marineris. While awaiting logistical support from Marc Bowles, Asshur cut a deal with Sam to use *Saracen* as a transport to get the equipment and supplies from Mirs and from Iapetus to Nachal Rachaf.

Aram recruited fifty adventurous Israelis consisting of some of the toughest, battle-hardened men and women in the country. They spent a couple of weeks at Mirs acclimatizing to the pressure suits and learning how to work in reduced gravity under the iron-fisted control of grizzled Israeli Army veteran Mordecai Rochlin—Rasam or *Sergeant Major* to all those who knew and respected him. He had spent twenty-five years fighting insurgents and building settlements in the Negev, rising to the top of his profession. His initial reaction to Nanedi Valles and Nachal Rachaf was, "Piece of cake!"

In the first two days, Rochlin's team raised a thirty-meter dome to house themselves while they stretched polymer across the top of Nachal Rachaf and draped both ends. It took them just under a month to enclose the canyon. Then they added a second, smaller dome for equipment repair without having to wear their pressure suits.

As the team was preparing to tunnel into the canyon walls, Asshur and Aram departed on Saracen for Lone Star, thirteen hundred kilometers to the south, to bring back a large load of Q-carbon on a rover. Q-carbon was artificially created on Earth in North Carolina in the early part of the twenty-first century. It was harder than diamond, an amazingly resilient and robust construction material. Sam Houston and his team at Lone Star Mars discovered that it had formed naturally near Mars' core long ago and extruded into the deeper levels of Valles Marineris. Asshur intended to line the Nachal Rachaf excavations with the material.

MARS—COPRATES CHASMA

Following their meeting with Sam after the rockfall, Asshur and Aram appropriated one of the rovers that mimicked the design of the *Cassini II* lander/rovers. The rover was constructed of aramid polymer, lightweight and robust. The machine was a four-and-a-quarter-meter long, three-meter wide cylinder sitting horizontally atop three sets of sizeable foam-filled rubber tires. The front end was capped with a tough radiation-resistant transparent polymer, and the cylinder contained three sapphire matrix ports down each side and three along the top. The rover's three-and-a-half-meter-long interior configuration was split by a deck running the length of the cylinder with a two-meter space above and storage below the deck, accessible from both inside and outside. The main deck consisted of a front section that sat six passengers three across with storage behind them. A three-quarter-meter chamber behind the rear bulkhead contained a compact variable output gas core reactor. This smaller version of the Cassini II reactor was fueled by gaseous uranium-hexafluoride fissile material (or Hex, as everybody called it) stored in saddle tanks around the rear of the rover. The gas was injected into a small fused silica vessel where it produced extremely high-energy ultraviolet light that generated prodigious amounts of electricity with photovoltaics that surrounded the outer wall. This electricity was directed to the electric motors on the six wheels and the vehicle interior. The rover had a one-atmosphere interior, accessed through a lock on the vehicle's left side. Also, there were emergency exits in the overhead and undercarriage that opened directly to the outside without benefit of a lock. A large, white numeral six was painted on the top, both sides, and the back of the vehicle.

Two reels of immensely strong, twisted, diamond-fiber rope one millimeter in diameter were located just below the transparent nosecone, and two more were centered on the back end of the cylinder. Over the years since fiber-optic cable had been invented, it had evolved into an ultra-high-bandwidth carrier. Nanotechnology had created continuous diamond strands from an engineered diamond that bore only a superficial resemblance to its namesake. Nearly invisible mono-filament strands were used for ultra-broadband communications by the Cassini II crew during their exploration of Iapetus. The ropes carried by the rover were constructed of 243 individual strands twisted in cascading groups of three with a tensile strength stronger than anything else known to humankind. The four reels carried by the rover each held twenty-five kilometers of this diamond rope.

"Pretty it's not," Aram said as they loaded the cargo bay below the main deck with bags of Q-carbon. Asshur grinned at him and tossed another bag of the microscopically fine black powder.

"So, tell me again why we're dragging this shit across thirteen hundred klicks of hostile Martian surface to Nachal Rachaf," Aram said as he caught another bag.

"This shit," Asshur answered, "is harder than diamond. We're digging kilometers deep into the Mars bedrock where we intend to create a new home for the Israeli people..."

"If we can get them to come," Aram interrupted.

"Yeah…anyway, we're going to line our excavations with this shit to ensure they never collapse."

"This is for real, right?"

"It's the same material that our ancestors used to line the hollowed-out core of Iapetus," Asshur said. "I didn't find out about it until Sam told me about the Q-carbon here in the Valles Marineris. I checked the Founder databases and learned all about it." He used the term Founder like everyone else—it was just easier.

They finished loading the cargo bay and then commenced filling every available space in the cabin interior, leaving just the front row of seats for themselves. Finally, Aram used a forklift-like loader to pile three pallets of Q-carbon-filled bags on top of the rover. The two men strapped them down and then called Sam.

"We're ready to depart, Sam," Asshur said on Sam's private Link.

"I'm not going to cycle the lock just to look at your ugly faces," Sam responded with a chuckle. "You guys be safe!"

Since the rover interior was equalized to the exterior because of the loading process, Asshur and Aram clambered into their seats over the bags, still clad in their pressure suits.

"I'll take the first leg," Asshur said as he brought the reactor to full power and diverted most of it to the six wheels. He pointed the clumsy-looking vehicle toward the base of the fall that terminated at the northwestern foot of Nectaris Montes, thirty or so kilometers ahead of them. "Nectaris Montes is about as wide as the particle driver ring on Iapetus," he said.

"But that went all the way around Iapetus, some forty-five hundred klicks," Aram said. "This one is only…what? Two hundred klicks?"

"One-eighty-five, and about six high."

They rolled east along the Coprates floor north of Nectaris Montes for a couple hundred kilometers. The canyon floor was virtually flat, covered with a layer of coarse sand less than a meter deep, punctuated by an occasional rock pile or outcropping. They were able to average nearly 100 kilometers per hour. Two hours later, they reached the eastern extent of Nectaris Montes without incident and continued to follow the Capri Chasma northern wall for sixty kilometers more, this time along a gentle upslope that slowed their progress slightly.

"There it is," Aram said, peering through his binoculars. "Look at that, will you!"

Ahead of them appeared what looked like a fairly steep hill, fully thirty kilometers around at the base, sloping up against the canyon wall commencing with about a twenty-degree angle and finishing at a thirty-five to forty-degree angle to the surface nearly six kilometers above them. No one had yet attempted to climb it, let alone take a rover up its slope, but measurements from orbit indicated that it was a rockfall from long ago down which millions of tons of sand had flowed, pushed by the sometimes up to 300-kilometer-per-hour Mars winds. Twenty-first-century Earth-bound explorers had named it the Capri Fan. The twelve kilometers of thirty-degree slope was their shortcut route to the surface.

As they approached the Fan, they could see no definable base. The surface steepened as they approached, and Asshur, who was at the controls, turned to the right to lessen the steepness of their traverse. "We can go about fifteen klicks at this angle," he said, "and then do a hundred eighty and do about thirty back across the Fan. We'll keep the angle as steep as possible and play it by ear as we get higher, and the slope gets steeper."

Other than the sideway angle, the traverse was much like their traverse across the Coprates floor. Sand had filled the spaces between the rocks so that the surface was even and firm, although Asshur could see rivulets of sand flowing downslope from his wheels. When they reached the turning point, Asshur brought the rover about to the left slowly and carefully. The large, soft wheels prevented any slippage, even when pointed directly upslope. Asshur heaved a sigh of relief as he brought the rover back to a relatively horizontal aspect with respect to the slope.

"Okay, that worked well. Now let's see how much altitude we can gain during this next transit." Asshur looked around the cabin. "You take over," he said to Aram. "I want to do some sightseeing."

Aram took over, continuing the careful drive along the traverse. Instead of sightseeing, however, Asshur kept a wary eye on his younger brother. He didn't want Aram to take any shortcuts or set the traverse too steep. He knew his younger brother well and was more interested in a safe transit than saving a couple of hours. As he watched, Aram began to edge the rover to the right, making the transit ever steeper.

"Cut that out!" Asshur admonished Aram. "Just keep to the angle I set until we reach the next turn. Then we'll figure out what to do."

The transit took a bit less than an hour. Asshur noticed that the rover's side angle was steepening and that the rivulets of sand were growing larger. "Time to test the terrain," he said. "You helmet up, but remain at the controls. I'll lock out and see what we have."

Asshur cycled through the lock and then stepped backward out of the lock to the sloping surface, maintaining a grip on the lock frame. "Whoa!" he said as his feet slipped out from under him. "This shit's pretty unstable." His voice trailed off as he established a firm footing against an underlying boulder.

Asshur looked out over the vast expanse of the Coprates canyon, now some three kilometers below him. He estimated that they had covered about half the distance to the top of the Fan. He walked around the front of the rover, being careful not to lose his footing.

"The boulders are just below the sand surface," he said, "but between the boulders, you can easily sink down into the sand."

"The boulders are stable, but the sand isn't," Aram offered.

"I'm coming back in."

Once inside, Asshur said, "We really need to be careful. We could easily start sliding downslope, or even worse, tumbling down like a rolling cylinder." He slid in beside Aram. "I'm taking over again."

Asshur inched around his course reversal with even greater care than the first one. Rather than merely drive slowly around the bend, he moved back and forth, settling through the sand to the boulder surface below, looking for stability. Then he slowly pivoted in place by alternating the direction of his front and back and upslope and downslope wheels to bring about the pivot. Then, with infinite care, he set along the third traverse at the steepest angle he dared.

About halfway through the traverse, the rover was at nearly a thirty-degree angle down to the right. Asshur could feel the vehicle slipping downslope as he worked his wheels for traction. All around them, boulders were now protruding through the sand, making it virtually impossible to move in a straight path.

"That's as far as we go in this mode," Asshur said to his brother.

"We've got about two klicks of slope ahead of us," Aram said, "and a half klick of altitude left."

"Now comes the hard part," Asshur said as he clambered toward the lock. "As before, you stay here. Come on out when I call you."

Asshur made his way to the front of the rover and hooked one of the diamond ropes to his utility belt. "Find me what looks like a good anchor point up ahead," he said.

"Three hundred meters at three-four-seven."

Asshur called up his digital compass and sighted along that line. "Don't see anything," he said.

"Head that way—you will in a couple of minutes."

Asshur began to climb the steep slope, paying close attention to his footing. As he climbed the surface, his senses began to distinguish slight depressions that indicated sand only, compared to small protrusions that indicated a boulder beneath the sand. Shortly, he saw the anchor point, and fifteen minutes later, he stood beside a boulder that protruded out of the sand more than his height. He unhooked the diamond rope from his belt and wrapped it around the boulder as close to the sand as he could.

"Okay…reel her in slow and easy!"

Asshur watched the rope take up a strain, and then vibrate as the rover worked its way up the 300 meters. After a few minutes, Asshur said, "Okay…I see you…slow it down…easy…okay, stop!"

The rover came to a stop, tilted at a crazy angle, but securely anchored to the boulder with about five meters of rope between the boulder and the rover.

"Okay," Asshur said, "find me the next boulder."

"Zero-zero-four, about two hundred eighty meters."

Leaving the first anchor attached, Asshur attached the second rope to his belt and trudged up to the next anchor point where he secured the rope. "Take a strain," he told Aram.

"The rover has moved ahead about a meter," Aram told Asshur after he activated the second reel enough to tighten the rope. "I'll release the first anchor reel."

A few seconds later, he told Asshur, "We're ready to go."

"Watch out that you don't tangle the first rope in one of the wheels," Asshur said.

"That's all we need," Aram muttered as the rover worked its way up and to the right toward Asshur.

Fifteen minutes later, the rover's nose was a couple of meters from the second anchoring boulder.

"Now comes the fun part," Aram said as he exited the rover while Asshur climbed inside.

Asshur watched Aram attach a sliding link to the first rope and work his way quickly to the original anchor point. "Okay…I'm ready," he said.

Asshur reeled in the first rope slowly enough to allow Aram to climb up the slope with ease. "Okay, little brother, three-five-one at two hundred meters."

"Yeah, yeah," Aram muttered as he worked his way to the next anchor point.

They still had to climb 1,500 meters, and the slope was getting steeper with each meter. Fortunately, more and more boulders were exposed, making finding secure anchor points increasingly easy. Since the final 500 meters were reasonably level, they really had only about a thousand meters of difficulty left.

They were on their fifth carry. Aram had just reached the fourth anchor point below the rover and was about to secure the anchor to himself when Asshur shouted a warning. "The boulder is breaking loose up here! I'm coming down…the rover is sliding…!"

It was almost like slow motion. There was no doubt, though, the anchor boulder was no longer an anchor. "Get behind the biggest boulder you can find…hurry!" Asshur shouted to Aram, and then he turned his attention to his controls. He free-wheeled the reel to the loose boulder, set the other reel going to the anchor below him to maintain tension, and backed away from the situation as fast as the rover would respond. The boulder whipped past the transparent nose of the rover, dropping the rope as it passed. Asshur reeled in the loose rope as he gained some traction and turned the rover parallel to the slope, aiming for another protruding boulder several meters behind him. He and the sand were moving faster than he realized, however, and the boulder passed behind him before he could reach it. Ahead and below, he saw another large boulder and aimed the rover to intersect it. By the time he got there several seconds later, his downslope speed had increased significantly. He impacted the boulder slightly aft of his center of gravity and pivoted around the boulder, pointing straight downslope. Ahead and to his right, he saw the anchor boulder but could not see Aram. *He's just going to have to take care of himself*, Asshur thought as he concentrated on controlling the careening rover.

As Asshur's position reached the level of the anchor boulder, he put full tension on the rope. Immediately, he began to swing to the left as his forward momentum changed to circular. He frantically worked the wheels and steering and finally found himself and the rover thirty meters directly downslope from the anchor rock. He glanced around and saw Aram step from behind another boulder several meters away.

"Now, that's what I call a good save," Aram said with a wave.

Asshur caught his breath and let the adrenaline in his system subside. "Yeah…let's get on with it…" he said as he scanned above and to his right for the next anchor boulder.

MARS—SURFACE TREK TO NANEDI VALLES

Aram secured the second rope hook to its reel. "That's it," he said. "We shouldn't need you for quite a while."

While Aram cycled through the rover lock, Asshur called up their route as a three-dimensional image floating before him in the cabin. Aram clambered into his seat and stowed his helmet.

"Two hundred klicks due north across Aurorae Planum to the western edge of Ganges Cavus," their route appeared as a red line superimposed over the detailed surface, "and then about three-four-zero for a hundred eighty klicks to skirt the western end of Ganges Chasma." The red line traced this route and then turned northeast toward the western extent of Xanthe Terra with its many ancient river valleys and deltas, some 400 kilometers distant. "We'll have to detour around a couple of big craters, but it's mostly a gentle downslope." Asshur extended the red line, turning it west directly into a feeder canyon to Nanedi Valles. "From here, we head nearly due west into Nanedi Valles. We'll follow the eastern branch north until we reach Nachal Rachaf."

Fourteen hours later, Asshur and Aram pulled Rover-6 into the southern end of Nachal Rachaf. They navigated the meandering kilometers along the canyon floor, reaching the dome at the northern end about a half-hour later.

"Home, sweet home," Aram said as he stepped onto the surface, stretching his arms toward the half-kilometer-distant canyon rim. "This is where I want to live out my life," he said, lacking a crystal ball to see what the next few months held.

✳

Asshur and Aram had been working nearly continuously since their arrival at Nachal Rachaf. Aram's *Home—Sweet Home!* turned out to be *Work—Hard Work!* He seemed increasingly distracted, causing Asshur to confront him.

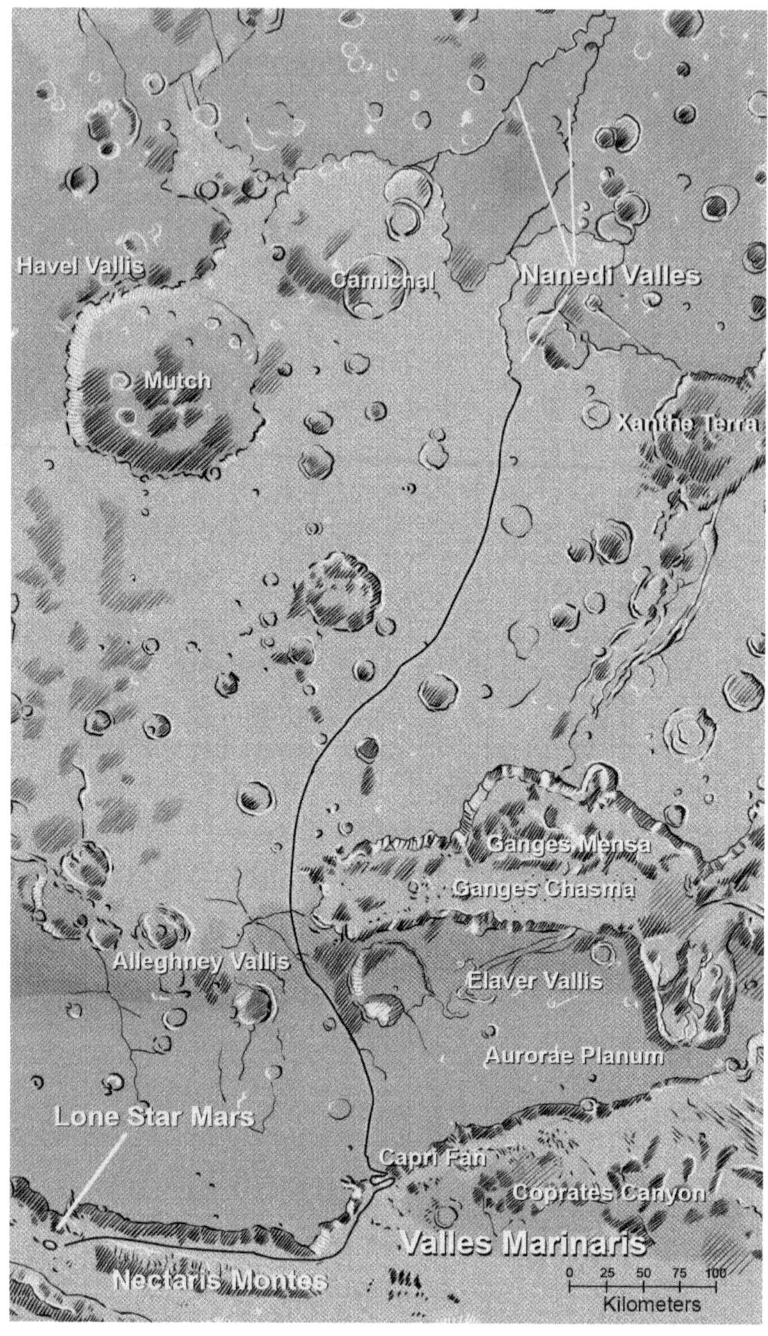

*IMAGE 1—The track of Founders Asshur and Aram
from Lone Star Mars to Nachal Rachaf in Nanedi Valles*

"What's on your mind, Little Brother?"

"I miss her, Asshur, I really miss Sari. Sometimes it just catches up with me."

"Hey…I miss Ishtar…I understand."

"It's different. Ishtar is alive, living her life doing what she wants to do. Sari is gone…" Aram sighed deeply.

"Of course, you're right." Asshur quietly considered his options. "We need some time off…just the two of us—*Us Time*—in the language of our new-found friends." Asshur wrapped an arm around his younger brother's shoulders. "And I know just the place…"

MARS—COPRATES CHASMA

Sam watched on the Control Center holodisplay as the Founder brothers departed in *Rover-6*. *What a life they've lived, he thought as they left in a cloud of dust. Born on a generational starship, crossed the galaxy and back (well, at least five hundred lightyears), traveled one hundred fifty thousand years forward in time, and now they're crossing thirteen hundred klicks of Martian desert…and yet they're regular guys and my personal friends.*

Several hundred people occupied hollowed-out Lone Star Station, although eventually, it would house thousands. They consisted of mining and structural engineers, skilled construction workers and heavy equipment operators, miners adept at handling heavy mining equipment, and several geologists, extreme environment agricultural types, chemists, and atmospheric specialists. Sam orchestrated their activities. Lone Star Mars was his dream, but every person in his crew shared that dream with him.

And a vast dream it was. The current project was 450 kilometers long, fifty kilometers wide, and six or more kilometers deep. When completed in several years, it would be filled with oxygenated air halfway up the canyon walls, so a person only needed an oxygen concentrator and a lightweight pressure suit. The canyon floor would be covered with transparent-dome-enclosed agricultural crops—grains, vegetables, fruit trees, and grasses for grazing, and the population would be in the tens of thousands. As the Lone Star Mars population grew, they could expand to the west in stages for about 1,500 kilometers and to the east for another 500 or so. Eventually, Sam hoped to terraform the entire surface of Mars, melting its polar ice caps, pumping free water from its vast aquifers, and extracting oxygen from its carbon-dioxide-rich atmosphere, creating a human-friendly surface pressure about ten times the present six millibar level.

Sam had a crew currently constructing a malgalith dam across a bottleneck in Valles Marineris 250 kilometers to the west. Another crew was building a dam at the eastern end of Nectaris Montes, effectively creating a 450-kilometer-long enclosed valley. Sam called up a holodisplay of the project and was studying the ledge that had collapsed under his feet when his second-in-command, fellow Texan Mattias McIntyre, entered the Operations Center.

"Matti," Sam gestured the red-headed Irishman over, "look at this." A portion of the display enlarged, showing a close-up of what remained after Sam's tumble into the canyon. "See those radial lines?" He pointed to a series of cracks emanating from a point now in mid-air, but that would have been in solid rock several meters below Sam's feet at the time of the collapse. "What do you make of that?"

"I'd say it ain't natural." McIntyre's voice carried a bit of an Irish lilt. "Not one of our crew. I'd stake my life on it!"

"Who else?"

"So, who else is there?" McIntyre sounded genuinely puzzled. "The Israelis over in Nachal Rachaf? That makes no sense at all."

"Not only that," Sam added, "it happened on the south rim." He stared at the holodisplay. "Nachal Rachaf is thirteen hundred klicks away…the other way. To get here," he indicated the collapsed cliff, "is at least another thousand klicks around the end of Marineris—or else down through." He zoomed to the Capri Fan on the north wall sixty kilometers east of Nectaris Montes. It displayed no wheel marks. "No one's come down here, and obviously, Asshur and Aram hadn't gotten there yet when the satellite got this shot."

"So, who, then?" McIntyre's puzzlement seemed to be growing. "Do we have a third party on Mars that we don't know about?" He pulled up a view of Lone Star's rover inventory. "We got nine rovers left since you sent one to Nachal Rachaf. We got three here, two at the western dam with another runnin' between there and here. That's six. We got two at the Montes dam and another runnin' between there and here. That makes a total of nine—our entire inventory." He called up an image of the parking bay. "Hey, Sam…There's only two rovers in the garage."

"Check the log," Sam told him.

McIntyre pulled up the log, read for several seconds, and then said, "A couple of our new guys, Chino and Rico, checked out Rover-two three days ago to bring some spare parts to the Montes crew."

Sam raised an eyebrow.

"They froze a bearing on the tall crane; had to rush one out to them, and these guys were available."

"So…where is *Rover-two* now?"

"Still out there. The guys probably stayed to learn and help."

Sam called the crew boss at Montes with his Link. Since Mars did not yet have a ServerSky swarm to support a planetary Link system, Sam had run optical lines from the central compound to each construction crew. The optical cables were identical to the ones used by the *Cassini II* crew during their initial exploration of Iapetus. They were made of mono-filament diamond fiber, were ultra-thin and flexible, and virtually unbreakable.

"Are Rover-two and crew still with you—Chino and Rico?" he asked the Monte crew boss.

"They pitched in for the rest of the day and then headed east to check out routes to the southern canyon rim. Haven't seen 'em since, but we've been pretty busy. They could have circled round north and returned on the other side of Nectaris Montes." He paused. "Why? Are they missing or something?"

"Something," Sam muttered. "Thanks."

Sam turned to McIntyre. "Please run a check of our entire inventory—especially explosives and tools."

✳

The following morning, McIntyre met with Sam in the Control Center. He looked tired. Sam motioned him to a seat. After making himself comfortable, McIntyre called up a display of the results of his inventory.

"This is kind of distressing, really," McIntyre commenced. "There's no easy way to tell you this, so here it is. We're missing the following items: Rover-two with backhoe and scraper attachments, one rover repair field kit, one tool pack, fifty liters of Hex, fifty kilometers of diamond rope on two reels, one trike with wagon, one laser drill, four Mars suits, two suit repair kits, four oxygen concentrators, one CO2/O2 converter, one water unit, two environmental tents, twelve months of concentrated rations for two, a hundred liters of water, shovel, rake, pickaxe, several boxes of hooks, fasteners, nails, and clips, and two tons of HE." McIntyre leaned back with a scowl.

"What do you make of it?" Sam asked, knowing full well what the answer was.

"Kinda obvious, don't you think?" McIntyre grimaced. "Chino and Rico ain't comin' back, and their names ain't Chino and Rico."

✳

Ra'id Kassab and Abdul-Hasid Naseri, aka Chino and Rico Delgado, pushed Rover-2 eastward as fast as the rough terrain would allow. Their immediate goal was a group of rounded hills with sharp outcroppings about thirty kilometers to the east of Nectaris Dam.

"Push her to the limit, Bro," Chino said to Rico, who was maneuvering their vehicle over the rock-strewn ground. Even out here, away from the others, they maintained cover.

"Goin' as fast as I can," Rico said, checking his rear-view scanner. "Those guys are way too busy to pay us any attention."

"See our old track yet?"

"Ground's too rough," Rico said. "Should pick it up the other side of the hills before we hit Aurorae Sinus…thirty minutes or so."

Chino called up a detailed terrain map. They had about a hundred kilometers to go past the hills in front of them before their old track turned sharply right. Before the brothers' arrival from Earth with the work crew, Mars experts from the Caliphate had pored over detailed terrain maps of this area of Valles Marineris and had discovered a heretofore unknown route to the surface from the floor of a still-unnamed crater, through the western crater wall. It was the route the brothers had used when they planted the explosives that nearly killed Sam Houston. This time, their route would take them to the east along the valley floor and then northeast along Eos Chasma toward Hydraotes Chaos. From there, they would head essentially due west, skirting various obstacles until they reached the southern extent of Eastern Nanedi Valles.

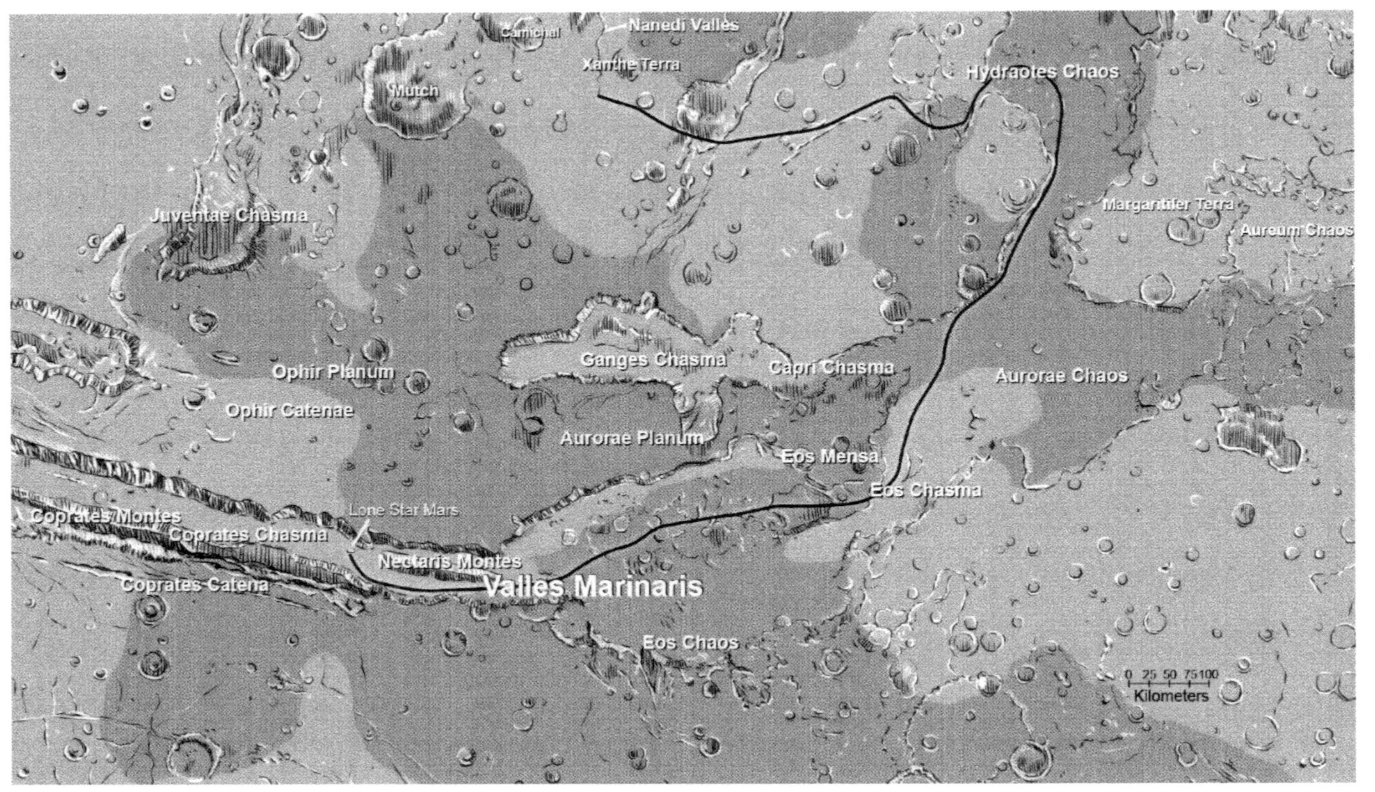

IMAGE 2—The track of Chino and Rico Delgados from Lone Star Mars to Nanedi Valles

In the confusion of the fast-moving Lone Star project, Chino and Rico had managed to place themselves as couriers to both dam construction teams. Their absence from servicing one team was merely assumed to be their presence with the other, and so they had managed to be absent sufficiently long to place the explosives on the canyon rim and return to Lone Star without being missed.

This time, however, was different. They had provisions for a year, barring any mishap, and they had everything they needed to carry out their mission. Chino sighed and then brightened.

"There!" Chino pointed. "Our old track." The surface had changed to heavy sand that clung together as if it were moist. Their outbound and return tracks were unmistakable. "A hundred klicks, and our old track turns south. Course, we keep goin' east, 'bout three hunnerd fifty kicks. You okay driving, Bro?"

"Shee-it, Chino! We got lots of driving to do. You'll get your chance."

Chino expanded the terrain map floating before them. Superimposed on the map was the route they planned to follow. Once they reached Eos Chasma, they would follow the upsloping valley for 600 kilometers and then skirt the southern edge of Hydraotes Chaos for 200 kilometers. After leaving the cinder cones of Hydraotes behind them, they would continue west, between Iamuna Chaos and Oxia Chaos, aiming for Nanedi Valles and the Israeli settlement of Nachal Rachaf, another 500 kilometers distant.

"You think the mullahs who planned this route really understood what we are facing?" Chino asked. "That's more than twenny-five-hunnerd klicks of completely unknown territory."

"Shee-it!" was all Rico had to say.

"I guess we got a job to do," Chino mused. "We gonna go down in history, Bro, you and me." His face broke into a grin. "This Jihad never been done before!" His face went solemn. "Allah will protect us 'cause we on a holy mission. Twenny-five-hunnerd klicks ain't nothin'."

Rico turned toward him. "We ain't prayed in a long time."

"We been undercover, Bro…."

Rico stopped the rover and donned his clear helmet. "Let's go pray," he said.

Chino also donned his helmet, and they both cycled through the lock to the cold surface. The sun was setting back over Nectaris Montes. The air was crisp and clear, and the sand crunched beneath their boots.

"Where's Earth?" Rico asked.

Chino pointed in a generally westerly direction. "Bow toward the Sun," he said. "Saeed explained that Allah allows prayer in the general direction of Earth for any Muslim who is off-planet. Remember what the Prophet went through during his trek to Iapetus. He prayed as best he could, and Allah kept him safe and prepared him for his ultimate Jihad. We," Chino said with considerable pride, "are part of that Jihad!"

They laid out their prayer mats on the frigid Martian surface and prostrated themselves, praying silently, reaching out to Allah for the first time in many months. Chino felt a warmth flow through his system as Allah's presence touched him.

"*Allahu Akbar!*" Chino said as he rose to his feet.

"*Allahu Akbar!*" Rico echoed as they reentered the rover.

CHAPTER FOUR

EARTH—WASHINGTON D.C.

Marc Bowles sat at his ornate desk in the Oval Office for the last time. President-Elect Stanford Jackson sat comfortably on the sofa to Marc's right, sipping from a cup of coffee—the cup emblazoned with the Presidential Seal on one side and the U.S. Navy SEALS Trident on the other. A Navy steward stood at parade rest by the door behind Jackson. Marc nodded to the steward who came to attention, did an about-face, and exited the Oval Office. Marc rose to his feet, motioning to Jackson to remain seated, and walked to the sofa on the opposite side of the antique coffee table, facing Jackson. He carried a glossy brown, well-worn, leather-bound notebook that he laid on the coffee table between them.

"This is a bit premature," Marc said with a smile, "since the inauguration will take place in about forty minutes. I suppose—hypothetically—that something could happen to you during that time that would prevent you from assuming office…but, let's tempt fate." He slid the notebook across the table. "My predecessor gave this to me, and his before him, to him, going back for God only knows how long. This cover," he tapped it with a finger, "is at least a century-and-a-half old."

Jackson set his cup and saucer on the coffee table but did not reach for the notebook. His regal features remained neutral.

"Only presidents' eyes have beheld what's inside," Marc told him. "Only presidents have recorded information on its pages." Marc stood up, and Jackson followed suit. "My only word of advice to you is to watch out for the Middle East. Something is brewing there, and we do not know what it is." He pointed toward the door. "Shall we?"

Jackson picked up the notebook, and they exited the Oval Office, Jackson in the lead. They were each picked up by their respective security details, and Marc noted that Jackson said something to an aide, handing him the notebook. The aide tucked it into his briefcase without looking at it. At that point, Marc's security detail whisked him off to the *Merkavah*.

EARTH—MINNEAPOLIS

Minneapolis was a great American city, progressive, tolerant, multicultural to a fault. Since the late twentieth century, it had welcomed peoples of every stripe, but as so often happens in the world, just as Boston became an *Irish* city, so Minneapolis became a tolerant haven for Muslims. Unlike many other places, in Minneapolis, Muslims lived side-by-side with Christians, Jews, and others in relative peace and harmony. As the war on terror developed in the early twenty-first century, there was a wave of resentment that swept across the country, even in Minneapolis. With time, much of the resentment against ordinary Muslims faded as the media focused their collective attention on the Muslim extremists who seemed to be the source of the problem.

Steven Brady would have been a Viking warrior had he lived a thousand years earlier. As it was, he was a captain in the Minnesota National Guard. Steve was a big man, with close-cropped blond hair and piercing blue eyes. He stood at relaxed attention on this frigid January 20th morning, watching his troops assemble into four thirty-four-man platoons under the guidance of his First Sergeant, Pollard "Bo" Bransom. The first sergeant was nearly as big as his captain, with a boxer's shoulders, medium brown features from his African heritage, and a smooth-shaven pate.

"Come on, you lackluster morons!" he shouted into the chill breeze. "It's too friggin' cold to drag out this formation!" He strode back and forth, slapping his gloved hands together to keep them warm. "Move your asses, Soldiers!"

Captain Brady watched with wry amusement as the four platoons formed up in front of the sergeant, three wide by eleven deep, on the snow-packed green just to the west of the main entrance to the Minnesota Army National Guard complex on Broadway in northeastern Minneapolis. Each squad leader reported to his platoon leader, and each platoon leader shouted his, and for platoon three her, readiness as First Sergeant Bransom came to attention, performed a practiced about-face, and reported with a snappy salute, "Charlie Company present and accounted for, Sir!"

"Thank you, First Sergeant." The increasing wind whipped the words out of the captain's mouth, and he could feel the chill beginning to penetrate his face. "Dismiss the troops and move them inside, Sergeant. We'll watch the inauguration without getting frostbite."

The National Guard soldiers hustled inside the Armory chow hall with more enthusiasm than they had shown forming up for roll call. Four stragglers with Middle Eastern features, one from each platoon, were the last to enter. They remained together and found seats near the back of the room, chatting quietly with one another.

Sergeant Bransom activated the raised holotank, and after a bit of random sparkling across the front of the room, a three-dimensional image formed of the U.S. Capitol Building, west side, viewed from the far side of the reflecting pool. The mall leading to the Capitol was filled with people, bundled up against the January cold. The entire west side of the Capitol was modified with a bleacher superstructure that accommodated several thousand dignitaries. There were no empty seats, despite the bitter cold.

Minneapolis time was fifteen minutes before one—fifteen minutes before Stanford Jackson would be sworn in as President.

The Chief Justice of the Supreme Court, robed in black for the occasion, stood to the right. A man of medium height with dark, wavy hair, bronze skin, and a full mustache, garbed in a dark suit and overcoat, approached from the left, accompanied by a smaller dark-featured woman, her head covered with a Muslim *Hijab* made of dark blue silk. The Chief Justice held out the traditional *Lincoln Bible* for the oath, but the woman smiled and handed him a tattered copy of the *Qur'an*. She said softly but clearly picked up by the microphones, "This *Qur'an* belonged to Syed Ata Ullah Shah Bukhari, my husband's ancestor and spiritual mentor. My husband wishes to take the oath on this." A startled expression crossed the Chief Justice's face, and then he nodded. Mrs. Bukhari held the 1898 *Qur'an* in her outstretched hands, and Dr. Syed Shah Bukhari placed his right hand on the book and repeated the solemn oath of office to become the new Vice President of the United States.

As the short ceremony concluded, the four Middle Eastern soldiers at the back of the Minneapolis chow hall jumped to their feet, shouting, "*Allahu Akbar!… Allahu Akbar!… Allahu Akbar!… Allahu Akbar!*"

EARTH—AUSTRIAN ALPS

Asshur tossed his younger brother Aram a wide grin and stretched out his arms to encompass the mountain panorama before them. "Have you ever seen anything like it?"

Ever since Aram had lost his beloved Sari during a stop-over on the Founders' hop-skipping journey forward through time, Aram had developed a reckless streak that so worried their grandmother, Vesta, that she charged Asshur with keeping him out of trouble. *I'll keep you out of trouble, Little Brother,* Asshur thought, a*nd enjoy myself the while.*

Asshur looked across a narrow suspension bridge that stretched 140 meters across a snow-filled gulch thirty meters below. The cable car terminal Stubnerkogel stood just beyond the suspension bridge, partially hidden by snowdrifts. Down a path on the other side of *Stubnerkogel,* its popular observation platform cantilevered out over the town of Bad Gastein in the valley a kilometer below separating the complex from the *Hohe Tauern* mountain range to the west that dominated this region of Austria. *Grossglockner* towered another kilometer above them, the highest peak in Austria, and the highest mountain in the Alps east of Brenner Pass.

"Not quite Mars," Asshur said. "Shall we?" Asshur pointed across the bridge to the terminal. They were the only ones left near the suspension bridge as twilight shadows sharply defined the nearby crags on that January 20th. It was approaching the sixth hour—too late to ski down the mountain to Bad Gastein, a kilometer below them. They would have to take the cable car's last run of the day—not something they wanted to miss.

About mid-span, Aram stopped and laid his skis across the meter gap that separated the light handrails. Nimbly, he boosted himself onto his skis, stretched out his arms, and shouted to Asshur, "Take a holo for Grandmother! She'll love it…"

"You idiot!" Asshur said with a laugh. "Get your ass down from there."

At that moment, a startled look crossed Aram's face. He looked at his brother in total astonishment, clutched his chest, and pitched silently backward over the rail, thirty meters above the snow-packed mountainside. At virtually the same instant, Asshur heard the sharp crack of a rifle, followed almost immediately by another shot. Still facing the cable car terminal, he dropped to the expanded metal walkway, peering through, trying to locate his brother in the gathering gloom. All he could see was a cloud of powder and the sluffing of the steep snow surface as it picked up momentum, the beginning of an avalanche that would end somewhere far below him, carrying Aram's body to an unmarked location that might not be found until May's snowmelt.

As he struggled to make sense of what had just happened, his Link activated in voice mode. "Asshur…?" The caller was using Founder Speak.

"Yes…"

"Stay as low as possible and return to the end of the bridge. When you get there, stay on the bridge. We'll meet you."

"Who are…"

Another rifle shot rang through the rapidly darkening snowscape as evening settled across *Stubnerkogel*. Only the *Grossglockner* peak stood out, still sunlit in the deepening sky. Keeping low, Asshur turned around to hurry in the direction from which they had just come. Then, from nearby, several rapid-fire bursts from what had to be automatic weapons shattered the stillness following the rifle shot.

"Quickly!" a voice said in Founder Speak from the darkness ahead. "Sprint around the hummock in front of you."

As he did, someone grabbed his arm and pulled him over a short rise as another shot rang out, followed by a brief, rapid-fire burst.

"My brother...Aram..." Asshur protested.

"Later...we'll retrieve him later. Right now, we need to get you out of here."

As they descended the rise, Asshur pulled back in astonishment. Floating just above the snow surface was the *Merkavah*, or a hyper-V craft identical to her. He looked over his shoulder as *Grossglockner* winked out and darkness enfolded them.

"Quickly!" his unseen companion urged, "Inside...quickly!" as another shot rang out and a bullet ricocheted off the craft's pitch-black hull.

As they mounted the ramp into the craft, a shot followed them, and Asshur heard the man behind him grunt in pain. The man pitched forward against them as they stumbled into the craft, and the ramp retracted.

EARTH—SAUDI ARABIAN DESERT

General Suleiman sipped a sweet mint tea, focusing his attention on the holovision image shimmering in the air before Saeed and himself. A quickening chilly January breeze ruffled the sprawling tent as the time approached 7 pm. Now and then, the wind carried a shard of human conversation through the canvas, the voice of one of the 2,000 warriors, huddled in their tents, trying to keep warm in the five-degree cold of the desert winter night. The holovision image steadied as Dr. Syed Shah Bukhari placed his right hand on the tattered *Qur'an* held by his wife.

As the ceremony concluded, the General's Link signaled. He called up the transmission in public form, and an image coalesced in the air before him. The view was dim, but he could make out the face of the German sniper he had assigned to the two warriors he had tasked with taking out Aram and Asshur. "Report!" the General ordered.

"Aram is dead." The speaker paused. He was blond and spoke Arabic with a heavy German accent. "And both my partners. Asshur escaped. He had help. They fired at us with automatic weapons and then disappeared into the night…made no other sound, left no tracks."

The General looked at Saeed. "It had to be a Founder craft, Sahib."

Saeed rose to his feet and defiantly lifted his leather-cupped right stump into the air. "Tomorrow, we commence moving our warriors into position across the region. In thirty days, we will strike at the heart of every capital."

IAPETUS—FEDERATION HEADQUARTERS

Unlike the inauguration of the new American president, Stanford Jackson, the ceremony that installed Rod Zakes as the new president of the Iapetus Federation consisted of a few formal words by Vesta and Rod to the small group assembled in her office. Present were Vesta and Rod Zakes, Dmitri Gagarin as both the outgoing and incoming Director of Security, Isidor Sokolov representing the Mirs Complex, Andrey Orlov representing Mirs Corp, and Marc Bowles, who had been whisked to the *Merkavah* immediately following his private conversation with Jackson in the Oval Office and transported to Iapetus in the shortest possible time. Jake was curled up in Vesta's lap.

Marc looked around at the small assemblage, still awed by how quickly and painlessly he had traveled from Washington to Iapetus in less time than it took to go by car from the White House to the Beltway. He felt honored to have been invited. Although he was not part of the new Federation Administration, he had accepted the offer to assume the directorship of the Starchild Institute.

Marc's life had been filled with twists and turns. He made it through Ohio State on an NROTC scholarship and as the captain of the football team—without injury. Following his initial military training, he was invited to become a Navy SEAL, initially as a junior officer and ultimately leading his own team. When the Russian president was taken hostage by Muslim extremists during a state visit to Kazakhstan, his team was the closest available special forces team with any chance of rescuing the Russian leader. Backed up by Russian Spetsnaz, Marc led a daring nighttime HALO raid on the complex holding the president and managed to extract him safely without any American or Russian casualties. For his heroism, Marc was awarded the Congressional

Medal of Honor and was designated a Hero of the Russian Federation. Following his Navy service, Marc entered Harvard Law School, but instead of becoming a lawyer, he joined a Wall Street firm, and within a year, had formed his own successful Wall Street trading company. Fabulously wealthy following several years on Wall Street, Marc sold his firm and turned his eyes toward Washington. After two years as a senator, Marc tossed his hat in the presidential ring. He won by a landslide larger than anything since the fabled Reagan days. His second term was marked by the Iapetus expedition and the destruction of the Persian Caliphate, and one would have thought that Vice President Wilfred Ames would follow in his footsteps.

Unfortunately, the mood of the nation had changed. The American people, tired of war, had turned inward. The American republic was now in the hands of Stanford Jackson and Syed Shah Bukhari.

God help us! Marc thought as he pulled himself out of his reverie and back into the Presidential Suite on Iapetus, some one-and-a-half billion kilometers from Washington. Vesta had just hugged Rod, and the others in the room were congratulating him with warm handshakes. Marc approached his old friend with outstretched hand.

"Your job is to carry forward what our country's founders started so long ago. This is a chance at a genuine fresh start." The room quieted as Marc spoke those words. "I fear for our ancestral home."

"My outlook is less gloomy than yours," Vesta said. "Azurad and I will be moving to a small Georgia plantation on the banks of the Savannah River. The Persian Caliphate is no more. The threat of Islamic terrorism has faded. The world looks pretty peaceful to me, and I intend to make the most of it for the remainder of my life."

Marc exchanged looks with Rod, and the two silently agreed to speak as soon as possible after Vesta left the room.

EARTH—AUSTRIAN ALPS

As his eyes adjusted to the interior lighting of the hyper-V craft, Asshur asked, "Who are you guys?" As soon as he saw the inside of the craft, Asshur knew it was not the *Merkavah*. "How and why were you right there...?" His voice trailed off as he remembered that a short time earlier, he and Aram were together on that mountainside.

"I'm Eli, this is Johan, and that," pointing to a third man lying on a built-in cot against the bulkhead holding a pressure dressing to his leg, "is Ori, malingering over a minor flesh wound." Eli grinned at Asshur. "We work for Daniel Ben-Gurion—Israeli Mossad. We're your guardian angels, but we really fucked this one up. We killed two of them who were getting ready to take you out from behind that hummock. We totally missed that sniper on the other side of the valley. He must have entirely buried himself in the snow."

"Slow down…take it easy! What do you mean, *guardian angels?*"

"You guys, all of you Founders, are extremely important to us… to the Israelis. The Knesset tasked Mossad with keeping all of you safe but surreptitiously in the background. We've had a tail on each of you when you are Earthside ever since you guys decided to stay in this century." Eli smiled with genuine warmth. "You and Aram have been the most challenging assignment." He hung his head, his grief apparent. "I am so, so very sorry about your brother."

Asshur was stunned at the revelation but simultaneously touched by Eli's apparent grief. He looked over at Johan, whose eyes dropped to the deck. Then he turned his attention to Ori on the cot. "I'm just a physics guy…don't know much about medicine, but we'd better take care of Ori's wound."

Eli and Asshur turned to Ori while Johan busied himself at the hyper-V craft's controls. Eli apparently had some medical training. Asshur watched him skillfully dress the wound. Antibiotics and a pain injection helped Ori to become part of the group again.

"Sorry we had to leave Aram's body back there, but with him gone, we decided to take no chances with you," Ori said as he sat up on the cot, sipping a cup of hot tea Eli handed him.

"Where are you taking me?" Asshur asked.

"We're not…we just arrived," Johan said from the controls. "Welcome to Tel Aviv!"

EARTH—TEL AVIV, ISRAEL

The hyper-V craft dropped Asshur in a meadow on the outskirts of Tel Aviv a few steps from a paved road and took off immediately. Within a minute, a gray late-model Fiat pulled over, and the driver motioned for Asshur to enter on the passenger side. The sky was dark, and he could see the lights of Tel Aviv in the near distance. They drove for about twenty minutes over a modern highway, turned off onto a city street and made several turns, ending up in the parking lot of an entirely unremarkable building in a generally commercial part of town. Nothing distinguished the building from several neighbors. Half the windows were lit, occupied apparently by office workers who had not yet finished the day's work. Asshur was ushered into a nondescript office that had no outward-facing windows. Mossad Director David Ben-Gurion rose to his feet from behind an ordinary desk and held out his hand in greeting.

The Director was about Asshur's height, with swarthy features and dark hair. He could have been Asshur's older brother. "*Shalom!*" he said with a warm smile and gestured to an overstuffed brown leather chair to the right of his desk. "Tea?"

"Thank you," Asshur said as he settled into the chair and gazed around the office. The walls were covered with framed holographs of Ben-Gurion shaking hands with this or that famous personage or pinning an award to the chest of somebody entirely unknown to the world at large. The only people Asshur recognized were the out-going American President, Marc Bowles, the *Cassini II* Captain Jon Stock, and Ari Rawlston, the Chief VASIMR Engineer on *Cassini II*, who—he had been told—was a former Mossad agent.

"I am so sorry about your brother," Ben-Gurion said. "Suleiman has his agents everywhere, and we know that he has targeted all of the Founders. Most of you are off-world, but you and Aram gave us fits since we never knew where you would go next. We thought we had identified all the agents following you, but we missed the shoot-er. We think he's a German national who specializes in long-range assassinations. He rarely misses as you discovered, but you are here because he isn't perfect."

The Director asked Asshur about the Mars project. "It's a full-time job keeping Israel safe," he said, "so that I have had no time to keep up with your efforts on Mars."

"We call it Nachal Rachaf," Asshur told him, although he suspected that the Director knew that and probably a lot more that he simply wasn't revealing. "It will be safe from terror."

"Israelis are a strange lot," the Director said. "They would rather live in their ancestral homeland with the terror threat than somewhere else and be safe." He held up his hand when Asshur started to comment. "On the other hand…now that you guys are here, perhaps you can persuade them that Israel is not their ancestral homeland after all." His eyes twinkled. "The man-in-the-street will be outraged by Aram's death. Perhaps you can use that to give his death meaning. The Israeli population needs someone to look up to, someone who can rally all the people in a non-partisan way." He stood up and walked around to the chair, putting his hand on Asshur's shoulder. "You just might be that person."

EARTH—SAVANNAH RIVER, GEORGIA

Merkavah settled through the air to just a few centimeters above the green grass slope that formed the front yard of a gracious southern mansion perched on a low hill about a hundred meters south of the Savannah River. Several dozens of white-robed people milled about the frontage between the mansion and river. Many held banners welcoming *Earth Mother*; others held up signs displaying the Wormhole of David that had become the universally recognized symbol of the Raëlians. The crowd was happy, boisterous, and nonthreatening as Vesta and Azurad descended the ramp onto the lawn, accompanied by Dmitri, who had insisted on being with them for added security. Jake had draped himself over Dmitri's left shoulder. A thirty-something woman who stood out from the crowd because of her business attire stepped toward the ramp, her hand held out in greeting.

"Welcome to Georgia and to Savannah Hills," she said, shaking Vesta's hand warmly. "I'm Sally King from the Governor's office. The Governor sent me to welcome you personally, to provide you with some crowd control, and to help you settle in any way I can."

As the ramp retracted and *Merkavah* departed, Dmitri eyed the young woman suspiciously, wondering why he had not been notified by the Governor's office that she would be there. For this occasion, he had chosen to wear a security vest under his shirt—just in case, he told himself. It itched in the humid Georgia afternoon, and Jake didn't much like the hardness of the vest's plates.

Vesta waved to the white-robed acolytes and smiled at the young woman from the Governor's office. "So gracious of you, Sally. I am honored by the Governor's solicitude." She gestured toward the entrance. "Shall we?"

As they walked, Vesta said, "I'm sure you know that my staff arrived early and has already set things up for Azurad and me. The robed greeters were a bit unexpected, but the Raëlians have always treated me with respect, and I'm certain that they present no harm. They should be gone before sunset."

Dmitri followed them, keeping a wary eye on the crowd, his senses on full alert.

They reached the door, and Vesta invited Sally in for a cup of tea. They strolled through the 200-year-old mansion, taking in the high ceilings, the beautiful crown moldings, and the nearly two-and-a-half meter high doorways (eight feet in the old English system when they were built). Once they settled down for tea, Jake settled in Vesta's lap while Dmitri walked through the rest of the mansion, making sure that there were no hidden dangers. He found nothing out of the ordinary, yet his sense of unease remained.

As Dmitri stepped into the tea room, surrounded on three sides with floor to ceiling windows, a flash from a wooded alcove several hundred meters along the hill crest from the house caught his eye. Instinctively, he stepped between Vesta and the window.

＊

Things had gotten a bit more complicated for Ben-Gurion when Vesta decided to settle down in Georgia. Since Asshur was now safely in Tel Aviv, regular Israeli security forces could keep an eye on him. This freed up his only hyper-V craft for other things, like sending Eli and Johan (Ori was still recuperating) to keep an eye on the Earth Mother at her Georgia plantation until they could come up with something better to keep her safe.

Johan dropped Eli off on the far side of a wooded grove along the ridge to the west of the mansion. They had picked this spot because, if they had an assassination assignment, that would have been their choice. They had also determined that the confusion of the arrival would be the best opportunity to take Vesta out. Eli crept through the grove, senses tuned to anything out of the ordinary. After several minutes, he could see the large trees demarking the edge of the grove closest to the mansion. He scanned the trees slowly, working his way up. Out of the corner of his eye, he saw some movement high up, too large to be a squirrel. As he brought his silenced rifle to bear, he heard a faint ratchet sound as the shooter chambered a round in his single-shot sniper rifle. Instinctively, Eli fired two quick silenced shots, but not before the sniper squeezed his trigger.

✳

Dmitri felt a sharp pain in his chest and dropped to his knees to watch—in astonishment—as the window shattered inward. He knew he had been hit but also knew that he was alive, and Vesta was in mortal danger. Dmitri staggered to his feet just in time to see Sally pull a small automatic from her purse, her suddenly hate-filled attention focused on Vesta. With a mighty effort, through a haze of pain, he threw himself across the table, shards of tea service flying everywhere.

Sally managed to place two well-aimed bullets into Dmitri's chest, just over his heart, before the full mass of his hundred kilos hit her. He crashed to the floor on top of her, with smithereens of chair protruding through her body in several places, including one entering the back of her neck and exiting through her mouth.

Dmitri looked down at the chair splinter protruding from Sally's mouth and then observed the hatred in her brown eyes dim until they stared lifelessly at the high ceiling. He shook his head and clambered to his feet, his chest beneath the vest feeling like a sledgehammer had struck him. Vesta huddled under the table with Azurad's protective arm around her shoulders while Jake checked out the damage to Sally. As Dmitri squatted down to determine their condition, a shadow passed across the transparent panes, and he heard the sound of running feet. Dmitri leaped to his feet, drawing his sidearm. As he did so, he recognized the distinctive disc shape of a hyper-V craft settling into a hover just above the grass on the western side of the mansion. The running feet belonged to a man wearing a camouflaged outfit carrying a sniper rifle at the ready. As Dmitri drew a bead on him, the man's Link projected a Star of David, and Dmitri relaxed. These apparently were the cavalry coming to the rescue.

Dmitri motioned to Azurad to move Vesta into the building interior. He kicked out the remaining glass from the broken window and leaped to the grass to meet the second man emerging from the craft.

"Vesta…?" Johan asked as he stretched out his hand in greeting.

"She and Azurad are okay…what happened?"

Eli joined them somewhat winded and told them about the sniper he had killed. Johan then explained how they had been assigned.

"You fellows stand by, please," Dmitri said as he turned toward the mansion front entrance. "I need to consult with Vesta."

Once inside, he located both women in a large sitting room adjacent to the master bedroom on the second floor. Vesta, looking pale and frightened, was sitting in a comfortable-looking chair sipping a glass of water with Jake happily curled up in her lap. Azurad stood behind her, stroking her hair and shoulders.

"Are you both okay?" He sounded brusque but didn't mean it.

They each nodded.

Dmitri took a deep breath. "I know we just arrived, Vesta, but this place simply isn't safe." His voice became soft and calming.

"But, I've waited a long time to settle down in this place," Vesta said, almost pensively. "I want to live out my life here."

"If you do, Vesta, unfortunately, yours will be a short life." Dmitri pulled up a chair so that he was facing her and leaned over, resting his elbows on his knees. "The Federation simply cannot spare the personnel right now to keep you safe here. Obviously, President Jackson has decided not to lend his assistance. The Israelis are stretched to the limit. We're very fortunate they had your back." He looked at her warmly but with real urgency on his face. "I can get you to a secure location that the Caliphate will not find for a while. Then we can figure out what to do."

"Can't we use that hyper-V craft," Vesta pointed out the window, "to go to Mirs or even Iapetus?"

"It's not configured for space flight yet," Dmitri said. "Asshur is working on that right now with the Starchild Institute." He smiled. "It can't take you to Mirs, but it can take you to the place I have in mind."

Vesta stood, unceremoniously dumping Jake to the floor, and walked to the window.

"Please," Dmitri told her as he gently moved her away from the expanse of glass. "That's not safe anymore."

Azurad walked over and took Vesta's hand. "Dmitri's right, Grand-mother; it's not safe here anymore."

From below, Jake rubbed her leg, purring loudly, having already forgiven the unceremonious dumping.

IAPETUS—STARCHILD INSTITUTE

Marc settled into his new responsibilities at the Starchild Institute without fanfare. The essence of his job was simple enough. The Founders had brought with them the vast knowledge databases of the entire Ectarian civilization. Marc was responsible for the continuing development of their technology and its eventual distribution to the peoples of Earth. The Founders themselves were an educated bunch, emphasizing biology and medicine on the one hand and physics and engineering on the other. Except for Lud and Shakbah, who were focused on their longevity research, none of them were actual scientists, however. While most people from his generation on Earth could use modern Earth technology, few really understood the inner workings of the machines they routinely used. So it was with the Founders and Ectarian technology. There was one exception: hyper-V drive technology and its underlying black-hole power source. Eber and his brothers had designed and built *Merkavah* from the ground up. This is what Marc concentrated on initially.

A continuing stream of scientists and technicians arrived almost daily from Earth and the Mirs Complex, seeking to work with this advanced technology or just wanting to get away from the increasing oppression that was Earth. Although Marc had no personal experience with high-tech manufacturing, he quickly discovered that Mirs was full of men and women with some of the best modern manufacturing experience available anywhere in the Solar System. Within a few short weeks, he had a fully functional manufacturing site, put together from the already-in-place manufacturing facilities on Iapetus married to the most up-to-date facilities that had produced the necessary elements of the gigantic Mirs Complex at L4. His people were like kids let loose in a vast toy store. Virtually every day, one of his senior people would come to him with another marvel. It fell to Marc to sort and prioritize.

"Rod…" Marc spoke at the lifelike holographic image of Federation President Rod Zakes seeming to sit in a chair opposite his desk. "We have the capability for building a small fleet of hyper-V craft similar to the *Merkavah*, but with a suite of effective weapons designed for the task." He paused to organize his thoughts. "We also can create another group of hyper-V craft, restricted to in-atmosphere transits." He smiled at the simulacrum. "This is worth billions!"

Rod snorted. "Until some smart guy reverse engineers the driver or power source."

"Well…not really." Marc smiled. "We're building into each craft a kind of deadman's switch so that if anyone actually tries to take apart the drive or power source mechanisms, the craft will blow up with sufficient force to kill anyone nearby."

"And this is a good thing?"

"Each craft will be sold with full disclosure, along with special warnings regarding the deadman switch. I think that's sufficient." Marc emphasized his next point. "What we don't want are Caliphate-owned hyper-V craft running all over the Solar System."

"So, why produce any at all?"

Marc couldn't tell for sure if Rod was serious, so he didn't respond.

"Okay, I agree," Rod continued. "*Merkavah* can't cover all the bases. But here's the thing. Scientists everywhere know about their technology. From my point of view, it's only a matter of time until someone somewhere figures it out independently. Between now and then is our window of opportunity. Just don't let it get out of hand."

Marc was struck by their reversal of power positions. Ever since he had known Rod, Marc had been his superior in whatever chain-of-command was operative. Now, however, Rod had the helm. And Marc agreed with him—you can't stop progress with secrecy. Delay it a bit, maybe, but you can't stop it. "I intend on supplying the first atmospheric unit to the Israelis," Marc said. "Dmitri will get the *Merkavah*, and the first fully functional unit will go to Sam. Then Dmitri will need a small fleet—say five."

Marc continued his discussion with Rod, outlining in a general way how hyper-V craft would be distributed. They also spent time discussing the development of weapons systems for deployment on Iapetus, the Mirs Complex, and at Udachny on the Moon.

"What about Mars?" Rod asked. "Settlement is proceeding apace, orchestrated by Asshur out of Israel and Mirs, and Sam Houston out of Texas and Lone Star Mars."

"That's why Sam gets the second craft. The Mars colonies have a combined total of a few hundred people right now," Marc said, "mostly Israeli and Texan engineers, Mirs construction people, heavy equipment operators, and miners, but in a year or so, I see significant expansion."

He manipulated his Link. A view of Sam Houston's Lone Star Mars appeared between them, also fully visible to Rod in his office. Lone Star Base was located on the eastern floor of Coprates Chasma, the deepest part of the vast Valles Marineris complex, about seven kilometers below the Martian surface. Fifty kilometers separated the northern and southern walls of the canyon. The walls were so steep that the canyon floor was nearly as wide. About fifty kilometers to the east of the base, a thirty-kilometer-wide mountain range filled the middle of the canyon, running for some one hundred eighty kilometers to the east. Nectaris Montes rose nearly to the level of the Martian surface. Its slopes were steep and rugged, but not nearly so much as the Valles Marineris walls. Lone Star Base was located in a two-kilometer-high rocky mound about three kilometers from the canyon's north wall. The bottom of the rocky mound was hollowed out, and as more space became necessary, the hollowing out would continue. Because of the depth of Coprates Chasma, Houston intended to generate oxygen from the vast aquifer located about a kilometer below the canyon floor and release it at the deepest levels of the canyon. He planned to dam the narrow western end of Coprates Chasma and at the eastern extent of Nectaris Montes, to retain the oxygen inside a seven-kilometer-deep, fifty-kilometer-wide, 450-kilometer-long trough.

"Initially," Marc explained, "once Sam expands beyond Lone Star Base, people will live in polymer domes on the canyon floor and in hollowed-out structures carved deep into the canyon walls. In a year or so, people will be able to function on the canyon floor dressed in light-weight pressure suits, breathing with oxygen concentrators."

Marc manipulated his Link again. A view of the Nachal Rachaf settlement appeared between them, also fully visible to Rod in his office.

"They're still living in a dome on the floor at the northern end of the canyon, but the roof and both ends are up and being sealed, and they are digging into both canyon walls," Marc said. "They've tapped into the local aquifer and are generating oxygen. Asshur tells me that the canyon will have a breathable atmosphere in another month or so." Marc dissolved the holoview. "Initially, just like Lone Star, people will breathe through oxygen concentrators, but pressure suits will not be necessary."

He called up another holoview that displayed a panorama of the Nanedi Valles system. From the northernmost point, it extended southward for 200 kilometers and then branched into a 400-kilometer leg to the west and a 930-kilometer leg to the east. Nachal Rachaf was located about 84 kilometers southward in the eastern branch. There the plateau separating the two Nanedi branches was sixty-five kilometers wide. The plateau widened to over 125 kilometers shortly before the western extension of Xanthe Terra 250 kilometers to the south. Total canyon floor area of the extended valley complex was about 7,600 square kilometers with an average width of four to five kilometers. The entire Nanedi complex, including the plateau that separated the two branches, totaled 40,000 square kilometers—about twice the size of Israel.

"In a couple of years," Marc explained, "polymer-domed settlements will be extending out north and south from Nachal Rachaf. Because Nanedi Valles is only five hundred meters or so deep, it will not be possible to build up local oxygen in the near term, but the individual settlements will each cover several square kilometers." Marc dissolved the holoview. "In several years," he added, "Nachal Rachaf will function as the major metropolitan center in an extended Israeli linear settlement running several hundred kilometers north and south along the valley floor. Eventually, settlements will push into the western branch, and the plateau between the branches will be covered with agricultural domes."

"That brings up another question," Rod said. "Aren't these long-term water-carved canyons?"

"That's the best guess."

"So, what happens when we get around to terraforming Mars? Will running water flood out New Israel?"

"Good question." Marc thought for a few seconds. "Dams can solve the problem in the near term. In the long term…well, I guess that's why they call it long term." He smiled. "To be solved later."

✳

Marc looked around at the assembled group in his SI office. Until this moment, he had not given his other *assignment* any real thought. Before *Starchild* departed on its shakedown cruise, Jon Stock and Eber had met privately with him in the Oval Office. They knew of his intention to assume the directorship of SI following Jackson's inauguration, and they wanted to ensure that part of his time would be devoted to learning as much as possible about HIP-84062, the G5-V star system in the constellation of Draco that was their tentative destination following the shakedown cruise.

The men and women in his office were the astronomers, astrophysicists, and cosmologists who chose to become part of SI, in addition to several people from related disciplines who were interested in the project.

Marc's office was obviously a working man's space. Subdued green walls covered with holographs from a long and storied career contrasted with a wood-grained desk that contained the electronic marvels suitable for the Director of the Starchild Institute. Marc occupied a comfortable, ventilated chair behind the desk.

"Here's what we know," Marc said, leaning forward, elbows on his desk. "HIP-eight-forty sixty-two is an unremarkable G5-V high proper-motion star, smaller and hotter than our sun, but radiating about the same amount of energy." Marc sat back and smiled at the group. "You guys have to remember that I am not an astronomer. In fact, I'm not even a scientist, so I'm not going to try and impress you with facts and figures about this star. Odds are that each of you already knows a heck of a lot more than I do about it anyway."

General laughter in the room.

"Here's the thing…back before the Founders arrived, actually, about the time *Cassini II* got underway, Earth astronomers received what seemed like coherent AM radio signals from what we will call Vesta's Star henceforth. The SETI people recorded it, but for a long time, there was no repetition…thus, no confirmation. Then, about the time of the Persian Caliphate Conflict, they received another signal. Similar, but not the same. Since then…nothing."

Marc slid his chair back and stood up, leaning his hands on his desk. "I want you guys to figure this out. You've got whatever resources you need. Two weeks from now, I want to meet with a delegation of representatives you have chosen to review a plan you will have drawn up for how you intend to solve this problem. When *Starchild* returns about a day from now for them, but nearly ten years for us, I want to have all the information Jon Stock and Eber need to justify their expedition to Vesta's Star."

MARS—NACHAL RACHAF

Following the loss of his brother and the first leg of an impassioned campaign in Israel to convince Israelis to emigrate to Mars, Asshur was ready to get to work on the project.

"Okay, Rasam, where are we?"

"We mapped out our first level openings on the west wall at the south end." Sergeant Major Rochlin fiddled with his Link, and a holodisplay of the west wall near the dome appeared above the table before them. "The engineers worked out the plans and have been programming the RVs…" He grinned at Asshur's raised eyebrow. "The Robotic Vaporizers," he explained. "We're installing the exhaust tubes now."

He referred to the large, impervious tubes that would carry the vaporized rock outside Nachal Rachaf. In the low-pressure cold Martian atmosphere, the vapor would condense as a fine powder. Since they would be vaporizing at least a cubic kilometer of rock, the waste volume would be significant. They intended to use the fine dust in many ways, including sealing the edges of the polymer canopy and sealing the ends of the canyon. The engineers had figured out a way to amalgamate the fine grit and were talking about building rock forms across the canyon openings and filling them with a slurry of the fine grit and local gravel that would form solid seals at each end.

"We should be ready later today," Rochlin said, "to commence digging."

"How fast will it proceed?"

"You probably learned this in school, but the builders of Iapetus used half a million RVs, each vaporizing ten thousand cubic meters of rock every day for over seventy-five years, to create the living space on Iapetus. They removed over thirteen million cubic kilometers of rock—we're going to remove one-twentieth of one cubic kilometer initially—that's fifty million cubic meters, and perhaps five times that by the time we're done." He grinned at Asshur. "We got a hundred RVs sitting out there. Give us fifty days—two months at the outmost."

CHAPTER FIVE

EARTH—WASHINGTON D.C.

President Stanford Jackson laid the ancient brown leather note-book on the ornate desk that was now his for at least the next four years. He carefully centered it on the leather desk pad and just looked at it for several minutes, thinking about the men who had handled it over the decades. His worldview was so different from his predecessor's. He was a diplomat and academic, schooled in the ways of the world's elite. He was on a first-name basis with most of Europe's leaders, having attended one or another private school or university with many of them. He chose to view America's position in the world as one nation among peers instead of the de facto leader of the world, as did his predecessor. He opened the notebook carefully, idly wondering what he would find.

The first thing he noticed was that the last entry consisted of several pages in Marc Bowles' neat handwriting and that it covered a time period that stretched from the first contact with the Founders, through the conquest of the Persian Caliphate, to the establishment of the Iapetus Federation. He learned, to his astonishment, that America had played a crucial role in the entire process; that it had, in fact, withheld critical information from its European allies and basically acted the international bully that it was for the entire eight years of the Bowles administration. He noted especially that America had materially assisted the Founders in violating the sovereignty of a dozen nations and had directly participated in the assassination of a score of Islamic clerics around the world.

The entry before that dealt with the journey of *Cassini II*, the discovery of the stowaway, Saeed Ismail, and the subsequent dealings with the Caliph. Jackson was deeply troubled by the rescue of Dr. Carmen Bhuta's parents from the clutches of the Caliph. He was gratified that they were set free but dismayed at how it was accomplished. Again, America—working closely with Israel—played the bully rather than taking the diplomatic path. Even the Iapetus expedition bothered him. It had cost America well over a hundred billion dollars, money that could have been better spent helping the less fortunate here at home. The subsequent events would not have happened, and billions more could have been saved, not to mention the out-of-proportion role Israel had played. And now that the Founders had positioned themselves with the Iapetus Federation and the Starchild Institute, America could do little to recover her investment. In fact, many of America's brightest were streaming out of the country to take up residence in the Federation.

President Jackson sighed as he closed the notebook and tucked it into his top desk drawer. It was time to embrace differences, he told himself. It was time to celebrate the human spirit as expressed within Islam, Buddhism, and the other world perspectives that differed from Judeo-Christianity that had dominated the American view for so long. He had already taken a gigantic step through his running mate, Dr. Syed Shah Bukhari. Images of his taking the oath of office on a *Qur'an* had flashed around the world, proving that America, finally, was headed in the proper direction.

EARTH—MINNEAPOLIS

The Minneapolis City Council was a diverse mixture of thirteen ward representatives presided over by Council President Ali Omar Elmi, from Ward 6, and a direct descendant of the first Somali representative to the City Council, Abdi Warsame, also from Ward 6, and the Mayor, Omar Elmi Dihoud, Ali Omar's father. Somali-Americans represented Wards 3 and 9, and a Middle Eastern man of Arabic extraction represented Ward 10. Of the four million people living in the seven-county region surrounding the twin cities of Minneapolis and St. Paul, more than a million had roots in either Somalia or the Arabic Middle East. Most were practicing Muslims, and in Wards 3, 6, 9, and 10, mosque minarets punctuated the cityscape every few blocks, and amplified calls to prayer could be heard five times daily throughout these four wards. Although Muslims predominated in these wards, many lived about the region served by a scattering of mosques throughout the seven counties.

For Christians, Jews, and people of other faiths—or even no faith—the ubiquitous sounds of Islam had become so regular a part of their lives that they hardly noticed them. Most of the citizens of all thirteen Wards paid little attention to what happened in the City Council. They went about their lives, earning a living, building a family, doing whatever people do in their daily lives. Individual citizens rarely came into contact with the authorities, perhaps only when receiving a parking citation or some other minor traffic infraction. Muslim, Christian, or Jew made little difference in daily living.

Ali Omar counted on this *laissez-faire* attitude when he introduced a resolution to the City Council at a sparsely attended meeting—only a minimum quorum of seven members was present, including the four Muslim Wards. His resolution was simplicity itself. Henceforth in Ward 6, a citizen could choose to submit to the current legal system, as had always been the case, or could choose to submit to Sharia Law. He made no argument. The other three Muslim Wards thought it would be an interesting experiment in dual jurisdiction, and the remaining three councilmen did not object since the resolution would not affect their Wards, and it would be interesting.

The following morning in Ward 6, women on the street not wearing some form of *hijab* were issued a citation and ordered to present it to the Imam of their local mosque. While this went far beyond the City Council's resolution, there were few complaints. Non-Muslim women were excused from meeting with the local Imam so long as they agreed to wear a hijab in the future. Disputes between citizens could be much more easily handled by the local Imam than the hassle of filing suit in the municipal court. Criminal matters that were subject to more draconian measures under Sharia Law were merely shipped to another Ward. Within two months, the traditional legal system in Ward 6 shut down completely, as Sharia subsumed every aspect of legal jurisprudence.

Within a month or so, Wards 3, 9, and 10 followed suit, but not without some genuine protests this time. Whereas Ward 6 was 95% Muslim, the other three Wards were closer to 60% or 70% Muslim, and many citizens did not like the idea of living under Sharia Law. Some just moved out, whereas others remained to fight the system and retain their way of life. Neighborhood police precincts in the four Wards already consisted of many Muslims, and with the shift in legal systems, the police officers who were unwilling to enforce the new policy were summarily dismissed. New Muslim enforcement officers were added so that within six months of the original resolution, the four Muslim wards were under the tight, heavy-handed control of the Imams throughout the Wards.

The rest of Minneapolis looked on these developments with increasing alarm, but the shift to Sharia Law had happened so quietly that in the rest of the nation, it went mostly unnoticed.

EARTH—MIDDLE-EAST

On the appointed day, in every capital city throughout the Arab and Persian Middle East, several thousand well-armed warriors, fanatically dedicated to the Prophet-of-Prophets, Saeed Esmail, viciously attacked the ruling establishments in each region. The attackers seemed to come from nowhere. The attacks were a total surprise. Within two hours, every single government official throughout the entire region was slain.

Saeed Esmail set up his provisional regime in the old Saudi government complex in Riyadh and tasked General Ismail Suleiman to establish a bureaucracy that would enable effective rule over the territory from his Riyadh headquarters.

In record time, General Suleiman kludged together a public works department charged with maintaining and integrating the existing infrastructure and a military department. He decided that he would deal with foreign rulers and dignitaries personally for the time being. He picked able officers from the former Persian Caliphate army to spearhead each effort. Suleiman chose his best commanders to form an army, a million-man army, and he set into motion initiatives that would result in a small air force and a coastal navy. These, he planned to expand later.

As Saeed consolidated his power through General Suleiman, the ancient divisions that had characterized Islam since its inception began to rise in protest. Saeed ruthlessly suppressed these uprisings, killing every Imam or other cleric who dared to raise his voice in protest.

Loyal Imams and clerics throughout the realm proclaimed in every mosque: *"There is but one God—Allah, and Saeed is his Prophet! There is but one Islam, and Saeed showeth the way!"*

Within six months of the inauguration of the new American President, the entire Arab and Persian Middle East was under the absolute control of Saeed Esmail, who exercised his power through his top military commander, General Ismail Suleiman. Any remaining protests were quashed within hours. Sunni, Shia, and the other dozen-or-so versions of Islam were no more. What remained was the Prophet-of-Prophets, Caliph Saeed Esmail.

EARTH—NEW DELHI, INDIA

Dr. Carmen Bhuta discovered that her job as Minister of Health for the Indian Government kept her occupied, or not, as she wished. She suspected that she was offered the position because of her celebrity status as the physician on *Cassini II*. She chose, however, to make it a full-time job, spending most of her time and efforts dedicated to upgrading India's marginal health system to modern standards. As the second most populated state on the planet following China, India still had difficulty keeping its rapidly expanding population healthy. Link technology had made a significant difference. Most educated Indians had a personal Link, but the isolated villages in India's vast interior were lucky to have one Link for the entire village. Medical personnel were even more scarce. Carmen's most significant task was finding enough physicians to make even one available for several villages. She initiated a crash program to educate physician assistants, independent duty nurses, and emergency medical technicians to enable each village to have at least someone with real medical training.

Carmen spent most of her time in her New Delhi offices located in the aging government complex built back in the initial years of the twenty-first century. Because of her celebrity status, the Prime Minister had located her personal office near his. From time to time, the Prime Minister would drop into her office with this or that dignitary to capture some of the aura that still clung to Carmen. She didn't mind since her proximity to the Prime Minister offered her many opportunities to push her medical agenda. Except for her immediate staff, an assistant, and three secretaries, the rest of Carmen's offices and personnel were located in a different wing of the complex. Fortunately, Link communications were first-class, so that she had eyeball contact with any of her department people. As she was very much a hands-on manager, this was important.

✳

The Indian Prime Minister was troubled. He reviewed for the hundredth time the holoimage of the encrypted intelligence communique he had received a week ago. Other than his intelligence chief, whom he trusted implicitly, no one in his government had seen or heard of the document.

The communique summarized the slaughter of government leaders and personnel throughout the Middle East. It detailed the surprisingly strong state of the Caliph's military forces, and it boldly predicted that Pakistan would take advantage of its common Islamic ties to the Caliph to push India from its prominent regional leadership position. It predicted a full-scale attack on India within a year.

He sat quietly for a while longer, considering his options. Then he sent an encrypted communique to the Caliphate requesting a private meeting.

✳

Carmen stepped into the small office that fronted her personal area to speak with one of the three secretaries that supported her efforts and those of her assistant. Despite modern technology, a secretary's desk was still a secretary's desk, with in and out baskets for the paper that no one had yet been able to get rid of, a built-in Link, and a holographic keyboard for those times when voice transcription was impractical. The front of the space consisted of a door and several vertical glass panels with a view of the ornate hallway leading to the Prime Minister's offices. Carmen was discussing the progress of medical equipment that had been shipped to remote southern Chhattisgarh but had not yet arrived, and no one knew where it was. She lifted her head at a commotion in the hallway.

To Carmen's utter surprise, two men passed the vertical windows. Both were swarthy but lighter-skinned than the typical Indian. One, dressed in a military uniform, was tall and sported a full close-cropped beard. The second was at least twenty centimeters shorter, had a full-length flowing beard, and wore a simple sackcloth robe. His right arm ended in a brown leather cup. Carmen started and turned her back to the windows.

It was Saeed Esmail!

✳

FFive-star General Ismail Suleiman walked down the ornate hallway leading to the Indian Prime Minister's offices at a pace that just exceeded the natural gait of the much shorter man walking beside him. The general's uniform was bedecked with medals that made a slight clinking sound as he walked. He wore a blue sash from his left shoulder to his right hip announcing his position as Chairman of the Caliphate's Council of Military Commanders. In stark contrast, the man at his side wore a plain sackcloth robe and sandals and carried a rustic staff.

Behind them strode two large bodyguards, dressed in black and displaying the Caliphate crest on their turbans—a severed hand holding a dagger. They were armed with steel scimitars and bejeweled daggers.

The general looked down at Saeed Esmail, his Grand Ayatollah, his Caliph, the Prophet-of-Prophets, and smiled inwardly. *He can call himself by any title he wishes—but I control him.*

They passed the offices of the Minister of Health without noticing the activity behind the windows. As they arrived at the entryway to the Prime Minister's offices, they were met by the man himself, dressed in traditional Indian attire, who greeted them with folded hands and a slight bow that somehow contained not even the faintest bit of deference.

"Please join me," the Prime Minister said in perfect Arabic, indicating that they should enter his offices.

"We are honored, thank you," the general answered back in perfect Hindi. They followed the Prime Minister into his large, comfortable office. As they settled onto a burgundy leather settee, the General spoke up. "At your request, we have come to you quietly and privately." The general looked around the office. "Is this meeting being recorded in any way?" he asked, gazing at the Prime Minister.

The Prime Minister silently looked at the general for several seconds before waving his hand toward the door. Someone closed the door, and the Prime Minister said, "Now we are in complete privacy."

General Suleiman leaned back into the leather, smiled, and said, "Now we will talk."

Initially, General Suleiman described how Saeed's desert warriors had simultaneously occupied every Muslim capital and overthrown the elite rulers who had been in place since the destruction of the Persian Caliphate by the Founders. He made sure that the Prime Minister understood that this was only the beginning of a global Jihad that would bring the entire world under the Caliph's rule. Suleiman then proceeded to outline a plan where India would supply the fledgling Caliphate with arms, munitions, aircraft, warships, especially those with tactical and strategic nuclear weapons along with long-range delivery platforms. India would provide all necessary training, including on-scene advisors. All these would be in exchange for unlimited oil at cost, unrestricted access to the Caliphate marketplace, and a non-aggression pact that would assure India's "neutrality" during the coming global conflict. "India," the general assured the Prime Minister, "will play an important background role during the Jihad, and thereafter will be a full partner with the Caliphate, sharing the spoils of conflict and benefitting from the role of ruler thereafter."

When General Suleiman had completed his presentation, he and Saeed sat quietly, awaiting the Prime Minister's response. The General was playing his hand close to his chest. He intended to intimidate the Prime Minister just sufficiently to cause him to sign the agreement without backing India against a wall that would force the Prime Minister to wage war on the Caliphate.

The Prime Minister slowly squared his desk pad, straightened an ornate silver pen on the pad, and then opened the top drawer of his desk and extracted a piece of parchment-like paper. He wrote carefully and precisely in English, the diplomatic language of choice, laying out the details of General Suleiman's proposal. He signed and dated it with a flourish, handed it to the general for his signature, and activated his desk Link to create a permanent record—one that General Suleiman was sure would remain private and secure.

"Thank you, Gentlemen," the Prime Minister said in Arabic. "My subordinates will work out the details with your staff." He handed the agreement to General Suleiman and ushered them to the door, where waiting personal guards escorted them to the building's general assembly area.

EARTH—WASHINGTON D.C.

Outgoing President Bowles had told him in this very room barely six months ago, "Keep your eye on the Middle East." President Jackson pulled the leather-covered notebook from his desk drawer and idly turned its pages. It had been a busy six months. Founder Aram had been shot, a fact not known to the world at large, that thought he had been killed in an avalanche. There had been a serious attempt on Founder Vesta's life, and now she had vanished, probably safely ensconced somewhere protected by Dmitri Gagarin's Iapetus Federation security force. Then there was the Sharia Law problem in Minneapolis. From Jackson's perspective, people should be able to live under whatever legal system they wished. It wasn't up to America, Jackson told his advisors, to impose its legal system on citizens who preferred Sharia Law. His White House Council, however, had informed him otherwise, that imposition of any jurisprudence but American constitutional law was illegal anywhere in the United States. To make his point, he referred the President to a Florida case back in the second decade of the previous century, where a local judge had cited to Shira Law in a decision. His reference was challenged in the Court of Appeals, where it was upheld. The U.S. Supreme

Court eventually overturned the Court of Appeals. Jackson made a mental note to address this inequality with congressional leaders in the near future.

And now, the Caliphate had reemerged in the Middle East. Intelligence reports were spotty, but his embassy staffs in every Middle East country except Israel had summarily been sent home. Satellite overflights showed nothing out of the ordinary, but something was seriously amiss.

Jackson leafed through the leather notebook, stopping at the pages describing the destruction of the Persian Caliphate navy and air force. It was pretty clear that whatever was happening over there now, was happening without warships and planes because when the Founders had completed their intervention, the Persian Caliphate had neither. Jackson was deeply worried about events over there, but he had made nonintervention his strongest point to the American people. In fact, to this end, in just six months, he had already reduced the country's offensive strike capability by over fifty percent. America no longer could launch an attack against another country that had any kind of defense capability. Fortunately, the new Caliphate was on the other side of the world and not a threat to the U.S.

On his Link, he called up his intelligence briefing from a couple of hours ago. Minneapolis was not included.

EARTH—SAVANNAH RIVER, GEORGIA

Dmitri set up a secure communication Link to Iapetus describing the details of what had happened at the plantation. Since it would take about three hours plus processing time on Iapetus before he received an answer, and Vesta's safety was utterly compromised at the plantation, Dmitri told Rod that he would take her to the Caspian Loop and place her with Lud and Shakbah at Mirs. If they could get the *Merkavah* to the Sevastopol Skyport before Vesta launched, fine, but he would not wait for the hyper-V craft to arrive.

Dmitri sat in an easy chair across an ornate coffee table from Vesta in the drawing-room of the stately mansion. Jake was out exploring the mansion. Vesta and Azurad sat together on an elegant couch. Vesta had recovered somewhat from the immediate ordeal, but her face was still pale. Azurad held her left hand. Vesta stroked a purring Jake, who had returned and discovered her lap, with her right.

"Vesta," Dmitri said gently, "we have no idea who else is out there. The Caliphate seems determined to kill you. The only safe place for you right now is back on Iapetus or at Mirs with Lud and Shakbah. *Merkavah* returned to Iapetus, so it will take at least an hour-and-a-half to get her back. I've informed Rod, but there's just no time."

Azurad squeezed Vesta's hand and put a comforting arm around her shoulders.

"The Israeli hyper-V craft out there," he pointed to the western window of the room, "has atmosphere capability only, but we can get anywhere on Earth in a hurry." He smiled warmly at Vesta. "I propose to take you to the Caspian Loop, run by some old friends of mine. We'll get you to Mirs before the Caliphate knows you left Georgia." Dmitri rose to his feet.

"This was going to be our final home," Vesta said wistfully. "What do you think, Azurad?"

"If we wish to live, Grandmother, I see no choice."

Sensing the imminent departure of his humans, Jake scampered up and clambered into his traveling cage.

Azurad assisted Vesta to her feet, and—arm-in-arm—they strolled toward the stained-glass-embellished entryway to the mansion, accompanied by Jake's satisfied purr.

✳

Vesta walked up the ramp with Azurad to enter the sleek, saucer-shaped hyper-V craft. Visually, it was almost indistinguishable from *Merkavah*, but its control module was designed for atmosphere flight only. Vesta had participated in the decision to give this limited craft to the Israelis, and now she wished she had championed giving them a fully capable craft like *Merkavah*. Over the years of their travel forward through the centuries of Earth's history, and then her close association with the *Cassini II* crew, and with Rod Zakes and Marc Bowles, Vesta had gained a great deal of sophisticated insight about the science and engineering of her own Ectarian culture and its interface with that of Earth. When they made a limited hyper-V craft available to Israel, it seemed the natural thing to do. Gradually introduce the interplanetary and then interstellar capability of the fully applied technology. From her current perspective, that decision seemed shortsighted.

While she, Jake, and Azurad took their places in the comfortable cabin seats, Vesta watched Dmitri speak softly with the two Israelis, Johan and Eli. They nodded, and Johan placed a secure Link call. From Vesta's position, the image was scrambled. Dmitri participated in the call for several seconds, and then Jon terminated it. Dmitri turned to Vesta.

"These boys work for Daniel Ben-Gurion, Vesta," he told her, "and he has just authorized me to use this craft to get you to safety." He called up his Link and then said to Johan, "Okay, you've got your coordinates."

Vesta was used to hyper-V travel, so she settled into her chair with Jake on her lap to await the end of the short trip.

EARTH—SEVASTOPOL, CRIMEA

The Caspian Loop was a joint project of Andrey Orlov and the Russian Government. Orlov rose from the ashes of the twenty-first-century business empire built by billionaire Roman Abramovich. He parlayed his wealth into a controlling interest in Mirs Corp and set about gaining control of the Baikonur Cosmodrome, which had been leased by Kazakhstan to the Russian Republic. Orlov initially used the Cosmodrome launch facilities to create the Mirs Complex at L4. When Slingshot in the Equatorial Pacific proved successful, he constructed his own launch loop stretching from the northwestern Black Sea to the Kazakh Steppe east of Baikonur. He used the Caspian Loop for the rest of the construction until Isidor Sokolov's Moon mining enterprise gave him a cheaper source for raw materials.

A sizeable nuclear facility on the Ukrainian coast south of Odessa powered the Caspian Loop's western end. A massive nuclear complex in the Kazakh Steppe powered the eastern end. The western skytower dropped to a socket just outside Sevastopol, so that this sleepy resort town transformed itself into the world's largest seaport/spaceport, eclipsing the launch activities of the Baker Island complex in the Western Pacific.

Dmitri had made prior arrangements with his old friend and mentor, Orlov, so that when the Israeli hyper-V craft flashed into the rainy skies above Sevastopol, hardly anyone noticed as the intensely black saucer-shaped craft settled its five legs softly on the socket's helipad. A hatch opened, and a ramp slid outward to the pad, met by a man and woman wearing pale blue uniforms of the Mirs Security Force. Vesta appeared at the head of the ramp with Dmitri gripping her right elbow and Azurad holding her left hand. Dmitri carried Jake's travel cage under his right arm. The three quickly joined the security guards and were hustled into a side door of the Launch Loop passenger terminal.

Since the early days of Slingshot in the Equatorial Pacific, the transfer capsules used to transport people to the launch loop skyports had changed. No longer were they intimidating, claustrophobic private cocoons for eight to ten people. Instead, they ranged from single-passenger modules to bus-like capsules that could carry up to twenty or more passengers in an environment ranging from minimal to outright luxury.

Stripped to its essence, a skytower consisted of a cable, a suspensor permanently anchored to the cable at points all along the cable, and a double lift cable that passed through spacers attached to the suspensor. The two-part lift cable consisted of a high-speed three-gee boost cable and a one-gee lift cable. The boost cable accelerated a capsule upward at three-gees for ten kilometers, handed it off to the lift cable for a seventy-five-kilometer, one-gee acceleration phase, with a final upward coasting freefall for the last fifteen kilometers. While the system was elaborate, with its double driving mechanisms, one to supersonic velocities, overall, it still consisted of a supporting cable and an elevator with a pulley-supported cable system.

The big difference between then and now was the evolving passenger modules and the size and luxury of the skyport itself. Initially, the Caspian Loop was used exclusively to transport construction materials for the L4 Mirs Complex. The skyport functioned only as a short-stop waystation for cargo-laden capsules destined for L4.

Cargo capsules stopped just sufficiently long to attach kick thrusters and transfer to the rail—a couple of minutes at most. The skyport was occupied by Mirs personnel, who maintained the facility and ensured that the kick thruster rack was stocked and available to keep the material moving on its way to L4. Once Sokolov's Moon mining enterprise could supply raw materials the Mirs complex needed, the Caspian Loop began to focus on passengers and upgraded its socket launch facility in Sevastopol and the skyport a hundred kilometers above the resort city. It still transported highly refined manufactured items, however, until the Mirs manufacturing facilities took over all manufacturing tasks. At this stage, the Sevastopol Skyport was a waystation to L4, the Moon, and beyond, but also was a top-of-the-line hotel for the well-heeled adventurous traveler.

Vesta had never seen a launch loop, let alone ridden one. The Ectarians had developed launch loops, but they had been entirely displaced by hyper-V technology that arrived on the scene less than a century afterward. She had learned about them when she was a schoolgirl as part of her history studies. Vesta felt safe with Dmitri at her side and comfortable holding her granddaughter-in-law's hand as they followed the security guards through a back corridor of the socket launch facility.

"We have arranged to transport you in a private capsule carrying only the three of you and one attendant," the attractive female guard said as they approached what appeared to be the side of a horizontal cylinder. When Jake greeted the attendant with a quiet mew, she added, "and one tabby cat." She said something into her Link that Vesta could not hear, and the side of the cylinder slid up and over the cylinder top, exposing interior and several easy-chair-like seats, looking much like the interior of a luxury private jet. An efficient-looking Ukrainian lass in her mid-twenties beckoned them to enter. She smiled at Vesta, her blue eyes twinkling beneath blond hair held in place with an ivory hairpiece, a pleasant contrast to her pale blue pants suit.

"Welcome aboard the Caspian Loop, Earth Mother," she said in flawless English. "As soon as you are settled in your seats, we will insert the capsule into the stream and get you underway." She pointed Vesta, Azurad, and Dmitri with Jake in his travel cage to their individual seats. "Once you are safely strapped in, we will move forward, tilt to vertical, and commence the boost leg of our journey. The acceleration is mild and will last for about twenty seconds. Then we will enter the lift stage, where you will feel normal gravity for about four minutes. During the third stage, we will coast for about two minutes—you will be weightless. Then, with the return of weight, we will tilt to horizontal." She smiled. "That's right, in about seven minutes, we will have arrived at Sevastopol Skyport." She checked each passenger's safety harness and cooed gentle sounds to Jake, who seemed a bit skittish. "At the skyport, you will feel some movement as the launch pouch and kick thruster are attached, and then you will once again experience acceleration as the magnetic rail brings us to escape velocity. Once we detach from the rail, we will be in free fall until we arrive at the Mirs complex, except for several short maneuvering bursts from the kick thruster." The attendant took her own seat. "Should anything go catastrophically wrong during ascent, your seat will encase you in a clear, impervious bubble, launch itself away from the capsule, and bring you to a gentle parachute landing where you will be met by safety and security personnel." She smiled at Vesta again. "This isn't Ectarian technology, but it's the best we have. You will be perfectly safe."

Vesta relaxed into her seat, allowing it to adjust itself to her small body. She smiled at Azurad and Dmitri. "I guess we're ready," she said as the door slid into place, sealing them inside, and the capsule moved forward and tilted to vertical.

A pleasant female voice filled the capsule, counting down the seconds to the launch—*...three...two...one...*

MARS—NACHAL RACHAF

The automated RV excavation progressed with virtually no delays. Martian rock proved no match for the advanced Ectarian technology behind the Robotic Vaporizers. Asshur followed the pattern used to hollow the Iapetus living space, except the cavern roof was only between 100 and 200 meters high, depending on location and purpose, instead of the two-kilometer-high Iapetus roof. The ceiling was supported by ten-meter-thick solid rock columns left in place every 200 meters as the vaporizing progressed.

Rochlin's crew worked on rotating shifts so that there was a nearly continuous stream of rock powder surging out of the exhaust tube. He assigned several crew members to the task of blending the hot rock vapor with the sandy regolith that made up the floor of the canyon beyond Nachal Rachaf into a cement-like slurry that they used to build the wall that would eventually plug the canyon end.

During the original outfitting back in Israel, Asshur had procured several sandblasters. Two of Rochlin's crew had modified these to accommodate Q-carbon dust. One of Asshur's engineers developed a mechanism to give the Q-carbon a static charge as it exited the blaster nozzle, causing the fine powder to stick to the rock surface inside the ever-growing cavern.

"So, how does this work?" Rochlin asked Asshur as they walked into the cavern entrance directly opposite the dome.

"Like this," Asshur said as he tugged on the hose trailing behind him, indicating that the guys outside should feed him more hose. Asshur squeezed the trigger, and a stream of black powder exited the nozzle to splash across the wall. Asshur adjusted the width and strength of the stream until he was able to move the nozzle back and forth like an oversized airbrush, leaving a dark black layer on the wall.

"That black layer," he said, "is just a couple of atoms thick, but it is the hardest known substance. It forms a matrix harder than diamond." He grinned at the Sergeant Major. "This stuff lines the hollow sphere at the center of Iapetus, where a mini-black-hole provides power for their entire kit-and-caboodle."

"So, the whole interior will be coal black?"

"That would be depressing." Asshur laughed. "We can coat this with anything we want, giving it any color we want, make it look like anything."

"I've studied the overall plans, of course," Rochlin said, "so I understand where we are headed. But I still don't really see the big picture. We have these hollowed-out large caverns interconnected by spacious passageways. Why didn't you just hollow out a whole bunch of smaller, house-like, or apartment-like openings that people could use for living? Why all this open space?"

Asshur and Rochlin had been so preoccupied that they really never had the chance to have this discussion. Old military guy that he was, Rochlin had no problem following directions, but it was evident to Asshur that it was time to explain the entire concept to him.

"The Iapetus living space is so realistic," Asshur said, "that it is virtually impossible not to think of it as earth and sky. We do not intend to do precisely the same thing here, but we want a reasonable approximation of what Iapetus has. We want the caverns to feel like open space. We want villages with houses and gardens and trees. We want towns with apartment buildings and office structures. We want a changing sky, flowing water, birds and bees—basically, we want to reconstruct a mini, Earth-like ecosystem inside these canyon walls. When we have completed the canyon containment, we will have an Earth-like atmosphere inside the entire canyon. We will fit the openings into our caverns with automatic closures for safety should a cataclysmic event disrupt the canyon environment.

"There's more, too. Eventually, we will terraform the entire surface of Mars. Among other things, this means an ocean, flowing rivers, the whole drill. Nanedi Valles is pretty well isolated from the sea's edge that will cover much of Mars' northern hemisphere, but we're taking no chances. We'll install a quarter-kilometer-thick malgalith dam at the northern leg of the East and West Nanedi Valles juncture."

Asshur gripped Rochlin's shoulder. "You guys are laying the foundation for all this."

✳

True to Rochlin's prediction, two months after they started, the main cavern complex was hollowed out and ready for refinements. The walls were coated with Q-carbon, and Rochlin's team was making good progress on the ceilings and pillars.

Using Sam Houston's *Saracen*, Asshur brought several Israeli urban planners to Nachal Rachaf so they could commence the process of turning hollow black caverns into livable space. Then he began to bring others with skills covering the vast complex of human habitation. They arrived on an almost daily basis, bringing their dreams and the talents to make those dreams a reality. All too soon, the project grew beyond his ability to manage it by himself. The complexities were too many and daunting. Asshur stepped back from his prior close management and passed most of his responsibilities to people he viewed as more capable than himself.

Within a month or so, the atmosphere within the enclosed canyon was breathable, using oxygen concentrators, and the pressure was sufficient for the population to stop using pressure suits.

Late one afternoon, Rochlin approached Asshur. "We got a problem, Boss."

"And exactly what kind of problem could possibly worry my Sergeant Major miracle worker?"

"Things are happening outside…"

"So…?"

"Well, a stone retaining wall for the rock powder was destroyed, and the powder in that stash was disbursed over a wide area. I found vehicle tracks where none of my vehicles has ever been. Two of my guys followed them north into Nanedi but lost the track on rocks near the eastern valley wall." Rochlin spread his weathered hands. "Somebody's out there, Boss, and they're up to no good."

Asshur told Rochlin about the incident back when he and Aram had picked up the load of Q-carbon at Lone Star. "Sam is convinced that the cliff collapse was no accident."

"Who would want to do something like that?" Rochlin asked, perplexity evident in his furrowed face. "I mean, we all got to work together to survive here."

"I ran into several people during my travels in Israel who thought Mars should be left as it is," Asshur said thoughtfully. "Could some of them have found their way here…or perhaps to Lone Star back when they were bringing in workers wholesale?" He stopped talking to think about the problem.

The who, how, and why escaped him entirely. To sabotage human activity on Mars…it was almost unthinkable. Israelis…Texans? It just didn't seem possible. The only party he knew about that might have such an agenda was the Caliphate, but there was no way they could be on Mars. Every space-worthy hyper-V craft was accounted for, of that he was confident. It was an immediate problem that needed to be solved.

Asshur checked his Link to see if he had satellite coverage to Lone Star. As luck would have it, he still had ten minutes left of a thirty-minute window. "Sam…" He spoke to the figure that coalesced before him. "We have a problem here." Asshur then described what Rochlin had told him.

"We've identified the culprits," Sam told him, and he related how Chino and Rico had ripped off equipment and supplies. "We lost them a hundred klicks east of Nectaris Montes on the floor of Marineris, headed east." Sam's holoimage touched his Link. "I just sent you a list of what they took. We haven't connected them with any organization yet, but I'm certain that they are not Israeli."

"We're running out of sky," Asshur said. "We absolutely need to orbit a ServerSky swarm…" The holoimage of Sam flickered several times and winked out.

CHAPTER SIX

MARS—NEW ISRAEL

Three full years had passed since *Starchild* departed on her historic voyage. Nachal Rachaf was up and running. In fact, except for the lighter gravity, inside the carved-out canyon walls, Nachal Rachaf was indistinguishable from anywhere in Israel. Outside, on the canyon floor, one had to wear a ubiquitous oxygen concentrator that fed pure oxygen into each nostril. The pressure was about 750 mbar, or about what one would experience on Earth at 2,500 meters, and the temperature averaged about 25 degrees Celsius. Consequently, shirt-sleeves were the order of the day. Up near the translucent cover, artificial lights filled the canyon with daylight-like brightness that mimicked the diurnal cycle at Israel's latitude on Earth.

Out on the floor of Nanedi Valles, spreading north and south from the curtain-enclosed canyon, rose hundreds of transparent domed habitats, many interconnected by enclosed walkways. Typical size of these domes was 100 to 200 meters across. They housed a myriad of crops and grazing animals that supplied virtually all the nutritional needs of New Israel, as the entire settlement was now called. As inside Nachal Rachaf, the dome interiors required neither oxygen concentrators nor pressure suits. On the floor of Nanedi Valles outside the domes, however, pressure suit protection with full breathing gas was still necessary.

New Israel's population had passed the one million mark and was increasing daily as transports from Earth disgorged thousands of permanent settlers from Israel. A specially built hyper-V transport that could hold 500 passengers made daily trips from each of several Launch Loops on Earth. Israelis, and people who identified with Israelis and who wanted to settle in New Israel, found their way to the nearby launch points of the Sahara Loop at Atar or the Mediterranean Loop at Mallorca, or to the launch points of six of the seven other launch loops that had been built following the success of Slingshot and the Caspian Loop. Caliphate rules prohibited Israelis from using the Saudi Loop at Mecca.

Asshur still was the titular head of New Israel, but the settlement actually ran itself in much the way the old Israeli Moshavim ran themselves, with an added collectivist element borrowed from the Kibbutzim. Unlike New Israel, the typical Israeli Moshav had relatively few members and, in its original conception, ran as a co-operative farm where the land was equally divided among the family units, and was worked cooperatively or individually as the situation dictated. This was in contrast to the Kibbutzim, that were conceived as perfected socialist communes, where everything was owned by the community, and profits were shared equally. Moshavim purchasing and sales were on a co-op basis so that better farmers and harder workers received greater gain. These Moshavim evolved from their simple origins in the early 1920s into complex communities that appeared much like modern gated co-housing communities in the United States. Mutual interdependence for sheer survival gave New Israel some of the original socialist trappings of the first Kibbutzim, and the universal Link made it possible for the community to make many decisions collectively, despite a population that exceeded a million. On the other hand, land was parceled out equally to all new arrivals, insofar as they wanted land, and what the new arrivals did with their land was entirely up to them individually.

"Rasam, when Aram and I conceived of Nachal Rachaf," Asshur told Mordecai Rochlin, "neither of us really thought past creating the habitat, creating a place where Israelis could live free of terrorism and fear." He smiled warmly and gripped his grizzled friend's arm. "And you did most of that." He leaned back in his chair, hands interlocked behind his head, and glanced around his spare office space. "And now, Aram's gone, and I am saddled with hundreds of committees, dozens of counsels, and I hear they're forming a Knesset." He sighed. "I do physics and communications…I don't do governance…" His voice trailed off.

"The hell you don't!" Rochlin said. "You created all this." He waved his hands around.

"You know better," Asshur commented with a smile. "But, there's still fourteen million people back in Israel, ripe for a Caliphate attack." He paused in thought. "My job is to get them here. You, my friend, have the mentality to govern those already here. Soon enough, the Knesset will take over, and you can focus on further expansion."

"We can accommodate three to four million in Nachal Rachaf itself," Rochlin said, "once we have fully completed the excavations. The Nanedi Valles complex can take all the rest, and their offspring for several generations."

MARS—NANEDI VALLES

Ra'id Kassab and Abdul-Hasid Naseri (aka Chino and Rico Delgado) slipped *Rover-2* along the floor of a narrow canyon extending southeast twenty-five kilometers from Nanedi West up to the plateau. Their goal lay forty kilometers eastward on the western rim of Nanedi East, overlooking the most recent Israeli dome complex, 700 meters below. The afternoon sun behind them cast long shadows from the rocks strewn along their path on the plateau, and their own shadow stretching ahead of them grew longer as they progressed.

"You drivin' good, Bro," Chino said as Rico turned south to avoid a kilometer-wide crater that blocked their path halfway to their destination.

"Wait'll I thread the needle," Rico retorted, referring to two slightly overlapping craters twenty kilometers ahead of them. A narrow, five-kilometer-long ridge of loose rubble and impact leavings separated the two craters. "I gonna show you some real drivin' then."

Thirty minutes later, Chino leaned forward as Rico came to a halt at the western end of the needle. "You sure you can do this, Bro?" Chino asked with a hint of concern in his voice.

To their left, the crater wall dropped nearly vertically for several hundred meters and then shallowed to the crater pan. To their right, loose rock piled at the smaller crater edge formed an unstable support structure for the narrow path. One wrong move, and they would end up sliding or even tumbling into one of the craters. They would probably be able to climb out of the smaller crater, but a tumble into the larger one could cripple their vehicle or even kill them, and if they survived, getting out would be a real problem.

"Whad'ya mean? Course I can do it!"

"We can go 'round the small crater, Bro. Don' wanna fail our Jihad before we really get goin'."

Rico turned scornfully. "Shee-it!"

"I know you ain't afraid, Bro, but our Jihad's bigger'n us. Let's be safe."

At that moment, the front right wheel dipped sharply down as the underlayment gave way. Rico slammed *Rover-2* into reverse and poured power to the middle and back wheels. Rock shards spit forward as the giant wheels spun, looking for traction. The rear right wheel began to dip as it eroded the underlying loose rock, and the entire rover tipped to the right. Rico increased power to the middle and back left wheels as the rover heaved backward and the front wheels regained traction on the loose surface.

Rico lifted his hands from the controls and grinned at Chino. "Looks like Allah tellin' me sump'n."

"You ain't wrong, Bro."

"Okay," Rico said, matter-of-factly, "let's go south."

✳

Two hours later, *Rover-2* pulled up to the edge of a drop-off that overlooked the newest Israeli settlement 700 meters below on the valley floor. The sun was about to drop below the horizon, but a domed sky full of stars illuminated the stark Martian terrain. Chino and Rico, in their pressure suits and spherical helmets, stood at the edge and took in the vast panorama of the valley below, illuminated not only by starlight but also by the artificial illumination from the settlement. They counted at least two-dozen domes, the largest about 200 meters across.

"Let's do it, Bro," Chino said and turned toward the rover.

During the next hour or so, they each drilled three holes down to a depth of three meters across a section of the ledge that jutted over the valley. Then they packed the holes with high explosives and set detonators designed to trigger on a CDMA signal from *Rover-2*.

"Okay, Chino, let's back off and blow it!"

MARS—NANEDI VALLES EAST

Mordecai Rochlin exited his rover dressed in regular street clothing, breathing deeply the moisture-laden air filled with pungent odors of livestock and growing maize. The sun, visible through the transparent dome, was approaching the western rim 700 meters above this newest Israeli settlement, some thirty kilometers south of Nachal Rachaf along the eastern Nanedi Valles floor. The valley floor was about seven kilometers wide here, and this dome was one of several placed on a rise along the valley spine. Several dozen similar domes occupied the valley floor, many connected by two-meter high transparent archways. Most were agricultural, but a half dozen along the valley spine, including this one, held living quarters. Where canyon wall met valley floor both east and west, mining and refining operations filled two strings of domes. The vast array of minerals available to these mining operations resulted in virtually everything the settlers needed to construct their domes and forge a living community out of the valley's sandy surface. As Rochlin gazed about, it was genuinely difficult to realize that he was on Mars and not inside one of the Negev Desert dome settlements the Israelis had erected during the last ten years. If it weren't for the lower gravity...

As the sun passed over the western canyon rim, Rochlin thought he saw the silhouettes of two individuals outlined against the still bright sky. It was difficult to be sure because the wall was some three kilometers away, and the rim was 700 meters above that. He turned to Levi Bar-Lev, the settler who oversaw the activities at this southernmost outpost.

"Did you see that?" he asked in Founder Speak. "On the rim…do you have anyone up there? Are you guys doing anything up there?" A majority of the population was fluent in Founder Speak, and there was even a movement to make Founder Speak the official language of Nachal Rachaf and the entire Nanedi Valles.

"Not that I'm aware of…and, nope, I didn't see anything. There are just a few of us here, and we have no business up there. We have enough to do right here." Levi spread his arms out to encompass the broad valley with its scattering of domes.

They stood together silently, watching darkness spread across the valley as bright stars filled the deepening, cloudless sky between the canyon walls.

As the night deepened, they turned to the entrance of the Levi's home, a few meters from the dust-covered rover. Suddenly the western sky lit up with a brilliant orange-white flash, followed by a roaring sound that reached them through the thin Martian atmosphere and the dome skin.

"Grab your people and get into the rover," Rochlin shouted at Levi as he sprinted to the rover. "Saboteurs did this at Lone Star, from the southern rim. It created a huge rock slide that traveled more than thirty klicks across Coprates Chasma. Of course, that rim was six klicks high, but still…better to be safe than sorry."

The falling cliff must have been deafening nearby, but Rochlin could barely hear it through the open doors of the rover. He did not anticipate that the slide would reach the valley spine, but he was concerned about flying rocks penetrating the domes. This settlement had two rovers, but he didn't know where they were stored. Every settler knew how to respond to an air emergency, but their established routine would most likely cause people to let their guards down.

Levi's family crowded into the rover, and Rochlin turned it to the west so they could observe the happenings through the transparent dome. He had his headlight beams on full strength and widest dispersion. After several minutes, they saw a shadow enter the light beams. The shadow resolved into a large boulder rolling rapidly up the slope toward the dome.

"Will it hit the dome?" one of the kids shouted.

"Might," Levi said. "Then again, might not," he added as it came to a rolling stand-still several meters from the dome.

That's when a smaller boulder hit the sandy ground next to the large boulder and bounced right over the dome. An even smaller one hit the dome and bounced back to roll down the slope. Then one crashed into the large boulder, splintered into many smaller pieces; several penetrated the dome. They landed in a maize field fifty meters short of the rover. Dome atmosphere began rushing through the cuts, threatening to tear them larger.

"Suits!" Levi and Rochlin shouted nearly simultaneously.

While Levi's family members scrambled, Rochlin told Levi, "My suit has TBH boots. Do you have patch material nearby?"

Levi pointed to a shed at the near edge of the maize field.

"Quickly," Rochlin told him, "pull out some sheets and follow me to right below the rips."

Levi extracted several light-weight sheets from the shed and caught up with Rochlin, who was already halfway to the point below the rips.

"Hand me a sheet," Rochlin said, the air whipping past him toward the rips.

With sheet in hand, he activated his TBH boots and rocketed toward the rips, ten meters above him. He knew he could not sustain the upward momentum very long against the Martian gravity but hoped to get enough out of the thrust to put the patch in place. Gravity slowed him as he approached the first rip, held the patch horizontally in front of him, and let it go as gravity pulled him to a stop two meters short of the rip. As he began to fall back, the wind picked up the patch and sucked it against the dome surface, effectively sealing the first rip.

"Hand me the next one," Rochlin said as he touched ground.

Three more times and the rips were sealed. Molecular and solar action would work on the seals, integrating them into the dome material and eventually bringing them to full transparency. Nothing further needed to be done.

Levi activated his local Link. "Report your status!"

"That was a close one," Rochlin said as he stripped out of his suit in the rover. "What would you have done had I not been here?"

"I have a scissor lift in the barn." Levi pointed. "Say a half-hour to position it, and then another half-hour to ride up, position the patches, reposition, etc." He grinned. "We would have survived, but thanks for your help."

Rochlin shrugged with a smile.

Levi turned his attention back to his Link. "It looks like the other spine domes are okay. Mine was the only one damaged. So, what's this all about?" he asked as they entered the house.

Rochlin told him about the attack at Lone Star and the attacks near Nachal Rachaf during its construction.

"There's clearly a group of unknown size deliberately sabotaging our efforts here and at Lone Star," Rochlin said. "We don't know who they are, their motive, who's backing them (if anyone at all); all we know is that they are like ghosts, giving no warning before they strike."

"Hold it! I've got a report coming in from the mining sites directly beneath the rock slide." Levi held his hand up, paying close attention to his private Link audio connection. "No one was killed… there are some minor injuries, and five guys are pinned under the rocks in their rigs. They're okay, but it will take some time to get to them." He looked around the room. "I'd better get over there to help rescue them."

"Need some help?" Rochlin asked.

"Need all the hands we can get," Levi said as he donned his suit, his two older boys joining them.

IAPETUS—STARCHILD INSTITUTE

Maarc Bowles activated his Link and watched the image of Rod Zakes materialize before him. Although he had been using Link technology most of his life, it still amazed him every time he found himself talking with an image that appeared as real as life.

"Three years," he said. "I wonder if I will ever get used to the concept. They're out there, time virtually at a standstill, while we get older every day…" His voice trailed off, and Rod kept his silence. "I think it's time for a change, Rod," he said finally.

Rod raised his eyebrows, and Marc continued. "Sam Houston is still running VASIMR driven freighters to Mars. They're fast enough compared to four years ago, but you know they're ancient technology next to hyper-V craft. We built a hyper-V freighter for Asshur to transport Israelis to New Israel, but except for a couple of Earth-bound craft and the *Merkavah*, *Saracen*, *RH*, and Dmitri's five, there are no other operational hyper-V craft." Marc paused and looked at Rod. "I think it's time to open the market to space-worthy hyper-V craft."

Rod started to interrupt, but Marc held up his hand. "I know where you're going, Rod. Besides the deadman switch, we would build in a remote kill switch in each unit that would deactivate the hyper-V drive on our command, and that would return the craft to Iapetus automatically should it range more than a light-month out." He looked at Rod, with his hands held out, palms partially up. "And," he added, "we would be selective to whom we sell."

"Who do you see as your initial customers?" Rod asked.

"Several to Mirs Corp, several to the U.S. government and to other well-heeled nations, New Israel and Lone Star, even wealthy private individuals."

"The Caliphate?"

"Not planning on it." Marc paused. "There is the secondary market, of course. We probably want to establish some controls."

"I'm not sure we want to control it," Rod said with a thoughtful tone. "It goes against everything we stand for."

"So, you'd rather see the Caliphate moving about the Solar System with impunity, striking at will, and impossible to track?"

"When you put it that way…"

"How about a long-term, non-transferrable lease?" Marc leaned forward, counting off points on his fingers. "We control to whom we lease, we control the kill switch, we control the outbound limits, and we control the lease itself."

"You do know about Murphy's Law, right?" Rod said with a smile.

"Unfortunately, I do…"

"So, how long do you think it will be until the Caliphate gets its hands on a hyper-V craft?"

EARTH—MINNEAPOLIS

Steven Brady hoisted a mug of Bauhaus Brew in the direction of his First Sergeant. "To good times, Bo!" He wore jeans, square-toed black boots, and an open shirt displaying a tank top with no visible markings stretched across his well-muscled chest.

Bransom hoisted his own mug and grinned, his dark face split by a wide, toothy smile. He also sported jeans and biker boots, topped off with a white tee-shirt, a pack of smokes rolled into his left sleeve. The bulging muscles of his arms stretched the sleeves to their limit. He was joined in the general toast by the four platoon leaders, including Sergeant Jerri Smyth in cut-offs, feet shod in brass tipped fancy western boots that extended her 178-centimeter height by five centimeters, and a tank top that displayed an upper-body musculature that belied her unsupported femininity.

It was Friday night at the Bauhaus Brew Labs, a venerable drinking establishment that had been there long before any of the Guardsmen had been born. Brady enjoyed spending quality time with his troops. He grinned at the guys and winked at Smyth. Two platoon leaders set up for an arm wrestle, and the soldiers gathered round. The larger, Sergeant Norbert Jacobsen or "Nor," as the troops called him, was a Viking-like warrior who looked a lot like Brady. The second was a seasoned Guardsman, dark, shorter, and ten kilos lighter. They both were tough and experienced, but the outcome was practically predetermined. Nevertheless, the troops whooped and hollered, cheering on their favorite. Then, one by one, the troopers stepped to the table, and one by one, the big Viking defeated them.

"How about it, Jer?" Brady said, lifting his mug in Smyth's direction. "You're pretty good at this…" He left it hanging.

"Wrestle a girl? You're kidding, right?" Jacobsen had joined the National Guard company recently and had not seen Smyth off-duty.

Brady could see Smyth bristle as she stepped to the table and adjusted its position to her liking. "You scared of a woman?" Her voice was soft and low.

Jacobsen blushed at the soft put-down. "Not hardly, Sarge…let's do it!" He placed his left arm flat on the table and parked his right elbow against his little finger.

Smyth took the chair opposite Jacobsen and positioned her arm next to his. Her wrist met his, but her hand was somewhat shorter.

"On my mark," Brady said. He saw Smyth catch Jacobsen's gaze and hold it. "Mark!"

At first, there was no movement, although the strain was evident in both their upper arms. Then Smyth smiled at Jacobsen, and in one smooth motion, laid his arm on the table.

Jacobsen looked at her in astonishment. "How'dyu do that?" He put his arm back up, elbow firmly planted. "Show me again…"

And she did.

✳

A holotank occupied the upper wall at the end of the room. It had been playing a football rerun of a game that everybody had already seen. Suddenly, the game dissolved into sparkles, and the words "NEWS FLASH" flowed across the space before the wall. The image of a well-known and popular male news anchor replaced the flowing words.

"Ladies and gentlemen…we are switching to a just-announced holovision broadcast out of the Middle East." His image faded, replaced by a light-blue flag fluttering slightly in the wind. The flag displayed a severed fist holding a dagger. A few centimeters from the wrist, a truncated arm flowed red blood. The image of a uniformed man coalesced before the flag. He was tall with a full head of close-cropped curly black hair under his peaked military cap. Prominent cheekbones highlighted Aryan features with large, dark eyes, and his short, nearly black curly beard carried streaks of grey. Beneath the image were the flowing Arabic words: اللواء إسماعيل سليمان، القائد الأعلى للخلافة.

The network quickly displayed the English version of the Arabic script: *General Ismail Suleiman, Caliphate Supreme Commander.*

The General began to speak in Arabic. Almost immediately, his voice faded, and a male voice speaking English superimposed over the General's words.

"I am General Ismail Suleiman, Caliphate Supreme Commander. Where once the Middle East was a scattering of countries, weak and ineffective, practicing many forms of Islam, fighting one another and the rest of the world, under the beneficent guidance of Allah's Holy Prophet Saeed Esmail, the Arab and Persian peoples have united under one flag and one Islam. We do not threaten the world. We do not threaten the State of Israel, with whom we have many differences. We intend to work through these differences diplomatically, without violence, to the benefit of our people and the people of Israel.

"We proclaim our full citizenship in the world community of nations, declaring our sovereignty as a nation, our right to traverse the international waters of the world and the void between the planets. We declare our right to defend our sovereign borders and to use whatever means necessary to maintain our sovereignty—including our arsenal of nuclear weapons. We do, however, pledge never to initiate the use of these terrible weapons of mass destruction. We wish to live in harmony and peace with the rest of the world."

As the General's words faded away, his image was replaced with the image of a man, small of stature, standing on a sand dune, robed in sackcloth, his full-length flowing beard fluttering in a slight breeze. As the man began to speak, Arabic script filled the bottom of the tank: سعيد اسماعيل—رسول الله الحرام, which the network translated as *Saeed Esmail—the holy messenger of Allah*.

"*Allahu Akbar!…Allahu Akbar!…Allahu Akbar!…Allahu Akbar!*" As the sound of his voice faded into the surrounding sand, he raised his arms; his right arm truncated in a leather cup. His voice rang out again across the dunes: "*Ashhadu an la ilaha illa Allah.*[4]" He repeated it, and then spoke in a slightly softer, sing-song manner: "*Ashadu anna Saeedan Rasool Allah Alhram.*[5]" Saeed repeated the phrase and smiled as his words echoed across the sand.

Saeed's image faded so that only the flag remained, and then it, too, faded to black.

The four Muslim members of the company jumped up and shouted in unison, "*Allahu Akbar!…Allahu Akbar!*" and then sat down abruptly when Bransom scowled at them.

"Enough of that crap!" Bransom said and waved them over.

Brady watched the four Islamic Guardsmen gather around his First Sergeant—displaying both fear and palpable excitement. He really had no complaints about these four. They tended to keep to themselves, but they did their duty, carried their share of the load, followed orders…in short, they were good Guardsmen.

---

4 *I bear witness that there is no god except Allah*
5 *I bear witness that Saeed is the holy messenger of God*

"No more terrorism," one of them said.

"The Prophet will lead the Earth to World peace," said another. All four beamed.

"Fat chance," Bransom muttered, catching Brady's eye.

Brady leaned over and whispered in Smyth's ear, "Watch your guy, and get the word to the other platoon leaders."

Smyth punched him in the arm as she left.

EARTH—MINNEAPOLIS

Minneapolis City Council President Ali Omar Elmi called the Council to order. Council members from Wards 3, 6, 9, and 10 were the only representatives present, three less than a quorum. The three non-Muslim councilmen who had acquiesced to imposing Sharia Law on Ward 6 had found themselves in serious political trouble in their own wards and were fighting recall movements in the three wards. Both Muslims and those opposing Islam wanted them out, to be replaced by proponents of Sharia Law on the one hand and by principled non-Muslims on the other. They didn't have time for hastily called Council meetings. They were fighting for their political lives.

TThe four councilmen and their leader focused their collective attention on the holotank dominating the front of the meeting chamber, as the shimmering display of multicolored dots coalesced into the image of Ismail Suleiman, Caliphate Supreme Commander. The five controlling members of the Minneapolis City Council watched in silent, rapt attention as the General uttered his historic words. When the Prophet's image replaced the General's, they rose in unison and, with one voice, echoed the Prophet's words, "*Allahu Akbar!...Allahu Akbar!...Allahu Akbar!...Allahu Akbar!*"

EARTH—WASHINGTON D.C.

President Jackson looked up from his desk in the Oval Office as an aide knocked and entered. He held out a thin folder.

"Intel briefing, Mr. President. It's an assessment of the Caliphate's military strength following their global announcement this evening."

Jackson glanced at the built-in time display on his desk. 11 PM. He reached for the folder.

"Thank you."

Jackson absorbed the brief from his national security team. It listed the Caliphate's known military assets, followed by an outline of their offensive capability. When done reading, he leaned back with his hands clasped behind his head. *One hundred fifty aircraft, of which one hundred are carrier-capable fighters, a nuclear-powered carrier, one hundred destroyer/cruisers, a thousand tanks and other armored vehicles, five hundred tactical nukes, one hundred fifty strategic thermonuclear weapons and three hundred long-range missiles to carry them, and a million-man army.* Jackson sighed. *How did this happen without our knowing? What else don't we know?*

Jackson paged through the brief again, his eyes landing on a breakout of the territorial description. He called up a map of the region on his Link and zoomed in on *Al Hadd* at the eastern tip of what used to be called Oman on the Arabian Peninsula. Then he connected it with a dotted line to *Pasabandar* at the western end of the bay split by the border between Pakistan and what used to be Iran. The line cut straight across the mouth of the Gulf of Oman, completely isolating both the Gulf of Oman and the Persian Gulf. He sat back, contemplating the situation. American warships routinely traversed the Persian Gulf—it was a matter of principle. He summoned Syed Shah Bukhari by Link and then reread the brief while awaiting the vice president's arrival.

Because of the hour, it took Vice President Bukhari less than a half-hour to arrive at the Oval Office a bit breathless. He smiled and shook the president's outstretched hand.

"Please sit and read this brief." The president handed the folder to Bukhari.

A few minutes later, the vice president looked up, and the president directed his attention to the holodisplay over his desk. Bukhari moved so he could see an unrestricted view.

"We have warships here and here," Jackson indicated two points in the Persian Gulf. "What is your advice as the American Vice President and as a Muslim?"

"Move them, of course," Bukhari said, with some emphasis. "The Caliphate is declaring these waters to be its sovereign territory. If we remain, we risk a shooting war. We cede nothing by leaving, and we can take the matter up with the United Nations."

Jackson nodded. This was aligned with his own thinking. Give the Caliphate sufficient room to flex its muscles. Do nothing provocative, and then address the situation with the world community at the negotiating table.

The president smiled and thanked Bukhari for showing up on such short notice so late at night. *After all*, he thought as the vice president closed the Oval Office door behind himself, *we have a substantial arsenal to defend against incursion on our territory. Why should not the Caliphate have a right to the same?* He smiled with self-satisfaction. *Besides*, he reminded himself, *the Caliph has promised peace. We should give him the chance.*

CHAPTER SEVEN

SOLAR SYSTEM—ASTEROID BELT

As the Solar System entered its fourth year since *Starchild* departed on her historic voyage, Humanity was rapidly expanding away from its second home—Earth. Ectaris was a long-forgotten memory, newly brought to the fore when the Founders made themselves known to the *Cassini II* crew during its epic voyage of exploration to Saturn's moon Iapetus. By this time, every soul on the planet knew that humans descended from the Ectarians who long ago fled their world shortly before their sun went nova. Every Earth schoolchild knew about the remarkable sequence of events that eventually led to the *Starchild's* departure on its ten-year shakedown cruise. A half-millennium earlier, the gold-seeking soldier-of-fortune, the adventurous sea captain and crew, the religiously or politically oppressed family, virtually anyone who wanted to escape from what was, made their way to the New World. Now, these same people were spreading throughout the Asteroid Belt.

Getting out of Earth's gravity well was easy and relatively inexpensive. For little more than the cost of a rail trip across the American continent in the twentieth century, anybody could book passage on one of the nine space launch loops scattered around the globe to arrive at the Mirs Complex at L4 several hours later. From there, the possibilities were endless.

Venture capital at L4 flowed like water. Anyone with money wanted a piece of the expansion into the Asteroid Belt. A small group of people intent on mining asteroid-X would have no trouble obtaining financial backing. And while many of these ventures went broke, those that prospered *really* prospered. A small constant acceleration VASIMR freighter on the resale market was easily within reach of any small group. Well-organized, well-funded ventures could lease a hyper-V craft for the initial exploratory runs, although at this stage, the Starchild Institute was not building hyper-V freighters for public use. Literally, hundreds of thousands of asteroids were available for the simple taking. A registry on Iapetus recorded claims. Physical presence on Iapetus was not necessary to register a mining or residential claim—just a permanent presence on the asteroid itself. Registration automatically joined the claim to the Federation, giving it legal protection. Belters filed claims daily, and the Asteroid Belt population quickly grew to hundreds of thousands.

SATURN'S MOONS

By year five, the Mirs Corporation had set its sights on Saturn's moon Titan as a potential place for human expansion. It established a domed colony of scientist-settlers whose purpose was to determine if Titan's subterranean water sources could be used to liberate oxygen into the atmosphere in sufficient quantities to make Titan's atmosphere breathable for humans. It was a long-term project looking forward to when Titan's vast surface might become necessary to accommodate humanity's exponential growth.

Simultaneously, the Starchild Institute created a division to exploit the vast water resources of Saturn's moon Enceladus, whose water geysers are responsible for Saturn's E-ring. SI scientists placed people on the surface near the south pole geyser field to determine if water could more easily be mined at the surface or by tapping into the vast underground ocean that lay about thirty kilometers beneath the ice at the pole.

SOLAR SYSTEM

Year six opened up the vast potential of space commercialization. Initially, and for years thereafter, the Mirs Corporation had dominated most commercial space activities. By year six, however, Mirs had several viable competitors, with the Europa Group leading the pack. The Europa Group was actively pursuing research into the eventual placement of a human habitat on the ocean floor under the ice surface of Europa, one of Jupiter's moons. The big move in year six, however, was to another of Jupiter's moons, Ganymede. The Ganymede Consortium formed with significant financial backing from the Starchild Institute to establish human habitation on Ganymede's surface. With Ganymede's minimal oxygen atmosphere and high radiation levels, the challenges were enormous but not insurmountable. The goal was a breathable atmosphere with sufficient pressure to enable unsupported life on Ganymede's surface.

Mirs and the Ganymede Consortium were in a heated race to determine whether Titan or Ganymede would first reach the goal of unsupported habitation. In the meantime, the Asteroid Belt population reached several millions. Dozens of smaller asteroids had been hollowed like Iapetus, using some of the Robotic Vaporizers stored on Iapetus that originally were used to hollow Iapetus itself. They were still works-in-progress, but with the artificial gravity fields derived from Founder technology, and Q-carbon liners from Mars, they rapidly became self-sufficient habitats that catered to groups with common goals, perspectives, religions, or philosophies.

In particular, the asteroid Daphne was coopted by the Raëlians, whose free-loving, open communities rubbed many of the Earth's traditional religious communities the wrong way. At 174 kilometers in diameter, with its own two-kilometer-wide moonlet and exotic name, the Raëlians thought of it as an ideal home for their growing number of acolytes. Its surface area of 95,000 square kilometers was somewhat smaller than Wyoming, so there was more than sufficient room, looking far into the future. The task of removing some 190,000 cubic kilometers of rock to create a two-kilometer-high interior space was daunting, but the automatic RV machines were certainly up to the task, and the Raëlians had a very substantial cache of available funds from their worldwide activities to get the project underway. They had already established that the carbonaceous chondrite making up most of Daphne was laced with significant amounts of relatively rare minerals that were in demand throughout the Solar System. Thus, the Raëlians were able to finance their ongoing operation by making these minerals available to interplanetary trade.

Elysium, their central city, was already an established destination for those who wanted to experience the Raëlians' peregrine best. If one could imagine an exotic or erotic pastime, it probably was available somewhere in Elysium. As the developed parts of Daphne expanded, so did the available pleasures. The population was pushing a quarter-million and was expected to pass one million before the *Starchild* returned. The Raëlian belief system, a strange hybrid of mainstream Catholicism, Pentecostalism, and Buddhism, with a healthy dose of the mid-twentieth century Raëlian Church, held that all life on Earth, humans included, was created scientifically by an alien race, the Elohim, whom the Raëlians more recently equated with the Founders. They especially honored the Founder matriarch, Vesta, as the *Earth Mother*. Their slab-sided churches, topped with the Wormhole of David, could be found in virtually every city and town on Earth, and their meeting places were everywhere in the Solar System that humans put down roots. Any large assemblage of people anywhere always included a contingent of white-robed Raëlians showing their white flag displaying the Wormhole of David, spreading peace and love like the flower-children of mid-twentieth-century America.

IMAGE 3—Wormhole of David

EARTH—MINNEAPOLIS

Steven Brady sat in his office in the Minnesota Army National Guard complex on Broadway, staring at the empty holotank. *The Guard is not like the Army*, he thought. *In times of conflict, it IS the Army, but now it's…well…The Guard.* He had recently earned his gold leaves, but he suspected it would be a long dry spell before he pinned on silver ones. Unlike the Army, his unit had stayed substantially the same. In the seven years since the *Starchild* departed on her shakedown cruise, a few guys came and went, even some gals, but for the most part, he still had the same people doing the same jobs. His First Sergeant, Bo Bransom, was up for Command Sergeant Major. Scuttlebutt said he was a shoo-in. Newly minted Staff Sergeant Jerri Smyth was still with him, as was Sergeant Nor Jacobsen, who needed more time in rank before promotion. Eighty percent of his troops were still with him, including the four Muslims.

Guard duty in modern America tended to attract single men with no permanent ties to the community. Charlie Company had several married men, two with families, but for most of the troops, an occasional one-night-stand was the best they could hope for. Bransom recently broke up with his long-time squeeze, and Brady simply had not yet found the right woman.

Brady was disturbed by what seemed to be happening in Minneapolis. He was not particularly political, but he could not help but notice the significant changes his city had undergone over the last three years. This thing about Sharia Law…that was particularly exasperating. He wasn't a constitutional expert, but he was pretty sure that imposing Sharia Law on American citizens was unconstitutional. Everywhere he went in the region, he was picking up rumblings. People were arming themselves despite the draconian gun rules the City Council had imposed on the community. Ammunition sales were through the roof.

Then there was the thing about presidential term limits—the 22nd amendment to the U.S. Constitution. Two years earlier, President Jackson's party under the leadership of Vice President Dr. Syed Shah Bukhari had proposed repealing the presidential term-limit amendment. With their overwhelming majorities in both houses, the repeal was passed and put to the state legislatures on an accelerated schedule. Only one more state was required for ratification, and Brady was pretty confident that Minnesota would be that state within the month.

Several months earlier, Brady had started training his troops in urban warfare. Every week they practiced close-in hand-to-hand combat and door-to-door search. Each of his platoons had a sniper and spotter. He trained them in urban tactics—how to find a safe perch and how to pick off enemy leaders quietly and efficiently. He used his four Muslim troops, who were fluent in Arabic, to teach the others enough Arabic to get by in an emergency when no one around spoke English. Surprisingly, his troops took to the language training, several becoming quite proficient in Arabic, including Smyth.

Brady had no idea what was coming, but he did his best to prepare himself and his people for whatever it was.

MARS—LONE STAR

Year eight found Sam Houston at Lone Star and Asshur at Nachal Rachaf coordinating their activities, working closely with Mattias McIntyre and Mordecai Rochlin. Lone Star was at a point where any of its nearly one million settlers could travel anywhere within the boundaries of the great eastern and western dams with nothing more than a light-weight pressure garment and an oxygen concentrator integrated into a transparent globe with a neckdam that maintained adequate pressure for the face, sinuses, and lungs. Nachal Rachaf had reached shirt-sleeve well before. Now, the first five kilometers of both the northern and southern Nanedi Valles had been covered with transparent polymer that retained a significant atmospheric pressure and oxygen content. The domes in these areas remained, but once oxygen reached normal levels, they were kept open to the surrounding atmosphere. The rest of settled Nanedi Valles, however, still required full pressure suits outside the ubiquitous domes that were everywhere.

Sam was being pressured by fellow Texans to return to Texas to run for governor. With the election about a year away, they had already commenced the campaign in his absence. Asshur was being pressured by Daniel Ben-Gurion, the secretive head of Mossad, to run for the Knesset on a platform of a wholesale migration to Mars. Asshur made it clear to Ben-Gurion that his home was Mars, but he agreed to travel the length and breadth of Israel with his message of hope—a new life for every Israeli in New Israel on Mars. Consequently, the day-to-day affairs of both Lone Star and Nachal Rachaf were being handled by McIntyre and Rochlin.

EARTH—JERUSALEM

Asshur stood at the dais, looking out over the 120 members of the Knesset, seated to his right, his left, and in front of him. The great Israeli parliament building in which he stood had been built way back in 1966 through the generosity of James A. de Rothschild on a hill in central-western Jerusalem, in the *Givat Ram* district. Over the decades, it had been modernized, but the layered, colonnaded, cubical building still appeared much as it had for more than a hundred years.

On this occasion, Asshur stood before this august assembly by invitation. Since his private conversation with Ben-Gurion following his brother's death, Asshur had traveled the length and breadth of this small country, speaking at assemblages, schools, factories, synagogues, churches, and mosques, talking about the real Jewish heritage. He spoke of Ectaris, about a 500-year journey through interstellar space, about civilization reestablishing itself, about disaster and a plunge into barbarism, and the slow, steady climb back to the modern world, and always, always he emphasized the unique role of the Semitic people. He knew intellectually that the Semites encompassed virtually all the peoples of the Middle East, but he found himself drawn to the Israelis. As a people, they seemed closest to what he had grown up with on the Ark, on Iapetus.

During his travels throughout the country, Asshur came to understand just how much the Israeli homeland—Israel—meant to these people. He also realized that, more and more, he was thinking of the Israelis as his people. They still existed as a nation only through the direct intervention of himself and his brothers, the Founders, as everyone liked to call them. It also seemed clear to him that their status as an independent nation situated between the Jordan River and the Mediterranean was, at best, temporary if left to their own devices. The sheer numbers surrounding them would eventually prevail.

The current Israeli population was near 15 million, at or near the limit that their 21,000 square kilometers of land could sustain. This was evident everywhere Asshur went. Israel would soon be forced to curtail internal growth, something intrinsically contrary to the Israeli mindset, or find new territory, a concept equally inimical to most Israelis. Asshur saw things from a different perspective. Restriction of population growth was inherently part of his thought process since he was born in, and spent most of his life in the Ark, or Iapetus, as he increasingly thought of it. From his perspective, Ectaris was the ancestral home of the Israelis, not the 10,000 or so square kilometers north of the Negev Desert. Asshur had traveled through the Negev and had seen what the Israelis could accomplish in this arid, inhospitable environment.

As he stood before this body of people chosen to represent the Israelis on the national stage, Asshur gave them the same message he had been giving as he traveled the length and breadth of Israel. He emphasized the similarity between the Negev and Mars and made it as clear as possible that while Palestine was the immediate home of the Israelis, their genuine ancestral home lay 500 lightyears distant, and was now completely and forever lost to history. He explained that time was short and that their options were rapidly shrinking.

"Get to Mars while you can," he told them, "Before the door closes forever."

Modern Israelis were as well educated and technologically sophisticated as the Knesset members. Most of Asshur's listeners were able to see the connection immediately. On an intellectual level, forward-looking Israelis got it—their future lay on Mars.

MARS—LONE STAR

A smiling holoimage of the statuesque blond CEO of Launch Loop International (LLI) materialized over Sam's desk. "Margo," he said warmly, "it looks like life is treating you well."

Margo Jackson was in her mid-sixties but appeared to be in her early forties at most. She started her LLI career over three decades earlier as the engineer in charge of underwater operations during the construction of the world's first launch loop, Slingshot, between Baker and Jarvis Islands in the Equatorial Pacific. Following Slingshot, Mable Fitzwinters, LLI's fabled founder, had put Margo in charge, along with Klaus Blumenfeld, the power systems engineer at Slingshot, of constructing the Atlantic Loop. Then it was the Sahara Loop at Atar in Mauritania, the Mediterranean Loop based out of Mallorca, followed by the Outback Loop at Coral Bay, Australia. By this time, launch loops had entirely taken over Earth-to-space launch operations. When Fitzwinters' heart gave out during the dedication ceremonies for the Outback Loop, the Board immediately installed Margo as the new CEO, following Fitzwinters' final wishes. Mirs' Andrey Orlov had built the Caspian Loop out of Sevastopol within a year of Slingshot's successful debut, the South Africans built the South African Loop out of Pretoria shortly thereafter, and the Caliphate was building the Saudi Loop at Mecca; otherwise, LLI was responsible for the remaining six launch loops. Additionally, Margo had worked closely with Isidor Sokolov to construct a space elevator from Udachny on the Moon's far side to L2, some 61,500 kilometers out from the Moon—Port Udachny.

Sam did not await Margo's response that would have arrived twenty-two minutes later. Mars and Earth were on the same side of the Sun at that point, and the transmission took just under eleven minutes, one way. There was no practical way to compress this delay, which made face-to-face communications over interplanetary distance tedious by usual communication standards and generally eliminated chit-chat.

"I'm not used to these long delays," Sam continued, "so let's cut to the chase. Funding for the Mars Launch Loop is in place, thanks to your efforts. Your engineering team will arrive at Lone Star," he glanced at something outside his Link pickup, "just after noon tomorrow, my time. Materials have been arriving daily at the Juventae and Margaritifer Sockets. SI engineers and technicians have been installing the Founder power sources beyond both socket locations. They should be ready to supply power to the linear drives in two months. In the meantime, power is being generated by variable output gas core reactors at both locations.

"The MagLev routes to Lone Star and New Israel have been cleared, and the magnetic base is being laid. This is a difficult situation because the lines are vulnerable to attack, and we have had several—at Lone Star and Nachal Rachaf. We're incorporating optical fiber eyes along the entire route with automatic monitoring of any movement. We're hoping that we can forestall any hits on the MagLev system this way.

"Asshur is in Israel stumping for maximum emigration. You should try to touch base with him before he leaves. Mordecai Rochlin is handling things at Nachal Rachaf and doing a damn good job! His launch loop team is working out the details of emplacing the tensioners along the ribbon. My guys—well, actually, Matti's guys—are preparing to install the four linear drivers. I think back to Slingshot and the Atlantic Loop and am amazed that you guys could do it at all. Doing this task on land is hard enough…doing it at sea is almost unimaginable. Andrey has lent us his team of experts, so we don't reinvent too many wheels. Of course, the Mars Loop will carry an order of magnitude more freight, and when he built the Caspian Loop, he didn't have the advantage of Founder technology. Marc's SI people are making a world of difference.

"The real problem we have is communications. You and I are stretching the limits with this conversation (if you can call it that). Mostly, we grab an available hyper-V craft and meet to talk face-to-face. I wanted you to know, however, before any rumors reached you that Asshur and I—with the full blessing of Rod and the Federation, Marc and SI, and Earth Mother, Vesta—have decided to name Mars' first launch loop the *Margo Jackson Loop*. We think it only fitting that the first space launch loop on another world be named after the woman who made Slingshot happen and who found Amelia Earhart's resting place.

"So…I'm going to busy myself with other things while I await your response." Sam turned to review progress reports on oxygen and pressure levels in Lone Star and materials stockpiled at the Juventae and Margaritifer Sockets.

While he busied himself with these reports, his Link flashed some good news. The first Martian Server Sky swarm was finally in position over the equator giving Lone Star and Nachal Rachaf direct Link communications. Sam called Rochlin on his Link.

"Rasam…nothing critical. Just wanted to touch base with you about the Server Sky Link."

"No shit! It's finally up and running…no one told me." Rochlin's craggy face broke into a big smile. "This'll make it a damn sight easier keeping things going here, and especially staying on top of the Jackson Loop." He was part of the naming convention. "When are you leaving for Texas?"

"In a day or so. Things are heating up down there."

"Stay safe, my friend!"

They signed off as Margo's image flashed into holographic solidity. "What a wonderful and undeserved surprise!" Margo said, her voice firm and rich. "So, all that other stuff was just a lead-in to your announcement? I'd kiss you, but this will have to do." She kissed her hand and waved it toward him, or so it seemed to Sam as he admired the self-effacing woman with a high profile throughout the Solar System second only to Vesta herself.

"Klaus has decided to visit the Mars Launch Loop, errr…the Jackson Loop (that's hard for me to say), next week to lend a hand with the linear drivers. He probably knows more about these behemoths than anyone else in the System. He won't jump into the project but will make himself available so your guys—Matti's guys—can tap into his expertise. Besides, he's never been to Mars, and a team of horses couldn't keep him away." She paused. "Thanks again for the honor…I'm completely overwhelmed." Her image faded as she signed off.

※

Sam watched as a fifty-meter hyper-V freighter settled its ten legs and three central foot stubs on the malgamac apron in front of Lone Star Base on the floor of Coprates Chasma. Overhead the sky was a pale, pastel blue streaked with faint cirrus-like clouds ripped by upper atmosphere winds. The northern canyon wall three kilometers to his left towered over seven kilometers above him. To his right, some forty kilometers distant, the southern wall loomed, but at that distance, it looked more like a ridge than a seven-kilometer-high wall. Sam's eyes picked out the dimple that identified the spot where the cliff had collapsed beneath his feet and traced the path of the rock slide as it nearly impacted Lone Star Base. Sam wore jeans, western boots, and a long-sleeved, red-checked shirt. Underneath his clothing, he still wore a lightweight pressure garment. His neckdammed bubble helmet maintained the pressure his face, sinuses, and lungs needed and protected his eyes from Mars' excessive UV, and an oxygen concentrator clipped to his belt supplied oxygen to a transparent tube inside his helmet that serviced an inconspicuous nasal cannula. The air was a crisp 18°, almost cold enough for a jacket.

Sam rubbed his hands together as the hyper-V craft dropped a ramp to the malgamac. It was one of three hyper-V freighters SI had made available to Lone Star and Nachal Rachaf to facilitate their individual projects and their joint construction of Jackson Loop. This particular craft contained a load of preformed polymer material that would become part of the linear driver housing to the west of Juventae Socket. The polymer had the characteristic that when inflated and exposed to direct UV light, it hardened to be stronger and much lighter than steel. Substantively, it was very similar to the material from which the rovers, and even many spacecraft, were constructed. Eventually, Mars would be able to manufacture its own structural polymer, but for the time being, it had to be imported from the Mirs Complex at L4.

Thirty technicians and two engineers arrived with the polymer. All were slated to join the crew already housed at Juventae. Sam wanted them to spend a couple of days at Lone Star to acclimatize themselves and to gain a sense of the overall operation—and to have some relaxed fun at White Elephant, located in a transparent cupula at the top of the three-kilometer-high rocky mound that housed Lone Star Base.

✳

The White Elephant's polymer dome was transparent to the human eye so that only stars were visible overhead, cut off sharply to the north by the canyon rim, and less noticeably by Nectaris Montes, blocking Valles Marineris to the east. The room was oval-shaped, running east to west. The entire northern side was an exact duplicate, insofar as was historically possible, of the 12-meter White Elephant mahogany bar from late-nineteenth-century Fort Worth. Lone Star Beer—brewed on Mars—flowed from its many beer spigots. Whiskeys, Scotches, bourbons, and ryes, many from Earth, graced the wall behind the bar, along with exotic Russian vodkas, Mexican tequilas, and peregrine beverages from across the Solar System.

Testosterone filled the air, muted by the presence of several females ranging from tough, stalky oil-rig mamas straight from the Texas Gulf Coast to willowy space-age technicians sporting stratospheric IQs, but with one common factor—they were outnumbered ten-to-one by their male counterparts. All were on Mars by choice, with a lust for adventure and the high wages Lone Star paid.

The settlers, on the other hand, who now occupied a large part of Valles Marineris between the retaining dams, avoided the White Elephant, preferring instead to focus on survival and transforming the hostile Martian environment into human-friendly living space.

✳

Unbeknownst to the revelers in the White Elephant, on the northern rim, five-and-a-half kilometers distant on a line vector from their transparent dome, Chino and Rico Delgado parked *Rover-2* a hundred meters back from the canyon rim, connected diamond fiber cables to their utility harnesses, and crept to the edge of the canyon wall. Using their suit optics, they zoomed in on the crowd in the White Elephant.

"How we gonna get them bastards?" Chino asked over their short-range circuit.

"Don' know, Bro. Gotta be sump'n tho, gotta be." Rico crouched, staring over the rim. "We ain't gonna get inside there," he added, "that's fo' sure."

"We gotta send sump'n in," Chino said. "You know, sump'n goes BOOM!"

"That's straight thinkin', Bro. These guys goin' to Juventae, and they be comin' back." The brothers bumped pressure-suited fists.

"We'll put a bomb in their stuff," Chino added. "That's cool, Bro!"

MARS—NACHAL RACHAF

Mordecai Rochlin sat at his desk in the government section of Nachal Rachaf, reviewing the returns from the Nanedi-Valles-wide referendum on establishing self-rule. Not that self-rule had not been in effect from the start of the settlement, but Asshur sat at the top, administrating the settlement and exercising the final say on everything. When he left for Earth to spearhead a push to convince Israelis to emigrate *en masse*, the job of administering New Israel fell on Rochlin's shoulders, not something the grizzled army veteran had ever anticipated. He had to admit, however, that Asshur was right. He was good at it and had managed to govern the nearly two million residents with virtually no serious altercations, stretching from Levi Bar-Lev's settlement some twenty kilometers south where the Delgado brothers had created the rock slide, to the new settlement erecting domes where Nanedi Valles widened some fifteen kilometers to the north.

With the Server Sky swarm providing continuous Link coverage, the referendum process was nearly painless. It wasn't unanimous, but nearly so. Knesset members had been selected and would convene in a month to choose a prime minister. Asshur was the titular president, and Rochlin was the designated administrator. I*n other word*s, he thought, grinning to himself, *I still run everything.*

"President Asshur," Rochlin spoke to a system-generated image of his Earthside friend, "here are the results of the referendum. And, yes, you got that! By virtually every measure, you are the New Israel President by acclamation. We have a twenty-seat Knesset, with each seat representing approximately one hundred thousand residents. By the time you return, the Knesset should have selected a prime minister—I suspect Levi Bar-Lev will get the nod. I think you know that he heads the Terraform Party; its members cast significantly more votes than the Greens or the Reds. Terraform holds twelve seats, the Greens have five, and the Reds, one. Someday, you need to explain the difference between the Terraforms and Greens. The Reds are nuts.—I think we need to watch them. They may actually invite the Delgado brothers to their next caucus!

"I may be missing something here, Asshur, err…Mr. President," he smiled, "but given that all of us are dependent on the integrity of our life-support systems, how can we legitimize the Red perspective that we should leave Mars as we found it?

"You know what? I hate these delayed conversations. There's no need for you to respond to this. I just wanted to bring you up to date, personally. Get my holdout countrymen to pack up and get their butts out here!"

EARTH—WASHINGTON D.C.

On an unusually warm and pleasant January 20 morning, President Stanford Jackson and Vice President Dr. Syed Shah Bukhari took their oaths of office for an unprecedented third time—at least since 1941.

EARTH—SAUDI ARABIAN DESERT

As year nine of the *Starchild's* absence got underway, General Ismail Suleiman gazed around the sprawling tent pitched atop the same low mound overlooking the dry lakebed near the center of Rub' al-Khali in the Saudi Arabian desert. The towering dunes surrounding the lakebed had completely shifted their positions since Saeed had first pitched his tent here, but from the first day over ten years ago, Saeed's tent had remained in the same position. The General shook his head with a mixture of amazement and admiration. This was the seat of government for a Caliphate that stretched from Afghanistan in the east, to Somalia in the south, across Mediterranean Africa to Morocco—everything, except Israel. Sure, the government administrative offices resided in Riyadh, but control originated right here, under his iron fist. Suleiman let his gaze fall on Saeed Esmail, lounging on a stack of cushions, leather-cupped right hand in his lap, studying a copy of the *Qur'an*. Somehow this little man, slight of figure, with no education beyond the *Qur'an*, had carried his Jihad to Iapetus, had met the Founders personally, had nearly succeeded in destroying them, and had survived the ensuing conflict and destruction of the Persian Caliphate to become the spiritual leader of a unified Islam. And, General Suleiman was certain, he was destined to rule the entire planet.

"Sahib…"

Saeed looked up from his reading. The General cleared his throat.

"My people in Pakistan informed me this morning that the Pakistani government is ready to integrate itself into the Caliphate. My generals control their army and air force, we control their nuclear weapons, and all forty of their naval vessels are captained by officers loyal to the Caliphate. This is important, Sahib, because it gives us complete access to the Pakistani nuclear manufacturing facilities. We will no longer be dependent on India."

Saeed gestured to a pile of cushions near him, and the General sat. "Excellent, General. When do you think Turkmenistan and Azerbaijan will join us?"

"Soon, Sahib, and Tajikistan and Uzbekistan as well. Your Jihadi army is moving into the Sudan and Chad as we speak. For the most part, our troops are greeted with enthusiasm. Resistance is put to the sword immediately. The word has preceded us, so there is very little resistance."

"And Israel?" Saeed looked directly at the General.

"We made a public pledge not to attack Israel, Sahib. Until we are certain that there will be no retaliation, we must staunchly protect Israel's independence." He smiled warmly at Saeed. "We have much to do yet. We must annex Kyrgyzstan to the east and Turkey to the north. Then we can move down the coast of the Bay of Bengal to annex Indonesia and everything in between, thus uniting virtually all the world's Muslims under your blue banner, except for India—which comes later."

"Have you given thought to obtaining a hyper-V craft?" Saeed asked. "We will need it for our planned asteroid outpost."

"Indeed, Sahib. I have set up a series of shell corporations through connections in India that ultimately lead to the American Vice President, Dr. Syed Shah Bukhari. Shortly, we will take possession of a space-capable hyper-V craft that no one will be able to connect to the Caliphate." The General's smile was broad. "No one," he emphasized.

CHAPTER EIGHT

MIRS COMPLEX—RING KIEV

Vesta looked around the expanded Great Room in the old Ring Kiev with an overwhelming sense of *déjà vu*. Could it possibly have been ten years since she and her friends and family watched the *Starchild* depart on its historic voyage? She gripped Azurad's hand as a personal shuttle passed in front of the great window, emblazoned with the logo: *L&S BioLabs*. Even though she and Azurad lived in the new Ring Samara where Lud and Shakbah lived, they didn't see each other very often because Lud and Shakbah were so involved with their longevity research. The shuttle disappeared over the window top on its way to the hub. She caught movement to her left and turned to see Henri and Michele Deville, France's new President and First Lady, moving through the crowd toward her. Deville was formally proper, as always, but still retained the twinkle in his eyes, and Michele was dazzling in a white gown that displayed her still youthful figure to its best possible advantage. She seemed not to have aged a minute.

"*Mes Chéries!*" Michele tripped toward the Founders and enthusiastically kissed each. "I have not seen you in so long, and I missed you, truly, I did!"

Henri raised each woman's fingers to his lips, his eyes sparkling. "So good to see you again, Earth Mother. Michele speaks the truth—she talks of you often, and on more than one occasion, has urged me to schedule a state visit to Mirs." He stepped back and offered a Gallic shrug. "But I am sure you know about the problems I am having with the French Muslim population." His eyes lost a bit of their twinkle.

"I have followed the French situation closely," Vesta answered. "I wish I could offer you some meaningful advice." She smiled up at him warmly. "I am, however," eyes twinkling back at him, "delighted that you could bring Michele for this auspicious event. We would have missed her terribly."

"*Mes Chéries...Mes Chéries!*" Michele pushed past the group and ran to embrace Rod Zakes and Marc Bowles, green eyes flashing. "You have just arrived from Iapetus, *non?*" She kissed each of them without ceremony, linked arms and pulled them toward the group.

Henri straightened formally. "Mr. President...Director....," but his eyes never lost their twinkle.

"Please, Henri," Marc said, shaking his hand. "We're among friends."

The surrounding crowd knew who each of these celebrities was and also understood what tied them together. Although the Great Room area was limited, the celebrants allowed them their space.

Through the crowd of ordinary people back-stopped by white-robed Raëlians holding welcoming banners, Vesta spotted a diminutive sari-clad figure making her way toward the group. Carmen Bhuta, India's Minister of Health, stretched out her hands to accept Vesta's embrace and then made her rounds, paying special attention to each person, friend or colleague, with genuine warmth but without Michele's exuberance. To Vesta, Carmen embodied the class and grace she still remembered from her long-ago days aboard the *Ark*—Iapetus—on the final stages of its interstellar voyage. When they first met, what seemed like a lifetime ago, Vesta quickly sensed the difference between Carmen and the other women on Jon's exploratory crew. The crew's free-wheeling sexuality mirrored her own culture's attitude, but Carmen more closely matched her earlier generation's more reserved approach to intimate human interactions. Vesta was fine with the modern but more comfortable with her own generation's values.

After greeting everyone, Carmen settled herself between Vesta and Azurad, arms linked in a show of closeness. Then her face broke into a bright smile as Noel Goddard arrived with Chen Lee-Fong in tow, Noel towering over his shorter friend.

"We're safe, now that the engineers have arrived," Marc said with a chuckle, gripping both men by their forearms.

Noel accepted Michele's ministrations with a touch of formality, and Chen blushed while clearly enjoying her sincere warmth. Noel explained that he had only recently reconnected with Chen when Chen had contacted him through his newly appointed position as head of China's Science Directorate. The Directorate was deeply involved with developing applications for Founder black-hole technology

That leaves only Dmitri and Asshur, Vesta thought, *and Aram*, she added wistfully. *Even an Earth Mother should not outlive her grandchildren.* With that thought, some of Vesta's joy at reuniting with friends evaporated. Lud's and Shakbah's arrival from the Hub restored some of her gaiety, and then Dmitri and Jake showed up with Asshur and Sam Houston in tow. Asshur hugged his grandmother warmly, and then Dmitri shoved him aside with friendly gruffness.

"Mirs suits you well, Earth Mother!" he said with a rumbling laugh, holding her small frame gently, and then gripped Azurad's hands and swung her around. "And you, Little Sister!"

And this time, Asshur pushed Dmitri aside to greet his sister-in-law properly. "Sis…," he said, kissing her warmly. Somehow, Michele got mixed up in the greeting, but nobody minded.

Asshur placed his arm around Sam Houston's shoulders, an upward reach to overcome Sam's height advantage. "You've all heard his name, folks, but let me make it official. This is Sam Houston, founder of Lone Star Mars and soon to be governor of Texas."

Sam acknowledged the introduction and then turned to Vesta. "It is my distinct honor, Earth Mother, to meet you finally, face-to-face." His large hands swallowed her small ones, and Vesta experienced what everyone else experienced when meeting Sam for the first time.

My kind of leader, she thought as she passed him on to Azurad before Michele pulled his head down for her version of the traditional French greeting.

My circle is almost complete…and as soon as Starchild *materializes…*

✳

Sam was in his element surrounded by people, good people, expert at what they did, confident leaders, explorers, adventurers, doers in every sense of the word. Michele's exuberance took him aback initially, but since nobody seemed to mind, he gave as well as he received. Because of his time with Asshur, he felt like he already knew everyone, but to see them all together was somewhat overwhelming.

As Sam glanced over the crowd from his personally elevated position, he let his gaze rest on the small group of Raëlians at the back of the Great Room. He remembered Matti McIntyre telling him about the latest arrivals at Lone Star and the contingent of Raëlians that debarked in full regalia. Matti had told him they turned out to be a productive addition to the Lone Star population, adding a well-deserved diversionary element to their still somewhat austere society. He didn't know about any Raëlian presence at New Israel but made a mental note to find out.

Sam was not easily awed or intimidated by people he met, but when he considered the collected talent in this group, it gave him pause. The woman who nurtured her family for a hundred fifty thousand years, and finally rose to become the first president of the Iapetus Federation—and Earth Mother to nearly ten billion souls; her grandchildren manning essential roles on the starship *Starchild*, or holding prominent positions in today's interplanetary civilization, and the man who created New Israel on Mars; the man who held the United States together against all odds and now guided the Starchild Institute research efforts; the man who orchestrated the *Cassini II* expedition and then succeeded Vesta as president of the Federation; the man who was holding France together against unbelievable outside pressure; the Russian who had stabilized the security of the entire Solar System beyond Earth; those *Cassini II* crew members who were now embarked on the *Starchild*, who discovered the connection between Iapetus and the Founders—it was an impressive list of accomplished people, and he felt honored to be included in their group.

Sam scanned the crowded room and then turned to former U.S. President and current director of the Starchild Institute, Marc Bowles. "Where is the U.S. delegation?" He continued scanning the crowd. "I would have thought that President Jackson would be here to celebrate the Starchild's return."

"Pretty unlikely," Marc answered. "He has pulled America way back from the world stage." The former president's eyes saddened. "Things are not going as he expected. I tried to warn him before the inauguration, but I fear he wasn't listening. The resurgence of the Caliphate has his full attention since he cut back America's defense capabilities by more than half. His low-level delegation left Slingshot in time to get here on time, but barely."

Sam could feel the former president's anguish as he talked about what was happening to his homeland. A disturbance at the back of the crowd caught both their attentions as the two-person American delegation made its way to the front. Both Sam and Marc recognized the two senators comprising the delegation and greeted them warmly.

Not their fault that their Commander-in-Chief doesn't get it, Sam thought as he turned his attention back to Marc and the rest of the celebrities grouped in front of the crowd.

✳

No one actually saw *Starchild* materialize. One moment the Great Room was alive with excited chatter, Raëlian chants, and the general buzz of an expectant crowd, and the next, it was totally silent except for a collective gasp as the window of the Great Room filled with the presence of the saucer-shaped starship. A cheer from the assembled Raëlians shattered the silence as they waved their white flags displaying the Wormhole of David, dancing with joy. The rest of the crowd joined them as Vesta withdrew slightly from the group with a shudder of relief.

A tug glided to *Starchild's* hatch, and within a few minutes, Jon Stock entered the Great Room, followed by Eber and the rest of the founders—Arpachshad, Rasu'eja, and Ishtar, who headed straight to Vesta, clasping her warmly. As the crowd cheered, Ginger Steele, Ari Rawlston, and Elke Gratz entered the room, Ari between the women, holding their hands high in salute. Then the seven new crew members entered, having graciously held back to let the original eight receive the initial limelight. Four women and three men who, like the other crew members, had become household names throughout the solar system in the intervening years.

"Who's in charge here?" Jon said with a broad smile as he approached the group of celebrities.

"In charge of what?" Marc quipped as they shook hands.

For these guys, it's been just a few hours, Marc thought as he gripped Jon's hand. *Has it really been ten years?*

"You carry the decade well," Jon told him, his craggy face filled with humor. "Seems like we just left, though."

✳

"In a pig's eye," Asshur said, feeling a deep rage well up inside him as he watched the heroic reception of the man he held responsible for his brother's death.

Conversation within earshot stopped as eyes turned to Asshur.

If this man had not been such a bullheaded jerk and spaced Saeed when he had the chance, my brother would still be alive and with me here. Asshur trembled with fury and stepped toward Jon. As he did, Vesta edged into view. She shook her head slightly, her eyes full of sadness.

"Where's your brother?" Jon asked, clearly sensing something was wrong. "No way he would miss this."

Asshur clenched his fists and gazed up at the taller man, rage threatening to overcome reason. Vesta shook her head. Asshur opened his mouth to call Jon out, to expose his deed, when Vesta stepped up to the two men, her eyes filled with tears.

Just before he launched himself at Jon, he glanced at Vesta. Once more, she shook her head. Before he could do anything, his grandmother moved between Jon and him.

"Saeed's agents got Aram—killed him in the Austrian Alps," she said. She leaned her head against Asshur's chest and reached out to grasp Jon's hand.

"Saeed…?" Jon's voice filled with astonishment.

Asshur clasped his grandmother and felt his anger dissolve as she wept against his chest. Then she pulled Jon's hand to Asshur's shoulder and slipped her arms around each man's waist.

Asshur took a deep, shuddering breath and managed to regain his composure. All around him, he heard guests murmur in relief.

"Saeed's back," Asshur said to Jon, "with a vengeance. He's the new prophet of a united Islam—mounting a global Jihad, I'm afraid."

Jon looked stricken. "What do you mean—'Global Jihad'?"

Marc moved forward and gave him a quick overview. "I'll brief you later," he concluded, "but let's carry on right now."

The Commander of *Starchild* shook his head in dismay, and Asshur heard him mutter, "A global Jihad… Dmitri was right, after all. I should have spaced the little terrorist."

Jon's words brought Asshur to his full senses, and he gripped Jon's arms with renewed warmth and friendship. Vesta stepped back, her face bright with hope, and this time she smiled to herself.

✸

As tension dissolved and people began to laugh again, Marc's thoughts returned to the immediate situation. The rest of *Starchild's* crew joined them, and things got a bit messy with Michelle doing her Gallic best to greet each arrival personally.

Deville joined Marc and Jon. "As you can see," he said with a barely discernible accent, "she hasn't changed one bit. That's why the French people love her so."

Arpachshad and Rasu'eja approached Marc, a powerfully built, compact, bronze-skinned warrior and a raven-haired athletic Amazon fully six centimeters taller than her mate—both obviously armed. Marc greeted him with a two-armed grip and received a warm kiss from her. Despite the space-age trappings of the Mirs Complex, the starship, and all the incredible technology that surrounded them, in these two, Marc saw the epitome of Boris Vallejo—warriors from a different age.

Then Ishtar approached him, a tall golden goddess who took his breath away. She clasped his hands to her bosom, leaned forward, her green eyes filled with mirth, and brushed her lips against his. "Mister President…," her voice a rich contralto.

"Director…" he responded, unable to take his eyes off hers, "… of the Starchild Institute." As tall as he, with oval face and nearly translucent skin, Ishtar was easily the most beautiful woman Marc had ever seen. She and Elke Gratz were the *Starchild's* historians, which created a clear link between them and the Institute, but Marc failed to see the personal connection that Ishtar had clearly expressed. He set it aside as something to ponder later and turned his attention to the approaching Ginger Steele, her statuesque blue-black features and green eyes filled with affection.

"Marc," she said, kissing him lightly, "I trust you missed me, too!" She brushed Ishtar's cheek with the back of her hand. "We really wanted you with us on *Starchild*…actually, *want*," she added as an afterthought.

"The Starchild Institute needed me." He grinned at the two women. "You gorgeous creatures will just have to continue without me!"

Eber and Ari made their way to Marc. "Stop hogging him!" Ari said to Ishtar and Ginger while shaking Marc's hand.

Marc gripped Eber's forearms. "It's good to see you, my friend," Marc said. "For you, it was just yesterday, but for me, it's been ten years. I'm glad to see your face again."

"I know how it feels," Eber said. "Remember, my brothers and I took turns remaining on Earth for ten-year stretches during our hundred fifty-thousand-year hopscotch journey to meet Jon and his crew on Iapetus." He paused in thought. "It's disorienting, to say the least."

Elke joined them, greeting Marc formally with a firm handshake and a little bow. Then she blushed and kissed him lightly. "Friends should not be too formal," she said in her slight German accent.

Ginger nodded her assent, slipping an arm around Ishtar's waist and gripping Elke's hand. "Come on, Girls, we got more people to greet."

IAPETUS

Following the celebrations, the reunions, the speeches—all transmitted throughout the solar system to human communities from the home planet to the Raëlian resort-asteroid Daphne and beyond—the *Starchild* crew brought the starship to its Iapetus home base.

"I know you guys understand this," Jon told his assembled crew, with an inclusive nod to Marc and Rod, Dmitri, and the non-crew Founders except for Lud and Shakbah. They lounged on the grass in front of the pyramid complex where Jon had originally set up his headquarters. "But it bears repeating. When we leave a month from now, we will be gone for a subjective year plus several days. When we return, one hundred eighty-five years will have passed here in the Solar System. Look back into our own past for two hundred years. Will we recognize the world we return to? Will our descendants remember us?"

Jon paused and swept his eyes around the group. *They all know this, of course, but I'm not confident they really understand the implications. Sure, they each are entirely capable of understanding it, but did they actually think their way through the consequences?* Jon pushed aside his musings and continued. "For the next month, each of us will collectively travel the length and breadth of this System, making sure that we get the personal support of as many movers and shakers as possible and of as many ordinary people as possible." He paused again. "We want our return to be the next pivotal event in human history. Our friends," he indicated the onlookers, "will do everything they can to ensure this. Marc and the Starchild Institute will do their collective best to keep the memory alive…but…," his voice took on an ominous tone, "one hundred eighty-five years is a very long time."

Eber stepped up. "We've done it before," he said. "Read your Biblical history and know the role we played, and see how it changed." He grinned at his immediate family members. "But that was then— no understanding of the universe and primitive technology, and this is now. We think we know a great deal about what's out there and how it works, and we have technology that seemed like magic to our Earth-brethren just a couple of years ago." He stopped talking and looked directly at the onlookers. "You guys just make sure we are remembered!"

✳

Dmitri called up the individual crew member itineraries. He shook his head in amazement. Jon had his fourteen people separately spread across the entire Solar System. That meant fifteen hyper-V craft. Dmitri had called in all his markers from across the System. He had assigned two of his security people to each craft—thirty people he really couldn't afford. He thought back to his days as a Russian Federation Aerospace Command Colonel. At one point, he had over 3,000 officers and airmen under his command, and that didn't include another 3,000 civilians. Now he was head of security for the entire Iapetus Federation—a planet, five moons, countless asteroids, L4 and L5, and all the vast space between, and he did it with just 300 people. And now, one-tenth of his staff was tied up with the *Starchild* crew. It kept him awake at night.

To top things off, Dmitri had disturbing reports of apparent terrorist incidents at both Mars settlements. It was only a matter of time, he was certain, until something dire would take place at L4. He had no practical way to control access and egress to the Mirs Complex. With the space elevator at L2 being the only real access to Udachny, Sokolov's Moon mining operation, and the other two outfits on the Moon, Dmitri had no concern for similar problems there. The Belter settlements were another thing altogether, however. Daphne was an obvious target, as were a couple of ultra-conservative Jewish settlements in the belt.

Like a sheriff in America's mythical west making rounds after dark, he regularly sent one of his agents to each of the settlements by hyper-V, since radio communications were haphazard at best. His agents exposed and eliminated a small Jihadist cell on Daphne, but finding that group was pure, dumb luck. How many other cells were on Daphne and spread throughout his vast area of responsibility was a complete unknown.

Dmitri did not have to worry about invasions by space fleets. His constant concern was one or two Jihadists on a specific mission, like when Aram was killed, or merely put somewhere to cause havoc, any kind of havoc, like the problems that kept happening on Mars. Right now, that was Matti McIntyre's and Mordecai Rochlin's problem, but sooner or later, it would become his as well. The Jackson Loop was well underway, a perfect target for the Delgado brothers or whoever the hell they were..

Kogda etot malen'kiy terrorist byl u nas, nam nado bylo yego vyki-nut' iz lyuka[6], Dmitri muttered to himself as he scratched Jake's chin. *Chert poberi!*[7].

✳

Marc Bowles sat at his desk at the peak of the pyramid complex that made up the sprawling Starchild Institute, several kilometers to the west of the government complex. He had been following the activities of the Starchild crew as they traveled the length and breadth of the Solar System, building goodwill, making sure they would be remembered, no matter where humans happened to settle.

---

6 *We should have spaced the little terrorist when we had him*
7 *Damn it!*

Hyper-V craft production was moving apace, although Dmitri had convinced Marc to make the entire current inventory of five available for the *Starchild* crew members. He had placed fifteen fully functional hyper-V craft and two freighters with various friendly parties throughout the Solar System. Another twenty that were restricted in multiple ways had been leased to anyone with the available cash—except the Caliphate. He had just learned from Dmitri, however, that despite his intentions, the Caliphate had managed to get its hands on two craft through a series of shell corporations and international political machinations. Fortunately, both were atmosphere restricted.

Marc leaned back, thinking about the next few days. He had a lot to cover before he met with the *Starchild* crew, Rod, Sam, and many others at Lone Star. This would be the last time many of them would see the crew members. There was no way he would miss it. Marc turned his thoughts to his primary responsibility as Director of the Starchild Institute. It turned out the Founders had no more in-depth understanding of the technology that drove their gadgets and equipment than did the typical tech-educated human understand modern human technology. Fortunately, the Ectarians had not built any deadman switches into their hardware. His scientists and engineers slowly but surely eked out the science and engineering behind the marvelous technology that had fallen into his hands.

In many cases, what they found opened doors they had been knocking against for decades. Particularly in the fields of artificial black holes and artificial gravity, they made significant progress. In effect, his guys had leap-frogged over 500 years of advancement in less than a decade and now faced the same scientific challenges as the Ectarians when they first arrived in the Solar System nearly a hundred fifty thousand years ago. Marc settled back to review the latest progress on the Link display above his desk.

MARS—WHITE ELEPHANT, LONE STAR MARS

Sam looked down the 12-meter mahogany bar at the fifteen Starchild crew members relaxing following a long day touring Nachal Rachaf, the Jackson Loop construction site, and Lone Star. Intermixed with them, he saw Asshur, Mordecai Rochlin—the Rasam, and Noel Goddard, who had arrived the day before to retrieve the *RH*, his personal hyper-V craft. At one of the tables, Vesta was huddled with President Rod Zakes and Margo Jackson. Earlier that day at the Jackson Loop, Sam had met with Margo and Klaus Blumenfeld, who was there to review the linear driver installation. Klaus stood off to the side with Matti McIntyre, talking shop, Sam presumed. Dmitri was in a back corner with Azurad in earnest, private conversation. Although the illumination in that corner was dim, Sam was pretty sure Dmitri was cupping Azurad's tiny hand in his large paw while Jake purred softly in her lap. Sadly missing were France's First Lady Michele deBois, India's Minister of Health, Carmen Bhuta, and head of China's Science Directorate, Chen Lee-Fong.

Sam had only met some of the assembled people recently and was well acquainted with only Dmitri, Rod, Marc, Matti, and the Rasam. Nevertheless, they felt like family. His eyes wandered from crew member to crew member when the thought struck him. **I'll never see these people ever again!**

Sam waved to the bartender. "Draw me another Lone Star, Billy."

"Klaus Blumenfeld just brought in a case of a special microbrew as a reward for naming the Space Loop after Margo. You wanna try that instead?"

"Why the hell not?" Sam grinned. "Set up the house!"

The bartender turned, opened the bottom middle cabinet in the wall behind the bar, and reached in to grab a case of glass-bottled microbrew. The case seemed stuck, so he gave it a tug.

At that moment, the domed room filled with a blinding flash and a deafening concussion. Pieces of bartender struck the overhead dome, sprayed the drinkers along the bar, and sailed across the room to hit the dome wall and several people sitting in booths. The massive mahogany bar splintered down the middle, knocking down four people on the other side. Glassware and bottles along the bar and in the wall shattered, glass flying everywhere. Then a loud crack broke the quiet following the explosion, and dome pressure began to drop precipitously.

Still on his feet, but cut from flying glass, Sam gazed about himself as the escaping air shrieked painfully in his ears. He saw Jon and Ari leap to their feet from the floor where they had been thrown. They each grabbed an edge of a piece of rubberized matting and together shoved it into the open cabinet where the microbrew had rested a moment before. Sam shook the blood from his vision, grabbed another piece of matting, and pressed it into the opening. The shriek dropped a couple of octaves, and the pressure loss slowed noticeably. Matti grabbed a cylinder that looked much like a standard fire extinguisher, but it was painted bright blue.

"Step aside, Gents!" he ordered as he pointed the nozzle at the open cabinet with its temporary rubberized stoppers. In seconds the entire cabinet filled with a tacky foam that sucked through the various openings and crevasses left by the matting and filled the crack at the base of the dome. Within a minute, pressure was restored, and Sam looked around to assess the situation. One of the new female crew-members and the Rasam were still down. Elke was checking the crew member, and Noel was reading the Rasam's pulse. Sam observed Elke carefully place the woman's head in her lap and then lean over to brush her lips as her eyes opened. Noel gave him a thumbs-up accompanied by a wide grin. Sam continued to look around the room. No one else appeared to be hurt, but there was a lot of blood—Billy's—and everyone was shaken up. He marveled at the swift, skillful action Jon and Ari took with whatever was available. Although both had been knocked to the deck, their reaction was immediate and resourceful. He turned as Dmitri walked up, Jake back in his traveling cage.

"The Delgado brothers?"

"Probably," Sam answered.

"Let's get this place cleaned up," Matti said to several Lone Star personnel who came when they heard the explosion. "And collect what's left of Billy."

IAPETUS—STARCHILD INSTITUTE

Marc looked at Jon and Eber, each occupying a comfortable chair in front of his desk. They came across to him as co-command-ers, although Eber had assured him that only Jon made the final decisions. Ari Rawlston, along with Ginger Steele, Elke Gratz, and Founder Ishtar, joined them, but Arpachshad and Rasu'eja had not yet returned from their goodwill tour. The other crew members still were out and about, lighting the home fires for the eventual return of *Starchild*.

"My team has worked on this problem the better part of your ten-year absence," Marc said. "I turned them loose right after you left, and it grew legs and took off on its own. Each of you, including the missing crew members, has received a detailed summary of our findings on your personal Links. The entire report is available in the general database, of course, but believe me, not one of you will want to wade through the hundreds-of-thousands of pages in that report."

A general chuckle passed through the group.

"Let me summarize what we found in terms that I can understand, so I'm sure all of you will too." He grinned at them, his eyes twinkling.

"The initial AM signal we received from Vesta's Star back before the Founders was too sketchy to determine much, although they actually deciphered a couple of words…in English!"

The group got very quiet.

"You did say 'English'?" Jon asked.

"English—'this' and 'it'—as best they could make them out."

"Nothing else?"

"Had a lot of trouble deciphering these two words. Not a hundred percent certain either. The next message was longer, very faint… one word—'by' or 'buy,' maybe even 'bye'—no way to tell, but more certain than the first message." Marc stopped, sipped from a glass on his desk, and continued.

"Our question was: Why English? How the Hell English? Only one way, we finally decided, only one. It had to be a reflected transmission from Earth. That implied something from one hundred eighty-four years before our reception. We obtained literally every AM broadcast that was still available in any possible format, starting with a hundred eighty-four years before the first reception, before the second, and everything between. We put Founder computers on the problem and set them loose. We reanalyzed the original two signals, taking them apart and reassembling them, microbit-by-microbit, and then we compared the result with the outgoing material.

"We obtained every single SETI recording—all of them—and put the computers on them as well, focused on the Draco sector.

We analyzed uncounted thousands of incoming signals, comparing them digitally to the corresponding outgoing signals.

"I could go on with all the things we did, but it's all in the summary. The bottom line is that we determined with a one-hundred-degree percentage of certainty that Vesta's Star has a transponder. It is on a planet orbiting the star between zero-point-nine and one-point-one AUs."

"A transponder…Who put it there?" Jon asked.

"You're serious? How could we know that?"

"Looks like we got a year to find it, and maybe…just maybe discover who…or what…put it there."

MIRS COMPLEX—RING KIEV

Virtually the same crowd that greeted the *Starchild* on its arrival a month earlier was present for its departure on its 185-year round-trip voyage to Vesta's Star. This time, however, the crowd was more somber since every person present would be long gone when *Starchild* returned. In addition to routine security measures, Dmitri had imposed container searches for every item being brought aboard Ring Kiev and body searches for everyone not personally known to his security people. This process slowed things down considerably, but nobody protested. The entire Solar System knew about the abortive attempt to take out the *Starchild* crew.

Dmitri's security people were everywhere. Outside the Great Room window, the *Starchild* hung suspended, moving in lock-synch with Ring Kiev's rotation so that to the crowd waiting inside, the backdrop seemed to be rotating behind the starship. Dmitri's three hyper-V craft, along with L4's two and the Moon's one, carefully arrayed themselves around *Starchild*. Dmitri was absolutely determined that nothing untoward would happen.

Speeches and farewells, hugs and kisses, tears and anguish—finally, a subdued crew filed into the shuttle that would transport them to *Starchild*. An hour later, Jon and his fourteen crew members were at their departure stations. Eber sat next to Jon at the control console. He looked at Jon. Jon nodded, and Eber pressed the launch button.

✳

The crowd in the Ring Kiev Great Room watched *Starchild* vanish in total silence. Then it heaved a collective sigh and disbursed.

The remaining *Cassini II* crew, the Founders, and their close associates stood silently while the crowd departed. Then Vesta pulled away from the group, walked to a window strut, and stood gazing out at the Mirs Complex. Azurad joined her, taking her hand.

"What is it, Grandmother mine?" she asked quietly in Founder Speak.

"Now it's just you, Asshur, Lud, and Shakbah…" Vesta's voice trailed off as a tear trickled down her cheek

EARTH—SAUDI ARABIAN DESERT

General Suleiman extinguished the holotank and turned to Saeed, ensconced in a pile of cushions. "They're gone, Sahib. I fear we will never see them again. Our agents on Mars, Ra'id Kassab and Abdul-Hasid Naseri, obviously failed their mission."

"I do not entirely agree, my General. They placed a bomb inside the room where the group assembled. The bomb detonated as they had planned. They killed one person and seriously disrupted operations at Lone Star." He smiled at Suleiman. "I think that counts for something, don't you?"

The General handed him a cup of strong, sweet mint tea. "You are correct again, Sahib." Then he activated his Link and called up an image. "Allow me to show you something." A shimmering image coalesced in the air before them. It was a large room, perhaps a hangar. In the middle, a hyper-V craft rested on its five extended legs. "You are aware, Sahib, that we obtained two such craft through our Indian connections. They were restricted to atmospheric travel, which made them of little use to us, but our Pakistani research team attacked the problem head-on. Unfortunately, during their initial investigation, they triggered the self-destruction mechanism of one craft. Several researchers were killed, and their facility destroyed when the core exploded." The image shifted to a bread-loaf-size module. Suleiman smiled widely and spread his arms. "Now, Sahib, they have learned to extract and replace this module at will. When the module is removed, the second craft will not operate, but when it is installed, the craft is fully atmosphere capable. We are now seeking access to a space-capable craft. The Americans have one, and I believe we can gain access through the Vice President, Syed Shah Bukhari. That will allow us to remove the controlling module and insert it into our own craft, making it space capable. This will give us at least temporary access to the Earth-Lunar space environment. Furthermore, they are now working on reverse-engineering the module." With a flourish, Suleiman bowed deeply. "Soon, Sahib, the entire Solar System will be open to you."

"Does our remaining craft have armament?" The image shifted back to the hyper-V craft, and Saeed lifted himself up to examine the image more closely.

"Not yet, Sahib." Suleiman shrugged. "It turns out making internal modifications to these craft is much easier than changing the outside." He sighed. "That may take a while, but I am confident that our scientists will eventually reach a solution."

CHAPTER NINE

MIRS COMPLEX

Marc watched Vesta withdraw into herself following the *Starchild's* departure. He knew she was hurting but felt unable to do anything about it. She was losing her immediate family piece-by-piece, and he was partly to blame. Azurad was there to comfort her, but Vesta had just lost two grandsons and two granddaughters-in-law forever. No amount of fixing would help. Dmitri stepped up and spoke quietly to grandmother and granddaughter-in-law, and then Azurad moved away with him. Marc took this opportunity to approach Vesta. She looked up at him with pain in her eyes, and he wrapped his arms around her and whispered softly into her hair, "Be strong, Earth Mother. We all need you; humanity needs you, and I need you."

Vesta heaved an immense sigh against Marc's chest, and then she stepped back and gave him a tentative smile. "Thank you, Marc…" She seemed about to say more but then simply took his hand and smiled sweetly. "Let's join the others."

A few minutes later, Marc and Rod, accompanied by several staff members, boarded Rod's hyper-V craft and departed for Iapetus. They all remained silent during the few minutes of subjective time their trip took. Marc was alone with his thoughts. Part of him wished he were aboard *Starchild*. The adventure of a lifetime, and he was stuck back here. The other part of him wanted to press forward with the black hole experiments. He was confident they were on the verge of a major breakthrough.

EARTH—OLD ISRAEL

Asshur looked out over the Plenary Chamber where he had spoken to the full Knesset two years ago. His thirteen-member security detail had dispersed itself unobtrusively in the chamber and its approaches, and in the U-shaped gallery overlooking the chamber. He could not see them but knew they were there. He deeply regretted their necessity, but Dmitri had insisted that a security team accompany Asshur on any trip to Earth, the more so when he visited Israel.

Over the years, the people of Israel had listened to Asshur's clarion call to join New Israel on Mars. By the time *Starchild* departed on her historic journey, only about 10,000 people were left in all Israel, mostly in and about Jerusalem, guarded by a military presence of about half the remaining population. Technically, as President, he was their commander-in-chief, but with the Israeli government officially located on Mars, all activity in the old government buildings in the *Givat Ram* district of Jerusalem had ceased. The local commander was on his own.

True to his promise, General Suleiman had allowed Israel to continue its existence. As Israelis departed for Mars, Palestinians moved in, and the landscape morphed from a lush, irrigated countryside to a wind- and water-eroded landscape. Representative government disappeared as martial law prevailed throughout the land. Asshur knew it was only a matter of time before the line broke, and Israel on Earth was no more. As he stared out over the Plenum, an elderly, stooped man with a flowing white beard made his way to the podium.

"Why have you done this?" the old man asked, lifting his head and speaking Hebrew in a surprisingly loud and clear voice, dark eyes boring into Asshur's. "Why have you destroyed everything we fought and died for?"

Asshur stepped down from the podium and approached the old man. "Who are you, sir?" he asked in Hebrew.

"My name does not matter…" The old man took a deep breath. "I fought in every Israeli conflict since I was fourteen. Four times I nursed burning desert sand to blooming garden. Four times I raised comfortable dwellings from arid wasteland. Four times I brought water to parched, cracked soil. And now it is all gone. It is as if I and my fellow settlers had never set foot on this land. Bedou tents have replaced houses I built. Arabic has usurped my native tongue…"

Asshur held up his hand and interrupted with a smile. "I understand, Old Man…" When the old soldier tried to continue his monolog, Asshur raised his other hand and then gripped the old-timer gently by his shoulders. "Hear me out, my friend, please…" The old soldier sighed and slumped his shoulders. "I know you believe this is your ancestral land…but it is not. Long ago, your forebears lived on the planet Ectaris, a world so distant that a radio signal broadcast to the Ectaris system today would not arrive there for five hundred years. It is an almost unimaginable distance. But that, my friend, was your ancestral home, not this strip of land along the Mediterranean. When Ectarian scientists discovered that their sun was going to nova—was going to explode—the Ectarian people came to Earth, a voyage of many lifetimes. My grandmother, I and my brothers and their wives… we are the only direct descendants of the original Ectarians…and we are your forebears."

The old soldier's face took on an incredulous look. "I know it's difficult to understand," Asshur squeezed his shoulders, "but it is true. My grandfather was the Noah of your *Torah*. My grandmother, Vesta, was his beloved wife." Asshur smiled warmly at him. "Your pioneering spirit and that of your compatriots kept Israel alive, and now Israel is flourishing in Nanedi Valles on the planet Mars with a bright and unstoppable future. New Israel needs your spirit; it needs you and what you represent. New Israel needs you and your fellow hold-outs. It's time to leave this strip of land to the Palestinians and join your brothers in the new Promised Land."

Tears streamed down the old soldier's cheeks. "This is true, what you tell me?" He reached beneath his shirt and brought forth a tattered copy of the *Torah*. "Will you swear to this on the Holy Scriptures?"

Asshur placed his hand on the old book. "I swear!"

As he spoke, a shot rang out from the junction of the left and rear galleries, followed by a volley of automatic fire and a scream.

Asshur watched the old man pitch to the floor, downed by a bullet apparently meant for himself, as two of his security team knocked him down, shielding his body with theirs. He lay on the cool floor, shielded by his protectors, watching the old man struggle to slide the tattered *Torah* toward him. Asshur reached out, grazing the book as his fingers touched the old man's trembling hand. "Devarim thirty-nineteen...*Shalom*," the old man whispered as life faded from his eyes.

Shouting, "*Allahu Akbar!*" a man rose to his feet in the right gallery, grenade in hand. A bullet pierced his arm, causing him to drop the grenade. The grenade exploded, shredding the would-be assassin, destroying part of the gallery, and killing a third fighter concealed several meters to the right.

"We have to leave NOW!" one of the security men said, pulling Asshur to his feet.

Asshur grabbed the tattered *Torah*, tucking it inside his tunic, and sprinted toward the back of the chamber with his two guards, keeping his head low. Automatic gunfire ahead of them mixed with the screams of dying men punctuated the seriousness of their situation. He and his detail had arrived on the *Merkavah*, which had been updated and outfitted with a new weapons suite developed by the Starchild Institute. It was waiting for them somewhere above the solar panel fields that covered most of the building roof.

"Faster!" his guards urged, "Faster!" They turned to enter a nondescript side door. "To the roof...hurry!"

As he reached the Knesset roof through a door in the central block structure, Asshur saw several hundred armed men crossing the plaza toward the main entrance in front and below him, and he was told of another group crossing the broad entrance to the parking garage at the back of the complex. They were being hit from the air by Gatling-style weapons mounted on Israeli helicopters and by RPGs fired by Israeli troops approaching them from the rear on both sides. A small cadre of fighters arrived on the roof from the opposite side of the block structure, discharging their weapons as they rounded the structure, running toward Asshur and his security team. With bullets flying from both directions, the two agents and Asshur crouched below the solar panel tops, running toward the ramp. As the agents pushed Asshur up the ramp into *Merkavah*, both took hits, one in his leg and the other to his shoulder. They pitched into *Merkavah* with Asshur, still clutching the tattered *Torah*, as three other security team members sprinted across the roof from the front of the block structure toward the hyper-V craft, dodging the solar panels and firing at the advancing fighters as they ran. One was hit as *Merkavah* fired a laser burst that took out the remaining sprinting fighters. The two security agents dragged their companion into *Merkavah*, and the hyper-V craft rose into the air as the ramp pulled up behind them. Two shoulder-fired missiles screamed upward from the attacking troops at the front and back of the complex, but *Merkavah's* automatic laser system took them out before they had traveled halfway, even though they would not have caused significant damage to the craft had they reached their destination.

"Status?" the detail Chief barked to his team.

"One killed, three wounded and onboard, seven making their way to the roof."

"They're together," his Coms said. "They'll be coming through the southeast access." He signaled the Israeli helicopters to cover the other accesses to the roof and instructed the remaining detail to sprint to *Merkavah* the moment they reached the roof. The Chief briefly instructed the hyper-V craft pilot. About a minute later, three airborne Gatlings opened fire on the doors of the block structure facing the rear as seven men hit the roof, running for all they were worth toward the hovering *Merkavah*. One man stumbled, hit by a stray bullet, and was dragged by two companions and hauled into the craft.

As the *Merkavah* rapidly rose into the sky and the three Israeli choppers dispersed in three separate directions, a mighty explosion shattered the air as the historic Knesset building belched a towering pillar of fire and smoke, and was no more.

MIRS COMPLEX

Lud's excitement was palpable to Shakbah as he strode into their living quarters in Ring Samara several days following *Starchild's* departure. He was centimeters taller than his brothers except for Eber, who towered over all of them. His blond hair was out of place, and his blue eyes flashed with excitement. "The test results are stunning, absolutely stunning!" He grabbed her svelte frame and swung her around.

"Put me down, Silly!" But ordinarily shy Shakbah began to catch Lud's excitement as he stroked a blond lock from her forehead and then gazed into her nearly purple eyes.

When the Founders first met the *Cassini II* explorers on Iapetus, two things had stood out to Shakbah. Their similarities were striking. Except for clothing and language, any one of the Founders could have blended in entirely anywhere in North and South America, Europe including Russia, and Australia and New Zealand. In Asia or Black Africa, they would have looked like a visitor from one of those regions. She was also struck by the differences in their technologies, but it wasn't across the board. Earth's Link technology and its associated holographic imaging were significantly more advanced than theirs. Longevity research even more so. When the entire population of the Ectarian solar system had left Ectaris on the *Ark*, that they now thought of as Iapetus, they were less concerned with living long lives and more focused on ensuring they had a viable civilization when they arrived at their destination. Shakbah was particularly impressed with the early twenty-first-century work of the Life Extension Foundation and its research partners. They had focused on parabiosis and the rejuvenating effect of young blood on aging microglia. Their landmark clinical study back in 2016 had set the stage for Shakbah's and Lud's current research. Now, apparently, their most recent test results had really excited Lud, to say the least.

"Tell me about it," she said, as she handed Lud a martini, something he had come to love since they settled in Ring Samara.

Lud relaxed in his favorite chair and described the details of the latest results.

"You're sure of this?" Shakbah asked.

"Absolutely," Lud said after pausing to refill his martini. "The aging process has entirely stopped, and, in fact, there is a significant age reversal."

"In all subjects?"

"Yep…"

"For real…no joke…you're positive…?"

"It is…it's not…I am!" He took another sip, his blue eyes twinkling. "We did it, Shakbah. We really did it!" He closed his eyes, savoring both their success and his martini. "We really did it!"

EARTH—SAUDI ARABIAN DESERT

As Saeed and General Suleiman watched the holovision broadcast of the destruction of the Knesset, Saeed said, "It's time to take Israel."

"There are perhaps ten thousand Israelis left in and about Jerusalem, and half as many IDF soldiers, scattered throughout the country," Suleiman answered thoughtfully. "Most of the land has reverted to desert crisscrossed by Bedouin caravans. The Israeli army holds back the Palestinian hordes, but they are slowly penetrating the interior anyway. If we bide our time, Israel will disappear of its own accord." The general smiled and poured Saeed some hot mint tea.

"Israel has NOT disappeared, and it will not unless we destroy it!" Saeed said with a snarl. "So, there are ten thousand here…but, there are some fifteen million in Nanedi Valles." He stood, raising his truncated arm. "I will not rest until the Israeli scum and the Founder vermin are forever vanquished!"

"A fuel-air burst would kill a lot of the hold-outs," Suleiman said softly, "and a well-placed nuke would destroy the Nanedi Valles complex." He paused, looking at the Prophet intently. "We can do the first, but we're not ready for the second; I think the Founders will interfere with any nuke delivery to Jerusalem by missile or aircraft. We could try overland, perhaps in several parts for local assembly. If we can get it to Jerusalem, we may be able to assemble and detonate it before the Founders detect and disable it." He poured himself a cup of mint tea. "We can deliver a small fuel-air device by hot air balloon and a couple of martyrs. We can sponsor a hot-air balloon

festival as a cover. This probably has the best chance of succeeding."
He paused, smiling broadly. "But it won't have much effect." Saeed
lifted his eyebrows. "A hot-air balloon cannot carry sufficient explosive fuel to have the effect we desire." He paused in thought. "If all
the balloons were ours…the effect would be much greater." Then he
looked straight at Saeed. "And, what about the Palestinians? Do we
sacrifice them for the greater glory of Allah?"

"No…we need their goodwill. Get the word out, quietly. Move
as many Palestinians out of Jerusalem as possible, but do it soon!"

IAPETUS—STARCHILD INSTITUTE

Noel Goddard sat in a comfortable chair, looking across a plain
desk at Marc Bowles. He had met Marc as President of the
United States shortly after the historic meeting with the Founders
and their subsequent interference with the Persian Caliphate's ill-con-
sidered assault on Israel. They met again when *Starchild* departed for
her shakedown cruise and twice more—for her return ten years later
and for her final departure. Those meetings were brief, however, and
since then, Noel had busied himself with his own research.

Nearly three years earlier, representatives from the Australian
government had approached Noel with a challenging proposition.
The Australians proposed establishing a large-scale O'Neill Cylinder
colony orbiting the L5 Lagrange position some 384,400 kilometers
behind the Moon in its orbit. They wanted Noel to head the project.

The Mirs Corporation had opted for the Stanford Double-torus
design at L4 and now had three rings, the original 3-kilometer Ring
Kiev and two newer 5-kilometer rings—Samara and Rostov. The Stanford design was ideal for smaller structures but was not well suited for
recreating an Earth-like environment. No matter how you did it, the
internal visual effect of the torus curving away from you was unavoidable. The Australians wanted something better, more earthlike. The L5
settlement was aimed at eliminating the torus problem by constructing
two 30-kilometer-long, 6-kilometer-wide linked O'Neill cylinders.
Each would have about 283 square kilometers of livable surface.

Noel had studied the project in detail for three years following
the initial proposal. Now he sat across from Marc Bowles, arguably the

most influential corporate director in the Solar System. Noel wasn't nervous, but he knew where the power lay in this meeting. All his life, Noel had held up his end, standing tall and confident in the face of herculean odds. This time was no different, except he felt a bond with the movie-star-handsome man on the other side of the desk. When they first met, when the American president had evaluated the unexpected presence of the Founders and then quickly made decisions that turned out to be the best possible under the circumstances, Noel was hugely impressed. As he watched Marc assume control of the Starchild Institute and turn it into the Solar System powerhouse it was, his esteem for this man grew even more. And now he was here as a supplicant, looking for something only the Starchild Institute could provide.

"Basically," Noel said, "the Aussies have followed the original O'Neill Island-three concept. This involves two linked cylinders rotating in opposite directions so that the cylinder end-caps will maintain their orientation toward the sun." He projected an image from his Link into the space between them. "O'Neill's calculations were based on 1970s technology. Today we have the Founder's black hole technology for power, diamond strand technology for cabling, and we have modern polymer technology for construction and radiation protection. This dramatically increases our options." The image shifted to a much larger single cylinder. "This cylinder is fifty kilometers long and ten in diameter. It has fifteen hundred and seventy square kilometers of livable surface—nearly three times the living space of Island-three. Its gyroscopic rotation causes it to maintain a fixed orientation in space. These three mirrors," in the holoimage three large mirrors off one endcap flashed, "will continuously adjust their orientation so that the sun will appear to rise and set in the cylinder's three window panels.

"This version of the O'Neill concept can comfortably accommodate over thirty million inhabitants—about the same as the population of Australia." Noel sat back with a smile. "It's not too difficult to see where these folks are headed." The space colony image collapsed, and Noel leaned forward. "This is way bigger than me or the Aussies. It will be the single largest structure ever attempted by humanity."

Marc lifted his eyebrows at this statement.

"Okay," Noel grinned, "aside from Iapetus." He leaned back. "For the most part, the funding will come from Aussie private sources, with significant inputs from their government. Their total funding will be about seventy percent. Mirs Corp. has agreed to cover ten percent. I am soliciting a twenty-percent investment from you in Starchild Institute funds and expertise." He spread his hands with a smile. "You see, Ayers Sky's internal volume of about four thousand cubic kilometers needs to be filled with about three thousand cubic kilometers of nitrogen and about one thousand cubic kilometers of oxygen—at STP. That's where you come in. There's a lot of oxygen and nitrogen out there, but I need it inside Ayers Sky at El-five."

"You've done the calculations, Noel. Give me some numbers."

Noel grinned and reactivated his Link display. "Internal volume, as I said, is just under four thousand cubic kilometers. That's just over five billion tonnes or cubic meters." Noel built an image of a VASIMR tug pulling a stylized load. "For simplicity, picture this pulled ice asteroid as a regular cube. If it is one hundred meters per side, the job will require about four thousand loads of nitrogen ice and one thousand loads of water ice." Noel smiled a bit uncertainly. "We are looking for SI to locate and get these to Ayers Sky."

"Your audacity matches your project," Marc said. "I presume El-five will join the Federation…" His voice trailed off.

"As soon as Ayers Sky meets Federation requirements."

IAPETUS—FEDERATION HEADQUARTERS

Despite being the chief executive officer of a federation that stretched across a significant part of the Solar System, President Rod Zakes retained much the same informality he had established when he was Mission Director for the *Cassini II* expedition to Iapetus. The Iapetus Federation had been in existence for well over a decade now, yet he still preferred not to assume the trappings of high office. Besides, as the man responsible for ensuring that the Federation actually functioned, he just didn't have time for any activity that did not directly serve to administer the vast realm he had inherited from Vesta. Sixteen- to 18-hour days were the norm for Rod. Nevertheless, his door remained open to any visitor whose business was sufficiently important to warrant his personal attention. He left it to his small staff to sort out the requests and handle matters not requiring his attention. Rod was well aware of the potential he had created for corrupt gatekeepers, but in the years since he assumed the president's office, this had not become a problem.

Rod's office was a study in minimalism. Light tan walls bedecked with holographs from his varied career blended unobtrusively with a darker carpet woven to handle the traffic of a busy working office. His desk was utilitarian with a full electronics suite and sufficient storage to keep things off his desktop, giving an impression of businesslike efficiency.

Rod was studying a summary of several reports from Dmitri on possible pirate attacks in the outer asteroids. Dmitri was unsure if these possible attacks stemmed from rival Belters or whether there was something more sinister at play. At this stage, there was little the Federation could do but monitor the situation. Rod looked up as Asshur strode into his office. "Mr. President," Rod said formally, with a smile.

"Likewise," Asshur answered, shaking Rod's hand. "Thank you for making time for me, Rod."

"For you, my friend, always!" Rod's tone was firm and resolute. "Dmitri briefed me on your close call in Jerusalem. Too bad about the old-timer. An ignominious end for a genuine pioneer and an inglorious end for a noble institution." Both men paused for a moment in silence, and then Rod said, sweeping his hand, "Please take a seat."

Asshur cleared his throat and then launched into the reason for his visit. "My sources tell me the Caliphate is about to abandon its pledge to protect Israel. New Israel is simply too distant to keep on top of the situation. If Suleiman attacks, I won't even know about it until it's all over. I could keep *Merkavah* stationed over Jerusalem, but to what effect? I can destroy several missiles or deactivate several nukes, but that wily bastard learned a hard lesson during the last conflict. He has sufficient firepower to completely overwhelm my defense capabilities. I have to stop everything he sends—while he needs to get only one through." Asshur gazed at Rod ruefully.

Rod sat silently in thought. On the one hand, the good guys and bad guys were clearly delineated. On the other, the hold-outs had remained of their own free choice. Furthermore, the Federation was in no position to take on the Caliphate without America's help, and there was little chance that would be forthcoming. Five years from now, things would be different. The Federation would have a well-armed fleet capable of defending any part of its vast realm…but not yet. He sighed as he carefully constructed his response.

"You know where my—our—sympathies lie, Asshur. But…" he sighed again, "if we take on the Caliphate right now, I'm not sure I can predict the outcome." He placed his palms on the desk. "Without America's help, I can't take that risk." He felt inadequate as he spoke, and his body language betrayed this.

"I'm not asking for Federation intervention, Rod, only for as many weapons-equipped hyper-V craft as you can spare. With ten craft, I can seek out and neutralize his nukes and simultaneously provide cover to prevent a fuel-air burst over Jerusalem.

"Ten thousand people are holed up in or near Jerusalem, plus half as many troops. I need to protect them during evacuation…"

"If you can talk them into leaving, my friend, and that's a big if."

"I've got to try, Rod, I've got to try!"

"How soon do you need them?"

"The Caliphate has moved nearly all Palestinians out of the area. They think we don't know, but…"

"You have two fighters at Mars, no, three—use one of Lone Star's, plus *Merkavah*. There are three at Mirs; you can use two. That's six. I've got four you can use. That's ten. That will have to do." Rod stood with a smile. "Dmitri will coordinate getting the fighters to you. You concentrate on setting up your protective shield." He held out his hand.

"I am in your debt, Rod. Thank you!"

EARTH—200 KM ABOVE OLD ISRAEL

Asshur checked *Merkavah's* screens, noting the positions of the nine other hyper-V fighters and the two transport craft hovering in place 200 kilometers above the surface, fanned out so that most of Israel was covered except for the Negev. Each fighter carried an experienced pilot, a co-pilot who was also the Astrogator, and a Weapons Officer. The Resident in each craft was programmed to protect itself and its personnel and fight the craft under the direction of the Weapons Officer or either of the pilots. Each craft was equipped with neutrino beams, high-energy laser disruptors, and anti-matter particle beams and carried full-spectrum receivers that could analyze virtually any type of incoming radiation, particles, or electromagnetics. The craft's accelerator ring generated a neutrino beam that could be focused down to about a meter at 61,000 kilometers. It could disrupt any biomaterial—specifically living matter, and would also shut down a nuclear reactor or disable a nuclear bomb. The laser disruptors were originally designed to protect Iapetus from incoming meteors but had been modified to provide both offensive and defensive capability to the hyper-V craft. They had a range of about 1,500 kilometers. The high-energy particle beam encapsulated a small amount of anti-matter from the core and transported it at very high velocity to a target location up to 3,000 kilometers distant, where it combined explosively with the target's normal matter, producing a prodigious explosion. The crafts' ability to maneuver radically and instantly was a significant element in their defense. In a battle scenario, each craft would maintain a continuous, erratic movement orchestrated by each Resident and coordinated with the others that would render them virtually impossible to target. Each craft was also outfitted with encrypted IFF transceivers to prevent friendly fire incidents, especially crucial with their relatively tight pattern over Israel. With their ability to translate from one position to another at near lightspeed, the IFF signals needed to be carefully monitored by the Residents to ensure the craft maintained safe distance from each other.

The transports were looking for troop movements and coordinating with the Israeli ground forces. Six of the fighters were probing Caliphate arsenals and launch sites for nukes being made ready. Asshur did not want to initiate hostilities by taking out the nukes unless they clearly were getting prepared for launch. Three fighters kept track of missile and bomber locations.

Asshur in *Merkavah* maintained station 500 kilometers above the shield, working through his Resident to coordinate all their activities.

"Gabriel, this is Lucifer, over."

Asshur turned his attention to his Communications Officer.

"Gabriel," the Communications Officer responded to the ground commander in Jerusalem.

"This is Lucifer…We got some unusual air activity…hot-air balloons moving west to east from the Med toward Jerusalem. There must be twenty or more."

"Roger that. Stand by. Gabriel out."

Asshur queried his pilots. They found nothing suspicious, just a typical hot-air balloon festival, nothing more. Nevertheless, Asshur's senses were on high alert. He motioned to his Communications Officer and took control of communications.

"Lucifer, this is Gabriel. Get your birds up and vector those balloons away from Jerusalem. Over."

"And how in hell do I do that, Gabriel? I can't stop the wind."

"Roger that!" *Dumb order*, Asshur said to himself as he rethought the matter.

"Lucifer, force them to the ground. Do not let them reach the city!"

"Gabriel, I've got five birds holding the line. The balloons are descending…omigosh! One just exploded…and a second…and a third! One of my birds is down in a cloud of flame a half kilometer wide. All the balloons have exploded…the sky is filled with fire…I lost another bird—the other three pulled up and away. What was that, Gabriel?"

"A distributed fuel-air burst, Lucifer. They intended to do it over Jerusalem, but you stopped them."

"Now what?"

"Get to as many of the holdout leaders as you can. Tell them that next time Jerusalem will go up in flames. Get them out of there. Tell them to use any launch loop they can reach. We will retrieve them from their trajectories. Tell them to show their passports, and New Israel will pick up the cost."

"Roger that, Gabriel. Anything else?"

"If they refuse the launch loops, get them out of the city, by force if necessary. I don't think we can stop the next attempt."

EARTH—SAUDI ARABIAN DESERT

General Suleiman briefed the Prophet on the misadventure. "The hot-air balloons exploded before reaching Jerusalem, Sahib. We downed two helicopters…that's it."

"Do you have a backup plan?"

"Yes, Sahib, it is being implemented as we speak."

Suleiman called up a bird's eye view of Jerusalem. "Normally, a fuel-air burst is accomplished by first releasing a massive explosive cloud over the target and then detonating the entire cloud at once. The ensuing firestorm sucks in the air from all directions, generating hurricane-like winds to fuel the firestorm. The result is much like the effect of a small nuclear bomb." He paused to let Saeed absorb the information. "Ideally, the blast is initiated from the air, but when that is impossible, there is another way." Moving points appeared on several of the roads leading into Jerusalem. "These," Suleiman said, "are tanker trucks filled with LPG—liquefied propane without the odor additive Ethyl Mercaptan."

Saeed raised his hand. "Ethyl Mercaptan?"

"I apologize, Sahib." Suleiman cursed himself inwardly. It was easy to forget that the Prophet had no formal education, except for his *Qur'an* studies. "You are familiar with the smell of a gas leak?"

Saeed nodded.

"Gasses like natural gas or propane have no smell. To know there is a gas leak, gas companies add Ethyl Mercaptan, which smells like rotten eggs—the smell of a gas leak."

Saeed smiled with comprehension.

The General continued. "Each refrigerated tanker filled with the odorless liquefied gas has been assigned a terminal location. Once they reach their terminals, on my signal, they will open their main valves and depart on predetermined routes, spreading odorless propane throughout metropolitan Jerusalem. The process will take about an hour. Once the tankers are clear, prepositioned firebombs will explode, igniting the propane, leveling Jerusalem—once and for all."

Saeed took in the images silently, in obvious thought. "When will your tankers be ready to roll?"

"We are refining and purifying the propane in the Saudi and Persian oil fields. I will need about two weeks to accumulate the LPG and load it into the tankers. Then a week to get them into position."

"Do not fail me this time!"

The General nodded, keeping his face neutral. He had killed the Persian Caliph, but only because it served his purpose. He approached this little despot cautiously. Somehow, despite all odds, Saeed had survived the journey to Saturn, the initial contact with the Founders, the destruction of the Persian Caliphate, and now was recognized worldwide as the leader of a singular Islam, the greatest prophet in Islamic history. No formal education beyond the Qur'an, this little holy man operated on pure instinct. That instinct, guided by the General's subtle hand, would place Saeed at the head of a worldwide Caliphate with himself actually running the show. He would become the most powerful ruler in all of human history. General Ismail Suleiman smiled inwardly, offering the Prophet a slight bow.

"We will succeed this time without fail, Sahib!"

✳

Two days later, Saeed lounged on his cushions in his sprawling tent complex, still pitched atop the same low mound overlooking the dry lakebed near the center of Rub' al-Khali in the Saudi Arabian desert. The evershifting dunes surrounding the lakebed provided Saeed with a continually changing view, but he was so used to it that he hardly noticed. Morning prayers were over, but his troops were still lounging in the bright morning sun outside their tents. He was about to immerse himself in the *Qur'an*, to ferret out the real meaning of a particularly obtuse passage when a soft whoosh brought him out of his tent. A hyper-V craft had landed in the space before him. Like the *Merkavah*, it was saucer-shaped and deep black, so black, in fact, that it almost looked like a hole in the air. A hatch opened, and a ramp extended to the ground. Moments later, General Suleiman walked down the ramp and approached Saeed. He bowed his head respectfully and gestured to the spacecraft.

"I bring you victory, Sahib—*Rasul Allah*[8], a fully space-worthy craft!"

Saeed lifted his right arm into the air, and his robe fell back revealing his leather-cup-covered stump. "*Allahu Akbar!*" His call rang across the encampment.

Two thousand voices answered back, "*Allahu Akbar! Allahu Akbar! Allahu Akbar!*"

8　*Messenger of Allah*

CHAPTER TEN

EARTH—PORT OF HAIFA, ISRAEL

At one time, the Port of Haifa was Israel's most significant commercial seaport. It could comfortably accommodate a dozen or more large container ships at the same time, and its passenger terminal could handle several cruise ships. Now, however, the gantries were silent, and the passenger terminal was empty. Closer inspection revealed that nearly every moveable item with any value had been removed, and what remained had been vandalized. The Port of Haifa was a shell of what it once had been.

Alam Abner Garlock let his gaze sweep over the decaying port facilities of Haifa, bathed in hazy sunlight filtered through dust off the Iraqi Desert 500 km to the east. As the Colonel in charge of the IDF in Old Israel, he was responsible for getting as many as possible of the remaining 10,000 Israeli citizens off-planet. It was like herding cats. The Israelis who, for whatever reason, had chosen to stay in Old Israel were a cantankerous, stubborn lot who would as soon spit in your face as give you the time of day. Somehow, he had to get as many of these as possible on a cruise ship docked along Haifa's loading wharf.

Under the best of circumstances, it was a crazy operation. A cadre of Garlock's officers and senior noncoms had traversed Old Israel, seeking out reluctant citizens from their hideouts virtually everywhere. By persuasive argument, bribing, and even coercion, he had been able to convince most of the holdouts to assemble at Haifa—nearly 9,000. It had been a logistics nightmare. Fortunately, Haifa's infrastructure was still capable of handling that many people, but there still was the matter of food. Israel no longer had sufficient capacity to feed that many people, and even if it had been possible, there was no way to get that much food into Haifa. New Israel ended up sending a hyper-V transport every third day crammed with MREs that were on an emergency production basis in a facility under Levi Bar-Lev's leadership in southern Nanedi Valles.

Hovering at 500 kilometers in *Merkavah*, Asshur followed the evacuation activities closely. He and Garlock maintained an open Link. As the last of the nearly 9,000 stragglers arrived in Haifa by truck, Garlock brought Asshur up to date.

"I have a cruise ship designed to carry three thousand passengers in relative comfort. I intend to cram five thousand people aboard to transport about half the holdouts to the Mediterranean Loop at Mallorca. I've got two large passenger planes, each capable of carrying nine hundred people. I intend to transport the remaining holdouts by aircraft to the base of the Sahara Loop at Atar in Mauritania.

"Since Palma cannot house nearly five thousand people, I'm retaining them on the cruise ship until they're called for transport. I'm told that the Med Loop can carry three hundred people per hour to the Intercontinental Skyport, but only if they're immediately launched along the loop. That's still a lot of capsules."

"We've got that covered," Asshur said. "Over the last week, my people delivered thirty extra capsules to both the Med Loop and the Sahara Loop on loan from the Margo Jackson Loop on Mars."

"How did you pull that off?"

"We used the two hyper-V transports we got from the Federation. They can each carry two fifty-passenger capsules."

"So, how do you get the passengers to Mars? I've been too busy to give it much thought, but I have wondered. I mean, I knew you had plans in place, but no one has briefed me on what happens after I get the refugees into the capsules." Garlock raised his eyebrows and smiled at Asshur's holographic image.

"The capsules carrying fifty persons each will be launched on a deep space trans-Mars trajectory as you indicated so that all the capsules from both Med and Sahara will be on a single known track. We'll use the transports to pick up the capsules with their passengers and transport them to Mars. Then we'll recycle the capsules as necessary until everyone is off Earth."

"Sounds simple enough," Garlock remarked.

"But a logistics nightmare," Asshur said with a grimace. "No more so, however, than what you're dealing with down there." He paused, and Garlock waited patiently, knowing that Asshur was juggling several balls at once. "How many holdouts are left, would you estimate?"

"Perhaps a thousand—no way to really tell," Garlock said thoughtfully. "A handful of Haredi or ultra-Orthodox types, probably hiding in the Beit Guvrin Caves about forty klicks southwest of Jerusalem. These caves have been used by rebel factions for over three thousand years—maybe longer, but we can trace archeological signs back at least that far. The rest will be in small groups in hidey-holes virtually anywhere in the Negev and Judean Deserts." He pulled up an image for Asshur. "Some of this region is more formidable than Nanedi Valles. It would take literally years to flush them out."

"Any chance some are still in Jerusalem?"

"A few…yes; Haredi types."

"Can you get them to leave?" Asshur asked.

"Possibly. What do you have in mind?"

"We suspect the Caliphate is planning some kind of fuel-air burst over Jerusalem. I'm not sure I can do anything about it. If you can persuade the Jerusalem holdouts to leave, the Caliphate's mischief will be a huge object lesson with few, if any, actual casualties."

EARTH—MALLORCA ISLAND, WESTERN MEDITERRANEAN

The sky over Palma on the western Mediterranean island of Mallorca was azure blue, hosting fluffy, white cumulus cloud clusters. The Intercontinental Skytower cables pierced the sparse cloud layer over the sleepy town at about 2,000 meters, their lacy parallel structure seeming to vanish somewhere above the fleecy clouds. Samuel Meisel was unimpressed with the view. He was unhappy as he and his wife herded their four children forward with the slowly moving line of people queued up to board the waiting space capsule at the Palma Socket Terminal. He had held out as long as possible, but the IDF sergeant who had located them in their modest home in a village on the edge of the Negev was most persuasive. The clincher was when the sergeant had made it clear that the only way Meisel's four children would grow to adulthood was for them to emigrate to New Israel on Mars.

The children were excited. Their mother Rachel had her hands full, keeping them in line. Meisel, however, was glum and despondent; everything he had worked so hard to give his family was back there. What did Mars possibly hold that could replace that? He looked up as they approached the capsule—a gleaming, aerodynamic, silver rail car with open clam-shell doors along the left side. Directly ahead of the capsule, another was just closing its clam-shell doors, and ahead of that one, a sealed capsule commenced movement along the track.

Meisel looked around. Most of the people were working-class, dressed much as he, in clothing that had seen its better days. Children shouted at one another, occasionally running away from the queue, but generally kept together mostly by their mothers. He recognized a couple of the men, but for the most part, his family had kept to itself back at home and did so on this journey as well.

At the capsule, they passed through metal detectors, and then attendants got them seated, Meisel and Rachel across the aisle from each other next to the youngest two children—both boys, Eldad and Ezra, and the two oldest, daughters Micha and Ester, in the seats behind his wife. Less than five minutes later, the clam-shells closed, and speakers for each pair of seats whispered instructions in Hebrew spoken by the pretty uniformed young woman at the back of the capsule.

"My name is Sarah. Welcome aboard the Med Loop, fellow countrymen." Her pleasant voice seemed to float through the capsule. "In a few moments, we will insert your capsule into the launch stream and get you underway." The capsule jerked slightly as it began to move forward. "On this, the start of the second part of your trek to Mars, we will move forward for a bit and then will tilt to vertical to commence the boost leg of our journey. The acceleration is mild, so don't worry about yourself or your children. It will last for about twenty seconds. Then we will enter the lift stage, where you will feel normal gravity for about four minutes. We will be weightless for about two minutes during the coasting third stage. Then, with the return of weight at the Intercontinental Skyport, we will tilt to horizontal. At the skyport, you will feel some movement as the launch pouch and kick thruster are attached, and then we will once again experience acceleration as the magnetic rail brings us to escape velocity. Once we detach from the rail, except for several short maneuvering bursts from the kick thruster, we will be in free fall until our capsule is retrieved by the New Israel hyper-V freighter."

The capsule tilted to vertical, and Sarah's soft voice commenced counting down the seconds to the launch—...*shlosha...shnyim...eh'ad...*[9]

The launch procedure pulled Meisel out of his funk, and he started to take an interest in his surroundings. He looked across at Rachel and Ezra and then at Eldad beside him. He could just hear the excited chatter of the older Micha and Ester right behind her. A quiet couple he did not know took the seat behind him. *Perhaps it is better this way,* he thought. *Now the children can grow up on Mars in peace.* As he pondered their future, he hardly noticed the transition from acceleration, to normal weight, to weightlessness, and back to normal weight. When acceleration returned, followed by weightlessness after a few minutes as the capsule released its magnetic grip on the rail and launched toward Mars, he had decided that it was a good choice and started to relax and enjoy the experience of free fall.

Meisel awakened with a start several hours later. He didn't know exactly how much time had passed while he had caught up on his sleep, but he was suddenly on high alert. Meisel brushed aside the tenuous remnants of a dream about a stealthy Palestinian invasion of his cottage on the edge of the Negev. As sleep fog left his brain, he distinctly heard soft whispers floating forward from the seats behind him—in Arabic.

---

9 *three...two...one...*

Back home, I would have a weapon, he thought grudgingly, *but not here*. He released his seat restraints and pulled his way to the cramped toilet facility in the rear. Moving in freefall was inefficient, and he felt foolish as he clambered past the seats. He managed to get a good look at the couple behind his seat. A young man and woman, looking much like the other passengers; they stopped whispering as he passed. Sarah was strapped to a seat against the rear bulkhead. He caught her eye, telling her quietly what he had heard. She acknowledged and withdrew a device from her pocket.

"Stun tube!" she said softly, releasing her restraints. She commenced pulling herself forward with considerably more grace than had Meisel, who followed, awkwardly trying to imitate her movement. As she approached the Arabic speakers' seat, the young man launched himself at the overhead, waving a 20-centimeter ceramic blade, shouting, "*Allahu Akbar!*"

Sarah raised the spark-spitting stun tube, but the man slashed at her arm, cutting deeply. She screamed and pulled back, leaving the crackling weapon and big droplets of blood floating in mid-air. Meisel reached for the tube and was rewarded by a slashing blow from another ceramic blade wielded from below by the young woman. He felt the knife slice into his arm, but his jacket took the brunt of the cut. He wrapped his fingers around the still active device and jammed it down against the young woman's neck. She screamed and went limp.

From the corner of his eye, Meisel saw her companion push off the overhead toward him, knifepoint aimed at his face. He tried to duck, but in free fall, all he accomplished was to rotate away from the point that still managed to slice through his hair into his scalp. As the air around him filled with more blood droplets, he lunged out with the still active stun tube, catching his attacker's knife hand. The attacker let go the knife, and as his motion brought him close to Meisel, Meisel jammed the electrodes against his torso. The attacker went limp.

Meisel looked around and saw that one of the women was binding Sarah's wound. Sarah pointed at a locker, from which Rachel retrieved a first-aid kit and dressed Meisel's head and arm wounds. Two of the other male passengers bound the hands and feet of both attackers with tape from the first-aid kit. Despite her youth and her rather severe cut, Sarah took charge of the situation, got the passengers back into their seats, and sent out a report of what had happened. Then she approached Meisel.

"Thank you for what you did," she told him. "You saved my life."

He reached over and hugged Eldad, his youngest, wondering how many more sleeper assassins were scattered among the refugees from Earth.

EARTH—ATAR, MAURITANIA, SAHARA DESERT

The sun still had to rise over the Mauritanian city of Atar in the western Sahara. At one time, Atar was a spot on the dusty road from Dakar to Algiers, but that was before Launch Loop International chose Atar as the western socket for its third Space Launch Loop. By the time the Sahara Loop had reached its hundred-kilometer altitude, Atar boasted three international hotels, five office towers, and an infrastructure that included single-family homes, parks, running streams, and green wherever concrete was not needed. A massive water pipeline originating in *Parc National du Bank D'Arguin* on the Mauritanian coast supplied Atar's water needs. LLI had towed a gigantic tabular iceberg from Antarctica, grounding it off the coast of the national park. A pontoon barrier skirt around the entire berg contained its melt, supplying fresh water from Dakar in Senegal to the south, north to Dakhla in Western Sahara, and east to Atar. The massive magnetic deflectors that turned the launch loop back on itself lay buried in the sand just east of the park, and the nuclear plant that powered the linear drivers squatted on the sand thirty kilometers further east.

Joseph Ephriam called Chaviva and Dalia to the small round window on the right side of the giant aircraft and pointed to the brightly shining oasis below them on the otherwise dark Sahara sand. Behind the large plane, the sun had just peeked over the horizon, generating a deep red glow through the dusty atmosphere. The transport turned northerly to join the flight pattern that extended several kilometers south of Atar.

"See the runway?" Ephriam pointed as the two teenage girls crowded around the small window, oohing and aahing. "There," he said, pointing to a low white building, its cables catching the sun a half kilometer above the squat building. "That's where we're headed." As he talked, the sun overtook their aircraft, and the golden oasis below them turned bright green in the early morning light.

"Ladies and gentlemen…" A pleasant female voice wafted throughout the plane, speaking unaccented Hebrew. "As you know by now, one of our Mallorcan capsules experienced a serious terrorist incident. No one was killed, but it was a close call. Fortunately, only the Attendant and one passenger were injured. We simply cannot effectively screen all of you for weapons, nor are we able to determine whether some of you may be bent on doing the rest of us harm. So, I ask each of you to be vigilant. Keep your family members close, and pay attention to everything and everyone. Immediately report anything unusual, and I mean anything!"

The aircraft cabin quieted as each adult looked around, fear evident in nearly every eye. Ephriam was especially vigilant. He had spent his life on the margins, settling in disputed Israeli territory and more than once defending his life with deadly force. He carried no weapons now. He wouldn't need them, the tough sergeant who had convinced him to join the emigrants told him. So much for that theory. Ephriam put himself on high alert. He, his wife Batya, and the two girls would not become victims of the fanatic extremist he was certain hid among them.

Landing at the Atar airport and assembling for passage up the tower to the Sahara Loop itself was almost routine. Even though the experience was new for Ephriam and his wife and very exciting for the girls, it still was a lot like waiting in line for the train. Batya told him as much, and he agreed completely.

As they were about to enter the waiting capsule, the Capsule Attendant strolled along the queue. She looked at Ephriam head to toe and then pulled him out of the line and surreptitiously handed him a small package. "It's a stun tube," she told him. "Just in case." She smiled ruefully. "I have another one."

The ride up the cable with its differing sensations of weight and their eventual transfer to the ribbon were experiences entirely foreign to each of them. The girls were excited, Batya nervous, while Ephriam remained stoic but ever vigilant. Once they injected into their trans-Martian trajectory and experienced free fall for more than a few minutes, the girls quieted down, his wife dozed, and Ephriam settled into his harness, letting his senses extend throughout the capsule, staying on high alert for any distractions. He fingered the device in his pocket and then surreptitiously withdrew and examined it. It looked like a small flashlight with two electrodes on one end. Simple instructions said: Press here and touch assailant with active end. *Simple enough*, he thought. *I can do that.*

"What's next, Poppa?" Chaviva interrupted his reverie.

"We continue like this until they pick us up, I guess." Ephriam had been briefed in a general way on the sequence of events, but hearing and experiencing were two different things. "We'll be moved inside a big space transport along with another capsule, and then we will be whisked to Mars." He smiled at his girls. "I don't understand much of this, but it's kinda like boarding a train in our village and then having our car attached to another train in Haifa to take us to Beirut. We enter our car in Atar and exit on Mars."

The girls turned their attention to a private conversation between them, Batya continued sleeping, and Ephriam remained on high alert.

It seemed like a very long time—several meals, trips to the washroom facility, fitful naps, and alert wakefulness. Then the Attendant announced, "NISS Abednego has pulled alongside. We will shortly be hauled into its interior. Abednego already picked up the other capsule, so once we are secured inside, we will get underway for Mars. Because of the relative positions of the Earth and Mars in their orbits right now—they are on opposite sides of the Sun—the actual time for our journey will be about thirty minutes. The passage of time you will experience, however, will be almost nothing."

Ephriam listened to the quiet babble around him as the passengers talked about this strange phenomenon. After several clanks, the Attendant announced, "Okay, everybody, we are ready to get underway." Then, seconds later, she said, "Welcome to Tiger Baily Skyport…" She paused and then said, "That's right, we have arrived at Mars. Shortly, your capsule will transfer to Baily Skyport control, you will tilt to vertical, and ride the cable down to Margaritifer Socket. From there, you will transfer to the Blumenfeld MagLev for your final leg to Nanedi Valles East and up the valley to Nachal Rachaf."

Ephriam was still getting used to the lighter Martian gravity as their capsule returned to horizontal. Beneath his feet, he could hear the MagLev base being clamped in place of the launch pouch that had accompanied them from the Sahara Loop. He looked around the inside of the capsule. *All this distance and still no trouble!* he thought as he maintained vigilance, fingering the stun gun in his pocket. He watched a young male passenger in the seat in front of him to his right idly pick at the seam of his jacket. He could have been no more than seventeen or eighteen. As Ephriam watched, the young man extracted a thin wire from the seam. He secured one end to what had to be a longish jacket button. Then he did the same to the other end.

My God! Ephriam suddenly realized. *That's a garrote!*

The young man lept to his feet shouting, "*Allahu Akbar!*"

Ephriam heard a scream that choked to a gurgle from the seat beside the man, and then Ephriam lunged with the stun tube in his extended hand. He caught the attacker's side as 100,000 volts surged through him, and he went limp. The moment Ephriam was aware of the second attacker was when a garrote whipped around his neck. The last thing he heard was "*Allahu Akbar!*" as the thin wire severed his larynx and jugular.

✳

The Attendant stunned the second attacker moments after he garroted Ephriam. There was nothing she could do for the father of two who hadn't wanted to be there in the first place. With help from two men, she secured the attackers and then calmed the rest of the passengers. Their reception at Nachal Rachaf was solemn and without fanfare. The passengers were directed to an auditorium for briefing and quarters assignment, two uniformed men took charge of the prisoners, and a sizeable Israeli woman took Ephriam's grieving widow and sobbing girls into her arms and led them off.

EARTH—OLD JERUSALEM

Alam Garlock had his work cut out for him. In his quick survey of the ancient city of Jerusalem, from time to time, he had seen furtive shadows flit across his peripheral vision—long black robe, black hat-box-like head covering, white stockings below black leggings. It was more of an impression than something Garlock actually saw. He had no idea how many were still in the city, but somehow, he had to reach them. He knew the group included several women, perhaps even children, but he had no idea of the group's number. Finding a way to communicate with them became one of his chief preoccupations.

Garlock finally came up with a plan that he thought might work. His Military Rabbinate Chaplain was forty-year-old Rabbi Abba Micula with the rank of Rasan, the equivalent of Major elsewhere. Over his objections, Garlock instructed Rabbi Micula to dress in the garb of the Haredi remnant still in Jerusalem, meet them in the inner city, and explain the situation to them.

✳

Rabbi Abba Micula felt uncomfortable in his disguise as he stood on a narrow street corner in Old Jerusalem. A quiet voice speaking Hebrew penetrated his awareness from behind.

"Do not turn around!" the voice commanded. "Who are you, and what are you doing here?"

Micula started to turn when he felt the point of a dagger pressing into his right kidney.

"Do NOT turn around!" the voice commanded again, more forcefully.

"I…I am Rabbi *Rasan* Abba Micula, of the I…IDF," he stammered. "I bring a life-critical message…"

"Why the subterfuge?" The voice sounded less threatening.

"I…I apologize…we could think of no other way…"

"What do you mean?" The ominous tone returned.

"I…I…must speak with…with your leader." Micula paused and then rattled out the words, "You are all about to die…I MUST speak with you!"

"Put this over your eyes," the voice said, softening a bit and handing Micula a black scarf.

Ten minutes later, Micula and his escort entered an ancient building through a low door, and the scarf was whisked from his eyes. As his eyes adjusted to the light, he saw arrayed before him seven men in Haredi dress, with five women sitting quietly against the wall.

"Speak!" the oldest of the men commanded.

"You know that most Israelis have departed for New Israel on Mars." Micula spoke rapidly but confidently now that he had the group's attention.

"Blasphemy!" one of the men uttered but was waved to silence by the Elder.

"The Caliphate is planning to destroy Jerusalem in the next few days using a fuel-air burst." He then explained the nature of such an explosion. "You cannot survive this," he ended ominously. "Nobody can."

He stood in silence, looking at the seven one by one. He had fully regained his confidence and was doing his Rabbinical best to persuade them.

"We will NOT go to Mars," the Elder said with finality.

"Fine, but you MUST leave Jerusalem for the time being." He used his most persuasive Rabbinical voice. "Afterward, you can return, but if you stay, all of you will die!"

The women looked at each other with alarm. The senior among them stood and approached the Elder, apparently her husband. She spoke quietly to him. He glanced at her sharply and then nodded at Micula. "Do you have a way for us to contact you?"

It was clear to Micula that these words were spoken with difficulty. "I do." Micula handed the Elder a Link unit. "Press this button, and we will contact you by holographic image." At the Elder's raised eyebrow, Micula found himself explaining the basics of Link communication. Then he pressed the button he had indicated. An image of Garlock materialized—he appeared to be standing on the floor in front of them. The twelve Haredi uttered astonished gasps.

"I am Alam Abner Garlock, commanding the IDF forces in Israel. Please, relax," he said with a smile. "You are viewing modern communications technology, something I understand full well that you eschew. I have no intentions of imposing any of this technology on you. All I ask, for your own safety, is that you carry the Link Rabbi Micula gave you until the immediate emergency is past. Do you have any questions?"

There were none, and Garlock's holoimage vanished.

EARTH—JERUSALEM

It was one o'clock in the morning; the sky was a moonless overcast, and there was only a fitful breeze that hardly moved the dust-laden air. Jerusalem was virtually empty and eerily silent, devoid of sounds that had permeated the ancient city for at least 3,000 years. Fifty heavily muffled tandem tanker trucks crept into the city, guided by personal Links individually programmed for each driver. Each cab carried a standard SCUBA tank with ninety minutes of air and a full-face mask. Without referring to street signs they passed—*Sderot Ben Tsvi, Natan Strauss, Shivtei Israel, Gershon Agron, Damascus Gate, Jaffa Gate, King David*—fifty drivers quietly delivered their lethal vehicles to fifty strategic locations throughout the ancient inner city, the westward-lying modern metropolis, and the surrounding suburbs to the north, west, and south. On a signal from General Suleiman, each driver donned his mask and opened the 20-cm ball valves at the rear of each trailer. Over the next sixty minutes, each driver followed his designated route while one hundred nozzles on all fifty tankers gushed clear, frigid, faintly blue liquid onto the pavement behind the tanker, where it formed rivulets and tendrils of icy omen before boiling into a dense, odorless fog. As the tankers moved through the nighttime streets of Jerusalem, this explosive vapor saturated every valley, nook and cranny, synagogue and mosque, church and store, hovel and mansion.

Forty-nine drivers made it out of the city safely before the incendiary bombs ignited their charges. The driver whose engine stalled on *King David*, and who was running north as fast as his heavy SCUBA pack would allow, perished when the fuel ignited simultaneously throughout the ancient region, sending a towering fireball through the low overcast, announcing the utter annihilation of a city that had endured over 5,000 years.

EARTH—BEIT GUVRIN CAVES, ISRAEL

From his command helicopter, Alam Garlock directed his small convoy of trucks to head west on Highway 1 out of the still smoking ruins of Jerusalem. With the morning sun behind them, shimmering in the smoke-filled air, they passed empty Moza Illit and stopped at the village of Telz-Stone. Garlock's helicopter landed in the town square, and he stepped out to speak with a small delegation that may well have been the entire population remnant of this Ultra-Orthodox holdout.

"I am Alam Abner Garlock, Commander of the remaining IDF in Israel," he said to the obvious leader of the solemn little group. "I am here to plead with you to join my caravan so that I can move you safely to New Israel."

"Why would we want to leave?" the somber Rabbi asked. "This is our home. We have lived here in peace and harmony for generations. We have nothing to fear—nothing at all." He spoke in an even tone with a rich baritone voice.

"Did you see what happened to Jerusalem?"

"We did. God has always punished those who turn against him. So it has been, and so it will be." The Rabbi spoke with finality.

"You are certain, then?" Garlock asked, discouragement creeping into his voice.

"Go in peace, my son. Do what you must. God will protect us." With that, the delegation turned and entered the synagogue bordering the town square.

"Carry on," Garlock signaled to the convoy and clambered into his helicopter.

The convoy continued past Neve Ilan Forest to the intersection with Highway 38. Then it traveled south on 38 past the empty towns of Mesilot Zion, Beit Shemesh, past the once-prosperous moshav Giv'at Yesha'ayahu with its popular Hans Sternbach winery, along the eastern border of Britannia Park, finally stopping at the ancient town of Beit Guvrin—the Place of Heroes.

By this time, the sun was high in the sky, hot and dry, as Garlock's helicopter came to a hover over the bleak landscape that concealed over a thousand caves and underground passages. He activated his external loudspeaker system and began speaking slowly and clearly. "I am Alam Abner Garlock, Commander of the remaining IDF in Israel. I am not your enemy. I am here to help…to save your lives. You all know the fate of Jerusalem. I deeply regret that I could not prevent that destruction. The Caliphate is now preparing to flush you good people out of your sanctuaries the same way. There will be no mercy. Those who survive the inevitable firestorm will be captured and put to the sword by Caliphate warriors. I cannot protect you. I say again, I cannot protect you!" He paused as his words echoed through the canyons below.

"I cannot protect you from the Caliphate barbarism, but I can offer you and your families safety…now…here…today!"

Slowly, in groups of twos and threes, figures began to appear at hidden entrances throughout the sprawling complex below him. Garlock identified several Rabbis, dozens of men and women of all ages, and a surprising number of children. When it was all done, he had collected 483 people who had made the difficult decision to leave their beloved homeland for an uncertain future on Mars.

✳

In the following days, Garlock's troops collected another 324 reluctant holdouts from a region that covered a significant portion of southern Israel. Altogether he transported just under a thousand desperate people to Atar. Finally, Garlock and his troops accompanied the last group of refugees to the relative safety and security of Nachal Rachaf on Mars—New Israel.

The next day, General Suleiman triggered a fuel-air burst over the Beit Guvrin cave system, smothering any holdouts still remaining in the ancient underground complex. He followed that with a systematic slaughter of the remaining inhabitants of Telz-Stone and the other villages generally surrounding Jerusalem from the north, around westward, to the south.

Within a month of the departure of Garlock and the IDF, Caliphate troops swept south from Morocco, attacked and leveled the unprotected town of Atar, and slaughtered its inhabitants. His engineers triggered an explosion at the top of the Atar Skytower that severed the Sahara Loop, sending it on a trajectory into the uncharted regions of the Solar System north of the ecliptic. The reactors supplying power for the linear drivers at both ends of the loop shut themselves down. The pumps that provided water from the grounded berg off the Mauritanian coast stopped pumping, leaving the African coast from Dakhla to Dakar bereft of fresh water.

MOON—UDACHNY COMPLEX

Noel Goddard looked around at the stark, utilitarian Udachny command center that controlled the space elevator stretching some 61,500 kilometers overhead to the L2 complex. Several kilometers to the west, the Udachny Lunar diamond mining and manufacturing facility was producing diamond rope 24/7. Noel, representing *Ayers Sky*, had contracted with Sokolov to produce the diamond-rope-based cables for the O'Neill habitat at L5. The cable consisted of 2,187 monofilament strands twisted in cascading groups of three. Basically, it was created by twisting together three standard diamond ropes used throughout the Solar System and then twisting three of those to get the final cable. Its theoretical tensile strength was astronomical, but nobody had yet found a way to make an actual measurement. Noel was at Udachny to ensure that the elevator facility could handle his load and volume requirements—that amounted to a solid cube of diamond material 20 m on a side.

Noel turned to the 10-centimeter shorter Isidor Sokolov who stood beside him, stroking his brown goatee. "So, I see this working, one freight pallet at a time, where we fill a hovering hyper-V freighter at the node and then whisk the load to El-five. If we run two freighters, realistically, that would be ten pallets daily. Can you keep up with the supply?"

"Not a problem, as I see it," Sokolov replied, his Russian accent barely audible. "Our calculations indicate we can meet your requirements until the entire cable web is in place. There is no way, however, that we can keep up with your rocky material needs once you commence the main cylinder structure."

"We came to the same conclusion," Noel said. "A mass-driver would be the best solution. If we commence construction now, it will be ready by the time we will need it."

"We split the construction cost, you use the driver to throw raw material to El-five, and when cylinder construction is completed, we continue as a Udachny-Ayers Sky joint operation supplying construction raw materials anywhere in the solar system." Sokolov's steel-blue eyes twinkled as he warmed to his subject. "Somebody's got to do it. Might as well be us!"

Noel could see no overriding downside to the cooperative venture and held out his hand.

"Calls for a drink," Sokolov said, opening a cabinet to retrieve a bottle of his favorite vodka. He poured two small goblets, handing one to Noel.

Noel tossed his drink back, following Sokolov's lead, and commented as he set his goblet down, "Next time we do this with Napoleon Brandy!"

IAPETUS—STARCHILD INSTITUTE

Lud and Shakbah worked feverishly since their successful longevity tests. They reran the tests with differing subjects and under varying conditions. The results were always the same: Aging stopped, and some age reversal was apparent. With virtual certainty in hand, they decided that Lud should pay Marc a visit at the Starchild Institute. Although Shakbah would love to have joined Lud, she chose to remain behind to be with Vesta.

At this juncture, Saturn was on the opposite side of the Sun as Earth, but that only made Lud's subjective travel time a few seconds longer. Since entry formalities were virtually nonexistent in the Federation, in no time at all, Lud found himself walking the short distance from the floater drop-off point to the base of the Starchild pyramid. As he took a seat in Marc's office, he realized that it had taken him longer to get there from the elevator base than for the entire 1.75-billion-kilometer journey from Earth to Iapetus. He chuckled to himself. *I grew up with this stuff, and it still amazes me.*

"What have you got for me?" Marc asked without preamble.

"You know what Shakbah and I have been researching, right?"

"I know you found Earth longevity research further advanced than Ectarian research." Marc smiled at him. "Something brought you all the way from El-four to here."

"Simple, really," Lud told him. "We did it! Look at these test results." He tapped his Link, and a series of charts and graphs materialized between them.

Marc studied them for a few minutes. Then he looked at Lud and said, "You sure of this?"

Lud nodded, grinning from ear to ear.

"What about human tests?"

"Not yet. We're not set up for that. It's one of the main reasons I'm here, though." Lud left the holographic images floating. "Iapetus has enough people, and you have the necessary facilities. I figure we can set up a human test protocol and get a test up and running fairly quickly."

"We have procedures, you know…"

"I know that, but this is different…isn't it?"

Marc sat in quiet contemplation. Then he smiled at Lud. "I agree, it is different!"

Later that day, Lud returned to Mirs, bundled up both Shakbah and Vesta, and brought them to the Starchild Institute before the day was over. They set themselves up in temporary quarters within the Starchild Institute complex and commenced constructing a human treatment protocol that would eliminate error and give them certainty.

✳

Almost immediately, it was apparent that their treatment actually did what they thought it might. The procedure was a bit cumbersome in that they had to withdraw blood from the subject, treat the blood according to their developed protocol, and then regenerate more modified blood from the treated sample. Finally, the subject's total blood was replaced with the newly generated blood. Within days, the subject's entire body began to rejuvenate itself. Within a month, the subject started to show signs of sluffing off age-related conditions. While the subjects stopped aging, they didn't appear to get any younger. It would take years to determine the eventual effect on total age.

After three months of testing, Lud spoke with Marc in his office.

"I can see no reason for further human testing of the Starchild Institute Longevity Protocol. We have had no negative results. There appears to be no downside to the SILP treatments. When something is this certain," he said passionately, "we should release it to the public!"

"I understand your point, Lud, and part of me agrees, but this thing is too big, and the consequences of being wrong are too overwhelming. As I see it, we can stop initiating new SILP test treatments, but we need to allow sufficient time for anything hidden to reveal itself before we release something this potent to the public."

"How much time?" Lud asked.

"You tell me, Lud—you're the scientist. You're the one who knows more about this than anyone. If we have missed something… how long until we know?"

"You're right," Lud acknowledged. "I've let my enthusiasm overcome my scientific common sense." Lud thought quietly for several moments.

Marc waited patiently, reviewing the options in his own mind.

"Right now," Marc said, "if we start making SILP available in its present form, each person will have to go through a lengthy process that cannot be hurried. It doesn't seem possible that SILP could be made available to people at large. It would overwhelm medical clinics everywhere."

"I'm working on changing that," Lud said. "I'm looking for a way to move the SILP process from *in vitro* to *in vivo*."

Marc raised his eyebrows.

"So, now we have to conduct the protocol on a sample of the subject's blood in the lab, then generate sufficient new blood from the modified sample to give the subject a complete transfusion, replacing his old blood with the protocol transformed blood. I'm researching how to bring about this change inside the subject's body."

"And I'm thinking that until you find that path, we need to hold off on any announcements. What is your timeframe?"

"Let's give it a year or so," Lud said. "We can convene a study group now to look at the SILP results thus far, and then it can delve into whatever we find with our present subjects a year from now and what my research produces. The review will be independent, removed from my personal biases."

"I think that's wise," Marc told him.

MIRS COMPLEX—RING SAMARA

Lud's instinct told him that there was no inherent reason to treat the blood *in vitro* and then transfuse the rejuvenated blood back into the body. He was convinced that he could modify the protocol that would allow *in situ* blood rejuvenation. Since neither he nor Shakbah were experienced parabiotic manipulators, and this was a skill they needed, Lud placed a Link call to Carmen Bhuta.

"Carmen, we haven't spoken since the *Starchild* departed…" They chatted for a few minutes, catching up on their respective careers and putting up with the annoying 1.3-second delay that L4's distance from Earth created. Finally, Lud took advantage of a break in their conversation and got down to the real reason for his call. "Carmen, I need some really expert research help. I simply can't do this by myself, and neither Shakbah nor I have the necessary experience."

"What, exactly, do you need?"

Lud explained the nature of the protocol and the kind of background that he thought he could best use and was rewarded a day later when Carmen sent him a CV from an Indian researcher whose credentials were precisely what he needed.

✳

Reyansh Acharya quickly became a valued partner in Lud's project. They worked closely together, and Acharya's parabiotic manipulation skills with a molecular microscope seemed almost magical to Lud. The obstacle they had to overcome was that every protocol modification they tried to inject into a host's blood was attacked and destroyed by the host's immune system. Somehow, they had to find a way around this problem.

About six months into their joint research, Lud observed Acharya gently nudge two immune-suppressing molecular components together on their high-resolution holographic display. The juxtaposition stuck, and when he tried it with another molecule, it, too, stuck. They mixed up a larger batch and injected a sample into one of their experimental lab hosts.

The following day, the host was not only alive and well, but frisky and playful to boot. A month's further testing demonstrated their successful suppression of the automatic immune system response to the SILP serum without any apparent immune suppression elsewhere in the host. It was time to change the underlying protocol.

What Lud didn't know was that when it came time for Acharya's return to India three months later, he left with Lud's goodwill, and surreptitiously with both the formula and several milliliters of the new serum.

✳

The day after Acharya returned to India, the Caliphate annexed Israel.

CHAPTER ELEVEN

SOLAR SYSTEM—ASTEROID BELT

The asteroid was one of many thousands of unnamed rocks orbiting the Sun between Mars and Jupiter. Shaped like a five-kilometer long potato, it was utterly unremarkable, except for one thing: It consisted of about 90% Q-carbon. Early on during the expansion of the Mirs Complex at L4, four young Ukrainian prospectors, brothers Danylo and Artem Orel and their Sevastopol college chums Mykola Bondaruk and Pavlo Kolisnyk, had picked up an unusual spectral reflection from the Belt that indicated the presence of carbon where there should not have been any. They followed up and pinpointed the location to a small, potato-shaped asteroid. In the free-wheeling Mirs economy, it wasn't very difficult to get financial backing for a small VASIMR driven spacecraft that could take them to the asteroid within a reasonable time. In the second half of the *Starchild's* ten-year absence, they discovered extensive Q-carbon deposits on the asteroid they christened *Spud*, set up an extraction facility and a small habitat, and proceeded to make a killing on the Q-carbon market for themselves and their investors. They had no need for a hyper-V craft. *Spudcraft*, their modern VASIMR driven spaceship, could transport three loaded bladders with their entire between-trip Q-carbon production to Mirs in just over five days at one-g all the way. It was a sweetheart deal.

Normally, it would be impossibly inefficient to conduct piracy operations in interplanetary space. Infrastructure cost would make it prohibitive. There were exceptions, however. An established Q-carbon mine was just such an exception.

The Starchild Institute had effectively controlled the distribution of hyper-V spacecraft for more than a decade. It was inevitable, however, that one or more groups would gain access to the control modules in the spaceship. This would pave the way for making every hyper-V craft fully functional. That still left the actual manufacture of the core drive and spacecraft hull entirely under the control of the Starchild Institute. There was little chance that any group, no matter its financial backing, would be able to reverse engineer the science and technology behind the drive and skin. This meant there was no chance that anyone in possession of a hyper-V craft modified for full space capability would be able to weaponize their craft.

One of the first to convert an atmosphere-restricted hyper-V craft to deep-space functionality was the Pakistani lab that converted the Caliphate's hyper-V—*Rasul Allah*.

Without armaments, *Rasul Allah* could only function as a very efficient method of traveling between any two points in the Solar System. When Suleiman's Mirs agents informed him about the Q-carbon mining operation, he sent a couple of Caliphate pilots to reconnoiter the asteroid. They reported back that the operation was completely unprotected and virtually automatic. The only time the four Ukrainians were present was during transfer of Q-carbon to their VASIMR craft. Otherwise, one lone miner occupied a small habitat on the asteroid.

Suleiman already had the *Spudcraft* shipping schedule from his Mirs agents. He supplied his pilots with small arms that could be fired through the hatch and gave them their marching orders.

❋

Danylo Orel had stayed behind this time, occupying Spud to ensure ownership of their claim in compliance with Federation rules. When the other three arrived, they tethered *Spudcraft* to their mining claim—the asteroid Spud. Technically, Danylo Orel—as the oldest—was in charge. But they had done this task so many times already that nobody needed supervision. During their absence, the automated system had filled three bladders with the fine black powder. All they had to do now was hook up the three empty bladders they brought with them and attach the full ones to their ship. The four split up, Danylo and Mykola, Artem and Pavlo.

Using their TBH boots to maneuver, Danylo and Mykola set to the task of pulling the folded bladders from *Spudcraft* and attaching them to the automated extraction nozzles on Spud. Artem and Pavlo tucked the three thirty-meter-long loaded bladders into the girdered framework separating *Spudcraft's* command module from its fuel and VASIMR engine module. The entire operation took the better part of a day. With the task completed, the four met at *Spudcraft's* main lock and passed out spacesuited high-fives.

Without warning, Danylo saw two holes appear in his brother's helmet, and the interior turned bright red as blood and brains sprayed out through the holes, spattering him and the others and the side of *Spudcraft*. Danylo turned to look past his brother's body to discern a darkness just at the edge of detection blotting out some of the stars. A flash from the center of the darkness caught his attention. He ducked instinctively as he watched Pavlo's head explode inside his helmet, red spray from the bullet holes adding to the mess around them. Danylo popped both big toes, letting his TBH boots carry him up and away from the hatch. Looking back, he saw Mykola's helmet shatter as a bullet passed through on a close tangent. He tucked and rotated and then extinguished his boots so that he glided at an angle that would bring him close to the other craft near the spot where he saw the flashes. He knew he was virtually invisible against the starry backdrop. He had one chance to get the shooter before the shooter got him. He tucked again and rotated before tapping his toes to bring himself straight over and down to the now slightly visible hatch with a dark figure crouched just inside.

Danylo caught the shooter entirely by surprise. He grabbed the shooter's gun, dropped his feet toward the shooter before activating his TBH boots again. When he was about a meter above the shooter, Danylo fired the weapon, penetrating the shooter's helmet and the top of his skull. Then he tucked and rotated to point directly at the top of the hatch. He tripped the TBH boots briefly and activated his headlamps on high, flooding the interior of the hyper-V craft with bright light. He saw a space-suited figure pointing a hand-held weapon at him and observed a bright flash. He felt a bullet penetrate his calf, but before he could react, the hyper-V craft vanished.

Danylo jetted back to *Spudcraft*. The entire sequence of events had taken only a few short minutes. He was still on an adrenaline high, but his heart was heavy. Artem, Mykola, and Pavlo were gone, and there was nothing he could do about it. He was alone, some 250 million klicks from Mirs. He had a loaded *Spudcraft*, ready to head for home, but if he left, he could lose his mining claim on Spud. His only real option was to send a distress call and hope that someone with a hyper-V would come to his rescue.

He secured the bodies of his brother and two friends to the girders that held the Q-carbon bladders. Then he made his way through the lock into the pressurized command module, where he stripped off his suit and attended to his leg wound.

"Mayday…Mayday!" His distress call commenced its twenty-two-minute transit toward Mirs. If his call were answered immediately, it would still take 45 minutes to hear back. "This is *Spudcraft*… Mayday…Mayday!"

Forty-five minutes later, his communicator bawled, "*Spudcraft*, this is *Merkavah*…Dmitri Gagarin here—Federation Security…look out your starboard viewport."

MARS

The population of New Israel had reached 15 million—3.5 million in Nachal Rachaf itself, and the rest scattered north and south along Nanedi Valles. The polymer cover extended several tens of kilometers in both directions with curtain dams every few kilometers, where canyon narrowing made it more accessible. The area inside the dams no longer required oxygen concentration or any kind of radiation protection, and the transparent covers maintained an acceptable atmospheric pressure and temperature just as in Nachal Rachaf. Old-timers still carried precautionary concentrators, but most

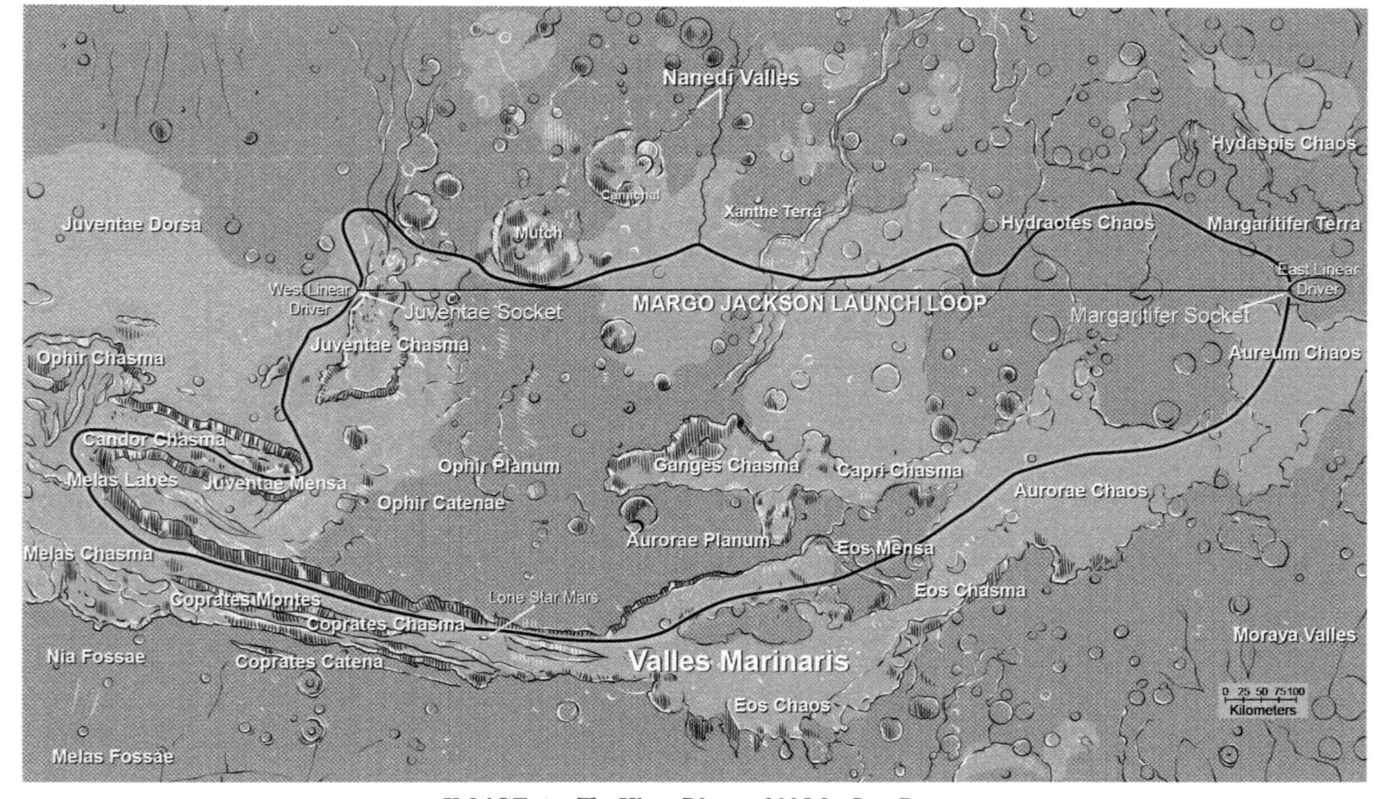

IMAGE 4—*The Klaus Blumenfeld MagLev Route*

of the population were comfortable relying on the infrastructure to keep them safe. The occasional breach was quickly repaired and didn't pose a risk to the general population.

New Israeli agriculture, in the open under the general cover and in domes north and south beyond that, was sufficient to make the entire settlement self-sufficient in every respect. In fact, some specialties unique to Israeli culture were exported to Lone Star, Mirs, and Iapetus, and there was even some fledgling trade with several of the asteroid settlements for luxuries not available from Mirs.

Lone Star had retained its original east and west margins, but both atmospheric pressure and oxygen content near the canyon floor had built up to the levels in New Israel, with one significant difference. Lone Star had no cover, not only because Valles Marineris was much too wide for an unsupported canopy, but also because the broad canyon was so deep that it could naturally contain the increased atmospheric pressure. Like New Israel, Lone Star had reached more than self-sufficiency and was beginning to export foods, material, and manufactured goods to New Israel, Mirs, Iapetus, and, like New Israel, to several of the asteroid settlements.

A MagLev line ran the full length of Nanedi Valles East. The southern-most point connected to the Klaus Blumenfeld MagLev, joining both the Juventae and Margaritifer Sockets and looping through the entire extent of Valles Marineris. The route went down Juventae Mensa, through Candor Chasma, around Melas Labes, along the length of Coprates Chasma, past Nectaris Montes, through Aurorae Sinus, up the Eos Chasma, through Aurorae Chaos, and finally Arsinoes and Aureum Chaoses to the Margaritifer Socket. Israelis and Martians, as the Lone Star folks preferred to call themselves, traveled routinely between the settlements and used both skytowers to access hyper-V transports that ran a schedule between Mirs, Mars, and Iapetus. Freight, rarely time-critical, used the launch loop facility to send it on its way or to capture and bring it down to the surface for MagLev distribution.

The two Martian settlements manifested dramatically different cultures, but their commonalities trumped their differences. The challenges of surviving Mars and prospering demanded of all the settlers a collective effort that far overshadowed any individual differences they might have had. The only exceptions were several outlying New Israeli communities that consisted nearly exclusively of the final holdouts to leave Old Israel. They kept to themselves for the most part, although even they participated actively in those activities geared toward common survival.

Both New Israel and Lone Star had limited expansion room, although for Lone Star, reaching any geographical limits seemed far in the future, given its total canyon floor area of about 600,000 square kilometers. Sam and McIntyre took the long view, planning for the day when Mars' arctic basin and the adjoining low areas were filled with water. This would inevitably bring water around the east from Chryse directly into Valles Marineris. They were already fortifying the Nectaris Montes dams to withstand the water build-up. Eventually, they would extend back into Valles Marineris for a quarter kilometer.

New Israel, on the other hand, would follow Nanedi Valles East northward for 140 kilometers to the junction with Nanedi Valles West and then turn south at the junction to follow Nandi Valles West for 360 kilometers. That totaled about 4,000 square kilometers, compared to about 20,000 square kilometers in Old Israel. Making the entire area habitable was a decades-long task, but the process was ongoing daily.

✳

"Ah…there you are, Rasam!" Matti McIntyre rose to his feet as Rasam Mordecai Rochlin approached his booth at the east end of the refurbished White Elephant. McIntyre waved to the bartender.

Rochlin interrupted, "Two Tubis if you please…straight…uh… if you have it, of course." He grinned at McIntyre and the bartender.

"Case shipped in last week," the bartender said, "from the Bar-Lev Distillery in southeastern Nanedi Valles."

"Ever try it, Matti?" Rochlin handed him a shot.

"But I been drinkin' Tullamore…"

"So, wash yer mouth with water and try this stuff. You won't regret it, I promise." They bumped glasses, and Rochlin tossed his back. "L'chaim!"

McIntyre brought the shot glass containing the cloudy drink to his nose. It smelled slightly lemony, slightly herbal. He tossed it back…It tasted like paint stripper…paint stripper mixed with a hint of lemongrass and maybe something like hand soap. And yet, he felt strangely compelled to take another shot. He waved his shot glass at the bartender. "So, that's your drink, Rasam?"

"Yep…Israel's favorite for more than a century. Created in Haifa way back in the early twenty-first century. I been drinkin' it since I was old enough to drink."

They settled into the booth and gazed out at the star-illuminated backdrop of Nectaris Montes dominating the eastern view. The White Elephant was mostly empty so that they could speak to each other in normal tones.

"So why the face-to-face?" McIntyre asked. "What do you have that we couldn't discuss by Link?" He grinned. "Besides this, of course," holding up a shot glass of Tubi.

"Old friendships must be nurtured," Rochlin said with a smile. "Something important came up, and I decided to discuss it in person," he held up his glass, "over this!"

McIntyre grunted his acknowledgment.

"We're making a lot of progress, you know, in Nanedi Valles. We've covered over a hundred running klicks of canyon, and the process is accelerating. We've even been giving some thought to putting a couple of domes on the surface between the valley branches."

"You're talking about some significant terraforming."

"Yeah, you could say so. Sooner or later, we all got to do it—bring up the surface pressure and add oxygen."

McIntyre nodded his assent. "At some point, I suppose, Nanedi and Marineris will be full of water…" He left the sentence hanging.

"And that's what I want to talk about." Rochlin leaned forward. "You know us. We'll argue about whether piss is yellow." He paused and leaned back. "You know how we govern, too. It's not as crazy here as it was in Old Israel…yet."

"So…"

"Back on Earth, we had two principal political parties, *Likud* and *HaAvoda*, Conservative and Labor, plus some thirty or so other parties, distributed over one hundred twenty seats. Here, we started with just twenty seats and no political parties, but not anymore. We're back up to one hundred twenty seats, but we have far fewer parties…and that's fine with me." Rochlin sighed and sipped his drink. "But…we got something new we never had before—the Red Party." He stopped talking.

"And…so…" McIntyre wondered where this was going. "The Reds…" He pushed a little.

"Yah…these yahoos want to keep Mars red, meaning no terraforming." He sighed deeply. "Oh…they're fine with what we have done thus far, but they oppose any further expansion. No domes on the surface. No expanding further north and south in Nanedi Valles. None of the advanced terraforming plans we have been talking about—the Soletta, melting the caps, you know the stuff we've talked about." He paused for another sip. "These guys have secured a Knesset seat… they're serious…threatening sabotage if we continue expansion."

"Tell you how we would handle that down here," McIntyre said laconically.

"I know, but WE don't do things that way," Rochlin said with a smile. "I guess we're more civilized."

"That's bullshit, and you know it!" A slight edge crept into McIntyre's voice. He really was good friends with the Rasam, but this was crazy. One disgruntled Red could do a lot of damage. "If they come down here and we identify them, they won't be a problem anymore—guarantee it!"

They clinked glasses and finished their drinks.

IAPETUS—STARCHILD INSTITUTE

Marc Bowles stood before the small group of space contractors who had gathered from Mirs, Iapetus, Mars, and even some of the settled asteroids. "The Starchild Institute did not originate the idea," he said. "That came from out of the past, a science fiction trilogy by author Kim Stanley Robinson, *Red Mars*, *Green Mars*, and *Blue Mars*—he called it the Soletta." Several people in his audience nodded familiarity with the works. "Robinson didn't get it entirely right," Marc continued, "but he was close enough." Marc triggered a holodisplay that filled the air beside him, a diagram of the Sun-Mars Lagrangian points. "The concept is to place a ten-thousand-kilometer disc at the Mars-Sun Lagrange point L-one, about a million klicks toward the Sun from Mars." The L1 point illuminated, and a larger-than-scale disc filled the spot. "The disc is constructed of a series of automatically activated circular louvers that make it function much like a Fresnel lens." A close-up of the disc replaced the larger image so that the individual circular louvers were clearly visible. "The effect is to capture some of the sunlight that would pass Mars and focus it on the Mars surface." The view shifted to a point between Mars and the Soletta. The Soletta moved to cover the solar disc so that the Sun disappeared, except for a ring around the Soletta edge. Then the louvers tilted, and the sun reappeared apparently larger and brighter than before. The image shifted to a view of Mars from space. "A ring of mirrors in polar orbit around Mars captures more of the sunlight that would otherwise bypass the planet and sends it back to the Soletta, where it gets focused back to Mars." The view shifted back to the point between Mars and the Soletta, and the solar image became even brighter. "One more thing, Mars used to have a magnetic field that kept the solar wind from stripping the atmosphere. Obviously, that's been gone for a long time. We're going to restore it by installing a two-Tesla magnetic dipole near the Soletta." The holoimage showed magnetic lines of force emanating from near the Soletta, encompassing Mars, shielding it from the Solar Wind.

"We have worked out the technical details. All you guys have to do is build it!" Good-natured laughter filled the room. "Author Robinson didn't have access to hyper-V technology to facilitate construction of his Mars-altering concept. In his trilogy, it took several decades. You guys are going to build this entire system in about three years." The room filled with applause, and Marc held up both hands. "Now...I give you Margo Jackson!" The applause from the small group was nearly deafening. "Margo is the engineer in charge of the Soletta Project. Most of you know that she was the underwater boss for Slingshot and the engineer-in-charge of the Atlantic and Sahara Loops. She knows more about building ultra-large structures than any human alive...Margo..."

Margo Jackson stepped to the front of the podium. She was tall and slender with deep green eyes and long tawny hair braided in coils atop her head. Although in her mid-sixties, she looked two decades younger. She raised a hand to quiet the group.

"It humbles me," her voice was a rich contralto, "to be standing before this group. You guys represent the very best the human race has to offer." There was an embarrassed shuffling of feet; otherwise, one could have heard a pin drop. "I am here not because I am better than you or know more than you, but simply because I've been there and done that more than most of you. And I guess that means something. You all know the drill at least as well as I do." She stopped talking and glanced around the room.

To Marc, she seemed to have every person there in the palm of her hand, even Noel Goddard, standing quietly at the back, fresh off his hyper-V trip from L5. *She is right*, he thought, *this is an amazing assemblage.*

"Alex Regent, my old boss on Slingshot, will head up the Soletta and dipole projects. Klaus Blumenfeld, whom you know from the linear driver construction at the Jackson Loop," she blushed slightly, "will head up the orbital mirror project. And I," she smiled and blushed slightly again, "will remain here on Iapetus and flirt with Marc." A general chuckle moved through the assemblage. "Actually, I'll have my office here at SI but will spend most of my time moving around the project and fixing the inevitable logistics logjams. You can count on seeing me every once in a while." As a murmur rose from the group, she raised a hand. "Any questions?"

She answered several and then added almost as an afternote, "Your asteroid teams have been moving the two asteroids we will use for raw material into their respective positions. They should be onsite within the week, with station-keeping engines already installed." She raised both her arms. "The rest is up to you guys!"

A rowdy cheer filled the room as Margo stepped down and wandered into the group, shaking hands, chatting, and making herself generally available.

EARTH—SAUDI ARABIAN DESERT

The black, featureless hyper-V craft extended its five legs and settled on the hot sand next to the Prophet's sprawling tent perched atop the same mound it had occupied since Saeed Ismael's warriors had first pitched it at the beginning of what the world now knew simply as the Caliphate. As soon as the ramp touched the sand, General Suleiman strode down and into the Prophet's tent.

"Sahib," he said with a curt bow, "I have excellent news… excellent news! We have now exceeded the size of the old Persian Caliphate." He brought up a large Link display. "Our territory extends from the northwestern tip of Africa, across all of the continent to the South African border, north through Turkey, Greece, Bulgaria, and the Balkans, to the Austrian and Hungarian borders, and then east through Azerbaijan and all the Stans. We've also annexed every country around the Bay of Bengal except India and Sri Lanka, and we're marching into Vietnam as we speak." The General smiled broadly and extended his arms toward the diminutive Prophet. "You, Sahib, are the ruler of the mightiest nation in the history of the World!" The General bowed deeply with a sweeping gesture.

Without a word, the little man dressed in sackcloth and sandals walked out into the hot afternoon sun and raised his leather cupped arm to the hazy blue sky. "*Allahu Akbar!… Allahu Akbar!… Allahu Akbar!*" As his voice floated across the dry lakebed, tent flaps across the compound flipped open, and Caliphate warriors emerged into the bright sun. Within thirty seconds, 2,000 voices filled the entire dry valley with a lusty response: "*Ashhadu an la ilaha illa Allah—Ashadu anna Saeedan Rasool Allah.*[10]"

MARS—NORTHERN NANEDI VALLES EAST

Samuel Meisel with Rachel and their children settled quickly into a small enclave at the northern extent of covered Nanedi Valles, about a hundred meters inside the northern-most curtain. They had met Joseph Ephriam's widow and two girls at the welcome center when they arrived and formed a friendship of sorts. Batya and the two girls moved to the enclave with them. Using materials donated by the community, Meisel built a modest home inside the northern-most dome and added two extra rooms, one for Batya and one to be shared by Chaviva and Dalia. Life was hard, but no more so than the Negev back on Earth, where they had eked out a living. The big difference was the canopy and the domes. On several occasions, Meisel had donned his pressure suit (everyone was

---

10 *I bear witness that there is no god except Allah. I bear witness that*
   Saeed is the messenger of God.

issued a suit upon arrival) and exited through the curtain lock to the stark, unprotected surface of the *real* Mars. It was like nothing he had ever experienced. Cold, bleak, arid, lifeless—so different from inside New Israel. He loved it, absolutely loved it. Had he been able, he would have remained in the haunting wilderness…but Meisel had obligations, a family…no, two families to look after, and so he always returned to the safety of the canopy.

One evening about a week-and-a-half after he had finished their dwelling, Meisel answered a knock at his door. It was his neighbor, Menachem Dubro.

"Dubro…what brings you out so late?"

"Call me Menachem, please. Can you join me for about an hour?" Dubro looked about furtively.

Meisel let Rachel know he would be out and left with Dubro.

"I've seen you exit the curtain several times," Dubro said. "Do you like it out there?"

"It is absolutely magnificent!"

"You know that our next expansion will be to the north, and all that will become just like in here…" The sentence ended with a question in his voice. "You know about the terraforming project?"

"That it exists, yes, but nothing else. Tell me."

Dubro commenced telling Maisel about the Soletta and the orbital mirrors. "They're even going to create an artificial magnetic field for Mars," he added as he finished his explanation.

"By God, I don't want that!" Meisel exclaimed angrily. "We got the settlement, and we need it. Let's leave the rest as we found it. What right do we have to make it like Earth?"

✳

""We gotta be careful, Bro," Ra'id Kassab (aka Chino Delgado) said as Abdul-Hasid Naseri (aka Rico Delgado) eased Rover-2 past an outcropping a couple of kilometers north of the northernmost New Israeli curtain. "Don' wanna be detected down here."

"You got that, Bro!" Rico answered, both men staying within their Mexican-American identities.

Should they be stopped anywhere on the plateau, they could claim they were prospecting out of Lone Star. *Rover-2*, along with their Hispanic personas, was proof enough, unless someone did a

Link verification, unfortunately, easy to do now that the ServerSky swarm was enabled and functioning.

They crept to within one kilometer of the curtain and settled in to await the fall of darkness.

"You think this is gonna work out, Chino?"

"The boss says to make it work, Bro."

Rico leaned the driver seat back and shut his eyes. "Might as well get some shut-eye while we wait."

An hour later, they started up and crept nearer the curtain, keeping as close as possible to the eastern canyon wall. About a hundred meters from the curtain that loomed high above them, they found a place of concealment, shut *Rover-2* down, donned their suits.

"You up to this, Bro?" Chino asked as they walked toward the lock.

"Sure, Man…we supposed to connect with the Reds that live on t'other side, right?"

"Yep."

They entered the lock, cycled it, and then removed and hung their suits and helmets on the available hooks.

"Lookie see!" Rico said, pointing to the glowing dome a hundred meters from the lock. "Let's check it out, Bro."

They knocked on the door and greeted Meisner in English when he opened it. "We been sent to help you guys out," Chino said, shaking Meisner's hand.

"How so?" Meisner questioned.

"You know," Rico answered, "keepin' things from getting outa hand."

"Messin' up the outside," Chino added.

Meisner smiled and waved them inside.

L5—AYERS SKY

Pallets of diamond cable arrived at Ayers Sky from Udachny ten times daily, and pallets of collapsed polymer beams came from the Mirs manufacturing facility as required. Noel's crew kept busy interconnecting polymer girders and rings and stretching diamond cable across segments along the 50 km length the giant cylinder eventually would occupy. Polymer rings 10 km across marked the end-caps and ribs every 5 km. They were connected with rigid 5-km-long polymer beams held in compression by diamond cables. Each pair of rings had six interconnecting girders around its circumference at about 5.25 km separation. Each pair of girders was braced corner to corner by crossed girders held in compression by diamond cables.

Noel assigned fifty men to assemble each of five ring pairs, one of which was connected to an endcap. Once these ring pairs were completed, each crew shifted focus to connect its ring pair to the next ring pair across the 5 km gap. With the interconnection of the last ring pair to the opposite endcap, the basic skeleton of the O'Neill Cylinder was completed. This had consumed 1,170 km each of diamond cable and polymer girders and 346 km of polymer ring material.

Next, the crews wrapped polymer sheeting over every part of the cylinder that would eventually become an interior surface, and placed transparent polymer sheeting over the three windows that ran the entire length of the cylinder. This used 785 square kilometers of opaque sheeting and another 785 square kilometers of transparent sheeting.

Next came diamond cable wrapped around the exterior of the cylinder to counter the outward force created when the structure was eventually rotated to generate Earth-normal gravity inside. These diamond cable rings were placed every ten meters along the entire length of the cylinder. The length of diamond cable for just this portion of the construction was over 157,000 km.

About the time the last diamond cable ring was cinched tight, the Delgado brothers were contacting Samuel Meisel and the Reds, and Dmitri was hailing *Spudcraft*.

SOLAR SYSTEM—ASTEROID BELT

Dmitri picked up *Spudcraft's* distress call just as he arrived at Iapetus from Mirs. "Locate the signal and take me there ASAP!" he instructed the Resident. His gray tabby, Jake, a constant flight companion, jumped into his lap, purring loudly.

Moments later, subjectively, *Merkavah* came to a hover alongside *Spudcraft*, and Dmitri signaled, "*Spudcraft*, this is *Merkavah*…Dmitri

Gagarin here—Federation Security…look out your starboard viewport." Dmitri could plainly see three spacesuited bodies strapped to the craft's superstructure. A face appeared in the viewport. "Set your Link to…" Dmitri gave Danylo Orel connection instructions, and shortly a holoimage of Orel appeared in the air before him. "Dmitri Gagarin, Federation Security."

"Danylo Orel, mining a Federation registered claim for Q-Carbon."

"What happened, Orel?" addressing him in Russian.

Orel told Dmitri about the attack and the deaths of his brother and friends. "We didn't have a chance, and I'm lucky to be alive."

"Any idea who the pirates were?"

"Not really. It all happened so fast…. It was a hyper-V craft like yours, only smaller. Two guys…dark hair and features. That's all I can tell you."

"What's your destination?" Dmitri asked.

"Mirs."

"How long?"

"Five days or so."

Dmitri contemplated the situation for a few moments. "Okay… here's the plan. You head back to Mirs. I'll jump ahead and have my people meet you. They'll take care of the legal requirements."

"What about occupying our claim?" Orel interrupted.

"I'll handle that as well. You just get back and take care of your people. We'll get to the bottom of this, I promise."

Orel's image vanished, and *Spudcraft's* VASIMR engines ignited. Dmitri stroked Jake as he watched the lumbering craft gain speed and fade into the star-studded background. As he considered what had happened, he could see only two possibilities. One was pure piracy, but the cost of obtaining a hyper-V craft was so high that there really were few operations that would warrant it. The other possibility sent a shiver through him. It seemed apparent that the Caliphate had acquired a hyper-V and was attempting to bully its way into Federation commerce. *We really should have spaced that little terrorist!* was his concluding thought.

Dmitri remained near Spud for an hour, scanning the asteroid surface and monitoring the frequency spectrum. "There's nothing here, Jake," he said as he anchored a beacon on the surface and instructed the Resident to take him back to Mirs.

Upon arrival, Dmitri wasted no time. He gathered his chief deputies by Link, briefed them on the attack, and told them his suspicion that the Caliphate was behind it. He instructed one deputy to assist Orel upon his arrival and set the rest to ferreting out the true nature of the attack.

"Go to records and identify every mining claim in the Belt. Assign a two-man team to carry a beacon to each claim and warn the claim holders. They're an ornery bunch, so use petty cash to load up on enough crates of the good stuff to leave a crate with each holder. That should mollify them a bit. IFF any hyper-V craft you encounter. If you don't get a positive response, neutralize the craft. Don't let this get out of hand!" he urged them.

With Jake quietly purring in his lap, Dmitri pulled up central hyper-V registration on his Link. He found several hundred craft scattered over the Solar System, including several on Earth. The US had a couple, as did the Israelis, although theirs were now on Mars at New Israel. The Russian Federation had acquired one, as had the Chinese and India. These were supposed to be atmosphere-limited versions, but by now, Dmitri was confident they were all space capable. He initiated a correlation search, trying to match original acquisition to present ownership. Transit times dramatically slowed the search, but several hours later, Dmitri had a partial answer. He had located all but two hyper-V craft.

"The Caliphate has two of them, Jake. I'm certain."

MARS—NORTHERN NANEDI VALLES EAST

Samuel Meisel was more than surprised when the two strangers presented themselves at his door. Their English was somewhat difficult to understand since his own English was not that good. They obviously were Hispanic, probably from Lone Star. In the few weeks Meisel had been on Mars, he had learned very little about Lone Star. He knew they were Texans, and he knew Texans did things in a big way. On the other hand, he wasn't entirely sure what a Texan was. In any case, his visitors quickly convinced him that they understood his perspective on Mars. In fact, they let drop a surprising piece of information.

"We skipped out on Lone Star," Rico said with a degree of bravado.

"S'right," Chino added, "that we did. Took a rover, bunch of food and water, explosives and stuff."

"Yeah," Rico chimed in, "we like Mars the way it is…mostly."

"Gotta have food to eat 'n air to breathe," Chino said, "but leave the rest t'way it is."

These guys are speaking my language, Meisel thought as he poured a glass of water for each of his strange guests. "So, why are you here?"

"We heard 'bout you guys here at the north end. You ain' gettin' much support from t'other guys."

"I guess that's true enough," Meisel said thoughtfully. "But why visit? Seems you are risking a lot."

"True, but we wanna help," Rico said. "Thought we could give you some explosives, maybe you can use…"

"They gonna push north of here," Chino added, "maybe you stop em."

Meisel sat quietly, pondering the possibilities. "Can I get you anything else?" he asked as they finished their water.

"Naw, that's good. We stash the explosives one klick out on the east side by a big outcropping. Ya can't miss it," Rico said as they rose to their feet. "Let's go, Bro."

Meisel let them through the door, and they disappeared in the darkness toward the curtain.

CHAPTER TWELVE

MARS—NEW ISRAEL

The canopy crew had been stretching transparent polymer sheeting across the northern extent of Nanedi Valles East for several weeks. The process was complex. First, the canyon edge had to be stabilized. Using the same Robotic Vaporizers (RV) that hollowed out the underground portions of Nachal Rachaf, they smoothed out the canyon walls and floor, piping the hot rock vapor to the edge where they forced it into the cracks and crevasses.

A large roll of sheeting was laid across the canyon at the end of the previous piece and rolled along the canyon with mechanized crawlers as work progressed. The sheeting was edged with two lengths of 243-strand, millimeter-thick diamond rope spaced a meter apart, with each rope molded into the polymer material. The rope looped out every meter, with the loops from each rope offset along the length by half a meter. Two-meter-long, harder-than-steel, hooked polymer spikes were driven through the loops into the stabilized regolith. Every ten meters, a millimeter-thick diamond rope crossed the canyon on top of the polymer cap. Finally, the interface of polymer edge and regolith was covered with a meter-thick layer of the amalgamate made from the RV-produced rock powder and sand-like regolith found a short distance to both the east and west of the canyon. Teams worked both sides of the canyon simultaneously, covering several hundred meters each day.

When the new canopy reached the one-and-a-half-kilometer mark, Meisel and the Reds decided to make their move. The Delgado brothers had informed them that they had buried explosives against the base of the southernmost curtain on the other side of New Israel. Meisel spent several nights moving the explosives into a trench at the bottom of the northernmost curtain. He dug a trench section right after leaving the lock, retrieved sufficient explosives to fill the ditch, and then covered it with regolith. The curtain bases were secured much like the canopy top, except with only one diamond rope along the bottom edge and the seal just a half meter thick. Meisel dug the trench about a meter deep, angled toward the seal. The idea was to break the seal upwards, pulling the spikes out in the process. This would result in a significant outward atmosphere flow and might even rip the curtain.

An hour before the planned coordinated explosions, Meisel and his comrades sealed their agriculture domes and retreated into their residential domes. As an additional precaution, Meisel and his family donned their individual suits, but he expected them to be just fine.

The explosion was surprisingly powerful. The ground beneath Meisel's dwelling moved with a wave-like motion as the force of the explosion worked its way through the solid rock underlying the regolith. Eldad and Ezra screamed in terror and then huddled together under the kitchen table. Ester grabbed Chaviva and Dalia, and Micha did his teenage best to protect the girls. Rachel and Batya reached out to Meisel, and he put a comforting arm around each.

Meisel had placed the explosive charge near the middle of the two-kilometer-wide curtain. The bottom edge rupture extended for over a hundred meters and was just over a meter high at the center. Pressure dropped rapidly in the northern section. Within a half-hour, internal pressure had equalized with Mars-normal. Oxygen content percentagewise was still Earth-normal, but the oxygen partial pressure had dropped to asphyxiation levels. Survival outside the individual domes was only possible in a pressure suit. Seven men, two women, and a child were caught without access to their suits. Their painful deaths resulted from a combination of depressurization and asphyxiation. The child's little body had actually ruptured.

Conditions were no better at the southern end of Nanedi Valles East. There, the breached curtain was nearly five kilometers wide, so it took somewhat longer to depressurize. Because this section had been established longer, more people lived there. The death toll reached thirty-four, including five children and seven women.

✳

Rasam Mordecai Rochlin had teams investigating the two breaches even before pressure had equilibrated. A team pulled from the canopy crew at the northern breach was on site within ten minutes. It took a half-hour to get the southern team in place while atmosphere continued to rush through the rupture. Rochlin kept in close Link contact with each team as they moved equipment into place to seal the breach as soon as the flow ceased.

Asshur entered Rochlin's office during the emergency response but wisely remained in the background while the Rasam did what he did best. Once things were fully under control with both breach repairs underway, Rochlin turned to Asshur, anguish showing on his face. "Forty-four souls," he said quietly. "Twenty-nine men, nine women, and six children, dammit all!" He fought back tears, and Asshur swallowed hard. "There is no doubt the breaches were deliberate." Rage replaced sadness in the Rasam's face.

A soft tone announced the Link presence of Mattias McIntyre from Lone Star. "Is there anything we can do to help?"

"We got it under control, friend—what a goddamn mess!"

"Thanks for the offer, Matti," Asshur said. "We're scrambling to find out who did this."

"Do you think the Delgados had a hand?" McIntyre asked.

"Probably," Rochlin said, "but it's bigger than just those two. We got something going on in our own population."

"I heard about your Reds…"

"It's difficult to understand people who would put the Martian wasteland ahead of their own kind's survival," Asshur said, thinking about his ancestor's exodus from Ectaris. "I don't think the Ectarians had any holdouts when they left their system."

"Are all the holdouts Reds?" McIntyre asked.

"Not really," Rochlin answered. "After seeing what happened to Old Israel, most are grateful to be here. Meisel's and Ephriam's families up north are exceptions. They fell in with Menachem Dubro from the get-go. Dubro was a pain-in-the-ass pro-Palestinian activist back in Jerusalem, and he got busy the moment he arrived here." Rochlin stopped, visibly upset. "He won a Knesset seat, you know…"

"Yeah, you told me your last visit but didn't say who."

"Thanks for your offer to help, Matti," Asshur said with a tone of finality. "But we got work to do."

"Got it!" McIntyre signed off.

"Now we gotta get the guys who did this," Rochlin said to Asshur.

While Rochlin busied himself with the immediate aftermath of the breaches, Asshur went back to his office in a contemplative mood. He had no doubt that the perpetrators would turn out to be Reds, probably controlled by Dubro. Asshur was equally sure that the Delgados were involved. *Being certain and proving it are two different things*, he thought as he leaned back in his desk chair.

Asshur pulled up Israel's legal history on his Link. He was particularly interested in the Israeli concept of Capital Punishment. Ectarian Jurisprudence was far simpler than modern human jurisprudence. It boiled down to the concept of personal responsibility—if you did it, you paid for it. There were no provisions for some of the odd defenses he had discovered in modern Earth justice, such as pleading insanity or being under the influence of narcotics. Ectarian courts were non-adversarial. They used a jury system, but there was no prosecutor or defense. Instead, the state and the accused's legal representative worked together to discover all the facts. Within this framework, the state representative ensured that what facts it had were sufficient to justify an arrest. The accused's representative ensured that the state had all the available evidence. Together they established a preponderance of guilt or innocence, which they presented to the jury. There was no gamesmanship or one-upmanship. The court did not rule on whether or not evidence could be admitted. Everything was admitted. The accused had the right to admit to the crime and offer a justification, such as self-defense, in which case the state and the accused's representative would collect any evidence showing the veracity of the justification. Justifications like "I was not responsible because…" were never allowed, and the court would enforce this. The bottom line was that every participant in the process was obligated to find the truth. If the accused "did it," and almost always this was the case, the sentence was carried out.

The deeper Asshur delved into Israeli jurisprudence, the more troubled he became. Capital punishment was allowed only during wartime for genocide, crimes against humanity, war crimes, crimes against the Jewish people, treason, and certain crimes under military law, but it was rarely imposed. It seemed that shortly after Israeli independence, an Army officer was found guilty of espionage against Israel and was executed. Later he was found to be innocent and was exonerated. This burden apparently became a millstone around the neck of Israeli jurisprudence. Adolf Eichmann, the notorious Holocaust architect, was executed in 1962, but that was the last execution in Israel.

Things are different here, Asshur pondered. Will the Israelis continue their old jurisprudence ways, or will they see things in the new light of harsh Martian reality? The former legal system arrived when the Earthside Knesset dissolved itself, and the Nachal Rachaf Knesset took over. We are at war in a serious way. By any measure, these explosions were crimes against the Jewish people. He sighed and took a sip of water from a glass one of his aides had brought. We will find them…we will convict them…what happens then?

✳

Asshur watched in fascination as the Rasam collected evidence, traced it to explosives stolen from Lone Star, connected that to Meisel through explosives residue on his clothing, and extracted a confession from Meisel implicating Menachem Dubro. Arrests followed, and a dramatic trial that was broadcast throughout New Israel and Lone Star by holovision. Inevitable convictions for war crimes, crimes against the Jewish people, and treason followed. There were no appeals.

During Rochlin's investigation, the Knesset met in special session to enact a particular punishment for crimes against the Jewish people that involved the wholesale destruction or attempted destruction of New Israel. This punishment was given the name

Banishment. It involved a simple process. The Banished was given a pressure suit and five hours of air, and was taken to a location on the Martian plateau midway between Nanedi Valles East and Nanedi Valles West. There the Banished was left, alone and without resources. The site was significantly greater than five hours by foot from any refuge. Death within five hours was certain and absolute, and the wait brought the horror of the offense and its consequence into sharp focus—unless the Banished chose to end it sooner.

Following sentencing of Banishment for Dubro, Meisel, and two others under Dubro's control but unknown to Meisel, Rachel and Batya appealed Meisel's sentence directly to President Asshur. Asshur had not anticipated this and was in a quandary. It was absolutely essential that similar future actions be deterred. On the other hand, here was a man who never wanted to leave Earth in the first place. This was a man who had saved the lives of his fellow passengers on the way to Mars, a man who had taken in the widow and daughters of another holdout who never made it, a man who—in his own elegant words—fell in love with the magnificence that untouched Mars represents.

It turned out to be an easy decision. Asshur commuted Meisel's sentence to five years detention and constructive community service for the remainder of his life.

✳

"Put on these pressure suits," the pressure-suited guard told Dubro and his two companions.

The three men glumly did as they were ordered. The guard strapped them into the back seats of a rover so they could not get loose to interfere with him. Asshur and Rasam stood by, but there was no ceremony. The guard drove the rover northward, through the northernmost curtain, and then ten kilometers farther north to a ramp that had been carved into the chasm wall. Then he headed south for three hours, to a point about midway between Nanedi Valles East and Nanedi Valles West. He stopped the rover and unstrapped the prisoners.

"Alright, you three. Get out…this is as far as you go. Your individual air supplies will last about five hours. Even if two of you removed your helmets and sacrificed yourselves for the third, he still would not have sufficient air to make it back. You guys love raw Mars…so enjoy it!"

He entered the rover, spun it around, and departed for home.

✳

Off in the distance, out of sight of the guard, the Delgado brothers watched quietly as the Israeli guard abandoned the three condemned men to Banishment.

"Hey Bro', that's cold," Chino said, maintaining his Hispanic cover.

"Truth, Man!" Rico said. "But fitting, I guess."

"Could be us, Bro'," Chino said.

"You know it. We gonna do sump'n?" Rico magnified their view. "Whadya think? Two of 'em buy it ta save the third?"

"Naw…them Israelis too smart for that," Chino said. "These guys ain't got a chance."

"Les' we do sump'n, Bro," Rico said. "Les' we do sump'n." Rico started up *Rover-2*.

"What they doin', Bro?" Chino said. "They fightin'…they really fightin'!"

As they watched, one figure managed to smash the helmet of one of the others with a rock. The third dropped to his knees to render aid, and the first smashed his helmet as well.

"That guy a survivor, fo' sure, Bro," Chino said.

"Yeah," Rico said. "He know the three got no chance…but he, alone…maybe he got a chance."

"Does if we get him," Chino said.

"We gonna!" Rico accelerated *Rover-2*.

EARTH—MINNEAPOLIS/ST PAUL

Once Sharia Law was firmly established in Minneapolis Wards 3, 6, 9, and 10, it was only a matter of time before the remaining nine Wards voted Muslims to the City Council. At the very next council meeting, the City Council established Sharia Law for the entire city, and shortly thereafter, the city voted for a Muslim mayor.

Quietly and almost without fanfare, St. Paul's Wards 5, 6, and 7 voted for a Muslim as councilmember during the same time that across the river, Minneapolis shifted to Sharia Law. Surreptitiously, several thousand Muslim residents of Minneapolis moved their residence across the river to St. Paul Wards 3 and 4 so that the next election placed a Muslim majority on the St. Paul's city council. Unlike the gradual shift to Sharia Law in Minneapolis, the change happened almost overnight in St. Paul. As winter closed in over Minnesota, the St. Paul city council relieved the sitting mayor of her duties and installed a Muslim cleric as the new mayor.

Encouraged by Muslim successes in Minneapolis/St. Paul, 660 km to the southeast, Chicago declared itself an independent Muslim city and established Sharia Law within its boundaries. Emboldened by these successes and undaunted by increasingly colder weather, militant members of the large Muslim population in Dearborn, Michigan, stormed city hall, killed the non-Muslim councilmembers and the mayor, and proclaimed Dearborn as an independent Islamic state.

News services simply could not ignore events of this magnitude. Holovision images of Muslims dancing in the snowy streets of Minneapolis/St. Paul, Chicago, and Dearborn flashed across the world. Seeing these events on the evening holovision news, non-Muslim citizens of the Twin Cities grabbed the weapons and ammunition they had accumulated during the past year and took to the chilly night streets. The first shootings were erratic and unplanned, but as news of the shootings flashed around the world, gun owners in Chicago took up arms and then in Dearborn.

Within hours, the shootings were no longer erratic, isolated events but came from organized citizen gangs roaming the streets, looking for Muslims to kill. By first light, 10,000 Muslims lay dead in the snow-covered streets of Dearborn, and thousands more had been slaughtered in Chicago and the Twin Cities.

The governors of Minnesota, Michigan, and Illinois called out their National Guards attempting to quell the violence, but when confronted with gangs of armed fellow citizens, many Guardsmen refused to fire on them.

✷

"Muster the troops and issue vests, rifles, and ammunition—the full urban combat kit," Major Steven Brady ordered Command Sergeant Major Bo Bransom. "We got major rioting downtown…we've been ordered to quell it."

Pulling the troops in was not a trivial operation, but an hour-and-a-half later, Bransom notified Brady that Charlie Company was waiting for him on the frozen Green—four absentees—all married guys, but that was an excellent showing for such short notice.

"We got a bunch of civilians running amok downtown," Brady told the assembled troops. "Seems they're on an anti-Muslim rampage. They're armed, and a lot of people have been killed. We're gonna spread out along the northern and western perimeters, grouped by twos under squad leader Link command. Squad leaders, Link to your platoon leaders. Platoon leaders, Link to Bransom—I'll be on that circuit as well. Move generally south and east. I'll coordinate the movement through your chain of command. Don't break pattern without specific permission. We'll deploy the Mosquito Swarm above and ahead of you, so I'll have the big picture. Bo and I will direct you through your platoon and squad leaders. Keep your safeties on, and don't shoot unless fired upon. Stay alert and stay alive! Lock and load!"

✳

Sergeant Jerri Smyth held up her right hand in a clenched fist and signaled *freeze* on her Link, halting the movement of the eleven members of Third Platoon, Squad 1, spread up and down both sides of icy North Washington Ave. She examined the holographic combat display seemingly projected in front of her but actually contained within her polymer full face shield. *Bar La Grassa* was just ahead to the left; they were approaching the Warehouse District on the northeast side of Washington Ave., where several burning structures illuminated the frigid night air. A bullet ricocheted off the wall just ahead of her, and she dropped to the pavement along with her squad leader.

"This is Three—I see the shooter!"

Smyth gave a thumbs up to her squad leader.

"This is One—take him out, Three!"

Smyth heard a barely audible muffled shot from several meters behind her, and a yell as a body tumbled from the flat roof of the three-story brick building across the street from her position.

"Forward!" Smyth ordered on Squad 1 circuit. To her right, a group of snow-covered parking lots opened up, and just ahead on her right was the *Freehouse Bar* and a multistory warehouse. While she watched, a group of women in burqas and men with what appeared to be AK-47s sprinted across a lot to a concrete wall shelter, peppered by bullets as they ran. A man and two women took hits and lay where they fell. The men commenced a continuous barrage of gunfire sweeping the street in front of her, the *Freehouse*, and several windows in the warehouse. Before she could act, a flash and a streak from one of the warehouse windows announced a rocket-propelled grenade that hit the barrier and took out the entire group of Muslims.

Smyth pulled the squad around to the *Freehouse* entrance and sent them into the building by twos. Within minutes the squad leader reported that they had captured seven men armed with automatic weapons. He said that as soon as they saw the Guardsman uniforms, they surrendered their weapons.

"I'm on my way up," Smyth told him.

When she arrived, she found the seven men standing together with morose looks on their faces. "Why?" she asked.

One of the men stepped forward; two Guardsmen raised their weapons.

"No need for that," he said. "We would never fire on you guys. You're part of us." Then he looked directly at Smyth. "You asked *Why?* These people stole our town, usurped our city council, replaced our mayor, and turned our hometown into a Muslim Sharia Law hell."

"What about the warehouse fires?" Smyth asked.

"We had to flush them out. They were ambushing us from inside."

"Women?" Smyth's voice conveyed her anger.

"Check them out; most have forty-sevens under their bur-qas...I'm not lyin'...truly!"

"Squad two, check out the dead combatants on Washington between seventh and eighth," Smyth ordered. "Count the weapons." She turned to the seven fighters. "You gents are my captives!"

"We know that. We won't resist. But you guys got to get a handle on this mess. They're gonna kill us all before this is over...unless you do something."

✻

Brady scanned his Link overview showing the placement of each platoon and their squads in the snowy cityscape. His Mosquito Swarm integrated image superimposed on his battle view allowed him to vector his assets as necessary to separate the combatants and herd them toward the river. He watched the slaughter of the Muslim group near Platoon 3 and Smyth's takedown of the vigilante group that did it. He noted Smyth's second squad report that all the RPG casualties were armed with AK-47s. He sent a transport to pick up the prisoners, along with three other groups that surrendered to other squads without a fight. That was the weird thing; some of these guys avoided any contact with his troops and gave up without resistance when cornered. Others tried to fight it out, resulting in twenty-six body bags.

As frigid night slipped into chilly dawn and the sun edged above the far side of St. Paul, numbers started coming in on Muslim civilian casualties from the Twin Cities. Fifty here, a hundred there…even members of the city council. By 5:30 AM, the total Muslim casualties had passed 10,000. There were a hundred non-Muslim dead and 250 captured. It was a one-sided massacre.

As Brady shook his head in disbelief, Smyth came through on the Link emergency override. "Major, look east toward the city, the sky…!"

Brady directed his Mosquito Swarm to tilt upward. What he saw stunned him almost beyond belief. Then he looked up for himself, just to be sure. Thousands of blue parachutes filled the entire sky to the east and south. He zoomed in on one of the closest. His left shoulder was emblazoned with a light-blue flag displaying a severed fist holding a dagger; below the wrist, a truncated arm flowed red blood. He activated his override and spoke directly to every Guardsman in Charlie Company. "This is the Major…Suspend all activity immediately. Retreat as rapidly as you can, and exfiltrate back to headquarters! Do it now! DO IT NOW!"

EARTH—CHICAGO

While bullets flew in Minneapolis/St. Paul, Muslims continued to dance in the snowy streets of the Independent Muslim City of Chicago. Despite the superficial change to Chicago's governance, Chicago still was Chicago, a city that had not changed all that much in more than 150 years. With the freeing up of gun ownership in the early twenty-first century, the terrible gun violence for which Chicago had become known back then dissipated—for the most part. A new administration with a different perspective cleaned up the gangs throughout the city. A corrupt police department cleaned itself up, and the city finally opened up to tolerance. That was when North African Muslims poured into the city, virtually taking over much of the business and eventually city government itself. When Sharia Law was imposed on the city, most non-Muslims sat back to await change because they were convinced, for the most part, that this was just a phase and that things would get back to normal sooner or later.

When the Minneapolis/St. Paul massacre was broadcast around the world by holovision, non-Muslim Chicagoans looked around and asked themselves what they were waiting for. Armed citizens spread from the snowy suburbs into the icy city center—white, black, Latino, Asian—they exchanged high-fives as they passed one another. They had one focus—they would take back their city.

As in Minnesota, the slaughter was terrible. As in Minnesota, the National Guard had some success herding the combatants toward the lake, but resistance by armed non-Muslim citizens was much stronger. At least a hundred Guardsmen were killed, along with over 10,000 Muslims and several hundred non-Muslims. As in Minnesota, however, it all ended when over 10,000 Caliphate paratroopers appeared in the winter sky over Chicago.

EARTH—DEARBORN

Even though, for all practical purposes, Dearborn, Michigan, is part of Detroit, Dearborn has always gone its own way, and even here, Dearborn did it differently. Because of the slaughter of the city council and mayor, the Michigan Governor activated the Michigan National Guard with orders to shut down the Islamic State of Dearborn and reestablish civil control over the city. The Guard surrounded the city except for a corridor bounded to the north by the Rouge River and to the south by West Outer Drive. They entered with guns blazing and a take-no-prisoners-attitude, herding the combatants toward the Detroit River. Militant Muslims put up a ferocious resistance, making every block the Guard advanced as expensive as possible in human casualties. The militants killed several thousand civilians as they retreated toward the river. By the time the Guard had driven them out of Dearborn proper into the narrow corridor, 300 Guardsman were dead or wounded, and well over 12,000 Muslims were dead. The Detroit police assisted by ensuring that no militant escaped to the north through Detroit.

Just when victory seemed assured, however, the frigid skies over Greater Detroit filled with the blue parachutes of Caliphate airborne troops—over 10,000 strong—firing automatic weapons as they descended. There were no Guard survivors, and civilian non-Muslim casualties approached 10,000.

EARTH—WASHINGTON D.C.

President Stanford Jackson gazed around the table at the members of his National Security Council. The Council members presented a textbook example of inclusive politics. Vice President Dr. Syed Shah Bukhari sat opposite the President. His black National Security Advisor was a nationally acclaimed female graduate of Columbia Law School who many thought would fill the next vacancy on the Supreme Court. The balance of the Council included the Secretary of State, a Native American policy expert and Chief of the Iroquois Tribe, the Defense Secretary, a flamboyant retired Army General who had been forced into retirement by former President Bowles for his public opposition to President Bowles' policies toward the Founders, the Chairman of the Joint Chiefs of Staff, a female Air Force General appointed by the President over an active list of more senior generals and admirals because her political stance mirrored the President's, the Energy Secretary, an Asian American physicist and political activist who, many believed, was on track for her second Nobel Prize, the Treasury Secretary, a Hispanic legislator and grape grower from Central California widely respected for his labor organizing activities among so-called undocumented immigrants, the CIA Director, a Pulitzer Prize winning investigative reporter whose exposés garnered fame for her across the globe, and an Islamic cleric and playwright, known popularly as *The Imam*, whose works glorified fundamental Islam and Sharia, and who, as a personal friend of the Vice President, was appointed to the NSC as a favor to the Vice President.

"We are meeting today," the President said solemnly, "because of the terrible events that have transpired in Minneapolis, Chicago, and Dearborn over the past several days." His regal face looked tired and drawn. "Three northern cities are occupied by foreign troops. Dr. Bukhari tells me from sources available to him that each of these cities specifically requested help from the Caliphate." He nodded to the Vice President. "Dr. Bukhari…"

Bukhari spread his hands flat on the table in front of him. "It's like this," he said in perfectly enunciated English, "Minneapolis and St. Paul are governed by legitimately elected city councils and a mayor, as is Chicago. Sharia Law was not imposed, so much as put in place experimentally by the Muslim majority, and has generally been accepted by the non-Muslim minorities in all three cities. This has precedence in England, France, Belgium, and even in our State of Georgia." He paused while murmurs went around the table. "We do, after all, live in a democracy," he pointed out. "People have the inherent right to be governed as they wish." He leaned forward, elbows and forearms on the table. "Dearborn is different, and I'll get to that in a moment. But first, the Twin Cities and Chicago experienced unprecedented civil uprisings, far beyond their city police departments' ability to quell. The mayors went to their respective governors for help, but neither governor would take the calls. It was only when the civilian revolt got out of hand that the National Guard was brought in. As Muslim civilian casualties began to mount, the mayors turned to the only source they were sure would help—the Caliphate." The Vice President sat back with a grim smile.

"Your timeline doesn't make sense," the Joint Chiefs Chair said, pushing herself back from the table. "Flight time from the Caliphate to the Twin-Cities is at least thirteen hours; from there to Chicago, another hour; and then a bit less than an hour to Dearborn. To get ten thousand troops in the air at each city would require at least thirty jam-packed troop transports, ten or more mid-air refueling craft, and a dozen or more protective fighters that will need to be refueled at least four times each way." She stood up, exasperated, and leaned forward, hands on the table edge. "Nobody does this kind of operation without weeks of preparation. It certainly doesn't happen following a frantic phone call of an American mayor!"

The Defense Secretary looked at his Chair of the Joint Chiefs and nodded. "The general makes a good point, Mr. President. This had to be a planned operation."

"I disagree," Dr. Bukhari interjected. "Dearborn, perhaps, but not the Twin-Cities or Chicago. These are clearly spontaneous democratic transfers. Dearborn, on the other hand, was a violent take-over that may have had Caliphate troops as a backup. Since the Twin-Cities and Chicago uprisings were so close in time to Dearborn," his face took on a quizzical expression, "perhaps the Caliphate simply took advantage of the situation and timing…"

"Ridiculous!" the Joint Chiefs Chair said. "That would take another twenty planeloads of troops and all the backup…"

President Jackson looked sharply at his Defense Secretary. "That's enough, General!" the Defense Secretary snapped. "Mr. President, what do you need from us?"

Around the table, heads nodded in agreement.

The President looked at his Secretary of State. "Find me an honorable path out of this mess."

✳

Over the next several days, State and Defense worked closely together to craft a solution. Diplomatic messages flew back and forth between Washington and the Caliphate, while in the Twin-Cities, the Caliphate on-scene commander consolidated his position and placed his troops strategically throughout the Wards of both cities. Chicago maintained an uneasy cease-fire as both National Guard and Caliphate forces jockeyed for position.

Right in the middle of negotiations, troop transports suddenly docked at the Detroit river docks, and in two hours, the Caliphate occupation of Dearborn ceased. The troops boarded the transports or seemed to melt into the landscape, weapons disappeared, and city hall was left empty. The Caliphate quietly informed State that it had unilaterally abandoned Dearborn and that it would evacuate Chicago on the condition that Minneapolis/St. Paul remain a Caliphate protectorate, controlled and governed by its own Muslim majority under the umbrella of Sharia Law.

State and Defense reported the compromise to President Jackson and Vice President Bukhari in the Oval Room that afternoon.

"Caliphate protectorate?" President Jackson asked, his voice strained.

"Technically," the Vice President said, "but since Sharia Law is already their choice, and since we have no intention of imposing something else on them, in reality, there is nothing for the Caliphate to protect. It will remain an American city. We get Dearborn and Chicago back, and we keep the peace. It seems a small price to pay."

"Madam Secretary…General…?" The President looked earnestly at his Secretaries of State and Defense. "You both see this as a workable solution?"

They nodded.

EARTH—AUSTIN, TEXAS

Sam Houston had a lot on his mind. On the one hand, he was worried about the terrorist activities on Mars. True, they seemed mostly limited to New Israel lately, but it was difficult to forget the White Elephant explosion. He thought about the Israeli concept of Banishment for crimes against the Jewish people that involved the wholesale destruction or attempted destruction of New Israel. *Talk about the punishment fitting the crime!* Sam thought as he affirmed in his own mind that it was what he would do in similar circumstances. He had always wondered why Jon had not spaced his terrorist stowaway. It certainly would have prevented a lot of subsequent problems.

He had regrets about leaving Lone Star Mars, but the settlement was in good hands. McIntyre was an able administrator. During the past few months, while Sam was campaigning for the governorship, McIntyre had kept things shipshape and on course. Sam had no complaints.

On the other hand, Sam was closely watching things up north. He simply could not believe the solution the Jackson administration put in place. To cede, in effect, the territories of two cities to a hostile foreign power was beyond belief—more than that, it was intolerably unacceptable. It made his blood boil just to think about it, but at this moment, he had something even more important to do. In the next few minutes, he would take the oath of office as Governor of the State of Texas.

The ceremony was short and sweet. After being sworn in, Sam watched his Lt. Governor Jim Grayson take the oath of office. It was over in fifteen minutes, and everyone retired to the park for the traditional barbeque picnic that had followed every gubernatorial inauguration for at least a hundred years. Then to the changing rooms to get ready for the black-tie inaugural ball that signified the *official* start of the new governor's term.

Sam was enjoying a traditional dance with his Lt. Governor's wife when an aide signaled him from the side of the dance floor. "Excuse me," Sam said, bowing low with a twinkle in his eye. "Duty already calls."

Sam strode to his aide and leaned over to hear what she had to say. After a few moments, he looked at her sharply and straightened up as the blood slowly left his face. "You're certain?" he asked quietly.

The aide nodded.

Pàrt Twö

Allàhü Akbàr!

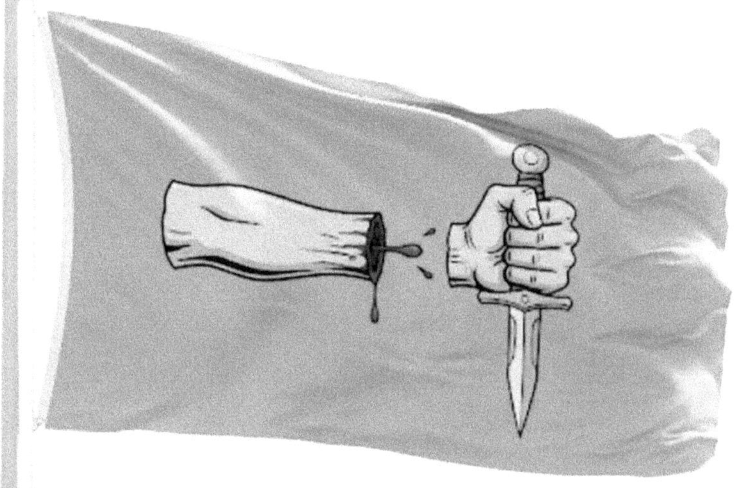

CHAPTER THIRTEEN

EARTH—PENTAGON, WASHINGTON D.C.

They said it couldn't happen in America. But, on a cold Tuesday at 7:00 PM Washington time, just as festivities were getting underway in Austin, President Jackson climbed the steps of *Marine One* for the short trip to Camp David where he was to meet again with his National Security Council about the Caliphate insurgency. *Marine One* never made it to Camp David. Instead, it set down in Ground Zero—the Pentagon's open central plaza, while the President—without his Secret Service bodyguards who were kept on board at gunpoint—was whisked away to a specially prepared chamber that was part of the National Military Command Center (NMCC). One minute after landing, without changing its designation, *Marine One* announced it was returning to the White House—with the President on board, the outside world believed.

A four-star Army general who had been passed over by President Jackson in favor of a younger, more politically aligned officer, greeted the President, offering him a comfortable chair. The President refused, and the Air Force general and Navy admiral, the balance of the triumvirate, remained standing as well.

"What is this outrage?" the President demanded.

"It's very simple, Sir," the general answered. "You are my guest here at the NMCC. We are in the middle of a national crisis. You and your National Security Council have botched things so badly that we have taken over."

"You what?"

"You heard me, Sir!" The Army general, who was clearly in charge, walked toward the door. "I've notified your National Security Advisor. We've activated the NMCC Backup Protocol. Your Situation Room is out of the circuit; it's all run from here now."

"You can't do this," the President protested.

"But we have…Sir!"

EARTH—WASHINGTON D.C.

Two hours after the triumvirate announced its coup, the National Security Council convened in the White House Situation Room that was now nothing more than another room in the White House. Vice President Dr. Syed Shah Bukhari sat opposite President Jackson's vacant seat. The National Security Advisor was speaking. "Constitutionally, Mr. Vice President, you are the acting president. You need to assert your position and ask the other cabinet members to write a formal statement declaring you the President in fact."

"I can't do that…not yet anyway," Bukhari said quietly. "All we know for sure is that they have the President, and they have removed Command and Control from this group. No one has been killed, no one has been injured. I believe we can negotiate our way to a compromise that will be in the best interests of the Country." The capital C in Country was clearly audible. He stood up and excused himself. "I must speak with the generals privately," he said as he stepped out of the room and contacted the NMCC triumvirate.

EARTH—LOW EARTH ORBIT TO GEOSTATIONARY ORBIT

About 150 km above the Earth's surface, a swarm of communications satellites transited their designated polar orbits approximately every 90 minutes. Nobody actually knew how many there were, since hundreds, perhaps thousands, were no longer active, yet continued in their orbits because it was cheaper to let them eventually burn up in the atmosphere than to send something or somebody up there to clean them out. Farther out, from roughly 10,000 km to 20,000 km, a similar swarm of satellites went about their daily business of monitoring, controlling, signaling, spying.... The list was endless, but they all did something useful for somebody somewhere on the planet beneath. In geosynchronous orbit, some 32,800 km out, hundreds of satellites maintained positions over small patches of the Earth's equator, functioning in their assigned capacities.

Returning to Earth from the Moon, L5, Mars, or Iapetus required a certain caution because no one really knew the orbits of every one of these moonlets. A certain number of these machines were controlled by the United States NMCC. They supplied intelligence, coordinated military activities and communications worldwide, and generally made sure the vast U.S. military complex functioned as flawlessly as humanly possible.

The satellite links were backed up by secure fiber-optic cable that formed a web across the United States and around the World.

Once the Caliphate had re-established itself as a world power, General Suleiman commenced launching his own satellite network so as not to be reliant on any other nation's capabilities. Suleiman put his satellites into every known orbit region occupied by the command and control satellites of any other country with such capability. Since such satellites had become a routine part of any nation's military stance, nobody took particular notice of this activity, except for logging and cataloging these satellites for future reference.

When Caliphate paratroopers loaded into the troop carriers along the Detroit River following the evacuation of Dearborn, several thousand just faded into the snowy landscape. With a change of clothing and hair trimmed to American standards, they became indistinguishable from millions of Hispanic citizens scattered across the country. Each had a specific mission, a designated spot to locate, and was prepared to act when the order arrived by Link.

When President Jackson was taken hostage by the triumvirate, Vice President Bukhari seized the opportunity to set in motion the next stage of Prophet Saeed Ismail's audacious plan. He broadcast an encrypted Link signal that notified General Suleiman the plan was underway. General Suleiman, in turn, sent a highly encrypted message to the President of Mexico. Bukhari's signal also activated the paratroopers who had disbursed across the nation. Each commenced his specific task.

High above the Earth, wherever Caliphate satellites were located, each moonlet ejected a swarm of small, explosive pellets that spread out behind the satellites in a cone of destruction. Everything orbiting behind the satellite down to the top of the Earth's atmosphere and out to several hundred kilometers was destroyed when impacting a pellet. Each Caliphate moonlet emitted a signal that caused any pellet approaching it to self-destruct, so that ninety minutes later, the only satellites in low-earth-orbit belonged to the Caliphate. Further out, the Caliphate's destructive moonlets took out every nation's satellites, including the command and control elements of the U.S. NMCC.

On the Earth's surface across the United States, 2,000 specially trained Caliphate warriors located 2,000 optical cable trunks, and with nearly simultaneous synchronicity, truncated the NMCC's landline backup system.

EARTH—WASHINGTON D.C.

Two hours following the Vice President's conversation with the triumvirate, President Jackson was back in the Oval Office. Command and Control—what there was left—reverted to the White House Situation Room, but the President agreed officially to defer all military decisions to the NMCC. The triumvirate agreed to grant the National Security Council a say in any national security-related decisions, but it retained veto power over any matters. In any case, regaining its worldwide ComCon ability had the triumvirate's highest priority.

President Jackson was unhappy with the outcome, but under the circumstances, he considered it a workable compromise. He was back in control of the government, and since he did not contemplate any military action in the immediate future, he did not care what happened over in the bowels of the Pentagon. The command and control matter was the Pentagon's purview in any case, so let them solve it. Besides, he still had to deal with Minneapolis/St. Paul and—now—the curfew the triumvirate had imposed before they let him return to the White House. He checked the time—it was approaching midnight. He activated a Link to the Vice President.

"You handled that well, Dr. Bukhari," Jackson told him, unaware of Bukhari's role. "I need you to remain on top of the Twin Cities while I have The Imam address the curfew problem. We don't need dead citizens littering the capital streets."

At that moment, Jackson's Link Emergency Call signaled him. He activated the Link to see his Defense Secretary and National Security Advisor, both in a state of agitation. Before either could speak, the NMCC broke in on an executive override, so that the Oval Office was filled with holoimages of the Vice President, the three triumvirate members, and his two Cabinet secretaries, all trying to speak at once.

EARTH—AUSTIN, TEXAS

Sam Houston stood in his office looking out over the darkened grounds of the Texas Capitol. It was a beautiful building that had been refurbished several times since its construction back in 1885. The moon glowed brightly on the evening grounds, casting long shadows across the greenery that was washed out by the gay inaugural lighting strung up around the open spaces. It made the problems in Europe and Washington seem remote.

Closer to home, however, was a much more immediate problem. At the inaugural ball a few minutes ago, his aide had put it quite succinctly. "There has been a coup in Washington!" she told him.

His Lieutenant Governor, Jim Grayson, entered his ornate office somewhat breathlessly. "What's up, Sam? Why the urgency?"

Sam activated the holotank that occupied one corner of the room. A pretty blonde with wide blue eyes was talking in hushed tones. "President Jackson is missing, and a group of three generals, one from each service...ahh...two generals and one admiral, has announced that they have assumed temporary control of the government." She put a hand to her ear and then looked up at the holocams. "They have imposed martial law on Greater Washington D.C." Her eyes got even wider. "They say that anyone on the Washington D.C.

streets after eleven PM will be shot on sight." She looked away from the holocams. "Oh my! It's ten-fifty…"

"Whadya think, Sam?" A wave of concern passed over Grayson's face.

"We got a problem…that's what!" Sam snapped. Then he smiled at Grayson. "Sorry…it's not you; it's that." He pointed at the holotank. Then Sam fielded an urgent call on his Link. "What? You've got to be kidding! Wait a sec…" He shifted the call to a holodisplay. The image of Major General Gregory Samuelson, the Texas Adjutant General who controlled Texas military forces, appeared before them, crisply uniformed, balding head uncovered. "Repeat what you just told me, Greg."

"Sir!" The general nodded at Grayson. "Mexican troops just crossed the borders of California, Arizona, and New Mexico. Initial estimate is about fifty thousand infantry backed by artillery and light armor—no tanks…mostly late-twentieth-century stuff." The general glanced at his desk. "No jet aircraft…they never replaced the last five fighters they retired in the early years of the twenty-first century. The motive seems to be reclaiming territory Mexican conservatives believe was stolen from Mexico in the nineteenth century. With Washington in disarray, I guess they think now is a good time." The general looked at a display invisible to Sam and Jim. "It appears that ComCon links worldwide have been severed—satellite and ground links…everything!" He shook his head. "No way Mexico did that! My ComCon aircraft are already airborne. We have had no interruption of our strategic control. Can't say the same about the national level. They're offline." He looked at another holoimage out of holocam view. "Mexican marines have just landed at North Island in San Diego, and Long Beach south of Los Angeles. Heavy casualties on North Island—a slaughter, actually…they took no prisoners. They're occupying the Port of Long Beach. Los Angeles is in a panic. Outbound freeways are jammed, and Hispanics are rioting throughout the city… civilian casualties everywhere.

"Border Patrol in California, Arizona, and New Mexico has been wiped out. The wall is completely demolished. Right now, fifty Rangers are holding off the Mexican army at El Paso with light resistance. I got armored troops headed that way—should be there in a half-hour. Mexican commanders apparently are not looking at Texas right now. Every town west of Texas for a hundred kilometers north is occupied, but they've stopped their movement for the time being. Supply lines too thin—they need fuel, ammo, and food."

"What about the U.S. Army?" Sam interrupted. "Link…holo-vision cables…Hell, tin cans and string…"

"Like I said, Sir, ComCon out of Washington is down. Nobody is doing anything…we're on our own, Sam. We're fucking on our own!"

"How much time do we have?" Sam asked.

"Twenty-four hours…forty-eight max…"

Sam sat at his desk thinking furiously. Perhaps two minutes passed while he scribbled notes on a pad. "Stand by, Greg. Keep this link open. I want you fully aware of the steps I am taking. As you listen, commence any appropriate actions you understand to be a logical consequence of what you see and hear from this office."

"Sir!"

"Jim…roust every member of the Texas House and Senate. Get as many as you can seated in the next two hours. Set up Links if necessary." He opened a second Link channel. Brad Comex, Texas Secretary of State, appeared, tall, slightly overweight and balding, but cutting a fine figure in his Inaugural Ball formal attire. Sam briefed him quickly on events. "Brad, have your people draw up papers of secession from the United States, ready to present to the House and Senate in two hours."

"Secession…two hours…you're shitting me?"

"Brad, I appointed you because you are the best man I know for this job." Sam smiled at the Secretary of State's holographic image. "Now you get to prove it!" Sam broke the Link. He looked over at Grayson, busy initiating the emergency recall system for the Texas Legislature, and raised his eyebrows.

"I'll have most of them in the chambers in two hours," Grayson told Sam.

How can this be happening? Sam thought. *My first day as Governor, and I'm declaring Texas independence and getting ready to go to war with Mexico.* He turned to the holoimage of his Adjutant General. "Status?"

"I have ordered the Commanding Officers of all twenty U.S. military facilities in Texas to transfer chain-of-command to the Texas

Military Department—Me! Eighteen did so immediately and are mo-
bilizing as we speak. I relieved two Commanding Generals, replacing
them with their Seconds, and put them under guarded house arrest.
Nine of the ten Coast Guard Facilities have put their facilities, ships,
and weapons under my control. One small station is commanded by
a Master Chief Petty Officer, who was reluctant to comply without
confirmation. I dispatched a Coast Guard Commander to his station
to get things moving. I think the Master Chief will be fine once he
and the Commander finish talking. There are no Navy bases with
warships in Texas, but two fast-attack subs, a frigate, and a cruiser are
making port call at Galveston. I spoke personally with both skippers
of the ships; because they lost ComCon, they have reluctantly joined
us. I am in communication with both subs. One skipper is talking
with my staff. The other is being a bit difficult, but I see some light
by tomorrow morning." The general tossed a lopsided grin at his
Commander-in-Chief. "This shit ain't in the command general orders,
Sam. The Skipper has to work through this.

"I activated the fifteen-thousand-strong Texas Army National
Guard. They completed a state-wide drill a month ago. They'll be up
to full complement and ready to fight in less than twenty-four hours. I
activated the twelve-thousand-strong Texas Air National Guard. I have
a hundred close-support aircraft ready to fly in less than thirty minutes.
And ten of the twenty military facilities are either Air Force, Naval Air,
or Army Air. They put another five hundred aircraft at my disposal,
including a hundred close-support choppers. The ten-thousand-strong
Texas State Guard has been on maneuvers for the past week. They are
disbursing to every Texas State border crossing as we speak. Finally,
I pulled the Texas Ranger Division from the Department of Public
Safety and incorporated it into the Domestic Operations Task Force,
making all two hundred Rangers available wherever they are needed."

"Okay, Greg, you've impressed the hell out of me!" Sam checked
the time. "I'm talking to the legislature in twenty minutes. Set up a
conference Link with your commanders, senior staffs, Jim, and me
for two hours from now. Tell your people to be ready to brief me on
how we can, one—preserve Texas sovereignty, two—stop the Mexican
advance, three—drive the Mexicans back to Mexico, and four—set
up an alliance with New Mexico, Arizona, and Southern California."

EARTH—AUSTIN, TEXAS

Sam Houston strode purposefully into the Texas House Chamber filled with virtually all the Texas representatives and senators. Ten holoimages occupied a section near the left front of the chamber, the only members unable to get to Austin in the short time the Lt. Governor had given them. Since most were already in Austin for the inauguration, the task of getting them there was easier than it might have been.

"Thank you all for making the herculean effort to be here on such notice," Sam commenced, glancing at the secession papers on the podium before him. "To the extent possible, you all have been briefed by Link before you got here. Nevertheless, let me take just a few minutes to fill you in."

Sam then launched into his carefully prepared monologue of all that had transpired in the last several hours. As he spoke, the room got very quiet.

"So, that's the long and short of it. We are cut off…on our own, and there is little likelihood that any kind of national command and control will be reestablished any time soon. The Mexican attack happening simultaneously with the coup in Washington and the loss of national command and control was no coincidence. We—Texas—will be at war with Mexico in a matter of hours. Bullets are already flying.

"It's time we recognize who and what we are!" Sam raised his voice so that it filled every corner of the chamber. "It's time we establish ourselves as a free and independent nation. There is no time for debate as we will be in a real shooting war within hours." He lifted up the secession papers, waving them at the representatives and senators arrayed before him. "I give you the Lone Star Conservancy!"

To a person, the assembled representatives and senators stood and cheered their approval. Shouts of "Texas!" and "Lone Star!" filled the chamber and the halls beyond. The Lt. Governor stepped to the podium.

"I call the question!" he shouted at the crowd. "All in favor?" *Ayes* drowned out his voice.

"All opposed?" Silence… "The Ayes have it! Welcome to the Lone Star Conservancy!"

The crowd went wild.

L4—MIRS COMPLEX

Word of the destruction of Earth's halo of artificial satellites flashed to the Mirs Complex as it happened. The coup in Washington was just a footnote, and the Texas secession went almost unnoticed, although the Mexican invasion of the Southern United States caught Dmitri's attention. He saw this as a big deal because, to him, it seemed to signal the end of a great nation.

As Director of Federation Security, he was morally certain that the Caliphate would soon export its mischief to the Federation. He could slow down the progress but saw no way to prevent it altogether. He decided to meet with Rod to work out whatever procedures they adopted to hem in the Caliphate. He briefed his staff and then boarded his hyper-V craft for the trip to Iapetus, carrying Jake in his travel cage.

It had been more than ten years now, but Dmitri still was amazed that it took more time to drop down the five-kilometer shaft into the Iapetus interior than to get there from Mirs. An hour after his staff meeting subjective time, however, Dmitri was sitting in front of Rod's desk in the Iapetus government complex.

"I received your summary about a half-hour ago," Rod told him. "The situation is pretty serious."

"It looks like the Caliphate satellite wipe took out a significant portion of Earth's ServerSky swarm as well," Dmitri said. "That puts Link service in jeopardy—at least worldwide." He spread his hands. "Sam will get something going over Texas pretty soon. I'm certain of that."

"The Mexican invasion will keep him busy for the time being," Rod added. "You know they invaded with a Twentieth Century army?"

"They obviously know something we don't." Dmitri pulled up a graphic of the U.S. Southwestern border. "Look at their supply line… Chihuahua is three hundred seventy klicks south, and it's the largest supply center. They've moved about a hundred klicks into the U.S., so we're talking about a five hundred klick supply route for everything except water, and there's damned little of that where they are."

"They've left Texas alone," Rod mused. "I wonder why?"

"For the time being," Dmitri said. "Sam's going to be in the middle of it in no time. 'Course, they got a good supply line from San Diego and Los Angeles. Long way from Sam." Dmitri placed his hands on Rod's desk. "We gotta contain them, you know." He smiled grimly. "We can't let them bring their crap out here."

"Problem is," Rod said, "nearly everybody's got space-capable hyper-V craft, including the Caliphate."

"Yeah, but they can't weaponize them…yet."

"I think I will issue a decree restricting Caliphate movement off Earth to specifically authorized missions that the Federation okays upfront." Rod leaned back in his chair. "How does that sound to you?"

"Fine…How do we enforce it?"

"That's the rub, isn't it?" Rod scrunched up his face. "I guess if you catch them, you destroy the hyper-V craft. They can't have too many…two or three max."

"Make it official, my friend, and my people will do their damnedest to make it happen!"

EARTH—SAUDI ARABIAN DESERT

General Suleiman bowed deeply, saying, "You now control the skies over the entire planet, Sahib." He touched chest, lips, and forehead as he straightened. "Even the Great Satan's command and control system is no more." He swept his gaze around the sprawling tent still pitched atop the same low mound overlooking the Rub' al-Khali lakebed where towering dunes presented an everchanging vista. Saeed Ismail sat quietly in his cushions, sipping strong mint tea.

"Do we control the space pathways between the planets?" Saeed asked.

"Not yet, Sahib." The general stood tall and silent, a far-away look in his eyes. "First, we keep their small security force busy with hit-and-run raids while we consolidate our control of Planet Earth, and then we sit down with the Federation as equal partners."

IAPETUS—STARCHILD INSTITUTE

Deep in the bowels of the Starchild Institute, a young graduate student working with Dr. Kristopher Lambin, a senior physicist on a project derived from Founder black hole technology, carefully measured the Casimir forces between two plates of the same exotic material that formed the skin of modern hyper-V craft.

"That can't be!" he muttered to himself and set about repeating the measurement. A half-hour later, he stared at the same result within seven significant figures, and then he called Dr. Lambin, his hands trembling.

EARTH—MEDITERRANEAN & EUROPE

The World watched as Caliphate forces swept across Africa. For the most part, there was no resistance. Rebel forces joined the Caliphate army, abolishing what little real civil government existed in each territory, replacing it with the local Imam and strict Sharia Law. More often than not, once Sharia was in place, the Caliphate forces turned on the cooperating rebels and slaughtered them. Europe remained unconcerned—it had its own problems with constant internal Muslim insurgencies resulting from misguided immigration policies during the previous century. North America was too far away, and it, also, was having its own problems. South America seemed not even to notice.

As Caliphate forces swept around the Bay of Bengal, India looked to its secret agreement with the Caliphate and felt only the slightest twinge of anxiety as she was side-stepped. Australia, on the other hand, massed its land, sea, and air forces along its northern shores, waiting with bated breath for the inevitable invasion—that never came, as Caliphate forces turned north through Vietnam and the rest of Southeast Asia. The Caliphate met its greatest resistance in the jungles of Vietnam, but unlike France and the United States during the past century, the Caliphate simply bypassed this resistance, for the time being, relying on its future China plans to solve that problem.

Unlike extended invasions from Earth's past, such as Napoleon and the Nazis in Russia, or Genghis Kahn even further past, where extended supply lines spelled certain disaster, the steppes of Central Africa readily supplied the African portion of the conquest, and Indonesia with its 25% Muslim population underwrote the entire Southeast Asian conquest.

Simultaneously with the push southward, Caliphate forces had overtaken Turkey, Greece, Bulgaria, the Balkans, and the Stans. It was now pressing through Rumania and Hungary and from the Balkans into northern Italy. Caliphate warriors surged across the Aegean Sea, attacking along the length of eastern Italy, and from what used to be Algeria north around Sicily to Italy's west coast. Rome fell in two days. The Vatican was leveled to the ground, the Pope and everyone inside the walls slaughtered.

With the fall of Italy, France and Spain belatedly mobilized their militaries, but coincident with that mobilization, internal Muslim insurgents attacked in full force throughout southern France and all of Spain and Portugal with predictable results. Two weeks following the fall of Rome, southern France from Geneva in Switzerland through Lyon, Clermont-Ferrand, and Limoges, to La Rochelle, and the entirety of Spain and Portugal had fallen under Caliphate rule.

This was a wake-up call for the rest of Europe—the British Isles, the Lowlands, Germany, Poland, and the eastern lands not yet under Caliphate rule, although Scandinavia seemed blissfully unconcerned with the events below its southern borders. The Europeans consolidated their forces, but under threat of internal attack, they hesitated to confront the overwhelming swarm of Muslim warriors who formed an unbroken line from the Kazakhstan-Russia-China border to La Rochelle, France. It was a classic stand-off that the Caliphate used to consolidate its gains and the Europeans used to strengthen their opposition.

Along the way, Caliphate forces employed a simple but effective technique for eliminating opposition. In every community they entered, the population was brought to a central location and given a choice: Convert to Islam or die. There was no discussion, no debate, no equilibration. Millions of the slaughtered lay on the ground in the wake of the advancing Caliphate forces, to be interred by those left alive. Caliphate governors replaced local authorities. Imams and mosques replaced priests and ministers, churches, temples, synagogues, and other religious edifices, such as the Raëlian slab-sided places of worship. By the time Caliphate forces reached La Rochelle, at the onset of the harshest winter Europe had experienced in the last several decades, nearly a billion human beings had been slaughtered, and over five billion had been compelled to accept Sharia Law.

By mid-winter, General Suleiman had resupplied his armies along the entire European front from La Rochelle to the Black Sea. He issued an ultimatum to the leaders of Hungary, Austria, Germany, the Benelux countries, Great Britain and Ireland, and what was left of France: "Submit or face nuclear annihilation!"

*

"Dmitri, it's Michele…I need you, *mon Cher*…we need you!" The transmission made its way from Paris to L4 via a direct dish link Dmitri had set up when the world's communication net disappeared.

"Explain…please…" The slight transmission delay between Earth and L4 caused the conversation to be choppy, something Dmitri never got used to.

"Henri refuses to leave France," she said, breaking into tears. "They will kill him, Dmitri…they will kill us both." She took a deep breath and then rushed on. "Muslim rioters have overwhelmed the Paris police. They destroyed the *Louvre*, *Tour Eiffel*, *l'Arc de Triomphe*…Oh, Dmitri, I'm so scared. They will be here soon…*mon Dieu!* They will kill us for sure!"

"I'm on my way, Michele, I'm on my way! Get the word out that I am coming, and to let me land in the main court…hurry!" Dmitri turned to his office interior. "Who's available right now? I mean right now…this very minute!"

To his surprise, Danylo Orel stepped forward, all seventy-five kilos of Cossack tough. "What are you doing here?" Dmitri asked.

"Checking records; trying to find the bastards who killed my brother and Mykola and Pavlo."

"I need some help, Dany. It's dangerous, but we need to rescue a beautiful woman…"

"I'm in…!" His dark eyes lit up.

"And her husband," Dmitri finished with a grin.

Orel's face dropped, but he said, "Really, I'm in…let's go!"

"Grab that travel cage," Dmitri said, pointing to Jake's favorite place when not in Dmitri's lap. "Lock it, please."

Five minutes later, they activated *Merkavah's* controls, and in mere seconds were hovering above the French presidential residence, Élysée Palace. From above, Dmitri saw rioters surging from both sides of the palace along *Rue Saint Honoré*. Palace guards were firing live bullets into the crowds from the roof of the front wall and from the ground just outside the locked steel gates.

"I'm here, Michele. You and Henri get out now. Your guards are nearly overwhelmed. You have to get out now!"

"Henri refuses to leave with me!"

"Let me speak with him, Michele."

"Henri, you're a stubborn bastard, but you cannot let Michele die…you hear me?"

"I agree, Dmitri, but I simply cannot leave myself. I would be shamed for all eternity."

"I got it! You and Michele get into the court right now! The rioters are breaking down the gates…now, Henri…now!"

Dmitri turned to Orel. "Get ready to open the hatch and grab Michele! You'll have only seconds. Keep a low profile; they'll be shooting at you."

Dmitri ordered his Resident to bring the hyper-V craft into the court and be ready to leave immediately. As they dropped and came to a hover, the main gates crashed inward, and the angry crowd swarmed into the court. The main doors opened, and Dmitri saw Henri grab Michele's hand and run toward *Merkavah*.

"Run, Henri! Run!" The crowd was meters behind the craft. "Faster!"

Deville picked Michele up and bodily tossed her into *Merkavah* as the crowd overwhelmed him.

"Got her!" Orel said as he grabbed the terrified woman and signaled the hatch closed.

"Gotta save Henri!" Dmitri shouted as he brought the craft to a hover fifty meters above the angry mob. He instructed the Resident to identify leaders and hit them with Neutrino Beams. Those selected collapsed beneath the mob's feet, but it made no difference. In less than a minute, they had torn France's last President, Henri Deville, limb from limb.

✳

It took only a day for the remaining European leaders to signify their capitulation. Over the next few freezing days, thousands of Imams throughout Europe converted Europeans by the hundreds of thousands to Islam in mass assemblages. By week's end, Europe's nearly one billion citizens professed only Islam as their religion and only Allah as their god, at least superficially. Cathedrals, churches, synagogues, and distinctive slab-sided Raëlian churches all but disappeared as indigenous Muslims throughout Europe destroyed the structures, from the smallest slab-sided Raëlian church in the Scottish Highlands, to Canterbury Cathedral in England, Notre-Dame in Paris, to the Dohány Street Synagogue in Budapest—all gone.

The World's four most powerful nations took no action. India was secure in its nonaggression treaty with the Caliphate. Russia relied on its size and history of aborted attacks that succumbed to impossibly long supply lines and upon the indomitable will of its people. China relied on its multi-million-man army, nuclear navy, and modern air force to keep the marauding forces at bay. And the United States was too busy sorting out Muslim incursions into several of its major cities, dealing with a blind-side attack on its southwestern border by Mexico, accommodating a complete loss of its Central Command and Control, and now, the secession of Texas from the Union.

EARTH—SOUTHWESTERN USA

The situation could not have been more urgent. Link communications were shaky at best and entirely nonexistent beyond the borders of Texas. Sam exercised command and control through his fleet of ComCon aircraft blanketing the skies of Texas. This did not, however, give him any communications beyond this. He desperately needed to speak with the governors of New Mexico and Arizona, and he had to reach somebody in southern California who exercised a measure of control.

Sam called his Adjutant General, Gregory Samuelson. As the trim and fit tough-guy image coalesced before him, Sam said, "Greg, can you stretch your ComCon resources so I can speak with Santa Fe and Phoenix? Also, do you have a solid contact in southern California?"

"Yes and yes! Gimme a half-hour for Santa Fe, another twenty for Phoenix, and an hour or so for California." The General saluted, and his image vanished.

Thirty minutes later, Sam spoke to the holoimage of the besieged governor of New Mexico. "This is more than a social call, my friend. I suspect you have been pretty much out of the loop since loss of ComCon." The New Mexico governor nodded but said nothing. Sam briefed him on the Texas secession and his consolidation of all military forces in Texas under his command. "Are your forces able to counter Mexico?" Sam asked.

"Not a chance."

"Will New Mexico join the Lone Star Conservancy under my command? You'll retain your state sovereignty as before."

"Do I really have a choice?" the belabored governor asked. "I'll have my people draw up the papers…"

"We already did that," Sam said. "I'll transmit them to you. I need you to put your forces at my command ASAP!" He grinned. "I'm talking to Phoenix next. General Samuelson will coordinate with your people." Sam cut the Link and called Phoenix.

Sam conducted virtually the same conversation with the Arizona governor, with substantially the same results. As he terminated the connection, his Link announced a call from General Samuelson.

"Sam, er…I mean, Governor, I'd like to introduce General Bob York, Commanding General of Camp Pendleton. Bob came up through the ranks…he's the toughest marine I know. Somehow, the Jackson Administration overlooked him and didn't boot him out with the other competent general officers."

General York saluted. "Sir!"

"Glad to have you aboard, General." Sam sighed and sat back in his chair. "Have a seat and get comfortable. We have a lot to cover." As General York sat, Sam outlined the events of the past few days. During Sam's monologue, York's countenance remained poker-faced. "How many fighting forces do you have at your disposal?" Sam asked as he finished.

"About a hundred thousand, Sir. Five hundred or so are raw recruits. The rest are seasoned marines from Pendleton and Twenty-nine Palms, sailors in San Diego, and Seal Teams One, Three, Five, and Seven. Right now, San Diego forces are scattered, but if you can get me reliable coms, I can assemble a pretty decent force in a few hours. These guys want a real fight more than anything!"

"What about armor and air power?" Sam asked.

"A hundred fifty close support choppers, fifty troop carrier and logistics rotorcraft including ten Ospreys, twenty-five Warthogs; a hundred light tanks and other mobile armor, and a lot of close-in artillery and other small armor." General York smiled grimly. "We can handle things here…if we regain ComCon."

"Here is the difficult part, General York," Sam said earnestly. "As I explained earlier, I have taken Texas out of the Union, and with New Mexico and Arizona, formed the Lone Star Conservancy. I need you to assume government control of southern California, formally secede from both California and the Union, and join Lone Star." Sam raised his eyebrows and held out his hands, palms up. "It's a big step. Are you up to it?" To his surprise, General York gave an immediate answer.

"Things are way out of control, Sir. Until this conversation, I've been helpless to do anything about it." He stood up and saluted. "I'm on board, Sir! Hell yes, I'm on board!"

EARTH—SOUTHWESTERN USA AND MEXICO

One week after formation of the Lone Star Conservancy, Lone Star fighter-bombers destroyed the industrial base of Ciudad Juarez, Tijuana, Mexicali, Nogales, Chihuahua, and Monterrey, and took out the supply caravans feeding Mexican forward troop emplacements. Coordinated Seal Teams eliminated the entire Mexican force occupying North Island and Coronado in San Diego, and Marine forces swept through the rest of the city, taking no prisoners.

In the Los Angeles area, 10,000 marines stormed the Port of Long Beach and other Mexican military force concentrations. Within seven hours, Mexican resistance ceased, and the fighting stopped.

The next day, Lone Star aircraft hit Mexico City industrial installations. Lone Star mobile forces raced south on Baja to Cabo San Lucas and south through mainland Mexico to Mazatlán in the west, Durango, Torreon, and Monterrey, to Matamoros south of

Brownsville and Playa Bagdad on the coast. For the next several days, Lone Star forces consolidated their southern positions and established reliable supply lines to feed each of the major and minor population centers along what they now called the Monterrey Line.

The Mexican government was in total disarray, but it finally sent a delegation to Austin to sue for peace. In Sam's mind, he and his people—the populations of Texas, New Mexico, Arizona, southern California, and even northern Mexico—had not asked for this confrontation. He discussed the matter with his fellow governors and his military staff. As he met the Mexican delegation formally in his office on the Texas Capitol second floor, he did so with the full backing of his own senior advisors. The Mexican delegation consisted of the President, his military Chief, the *Secretaría de la Defensa Nacional*, and the *Secretaría de Relaciones Exteriores*, the Mexican Foreign Minister. As with all educated Mexicans, they spoke English fluently.

"Gentlemen," Sam said, indicating three straight-backed chairs around a table placed in the center of his office. Sam took the fourth chair, also straight-backed. "We are a young nation," Sam continued. "We have no history like Mexico, no traditions, and no illusions about who we are and who you are." Sam kept his countenance neutral, being careful not to smile. "Mexico started this war. We believe we know why, but we want to hear it from your lips." Sam sat back and waited.

An awkward silence filled the office as the Mexican President looked from his Defense Minister to his Foreign Minister.

"Well," Sam said, letting a bit of irritation creep into his voice.

"We have had friendly relations with the United States…" The Mexican President looked embarrassed and corrected himself. "…with you, for a very long time." He extracted a handkerchief from his inner breast pocket and wiped his face. "We were…we were pressured into our actions…" He hesitated and took in a deep breath. "We were pressured by the Caliphate." His words tumbled out quickly.

Sam raised his eyebrows.

"We all know what is happening in Washington…" The President took another deep breath and wiped his face again. "It seemed only a matter of time until the Caliphate took over the U.S." Another sigh. "We were promised an accommodation…to keep our sovereignty, even to regain what was taken from us in the past." He splayed his hands on the tabletop. "We really had no choice…since the alternative was total destruction of our nation and people."

Sam was sympathetic, but he didn't let it show. "And so, you launched an unprovoked attack, killed thousands of our citizens, occupied our lands…for an empty promise. And now you justify your actions?" Sam let anger enter his voice. "How dare you?" Silence filled the room as all three men wiped perspiration from their faces. "You are here suing for peace…Here are our conditions.

"Our southern border will remain at the Monterrey Line and will include all of the Baja Peninsula. Any Mexican citizen within this territory who wishes to remain a Mexican citizen will be transported to one of the towns south of the Monterrey Line to be resettled by your government. The Lone Star Conservancy will grant every such returning citizen $1,000 in compensation for the land and personal property left behind. Any Mexican citizen wishing to remain will first be vetted to eliminate those with criminal backgrounds and then will be required to renounce Mexican citizenship and swear loyalty to the Lone Star Conservancy. Each of these former Mexican citizens will then be granted a one-time $2,000 stipend." Sam allowed himself to smile slightly at this point. "The entire Mexican government—all elected and appointed senior officials—will resign their positions, and new elections will be held. None of you may ever serve again. Once the Mexican government is reconstituted, it will pay the Lone Star Conservancy one hundred million dollars in reparations." The three men's faces blanched. Sam stood up, followed immediately by the three Mexican officials.

"These terms are non-negotiable. If you do not accept them, we will remove every Mexican city from the face of the Earth, destroy your entire industrial base, and let you exist as best you can on the edge of survival." Sam strode away from the table and turned around to face the three. "If you accept these terms but then do not pay the reparations, you will face the same fate." Sam put his features in neutral and said quietly, "Now…sign the papers!"

They did.

CHAPTER FOURTEEN

EARTH—WASHINGTON D.C.

President Jackson held up a hand to silence his Defense Secretary and National Security Advisor. Then he looked at the general he had canned, who now headed the triumvirate that had effectively taken over his government. "What is it, General?" the President snapped.

"Mexico has just invaded along our southwest border…" the general answered, clearly himself agitated.

"Mexico what?"

"And Texas just announced its secession from the Union," the general added.

President Jackson looked around the Oval Office and muted his outgoing transmission to everyone but the Vice President. "Dr. Bukhari," he addressed the holoimage, "how quickly can you get over here?"

"Twenty-thirty minutes, Sir."

"Figure out what is really happening and get back to me within the hour," the President ordered and disconnected the remaining Links.

✳

Before he left his residence just over 3.5 kilometers from the White House, Vice President Dr. Syed Shah Bukhari sent an encrypted signal over a still operating landline that only he knew about. The signal set into motion a plan conceived before he assumed office as the Vice President of the United States. Within a few minutes, a jumbo troop transport specially modified for rapid paratroop deployment took off from Minneapolis-St. Paul International Airport. Packed inside its belly were a thousand Caliphate paratroops ready to disgorge over two points at the nation's capital, the White House and the Pentagon. The troops were heavily armed. Following closely was another aircraft filled with air-drop-ready mobile armor, ammunition, communications gear, and everything else a mobile strike team might need far from its operating base.

In a scant nine minutes, the Vice President's limousine pulled up to the White House service entrance and was granted routine entry. Five minutes later, Dr. Bukhari strode into the Oval Office. He glanced around the room, noting that no holographic images were present. The President sat at his desk, staring at a communications sheet.

"What is it, Sir?" The Vice President stepped around the desk to peer over the President's shoulder.

"It's all coming apart, Dr. Bukhari."

"Actually, Sir. It's all coming together," Dr. Bukhari said as he extracted a thirty-centimeter blade and drew it across the President's throat. "*Allahu Akbar!*" he muttered quietly as he wiped the blade across the President's jacket. "*Allahu Akbar,* you heathen infidel!" He pushed the President's body to the floor and sat in the leather chair behind the President's desk, waiting patiently.

The President's Link announced an incoming call from his National Security Advisor—Dr. Bukhari ignored it. Another call from the triumvirate. Dr. Bukhari ignored that as well. About an hour later, he thought he heard distant gunfire. Then it was closer…then it was outside the Oval Office. The door opened, and a Caliphate commander entered. When he saw Dr. Bukhari sitting behind the desk, he relaxed.

"*Al-salāmu 'alaykum*[11]," the commander said with a sweeping gesture.

"*Wa rihmat Allāh wa barakatuhu*[12]," Dr. Bukhari answered with a smile.

✳

President Jackson's assassination would be reported the world over, but the how of his death was known only to Dr. Bukhari, the Prophet Saeed, General Suleiman, and for about an hour, the Caliphate commander who walked in on the Vice President. A sniper's bullet took him out immediately after he had personally supervised staging the Oval Office for the next act. The press release that went out about an hour later told how a desperate United States President had reached out to Caliphate forces in the Twin Cities for assistance in suppressing the military coup that had swept the U.S. Capital. It told of a staunch and brave world leader personally holding off two general officers and a flag officer at gunpoint in the Oval Office while he summoned help, only to be overcome by the three, who slit his throat before help arrived in the form of Caliphate paratroopers who immediately dispatched the three officers. The press release failed to mention that the paratroopers who had dispatched the three officers were themselves dispatched shortly thereafter.

In the sorrowful aftermath, Dr. Syed Shah Bukhari was sworn in as the next President of the United States, taking the oath on the same 1898 *Qur'an* that had ushered him into the Vice Presidency.

EARTH—SEATTLE, WASHINGTON

Washington governor Percival Enderly, short and pudgy, with brown hair cut in a fringe around a balding pate, focused his piercing brown eyes on the images of the Oregon and Idaho governors, and the woman who was left in charge of California's government following the Mexican invasion, California's Lt. Governor. He spoke rapidly, his words tripping over one another. "I called this emergency meeting because we are facing the most critical emergency in our collective history." He took a deep breath and slowed down a bit.

---

11 *Peace be upon you*
12 *And Allah's mercy and forgiveness*

"Individually, we cannot survive…cannot survive." He stopped talking to let his words sink in. "Sam Houston down in Texas did the right thing. His Lone Star Conservancy is a going concern. If we don't copy his ways, we're goners…I mean that…literally!" He sat back, awaiting a response.

"Command and control are gone, the President's dead, the Caliphate occupies D.C.," Idaho offered.

"I got subs and warships…if I can convince them to cooperate," Enderly said.

"I can't help much with military," Oregon said. "Research ships, maybe," he added.

"We're pretty shy in that department as well," California said, "military, I mean."

"I got some training facilities," Idaho said.

"We gotta follow Houston's example," Enderly said forcefully, "or we're dead." He stood and picked up a sheaf of papers from his desk. "This is my proposal to form the Columbia Freehold. Let's declare our independence and find a way to make this work!"

"Perhaps we can invite Montana, Wyoming…some of the others to join us," Oregon said. Everyone nodded.

"We have to do this right," California's Lt. Governor said. "We need to talk with our legislatures…it's a big job…it'll take a long time…"

"Not do it right…just do it," Enderly snapped. "Put the pieces in place afterwards."

And so, the Columbia Freehold was born.

EARTH—ALASKA

Seen from the air, Juneau, Alaska, is a beautiful town nestled between the Alaska Inland Waterway that separates the mainland from Douglas Island to the west and the impossibly green, steep slopes of Mt. Roberts to the east. Juneau makes up everything between the steep slopes and the water—there isn't room for anything more. Up close is a different story, however. As the twenty-first century marched on, most American towns managed to hide their cables and transmission lines underground so that the eye was not offended by copper-matrix-filled sky views. Not so Juneau, where the overhead view remained a tangle of wire and cable that hazarded migrating birds, and only a bat could navigate safely.

The Alaska legislature was in emergency session when Columbia Freehold formed, having been called into session by the governor when Sam pulled Texas out of the Union. Nearly all the House and Senate members held outside jobs of one kind or another. They normally served their districts for ninety days each year. While they understood the urgency of what was happening in the lower forty-eight, their individual job-related requirements naturally took precedence.

The governor posed the obvious question: Should Alaska remain in the Union or secede and go it alone, or should it become part of Columbia Freehold? For most citizen lawmakers, Columbia Freehold was just another rendition of the lower forty-eight. The answer seemed clear.

EARTH—NEW ENGLAND

Unlike Alaska, that was pretty much on its own from its inception in 1876, when U.S. Secretary of State William Seward purchased the territory from Russia, the northeastern states had been part and parcel of the country from the beginning, back in 1776. The people of the New England states, south through New Jersey, and east to Ohio, and even parts of Canada south of the St Lawrence River, however, had a long shared history, culture, and mores that differentiated them from the rest of the United States and Canada.

These good people watched the crumbling of the national government and the loss of command and control over American military resources. They observed the breakaway of Texas and the southwestern states and formation of the Lone Star Conservancy, the Columbia Freehold, and the Nation of Alaska. They saw the scourge of war creep ever closer to their long-protected environs, and they were frightened as never before. They saw salvation in pooling resources and separating their united interest from the rest of the country.

Two months after the Nation of Alaska went its separate way, the Federated Nation of New England announced its presence on the world stage, determined to preserve its sovereignty and the individual freedoms its people had enjoyed since even before the formation of the United States in 1776.

EARTH—SOUTHEAST UNITED STATES

The formation of the Federated Nation of New England was a wake-up call for the rest of the United States. The presence of Islamic troops in Minnesota, and recently back in Illinois and Michigan, and now in the District of Columbia, brought little comfort to the people living in these areas. The surrounding states, Virginia, Maryland, Delaware, had little to offer by way of protection for their citizens. Near total reliance on their proximity to the nation's capital brought about their nearly complete subjugation to the growing Islamic virus spreading out from the White House itself, where President Bukhari increasingly seemed linked to the Prophet Saeed and his minions halfway around the world.

By the mid-twenty-first century, the last stigma left from the then 200-year-old American civil war had finally been erased from American culture. With the Balkanization of America's west and northeast, however, the *Stars and Bars* appeared spontaneously throughout the south from the Texas border to Miami and north to Pennsylvania, excepting those parts of Virginia and Maryland under virtual Caliphate control. Similar to what happened leading up to the 1861 Fort Sumter attack, the southern states jockeyed for position and advantage and finally declared themselves the Confederate States of America and closed their northern border.

EARTH—WASHINGTON D.C.

Yielding to what he considered inevitable, President Bukhari did not militarily resist any of the secessions but instead set about consolidating his power in Washington and surrounds and throughout the north-central portion of the nation. His first act as President was to declare a National Emergency and set Martial Law throughout the country. Then he called a joint session of Congress on the pretext that he needed to meet with lawmakers to decide how to move forward under these extraordinary times.

President Bukhari arrived at the Capitol in his limousine with a rolling contingent of 100 Islamic warriors that formed his personal bodyguard. They killed the Capitol police on the grounds and around the building and then blocked all the doors with armed guards. Once inside the House chamber where House and Senate members awaited his presentation, Bukhari signaled the major in charge of his bodyguard contingent, and they opened fire with automatic weapons, slaughtering everyone in the chamber. The bodyguards then methodically went from room to room on every floor, killing anyone they found until no one was left alive in the U.S. Capitol.

While the slaughter in the Capitol was underway, a jumbo aircraft with Caliphate markings landed at Reagan International. The occupants were quickly ushered by armed Caliphate warriors into busses and transported to the Capitol. By the time they arrived in the House chamber, the bodies and blood had been removed. The arrivals, formally attired in robe and turban, were each handed credentials identifying which part of the country the recipient represented. They were directed to take their seats, and Bukhari mounted the podium and tapped on the mike.

"I bid welcome," President Bukhari said with ringing voice, "to you, the representatives of the ISA—the Islamic States of America."

IAPETUS—FEDERATION HEADQUARTERS

Iapetus president Rod Zakes sat at his desk in the presidential office atop the governmental pyramid waiting for Dmitri, who had promised to drop by when he returned from the latest asteroid pirate debacle. Over the years since the election of Stanford Jackson, his reelection, and then the radical restructuring of the 22nd Amendment to the U.S. Constitution that enabled his third term, Rod had kept a wary eye on things Earthside. Iapetus was his home, more so than any place had ever been. Nevertheless, Earth, the United States, was where he was born, and in some ways, it would always be *home*.

On the one hand, he watched the Caliphate spread its insidious doctrine across much of the planet. On the other, it seemed as if political correctness and inclusiveness had prevented any counteraction until it was too late to do anything. Some of his personal advisors had urged him to take some action, any action, to limit the loss of human life, especially when those losses climbed above two billion. Dmitri pressured him every time they were together, yet Rod was reluctant. The Federation had a great deal of firepower, perhaps even sufficient to halt the Caliphate's advance, but at what cost? One way or another, the Caliphate held hostage the Earth's remaining billions. Rod had no illusions about what would happen should the Federation interfere in the Caliphate's advance.

The Federation had a lot at stake. Many of its structures were fragile at best, not designed to withstand a direct assault. Iapetus was secure, but the Mars settlements, especially New Israel, were subject to devastating destruction from space, to say nothing about the spaceborne Mars terraforming projects. Ayers Sky at L5, although not yet ready for occupancy, could be damaged easily. Ganymede and Titan had many vulnerable structures; Daphne, because of its tourist trade, was subject to sabotage, and Ceres would increasingly be open to damage from space as its transformation progressed. Rod ticked these off in his mind as he considered the consequences that Federation interference could bring about.

Thousands of people were leaving Earth every day. Every operating launch loop had long queues, but the Sahara Loop was permanently down, and it looked like the Saudi and Jakarta Loops might fail next. It was just a matter of time. The Kiwis were preparing Ceres as quickly as humanly possible. Rod figured they saw the eventual handwriting on the wall. The Australians were well on their way to completing Ayers Sky, but both the Aussies and Kiwis had a major logistics challenge to get any significant part of their populations to these locales. One launch loop each was not really sufficient for that task, at least not if they were under pressure from the Caliphate.

Rod was deep in thought when Dmitri strode into his office, flush with his latest victory, placing Jake's cage on the floor and opening it. "One more pirate asshole bites the dust!" he said as he took a chair in front of Rod's desk.

"How many is that now?" Rod asked. "Six?"

"Seven! And these guys had no stomach for a fight. The problem is, we don't have any way to chase them. We got one of them, however. These guys definitely are Caliphate. Their mission—to keep us too busy to interfere on Earth."

"Why do you think that?"

"I used a little persuasion, and the captive told me," Dmitri said with a wide grin. "Don't ask what I did," he added as Rod appeared ready to speak. "He's alive with all his body parts." Dmitri stood and placed his hands on Rod's desk, looming over Rod. "We have to do something about what is happening on Earth!"

"And what do you suggest?"

"We can disrupt individual commands. We can even play havoc with their munitions, ground their planes, sink their ships—like the Founders did the first time."

"Have you looked at the size of their army? The one that just passed through southern Europe and Spain like a hot knife through butter?" Rod sighed. "That army consists of more than a million warriors. Sure, they have guns and ammo, but their weapon of choice is the scimitar. How do you stop that with neutrinos and lasers?"

"But we gotta do something…before they take out Russia and China…"

As if to emphasize Dmitri's point, Jake leaped to Rod's desktop, emitting a clickity chirp.

EARTH—ISLAMIC STATES OF AMERICA

More than half the country was gone, but this presented no real concern to President Bukhari because he knew that in time he would regain everything lost, and then some. As the worst winter in decades deepened, his immediate task was to change the demographics of the North American continent. To do this, passenger ships landed daily in Chesapeake Bay and Great Lakes ports, disgorging tens of thousands of Muslims from around the world. As these new arrivals moved north, south, and west from their debarkation points, they had the benefit of Islamic warrior escort so that they were able to displace current residents by merely showing up. When news of the imminent arrival of a Muslim group reached a community, mass exodus followed because the only alternative was either forced conversion to Islam and subsequent second-class status, or beheading.

In the Muslim-occupied territories around the Great Lakes, new arrivals assimilated in a virtually identical manner, resulting in hundreds of thousands of displaced Americans pushing south and west, and even north into Canada. Winter highways became impassable, fuel was scarce, and food outlets ran out of supplies. With no reliable mechanism for resupply, within a week, this wholesale migration of millions of once-proud Americans became a desperate push for survival under harsh winter and near-starvation conditions. Any remaining human decency was overwhelmed by the fundamental need to keep a child or a spouse alive another few days.

Always a short distance behind the starving refugees, driving them on like a herd of cattle, scimitar-wielding warriors killed stragglers, the weak, the sick, the young. The marauders consumed everything in sight—livestock, warehoused crops, whatever was left after the refugees passed through. And behind them, tens of thousands of Muslim arrivals settled in on whatever remained and prepared to start a new life. Supplies for the new settlers arrived daily on a continuous convoy of freighters arriving at Caliphate-controlled ports in Chesapeake and the Great Lakes.

The Midwest and Mountain states did what they could to accommodate the refugees, but the influx was simply beyond their capacity. They had no fuel for emergency aircraft, the winter roads clogged by refugee vehicles were all but impassable. The only practical way to move anything was with tracked vehicles across open fields. But tracked vehicles were in short supply as remaining viable military units appropriated every available one. Furthermore, even where some local government agencies managed to commandeer one or two vehicles, fuel was so scarce that they had to use them under strict rationing.

The Midwest and Mountain states traditionally counted more preppers and gun owners among their citizens than otherwise in the country, except for the states that now made up the Lone Star Conservancy. The calamitous circumstance of the mass exodus of people fleeing the Muslim invasion found these individuals in a more advantageous situation. Weapons and ammo, where gun owners had sufficient foresight to accumulate significant amounts of ammo, and a supply of readily transportable food, gave these individuals an unassailable barter position. Under the circumstances, however, most chose to hoard rather than trade.

Refugee leaders rose up from the ranks, promising people safety in the mountains of Montana, Wyoming, or Colorado. How to survive the winter once they got there did not come up. Others promised refuge in the vast camps springing up just inside the northern Lone Star borders. The simple truth was, however, that nobody could promise anything with certainty. The mass of suffering humanity sweeping south and west, and to some extent north, was beyond the scope of anyone or any organization to assist, let alone control. The surge was nearly continuous as Muslim warriors constantly nipped at the heels of the masses, grabbing any who hesitated or stopped. Forced conversion to Islam and secondary citizenship seemed viable when the alternative was certain death by scimitar or probable death by starvation or mishap along the way to an unknowable future.

EARTH—MINNEAPOLIS

As the sun set over the snow-covered parade field just west of Armory Hall, Major Steven Brady looked around the spare wooden table at Command Sergeant Major Pollard Bransom and Staff Sergeant Jerri Smyth. The holotank on the platform in front of them was carrying a mix of local and national news—all about the intense fighting in the Twin Cities, Chicago, and Detroit, with cut-ins covering events in Washington and along the southwestern border. A dozen troops were lounging in chairs scattered around the hall, and every few minutes, another two or three would slip in through the back door. The men were cold, tired, bedraggled, and dirty, but no one seemed in a hurry to get cleaned up.

"You know what this means, Bo?" Brady gestured at the holotank.

Bransom wiped his pate with a checkered cloth. "Not entirely sure I do, Major."

Brady turned to his newly minted Staff Sergeant and Communications Adjutant, her good looks hidden behind olive-drab paint splotches and the dirt and grime of battle. "Any thoughts, Jer?"

"That's why they pay you the big bucks, Major," she answered with a grin that revealed straight, white teeth.

Brady grinned back. "Bo, gather the platoon and squad leaders around the table, please."

The Command Sergeant Major pushed his chair back to comply. "You got sump'n in mind, Boss. I know that look." He turned to face the auditorium. "All right, you people, listen up!" His voice filled the hall without amplification. Heads bobbed up around the room. "Platoon leaders, squad leaders…front and center!"

After some shuffling and good-natured heckling, the four platoon leaders, including Sergeant Norbert Jacobsen and seven of the twelve squad leaders, pulled up to the table. Brady raised his hand, and their chatter died down.

"Do you guys know what's happening out there?"

"Not really…"

"Lot of fightin'…"

"Fuckin' snowstorm…"

"Sump'n bout Chicago…"

"Detroit…"

Brady held his hand up again. "A lot has happened. You guys experienced part of it up close and personal, but it's way bigger than us." He paused and looked around the table. "Where are the rest of your people?" He was met with shrugs.

"Okay…soon as it gets dark, I want you guys to pair up, keep your coms live, and find everybody. Report back here by midnight. We're gonna bivouac here…" Several eyebrows lifted. "Okay, guys," Brady interrupted with a grin, "so we got cover here…let's not mince words. We're gonna bivouac, so everyone gets a bit of sleep, and we'll figure out what to do in the AM." He paused. "Any questions?"

"What if we find, you know, casualties?"

"The Command Sergeant Major'll send someone out to pick them up," Brady said. "Now, look sharp and see how many stragglers you can bring back here by midnight."

In their urgency to locate the missing people, both Brady and Bransom missed the holovision announcement that two generals and an admiral had assumed control of the national government.

✳

As midnight approached, exhausted troops began straggling into Armory Hall. Bransom dipped into their MRE stores to put some nutrition into the weary guardsmen. The platoon leaders reported twenty-eight troops missing—the married guys, the singles with live-in girlfriends, and the four Muslims. They reported no casualties. He figured the Muslims were gone for good; too bad, they were good troopers. He hoped the others would make it back. "Bed down where you can," he told everyone. "Get a few hours of shut-eye."

Bransom then assembled Smyth and the four platoon leaders at the table and waved to Brady. Brady walked to the table and said to Bransom, "Set a two-hour watch schedule so people can get some sleep. All of you, meet me here at oh-six-hundred with coffee and MREs." He pulled Bransom aside. "Get some sleep, Bo. You're gonna need it."

"What about you, Major?"

"In a few…I have to check on some things."

Bransom placed himself in a position where he could keep an eye on the Major, then set his internal system for light sleep and dozed off.

※

Brady watched Charlie Company settle down, one man setting up a watch station just outside the back door. He was relieved that everyone had made it back but was disappointed about the four Muslims. No surprise, however. He had figured that would happen. He poured a cup of coffee and focused on his task; he had a lot to do before morning, and he needed to get some sleep as well.

He checked into national ComCon by Link, attempting to fill in the gaping gaps in his understanding of what had happened and where things were going. That's when he learned about the coup. His training, his experience, everything he had learned during his time in the Guard…nothing had prepared him for this. Since ComCon seemed to be functioning, he began to look for other operational Guard companies in the Twin Cities. There were none—they were all wiped out, slaughtered to a man. He moved up his chain of command. His battalion colonel was gone, as were the other three in his brigade, along with their entire battalions. Brady found remnants of the other two Guard brigades in Minnesota but no command structure. He put out the word that Charlie Company, First Battalion, Second Brigade was still functional, gave his coded location, and invited any stragglers to join him ASAP. He said they would move out shortly after nightfall the following day.

"Bring armor," he said, "tracked vehicles…fuel…ammo… everything you can carry, and Godspeed!"

That was when ComCon disappeared, his Link stopped working, and the lights went out. Working from an emergency generator powering the holotank, Brady learned that Mexico had invaded the Southwest, and Texas had seceded from the Union.

"Command Sergeant Major!" Brady shook Bransom's shoulder. "Wake up, Bo, we got a big problem." He handed Bransom a steaming cup of black coffee and briefed him on what he had learned. "We can't wait for tomorrow night," he said urgently. "If we don't leave right now, we'll never get out of here!"

EARTH—CALIPHATE FORCES WORLDWIDE

The building looked like a slab-sided cube, with an arched tall front entrance and arched windows on both sides. The back was bare. Rising from the icicle-edged roofline above the arched entry was a white flag displaying a black Wormhole of David. This Raëlian church occupied the western end of Wells Point, a finger of land jutting out into Chesapeake Bay several kilometers north of Baltimore.

As Caliphate forces swept through Chesapeake Bay and surrounds, virtually every religious structure was burned to the ground, its possessions confiscated, and its congregation scattered. In the grand sweep, this small, isolated Raëlian center was overlooked. Many locals regularly attended gatherings, some because they professed to be Raëlians, and others because it was there, and the free-wheeling sex was a great way to spend an evening.

This out-of-the-way bohemian center remained off the Caliphate radar until a group of young Muslims spent an evening at the venerable Sue Island Grill and Crab House on Wells Point and then wandered east along snow-covered Holly Neck Road for about a kilometer. They landed in the middle of a particularly intense evening of Raëlian activity and fled in utter terror and disbelief. The following day, Caliphate forces herded Wells Point residents into the slab-sided cube and set it afire.

❋

Elsewhere throughout Caliphate occupied territories anywhere in the ISA, warriors stormed remaining church, synagogue, or temple structures, dragged occupants outside, and demanded their immediate conversion to Islam, or they were beheaded on the spot.

With the phenomenal rise of Raëlians around the world following the arrival of the Founders, the primary focus of the Caliphate's war against other religious beliefs zeroed in on this happy cult of pleasure worshipers. But the Caliphate also focused on Jews who had not relocated to New Israel on Mars, on Christian believers wherever they found them, and on the myriad of other non-Muslim faiths practicing their beliefs throughout the world. With the passage of Caliphate forces, only the Prophet Saeed's brand of Islam remained. Planet-wide, except for areas not yet controlled by the Caliphate, believers were put to the sword as quickly as possible. In deeply Christian cities in Spain, Portugal, and Italy, the streets literally flowed red with blood. The more secular and urban populations smiled indulgently, converted to Islam, and then found themselves in servitude to their Muslim conquerors. They lived, but in abject subjugation—virtual slavery.

CHAPTER FIFTEEN

EARTH—MINNEAPOLIS

Command Sergeant Major Bransom seemed to be taking it easy on Charlie Company. Major Brady appreciated that, considering the long day behind them and the still longer one that would start as soon as Bransom got the troops up and about. Too bad he couldn't serve them a hearty breakfast, but black coffee and MREs were all they had. Sergeant Smyth handed him a sheaf of comms, such as they were, and he sipped his coffee while he read them.

"You up to this, Jer?" he asked the pretty sergeant, who had somehow managed to clean herself up and find a pressed set of fatigues. She nodded while sipping her own cup, her intense blue eyes drilling into his. "You got the drones ready and all the comms set up?" It was a *pro forma* question to which he already knew the answer. Jer was as good as they got, and she was ready. She nodded with a smile.

While the troops ate, Brady briefed them.

After outlining the national situation and the status of the Minnesota Guard, Brady went into detail about their equipment, fuel, and food status. "There you have it…now you know as much as I do. So,

238

here's the problem. There are one hundred twelve of us…there are at least ten thousand of them, and they're looking for us right now. They're taking no prisoners…they've slaughtered every unit they have engaged, down to the last man. I know you men. Every one of you is brave and would die to protect your squadmates. But now is not the time to die uselessly.

"Caliphate soldiers are slaughtering everyone they find who won't convert to Islam on the spot. People will be streaming out of here in every direction. If we don't leave now, we'll be bogged down in the largest refugee evacuation in human history." He paused and looked from man to man for a few seconds. "Texas has seceded from the Union and formed the Lone Star Conservancy with New Mexico, Arizona, and Southern California. They have an active military, and I bet they can use our help.

"So, here's the plan. We're gonna load up our personnel tracks with all the MREs, ammo, and fuel they can carry. Take your Links; national Link is down, but Jer will keep a drone up so we can stay linked together. Wear sidearms and carry rifles. Wear vests.

"Load the tracks, one platoon per track—yeah, I know it's crowded, but we gotta save fuel. Since we're down twenty-nine, Command Sergeant Major Bransom has redistributed the squads, so get to know your new squadmates. The Command Sergeant Major, Sergeant Smyth, and I will take the Command Track. Now move your asses. We depart in an hour!"

"Get the platoon leaders moving, Bo, and then grab Jer, and come and see me," Brady said to his Command Sergeant Major.

A few minutes later, the big man pulled a chair to Brady's table while Smyth perched herself on the table corner. "What's on your mind, Major?" Branson asked.

"We got a big problem here, Bo, and I'm not sure I fully communicated it to the troops." He looked at Smyth and took a deep breath. "Hell…I'm not sure I understand it myself…" Bransom sat listening quietly, his black pate glistening slightly; Smyth focused her attention on Brady's tired features. "The national command structure is gone, guys. We got no backup…we're the only viable military unit within a couple hundred klicks. There's an army of fanatics looking for us—several thousand or more. There's millions of civilians heading out in all directions. It's friggin' cold, and they'll run out of food in just a few days, and water and fuel. No way we can help them; what we got wouldn't last an hour. They get hungry, they'll turn into a mob, and I sure as hell won't fight our own people. We got to get our troops to understand that our only job is to get to the Texas border as fast as possible. We can't be stopping to help, or we'll submerge into the quagmire that will be everywhere in a few days." He stopped talking and looked earnestly at his Communications Adjutant and his Command Sergeant Major. "Give me your thoughts on this—as soldiers, as senior non-coms, and as my friends. Please be honest and straightforward."

"We can try to hold the troops together, Steve, but I don't think we can do it for long." Bransom whipped out his checkered cloth and wiped his pate. "We got good guys who follow orders, but when the orders say to ignore human suffering around them, I don' think they will…Hell, maybe I won't…"

"We're no good to anyone if we're dead," Brady said.

Smyth reached out and laid her hand on Brady's shoulder but said nothing.

"I know that, Sir," Bransom said, "but that's intellect stuff. When we're face-to-face with all that, what're we gonna do?"

"We been together a long time, Bo…Jer. When the chips are down, we—you and me—will do the right thing, no matter the cost. I'm not worried about you, Bo, and you, Jer, but the guys…we need to hold them together 'till we can do something that matters in this goddamn mess. I don't know what that is yet, but it sure as hell ain't up here." He called up a map of the United States and highlighted Interstates 35 and 80. "People gonna be headin' south and west…these routes will be chocked solid. We need to get in front of the masses as we head toward Texas." A dotted line connected Minneapolis with Austin. "If we head south, we'll be crossing the main western movement of refugees. That won't be good." Another dotted line appeared connecting Minneapolis with Denver. "So, we head west in front of the crowd, and we stay in front all the way to Denver. If things aren't totally nuts there, we can reprovision and then head south." He indicated a swath west of I-35 and north of I-80. "We keep off the roads and move as fast as the terrain will let us. Then we head south into New Mexico and check in with the Lone Star command."

"Sounds simple sittin' here, Major. Ain't gonna be so simple for real." Bransom grinned at Brady.

"But we gotta try, Sir," Smyth added, slipping her hand from Brady's shoulder, "No other way!"

✳

Thirty minutes later, five tracked personnel carriers headed west on darkened, snow-covered Broadway from the Minnesota Army National Guard complex in northeastern Minneapolis. The outside temperature was frigid—more than thirty degrees below freezing—in this, the coldest winter in the current global cooling cycle. Inside the toasty-warm small lead command vehicle, Bransom sat at the controls, Smyth coordinated the drone a thousand meters above the double column, and Brady concentrated on the larger picture he assembled from the drone and sporadic news feeds. Because he was moving rapidly, he could not deploy his Mosquito Swarm. The four larger carriers followed two by two, hard rubber treads generating a clicking, muffled hiss on the snow-covered pavement.

"Incoming!" Smyth suddenly announced on the general circuit. "Two of 'em!"

Standard protocol was to spread a column as widely as possible. Bransom accelerated and swerved left. The two trailing carriers slowed dramatically and pivoted left and right, opening distance between them. The middle two also accelerated and swerved outward in both directions. The first incoming round struck the National Guard complex main building, collapsing the roof. The second exploded on the pavement right where the two middle tracks had just been.

Up to this moment, the reality of the situation apparently had not yet sunk in for the residents in this mixed neighborhood, as nobody was out and about. Following the mortar rounds, hand-held lights began to appear near the darkened houses as Brandon increased his speed to 120 km an hour, needing to cross the bridge before a round took it out. He throttled down his mufflers, so the sound they emitted was barely audible, blending in with the hiss of the treads, and he shuttered his headlights, so they barely illuminated the white road surface ahead. He signaled the other units to do likewise. Any onlooker would not have been aware of the speeding behemoths until they were alongside and would have quickly lost them.

A minute later, they rumbled across the Mississippi, moments before three rounds found their mark, collapsing the Broadway Bridge behind them. They passed under the train overpass, over the interstate, into the pitch dark, snow-covered western suburbs along Golden Valley Road and finally turned southwest into the Golden Valley, where they could make out isolated lights glistening in the frigid, snowy landscape. Explosive charges followed them, landing on the pavement behind them and to either side, but it seemed as if the Caliphate forces were underestimating their speed of progress. The pursuers obviously had no airborne radar, so they were firing blind, based upon their best estimate of the escape route.

Smyth launched a second drone and vectored it toward whatever was pursuing them. "Major, it looks like we're being chased by fifteen tracks, half of them with long guns. I don't see any drones, but I'm jamming the frequency band just in case."

"I don't think they brought any tracked vehicles with them, at least not yet," Brady said through clenched teeth.

"The tracks look like National Guard units," Smyth said. "They're using our own goddamned equipment!" She was silent as she tracked the pursuing vehicles. "Omigosh! They're running right over people! Major, we got to do something…Major!" Tears streaked her face. "We got to do something!"

"Take it easy, Jer…there's nothing we can do. Your drones can't drop charges. We don't carry any artillery. If we turn back now, we'll do nothing to stop them, and we'll all die. That does nobody any good!" Brady reached out to touch Smyth's arm. "Keep close tabs on them…make sure they don't get any closer."

They left the explosive rounds behind them as Brady kept them moving at high speed on public roads for the remainder of the night. They rolled through frozen Sioux Falls as the sun began to hint an overcast morning behind them to the east. By the time the sun was up, but not nearly warm enough to melt the ice on Interstate 29 south toward Sioux City, the highway began filling up with people fleeing southward. Brady headed the carriers off the road, pointing them toward Vermillion near the Missouri River border of South Dakota. They slowed to about 80 km an hour, crunching through a brittle snow crust on the frozen ground, but faced no serious obstacles as they headed to the Highway 19 Missouri River crossing into Nebraska.

"How you holding up, Bo?" Brady asked. "Need me to take over driving for a while?"

"Thanks, Boss. I can use a break."

"Signal the others to keep a fresh driver at the controls," Brady told Smyth. "Let's keep moving 'till we need to stop for fuel." He smiled at her. "How far behind are the pursuers now?"

"Almost fifty klicks," she answered. "They passed through the first wave of refugees. The next bunch is about twenty klicks ahead of them."

As they continued southwestward, every road they crossed was filled to capacity with vehicles, all lanes moving west and south. Already, many cars were stalled alongside the roads, out of fuel or broken down. The lines of vehicles opened up to let the convoy cross so that they were able to continue their relatively rapid pace through the white landscape. By nightfall, they reached the outskirts of North Platte along Interstate 80 near the Colorado border. They were low on fuel, and one of the carriers was overheating. The panic-exodus had not yet reached full crescendo in this prairie community of 30,000, and without Link access, they had no idea what was coming their way.

Brandon found a truck stop at the west end of the town that still had sufficient fuel to fill their tanks completely and even fill their spares. Several Charlie Company mechanics opened the overheating carrier engine space and found a leaking head gasket. While this was going on, Smyth launched a loud-speaker-equipped drone and flew over the entire town, announcing the imminent arrival of the Caliphate pursuers. The mechanics replaced the head gasket in a couple of hours, so that three hours after the convoy arrived in North Platte, they were once again underway, this time on I-80 and then on I-76 toward Denver.

Moving down the snow-free Interstate toward Denver, Brady almost had the feeling that everything was back to normal. With Denver in his sights, Brady passed right through Sterling, hardly slowing down as the convoy continued along the Platte River valley. By staying on the snow-free roadways, Brady hoped to confuse their pursuers.

"Major," Smyth interrupted his musings, "we got something ahead. GPS says it's at the entrance to the town of Fort Morgan."

"Take the drone in for a closer look," Brady told her. "Stay a hundred fifty meters behind me," Brady ordered the others.

"It's some kind of barricade…manned by State Patrol and civilians…there's no military nearby," Smyth commented as her drone hovered a few tens of meters above the barricade. "They're waving at the drone."

Brady slowed as he pulled up to the barrier, stopping a few meters away. He loosened his holstered pistol and stepped through his door. The barricade guards kept their weapons pointed toward the ground, and one of them stepped out.

"Who are you, and what do you want?" The challenge was firm but friendly.

"Major Steve Brady, commanding Charlie Company, First Battalion, Second Brigade, Minnesota Army National Guard. We're bound for Lone Star—Texas—via Denver, where we intend to refuel and reprovision."

"Denver is a no-go…rioting throughout the city core. Muslim population went berserk a couple days ago, rampaging, killing any non-Muslim they found. The city is quarantined by the National Guard—nobody in, nobody out. You can still get fuel at the Suncor Refinery, south side of I-76 just past Rocky Mountain Arsenal…" He stopped talking as Brady's eyes opened wider. "Naw, Major, no munitions there—it's just a national park now. But there's a large Safeway distribution center about three klicks south of there. You should have no problem supplementing your provisions." He presented a broad grin. "Ain't nothin' for you here, Major. Soon as yer provisioned, take I-70 east to E-470, and follow that to I-25. That'll take you around the Denver mess and get you to the New Mexico border."

"Thanks for the info and advice," Brady said warmly. "You guys know I've got a friggin' army on my tail?" He pointed back the way they had come. "And every street, every road, every highway is clogged with refugees scrambling ahead of that army. They'll be here in less than a day. They're hungry, they're pissed, and they're scared as hell. You guys aren't up to shooting Americans—at least not yet. I know that. But if you stay here, that's exactly what will happen. And then you'll be facing at least fifteen tracks, half of them with long guns, and thousands of scimitar-wielding crazies somewhere behind them." Brady stopped and took a deep breath. "Your chance of surviving that is flat zero." As he turned back to his carrier, he added, "You guys may want to follow us to Lone Star. You'll have a fighting chance there, I'm sure of it."

✳

An hour-and-a-half later, Charlie Company pulled into Suncor Refinery. The facility was abandoned, but one of the gasoline tanks still held more than sufficient to fill their tanks and reserves. It took another half-hour to locate the Safeway distribution center by drone and get there. It, too, was abandoned, but several pickups were parked on the snow-veneered lot, and people were grabbing whatever they could.

"Three men from each squad…in and out in a hurry. You guys know what we need and what we can't use: preserved meats, cheeses, bottled water, bread and rolls, canned goods, but not too many…you get the gist…Go!"

Twenty minutes later, they were back on Interstate 70, heading east. Ten minutes of dodging traffic, and they turned south on E-470. A half-hour later, after E-470 turned west, they headed south on Interstate 25.

"The first refugees just arrived at the Fort Morgan barricade," Smyth announced. "They're being welcomed." She paused to adjust her controls. "Oh, Shit! Someone's shooting at the drone!" She sent it into wild aerobatics and pulled it up to a thousand meters. "Omigosh! A Jeep with a mounted fifty-caliber just broke through the crowd. It has no markings; the guy manning the gun is wearing cold-weather fatigues. The barricade guards are challenging him. Oh no! He's firing at them…they're down…the crowd is surging forward. Two more Jeeps have pushed through the crowd. They're firing too…at me!" Smyth focused on her drone controls. "Shit…they got me!" She turned to the other drone, high above the Caliphate tracks. "The Caliphate long guns are nearly in range of the barricade. They're pushing through the crowd but not running them over this time. And it looks like they have brought in a bunch of trucks carrying troops. I can see at least several hundred trucks."

"Check the regular HF bands, Jer," Brady said. "I think they got coms with someone in Denver."

"You nailed it," Smyth said several minutes later. "They're speaking Arabic with a spotter on one of the tall office buildings." Suddenly her eyes widened. "Major…someone a lot closer to us just reported our position to the long guns!"

"Spread it!" Brady ordered on the general circuit. "Change your heading continuously…speed up and slow down. Don't let yourselves be a target!"

Explosive shells began falling near them, cracking the concrete pavement and gouging large holes beside the roadway.

"Jer, can you spot the spotter?"

"No way, Major!"

"Okay…check out ahead…what do we have ahead of us?"

"Things flatten out in a few minutes, and there is little chance of a spotter directing anything from there on. They haven't pushed out of Denver this far, I'm sure," Smyth said as she scanned the drone images.

✳

"We got Colorado Springs ahead of us—Air Force Academy, Peterson Air Force Base, and Cheyenne Mountain Air Force Station," Smyth said.

"Cheyenne Mountain used to be the control center for a missile shield that protected the entire North American Continent," Brady said. "That shifted to Peterson but was shut down by President Jackson soon after his inauguration as an international de-escalation measure, according to what I got on my Link archives. See if you can reach the Air Force Academy. They may have something going."

"I've been trying, Major…nothing…nothing at all."

"Where are the bad guys now? Can you see them back there?"

"I got drone scanning, Major…Shit! They spotted me. I got a whole bunch of incoming." Smyth sounded almost breathless. "I think they know we're on I-25. We're about forty klicks out of Pueblo, and then we got another hundred and twenty to the border."

Somewhere south of Pueblo, a half-hour later, Brady said to Smyth, "Push ahead and try to interface with Lone Star ComCon." And on the general Link, "How is everybody? I think things will get a bit dicey shortly, but we're close to the border. Hang in there!"

Smyth flew her drone ahead to somewhere near Starkville. She interfaced her drone with Lone Star ComCon and indicated to Brady that he was on.

"This is Major Steve Brady, commanding Charlie Company, First Battalion, Second Brigade, Minnesota Army National Guard… We're all that's left. I've got one hundred nine troops and two senior non-coms. We got four armored troop tracks and my command track, several drones, and lots of ammo, but precious little food and fuel. I've got fifteen or more Caliphate tracks with long guns on my tail, and thousands of infantry are following in truck transports. They will be restricted to the highway, but the tracks can go anywhere—they got them from the battalions they overran in Minneapolis/St. Paul."

Smyth handed him a note. "The road is jammed from a few klicks ahead of me to the border," he continued. "I don't think I can get through before the bad guys get here."

"We got you covered, Major. Get off the highway and follow it along the fire-gap through Raton Pass, and then break left to the southeast. You'll break out into Bartlett Mesa, and things should be obvious from there. Good Luck!"

Two minutes later, three Warthog ground control fighters screamed low over their position, rocking their wings as they passed. Smyth brought another drone to their rear and located the pursuing column of captured tracks. The Warthogs had slowed to minimum airspeed and were raking the enemy tracks with withering Gatling cannon fire. Within seconds, all fifteen vehicles transformed into fiery coffins for their occupants. Smyth pushed her drone further back, taking it a thousand meters above the landscape. Using her telescopic lens, she watched the Warthogs tear into the troop transport trucks as they spilled dead and dying Caliphate warriors onto the cold highway.

It was over in minutes. Brady's column passed Starkville, where the Interstate jammed tight with traffic. The tracks turned off the highway, keeping to the fire-gap along the road, and traversed the remaining ten kilometers to the Raton Pass approach. Shortly thereafter, they followed a narrow road to the southeast and then broke out onto Bartlett Mesa, across the border in Lone Star. Ahead lay the beginnings of Camp Bartlett, where already thousands of refugees were housed in RVs, tents, pickups, and whatever else was available.

The red, white, and blue Lone Star flag flapped in the brisk wind as Brady and Charlie Company rolled up to the low-lying one-story headquarters, where a full colonel stood waiting. Brady stepped from his command track and saluted.

"Welcome, Major, to the Lone Star Conservancy!"

EARTH—THE FEDERATED NATION OF NEW ENGLAND

Over the last several decades, winters had gotten much colder. The sun had been in a quiescent mode for nearly a century, producing significantly fewer charged particles than in the previous two centuries. Consequently, Earth's magnetic field had been drained of most of its circulating charged particles that would normally stop all but the most energetic cosmic rays, leaving Earth open to a much larger influx of cosmic radiation. Early twenty-first-century scientists had finally determined that it was not human activity but solar variability that caused periodic global climate changes. Cosmic radiation influx into the atmosphere had been found to be responsible for about 30% of cloud formation. Consequently, the increasing flux had nearly blanketed the planet with clouds, significantly reducing solar radiation influx, and Earth had cooled. Earth's climate from the 16th to the 19th centuries had come to be called the mini-ice age, and current conditions reflected those from that time.

The Federated Nation of New England was hunkered down for the frigid winter. Rivers and fresh-water lakes froze, and the population stayed indoors as much as possible. Shopping by Link had disappeared with the destruction of Earth's satellite swarm, and the large chain stores, warehouses, and food suppliers could no longer resupply through their automated systems. Independent stores and mom and pop grocers found that they could maintain a reasonable flow of goods by contracting directly with independent truckers to supply their needs from regional centers. It worked so that, in many ways, modern New England resembled New England of the late 19th century.

The main problem, however, was coordination. With the destruction of Link coms, long-distance communication was either by landline or old-fashioned radio. The Mob, that had previously entrenched itself into twenty-first-century society, found new life when it discovered that by controlling New England communications, it controlled virtually everything. Within months of creating the Federated Nation of New England, the Mob had gained control of every significant communications hub in the new nation. Unlike their predecessors, these modern mobsters quickly discovered that their continued flow of wealth depended on the public's continuing acceptance of their control of communications. Consequently, they did their job well, and New England citizens were satisfied, for the most part.

✳

President Syed Shah Bukhari was generally pleased with Caliphate expansion from Minneapolis/St. Paul and the Washington region. Lone Star and the West Coast were problems that he intended to deal with at the appropriate time, but right now, his biggest headache was New England. General Suleiman wanted Caliphate forces to push northeast, at least as far as the St. Lawrence River, but Bukhari disagreed.

"Your warriors have done a magnificent job thus far," he told Suleiman over the only international Link connection between the Americas and the Middle East, "but they do not understand the cold conditions they will encounter here. Minnesota is colder than anything they have experienced thus far in any of your conquests, however, New England is as cold but accompanied by deep snow. As good as they are, your men are not equipped to handle these conditions." Bukhari paused and smiled slightly. "I have a plan that will give you control of New England without any of the losses you would otherwise sustain."

He then outlined how the Mob had wrested virtual control of the new nation from its leaders and explained how it depended on antiquated equipment and a shortage of spare parts and replacements. "Even as we speak, one of my agents is in contact with the Mob leadership, posing as a Roman Catholic priest attempting to gain inroads into the hearts and minds of the New England population."

The general started to interrupt, but Bukhari raised his hand and continued. "The Mob is one hundred percent Roman Catholic. They will welcome my agent, never suspecting anything. My *priest* will arrange for a reliable and inexpensive source of spares and replacements and will sponsor a gala fest to celebrate the event—a fest that will be attended by all the senior mobsters." Bukhari allowed himself a big smile. "That's when we will take them out—all of them. My people will immediately take control of every communications hub in the region, eliminating as many lower-level mobsters as they can find. With the spring thaw, our warriors will sweep New England, and we can bring in our people to settle the region."

Two weeks later, no senior mobster survived anywhere in the Federated Nation of New England.

EARTH—THE CONFEDERATE STATES OF AMERICA

It was a noble attempt, but unlike Lone Star, the Confederacy did not have the coherent military infrastructure of the Conservancy. Several of the world's largest military bases called the American Southeast home, but with the collapse of national ComCon, the Army in Ft. Bragg could not communicate with the Marines at Camp Lejeune, and neither of them could talk with Ft. Benning in Georgia, and forget about Fort Campbell on the Kentucky-Tennessee border. Between them, they had well over 150 thousand fighting men, including the 82nd Airborne and the Special Forces Command, and a significant portion of America's rolling armor. Because of the military's complete conversion to Link command and control, when that was gone, there was no way to move the troops, let alone coordinate their movements. Elgin Air Force Base in northern Florida made a half-hearted attempt to establish ComCon like Lone Star, but with the disparate facilities scattered over nearly one-quarter of the country, the effort was doomed before it started.

The Navy's 44,000 sailors in the Norfolk area were effectively neutralized immediately following the coup and the subsequent take-over of Washington by Caliphate troops. Charleston's heavy Navy presence could do little more than remain tied up to the various piers and await a hopeful reestablishment of sufficient command and control functions to allow ships to get underway, coordinate their movements, and—perhaps—take on the massive Caliphate presence off Chesapeake Bay.

There was no lack of will…just an inability to act without effective ComCon. The Confederacy never was able to establish itself convincingly. When it became clear that nobody was in charge, the individual states began to turn inward, doing whatever was possible to relieve the suffering of their citizens. Before the end of winter, the Confederacy had crumbled, and one by one, the individual states fell to Caliphate forces.

EARTH—THE COLUMBIA FREEHOLD

Chairman Percival Enderly had lost a few pounds since cajoling and bullying his fellow governors into forming the Columbia Freehold. Since then, he had managed to convince Montana, Wyoming, Utah, and Nevada to join the Freehold. The Muslim uprising in Denver had crashed Colorado's government; the Caliphate was firmly in control there. Initially, North and South Dakota were left to their own devices, but with the fall of Nebraska shortly after Charlie Company passed through, and then Colorado, the Dakotas slipped into the Caliphate fold without a whimper. For the most part, Dakotans continued to be who they were without subjugating themselves to Islam; but that was due to change within a few months. They just didn't know it yet.

Enderly was deeply worried about protecting the Freehold from what was sure to come. He had the provisional cooperation of the Army at Joint Base Lewis-McChord and the Navy at the Bremerton submarine facilities. Montana and Wyoming had little to offer militarily because what they had consisted of obsolete intercontinental missile silos and their associated command and control systems, none of which functioned anymore due to the Caliphate's intervention. Utah's Hill Air Force Base working with Nellis Air Force Base in Nevada established limited ComCon, but Columbia Freehold covered such a vast region, and fuel was sufficiently scarce, that Enderly needed a secure backup.

Working closely with management of that Seattle fixture, REI, and the 87th Mountain Infantry out of Fort Lewis, Enderly sent expeditions to the peaks of the eight major volcanoes in the Cascade Mountain range—Baker, Rainier, Hood, St. Helens, Adams, Jefferson,

South Sister, and Shasta—and Mt. Olympus on the Olympic Peninsula. Their purpose was to emplace a beacon on each peak to establish command and control over as much of Columbia Freehold as possible.

Submarines from Bremerton began patrolling Pacific waters several hundred kilometers off the West Coast, forming a screen to prevent the intrusion of any Caliphate ships. Command and control was exercised through the Very Low Frequency (VLF) antenna array at Jim Creek. Enderly asked his specialists why the VLF array could not be used for ComCon. They explained that at such a low frequency, transmission rate would be about 38 characters a second, far too slow for active command and control of jet aircraft or even troop ground movements. He would have to live with his mountain-top transceivers and airborne relays. In any case, it was better than the Confederacy disaster or the New England take-over.

MARS—LONE STAR

Matti McIntyre looked up from his Link projection of the latest reports on the terraforming efforts in orbit around Mars. He smiled as Sam Houston strode into the room closely resembling a thousand other offices scattered throughout the Solar System. It was a simple, utilitarian workspace with light green walls covered with holographs, contrasting commercial carpet, and a spectacular shot of Valles Marineris from orbit.

"I like what you've done with the place," Sam said, "Lone Star, I mean, not the office."

McIntyre stood and shook the much larger man's hand. "We miss you around here, Sam."

"I got my hands full, as I'm sure you know," Sam retorted. "But I came here to talk with you and Rod about what's happening back on Earth." He paused and looked around. "Where is Rod?"

"He landed right after you. Should be here any minute." As he spoke, Rod Zakes entered the office. McIntyre reached across his desk for a handshake, eye to eye with the Iapetus Federation leader.

"It still takes my breath away that a face-to-face meeting with people from across the Solar System is easier than a Link conference," Zakes said as he took a proffered seat. "You called the meeting, Sam. Bring us up to date."

"It's a complicated situation on Earth. The Caliphate is on a rampage. Most of Europe has fallen. Africa has fallen—except South Africa. Southeast Asia has fallen. North America is collapsing. What's left are South America, several Eastern European States, Russia, China, Japan, India, Australia, and New Zealand. We're holding our own in Lone Star. The Pacific Northwest has reorganized as the Columbia Freehold and seems to be keeping it together for now, but the rest of the country is gone, and the refugee problem is horrendous.

"The winter is even colder than projections for the cooling planet. There's starvation in Central Europe, and North America is not far behind. We can feed our own Lone Star Conservancy citizens right now, but the millions pressing on our borders from all sides except Mexico will overwhelm us sooner or later. We've got to find a way to move people to here." Sam pointed out the window. "If I can get people here, Matti—not just a few, but hundreds of thousands… millions actually—can you accommodate them?"

"The quick answer," McIntyre said, "is *Yes!*" He called up several diagrams on his Link. "We can erect multi-housing units very quickly—in days literally." He pointed to the sequential construction plans suspended in the air between them. "Furnishings will take a bit longer, but with sufficient advance notice, we can keep ahead of it." He paused. "How many people?"

"That's the problem," Sam said. "The Caliphate seems determined to conquer the entire planet. We can hold them off for some time, but the end is inevitable. We're talking millions of people… although right now, I don't have a clue how to get them here."

"I have a couple of thoughts," Zakes said. "First, the Israelis pulled off something similar just before the Caliphate shut down Israel. The numbers were lower, but still in the millions. Second, we've got a lot of room on Iapetus. Remember, it was built to accommodate billions of inhabitants, and it has a complete infrastructure. So, if we're going to move people en masse by hyper-V craft, Iapetus might be a better destination than Mars, at least initially."

"That still leaves the question of how we move so many people," McIntyre said.

"Well…we're working on that," Zakes said with a slight smile. "Don't have a lot to report yet, but some of Marc's people have opened a door we did not know existed. I'll have more soon."

IAPETUS—STARCHILD INSTITUTE

Within a month following the initial discovery of the much larger-than-expected Casimir effect between the two plates of hyper-V skin material, more than a thousand researchers under Dr. Lambin's leadership were coaxing new bits of knowledge from the juxtaposition of these pieces of exotic material. Five short weeks following the initial aberrant measurements, Marc Bowles in his office atop the SI complex Linked into Rod Zakes' office perched at the zenith of the Government Pyramid.

"I want to show you something extraordinary," Marc said without preamble. The image he flashed looked like two oblong 20 cm long vertical plates, separated by 20 cm. Between the plates shimmered a pitch-black worm-like object about 5 cm long. "This," Marc said with a theatrical voice, "is a Morris-Thorne Wormhole."

"Okay…" Rod said with lifted eyebrow since his Duke University aerospace engineering degree did not really give him a theoretical physics background.

"For over a hundred fifty years, this has been a theoretical construct, something the physics boys and girls played around with on whiteboards, computer screens, and Link projections." Marc dropped the theatrics.

"And…"

"We actually built one! The top and bottom of that worm occupy the same physical position and time…"

"You mean," Rod interrupted, "you can go from the top to the bottom instantaneously, without traversing the intermediate space?"

"In principle, yes, but we haven't done that yet." Marc settled back into his chair. "You know what this means, don't you?"

"I don't have a degree in theoretical physics, but I do keep a finger on the pulse. Are you implying we are on the doorstep of faster-than-light transportation?"

"FTL…could be. I'll have an update for you in a few days." Marc cut the Link but continued to stare at the image. Just step one, he thought. *We have a long way to go, but it's happening far faster than I ever imagined. It's stable, but we have to find a way to pass something through it. Then scale it up…larger objects…living objects…humans…find the limits… make it portable….* He leaned back and let his imagination take over.

EARTH—LONE STAR CONSERVANCY

Sam Houston relaxed in the governor's office following his return from Lone Star Mars. His conversation with McIntyre and Zakes was still fresh on his mind when Lt. Governor Jim Grayson strode into the room and dropped his lanky frame in a chair opposite Sam's desk.

"We got a problem," Grayson said.

"Tell me something I don't know." Sam smiled wearily at him.

"Seriously," Grayson leaned forward with his elbows on his knees, "since the Mexican peace and the Caliphate rampage, the drug cartels have shifted into high gear. Columbia and us are the only realistic markets for these scumbags. They are taking full advantage of our preoccupation with the Caliphate. It's time we put an end to it."

"I don't disagree," Sam said cautiously, "but that's easier said than done." He called his Adjutant General. General Gregory Samuelson's tough-guy image flashed into the office space. "Greg, Jim tells me we have a drug cartel problem…"

"He's right, Sam, we do."

"It's demand and supply," Grayson quipped. "No users, no cartels."

"Can't do much about the users," Sam said, "at least in the short run. What about the sources…the refineries…the supply lines?" He looked from Lt. Governor to General. "Jim…Greg…?"

"We can find their growing fields, their manufacturing facilities, their mansions…. With satellite surveillance gone, it's just a matter of several overflights with cameras," Samuelson said. "Two or three days should do it."

"And then?" Sam asked.

"We take them out—permanently," Samuelson said with a shrug. "Should have done it long ago, but no one had the guts."

✳

The next day three high-flying surveillance aircraft blanketed the known drug-growing regions of Southern Mexico and Central America. Sam connected with the former Mexican President, and following suitable inducement, found him more than willing to disclose the locations of the residential compounds of the cartel leaders in Mexico. Discreet questions by Lone Star agents in Central America and a bit of quiet monetary inducement also disclosed the locations of the major drug cartel heads outside of Mexico.

"Okay…we've got the information we need," General Samuelson told Sam and Grayson several days after their meeting on the drug cartel matter.

"What remains?" Sam asked.

"Missiles to the facilities and mansions, napalm to the fields." His face was grim. "It's over in an hour, and the drug cartel problem will be gone for decades. I've code-named it *Iron Fist*."

"You understand the risks?" Grayson asked.

"Sure. Civilians will die; livelihoods will be destroyed; lots of people down there will hate the Lone Star Conservancy." He paused, looking thoughtful. "On the other hand, the drug flow into Lone Star will effectively cease for the time being. Thousands of our citizens' lives will be saved—despite themselves. We can keep a thumb on the problem down there and hold off any reestablishment of their infrastructure for maybe a decade."

"And," Sam interjected, "if we decide to let people here take charge of their own lives, we might want to consider removing restrictions on the cultivation and sale of this stuff in Lone Star—make it legal, and remove any reason for the cartels coming back."

"You're shitting me!" Samuelson said. "Make it legal?"

"Consider it," Sam said. "They do it anyway, giving a reason for, and sustaining the cartels. If you can grow your own or buy it at the corner drugstore, where do illegal drug cartels come into it?"

"The black market…?" Grayson's voice carried a question.

"Only if there is a reason to sell it under the table," Sam said. "Don't tax it. Don't regulate it. Leave it alone. If you do this, there simply is no room for the cartels."

"I don't like it," the general said with a frown.

"Why not?" Sam asked.

"I don't know. I just don't like it."

"Let's address it again after you've had some time to think about it," Sam said. "For now, you're Go for *Iron Fist*."

CHAPTER SIXTEEN

IAPETUS—STARCHILD INSTITUTE

Marc Bowles fixed his eyes on a holographic poem attached to his office wall where he could see it from his desk. The words were in English, although originally, they had been written by Lucretius Carus in Latin around 55 BCE.

> *No single thing abides, but all things flow.*
> *Fragment to fragment clings, and things thus grow*
> *until we know and name them.*
> *By degrees they change,*
> *and are no more the things we know.*

He pondered how so long ago a man could have written something so acutely relevant to the moment. He dropped his gaze to the holoimage floating over the right side of his desk—an elongated, profoundly black worm floating between two plates of hyper-V skin material. His mind drifted back over a hundred fifty years to 1935, when Einstein, working with his assistant, Israeli physicist Nathan Rosen, worried out the mathematical basis for the Einstein-Rosen Bridge, an unstable theoretical object that seemed to connect two distant parts of the physical universe. Then in 1988, Kip Thorne and his graduate student Mike Morris found a stable theoretical version—the Morris-Thorne Wormhole—that incorporated exotic matter, matter that was theoretically possible but that had not yet been discovered. Enter the Founders, with their hyper-V craft skinned with material derived from exotic matter. And now…

SI scientists had just this morning passed subatomic particles through the wormhole that appeared over his desk. The transit time was instantaneous. Taking it from the subatomic to the macro world was just a matter of scale, Dr. Lambin told him, and power, prodigious amounts of power.

Marc glanced back at the ancient poem. Until we know and name them, he thought. Until we know and name them… He cut four squares of paper and wrote a letter on each, the initial letters of the names of the wormhole pioneers—E, R, M, T. Then he slid them around on his desk, looking at various combinations. One stood out: M E R T—Morris-Thorne wrapped around Einstein-Rosen. He liked it…the MERT something—bridge, portal, drive…whatever it turned out to be.

EARTH—SAUDI ARABIAN DESERT

Wind-whipped sand created a background staccato of sound against the double-walled desert tent headquarters. "It's time," General Suleiman said to the Prophet.

"Time for what?" Saeed asked, sipping his strong mint tea.

"To take India," Suleiman answered, "and Bangladesh and Sri Lanka." He sipped his own tea. "And South Africa," he added. "The rest of Africa is completely subdued. All we have to do is move the warriors south…the South Africans will not be able to resist."

"What about India's nuclear weapons?" Saeed asked. "And its formidable navy?"

"Since our initial treaty with India, we have moved Muslims into every responsible position in India's nuclear weapons program. To a man, they are loyal to you. Every ship is captained by a loyal Muslim, and virtually all second-in-command posts are held by Muslims. The crews will do as ordered."

"Then make it so."

EARTH—NEW DELHI, INDIA

Carmen Bhuta had consolidated her position as India's Minister of Health. Her people had made great strides in bringing modern medicine to the interior, backward sections of the Subcontinent. As she watched the world beyond India collapse into chaos, she felt a growing dread that all was not well in the homeland either. It was clear to her that the Prime Minister had cut a deal with the Caliphate. She vividly recalled the visit of Saeed and General Suleiman. It was apparent to her that the Prime Minister felt secure in his arrangement with them, but Carmen could see what happened to non-Muslims in the countries the Caliphate had ravaged. She knew it was only a matter of time, and part of her wanted desperately to leave India, leave Earth, to be with her friends at Mirs. The doctor-part of her wanted to stay, to help with what she believed was inevitable, and the inner conflict was tearing her apart. Despite herself, Carmen made plans to get to the Sri Lanka Loop in Colombo as a fallback if everything collapsed.

Carmen was sitting in her office reviewing inoculation reports from the more remote villages when a disturbance caught her attention. She looked out the window to see throngs of people milling in the streets around the government complex. Several buildings were on fire, and she could hear muffled shots through the glass. With the destruction of the worldwide satellite Link system, the Indian government had reverted to landlines to keep government agencies coordinated. Carmen tapped her landline to call the Prime Minister, whose offices were just down the hall.

"What's happening?" she asked the holographic image, clearly seeing fear in his eyes.

"The Caliphate has invaded from Pakistan, I have lost control of our nuclear weapons, the Navy has mutinied en masse, and is supporting the invasion..." He caught his breath. "And Muslims are rioting in every major Indian city. The rioters are killing non-Muslims everywhere. Caliphate troops are converting the population of every village they pass to Islam by force or beheading those who resist. Tens of thousands are already dead.

"You must leave, Dr. Bhuta! I know you have friends at Mirs. Take my jet to Colombo, to the Sri Lanka Loop, and save yourself."

"But…but…"

"There is nothing you can do, nothing at all. This is all my fault; I made a deal with the Devil, and now everyone is paying the price. I will hold things together as long as possible, but you need to leave. India is no longer your problem."

At that moment, Carmen's Link connection with the Prime Minister was interrupted, and to her astonishment, Saeed Ismael appeared to be standing before her desk, dressed in sackcloth with a leather cup capping his stump.

"Dr. Bhuta," Saeed said to her. "I have not forgotten that I owe you my life. Though you are Christian, you treated me with dignity and respect when I was at death's door on Cassini II. I will now repay that favor. Do as the Prime Minister told you. His pilot is one of my men. He will fly you to the Sri Lanka Loop. I have arranged the details of your trip to Mirs. Do not delay, for as soon as you have cleared the Sri Lanka Loop rail, my people will bring down the loop.

"My debt to you is paid. May your life be long and filled with happiness." Saeed's image was replaced by the Caliphate flag, and then the image collapsed.

✳

Two men Carmen did not know entered her office, grabbed her arms, and whisked her out of the building into a waiting helicopter. Thirty minutes later, she was on the tarmac of Indira Gandhi International Airport, entering the Prime Minister's private jet. Three-and-a-half hours later, she climbed down the aircraft steps at Bandaranaike International Airport, entered a black limousine, and shortly thereafter boarded a waiting helicopter. After fifteen minutes, she found herself at the launch socket of the Sri Lanka Launch Loop. A capsule was waiting for her, hatchway doors swung up; she was the only passenger. She entered, and the doors closed; there was no attendant. Her trip up the tower was without incident, and the automated attaching of kick-thruster and magnetic coupler was routine. In fact, she saw no one after she entered the capsule at the socket.

Carmen experienced some nervousness during the magnetic coupling to the rail, the acceleration, and the final kick-thruster course adjustment after her capsule left the rail. Then she settled into free fall relaxation for her ten-hour transit to Mirs. She did not see the explosion that destroyed the terminal atop Colombo Tower, nor the Sri Lanka soft-iron ribbon as it streamed away from Earth at about 17 km/s into solar orbit.

IAPETUS—STARCHILD INSTITUTE

Marc Bowles examined the three-centimeter disc Dr. Lambin handed him. It felt lightweight and cool in his palm. One side was a dull, silvery color, like a coin that had been in circulation for a while. The other was deep, featureless black, like the skin of a hyper-V craft.

"Tap the center of the silvery side." Dr. Lambin said.

Marc tapped the center of the silvery side.

"Now, instead of tapping like before, hold your finger against the surface. Use a light touch."

Marc did so, and a small spot in the air before him began to expand.

When it reached about thirty centimeters, Dr. Lambin said, "Lift your finger."

Several centimeters through the opening, Marc saw a human hand with a bright red cube slightly larger than a die nestled in its palm. Four fingers from a second hand appeared behind the cube, knuckles facing Marc. They flicked the cube so that it tumbled through the opening onto his desk. Marc blinked as a smiling face replaced the hand.

"Toss the cube back!" Dr. Lambin told Marc.

Marc picked up the red cube and tossed it through the opening at the face. A hand reached up and caught it.

"Okay," Dr. Lambin said, "now double-tap the silver side."

Marc did, and the opening collapsed and disappeared, leaving behind a faint odor of ozone.

"That, my friend, is a hyper-Disc—the untethered end of a tethered MERT-Portal. We haven't tried anything living yet, but that's next. Plants and then critters. Obviously, we have precise control of the location of the untethered end because we place it where we want it. Its size, how far we can project it, and how long it will remain open are functions of how much power we have available at the tethered end." He sat down facing Marc's desk.

"We create the MERT wormhole at the power source and then collapse the untethered end into a hyper-Disc like that one." Dr. Lambin pointed to the disc on Marc's desk. "It has controls to activate and size the link. Once activated, the hyper-Disc loses control, except to shut it down. So long as the tethered portal is powered, the hyper-Disc remains linked, and the tethered portal can control it."

Marc sat quietly, digesting what Dr. Lambin had told him. "So, we have what amounts to instant transportation from here to there, so long as we physically travel to there once."

"For now, anyway," Dr. Lambin said, "but we're just getting started."

EARTH—SAUDI ARABIAN DESERT

Bowing low with a flourish, General Ismail Suleiman said to Saeed Esmail, "Resupply of our European front is complete, Sahib. They are assembled along the German, Austrian, Hungarian, and Rumanian borders to the Black Sea." He manipulated his Link, and a map of Europe appeared with a red line marking the troop locations. "Tomorrow, we commence a rapid push eastward to the Russian border from Estonia in the north to the Russian Black Sea coast." The line moved eastward.

"And Russia?" Saeed asked.

"They shut their borders to refugees, so the eastward flow has all but stopped. Russia thinks it knows what is coming and has amassed a huge force along its western border."

"So, they do not suspect what really is coming?"

"Apparently not, Sahib. Our agents have placed Pakistani portable nuclear devices in every major Russian city, town, and military district. They will personally detonate the devices on my radio order, or spontaneously if they see devices exploding in their vicinity."

"When, General??"

"Not yet, Sahib, but soon."

IAPETUS—STARCHILD INSTITUTE

Marc stood in front of his desk chatting with the holoimage of his chief wormhole researcher, Dr. Kristopher Lambin. "My demonstration of the tethered MERT-Portal last week was pretty simple," Dr. Lambin said. "I brought the hyper-Disc into your office, and then you sent a cube back and forth through the portal to my lab. Today is quite different." He turned away to do something out of Marc's sight. The view shifted, and Marc could see a device on the floor beside the scientist. "I asked myself," Dr. Lambin continued, "what would happen if I passed a hyper-Disc through a MERT wormhole? So, we tried it."

"And…" Marc said.

"We deactivated both discs, moved them to different locations, and opened them again. They both still worked. Then we tried passing the first hyper-Disc through the hyper-Disc that had already been passed through it. Again, it still worked. Physically, we thought we had twisted the wormholes around each other through some kind of Klein Bottle dimension, but when we followed the math, the wormholes seemed to pass through each other by using a dimension beyond the one where they have their physical existence." Dr. Lambin shrugged his shoulders and smiled. "The end result is that by passing two hyper-Discs through each other sequentially, we could leap-frog a projected untethered portal many times farther than we could by itself with just its power supply.

"Then we went one step farther and passed both the tethered and untethered portals of a MERT wormhole through another untethered portal—through a hyper-Disc. It worked flawlessly. We began to shorten the timeframe until we were able to do a series of one-meter jumps, each lasting a picosecond."

Marc held up his hand. "Slow down, Kris. I need to wrap my mind around this. So, you're creating a portal, and then picking up another portal generator and carrying it through the first portal, setting up and opening the second portal, and then closing and packing up the first portal, and then carrying it through the second portal, and so on…but you're doing this very, very fast—a picosecond for each jump. Did I get it?"

"Yah…pretty much…"

"How far was each jump?" Marc's mind was moving ahead.

"We used a meter. Enough to accommodate the equipment size."

"And you're going to demonstrate it…"

"This untethered MERT is entirely self-contained." Dr. Lambin indicated a small unit beside him on the lab floor. "Stand by…."

A circular opening in the air appeared at floor level in front of Marc. Then the device itself appeared on the floor in front of Marc.

"You set this up for a hundred klick transit, right?" Marc said. "How many jumps was that?"

"A hundred thousand."

"Oh…sure…yah…that's obvious. And how long was the trip?"

"Ten microseconds."

"Obvious as well, I guess. You pulled this off in a week?" Marc said.

"Not really. We knew where we were going so that once we split off the untethered hyper-Disc, the rest was by the numbers, so to speak. By last week it was just iron out a few bugs, and we had this little guy."

"Can you show me again…do it in reverse?"

"In principle, yes, but we just used up all the available power in these portable units. I will need to retrieve them for a recharge before we can do it again." He said something to someone out of range of the pickup. "I'm sending someone with a hyper-Disc." He sat down at his desk, and Marc followed suit.

"Do you see what we have here, Marc? With sufficient power, this double unit can project a portal, transit through the portal, immediately project another portal, transit through, and so on, limited only by its power."

"Okay," Marc said, "remember, I'm a smart guy, but I am not a scientist. I'm still struggling with how the hyper-V works. I think I understand that a hyper-V gets to its destination about the same time light would, but that passengers experience virtually no passage of time…"

"In a nutshell," Dr. Lambin said, "that's it." He adjusted his glasses, muttering, "I hate these things.

"The hyper-V craft moves between points A and B at near light speed. With the MERT, portal A and portal B are the same thing—a bit like a door between two rooms. It looks like two portals, but it really is just one portal between two locations. Imagine you are in your office, and you step through a door into my office, and then you step through another door into President Zakes' office."

"But it's not teleporting…?"

"Not even slightly, and we have no idea how to do that," Dr. Lambin said. "Now, take it one step further. Carry a complete unit with you when you transit the portal, then open another portal, pick up the unit you just used, and carry it through the next portal, and then you generate a third portal and immediately step through it with the second unit under arm, and so on, and so on." Dr. Lambin made eye contact with Marc. "That's how the untethered MERT drive works."

"How do you project the portal to the final location you want?"

"We're working on that," Dr. Lambin said. "The parameters are controlled by how much power you have and the theoretical boundaries for the entire process. We're still working out those equations."

"What's the next step?"

"Next steps, actually."

"Okay…"

"Passing living matter through a tethered portal, and then scaling it up to something human-size."

"And the second?"

"Scaling up the MERT Drive. If we can do people—and we're virtually certain we can—we need a self-contained vehicle sufficiently large to carry all the people we want. I'm talking about a *Starchild*-sized starship with a MERT Drive."

"How long?" Marc was thinking about Earth.

"Sooner than you think."

EARTH—NORTH AMERICA

As Earth's northern hemisphere moved from frigid winter to chilly spring, President Syed Shah Bukhari sat behind his desk in the Oval Office conferring with General Ismail Suleiman and the four generals running Caliphate operations in North America.

"We have the country locked down from the east coast to the Lone Star and Columbia borders," Suleiman said. "We have fierce resistance in the Rocky Mountains, but with the thaw, we'll clean that up." He looked from general to general and then to President

Bukhari. "We can't do much about Lone Star and Columbia right now, but Canada is ripe for immediate conquest." He looked at his general in charge of the American northeast. "Follow the spring thaw north and west into Canada. You won't have much resistance." He looked at all the generals. "We'll talk Alaska after that."

President Bukhari looked down at his desk, deep in thought. *Millions of Americans dead in the last few months—over a billion world-wide…the world transformed forever…Sharia Law worldwide (more or less)…and I played a significant role…all because of a little, handicapped man, uneducated in the ways of the world, but deeply steeped in the* Qur'an *and his Allah-inspired interpretation. I never dreamed it could come to this.*

"*Allahu Akbar,*" President Bukhari said quietly. Suleiman and the other generals looked at him. "*Allahu Akbar,*" he said more forcefully, standing to his feet.

Coming to attention, the generals joined him, raising their voices together. "*Allahu Akbar…Allahu Akbar…Allahu Akbar!*"

✳

Eastern Canada fell to the Caliphate like a ripe fruit—New Brunswick, Nova Scotia, Prince Edward Island, and along the St Lawrence River into Ontario. When Canadians saw what happened to those who resisted in the United States, they had no heart to fight. Before the invasion, the highest population density outside urban areas was less than ten persons per square kilometer, so it was easier to become a second-class Muslim and then continue living as before in the sparsely populated countryside.

Southern Saskatchewan, Alberta, and British Columbia offered more resistance than eastern Canada; nevertheless, Caliphate forces swept to the Rockies in a matter of two weeks. Unlike eastern Canada, however, instead of converting, when defeat was inevitable, western Canadians quietly faded north into the Yukon or west into the mountains.

The Rocky Mountains proved to be a formidable challenge to Caliphate forces.

"We are unable to follow our plan into Alaska, Sahib," General Suleiman told the Prophet over their private Link. "These mountains are more than any of us realized…an uncrossable barrier. An individual can cross, even small groups, with full knowledge of the terrain or with guides, but our army will be stopped before it really gets underway."

"So, what do we do, General? We cannot let Alaska escape Allah's vengeance."

"Alaska has two major population centers," Suleiman said, "around the capital Juneau, and the Anchorage area, leading north to Fairbanks." He brought up a map illustrating his point. "We can move north from British Columbia to the capital relatively easily. There should be no real resistance. We can eliminate the leadership and put our own people in place."

"Do you really think that is necessary?" Saeed seemed genuinely puzzled. "It's a remote, sparsely populated land."

"It has much to offer—oil, minerals to mine, lumber, vast fisheries. We cannot afford to let Alaska revert to local rule once we have conquered." Suleiman's eyes bored into Saeed's.

"You are correct, of course, General Suleiman. What is the Muslim population of Alaska? Do they have a Mosque?"

"Four to five thousand, mostly in Anchorage, where they have the only mosque."

"Will they assist our invasion?"

"We will need to duplicate our Minneapolis operation in Anchorage and Fairbanks—a massive paratrooper drop. Unlike Minneapolis, we may find heavy resistance. We are passing word to the local Imam, who will instruct the faithful regarding their duties during the aerial invasion. If we can clear out the resistance quickly, the Alaskans will do like the western Canadians, and fade into the mountains."

"Military presence?"

"Air Force and Army, but without command and control, they are restricted to local operations. My contacts say they are mostly shut down."

"So…Alaska will not be a problem?"

"I think not, Sahib."

✳

"And Hawaii?" Saeed had never visited Hawaii, but he was aware of its strategic pre-Jihad importance to the United States.

"When the US broke up right after the beginning of your North American campaign, Hawaii quietly reestablished itself as a monarchy and resurrected a distant descendant of the Kamehameha Dynasty. Hawaii is maintaining a low profile, distancing itself from your global

Jihad. With our destruction of Earth's satellite net, it is virtually cut off from the rest of the world."

"How many Muslims?"

"About ten thousand out of a population of nearly two million."

"Imams?"

"Several hundred, scattered throughout the islands."

"Are we able to communicate with them?"

"Actually, we have the only regular communications with Hawaii, except for some amateur short-wave hobbyists."

"Then, let Hawaii Muslims take care of Hawaii," Saeed said with finality.

IAPETUS—STARCHILD INSTITUTE

Marc dropped his focus as Dr. Kristopher Lambin asked over their Link connection, "Can you please come down to my lab?"

"I'm pretty busy, Kris. I trust this is important." Marc scanned his schedule and groaned as he pushed his appointments forward by several hours.

"You won't regret it, I promise," Dr. Lambin answered with a smile.

Marc placed a couple of calls and then strode out of his office and dropped down the tube to the underground wormhole lab complex. As he stepped into the lab, his eyes were drawn to a door-shaped device commanding the center of the room. Several scientists and technicians in traditional lab coats focused their attention on pieces of equipment or holographic images of what had to be essential elements of the door-like device. Dr. Lambin greeted him.

"I wanted you to witness the first living creature to pass through a MERT Portal." He took Marc's elbow and guided him to one side of the portal. It looked exactly like an open door, but the space through the door was not the lab where he stood. Dr. Lambin steered him to the other side. As he stepped around the door, it disappeared, as if it weren't there. They returned to the front.

"Dmitri," Dr. Lambin said.

"Da, I'm here!" Dmitri's grinning face appeared through the door as he walked into full view. "Marc, good to see you."

Dr. Lambin turned to Marc. "When Dmitri was here yesterday, we gave him a hyper-Disc linked to this portal. He activated the portal in his Security Office at Mirs." Dmitri gave a little wave from his side of the portal. "I thought the security his office supplies would be a positive element in this exercise." Marc nodded. "We already have tossed several inanimate objects through the portal." He handed Marc a red cube, like the cube he had already used, or the same one. "Go ahead…Toss it to Dmitri."

Marc tossed the red cube at Dmitri through the door. "Catch!"

Dmitri did and tossed it back.

"You're at Mirs?" Marc asked.

"Yep."

"Yet, we're talking as if we were side-by-side…"

"Yep."

"Here…" Dr. Lambin handed Marc a potted plant. "Toss it."

Dmitri caught the plant and examined it. "Looks fine to me," he said and tossed it back.

Marc, who had a bit of a green thumb, examined the plant closely. "No difference at the macro level that I can tell." He shook his head in amazement.

"We've analyzed transmitted plants at every possible level, comparing portal and non-portal results. They are identical…there is no detectable difference all the way to the quantum level."

Marc stood quietly, contemplating what he had just seen and heard. He let his eyes wander to a feline traveling cage on the floor.

"That's Jake," Dmitri said through the door. "I dropped him off yesterday before I left for Mirs in *Merkavah*."

"Everyone ready?" Dr. Lambin said to no one in particular. He reached down to the cage and released the latch. Jake pushed the door open with his nose, stepped onto the floor, and stretched languorously, prominently displaying the characteristic dark tabby-M on his forehead.

"Jake…over here, boy!" Dmitri said through the door, squatting. Jake perked his ears but otherwise pretended not to hear. He nonchalantly strolled left and right for several seconds and then bounded through the door into Dmitri's arms, purring loudly. "Good boy," Dmitri said softly, scratching Jake behind his ears. Then he rose to his feet. "What the hell!" he said and strode through the door into the lab.

CHAPTER SEVENTEEN

EARTH—MERKAVAH HIGH ABOVE SOUTHWESTERN RUSSIA

Dmitri looked at Orel and asked, "Do you ever miss your Spud mining operation, Dany?"

"Sometimes, I suppose. It certainly had the potential for making me rich," Orel said. "Why?"

"Except for the pirates, it was a routine, ho-hum kind of operation, wouldn't you say?" Dmitri grinned at him. "Nothing like the excitement you've had since joining me…"

"There were other choices besides Q-carbon, you know," Orel said, setting his stocky frame firmly against the control panel. "Ayers Sky put out a call for water and nitrogen ice."

"Yeah, I heard."

"I looked closely at the profit margins before choosing Q-carbon. Problem with nitrogen ice is you either got to bring it up from some planet or moon surface, or you got to drag an entire asteroid from where it is to El-five. Same for water ice, except there's plenty in the asteroids. Real profit would have required a fleet of VASIMR tugs. Ayers Sky wasn't paying enough, and there was a lot of competition, which drove the profit even lower. Q-carbon was the better deal."

"Makes sense, I guess," Dmitri said, turning his attention to *Merkavah*'s screens.

"So, why are we here?" Orel asked.

"See those masses of troop concentrations down there?" Dmitri amplified the display on *Merkavah*'s main screen. "That's the southern border between the Ukraine and Russia. Those guys," he pointed to the troops west of the border, "are Caliphate. And these," he pointed to the troops east of the border, "are Russian." Dmitri pulled the view back to take in the entire western Russian border. "There are more than a million Caliphate warriors along this border…and half as many Russians. The Russians have better armor, better weapons, and they are fighting for Mother Russia."

"But the Caliphate has Allah," Orel said, "and he seems to be favoring the Muslims lately."

"You're not serious…"

"No, but they are." Orel gestured to the massed Caliphate troops. "They buy it hook, line, and sinker."

"That's what scares me," Dmitri said softly. "That's what scares the shit out of me!"

"Dmitri, look! Caliphate troops are pushing forward." He pointed to a surge just outside Luhansk on the Ukrainian border pointed at Volgograd.

Dmitri pointed to the Kazakhstan border east of Volgograd. "And Caliphate troops are moving westward here. They're going to pinch off the entire Russian southern force." He zoomed in to reveal brutal, hand-to-hand combat.

"The Russians are giving as good as they're getting," Orel said, excitement tinging his voice.

"Not good enough," Dmitri said. "Even if they keep this up, when they're done, all the Russians will be dead, and there will still be a half-million Caliphate warriors on the battlefield." He sat, shaking his head in dismay. "They've got to bring in the heavy stuff, and they've got to do it now."

They waited, watching, but nothing happened as the battle waged on.

"What was that?" Orel said, "And that…and that…?" pointing to several brilliant flashes that had suddenly appeared across the vast Russian landscape below them.

"Track and analyze," Dmitri ordered the Resident. As they watched, the bright flashes blossomed throughout the Russian landscape below them, all the way to the Bering Straits. "What are they?" Dmitri asked, although he already knew the answer.

"Thermonuclear explosions," the Resident answered, "twelve hundred ten of them."

"How is that number significant?" Dmitri asked.

"That is the number of cities and towns in the Russian Federation," the Resident said.

"My God, Dmitri. They hit every one of them."

"Must have been prepositioned," Dmitri said quietly. "It's over, Dany, it's over. One thousand two hundred cities and towns…millions and millions of people…factories, museums, commercial centers… all gone…everywhere…" He wept silently.

Below *Merkavah*, the fierce battle still waged, although the troops had to have seen the explosions in nearby towns. Soon, all along the sweeping border, Russian troops began to pull back as word of the extensive thermonuclear destruction reached them. From overhead, Dmitri and Orel watched in horror.

"Can't we do something?" Orel asked.

"What?" Dmitri snapped. "Neutrino beams work on individuals or nuclear devices, not on troop concentrations. Lasers don't work through an atmosphere; neither do the particle beams, except on a limited, focused basis." He looked at Orel's surprised expression. "Sorry, Dany, it's not you. I feel so damned helpless." He stepped to the drive console. "Let's check the Chinese border…see what's happening there."

Dmitri issued orders to the Resident, and shortly they looked down on the 4,209 km Sino-Russian border.

"Look, Dany, Chinese troops have crossed the border in hundreds of locations," Dmitri said as he swept *Merkavah*'s sensors along the divide. "Whatever Russia had there is either destroyed or took to heel. There's no opposition…"

✳

The world had never seen a more ferocious defending army. For 1,500 years, Russia had existed in one form or another, culminating with the Russian Federation following the demise of the Soviet

Union in the twentieth century. After the United States balkanized, the world's superpower mantle shifted to the Russian Federation. The half-million troops along the Euro-Russian border knew why they were fighting—especially following the destruction of the Motherland's cities and towns. Each soldier knew deep down that he or she was fighting for a lost cause. Nevertheless, not one man, not one woman along the entire front yielded so much as a meter. They fought courageously from Khasan on the Korean border to St. Petersburg on the Gulf of Finland—all 20,700 km, and died heroically, taking with them three Caliphate warriors for each Russian sacrifice.

✳

"Russia is yours, Sahib!" General Suleiman bowed low with a flourish. "We lost more warriors in Russia than with the entire rest of the world." Suleiman's countenance turned grave as he spoke. "Over three million faithful warriors are no longer with us. They await Judgement Day to be admitted to *Jannah*."

Saeed listened to his general carefully and then rose to his feet as he felt Allah's power surge through him. He stood quietly, hands raised in humble supplication. "No, General Suleiman. Allah in his infinite wisdom has revealed to me that our holy warriors who die prosecuting this holy Jihad are admitted to *Jannah* the moment life leaves their bodies." Saeed turned slowly, letting Allah's grace flow through his body into his command tent, through the double walls into the desert compound, and then outward until the entire world was awash with Allah's beneficence.

Saeed lowered his arms and turned to look directly at General Suleiman. "Make sure," he said evenly, "that every warrior understands what Allah has revealed this day!"

IAPETUS—NEAR THE STARCHILD INSTITUTE

Dr. Lambin leaned his ascetic frame against what looked like a 25-meter *Merkavah* Class hyper-V craft, except that it sported two long vertical fins attached to the craft tangentially on opposite sides. They were as long as the craft and had the same vertical dimension. The fins were covered with the same material as the rest of the craft— deep, featureless black. The top and bottom edges and the leading and trailing edges appeared to be razor-sharp. Marc and Dr. Lambin stood on the green outside the Starchild Institute pyramid. "I want to make sure I understood what you just told me, Kris," Marc Bowles said. "This is *not* a hyper-V craft."

"Well, yes and no…and I am not being coy."

"So…"

"Let's call this vehicle a *MERT Craft*," Dr. Lambin said. "It definitely started out as a plain vanilla hyper-V craft, but we made a couple of modifications. We liked the skin because it's impervious. We needed the singularity power source and the underlying hyper-V drive mechanism to hover in a gravity field and perform close-in maneuvers. We also really needed the Resident. But we needed to add the exotic matter fins to generate the MERT wormhole. Watch out!" he said. "The edges are razor sharp."

"So, this MERT Craft," Marc said, "knows how to create two MERT Portals, slip through one carrying the second, open the second, close the first, and carry it through the second, and so on…and so on." Dr. Lambin nodded his assent. "And it can hover and maneuver like a hyper-V craft." Dr. Lambin nodded again. Marc was satisfied that he understood the basic concept, but that was it. He had a lot of questions.

"How far can the MERT Craft project the untethered portal?"

"Wrong question," Dr. Lambin said. "Each jump is twenty-five meters—because that's how long the craft is—with a picosecond duration. The distance of the destination determines the number of jumps."

"How does the craft know where to go?"

"We're still working on that," Dr. Lambin said. "The calculations are massive and extremely rapid, which is the reason for the onboard computers and the Resident,"

"When Jake stepped through the MERT Portal from your lab to Dmitri's office, conditions on both sides of the portal were compatible. What if they weren't?"

"You mean like pressure differences, atmospheric component differences, gravitational differences…things like that?" Dr. Lambin said, ticking them off on his fingers.

"Right…like when Jon Stock first entered Iapetus from the elevator lock…the gravity difference he experienced?"

"Exactly! Each twenty-five-meter jump is on a specific vector, identical to the craft's fore-and-aft axis, and the craft maintains its internal environment, including gravity." Dr. Lambin's animated mood was catching, and Marc found himself really enjoying the conversation.

"Don't want to open a portal to the surface of Iapetus and suck all the air out of the interior," Marc commented dryly.

"Something like that…except that's a different subject—tethered portals. We're dealing with the MERT *Drive* here." Dr. Lambin stepped away from the MERT Craft. "In the real world, the Resident sets up a vector and determines when to take another look. At that time, the craft pauses sufficiently long to shoot the stars and set a new vector. The actual path to a destination will be curved, following a path that eventually catches up with the destination." He patted the craft.

"We programmed the Resident to run the test protocol without anyone in the craft. It will transfer to several locations within Iapetus and finally return here."

"How many jumps for each transfer?" Marc asked.

"For these distances, a few—divide the straight-line distance by twenty-five meters. Also," Lambin added, "we set up Link holocams at each location so we can monitor them from here." He pointed to four holodisplays of empty scenes, almost indistinguishable from the background.

"How much time do you allow for each jump?"

"That's a fixed variable, meaning we choose an interval and then run the course with that interval. Our default setting is one picosecond." Dr. Lambin looked at Marc expectantly. "Ready to do it?"

Marc nodded, and Dr. Lambin tapped his Link.

The MERC Craft vanished. Then it appeared briefly in each of the four holodisplays, and then it appeared before them again.

"That's it?" Marc asked.

"For now, anyway." Dr. Lambin had the look of a kid in a candy shop.

EARTH—BEIJING, CHINA

Carmen Bhuta looked at Chen Lee-Fong and Dmitri—Carmen's and Dmitri's holoimages appearing in Chen's office on the top floor of a stunning glass structure in central Beijing. "I've never seen anything like it," she said. "It's a flu virus variation, but, oh my…it's virulent!" She looked from face to face. "Where did you get this?"

"It's everywhere, Carmen…I mean everywhere." The head of China's Science Directorate wiped his forehead with a paper towel. "We're just beginning to understand what we are up against."

"By everywhere, you mean China?"

"China, Korea, Mongolia…It's genetically linked in some fashion we do not understand to the congenital Mongolian spots common among East Asian peoples."

"You mean congenital dermal melanocytosis?" Carmen asked.

"Yes…I think. It has a two-day incubation period, and it's nearly one hundred percent fatal." Chen wiped his face again; he was perspiring freely.

A tall, ascetic man in his early fifties entered the room carrying a stainless bowl of ice water and several cloths.

"My assistant, Ibrahim Mah Fung," Chen said weakly, wiping his face with a chilled cloth Ibrahim handed him.

Carmen nodded and asked in Mandarin, "Xi'an Hui? From Zhongyuan?"

"You have an excellent ear and fine accent," Ibrahim said to her. "I am a Xi'an Hui Muslim, and I work closely with Chen." His face took on a distressed look. "I received a vaccine from my Imam to administer to Chen, but I am afraid I am too late." He held up an inoculation vial. "My Imam said I would not need the vaccination—my Arabic genetic heritage." He wiped Chen's face with a cold cloth.

"My God!" Carmen said softly. "They've found a way to target Asian peoples." She turned to Dmitri. "I need samples. I've got to get them back to my lab in Mirs. We've got to put people on this right away…there's no time to lose…" Carmen's voice trailed off as Chen collapsed to the floor of his office.

Ibrahim kneeled beside him, stroking his fevered forehead.

"A hundred million people died today," Chen whispered from the floor. "In two days, we will all be gone…"

EARTH—AUSTIN, TEXAS

Percival Enderly reached across Sam's desk and shook his hand. "So, you're the famous Sam Houston I've heard so much about?" he said.

Sam examined the short, stout Chairman of the Columbia Freehold standing before him and realized that Enderly was no slouch. He had pulled most of the Northwest together and was even conducting submarine patrols off the coast. Sam gestured to a chair facing his desk but remained in his seat.

"Nice job pulling Columbia together," Sam said. "May I offer you a drink?"

"Thanks, but I try to stay away from the hard stuff. Wine with meals, that's about it," Enderly said.

"How about coffee, then?"

"Sure…thanks."

Sam poured two cups, took his black, but offered Enderly cream and sugar. Then he sat down and leaned back as they sipped their coffee.

Following a brief silence, Enderly said, "You have managed to maintain command and control. You have the fuel…we don't." He then described his mountaintop transponder solution. "Our VLF station at Jim Creek handles submarine ComCon so that we are keeping things together."

Sam nodded, sipping coffee as he watched conflicting emotions cross Enderly's face. "My worry," Enderly finally said, "is the massed Caliphate presence on both our borders. I'm protected by mountains to the north, but you are wide open." Enderly leaned into Sam's desk. "You know neither one of us can successfully take on the Caliphate, especially if they bring their European army here."

"They lost a lot of warriors in Russia," Sam said.

"Yeah, but there's plenty more where those came from."

"I don't disagree with that, but…"

"We need an alliance," Enderly said, rising to his feet. "I can extend my sub patrols along the coast southward. You can extend your ComCon far enough north to interface with my system." Enderly's eyes smoldered with intensity. "We can back each other up, move men and supplies, stop incursions before they start."

"I agree that we can be better by cooperating than going it alone, but I'm not ready to integrate forces." Sam held up his hand when he saw that Enderly was about to interrupt. "I've got southern, eastern, and northern borders to worry about. I welcome your sub patrols and am more than willing to supply ComCon and make needed supplies available to you, but I need to keep my troops here. I can run air interference for you if it comes to that, but I need my troops here."

Enderly sat down and nodded. "I can see that. The main thing is that we have each other's back…that the Caliphate doesn't overrun either of us."

"Our staffs can work out the details," Sam said, towering over Enderly as he rose to his feet, holding out his hand.

EARTH—SAUDI ARABIAN DESERT

General Suleiman bowed low with a flourish and said, "Allow me to update you on our progress in Asia, Sahib." Then he settled down on a pile of cushions opposite the diminutive prophet. They both sipped cups of sweet mint tea.

"Please do so."

"The modified flu our faithful Hui introduced throughout China's cities and countryside has been successful beyond our wildest dreams. Of three billion Chinese from a month ago, forty million survive, and thirty million of those are Muslim, led by Ibrahim Mah Fung, former assistant to Chen Lee-Fong, head of China's Science Directorate."

"What of Chen Lee-Fong?"

"He perished the second day."

"He was my friend, Chen Lee-Fong."

"I did not know that, Sahib. I am sorry."

"Allah moves in mysterious ways, may His will prevail." Saeed finished his tea and stood. Suleiman rose to his feet as well. "And the rest of Asia, General, and Japan?"

"The rest succumbed to our potion—as we expected. Only Japan remains, totally isolated and alone." The General refilled their cups. "May I tell you a tale from the past, Sahib?"

Saeed nodded his assent.

"Before the First World War in the early twentieth century, Muslims of mixed Persian-Chinese background, the Hui, made up about two percent of the Chinese population, some ten million people. Many held positions of stature and importance in the military and in government and commerce. In the previous century, the Empire of Japan had attacked China, perpetrating many atrocities, especially against the Hui, a people with a long memory. When the Empire of Japan attacked China again in what has come to be known as the Second Sino-Japanese War, almost all Chinese Muslims supported and fought for China against the Japanese invaders, and the Hui initiated a Jihad against the Japanese.

"This Jihad resulted in the Rape of Nanking by the Japanese, where tens of thousands of Hui—Muslims—were slaughtered by the Japanese invaders...they raped and tortured women and children, butchered young and old alike, leaving nothing alive in their wake—neither plants, animals, or people."

Saeed sat quietly following Suleiman's tale, deep in thought. He finally roused himself. "Make certain our warriors know this tale. Make sure every Muslim knows this tale. Make sure the world knows this tale." He stood to his feet and raised his severed trunk. "And most especially, make sure Japan knows this tale."

IAPETUS—FEDERATION HEADQUARTERS

Rod Zakes slid a Lone Star Bourbon across his desk. "Don't see much of you out here anymore, Sam," he said. "The bourbon is from Mars, the ice from here—mined outside, not from an icemaker."

They sipped quietly. "Pretty good stuff," Sam said. "Those Martians are...well...pretty good!"

"I guess things are getting pretty bad back on Earth," Rod said.

"You can't begin to understand the full impact of what is happening," Sam told him earnestly.

"What's your read going forward?"

"That's why I'm here, Rod. This thing won't stop until it's over...I mean completely over—the entire world in the Caliphate." He paused and took a deep breath. "There are still some holdouts. Us, of course, and the Columbia Freehold. I just came from a meeting with Enderly—tough little guy, and smart. Between the two of us, we can hold out for a while. There's Australia and New Zealand—mostly because they are isolated. It's not worth the Caliphate's bother yet."

"You know the Kiwis are terraforming Ceres, and the Aussies are building Ayers Sky at El-five?" Rod said.

"I know that. What is their status?"

"The black hole power core is installed in Ceres, and they are hollowing the interior living layer like here in Iapetus. It will be a while before any part is ready for habitation. Ayers Sky is nearing the point where people can live there—in a pinch. They'll be ready well before Ceres, but it's still more than a year out."

Sam acknowledged and then continued. "Scandinavia is holding out, but that's just a fluke. The Caliphate has merely not looked in their direction yet. When it does, it will be several days at most. The Norwegians will take to the mountains, and the rest will just give up—at least superficially. South America is untouched, but I think it's next and will be a roll-over. The Caliphate will replace the governments, kill the religious leaders, do some mass conversions with symbolic beheadings, and the nations of South America will be history.

"Then, there's Japan. When all this started, Japan completely isolated itself. They mined their own waters and shut down their airports. Nobody has any idea what's going on there. The Pacific islands are untouched and probably will remain so going forward. I suspect that sometime in the future, Imams will take over island by island until all are under the Caliphate umbrella.

"The thing is, Rod, Lone Star has about seventy million citizens, and Columbia has about thirty-nine. Australia has another thirty, and New Zealand about five. I've been moving people out of Lone Star to Mars daily. The problem is that we don't have a Launch Loop—all I have is Saracen to move them off-planet and several hyper-V freighters to get them to Mars. I've got space on Mars for everyone, but I'm not even beginning to make a dent in the numbers. Enderly has no way to get his people off-planet. The Aussies have the Outback Loop, and New Zealand has the Kiwi Loop. Both have been pushing people out as fast as possible—I understand they are operating twenty-four/seven. Even so, it's too slow!"

Sam stood and looked out the window over the pastoral visage of Iapetus. He turned back to Rod and said with desperation, "I can't have one hundred forty-three million deaths on my hands!"

"And you won't," Rod said.

❋

"Let's have some lunch while my people set up something I want to show you," Rod said, standing and walking toward the door.

They joined dozens of others in a cafeteria-style eatery with none of the trappings of power that were so common with government facilities on Earth. They spent a half-hour enjoying good but simple food while discussing these differences. As they were finishing, Rod's Link announced that the demonstration was ready. Instead of going back to the top of the governmental pyramid, they exited the building, boarded a floater, and traveled the short distance to the SI complex, where Dr. Kristopher Lambin met them at the door. Rod made introductions, and the three made their way to Dr. Lambin's lab.

An isolated doorway stood in the middle of the open floor space. Rod walked through the door and asked Sam to follow him.

"What the Hell…!" Sam said as he stepped into his own governor's office in Austin. He turned around, his eyes filled with disbelief. Dr. Lambin beckoned him through the doorway.

"Come on back, Sam…It's okay…" Dr. Lambin reached out his hand.

"What is this magic?" Sam asked as he stepped back into Dr. Lambin's lab.

❋

Since Marc Bowles' last meeting with Noel Goddard about funding Ayers Sky and generating its atmosphere, MERT Portal technology had progressed from successful lab demonstration to a full-fledged operating portal between Iapetus and Sam Houston's office in Austin. What it took behind the scenes to keep the untethered hyper-Disc in Sam's office on a rotating planet revolving around the sun, locked to the tethered end anchored inside Iapetus, rotating around Saturn, also revolving around the sun, was entirely beyond Marc's ability to comprehend, let alone calculate. Nevertheless, the portal was secure and being used multiple times each day.

Since his meeting with Noel, Marc had created an independent division of SI dedicated to locating and transporting nitrogen and water ice to L5, popularly called IceDiv throughout SI. His people had already discovered three nitrogen ice and two water ice asteroids that were well on their way to L5. As Marc reviewed his progress, he let out an exasperated sigh. *That's five out of a total of four thousand loads—better find a way to speed this up*, he thought as he contemplated the enormity of the problem. The matter nagged at him as he continued with other tasks, coming into focus every few minutes.

"Hello, Marc," Sam Houston said, suddenly walking through Marc's office door.

Marc looked up. "Hello, yourself. What brings you to my domain?"

"I wanted to discuss using this crazy portal mechanism to move people wholesale from Earth to here."

"Oh my God!" Marc said. "That's it!"

"I know," Sam said. "That's why I'm here…like I said…"

"Not what I mean, Sam." Marc stood and walked around his desk to stand in front of his taller friend. "Bear with me for a few minutes."

Marc then described the problem of finding and transporting sufficient breathable atmosphere to fill Ayers Sky. He ended up saying, "So, that's five thousand seventy-seven loads, but I just made a connection I had missed until now. You showing up triggered it." He sat back at his desk and manipulated his Link to produce an image above the desk. "Here's Earth and the Moon, with El-four leading and El-five trailing." A tube appeared leading from L5 to the Earth's north pole. "We install a large MERT Portal in Ayers Sky, and carry the linked hyper-Disc end into Earth's atmosphere near the surface at the North Pole, and then open the portal. Air from Earth's atmosphere will flow through the portal to fill Ayers Sky with virtually no effect on Earth's total atmosphere." He paused to enter some numbers. "If the portal is—say—twenty meters wide, equilibration will be… add half again… a bit over ten days; if the portal is ten meters wider, equilibration will be in about…four-and-a-half days." Marc looked up at Sam. "Let me get this into motion, and then we'll deal with your reason for being here."

L5—AYERS SKY

Noel Goddard sat before the controls of the RH, holding the hyper-Disc Marc Bowles had given him during their last visit, turning it over and over. He and Marc had activated his portal link and walked through the portal several times from several locations within Iapetus until he felt comfortable with the process. Noel hadn't used the hyper-Disc since then, but only because there had been no need.

He examined the vast structure floating in front of him. It wasn't that long ago that he had sat in Marc Bowles's office at SI, pitching his plan for filling Ayers Sky with breathable air. There was nothing wrong with his plan, except for the time and effort it was taking to make it happen. He looked at the hyper-Disc he was holding. Every Federation outpost was buzzing with the exciting potential these discs and the technology behind them brought to the entire Solar System. It was evident to Noel that they had forever changed interplanetary transportation. He checked the shipping schedule. The first nitrogen ice shipment was due in about a week. At least four more tugs were underway, and SI was scouring the Belt for more.

Filling Noel's screen, Ayers Sky stretched fifty kilometers from endcap to endcap. Its ten-kilometer-wide interior had been sealed a week ago and was now filling with atmospheric gas—all 3,927 cubic kilometers. A continuous stream of tugs ferried water ice from the mines at Udachny. Also, five VASIMR tugs were towing water ice and nitrogen ice asteroids from the Belt. When they arrived, Noel's External Crew would park them within the L5 gravitation zone pending processing. He watched transportation crew members emblazoned with fluorescent XCs flitting around the Udachny tugs under TBH boot control. At both endcaps, Conversion Crews emblazoned with fluorescent CCs were making breathable atmosphere out of the ice.

Converting the nitrogen ice was simplicity itself—break up the large nitrogen ice chunks, put them inside Ayers Sky, and let them evaporate. Water ice was a different matter, however. Ayers Sky needed water for streams and lakes—once the pressure was up. Otherwise, the Conversion Crew used sizeable solar-powered electrolysis units to break the water into hydrogen and oxygen. They pumped the oxygen into Ayers Sky and processed the hydrogen with some of the nitrogen to produce ammonia that they pressurized, froze, and eventually used as part of the outer covering of the massive cylinder. Noel had worked out these details during the three years he spent studying and modifying the Ayers Sky plans, refining them frequently as the project progressed.

Noel watched the outside activity, idly turning the hyper-Disc in his hand, first one side, then the other, thinking about its possibilities. That's when it hit him. Noel tapped the back and then oriented the growing portal as he kept his finger on the disc. "Marc, are you there," Noel said as he stepped through into Marc's office. "Marc, it's Noel…please don't be startled."

Marc stood, offering his hand. "What's up, Noel?"

"I just came up with the solution for transporting ice to Ayers Sky," Noel said with a big grin.

Marc held up his hand as if to say something, but Noel rushed on. "We install several MERT Ports at Ayers Sky by bringing them through this portal." He pointed at the door through which he had just entered Marc's office. "Then we place linked hyper-Discs with each of the craft looking for ice in the Belt. When they locate something, they pass it through the portal to Ayers Sky. We save months of travel time." He stopped talking and sat in the chair before Marc's desk.

"I would never deliberately burst a guy's bubble, but I have to tell you that we already thought of your solution, and discarded it…"

"What…?" Noel's face fell.

"Hold on!" Marc held up his hand again. "Hold on, Noel. We discarded that idea because we came up with something even better." Marc smiled warmly and leaned back. "MERT Portal development has accelerated beyond all our expectations," he said. "I know you are aware of what is happening on Earth. Sam wants to evacuate…"

"Evacuate? You mean leave Earth…everybody…lock, stock, and barrel?" Noel asked.

"That's what he's talking about—at least the Lone Star Conservancy and Columbia Freehold," Marc said.

A robotic server rolled into the office with two steaming cups, one coffee, one tea. "Want one?" Marc asked, taking the coffee for himself.

"Love one," Noel said. "Hey, it knows I like tea."

"You and your people have made herculean progress at El-five. I would never have guessed you would be so far along this early. Unfortunately, the Caliphate is further ahead with its worldwide Jihad than you are getting Ayers Sky ready for occupation."

"We're working on that," Noel said, "and what I came to tell you would speed things up."

"I know, but one Launch Loop does not a population of thirty million move, and several MERT Portals won't fill Ayers Sky that much quicker than using VASIMR tugs. We're close to solving the people transportation conundrum, but you need to have this place ready when we can get your people out."

"I see that and couldn't agree more. So, what's wrong with my idea?"

Marc paused in obvious thought. "I didn't see it at first, and I blame myself," he said, "but we're full steam ahead now. I presume you understand that that portal you just walked through really is a stable Morris-Einstein-Rosen-Thorne wormhole? By the magic of relativistic and quantum physics, this portal connects my office and the *RH* control room."

"I'm not sure anyone really understands it, but I do get your point. I can get to your office by flying *RH* to Iapetus, descending to the operations level, and go to your office, or I can walk through that door into your office. Obviously, one way is longer than the other."

"Okay," Marc said, "you got it. Now, follow me…" Marc used his Link to display an image of Ayers Sky. Some distance away, he projected an image of Earth, not to scale. "Earth has a fifty-kilometer thick layer of atmosphere that produces a surface pressure of a hundred kilo-Pascals or one bar, for all practical purposes." He connected the images with a tube. "What do you think will happen if we establish a MERT Portal between—say—Earth's north pole at sea level and the interior of Ayers Sky?"

Noel sat quietly for a moment. "I'll be damned!" he said. "How big a portal?"

"How about thirty meters," Marc said.

Noel tapped his Link. "We'd have our atmosphere in four-and-a-half days!"

"How soon can you rig one endcap for the portal?"

"What will it take?"

"We'll move this portal," Marc pointed to the door, "to the end-cap you designate and enlarge it to accommodate the larger MERT Portal that we'll transfer to you. You install it so that it can handle a thirty-meter cross-section of air rushing in at three hundred fifty meters per second. Then all you do is carry the linked hyper-Disc to Earth near the surface at Earth's north pole. From Ayers Sky, you can manipulate the portal on Earth, so it is about twenty meters above the ice, pointed upward, and then you expand it to thirty meters, and open it."

Noel sat, thinking about what he had just heard. "I think we need a second transfer point, one south of the equator," he said. "Between Baker and Jarvis Islands, about a thousand klicks south of Slingshot."

"Your reasons?" Marc said.

"Four-and-a-half days of supersonic winds entering the North Pole portal will create quite a maelstrom. Somebody will notice. Put another in the South Pacific, and run both for a bit over two days—people are less likely to notice, and the local effects will have smaller impact."

It was Marc's turn to think. He sat quietly doing so. He looked up with a smile. "I agree!"

"Send me the drawings, and give me a week."

CHAPTER EIGHTEEN

EARTH—WESTERN AUSTRALIA

Most of the world, as it was before Jihad, knew very little about Australia's Outback Loop. Coral Bay, Australia's westernmost outpost, was just that before the Outback Loop, about 200 souls operating mostly tourist businesses, protected from the sea by Ningaloo Reef, and landward by 3,000 kilometers of desolate, dry Outback. The launch loop changed everything for this isolated community. Coral Bay Skyport, 80 kilometers above the tourist resort, became the destination of choice for well-heeled Australians looking for a different kind of vacation. It was larger than most of the other launch loop skyports, comfortably accommodating 300 guests in the lap of luxury.

Ground facilities at Coral Bay expanded to service Outback Loop. Several hotels designed for the traveler, recreation facilities, restaurants, all catering to the temporary guest with exotic destinations like the Moon, Mirs, Mars, and especially Ayers Sky.

As worldwide panic set in following one Caliphate victory after another, more cautious Australians decided that Australia was no longer safe and queued up for somewhere else—anywhere but Earth. Generally, most Australians knew about Ayers Sky and the dream to reconstruct Australia in this heavenly orb. Actually going there, however, still seemed an unreachable goal for most. Ayers Sky Corporation worked hard with the Australian government to convince the man and woman on the street that their future lay on Ayers Sky, not Australia. The government promised free passage to Ayers Sky when the time came, free land, and free settlement assistance.

Nobody had any idea, however, in which direction Ayers Sky would develop once it had a stable population. Most people believed that sooner or later, the Caliphate would overrun Australia. This belief gave impetus to the government's and Ayers Sky Corporation's efforts to convince Australians that they wanted to live out their lives on Ayers Sky.

The queues at Outback Loop got longer, and tempers got shorter as people began to realize that Outback Loop could not possibly carry everybody to Ayers Sky. Australia's minority Conservative Party began to resist the government's efforts, saying the government was exaggerating the danger to scare people into submitting to Ayers Sky. It announced that a better way was to resist the imminent Caliphate invasion. Their mantra, "Don't let the ragheads steal our homeland!" was taken up by at least half the population.

The ruling party fell on a vote of no confidence, and the government collapsed. In the following election, the Conservatives won a significant majority and selected businessman Joe Ridden as Prime Minister. Riding this majority, the Conservatives intended to scale back the Ayers Sky project and turn the country's attention to pending war with the Caliphate.

Noel kept up with Australian politics and was dismayed at the change in direction Joe Ridden had taken the country. He was on the verge of activating the MERT Portals to transfer atmosphere to Ayers Sky. Noel needed to change the Conservative Party's collective mind to get Australia back on track for the eventual evacuation. He called the Prime Minister by having one of his technicians rig a radio connection from L5 to the Australian landline grid.

"Prime Minister Ridden?" An aide fetched the Prime Minister. "This is Noel Goddard, Sir, the engineer in charge of the Ayers Sky project. We are on the verge of the next big step in readying Ayers

Sky for occupation. Since you are new to office, I would like to invite you to meet with me, so we can review the project, and you can observe this big step."

※

Although it took some political maneuvering, the next day, Noel landed *RH* in the plaza outside the House of Parliament in Canberra. He was met by a small delegation consisting of Joe Ridden with two senior government officials and the former Prime Minister, Morten Obers. They entered the hyper-V craft and settled into comfortable chairs Noel had provided. None had traveled by hyper-V, so Noel explained.

"You will feel no acceleration because the propelling force acts on everything inside the craft," Noel said. "We will accelerate to near light-speed, head to our destination, and slow down, all within a few seconds." Noel put a world chart on the main screen. "First, we will visit Europe and Western Russia. Then we will swing over parts of the former United States." The chart followed Noel's words. "After that, we'll go to El-five to visit Ayers Sky. Then we'll step through a MERT Portal to visit with Marc Bowles, Chairman of the Starchild Institute." He collapsed the chart view. "Then, finally, we'll set ourselves up to view the next major step in the Ayers Sky project."

Noel reached for a hyper-Disc labeled *Australia* and handed it to an aide waiting outside the craft. "Please see to it that this is placed on the Prime Minister's desk. Thank you." He pulled up the ramp and closed the craft door, and then he activated *RH*.

A moment later, Noel announced, "We're over Central Europe." The screen displayed the desolation, the destruction, the terrible aftermath of the Caliphate sweep. "Throughout Europe, everywhere, it's like this—death and desolation."

His passengers gasped at what they saw. The bustling stainless steel and glass face that modern European cities showed the world was entirely gone. Noel jumped to Berlin, Brussels, Paris, London, Madrid, Rome, and several other metropolitan areas…they were all the same, a mass of rubble, burned-out hulks of once majestic buildings, and death everywhere.

"Are those stacks of bodies?" Ridden asked.

In response, Noel zoomed in.

"My God…" Obers said, his voice filled with pain.

"It's like this everywhere," Noel said, "everywhere."

Then he took them over Western Russia. "All these cities and villages were hit with nuclear explosions—all of them. The Russians took a lot of Caliphate warriors with them, but in the end, the Caliphate prevailed. Russia as a state is no more."

"It doesn't seem possible," Ridden said, "but the destruction here is even worse than in Europe."

They crossed the Atlantic in a flash and swooped low over several American cities. All were destroyed or clearly under Caliphate rule. "No one escaped except for those who fled to the Lone Star Conservancy or the Columbia Freehold," Noel told them. "Both these states have more refugees than they can handle. People are starving and dying of exposure."

Stunned silence filled *RH*. Finally, Ridden spoke up. "I had no idea it was like this." Tears filled his eyes.

Obers walked over to him and placed a hand on his shoulder. "We're in this together, my friend, all of us." Ridden nodded his agreement.

"We cannot prevail against them," Ridden said. His two ministers nodded. "Our only hope…"

"Is Ayers Sky…" Obers said, finishing his sentence.

A few minutes later, Noel parked *RH* in an L5 location about fifty kilometers away from Ayers Sky. His guests examined the vast structure on the monitors, asking questions about one thing or another.

"Reading about it…seeing holos is not the same," Ridden said. "This is astounding." He was all smiles. "And this will hold Australia's total population?"

"And then some," Noel said. "With comfort…and it's completely self-sustaining." He picked up his hyper-Disc, set it up, and activated it. The open portal looked into Marc's office. "Gentlemen, please follow me," Noel said, stepping through the door.

EARTH—NORTH POLE

Noel brought the RH to a hover a half meter above the frozen surface. He had measured the ice thickness at four meters, with a nearby mass at nearly twenty meters, so there was little chance of breaking through the surface. Turning to Joe Ridden, he said, "The five of you, please remain inside *RH* while I step out and set things up."

"I have a request, and I am certain I speak for the four of us," Ridden said as the hatch opened. Noel looked at him. "You're a traveled man, Dr. Goddard, but we aren't. Could we please join you on the ice for a few minutes? We would be ever so grateful."

It hadn't occurred to Noel, but he could think of no reason not to allow it. He handed them each UV-filter glasses. "Put these on. You'll have to wear what you are wearing. Stay close to the hatch, and be ready to load on a moment's notice!" He did not intend to extend the ramp.

Holding the hyper-Disc linked to one endcap of Ayers Sky, Noel hopped to the ice surface, followed by his four guests. The temperature was a crisp -40°C with no wind. The skydome was a clear, powder-blue, filled with sparkling ice crystals. The four Australians stomped their feet as the chill penetrated their soles and slapped their hands together to keep the circulation flowing. Noel turned toward the sun pointing, about nineteen degrees above the horizon. Their glasses darkened, but through them, they could clearly see two distinct halos around the sun, the outer one just touching the horizon. Left and right, above and below, they could make out vertical and horizontal shafts of light that intersected the halos, forming sun-dogs at the intersections. They could have watched all day, but the cold was overwhelming, and people in Ayers Sky were waiting for them.

Noel activated the portal and had Ayers Sky manipulate it so that it was pointing toward the sky, and then he and the others entered the *RH* hatch.

Ridden, Obers, and the other two officials were a bit overwhelmed. None of them had visited the Arctic, let alone the North Pole itself, this was only their second hyper-V trip, and MERT Portals were still a total mystery. Because they were who they were, they took it in stride, but Noel was amused by the incredulity their faces displayed. As he closed the hatch, they got one last glimpse of the sun-dogs, and then they arranged their chairs for a good view of the displays as *RH* rose to twenty kilometers above and five south.

"We're ready down here," Noel told his controller in Ayers Sky. "Bring the portal to one hundred meters."

"Done."

"Okay…expand to thirty meters."

"Done."

"Are you gentlemen ready?" Noel asked his guests.

They nodded, not knowing what to expect.

"Everyone ready up there?"

"Roger, standing by…"

"Open the portal!"

Although the *RH* was twenty-five kilometers away from the portal, the massive downflow of frigid air was clearly visible because of the sparkling ice crystals in the air. Noel flew around the Pole, noting the effect of the airflow. It did not seem to be picking up snow from the surface, but the air movement toward the portal was prodigious.

"It seems to be working well here," Noel told his controller. "What's happening up there?"

"Ice fog everywhere! Noisy as hell—high-pitched scream. Seems to be working, though. Nothing we didn't expect…just a lot more!"

"Everyone ready here?" Noel asked. He took their muted responses for a Yes.

"We're heading for the South Pacific," he told the controller.

"Catch you in a bit."

EARTH—SOUTH PACIFIC

As before, Noel brought the *RH* to a hover, this time about ten meters above the sea surface, and opened the hatch. The waves were rolling slowly from west toward the east, about two meters from trough to peak. The sun had passed its zenith but was still high in the northwestern sky. Filmy, streaked clouds filled the upper atmosphere, and off to the west, Noel spotted a couple of squalls. Humid, salty air filled the *RH* interior.

"Look a bit more familiar than our last stop?" Noel asked his guests to smiles and nods.

Holding the hyper-Disc linked to the other endcap of Ayers Sky, he activated it. The resulting still sealed portal was pointing downward. He shut the hatch and picked up the portal on his primary monitor.

"Ayers Sky, are you ready?"

"Standing by."

"First thing, flip it over—that's it. Now move it up to one hundred meters altitude, and expand it to thirty meters."

Noel moved *RH* up and to the side as he had done at the Pole.

"Everyone ready here?" he asked. Hearing no objections, he ordered, "Open the portal!"

The effect was much less evident over the water. As they watched, a seabird got caught up in the maelstrom and was sucked into the portal. Then another, and another.

"Looks like you are going to have some company up there," Noel told his guests, "if they survive, that is."

Noel asked his Resident to identify the birds, but before the Resident could answer, Obers said, "They're Lesser Frigate Birds."

The Resident added, "Capable of sustained flight of several thousand kilometers."

Noel informed his controller, who remarked, "Not enough atmosphere yet for their survival. I can see 'em, but they got no life. Maybe near the end, when the airspeed is a lot less, and the atmosphere is a lot more."

An unexpected addition to the Ayers Sky biosphere, Noel thought as he told the Resident to take them back to Canberra.

✳

"Thank you for allowing us to participate in this remarkable operation," Ridden said.

"I second that," Obers added, and the other two nodded their agreement.

"You are a remarkable man, Dr. Goddard," Obers said. "In a few short hours, you have managed to convince us that Ayers Sky is our future, and you have managed to unite our interests in making this happen. I think you knew when you set this up that it would be way more than a joy ride. I am certain that I speak for Prime Minister Ridden that we owe you a debt of gratitude that will not soon be repaid."

"More elegantly spoken than I am capable of," Ridden said. His voice took on a note of determination. "Together, we will make this happen!"

EARTH—NEW ZEALAND—NORTH ISLAND

New Zealanders had long taken pride in their nickname. When the Kiwi Loop went into operation with its base socket on the North Island just outside of Wellington, Kiwis everywhere took particular pride in being the smallest national group to have its own Launch Loop. New Wellington Skyport atop the Wellington Tower sported a hotel, but without the capacity and luxuries of Coral Bay Skyport. It was the jumping-off point for Kiwis leaving Earth. During the previous two centuries, Kiwis were employed in many construction tasks in Antarctica and had gained a reputation for being able to take on any construction project anywhere. When Mirs commenced construction, Kiwis formed a significant part of the construction crew. Kiwis played an active role in building Lone Star Mars and even participated at Nachal Rachaf. Kiwis were a part of every construction project throughout the Solar System. One project, however, was exclusively Kiwi—the Ceres terraforming project.

Ceres has about 41% of the surface area of Iapetus. The Kiwis decided to follow the Iapetus model but do only one-half initially. They used the Iapetus plans from the Ectarian library, obtained custody of most of the Robotic Vaporizers from SI, and spent the first year hollowing the core and installing the black hole power generator. Their calculations indicated that if they could vaporize 91 cubic kilometers daily, the interior of Ceres would be ready for finishing touches and occupation in about five years. This was doable if they could interest enough Kiwis to move to Ceres under the most primitive set of living conditions.

To everyone's surprise, Kiwis volunteered by the thousands so that the terraforming project was able to jump-start itself, exceeding its ambitious schedule.

Unlike the Australians, the Kiwis had no illusions about what would happen to them and their island paradise once the Caliphate turned its attention to the South Pacific. This understanding gave the Ceres project great impetus. Kiwis by the thousands had been leaving New Zealand to settle in Mirs, on Mars, or Iapetus. To the Kiwi mind, however, this settlement was temporary, pending completion of the Ceres project. With three million people to move, however, progress was agonizingly slow. At a thousand people per day, they were looking at more than eight years to get everyone away from Earth.

When Marc contacted Lynette Williams, the Kiwi Prime Minister, to set up a meeting between himself, the Australians, and the Kiwis, he received no resistance. He dispatched Dmitri and Orel in *Merkavah* to bring Williams and several of her cabinet members to SI. Before Dmitri departed with the New Zealand delegation, he left a hyper-Disc with the Prime Minister's personal assistant, who put it on Williams' desk.

Marc arranged the schedule so that Dr. Lambin could give the delegation a demonstration of the MERT Portal. Upon conclusion of the presentation, Dmitri led them to the portal between the lab and Marc's office.

"Please follow me, your Excellencies," Dmitri said as he walked through the portal.

IAPETUS—STARCHILD INSTITUTE

Noel met the Kiwis as they entered the office through the portal, giving Lynette Williams, who was just slightly shorter than he, an appreciative smile before settling the Australians and Kiwis in seats arrayed before Marc's desk. "Let's get the questions about how we got here handled first."

Each member of the party had questions. Noel and Marc took a full half-hour to answer as many as possible. Finally, Marc held up both hands.

"I know you still have questions—hell! I still have them—but let's get to the matter at hand, shall we?"

As a chuckle rippled through the group, he continued. "Both your nations have a serious problem. Stated simply, the Caliphate is coming, and it will win. I mean no disrespect to you or your long heritage as sovereign nations. The simple truth is, however, that the Caliphate will eventually subsume both Australia and New Zealand." He paused to let it sink in. "Sure, you can hold out for a while, but they will prevail. Anyone left in your countries will either be forced to convert to Islam and become a second-class citizen, or they will be killed."

Murmurs of protest filled the office. Marc held up his hand again. "This is exactly what has happened everywhere else. Where there was a significant indigenous Muslim population, the Caliphate used them to subjugate the rest. There have been no exceptions. Let me repeat that. There have been absolutely no exceptions at all! Please understand, this is exactly what has happened in every single nation that the Caliphate has overrun. Your only option—and I mean your only option—is to get your people off Earth. I know you realize this, at least in some intellectual sense. That's why you created both Ayers Sky and Ceres. The problem is, of course, that you cannot move people sufficiently fast to get everyone out before the Caliphate comes in. And that's why you are here today." Marc stopped talking to let his visitors absorb what he had said.

Joe Ridden rose to his feet. "We saw how a MERT—that's what you call it, right?—Portal works. It's great for a few persons, but I've got thirty million people to move. How is that possible?" He remained standing.

Williams rose. "I've only got three million, but three or thirty… how can it be possible?"

"Here's how we figured it," Marc said. "Typically, if you have a long queue, you can easily pass one person per second through a door…it's probably closer to a person per half-second, but we tried to stay conservative. For Australia, if you allow twelve twenty-four-hour days, it will take twenty-nine MERT Portals, and for New Zealand, five Portals." He stopped speaking to let the information sink in.

"It seems to me that you need to decide where to put the Portals and when to start the evacuations. You might also consider how you will protect the Portals from near-certain Caliphate attack."

"How do we distribute the Portals?" Williams asked, subconsciously touching her blond bun.

"We will give you five of these," Marc held up a hyper-Disc, "and show you how to activate them. You determine how to distribute them in New Zealand. If it turns out that you made a bad choice, you can easily collapse a portal and move it to another location."

"What about at this end?" one of Ridden's delegation asked.

"We will set up everything at this end. Incoming people will be distributed to the many different accommodations we have here in Iapetus. We will do our best to set up an appropriate infrastructure that will accommodate everyone."

"What about a Caliphate agent slipping through?" Ridden asked.

"That's the real problem as I see it," Marc said. "We're still working on that." Marc stood, walked around his desk, and sat on the edge. "That's really it…all we had to say."

✳

"A moment of your time Prime Minister," Noel said to the Kiwi delegation leader. He gestured to a chair. "How are you currently disposing of the rock vapor generated by your RVs at Ceres?"

"That's not exactly my purview, but my understanding is that we simply spew it into the surrounding space."

"Are you aware that I am the engineer in charge of the Ayers Sky project?"

"I am."

"We need to bring in a vast amount of rocky material from the moon as an outer layer for Ayers Sky. This process is enormously expensive and ridiculously inefficient. We could set up several MERT Portals with the power supplies at our end and the untethered ports at Ceres hooked up to your RVs. By coordinating our activities through an independent MERT Communications Port, we can spew your rock vapor directly onto the external parts of Ayers Sky, resulting in a structure that is far more secure and stable.

"Do you think we could do this?"

"My instinct is to say yes," Williams answered, her blue eyes boring into his, "but let me check with our technical support team."

IAPETUS—STARCHILD INSTITUTE

Marc walked up the ramp into the small craft. "Welcome to *Experimental MERT Craft One—XMERT-One* for short," Dr. Lambin said.

"Isn't this the same craft you demonstrated last time?"

"It is, but this time she is manned, and tradition going back as far as we can measure dictates that she be named before she can fly."

"Not very imaginative, Kris."

"No, but it'll do." Dr. Lambin handed Marc a hyper-Disc and slipped one into his smock breast pocket.

"In case something goes wrong, these may be able to bring us back."

"What do you mean, *may?*"

"Well, we're jumping to Mirs on this first jump. So long as we are in the Solar System, generally, these discs will remain linked, and we can use them to get back. So…if we don't end up at Mirs, but we are still in the Solar System, then these get us home."

"And if not?" Marc felt a bit of concern.

"*XMERT-One* has a built-in safety device. The diameter of the Solar System is approximately twenty-four hundred astronomical units. This defines a rather lumpy sphere surrounding the Solar System. Everywhere on the surface of this sphere, the inward pull of Solar System gravity exactly balances the outward pull of everything else in the universe. At every picosecond jump, the Resident measures these forces. Whenever the universe pull exceeds the Solar System pull, the Resident interrupts the jumps. So, the farthest we can stray is twelve hundred astronomical units. If this happens, we can give the Resident appropriate instructions and jump back to whatever destination we wish."

"What if the same problem happens again?"

"There is that, but we believe it won't happen in the first place. We've run the test twenty times on automatic without a hitch." Dr. Lambin grinned at Marc. "You nervous about going?"

"Not really—just askin'."

"Ready to do it?" Dr. Lambin asked.

"Let's do it!"

They withdrew the ramp, shut the hatch, and took seats at the console. "Activate MERT system," Dr. Lambin ordered.

"MERT system ready. State destination," the Resident said.

"Mirs holding bay," Dr. Lambin said.

"We have arrived," the Resident announced.

"Wow! Already?"

"The trip took six-point-seven hundredths of a second. That's because Earth and Saturn are on opposite sides of the Sun right now. Otherwise, it would have taken six-point-one hundredths of a second."

"I guess you can say that I am impressed."

"The interesting thing," Dr. Lambin said, "is that stepping through a MERT Portal would have been instantaneous, and thus faster—if you happen to have an untethered portal where you wish to go."

EARTH—SAUDI ARABIAN DESERT

General Suleiman bowed deeply. "China is consolidated, Sahib," he said. "This includes Mongolia, Nepal, the Vietnamese holdouts, and the Koreas. Virtually all non-Muslims have perished, and the few who remain are only too happy to convert."

"What remains, my General?"

"Japan, several South Pacific Island nations, Hawaii, and South and Central America."

"Where next?" Saeed focused his attention on General Suleiman.

"South America, Sahib. We strike simultaneously at Rio de Janeiro, Brasilia, and Buenos Aires with prepositioned nuclear bombs and hit Panama with a concentration of warriors. They have no satellite command and control, and this will take out their military leadership. Then we sweep north and west from Buenos Aires, south, and west from Rio, just like in the United States, and south from Panama. We will avoid jungle areas and high mountains, sweeping down both sides of the Andes. I do not expect much real resistance. We will control everything that matters and will conduct conversions as we did in Europe."

"How long do you think this campaign will take?" Saeed asked.

"In six months, we will have consolidated all of South and Central America and will be knocking on the southern door of the Lone Star Conservancy."

"When will we commence the South American Jihad?"

"On your word, Sahib."

"I give it!"

IAPETUS—FEDERATION HEADQUARTERS

Rod Zakes' voice filled the large room in the Federation government complex. "Okay, everybody…please come to order, please come to order!"

Feet shuffled, and chairs scraped as everyone found a seat. Rod had assembled representatives from Lone Star Conservancy, Columbia Freehold, Australia, New Zealand, Mirs, the Moon, Lone Star Mars, New Israel, Delphi, and his four immigration directors. The four Earthside and two Mars delegations included their Heads of State. Altogether, thirty-six people found their seats.

As the room quieted, Rod began, "I want to make sure each of you understands the enormity of what we are trying to accomplish here. You each have an outline of this presentation on your Links, but I want everyone to work with me on this.

"You all have a working understanding of the MERT Portal. In brief overview, each portal has a tethered end where the power supply and controllers are located and an untethered end linked to a hyper-Disc. The farther away the untethered end can be, and the physical size of the portal, depend on the power supplied at the tethered end. We have projected portals more than eleven astronomical units and expect no difficulties as far out as thirty AUs—that's the orbit of Neptune. So, distance doesn't seem to be a problem right now.

"What we want to do is evacuate everyone who wishes from Lone Star, Columbia, Australia, and New Zealand to somewhere off Earth. So, the problem is (1) how do we move them from Earth? (2) Where do we send them? And (3) what do we do with them when they arrive?

"Lone Star Conservancy has around sixty-nine million people. Columbia Freehold has thirty-eight-and-a-half, Australia has thirty, and New Zealand has five. No matter how you slice it, that's a lot of people! If you people can get things organized at your respective ends, we think we can move one person per second through each portal. If we allow ourselves twelve days for the entire exodus, we will need sixty-seven portals for Lone Star, thirty-seven for Columbia, twenty-nine for Australia, and five for New Zealand.

"We can distribute the hyper-Discs to whatever locations you decide will work best, but you people will have to coordinate where people go, how they assemble, how they eat and drink, how you handle human waste and garbage, and even what to do with their pets. And another thing…the Caliphate will most certainly learn of our plans. It will do everything possible to thwart them. You Kiwis will be least bothered by this, and you Australians will have a pretty easy go of it as well. I fear, however, that Lone Star and Columbia will be the focus of the most ferocious assaults Caliphate troops can muster. And be alert for the suicide warrior, and beyond that, for the surreptitiously embedded warrior who will try to cause his mischief at the other end.

"So…there is the outline of how we move people from Earth. The next question is, *Where do we send them?*

"We are still open on this one. Iapetus was built for, and can accommodate, several billions of humans. For obvious reasons, much of the interior has not been activated, but we can activate as much as needed. Lone Star Mars has set up accommodations for a whole lot of people, and I will leave it to the Lone Star delegation to determine how many of the sixty-seven portals will be installed on Mars.

"Ceres is not yet ready for a massive influx of people. So…unless there is a serious objection, Kiwis will be transported to Iapetus, and I will leave it up to your delegation working with my people to work out the details.

"Columbia Freehold will come to Iapetus as well. You can work out the details of who goes where. For the rest of you, please give serious thought to how many evacuees you can reasonably accommodate—and how many you really want, if any, for that matter. We can quickly set up several portals to Mirs, New Israel, the Moon, and even Daphne, if there is sufficient interest. That's why you are all here.

"You might also consider giving people an option to come here and then immediately depart for another location—like Daphne. I don't think this would cause too much disruption. And this segues right into the third question, *What do we do with them when they arrive?*

"No matter how you slice it, the arrival locations will be a complete and total zoo. Remember that we will be trying to direct and relocate one hundred forty-two million people. This is unprecedented in human history. When the Ectarians left Ectaris for Iapetus, it was a many-year, orderly process. We will be trying to move our people in just twelve days—one person per second, every minute of every hour of every day for twelve days. It's a tiny fraction of what the Ectarians did, but over a sliver of time.

"Get yourselves organized…my people will coordinate this. Then work together to find the best, most workable solutions to everything we know we will encounter, everything we think we will encounter, and everything we might possibly encounter. Each delegation has an established MERT Portal to your homeworld or country. You can use the portals freely and without worry, so you can coordinate things at both ends of your particular piece of the problem.

"My door is open, but I would appreciate one delegation member be selected to deal directly with me should the occasion arise. I will be following the big picture from my Federation office, and may, from time to time, insert my own thoughts. Other than that, however, it is up to you folks. It is a herculean task, but I know you are up to it."

EARTH—JAPAN

The Prime Minister of Japan sat at a bare desk in his minimally furnished personal office atop the Shushō Kantei. Arrayed before him stood thirteen of his most senior cabinet ministers and five of his closest personal advisors. The men were dressed in expensive business suits, and the four women wore clothing suitable for senior female executives in Japan. The PM looked beyond the assembled ministers through the glass wall behind them. The sky was appropriately gray and ominous.

"Thank you for your reports," the PM said at last. "Your staffs have conducted a most thorough research. I have read each report, and I find it interesting that you have produced no real conflicts in your understanding of Japan's role in what is happening in the world. My staff has summarized your efforts and produced a short statement that I will deliver to the Emperor tomorrow morning, a statement that he will deliver to the nation at noon, the day after." He shuffled some papers on his otherwise empty desk.

"Not being able to use the global Link system has seriously limited our ability to conduct business as usual." He picked up one sheet. "I will read the Emperor's statement." He sat back, holding the sheet in front of him, and adjusted his glasses.

"In the lead-up to World War Two, Japanese soldiers committed many atrocities in China against indigenous Chinese Muslims. Although in the ensuing years following the war, Japan officially apologized for these actions, nevertheless, they remain a terrible blot on Japan's illustrious history. We, the Japanese people of today, had nothing to do with these terrible atrocities, and the modern world has not held them against us or our nation. Unfortunately, Caliph Saeed Esmail, the Caliphate Prophet, disagrees. In his world perspective, Japan is guilty of an unforgivable act that must be avenged with blood—Japanese blood—our blood.

"The Caliphate is preparing to attack Japan. It has at its disposal the combined navies of most of the rest of the world. This colossal armada is making its way toward our islands. We can expect these thousands of ships to have surrounded us entirely by the end of next week. They do not intend to bombard us. Our intel informs us they plan to come ashore by the millions, with instructions to behead every man, woman, and child in Japan.

"Japan cannot allow this to happen, but we cannot stop it—we can only delay it for a short period. We are faced with only one honorable solution—Seppuku, an honorable death! I, your Emperor, therefore command each of you, every Japanese, to commit Seppuku if you are able, and otherwise to drink the potion that will be delivered to you shortly. The potion will put you to sleep gently, a sleep from which you will not waken.

"One week from today, at twelve noon, is when we all will forever take vengeance away from the Caliph. I will be the first to commit Seppuku; the Prime Minister will stand as kaishakunin. This will be broadcast by holovision throughout the country. Thereafter, all of you will follow me to Yomi, forever safely out of the hands of the Caliph and his minions.

"It is your sacred duty to carry out this, my final command!"

✳

General Ismail Suleiman, commander of worldwide Caliphate forces, had decided to come ashore in Japan like General McArthur when he returned to the Philippines during World War II. That morning, he arrived on the deck of his fleet flagship, aircraft carrier *ISS Saeed Esmail*, the former *USS Marc Bowles*. The Pakistani Admiral who met him on the flight deck apologized for the dismal weather.

"A stationary weather system has dominated Japan for nearly nine days," the admiral told him. "The wind and rain have hampered our reconnaissance overflights. Oddly, the Japanese air force has not challenged us in the air, and the coastal batteries have been silent.

On your orders, General, we have not bombarded the beaches, but we have not spotted massed troops anywhere along the coastline. None at all.

"The troops are ready to land on a moment's notice. When you give the word, fifteen minutes later, troops will hit the beaches along the entire coastline."

"Send up air cover, Admiral, and then send them ashore!"

"Aye, Sir!"

Suleiman watched the nearby amphibious troop carriers through image-enhancing binoculars. As his warriors hit the beaches near him, there was no opposing gunfire. He scanned the nearest beach. He could see no Japanese soldiers. "Is my launch ready?" he asked the Admiral.

"Yes, Sir. This way."

Fifteen minutes later, General Ismail Suleiman stepped ashore, followed closely by his immediate staff. As he strode purposefully toward a line of green a hundred meters from the water, the colonel in charge of this beachhead hurried up to him, saluted smartly, and said, "They're all dead, General…all dead…" His voice trailed off.

Suleiman and his entourage reached the street where the colonel gestured to the first house on his right. "Look inside, Sir!"

Suleiman, who at one time or another in his military career had seen everything, was shocked beyond words. A man lay on the floor, his intestines spewed out around him. Nearby was a woman, also dead, a small plastic bottle nearby, and in a separate bedroom, two small children lay dead in their beds, as if sleeping. On the floor, he saw another empty plastic bottle.

"It's the same in every house we have entered," the colonel told him. "Where there were two adult males, the one with the spilled intestines had a half-severed head, and the rest died, apparently from whatever they drank. Some houses had pets. They were dead as well."

"Clear this house and set up communications here," the general ordered. Within minutes he started receiving reports from all around Japan. Everywhere, the people had taken their own lives. He called for a helicopter and ordered it to fly to Tokyo.

The city below was strangely still. The general could see an occasional stray dog wandering aimlessly. The heavy sky above forecast what he knew he would find. The helicopter landed in the

Emperor's private patio. General Suleiman exited the helicopter, saying, "Follow me!"

Standing in the Emperor of Japan's private chambers, Suleiman contacted Saeed. "Look at this," he said to Saeed, directing holocams toward the carnage.

"And that is…" Saeed said, looking at the disemboweled body of the Japanese Emperor with partially severed head, the dead Prime Minister, and two dead holocam operators, a dead dog, and a dead cat.

"The Emperor, Sahib. It appears his suicide was broadcast by holovision around Japan. And all his subjects followed suit—all of them, including pets of all kinds. No one is left alive, Sahib, no one."

IAPETUS—STARCHILD INSTITUTE

Rod stood before his assembled refugee coordinators. "Let's make sure we are operating from the same page," he said. "I've brought in General Bob York, Commander of Camp Pendleton in California, on Sam Houston's recommendation to head up the Federation Immigration Department. Bob, please stand and be recognized."

General York, resplendent in Army Dress Uniform, stood to polite applause.

"For those of you who don't know, Bob was responsible for moving the Mexican invaders out of Southern California and Arizona. I think he's up to the task." Polite applause again. "Bob and I have assigned specific individuals to head up each of the major groupings—Lone Star, Columbia, Australia, and New Zealand. These individuals will coordinate with the heads of government for each area. The government heads will \assign their own coordinators and will be responsible for what happens Earthside. Bob and his people will set up appropriate procedures to move people quickly through the portals and get them to their intermediate destinations within Iapetus and then to their final destinations.

"Keep in mind that any slowdown through the portals can spell disaster for many evacuees as the Caliphate forces move in. Each area has the potential for surreptitious Caliphate infiltration by single individuals or small groups. It is absolutely imperative that each area develop appropriate procedures for filtering out these terrorists. An explosive shell penetrating a portal could also spell disaster. We will orient each portal to minimize this possibility, but the person in charge at each portal will have to coordinate with the Iapetus controller of that portal to change the orientation if necessary.

"I'm going to turn things over to Bob. Each of you has received a preliminary operational chart. Working with Bob initially, and then with directors further down the chain, continually correct the master chart so I can have a complete picture. Thank you for your attention."

✳

"I know that you know that I'm a general. You probably are saying to yourselves, *Oh no! Now, on top of everything else, I've got to deal with some military bullshit!*" Chuckles throughout the room. "I'm here to tell you I'm not that kind of general. Once we start, we will have just twelve days to complete the entire evacuation. We won't have time for bullshit! Each of you do the best job you can. Make any decisions you can as far down the chain as possible. If you make a mistake, fess up to it and correct it. You will NOT be penalized. This is a critical point for each of you in supervisory positions. Do not punish mistakes. Help the person who makes a mistake correct it quickly. Then move on. If you make a mistake, try not to repeat it. If you need a procedural change, suggest it and put it into the chart, or just put it in the chart.

"We're going to keep things as simple as possible, with the fewest possible supervisors. You are going to have problems on both sides of the portals. Handle them! If you cannot, if you need more than words—and this will happen from time to time—if you are Earthside, contact the nearest military authority. If you are on Iapetus, contact Security. Dmitri Gagarin has established people and procedures on Iapetus to get things under control quickly. Remember, we're saving lives—one hundred forty-two and a half-million of them!"

York then split the group into the four areas, gave them their marching instructions, and let them loose with the admonition, "You guys need to get this thing up and running ASAP! The Prophet is knocking at the door…"

EARTH—SAUDI ARABIAN DESERT

General Suleiman bowed low. "You rule most of the World, Sahib," he said reverently. "Never in history…"

"But not all of it," Saeed said. "What do we still not control?"

Suleiman straightened, remarking to himself again that this man of small stature and little formal education seemed to cut to the chase every time it mattered.

"The Lone Star Conservancy and Columbia Freehold in North America, Denmark, Norway, Sweden, and Finland, in Europe, Australia, New Zealand, and most of the Pacific islands.

"We are moving on Scandinavia as we speak. We are encountering little resistance. The Danes have been meeting us, asking to be converted. The Norwegians have, for the most part, faded into their impenetrable mountains. We will probably experience Norwegian raids from time to time, but we will put them down, and eventually, it will cease. The Swedes and the Finns are proving somewhat more difficult, but they are so outnumbered that we are certain to win. The Pacific islands are unimportant, except for the Kingdom of Hawaii. Although you did say to let the local Island Muslims handle the take-over, I think it better that we take that island group as soon as Scandinavia is consolidated. The rest we will take as the need dictates. Before the month is out, we will be pushing hard against Lone Star and Columbia and establishing a front in Australia. After Australia, we'll tackle New Zealand."

"Tell me more about Lone Star and Columbia," Saeed said.

"Lone Star will be our biggest challenge. It has nuclear weapons but will be reluctant to use them. We have no such qualms. Millions of refugees are streaming into Lone Star and Columbia. This is a big problem for them. They will have to feed and house them while trying to hold us off."

"What about developments off-Earth?" Saeed asked.

"The Federation has developed a method of instant transportation from one point to another. They call it a MERT Portal, and I'm told it is like walking through a door…"

"And you know this how, my General?"

"We have a man deeply embedded in the Starchild Institute research staff. He is of Pakistani extraction and blends in well. Nobody suspects him, and he keeps me informed. In time, he will supply us with what we need to build one for ourselves."

IAPETUS—STARCHILD INSTITUTE

Marc Bowles stood as the general entered his SI office. "General York, it's good to meet you in person," he said.

"Please call me Bob. Everyone else does."

"My people tell me you have done a remarkable job organizing the evacuation effort."

"I'll agree that I am good at organizing and getting things done, but an organization without willing people who actually accomplish the work is entirely useless. We are where we are precisely because of a group of very dedicated, highly capable people." York sat down facing Marc's desk, his gaze moving over the holographs within his view. "I am well aware of your background and what you did as President, so you fully understand what I mean."

"Of course I do, Bob, but without you…" Marc smiled warmly, realizing that a close friendship was in the making. "You're here to ensure delivery of two hundred MERT Portals. We've already set up portals to each of your ingress points around Iapetus. I understand that each of your ingress points has a portal to one of the four areas. How are you handling it from there?"

"Actually, we've split the ingress points by demographic population numbers in each area. For example, we're bringing in sixty-nine million people from Lone Star, thirty each from Texas and Southern California, and the other nine from Arizona and New Mexico. The thing is, we expect a lot more because of the influx of refugees from all over. Lone Star and Columbia will start evacuating people as soon as possible—well before the schedule.

"Columbia has thirty-eight-and-a-half—they'll have more as well, not like Lone Star, but a lot of folks are crowding across all the borders. People don't want any part of that Caliphate hell.

"Australia and New Zealand don't have the refugee problem, but Australia is a large area with thirty million people spread all over.

That's twenty-nine portals we need to space appropriately. I've got several guys working on it. I'll have an answer later today. New Zealand has two main islands. We'll distribute five portals appropriately.

"And this brings up an interesting problem. We will be dealing with a dynamic situation from the get-go. I have people assigned to monitor the crowd backups at each Earthside portal. On their own initiative, any one of these can collapse a portal, carry it back to the Iapetus ingress point, and back through to a portal that has greater pressure. It will take just a few minutes to do this and is much easier than transporting a few thousand people from Austin to Dallas, for example."

"That makes a lot of sense, and the automatic loggers will give us the current configuration at any time, so we know where we are. I like it." Marc said.

"More than that, really. We're moving a lot of people, and when we're done, a lot of people will want to find a lot of other people. Since most everyone has a personal Link, we've set up each portal into Iapetus with an automatic registration device that IDs and codes each incoming Link. This information feeds a monstrous database controlled by the Iapetus Resident—don't ask me how the Resident accomplishes it. Anyone entering without a personal Link is given a small ID disc to keep with them that accomplishes the same thing. We're going to have some glitches, but in principle, we know who and where every evacuee is within Iapetus."

Marc's face took on a thoughtful look. "What about Ayers Sky and Ceres?"

"This is where it really gets interesting," York said. "Ayers Sky has an atmosphere now, along with a full complement of Masked Boobies, Lesser Frigate Birds, and even several Albatrosses. They're getting pretty hungry, and Noel has set up a program to stock some of the larger lakes with fish.

"Joe Ridden, Australia's PM, has set up a program to train a hundred thousand construction workers on a fast-track. They're all volunteers. They will be building the Ayers Sky infrastructure commencing right now. He's got another two thousand biologists being specially trained in hydroponic and micro-g farming who will get the food production modules up and running. The bulk of the Aussies, however, will have to sojourn at Iapetus for a while yet.

"Ceres is another thing altogether. First, it's a long-term construction project. Remember that the Ectarians took three hundred years to build Iapetus. It will take the Kiwis another five years at least for even part of Ceres to be habitable. That doesn't mean they aren't working hard, however. We've already put a portal out there, and we are rotating crews weekly to keep the project moving rapidly."

"I know you've given security a lot of thought," Marc said. "Can you summarize it for me?"

"As far away from the portals as we can do it, we are dividing people into four categories. Group One consists of people with positive identification. Group Two consists of people positively identified by Group One people. Group Three consists of people positively identified by Group Two people. Group Four is everybody else. Evacuation is prioritized by group number. As I mentioned, we are getting a jump on the Group One people. By the time we get to Group Four people, we really will have to keep an eye on things because the Caliphate will undoubtedly know what we are doing by then.

"Our biggest fear is the suicide bomber. We have explosive sensors at each portal, but a determined guy could rush a portal and explode himself on either side or in the portal itself. Each way, a lot of people die." York sighed. "We will do our best, but it's going to happen, and we need to be prepared for it."

"Thanks," Marc said, "now let me fill you in on some other activities. The Titan colony established by Mirs is flourishing. It's not self-sufficient yet, and probably won't be for a long time. Their goal is to liberate sufficient oxygen from Titan's underground water sources to make the surface livable without protection. SI and the Ganymede Consortium are working together to make Ganymede habitable. Like Titan, it's long-term. One of our divisions is working to exploit the water resources of Enceladus. Now that we've figured out how to move atmosphere from one place to another, we are gearing up to do the same with water. Think about what that could mean. The Europa Group just recently placed a human habitat on the ocean floor of Europa. It's in the early stages right now, but it has an exciting potential. All the more so, now that we have portal technology," Marc said. "It changes everything, doesn't it?"

"One needs several lifetimes to experience it all," York said.

"We're working on that," Marc said.

York raised his eyes.

"For real…"

Marc stood up. "Let's get these people off Earth so they can share this future with the rest of us."

CHAPTER NINETEEN

EARTH—SAUDI ARABIAN DESERT

As Saeed and General Suleiman sipped cups of sweet mint tea, Saeed asked, "How goes the North American Jihad?"

"We are putting pressure on both Lone Star and Columbia by increasing the refugee flow. My resources tell me that Lone Star is reaching capacity to feed everyone. Because of the mountain barriers into Columbia, their refugee flow is lower, so they still have some room." Suleiman sat quietly for a few minutes contemplating how to bring the next bit of information to his Prophet.

"We mustn't let them get too established," Saeed said. "Remember, I've watched these people work in close quarters with them. They can produce effective solutions to problems with remarkable speed. They value human life—I live because of that—and they will go to great lengths to keep the refugees alive."

"You are correct, Sahib. We cannot wait for very much longer." He paused. "I do have something else to share with you. My contact at the Starchild Institute has sent us a batch of files that contain the information we need to construct our own MERT Portal." He sighed. "We still have a major hurdle to cross, however. To build a portal, we need to have a supply of the metal used to skin the hyper-V craft, and we will need to build or obtain a black hole power source like what drives the hyper-V craft. Once we have solved those riddles, we will be able to build a MERT Portal."

"Allah will meet our needs when his time is ripe." Saeed smiled with quiet certainty.

"Our Pakistani and Korean labs are working on the joint problems. The exotic skin material has first priority. We can modify *Rasul Allah* so that it has the necessary exotic metal walls and can use its power source to power the MERT Portal. This will give us only one portal, but since the base will be inside *Rasul Allah*, we can have a great deal of flexibility. Several small asteroids have installed black hole power sources. Perhaps when the time comes, we can take over one of these, which will give us an unlimited power source for further expansion."

"Dream big, General Suleiman, but keep your focus on the here and now." Saeed closed his eyes and seemed to go into a trance. With eyes still closed, he said, "Our Earthly Jihad is not yet complete. Allah compels us to fulfill our promise of worldwide Islam. We must not fail him."

EARTH—ABILENE, TEXAS

Command Sergeant Major Bransom boomed over the loudspeaker system, "Listen up, People! We got a job to do, and it ain't gonna be easy. You all know what's goin' on. We gonna help all them people," he spread his arms wide, encompassing several hundred thousand people around their open field just to the northeast of Abilene, "get the hell out of here. We gonna make sure we know who each person is, and we gonna push them through these portals just as fast as we can. One a second, if we can do it."

Lt. Col. Steve Brady watched Bo exhort his troops to action. Newly minted 2nd Lt. Jerri Smyth stood at his side, butter bars glistening on her collar tips.

"Did you ever imagine, Jer?"

"I'm just glad we can be here..."

"*We*, all of us, or *we*, you and me?" Brady asked with a chuckle.

"You figure it out, Sir!"

Bransom continued, "We got ragheads to the north and east. There's five thousand Lone Star soldiers out there movin' people toward us and fending off the bad guys. We got maybe ten, twelve days movin' people, then we tangle with the bad guys ourselves. You done it before, so you know what you're up against. But for now, let's get people moving."

The four platoons split up, one to each portal, half the squad members working to funnel people toward the rope-designated lanes, the other half pulling back to get some rest for the next four-hour shift that would arrive much faster than it had any right to. Children screamed, dogs barked, and people were scared. Brady had a clear view of Sergeant Norbert Jacobsen, the tall, lanky Norwegian who had replaced Jer as Platoon 3 leader. He quickly got his platoon organized, picked up a small, screaming girl, and handed her to her father, speaking quietly to him. Then he picked up a little dog and found its owner. Brady heard him say, "Hold onto him. Don't let him get away!"

The day was warm, with a light overcast. A steady breeze from the east kept things cool as the vast crowd queued up. A siren sounded, signaling the opening of the portals, and each platoon began urging its charges to a slow trot. "Go…go…go…go!" echoed across the field as people loaded with backpacks, suitcases, even garbage bags, trotted down the roped lanes and through the portals to safety—240 every minute, 14,400 every hour.

"You got the first watch, Bo," Brady ordered. "We'll rest up, and I'll relieve you, and Jer will relieve me. Call me immediately if something comes up."

✳

TThe evacuation went smoothly for the first three days. Everybody in line was Group One, and with very few exceptions, they were orderly and kept up the pace, even loaded down as they were. The weather held, but the wind died, making the heat oppressive. Brady figured by the end of day three, they had evacuated well over a million people. He and Jer were sharing a small breakfast when he received an emergency call from Bransom.

"You gotta get over here right away, Boss!"

Brady and Smyth left their breakfast and hurried down the makeshift walkway to the line of portals. A red pickup was pushing its way through the crowd. Five rough-hewn men in the pickup bed held rifles high, firing them into the air. A military Humvee followed their path through the crowd, red and blue lights flashing, siren screaming. Brady grabbed a mike.

"Stop now!" he ordered, loudspeakers set to their highest volume. He drew his firearm and aimed it at the pickup driver. The vehicle stopped.

"Positions!" Bransom ordered. Charlie Company unslung weapons and brought them into firing position.

One of the men in the truck bed pointed his rifle at Brady. With one quick movement, Brady brought his pistol to bear on the man and shot him twice through the torso. Another pointed his rifle but was cut down by Jacobsen. The others dropped their firearms, and the driver exited the vehicle.

"What's this all about?" Brady asked the driver.

"We ain't gonna wait." The driver slurred his words. "We got the same right as everyone else, and we're armed."

"You will, and you don't," Brady snapped.

The Humvee approached, and a middle-aged warrant officer got out, accompanied by two non-coms. "I'll take these bastards," he said, handcuffing them and shoving them unceremoniously into the Humvee. "We don't need this kind of crap." He saluted Brady and turned and left with his prisoners in the Humvee. One of the non-coms drove off in the pickup.

"What do you make of that?" Smyth asked.

"Some good old boys with too much beer in their bellies," Brady said. "We've been lucky thus far. We've had all Group One, and they have been orderly and worked well with us."

"Those boys on the outskirts are doing a good job," Smyth said. "I'm glad we pulled this detail instead of that one."

"Thanks for gettin' here so fast, Colonel," Bransom said. "I just wasn't sure about using deadly force." He grinned. "Glad it was you 'n not me."

"Give Nor an attaboy, Bo," Brady said, "and have the ongoing shift report to me first."

Thirty men jostled for position around Brady and Smyth as Brady got ready to brief them. First, he summarized the event that led up to the shootings. Then he continued, "We've had it better than I had hoped up till now, but that's going to change dramatically in the next couple of days. Stay focused on the task: pushing people through the portals as fast as they can move. We're one of the fast-track portal groups. A couple of groups are reserved for those with health problems or who are otherwise unable to move through at our pace. We're going to be pushing Group Two people through soon. I don't think there will be much difference since they will have been vetted by the guys out there.

"I just found out that Caliphate troops have crossed the border in several places; this will become a significant problem. We don't want them killing our people, and we definitely don't want them moving through our portals. Keep a sharp focus, and remember what you are doing. These people are scared to death. They've been run out of their homes, have lost everything they own, and are fleeing for their lives through a door that seems more magic than not, to a place they know absolutely nothing about.

"You guys are their only link to reality. Give it your best. That could be your mom or dad, your kid sister or brother sprinting through the portal."

As Brady spoke, three jet fighters made a low pass and headed northeast, followed by a squadron of battle-support helicopters. As he watched them fade into the distance, his Link delivered an urgent message. It was from his colonel. "Your portal group is being truncated. I'm sending you four choppers. As soon as each of your lanes has cleared, collapse the portals and take each hyper-Disc to one of the choppers. We're moving your company just behind the northeastern front line at Lake Diversion. We got a whole bunch of civilians trapped along the north shore of the lake. They're going to be slaughtered unless we can evacuate them. Charlie Company has the nearest portals, and your guys have already proved they have the balls to get these people out. I'll keep you informed on the fly, but don't wait to hear from me to do what you think necessary! One more thing, Steve…these civilians are not vetted. We don't know who they are or where they came from. The receiving guys on Iapetus know about this and are taking necessary precautions. Your job is to get as many as possible through the portals before the Caliphate shuts us down. Good luck!"

EARTH—LAKE DIVERSION, TEXAS

In 1849, Dan Wagoneer established what became one of the largest ranch spreads in the United States—comprising over 250,000 ha in northern Texas. In 1924, W.T. Wagoneer dammed the Wichita River 50 km southeast of Wichita Falls, where it ran through the W.T. Wagoneer Estate, forming Lake Diversion, about 10 km long with a surface area of nearly 1,500 ha and 50 km of virgin shoreline. Over the years, the Estate leased the lakefront property to about 1,500 people who built modest homes and lived on these leased properties. In 2016, the Wagoneer heirs sold the Estate to a Montana billionaire, who decided to hold Lake Diversion as an untouched nature preserve, and summarily terminated the leases and evicted all the people who had lived there for four generations. The modest houses and shacks remained where they were built, to be overtaken by the verdant regional vegetation. Over the years, the 50 km Lake Diversion shoreline became a nearly impenetrable tangle of brush and trees, brambles and vines.

Fast forward to modern times, a Balkanized United States with Caliphate warriors storming across America's heartland, driving tens of millions of terrified refugees ahead of their swinging scimitars. The land was relatively smooth, and modern American vehicles had proved remarkably able to handle themselves off-road. Caliphate commanders, frustrated by the mobility of the refugees they were ruthlessly driving southwesterly, needed a way to corral them into a natural funnel where their warriors could finally clean up, finally finish their holy duty—convert or slaughter the infidels. The Wichita River and Lake Diversion formed one such funnel. Caliphate troops, 200,000 strong, dropped rapidly south to the east and west of the lake in a pincer that forced the terrified refugees into the wild vegetation spreading several kilometers northward from the lake, trapping them against the lake's wild northern shore.

※

Within minutes after collapsing the Abilene portals, Lt. Col. Steve Brady and Charlie Company were speeding northward in five attack-modified troop helicopters at 300 kph. Brady addressed Bransom and Smyth in the command unit. "I know you tried to get each platoon in its own chopper, but it looks like we got a bit mixed up in the hurried departure."

"You got that right," Bransom quipped.

"How many hyper-Discs did we get, Bo?"

"We got twenty in each chopper and ten here in ours. They're all linked to a special staging area on Iapetus. We can literally toss people through the portals without hurting them. Also, each man has a personal hyper-Disc set up so that all he has to do is hit the rim, and it will open, snatch him to Medical Staging, and close behind him. If he's incapacitated, the disc will sense this and snatch him to Medical Staging without him doing anything."

Smyth called up the platoon leaders on their Links, coordinated by the ComCon aircraft several kilometers overhead. "Okay, everybody, here's a terrain chart of the area north of Lake Diversion. Take a few moments to let everyone get familiar with the general outline…Colonel…"

"This operation is a variation of the classic snatch and grab. Command says there are a million people out there being pressed into that mess. Those jets and combat choppers you saw a while back are bringing as much grief as possible to the Caliphate troops chasing these people, and they are opening pathways for the refugees to get through the thickets. ComCon topside will vector me, and I will give each chopper very short-time coordinates. The choppers will drop you off ten at a time. Four of you will set up an immediate safety perimeter. Caliphate warriors are chasing these people down. The four safety guys keep the path open and gun down any bad guys. The other six working in pairs will grab anyone you see and move them through the portal—that's anyone, man, woman, child…if a woman is holding an infant, move them both through. Don't explain anything, just move as many as possible through the portals. So long as you have people, keep the portals open, and move them through. If you no longer need all your portals, collapse the ones you don't need, and toss them through another portal. The staging guys will handle them and get them back to us. Lt. Smyth will handle the coordination. If you need more portals at any location, shout through any portal how many discs you need. They've got stacks of them standing by and will toss you what you need. Once everyone at your point is evacuated, let Lt. Smyth know so we can move you to the next staging area." Brady paused. "Any questions?"

"Guys, it doesn't get crazier than this. This plan is a work in progress. Don't hesitate to do what is necessary. If you take a hit, if you are at all functional, use your personal disc. We're going to be all over this like white on snow. Those bastards won't know what hit them."

"Steve," Smyth said quietly, "we're ten minutes out!"

✳

Sergeant Norbert Jacobsen dropped his first squad near the shoreline of a square-shaped peninsula a kilometer west of the northeastern corner of the lake. The entire 500-meter width of the land was covered with a mass of people who had trampled any existing vegetation into the mud. Jacobsen estimated the crowd at about 200,000. A kilometer to the north, 100,000 Caliphate warriors charged southward. A high-speed attack helicopter blazed past Jacobsen, hitting the charging line of fighters with a volley of anti-personnel missiles. An entire mass of charging warriors dropped—the wave stopped forward movement.

"Open portals and start moving people!" First Squad Leader shouted as he grabbed a young boy and pushed him through the portal next to him.

Up above, Jacobsen dropped his remaining two squads along the peninsula shore. "Perimeter teams…get your asses out there," he ordered through each trooper's Link into their headsets. "The attack chopper stopped them…you guys set up behind the crowd, and keep 'em stopped!"

Another volley of anti-personnel missiles swept overhead, slamming into the dazed Caliphate fighters before they had time to recover from the first blow. The twelve Third Platoon perimeter troops fanned out behind the crowd, spewing withering fire toward the oncoming Caliphate swarm. Eighteen troops manning the portals moved people through as fast as physically possible. As they did this, people near the ports got the idea, concluded that these strange troops were helping them escape, and started running through the portals without assistance. Third Platoon troops quickly realized they didn't have to push anyone. People were running through the portals as fast as they could without help. Within minutes, however, the crowd completely overwhelmed the portals.

Jacobsen sounded a shrieking, piercing sound that momentarily stopped everyone. Then he broadcast over his loudspeakers, "This is Sergeant Jacobsen, Lone Star Conservancy Army. We're here to help, but you got to work with us. Those that can help form up queues to get people through quicker. Don't worry about the other side. Someone there will take care of you. Stay orderly…NOW MOVE IT!"

Two jets swooped low over the Caliphate fighters, spewing a broad swath of napalm. Caliphate warriors died by the thousands, and yet others continued coming. Third Platoon perimeter fell back as the crowd diminished and the fighters drew closer.

"We're running low on ammo," the corporal in charge of the perimeter said to Jacobsen through the Link circuit.

"Okay…conserve your remaining ammo. Drop back to the crowd edge. Keep moving with them. Aim your shots, men, aim your shots!"

Up above, Brady watched the progress on his enlarged holo-image. Jacobsen had Third Platoon under control, but the Caliphate warriors were getting close. The other three platoons did not face such an enemy concentration. "Bransom, reinforce Third Platoon with First Platoon...ASAP!"

Brady turned to Smyth. "Open up portals between each chopper and Medical Staging." Then he opened the general circuit. "This is Brady…don't wait on your chopper for evac. Use your personal disc. Medical Staging will get you back to your bird."

✳

"Save me…oh God, save me!" the terrified woman whimpered, clutching an infant in a papoose to her bosom while gripping the hand of a four-year-old boy. Gunfire shattered the air behind her, strangers pressed in from all sides, and her husband had disappeared. A chanted shout, "*Allahu Akbar! Allahu Akbar!*" rose above the sounds of gunfire and screams of people. She moved forward, pushed by the throng, unable to set her own direction. Jet fighters screamed overhead, and the shouts of "*Allahu Akbar!*" stopped for a while, replaced by the screams of dying men. Then the chant resumed while the throng pressed her forward more urgently. "Hold tight!" she told her toddler. "Mommy's got you." And then the crowd in front of her parted, revealing an open door, standing in the mud.

Jacobsen, who had dropped down to supply another pair of hands for the evacuation, beckoned to her as she watched a young man sprint through the door, followed by a woman, then a youngster, and then another man. Jacobsen beckoned again. "Common, Lady… hurry!" he said. "You'll be safe."

She clutched her infant tightly and squeezed her boy's hand so hard he cried, "Ow, Mommy…that hurts!" And she ran through the door…

…into an area with only distant sounds of gunfire coming through the door, where everyone seemed to be moving with purpose, there was grass under her feet, and the air smelled sweet and clean. A young woman clutched her elbow, telling her, "You're safe now… come with me," and guided her away from the entrance to an area where other mothers and their young children had assembled. Some of the children played together while others clung desperately to their mothers. Sympathetic adults wandered through the group asking questions, entering the answers into a general database, supplementing the automatic logging that took place as people passed through the portals so that people could locate their loved ones.

"Where are we?" she asked her young guide.

"In due course," the girl told her. "You're safe now. No one can hurt you here."

"What about my husband?"

"If he's alive, we'll find him. When did you see him last?"

"An hour ago…we got separated in the crowd."

"In that case, he's here somewhere, or will be. You'll be together before you know it."

✳

Second and Fourth Platoons evacuated people from the mess of brambles and vines that dominated the shoreline going west. They dropped a squad, got people out, and the squad members escaped through their personal portals. Shortly thereafter, they popped back into their helicopters. They evacuated people by the hundreds, by the tens, and even an occasional individual or couple. Brady timed a drop by Fourth Platoon that evacuated about 200 people: ten seconds to drop and open the portals, fifty seconds to inform the evacuees, three minutes to get everyone through the portals and shut down the drop—four minutes total. Brady did a quick calculation. *Four hours at this rate to evacuate all seven hundred fifty thousand,* he thought as he watched Bransom vector Second Platoon to another cluster of people. He turned his attention back to the primary activity on the square peninsula.

Several thousand people still needed evacuating. Third Platoon gunfire held off the Caliphate fighters, but they were barely a hundred meters away now, waving their scimitars in the air, screaming *"Allahu Akbar!"* as they charged into the hail of bullets.

"Bo! Drop everything…get every possible man and portal down there right now! Those people are gonna die! Move it!"

"Second Platoon, reinforce the perimeter!" Bransom ordered. "Fourth Platoon, max portals…NOW!"

Within seconds, fifty troops with full ammunition packs manned the perimeter, hitting the Caliphate fighters with continuous gunfire. Two jet fighters screamed in from the east, once again smothering the Caliphate warriors with flaming napalm, and still, the fighters pressed forward. Dead Islamic warriors covered the ground, stacked in a sickening random array of legs, arms, torsos, and heads. Living warriors sought no cover. Instead, they charged into the withering fire, bringing them ever closer.

Brady concentrated on his battle display. *At least two thousand evacuees left down there…the warriors just gained another twenty-five meters…* "Shit, Bo, we must have killed ten thousand of 'em, and they still keep coming!"

"There's 'bout a thousand evacuees left…leavin' fast!" Bransom checked his personal battle display. "Shit! Caliphate fighters have fired a broad swath of ground cover near the west end of the lake. There's a bunch of people trapped against the water…Fourth Platoon…get the hell over to that smoke in the west and evacuate them people! Move it, guys!"

The last of the ambulatory evacuees on the square peninsula ran through the portals as the Caliphate troops burst through the withering gunfire, trampling on the bodies of several dozen dead civilians.

"Everybody!" Bransom shouted over his Link. "There's about a hundred wounded civilians on the ground. First and Second Platoons…lay covering fire. Keep them, bastards, back for three minutes. Third Platoon… Jacobsen… grab all the wounded you can…get 'em through the portals! Move it! We'll hold off the bad guys, but you got to move it…"

A volley of bullets dropped several lines of Caliphate fighters, stopping their forward movement at twenty meters, as Jacobsen pushed one and then another wounded civilian through the portal nearest him. As the next line of fighters pushed past their dead, the continuing volley stopped them cold, but the line didn't break. Meter by meter, the line moved closer to the portals, closer to Jacobsen. One by one, the portals collapsed until only Jacobsen was left, dragging the last wounded civilian to the last portal. Two bearded warriors leaped at him. He drew his sidearm, killing both. Three more came at him, scimitars whistling through the air, aiming for his neck. He fired three more shots, killing all three, but not before one flashing blade cut deeply into his right thigh. With his last remaining strength, he heaved his charge through the portal, and it collapsed before his eyes. Jacobsen looked up to see a scimitar about to split his head.

"First, Second, Third Platoons…I'm activating your personal portals," Brady announced as every Lone Star soldier on the peninsula disappeared. Caliphate warriors screamed through the mud, slashing the air with their scimitars, slicing at the muck, trying to skewer what had been right there a moment before. Finally, they came to a halt, looking around with bewilderment, wondering what had happened to the enemy that was right there a moment before.

✳

Jacobsen shut his eyes, expecting never to open them. When the descending blade didn't strike his helmet, he opened his eyes…to see fleeting clouds high above him in a blue sky. His heads-up display kicked in as he sat up and looked around him.

"This is Iapetus Medical Staging," a voice said in his ears. Blood spurted from his right leg. "Help will be with you in a moment." Two medics arrived at his side, applied a tourniquet, and proceeded to work on his leg.

"Nasty cut," the first medic said.

"Not the worst we've seen today," the second quipped, "but close." He grinned at Jacobsen. "You'll be fine, Sergeant." He applied a clamp, added some powder, removed the tourniquet, and watched the artery. "Fixed," he said, removing the clamp and closing the wound. "Give it fifteen minutes, and you can return to your chopper."

Jacobsen's face-up display changed, showing his surroundings, with everything appropriately labeled. Portal doors filled virtually all the open space around him. One flashed purple, displaying *Third Platoon*. He remained where he sat for fifteen minutes and then got to his feet warily. Other than a bit of stiffness, he felt nothing. He checked his display, found the purple door, and walked through it into his helicopter.

A moment later, three new arrivals tumbled into Medical Staging, not three soldiers, but three Caliphate warriors whose faces displayed total astonishment. To their credit, they recovered in less than a second, realized they were surrounded by hostiles, and commenced a coordinated swinging of their scimitars. As the medics scurried out of the way, one sustained a severe slash to his upper arm before the sergeant and his platoon guarding the Medical Staging opened fire and cut down the three warriors.

The sergeant ran to the nearest downed warrior and inspected him carefully. "This asshole has a personal disc!" He held the disc in the air.

"So does this one." One of his troops displayed the second disc.

"This one, too!" a third soldier said.

The sergeant checked in with the Medical Staging coordinator. "It looks like three of our guys lost their discs," he said, handing the discs to the coordinator.

After checking his system, the coordinator said, "They're from Charlie Company." Turning to his comm specialist, he said, "Tell Command Sergeant Major Bransom that three of his guys are down without their discs."

*

"Okay, everybody…get them choppers over to that smoke and get them civilians out!" Bransom ordered as the troopers streamed into their respective helicopters.

Four attack helicopters released a volley of antipersonnel missiles into the massed Caliphate warriors on the north side of the wall of fire they had created. Charlie Company troops disbursed throughout the tangled mess of bushes and brambles, moving people through the portals by ones and twos, by dozens, and by the hundreds.

At that moment, a medic stepped through the portal in the helicopter. "Command Sergeant Major, you got three men down there without discs. We just dispatched three warriors who entered Medical Staging using their discs." He gave Bransom their names.

Bransom put out a general Link call, but when the three did not respond, he sent their Link coordinates to everyone on the ground. "Find them, and take them to Medical Staging," he said.

Ten minutes later, Bransom took an emergency Link call. "We found them, Sarge, but it ain't pretty. All three lost their heads, but we found 'em—their heads. The bastards took everything they had. They're chopped up pretty bad. They're gone, Sarge, no chance of saving 'em."

Just then, the pilot yelled, "Incoming!" as a Manpad rocket slammed into the helicopter's tail rotor. The craft went into a wildly gyrating spin and then slammed into the ground. At the moment of impact, Bransom's personal disc activated, as did the discs of the others in the helicopter.

Bransom was fully awake and alert when he landed at Medical Staging. "Where are my people?" he asked the medic checking him. "There were six of us."

The medic did a quick Link check. "Only three of you made it," he said. "Sorry…"

An hour later, Brady made a thorough sweep of the entire north shore of Lake Division. "Colonel," he reported to field headquarters, "all civilians in the Lake Division quarter are evacuated." He paused in disbelief. "This is difficult to describe, Sir. I'm looking at the scattered bodies of at least a hundred thousand Caliphate warriors, many napalmed to a crisp, many taken out by anti-personnel missiles, and thousands by gunfire. They had no firearms, Sir—none. They appear to be armed only with scimitars and knives. And yet, with everything we had, Sir, we couldn't stop them…only slowed them down." Brady took a deep breath.

"How the hell, Colonel, do we win this war?"

IAPETUS—ARRIVAL STAGING

A severed soldier's head sailed through El Paso 9, bouncing on the green grass several meters inside the portal. Every eye followed the head, and no one saw what followed until it was too late. The warrior was huge by Caliphate standards, a full two meters tall. His right hand held a large scimitar, and his left held a bound-together package of what looked like clay bricks. With a mighty yell, the warrior threw the package at a group of refugees about a hundred meters from the portal. The explosion killed all of them.

For several seconds following the explosion, the giant warrior stood, laughing at the results of his handiwork. Then he turned back toward the portal, just as two soldiers ran through. They tucked and rolled in opposite directions, firing at the giant, five, ten, fifteen rounds, while the warrior twirled and spun, desperately trying to reach the shooters with his massive blade. Finally, two shots to his oversize head brought him down.

"It's over, folks," the local director's amplified voice filled the immediate area. "Tend to the living, and maintain your focus."

EARTH—AUSTIN, TEXAS

Sam Houston looked at his Adjutant General. "Give me some numbers, Greg," he said.

"Arizona and New Mexico are virtually empty. All we got are stragglers. Northern Mexico is empty because everyone pushed north and are either already out of here or are in southern Texas, awaiting evacuation. Southern California has massive problems. More than half are Group Four. They're rioting everywhere there are sufficient people to riot. Several thousand have been killed, and the hospitals are overflowing. Those who could fled to Arizona and New Mexico and are gone already." General Samuelson heaved a big sigh. "Instead of moving two a second, we're lucky to move two every minute. We are surrounding each portal with a ring of armed soldiers with shoot-to-kill orders for anyone who crosses the perimeter."

"At least," Sam said, "you're not dealing with the Caliphate yet in California. The Japan flotilla hit Columbia hard. Seattle and Portland are gone, and most of the coast is abandoned. Caliphate forces are moving from the east and striking northward through Nevada and Utah."

"We're cut off to the north," Samuelson said, "but you know that. We're still holding Dallas and El Paso, but when Dallas falls, be ready to shift operations to Houston."

"Do you have any information about Australia and New Zealand?"

"Only that they are evacuating. The Aussies sent a whole bunch of people to El-Five—construction types, mostly. They have fortified their northern shore. Anything within fifty klicks gets sunk. As to the Kiwis, there is not very much info. I can tell you this. New Zealand's Muslim population has increased over the years to over a hundred thousand, despite its isolation. Radicalism has been a growing factor during the past century. I haven't heard of any specific problems since the Caliphate Jihad, but it's almost inconceivable that local Muslims didn't act as they have done everywhere else in the world. The Kiwis are a tolerant people, but I would not put it past them to have interned every Muslim on the islands if there was any significant Muslim violence."

"Your breadth of knowledge always amazes me, Greg. See if you can set up a commlink via Iapetus portals or—perhaps—Ayres Sky, between me and both nations."

"I'll get on that right away. Bob York should be able to get it done almost immediately." Samuelson turned, opened the newly installed wood-grained, high-strength polymer security door, and stepped through the SI portal into Marc Bowles' office.

IAPETUS—GENERALLY

Samuelson opened the door and stepped through the portal into Marc's SI office, having first automatically announced his arrival on the brand new biosensing annunciator. "Greg, it's been a while," Marc Bowles told him.

"Hi, Marc. I'm using your office as a gateway. I need to talk with Bob York."

Marc casually waved a hand toward a wall behind Samuelson. Several wood-grained doors had clear labels: *Rod Zakes, Lab, Evac HQ, Mirs Security, Noel*…and there were others, each concealing a portal. "I ended up as a kind of hub," Marc said with a smile. "We'll get everything better organized someday…just not today. Take the *Evac HQ* portal. Its biosensor is programmed to let you through. The people there will find Bob."

Samuelson looked at the doors and grinned. "Are those what I think they are?" he asked, indicating a cat-sized hinged opening at the bottom of each door.

"You got it," Marc said, laughing. "Dmitri installed them in each portal where Jake has friends. The biosensor automatically controls them by sensing Jake's biomarkers."

Samuelson opened the Evac HQ door and stepped through the portal and within minutes was explaining Sam's communication need to General York. To his surprise, he felt Jake bumping his leg and purring.

"Bottom line is," Samuelson said while reaching down to stroke Jake, "that Sam believes the evacuation will go better if he can talk directly with Joe Ridden and Lynette Williams."

"Here's our basic problem," York said. "We can't set up a portal Earthside because of the prodigious power requirement. One portal would consume several times the entire Lone Star power generating capacity. Iapetus has virtually unlimited power, so whenever possible, we try to put portal base stations on Iapetus. The hyper-Discs draw their power from the portal. We could feed a power cable through a portal to Sam, and he could then set up portals to Australia and New Zealand. Problem with this is that it would be subject to capture in a worst-case scenario. So, we'll run two optical fibers from Sam's Link unit through his portal to Marc's office, and then through portals to Link units in Australia and New Zealand."

"We've got the appropriate Link units," Samuelson said.

"Good. Pass me two units, and we'll pass cable to Joe and Lynette so any unit can talk with any unit—full Link capability and reciprocity."

EARTH—AUSTIN, TEXAS

Sam's technician fiddled with the slim Link unit that occupied a small corner of Sam's desk.

"Okay, Sir, you got it."

Sam called up both Joe Ridden and Lynette Williams. Their images appeared near his desk. "It works at this end," Sam said.

"Here, too," Williams said.

"And here," from Ridden.

Sam told them, "I wanted these Links so we could coordinate our respective activities. There will be times during the coming hours where either of you may need additional discs. We have more than we need at this point and can pass them to you quickly."

"I feel more comfortable with this Link connection than the portals," Williams said. "They still seem like black magic."

"Can't say I disagree," Ridden said. "I'm still wrapping myself around what we are doing out there. It seems so incredible."

"What are you doing with your Muslims, Lynette?" Sam asked. "I know you have around a hundred thousand."

"We had some pretty serious Muslim rioting for the first time ever last month," Williams said. "Not all our Muslims. Many still see themselves as Kiwi first and Muslim second."

"So…?" Ridden said.

"I've interned all our Muslims for the time being. It's terribly embarrassing, but I see no way past it right now. My Parliament's mindset is to leave all Muslims on the islands as we evacuate. They should come to no harm, after all."

"We've got nearly a million, although many thousands have been killed during last month's rioting," Ridden said.

"Iapetus will not allow any Muslims into Iapetus right now," Sam said. "If you don't agree, they'll shut the portals."

"Really? Are you certain? Would they really do that?" Williams said, emotions flooding her face.

"It's not my call, Lynette. I run Lone Star Conservancy. For us, I see the writing on the wall. We've got no more than two weeks, and the Caliphate will control everything…and I mean everything."

"We're holding them off our north shore right now," Ridden said, "but if their Pacific Flotilla shows up, it's all over for us. Our evacuation is behind schedule. We could move more if we had more hyper-Discs."

"I'll have my people send two hundred within the next few minutes," Sam said and turned away to issue the order. Then he turned to Williams' image. "If you're certain about bringing Muslims to Iapetus, Lynette, I suggest you use your portal to get before Rod Zakes right away—within the hour, for certain. Present your case. Let him see your passion. But when he decides, you had better be ready to comply. If he cuts New Zealand off, you and everyone left on the islands will be slaughtered when the Caliphate arrives."

CHAPTER TWENTY

IAPETUS—FEDERATION HEADQUARTERS

Lynette Williams smiled furtively at Rod Zakes. "Thank you for seeing me on such short notice," she said and accepted the proffered chair.

"Sam alerted me, and I made room on my calendar." Rod did his best to give the New Zealand Prime Minister his full attention. He knew what she would say, and he knew what his answer had to be.

"Thank you! I understand that your policy is to exclude all Muslims from Iapetus at this time. Why?"

Good approach, Rod thought. "Iapetus is not a planet. We are a partially hollowed-out asteroid—like Ceres, only very much larger. There has never been conflict inside Iapetus since its inception well over one hundred fifty thousand years ago. Everywhere Muslims have gone at any time in the last two centuries, conflict has followed—everywhere.

"You want to transport Muslims to Ceres…we'll help you, but they cannot transit through Iapetus. Mirs is closed to Muslims as well, for substantially the same reasons. Mars? New Israel will not take them. Lone Star Mars will not take them. If you can set up and maintain a separate Muslim settlement on Mars, go for it. We'll get them there, but won't help you set it up. Ayers Sky? You'll have to talk to Joe Ridden about that.

"The bottom line is, there is no place anywhere out here for people who want to kill us."

"But, the Muslims I speak of are not that kind of Muslim. They will help make the Federation a better place, a safer place."

"I doubt that but grant the possibility that you could be right. Nevertheless, that does not change my mind."

Williams' face dropped. "You're certain?"

"Absolutely!" Rod stood, signaling the end of the meeting. "One more thing. If anyone anywhere within my large complement of people working the evacuation gets even a hint that you have let a Muslim come through a portal, we will immediately shut down every New Zealand portal, forever. There are no second chances on this…none!"

EARTH—LONE STAR CONSERVANCY

Lt. Col. Steve Brady pulled together the five company officers under his command, including his original Charlie Company. "We gotta hold the North-Dallas line till the civilians are evaced," he said. "We're not trying to beat the Caliphate fighters headed our way, just slow them down enough to get the civilians through the portals. We got a hundred portals set up in the old Toyota Soccer complex east of Louisville Lake, and will be pushing people through them as fast as possible. Since my old Charlie Company has done this more than anyone else, they will be handling the portals under my direct command through Command Sergeant Major Bransom.

"The rest of you will fight a holding action. The Caliphate warriors will be coming on fast to engage in hand-to-hand combat. You cannot let this happen—if it does, you will lose in a heartbeat. I don't care how good you think your people are, they cannot stand against a close-in scimitar onslaught. Take out the charging fighters with rapid gunfire. We'll try to give you some air support with anti-personnel charges and napalm.

"We gotta evacuate about a million civilians. If we can do one a second, and that's about as good as we've ever done, it's going to take about an hour-and-a-half. So, you gotta hold them for at least that long. We're talking about city streets, but the Complex is surrounded by a bunch of soccer fields, so you will have a lot of open space to work with.

"Buy us as much time as possible, but don't get killed in the process. Drop back as you take them down…and keep me informed."

The first wave of Caliphate warriors hit two hours later, just south of old U.S. Highway 380. The four Lone Star Conservancy companies were stretched out across the front, with one platoon from each company holding the front line and the second and third platoons holding positions 25 and 50 meters back. The first volley stopped the Caliphate advance, even as fighting-capable Caliphate fighters extracted themselves from the wounded and dead and formed up for the next charge. As soon as the forward platoons exhausted their ready ammunition, they dropped 25 meters behind the back platoons.

Brady observed the action from a drone 500 meters above the action. He called in an airstrike as the front line exhausted its ready ammunition. Two jet fighters screeched 50 meters over the Caliphate troops, leaving burning napalm and screaming warriors in their wake. In less than a minute, the sound of screaming men was drowned out by coordinated shouts of *"Allahu Akbar!"* and by renewed gunfire, as the first line dropped back and the second took over. The four companies kept up their coordinated slow retreat for an hour-and-twenty-minutes, although the fallback positions had stretched to 100 meters. Twice more, Brady called in airstrikes, but with attack helicopters carrying anti-personnel missiles. And still, the Caliphate warriors kept coming.

The last few thousand civilians crowded into the stadium waving identity papers, wads of money, and occasionally, a firearm. Taking no chances, Charlie Company snipers located strategically throughout the stadium took out anyone displaying a firearm or any other weapon. When the Caliphate fighters broke through the Lone Star line, they charged the gates after the civilians, mauling, killing, and beheading several hundred as they pressed behind the terrified civilians, screaming *"Allahu Akbar!"* Brady remotely evacuated all the line soldiers through their personal discs, but the melee at the stadium gates caught up two dozen Charlie Company troops before Brady could evacuate them. A dozen were severely wounded before he got them to Medical Staging. Four arrived at Iapetus without their heads. The last thing Brady saw before a Manpad destroyed his drone was several Caliphate warriors playing soccer on the field with the missing heads.

EARTH—AUSTIN, TEXAS

We're down to Group Four evacuees," Sam said to Rod Zakes' holoimage. He could have stepped through his personal portal and then through Rod's into his office, but the Link still was a better substitute. Since Link comms to Iapetus had not previously existed, he felt fortunate to have the capability.

"You didn't call to chat, Sam. What's up?"

"Well…the Caliphate has managed to infiltrate all our Group Four camps. Between Texas and California, we probably have more than a million. We're doing everything possible to vet everyone we can, but damned if I'm going to let hidden terrorists into Iapetus!

"I got agitators working every Group Four camp. These guys aren't preaching religion…just pure hate. They're saying the Anglos will leave them behind…things like that. They're passing out firearms and urging a rebellion. Many innocent people will die if we can't stop it now. I've been briefed on what the Founders did to Muslim agitators throughout the planet during the Persian Caliphate conflict. I don't really understand a neutrino weapon, but they were effective."

"I don't understand them either," Rod said, "but a concentrated neutrino beam will disrupt living cells. All you need is someone who can pinpoint the exact position of the agitator.

"I take your point, Sam. You want to take out your agitators. Why not simply use several snipers?"

"Because the crowds will tear them apart. No way to conceal their presence."

"Can you get someone with a locator and comms sufficiently close to identify the agitator to Dmitri in *Merkavah* topside?" Rod said.

"Shouldn't be a problem," Sam said.

"Then I think we have solved your problem. I'll have Dmitri contact you."

SOLAR SYSTEM—NEAR-EARTH SPACE

Dmitri briefed his young sidekick and former Q-carbon miner, Danylo Orel, on a bit of Founder history. "The Persian Caliphate threatened Israel directly. The Founders took a personal interest in the Israelis because they saw them as their direct descendants. The only hyper-V craft they had then was this one, the *Merkavah*." Dmitri patted the control panel. "It had never occurred to them to mount weapons on *Merkavah*, so they improvised. They already had Laser Disruptors on Iapetus that could destroy any incoming object out to about fifteen hundred kilometers. It was designed originally to protect Iapetus from incoming asteroids. They built an anti-matter particle beam that could deliver a packet of anti-matter to any point within about three thousand kilometers. And finally, they designed a focused neutrino beam that could take out biological systems, nuclear reactors, and nuclear bombs with an effective range of about sixty-one thousand kilometers with a ranging error of about a meter. That's what we got to work with."

"So, what do we use?"

"Particle beams are like using a sledgehammer on a fly. Lasers don't work through an atmosphere. Back then, the Founders used Neutrino Beams to take out individual agitators. Sam says they got guys in the crowds who can pinpoint the agitators without revealing themselves. We can take it from there."

Dmitri set up the Resident to locate the signals sent by Sam's agents. Dmitri wanted final control of the Neutrino Beam but let the Resident do everything else.

"There we go, Dany," Dmitri said as a point lighted on their enlarged display. "What is it?" Dmitri addressed the Resident.

"An individual standing on a small platform."

"Give me an image." Half the monitor displayed a man from directly above, standing on a crate. "Take him out!"

As the man crumbled to the ground, Jake seemed to give his tacit approval, mewing softly in his cage. Almost immediately, another man examined him and took his place on the crate, apparently continuing the harangue. Shortly thereafter, the Resident announced an incoming signal.

"It's that new individual," the Resident said.

"Take him out!"

Nobody stepped up after that.

✳

"That's hard to believe," Orel said as he looked at the magnified chaos on the monitor. "This used to be the land of dreams—Southern California." He shook his head in dismay.

They watched a massive crowd entirely surround the venerable downtown Los Angeles Sports Arena. Soldiers at the various access points held the crowd back, but it was evident that one or more barriers would soon fail, giving the crowd access to the portals ranged across the sports playing surface inside the arena.

"Those people are mostly dark-skinned," Orel said.

"You're right, but it's not what you think," Dmitri said. "Southern California demographics have changed dramatically during the last couple of generations. I understand that fully eighty percent of the population is Hispanic—as opposed to your typical North American Anglo. In California, Groups One, Two, and Three were predominately Hispanic. By the time you get to Group Four, the people down there, most of them have dark skin." Dmitri grinned. "It's not racist, Dany, just demographics."

Dmitri focused on the monitor. "We're looking for people agitating the crowd. Problem is, we're too late. They're already agitated."

As they watched, the crowd at the Chick Hearn access point began to surge down the broad steps into the complex. Dmitri directed the Resident to bring *Merkavah* directly over the entrance at thirty meters altitude. He activated his external speaker system, emitting an ear-piercing screech. The crowd halted momentarily, many looking up at *Merkavah*.

"Listen up!" Dmitri said to the crowd. "Inside, they're moving people through the portals as fast as possible. If you want out of here, you gotta wait your turn. If you break into the building, the portals will close, and you will forever lose your chance to get out of here."

The crowd started to surge forward again.

Dmitri cranked the volume to its maximum. "STOP!"

Startled, Jake leaped from his cage.

Bullets from several places in the crowd struck *Merkavah*. "Locate and eliminate the shooters!" Dmitri directed the Resident.

Several people in the crowd dropped to the pavement. Two more shots rang out, and two more people fell.

"You soldiers…keep the people moving into the arena…quickly. We'll try to tame the crowd out here."

A soldier wearing sergeant's stripes waved to the hyper-V craft as the crowd commenced moving into the arena in a more orderly fashion.

Dmitri directed the Resident to give him a panoramic view of their surroundings, centered on the arena entrance. Across the people-filled boulevard to the east, fifteen young men dressed virtually alike in what the Resident identified as one of the local gang uniforms were smashing windows in the bottom floor of a high-end hotel. Two of them had just grabbed two young women from the crowd and were dragging them into the building.

"Eliminate those men, but spare the two women," Dmitri ordered. The fifteen men fell in their tracks, and the two women struggled to their feet, looked around bewildered, and ran back to the crowd.

Dmitri reached the local military command center. He briefly explained the situation. "I need a couple of choppers out here right away. I don't want to leave till they get here, but I'm needed elsewhere."

When two helicopters arrived several minutes later, Dmitri vectored *Merkavah* further south to the evacuation center in the coliseum field just south of the University of Southern California.

Every square meter of open space around the coliseum was filled with people, every field, street, and parking lot. The freeway next door was jammed with abandoned cars.

"How many gates does the coliseum have?" Dmitri asked the Resident.

"Thirty-three," the Resident said.

People appeared to be moving with relative order through all thirty-three gates. Lone Star troops seemed to be keeping tight control. Dmitri pulled *Merkavah* higher and headed to the next extraction point, Markham Middle School in Watts.

As in the other areas, people thronged throughout the region surrounding the school itself. The portals were located in the main auditorium. Well-controlled lines of people led to the entrances.

"Look at that," Orel said, pointing to several well-dressed black men who seemed to be keeping the crowd under control, and the lines moving. Then he said, "Look! That line is moving away from the auditorium. What's going on?"

Dmitri reported the matter to Sam, and fifteen minutes later, got his answer.

"I sent someone down there through the portals," Sam told him. "Those well-dressed guys are members of the Nation of Islam, a group of black nationalists that has been around North America for quite some time. They volunteered to keep the evacuation process orderly on the condition that we let them witness to the incoming people and try to convince them to remain. They're telling them that as Black Muslims, they have nothing to fear from the Caliphate. What makes this particularly interesting is that they are separating out any Muslims for us—in effect, doing our job for us. They have been pretty tough on anybody who steps out of line. We're keeping a close eye on them, ready to pull the plug in an instant, especially if it appears that they might be starting a run for the portals." Sam thanked Dmitri and Orel for their efforts and had them continue their inspection of the extraction points.

Before they left Los Angeles, they quelled riots in three more areas, enabled the removal of portals in two, and beamed a dozen agitators before they were able to incite the people around them. In San Diego, they found things particularly well-controlled, with an armed Marine guarding every corner and people efficiently moving through portals. In Santa Barbara and smaller communities along the coast, people pitched in, neighbor helping neighbor, without need for outside intervention.

The farther north Dmitri and Orel ventured, the more urgent was the evacuation, as Caliphate forces had overrun San Francisco and were pressing rapidly southward. They headed inland, where here and there they saw helicopters bringing hyper-Discs to isolated individuals and small groups. For the most part, however, the countryside was empty of people, except for the occasional lone holdout, too stubborn to take the proffered help, believing instead in divine providence or personal fortitude.

EARTH—AUSTRALIA

Prime Minister Joe Ridden looked at his Defense Minister. "How many ships did you say?" he asked.

"At least a thousand…perhaps half again as many, off northern Queensland," she answered.

Ridden turned to his Minister for Home Affairs. "How many souls still to evacuate?"

"Five million, Sir, but it's a bit complicated. North of a line stretching from Rockhampton in the east to Coral Bay in the west, everyone that wants is cleared out. A few thousand have vowed to stay on, no matter what. There's a lot of folks around Coral Bay still escaping on Outback Loop. We have several portals on standby out there, but they are not in use at the moment. Nearly everyone else in Western Australia has pushed to Perth, where they're being evacuated as fast as possible. We've got portals scattered along the Bight, large concentrations in Adelaide and Melbourne, and Tasmania has portals in Launceston and Hobart. Every community between Brisbane and Melbourne has at least one portal. Australia will be empty in less than a week."

"In that case, Minister," Ridden said to Defense, "pull everything and everybody from the north coast, and clear Queensland to Brisbane. Don't leave anything the Caliphate can use. If you don't bring it with you, completely destroy it. As your troops move south, if any stay-behinds want weapons or ammo, give it to them—whatever they want."

"Even automatics?" she asked.

"Especially automatics. In the event we need it, they can slow down the bad guys," Ridden said. Turning to Home Affairs, he said, "Get everyone north of Brisbane out now and then work down the coast. Keep me informed of your progress. I don't want a soul left in Australia that does not want to be here."

✳

From the bridge of his flagship, aircraft carrier *ISS Saeed Esmail*, General Ismail Suleiman gazed out over the northeastern coast of Queensland at sloping white beaches, low, green hills, and clear skies. He had assigned several cruisers to each community along the coast from Port Douglas to Harvey Bay. Suleiman knew the Australians were evacuating, and he really didn't care anymore. Empty or not, he would shell the communities, commencing with Darwin on the north coast and down the east coast to Brisbane.

ISS Saeed Esmail kept station five kilometers off Port of Townsville, Australia's northernmost significant shipping port. The port was empty of shipping. The harbor was empty; the wharfs with their giant cargo cranes were empty; the roads leading to the harbor were empty. Through his binoculars, Suleiman watched a stray dog scurry after a gull. Otherwise, he saw no activity at all.

"Commence the bombardment!" Suleiman said to his fleet admiral standing on the bridge beside him.

Of the three cruisers accompanying the *Esmail*, one carried long guns, and two carried missiles. The gunship let loose as Suleiman watched Port of Townsville erupt in showers of splinters and sheets of metal roofing. It was over in five minutes. A community that had once housed over 200,000 people lay like a broken skeleton along the Queensland shore.

In that same five minutes, Darwin was wiped off the map, Port Douglas was gone, and the communities of Cairns, Arlie Beach, MacKay, Yeppoon, Gladstone, and Noosa Heads were destroyed by shells, and Brisbane roiled with the onslaught of 200 missiles.

Not leaving anything to chance, Suleiman ordered troops ashore all along the east coast, 10,000 landing at each bombarded community and 50,000 at Brisbane. He put 100,000 troops ashore at Darwin with orders to spread out and proceed south. The Australian troop deployment totaled a quarter-million warriors. As in the Lone Star Conservancy assaults, his warriors carried only scimitar and knife. They did not fear death. Every bullet fired against them by non-Muslim forces was one bullet less from the world supply of ammunition. The Caliphate controlled the only sources of weapons and ammunition anywhere in the world, except Australia and New Zealand, and Suleiman was about to put a stop to that.

EARTH—TASMANIA

Australian Prime Minister Joe Ridden looked out over the expanse of green that protected the east side of Tasman Government House. He lifted his eyes to the River Derwent bridge that accessed Montagu Bay and eastern Hobart. The late morning spring sun cast lengthening shadows across the green, filtered by high-level haze and occasionally blocked by fleecy white clouds that scudded across the sky, driven by cold winds off the Antarctic ice cap.

As of yesterday, at 6:00 PM officially, mainland Australia belonged to the Caliphate. Ridden and several of his top advisors had evacuated to Hobart in his official helicopter. Most of Tasmania was already evacuated. The only people staying behind were several hundred holdouts gathered in Queenstown, vowing to hold off the Caliphate forces, no matter what.

"Thank you for evacuating the mainland with me," Ridden said to the small group of ministers standing around his desk. "I know how difficult this has been for you, but keep in mind that we are not licked—we are going to a better place where we can live in peace while participating in the expansion of humanity into the Universe.

"I want to clarify a misconception that I have heard from media sources before they shut down yesterday. We did not…" emphatically, "DID NOT abandon our aboriginal citizens. The Minister for Aboriginal Affairs visited with aboriginal leaders several weeks ago, explained as best she could what was happening, and set in motion a program that would enable any aboriginal who wishes to accompany the rest of us. We have agreed to set aside a part of Ayers Sky as a new aboriginal homeland. Several days ago, we were told that virtually all aboriginal people wanted to remain on the mainland. The small numbers who want to go with us have already integrated themselves into our society so that they have been treated like any other citizen. Except for a dozen or so Tasmanian aboriginals, they have already departed for Iapetus—and a dozen are in Ayers Sky applying their particular skills to complete our new home. The Tasmanian aboriginals are leaving this afternoon with the rest of us.

"The Outback Loop operated until Caliphate forces were just a day away. Everyone still there passed through the portals, and the last person turned out the lights—dynamited Coral Bay Tower."

"Where is the Caliphate flotilla now?" one of the ministers asked.

"Our best intel says it has split up. The largest part is heading into the central Pacific to commence island jumping. Three ships with several thousand troops will land at Devonport sometime tomorrow. Fifty thousand troops will land here right after their bombardment, which should occur right after sunrise tomorrow.

"Hobart has been evacuating for the past five days. Tasmania will be empty of people at around five PM, except for the Queenstown holdouts. We've left them some heavy artillery and all our remaining ammunition.

"Any questions, folks? It's now or never…"

"Are we certain that we could not have held out against the Caliphate?" a minister asked. "Are we really certain?"

Several heads nodded assent.

"It's too late now, but consider this: Europe is gone. Russia and China are gone. The U.S. is gone. Do you honestly believe we would have done better?"

The discussion continued over tea and sandwiches, followed by a round of the oldest, finest scotch the Ginger Steele Distillery had in its storehouse.

*

At 4:00 PM in the green area, just east of Government House, the Governor of Tasmania shook Joe Ridden's hand and stepped through one of ten remaining portals. Immediately thereafter, Ridden's official helicopter landed, the pilot and crewman jumped out and began offloading the entire Ginger Steele Distillery stock. Ridden and the other ministers quickly moved them to the ten portals and then passed them through.

An hour later, Australian Prime Minister Joe Ridden shook the hand of each of the ministers who had accompanied him to Tasmania, as, one by one, they stepped from Hobart, Tasmania, into Iapetus, some one billion four hundred million kilometers distant. All the portals save one collapsed following their departure.

Ridden took one last look at the River Derwent bridge and Montagu Bay beyond that. Then he pressed the remote in his hand to activate a delayed destruction of his official helicopter and stepped through the last portal that collapsed behind him.

EARTH—COLUMBIA FREEHOLD

Chairman Percival Enderly examined a holographic chart of Columbia Freehold hovering over his desk. The entire coast had fallen to the Caliphate, from Seattle to San Francisco, eastward to the Cascades. Nevada and most of Utah were gone, as were the southern parts of Wyoming, Idaho, and Oregon, and eastern Montana. It was only a matter of time.

The mountainous terrain made evacuation difficult. Enderly's people found themselves hopping from location to location, minutes ahead of Caliphate warriors, to evacuate just a handful of people from each site. Finally, he was down to a few thousand people grouped in the Kennewick-Richland area, the Clarkston-Lewiston valley, around Salt Lake City, and in Great Falls.

The weather was overcast and windy outside Enderly's Lewiston headquarters in an old stone residence overlooking the Snake River near the bridge to Clarkston. It felt like snow in the air, but it was too early for a real snowstorm. The wind kicked up small waves in the confluence of the Clearwater and Snake Rivers. It would have been a good day for sailing, but nobody was left to sail. If things worked out, this could be his last day on Earth.

To expedite matters, a week earlier, Enderly obtained four hundred hyper-Discs from Sam. His people delivered the discs to each location using his only remaining combat helicopter. The rest had been lost in close-in battle with a Caliphate force that Intel said had no firearms. During battle, it turned out that they had several dozen ground-to-air missiles that took out all but one of his combat helicopters.

As the day drew to a close, the helicopter landed in his front yard. The pilot jumped out and told him, "We've got about three thousand folks lined along Main Street. That's it for here. We got another thousand in Clarkston, in the clear area north of the bridge. That's it—everyone who wants to come. We've distributed weapons and ammo to anyone who wants to stay."

"Thanks. Are you evacuating the folks along Main Street?"

"It's happening now."

"Okay, hop to Clarkston, and get those people out of there."

"Roger!"

A half-hour later, Enderly received word that every evacuation point was clear of people, and the portals were collapsed. He opened his personal portal, indicated to his pilot to enter, and commenced the destruct sequence for the helicopter. Enderly took one final look around and stepped through his portal that collapsed behind him.

EARTH—NEW ZEALAND

New Zealand Prime Minister Lynette Williams stood in her office in Wellington, looking out the window to the north. All she saw on this late spring afternoon were green trees and bushes crowding in on the north lawn of the complex. The sky was mostly clear, punctuated by small, puffy clouds driven to the northeast by a brisk wind off the Antarctic plateau.

Williams was filled with grief. Following her meeting with Federation President Zakes two weeks earlier, she had ordered her Defense Minister to round up the Muslims on both islands and put them in holding camps pending the evacuation of the rest of the Islands' population. Either the Muslims stayed, or there would be no evacuation from New Zealand, Zakes had told her in no uncertain terms.

The New Zealand evacuation had been underway now for ten days. The South Island was virtually empty of all but the Muslim population of nearly 49,000, who had been released from internment following the evacuation of the last Kiwi. The remaining North Island Kiwis would be evacuated within the hour, leaving only some 51,000 Muslims to await the Caliphate invasion. Williams drew in a deep breath, dried her eyes, pocketed her hyper-Disc, and called for her official car. She instructed the driver to take her to Maupuia Peninsula, where the North Island's 51,000 Muslims were temporarily located. After her car entered the gate, she stopped her driver and instructed him and the gate guards to make their way to the airport evacuation point.

"On the double!" she told them. "You don't want to miss the evacuation."

"What about you, Ma'am?" her driver asked.

"Don't worry about me," she said. "I'll be okay."

Williams walked briskly to the Roxy Cinema converted to a temporary mosque. There she located the Imam who had taken charge of the interned Muslims. He and several others watched three Caliphate cruisers move majestically into Wellington Harbor. As if on cue, all three vessels commenced firing, aiming their shells at downtown Wellington and the government complex Williams had just vacated.

"Why are no shells landing here?" she asked the Imam.

"When I first saw the warship, I contacted them by radio and informed them of our location. They promised not to shell us." Then he looked Williams in her eyes and said, "You must leave now, or you will miss the evacuation."

Williams smiled at the Imam and produced her hyper-Disc. "We can get as many through this portal as possible before they figure out what I am doing."

"That is very generous of you, Madam Prime Minister, but we will not be harmed by the invading forces. We view them as our liberators. You are their enemy—you must go!"

"If you won't go, then I must stay," she said and ground her hyper-Disc under her heel.

※

Caliphate warriors by the tens of thousands poured ashore at the foot of Evans Bay and spread throughout Wellington. Within a half-hour, troops and their officer arrived at the gates of the compound, opened them, and flooded onto Maupuia Peninsula. The Imam and Williams met the young Caliphate major as his troops reached the doors of the temporary mosque. The major addressed the Imam with deference, but when the Imam presented Williams, he looked at her blond hair and blue eyes and said in broken English, "Are you Muslim?"

"No, but…" she said.

"Will you convert?" he demanded of her, his voice growing shrill.

"Wait…I…ah…wait…," she said, fear causing her gorge to rise.

The major drew his scimitar, and with a single full sweep, severed her head and watched it roll into the gutter, eyes still showing total astonishment.

EARTH—LONE STAR CONSERVANCY

Sam Houston smiled at the small group surrounding him—Jim Grayson, Lt. Governor, Brad Comex, Secretary of State, and Gregory Samuelson, Adjutant General. General Bob York would have joined them, but he was off on Iapetus making sure the evacuation went smoothly. They had assembled in Houston's ornate City Council Chamber on the second floor of City Hall—just the four of them. Everyone else was gone. About a half-hour earlier, the last Texas evacuee had stepped through the last portal in Herman Square, abutted to the southeast side of City Hall. Houston was eerily quiet under a heavy overcast that blocked the sun, preventing lengthening afternoon shadows.

"Gentlemen," Sam said, "words cannot express my admiration for the job each of you has done during these chaotic months."

"Sam…" Grayson attempted to speak, but Sam held up his hand and continued.

"I want to ensure you guys really get it." He smiled at them again. "During the past three weeks alone, you have evacuated thirty million from Texas, another thirty million from California, seven million from Arizona, and two million from New Mexico." He paused, taking a breath. "And this doesn't even count the tens of millions who crossed our borders in a panic, just steps ahead of Caliphate marauders. Somehow you guys sent the ones we wanted through the portals and managed to screen out the rest.

"I don't know how many bad guys you killed, Greg, but it's a shockingly high number. Jim, you kept the machine running while I put out fires, and Brad, you kept the disparate pieces working together. Without the three of you, we would not be where we now are. Columbia shut down yesterday afternoon, about the same time that Australia and New Zealand turned out the lights. Unfortunately, Lynette Williams made a serious error in judgment, thinking she could deal with a Caliphate field commander.

"Thanks to Bob York, things on Iapetus went better than we could have hoped. There were some incidents; several people were killed; there was some infrastructure damage; but all-in-all, considering the magnitude of what we tried to accomplish, things went exceedingly well." Sam folded his hands as if in prayer. "You gentlemen have a choice. You can use my personal portal to step into Marc's office at the Starchild Institute, or you can leave with me on Saracen—destination Lone Star Mars."

※

Lt. Col. Steve Brady assembled his troops in the open area between City Hall and the Hermann Square pond. *Saracen* rested on her five legs between them and the building, ramp extended. Lt. Jerri Smyth stood to Brady's right, and Command Sergeant Major Bo Bransom to his left. Charlie Company stood in loose formation, backs to the pond, ordered by platoons. Ten additional men were missing, in addition to the twenty-nine who stayed in Minneapolis. Six who were killed at Lake Diversion, and four who were lost defending the Dallas evacuation portals.

"This is it," Brady told his men. "I don't know what will happen after we transit to Iapetus this last time. We will remain a military unit for the time being, but we are going to a place that has no military. And at least up till now, they haven't needed one. The problem is that Iapetus has been home to a relatively small number of people until all this started. Now it has millions. Even after many Texans leave for Mars, it still will have a larger population than it has had since the Founders first came here from Ectaris. If you get lost in the shuffle, contact the nearest uniformed person. One way or the other, we'll get back together again.

"Right now, you're on your last detail. Bo will position you to your best advantage to hold off the Caliphate warriors. They want to take the Saracen, but you're not going to let them. You need to hold them off until Sam Houston and his deputies board her and take off. That is your signal to evacuate through your personal discs. Lt. Smyth and I will board Saracen with them. Bo will evacuate with you guys. We're going to Lone Star Mars and will meet up with you all later."

At the far end of the pond, several Caliphate warriors crashed through the bushes, shouting "*Allahu Akbar!*"

"To your posts!" Bransom yelled as he took out three of them with his sidearm. "Don't let them get any closer!"

Brady activated his Link. "Governor Houston…you need to get down here ASAP!"

Within a minute, Caliphate warriors had the entire City Hall complex surrounded and were pressing ferociously to reach the hyper-V craft. Sam Houston and his staff, each with gun in hand, emerged through the heavy City Hall doors, shooting at charging warriors as they crossed the short distance to Saracen and scrambled up the ramp.

"Quick, Jer…up the ramp!" Brady said, grabbing her hand and running with all the speed he could muster.

One huge warrior broke through the defense line and charged up the ramp toward Brady and Smyth. Brady brought up his weapon to shoot, but the warrior slammed the gun out of his hand with a mighty scimitar blow and a shout of *"Allahu Akbar!"* Without hesitating, Smyth drew her weapon and placed a bullet between the warrior's eyes. The warrior stumbled and dropped his scimitar on the ramp as he fell to the ground. Smyth scooped it up and pushed Brady into *Saracen's* interior.

As the ramp closed and *Saracen* lifted to a hover, Brady activated the personal discs of his remaining Charlie Company troops, the sound of a thousand warriors shouting *"Allahu Akbar!"* still ringing in his ears.

EARTH—NORWAY

For months following the Caliphate invasion of Norway, the capital city of Oslo, and the cities of Bergen, Trondheim, and Stavanger became veritable ghost towns of their former selves. The remaining forty-seven towns and villages along the rugged coastline with populations ranging from 90,000 to 350 ceased to function as centers of civilization as the Norwegians faded into their mountainous terrain. Their Viking heritage and the resourcefulness of virtually everyone made it possible to continue living off the land while maintaining a semblance of their former high-tech existence.

With time, however, increasing numbers of Norwegians tired of their refugee life and yearned for the comforts of civilization. An occasional small group would make its way out of the mountains into one or another of the coastal towns. Not one of them was heard from again. Upon discovery by the occupying Caliphate forces, they were slaughtered without mercy.

Eventually, the low-level slaughter became too much for Norway's monarch, ruling in exile from a small, well-hidden northern mountain hamlet. He ordered his Chief of Defense to organize retaliatory raids on the small Caliphate garrisons occupying strategic positions along the entire coast. The Norwegian raiders employed an ancient tactic—strike quietly and quickly, kill everyone, leave no evidence of any kind.

At first, the Norwegians raiders were very successful. They killed several tens of thousands of Caliphate warriors. Then things changed. Raiders entered a village, killed the occupying warriors without any losses, but as they were leaving, they were set upon by several hundred warriors who had been waiting for them in ambush. The waiting warriors sacrificed the warriors in the village to kill the raiders. None survived.

The Caliphate continued this tactic until Norwegian raiders stopped descending from the mountains.

The Norwegian raiders then commenced water-born assaults against occupying warriors. This tactic was successful for several raids before the Caliphate started mining Norway's coastal waters. The standoff continued for several months. Isolated Caliphate warriors, singly or in small groups, were taken out by snipers. From time to time, the Caliphate would organize a raid into one or another mountain community, slaughtering everyone they found.

After months of back-and-forth killings, the Caliphate rounded up 100,000 residents from various coastal communities who had chosen to remain, accept Islam, and assume second-class citizenship. For two weeks, the Caliphate broadcast into the mountains that unless the king surrendered himself, the hostages would be killed. When the two weeks were up, all 100,000 hostages were beheaded. The Caliphate then collected another 100,000 hostages—this time, only women and children. Once again, the call went into the mountains.

At the deadline last minute, Norway's king surrendered himself and his entourage. The Caliphate immediately beheaded him and everyone with him. Then the warriors slaughtered the women and children hostages, beheading one every thirty seconds for thirty-five days. Before it was over, most of the mountain holdouts had surrendered. The Caliphate killed half of them randomly but allowed the remaining half to convert.

From that point forward, every time a Caliphate warrior was killed by a mountain holdout, or by anyone else for that matter, the Caliphate beheaded a thousand Norwegians. Within six months, the mountains were bereft of holdouts, and all resistance ceased.

CHAPTER TWENTY-ONE

MARS—JUVENTAE SOCKET

Dmitri Gagarin and his protégé Danylo Orel brought *Merkavah* to rest on its five extended legs on the smooth surface surrounding Juventae Socket. In the early afternoon, the Sun loomed in the southwestern sky, filtered a bit by a thin layer of wispy clouds.

"Sun looks bigger than it should," Orel said. "I guess they made a lot of progress with the terraforming project."

"Margo Jackson's been pushing everybody to the limit."

"Same gal they named this Loop after?"

"That's the one. What you see there is not really the Sun. That's an image of the Sun magnified by the Soletta—a ten-thousand-klick louvered disc at the L1 point, 'bout a million klicks toward the Sun. What you don't see is a ring of giant mirrors in Mars polar orbit that reflect sunlight that would otherwise bypass Mars back to the Soletta to be reflected back to Mars. They built the whole thing in about three years."

"What is this stuff?" Orel asked as they stepped onto the reddish-tinged surface in their pressure suits.

"They call the surface a malgamac," Dmitri said, "although it has nothing to do with tar as in tarmac back on Earth. It's made from malgalith, an amalgamate consisting of RV-produced rock vapor and sand-like regolith found a short distance in virtually all directions. They lay it down as a very hot, cement-like stuff. Gravity—even Mars' light version—smooths it out, and it cures to malgamac in a few minutes." They walked across the malgamac toward the building at the base of the socket. "The upper edges of the covered portion of Nanedi Valles are stabilized with this stuff," Dmitri added as they entered the low building through a set of locks.

"So, malgalith is the Martian equivalent of Earth concrete," Orel asked.

"Yeah, 'cept it's stronger and better. See that building?" Dmitri pointed to a low reddish building at the edge of the malgamac toward the Sun. "That's the MagLev station. Like this building, it's made of cast malgalith. The Klaus Blumenfeld MagLev heads a thousand klicks southwest to the western end of Valles Marineris, then seven hundred sixty klicks east to Lone Star Mars, then eighteen hundred klicks to Margaritifer Socket. From there, it goes fourteen hundred klicks west to Nanedi Valles. Finally, it heads six hundred klicks west back to here. All sixty-five hundred kicks of MagLev base are made of malgalith." Dmitri checked the time. "They should be here any time now."

The Juventae Socket Building housed the administrative functions for the Jackson Loop, dormitory facilities for the three-person, three-section watch, a dining facility, such as it was, manned by one of the watch members, and the drivers and other machinery that ran the Juventae Tower lift system. The socket building lacked the luxury tourist facilities that differentiated Alex Regent Skyport from every Earthly launch tower skyport except possibly Sevastopol Skyport before its destruction by the Caliphate. Nevertheless, the waiting room was comfortably outfitted and capable of handling up to fifty people in relative style.

As they looked through the window across the malgamac to the stark Martian landscape between the malgamac and the edge of Juventae Chasma, the Saracen settled on its legs beside the *Merkavah*. It extended its ramp like a tongue, and five pressure-suited figures strode down the ramp and walked toward the socket building, casting shadows behind them. The lock cycled, and the five entered the building. Dmitri knew Sam and had met the other two civilians. He had never seen the tall, Viking-like warrior and his striking female companion, blond, blue-eyed, tough-looking, and eye-to-eye with himself—both clad in military battlefield dress.

Sam stepped forward with hand outstretched. "Dmitri!" He smiled broadly. "Let me introduce my Lt. Governor back on Earth, Jim Grayson, and Major General Gregory Samuelson, my former Adjutant General—both between jobs right now. This is Dmitri Gagarin, head of Federation Security, and…"

"My sidekick, Dany Orel." Dmitri shook their hands. Orel reached out and shook their hands as well.

Sam turned to his uniformed companions. "This is Lt. Col. Steve Brady and Lt. Jerri Smyth, late of the Lone Star Conservancy Army, also between jobs."

Dmitri shook hands with the warrior, testing the strength of his grip. "Colonel," Dmitri said.

"Steve," the warrior said back with a smile, giving as good as he got.

"Lieutenant," Dmitri said to Smyth, taking her hand, unsure whether to shake, or bow and kiss it. He opted for a friendly squeeze and was surprised by a return grip that nearly rivaled Brady's.

"Jer," Smyth let his hand go, her eyes twinkling.

"Dany," Orel said, shaking both their hands.

"Now that we are through the formalities," Sam pointed to a set of easy chairs and a couch at one side of the room, "let's sit and talk."

Dmitri held back a bit to watch the others take their seats. Sam, who was used to power, and Grayson and Samuelson just took available seats. Steve seemed somewhat protective of Jer while trying not to show it. Jer seemed to accept as a natural right her position as the female in the room that everyone wanted. Dany, who was not yet comfortable being cast into the presence of powerful people, and who apparently did not see himself as a rival for the affections of Jer, took a seat away from Jer and tried not to make eye contact with anyone. Dmitri joined the group, taking a seat where he could see everyone, and released Jake to roam free.

"The last few hours must have been tough," Dmitri said.

Sam nodded. "If it hadn't been for Steve here and his Charlie Company troops, I don't think the three of us would have made it."

"Where are your guys?" Dmitri asked, looking at Brady.

"Twenty-nine remained in Minneapolis—twenty-five family guys and four Muslims. I lost ten killed during the evacuation. The remaining ninety-nine evaced through portals with Command Sergeant Major Pollard Bransom—I call him Bo. They're somewhere on Iapetus." Brady's face took on a tortured look. "I promised them we'd keep Charlie Company together." Smyth reached out and squeezed his hand, a gesture noticed by all present.

"And you shall," Sam said. "We have a growing terror problem here on Mars, both at Lone Star and New Israel. There's a group in New Israel—they call themselves the Reds—who want to return Mars to its pristine condition before humans arrived."

"Really," Brady quipped, "and how would they live?"

"They're okay with Nachal Rachaf as it is now, but they want to dismantle everything else—the polymer covers and curtains in New Israel and the megalith walls retaining atmosphere in Lone Star Mars. To make matters worse, they've joined forces with the Caliphate. There are at least two Caliphate-controlled operatives out there," Sam pointed in a generally northerly direction, "who are well-equipped and know what they are doing."

"It's idiotic," Dmitri added, "but the Red movement seems to be growing. The Israelis Banished three Reds a while back..." He interrupted himself at questioning looks from the others. "Basically, they marooned them out on the Martian surface in pressure suits, but with no extra air. Anyway, the Delgado brothers—the Caliphate operatives—rescued one of them."

"We need to put a stop to this before it grows out of hand," Sam told the group. "Dmitri's security forces are not set up to handle something like this."

"And that's where you come in," Dmitri said to Brady. "you and Charlie Company...if you're willing, of course. The Federation does not compel people."

✳

"We need to speak with President Zakes, but I don't want to inconvenience all of you with having to don and remove your pressure suits," Dmitri said. "Will you excuse me for a moment?" He donned his pressure suit as Jake found a place in Smyth's lap and then cycled through the lock to the malgamac. He entered *Merkavah*, closed and pressurized the craft, and removed his pressure suit. Then he activated his MERT Portal to Rod Zakes' office and stepped through, the annunciator stating his presence.

Rod looked up, briefly surprised, and asked, "Dmitri…what brings you here?"

"I have Sam and two of his people, and Charlie Company commander and his lieutenant, at Juventae Socket. I want to take a MERT Disc to the socket to bring them here without a bunch of pressure suit donning and doffing."

"No problem, Dmitri." Rod handed him a disc. "Just don't leave this there."

Dmitri accepted the disc and returned to *Merkavah*. A few minutes later, he was back in Juventae Socket Building.

IAPETUS—FEDERATION HEADQUARTERS

The five evacuees from Earth stepped through the portal into President Rod Zakes' office in Iapetus Federation Headquarters. Rod stood, greeted his old friend, Sam, and then went through the introductions of the other four. He noted with a smile that Brady and Smyth both came to attention when he shook their hands, and when he indicated that they should relax, they came to parade rest.

"Okay, everybody," Rod said, "please take seats, relax, and let's have some refreshments while we get acquainted and decide how to move forward."

A ubiquitous mechanical server floated through the room, silently taking verbal orders, while Rod asked for and listened to information about the final hours of the evacuation from Earth.

"So, most of the Caliphate fighters did not carry firearms?" Rod asked.

Brady spoke up. "The ones we encountered during the airdrop obviously had everything such an invasion would require. So far as I know, they wiped out every unit except ours, and our survival was more luck than skill."

"I'm not sure I would agree," Rod commented to nods from Sam, General Samuelson, and Dmitri. "But please, continue."

"The Caliphate troops we initially encountered during our evacuation from Minneapolis and our southwestward flight certainly had mortars and long guns, probably captured from the National Guard units that didn't make it, and they had mechanized troop carriers," Brady said. "After Lone Star air support took out our mechanized pursuers just north of the Texas border, the only Caliphate troops we encountered were armed with scimitars and knives, nothing else." Brady shook his head. "You had to be there to really understand. Thousands of men charging into a solid wall of lead, gaining ground with total disregard for their lives. They didn't take cover, they didn't feint or hesitate, they just kept coming until we killed them—by the tens of thousands. It was horrible…" Brady bowed his head. Smyth touched his shoulder sympathetically.

"You may not be aware of this," General Samuelson spoke directly to Brady, "but you and your troops are the only intact military unit that made it to Lone Star, the only one. That wasn't luck, Son, that was pure skill on your part and dogged determination and incredible bravery by Charlie Company personnel. In all my long career, I've never seen anything like it!" The general came to his feet. "I salute you, Sir!"

Brady came to his feet after an embarrassed silence, coming to attention. "Thank you, General!" He saluted back.

"I hate to say this to an old friend, Rod," Sam said after Samuelson and Brady retook their seats, "but you need a military. I know you have resisted it on philosophical and practical grounds since the founding of the Federation, but we are facing an enemy like nothing ever seen in Earth's history." Rod started to speak, but Sam held up his hand. "A moment, Rod. I know the Caliphate is isolated to Earth, but you know as well as I that this is just temporary. Saeed has to consolidate his worldwide gains and put his house in order. Suleiman will do that for him. He's a brilliant tactician and a skilled manager;

that's obvious, given what he has accomplished. But…we're gonna face him sooner or later, and we better be ready."

The room was quiet as everyone digested Sam's words.

"Sam's right!" Samuelson finally broke the silence.

Rod's face took on a drawn, tortured look. "Your logic is impeccable," he said to Sam with a nod to Samuelson, "but I simply cannot take a step that goes against everything I have believed all my adult life." He looked at each face. "I have held this seat for too long anyway. Vesta got this magnificent enterprise underway. I've brought us to second base, but someone else will have to carry forward from here, and I think I know who." He paused and then stood up. "Give me a few minutes, please," and he opened a door and stepped through a portal behind his desk.

With stiff tail, Jake suddenly appeared seemingly out of nowhere and scampered after Rod through the cat door.

✳

For a half-hour, Sam and the others checked out the holographs on Rod's walls, chatted about his extraordinary career, and talked about the Exodus. They queried Brady and Smyth about their roles and their thoughts as the Exodus unfolded. Samuelson answered questions about how he handled the Mexican invasion, and then how he managed to coordinate the interests of the Columbia Freehold and the varied interests of the members of the Lone Star Conservancy, and—of course—how he held off the Caliphate. Jim Grayson listened quietly, for the most part.

Then, Rod stepped through the portal, followed closely by Marc Bowles. "I think most of you know Marc," Rod said and then introduced Marc to Brady and Smyth. "Sorry I took so long, but I had to bring Marc up to date." He smiled at the group and then turned to Marc. "I now have the pleasure of announcing that Marc Bowles has agreed to assume the Presidency of the Iapetus Federation. I know of no one, and I mean absolutely no one, better qualified to head the Federation at any time, but especially now." He took his seat behind his desk, leaving the floor to Marc.

"Well…" Marc said, "how's that for an entrance?"

Everyone chuckled.

"We must have an election, of course, but I do not expect any opposition. Rod has agreed to stay on, making the official decisions until I am inaugurated. I will need a replacement at the Starchild Institute, and I am relatively certain that Margo Jackson will be happy to take up where I leave off." Marc looked directly at Brady and Smyth. "Margo was in charge of underwater construction for Slingshot and then became CEO of LLI—Launch Loop International. She built most of the Earthside Launch Loops and was in charge of the space-based terraforming projects for Mars."

Marc looked at Samuelson. "You, General, will head up the Iapetus Federation Defense Force—the IFDF if you are willing. And you two," he looked at Brady and Smyth, "along with every Charlie Company member who volunteers, are immediately assigned to General Samuelson to work with him to organize and fill the ranks of the IFDF—if you are so willing, of course."

"IFDF or IFSF?" Samuelson asked.

"What do you mean?" Rod said.

"*Defense* Force or *Strike* Force," Samuelson said.

"Defense Force, of course," Rod said indignantly.

"There's something to be said for the name *Iapetus Federation Strike Force*," Brady said. "*Defense Force* implies a defensive posture to attack, whereas *Strike Force* implies striking out at an attacker, an enemy, preemptively, if necessary."

"Steve has a point," Marc said.

Samuelson nodded assent.

"So…What is our posture?" Marc asked the group.

"Strike," Brady said without hesitation.

"Strike," Smyth said, looking at Brady.

"Strike," Orel said, looking at Dmitri.

"Strike," Dmitri said, smiling at Orel.

"Strike," Grayson said slowly, looking at Sam.

"Strike," Sam said, nodding.

"Defense," Rod said quietly, his face nearly drained of color.

"I think that settles it," Samuelson said.

"Are you sure?" Rod put the question to the room. "Is the Federation to become just another intimidating bully?"

"You don't mean that," Marc said.

"I do," Rod answered. "And history is on my side. My reasons for not interfering in Earth were, one—we do not really have the ability, and two—it's not our problem."

"But you did interfere," Marc said, "with the Exodus."

"That was different—the Exodus was an emergency evacuation," Rod said.

"What about my interference with *Merkavah*?" Dmitri asked.

"We had to do that to ensure the success of the Exodus." Rod sounded a bit frustrated.

Marc stepped in. "Look, Rod…the Federation will never become the kind of bully you fear because we will never let it go there. We're going to be around for a long time, and we're not going anywhere—at least most of us are not."

Rod smiled at his long-time friend. "You've made your point well, and I accept the decision. IFSF it is."

"I agree," Marc said and looked at Sam. "I need a Vice President, Sam, somebody who thinks like I do, who can govern, and who can effectively take over part of this task that is far too big for one man."

Sam looked over at Grayson. "Will you join me, Jim? We're the best team I know, and I'm gonna need all the help I can get."

Samuelson looked at Dmitri. "You know the ins and outs of Federation security better than anyone else, and you are an experienced military commander. Will you join me to help make this thing work?"

Dmitri came to his feet with a snappy salute. "Thank you, General, but I have created and shaped Federation Security. I know more about it than anyone. As much as I would like to be in your IFSF, I belong as Director of Federation Security." Then he looked down at Orel and said softly in Russian, "Do you like what we have been doing?"

"Da!" Orel said.

Dmitri looked at Marc. "Danylo Orel is the best man I know to back me up at Federation Security."

"So be it."

✳

The surviving ninety-nine members of Charlie Company crowded into a large room on the bottom floor in one of the ubiquitous pyramid buildings scattered across the Iapetus interior. They had all received a Link signal and were picked up individually and in groups by floaters and transported to the building. Command Sergeant Major Bransom checked each man personally to ensure that he was not injured and in good health. Some of the men had done some exploring between the time they arrived in Iapetus and their call to the meeting. They were excitedly exchanging experiences and their wonder at this strange place.

After about a half-hour of informal chit-chat, Bransom called Brady by Link. "We're ready for you, Sir."

Within moments, Brady and Smyth stepped through an unobtrusive portal at the head of the room.

"Atten-hut!" Bransom called out as all ninety-nine troops came to their feet.

"At ease," Brady said. "Take your seats." He motioned for Smyth and Bransom to take seats behind him. "Welcome, Guardsmen!" Brady shouted into the room to the cheers of his men. "I see that most of you made it. We mourn the loss of our comrades but know that they died fighting for all of us." He was interrupted by cheers and applause.

"First, let me bring you up to date about Captains Smyth and Bransom…you heard me right. Jerri Smyth has been commissioned a captain in the IFSF—the Iapetus Federation Strike Force. And so too, Bo Bransom. Front and center, both of you!"

Brady pinned the glistening twin silver bars on their collars and then stepped back and saluted both. "Congratulations, Captains!"

Brady then proceeded to brief Charlie Company about the big picture back on Earth and in Iapetus. He outlined the new IFSF and explained that each of them had the opportunity to join while remaining part of Charlie Company. He laid out pay and benefits and then dropped the big piece of information.

"As most of you probably know by now, Mars has two settlements, New Israel and Lone Star Mars. Unfortunately, members of the Caliphate have infiltrated the Martian settlements and are also running loose on the Martian surface. The Martian settlements are taking care of their internal problems, but Charlie Company's new assignment is to go to Mars and rid the rest of that planet of those suckers."

Charlie Company rose as if one person, whooping and cheering and stamping their feet. Pandemonium reigned.

"Any of you want out," Brady shouted, "now's the time."

A general "BOO" emanated from the troops. No one stepped forward.

IAPETUS—LONE STAR COMPOUND

Sam looked at Matti McIntyre across the utilitarian desk in his Lone Star Headquarters office located in a part of Iapetus McIntyre had never seen. "Matti," he said, "I've got more than seventy million people here. When can you start moving people to Mars, and how many can you take?"

"I wish I could make a big dent in your population, but that ain't gonna happen. You know that already." McIntyre shook his head in frustration. "We been workin' our butts off getting ready for you, but the project is too vast, too overwhelming." He sighed. "We're just gonna have to take it one step at a time."

"So, when, and how many?"

"I can start in a week, but you gotta take it slow. I've got room for two million right now, but we need to bring them in to keep the process orderly—say, a month to bring them in and get them settled."

"Well, that's about one-and-a-half percent—it's better than nothing."

"Actually," McIntyre said with a broad grin, "I can do you better than that. Once we get these people settled, and once they understand what's going on, what's at stake, they're gonna pitch in and make a big difference. Two weeks or so after they are settled, we can start a continuous transfer to a total of about ten million."

"That's the kind of number I like to hear," Sam said with a sigh as Jake suddenly passed through the portal cat door, jumped into his lap, and settled down purring softly.

"We keep the process going, and I can take another ten million within six months. That's twenty million people makin' hay down in Lone Star Mars."

"That many people will require that we change how we govern. It's got to be more like Texas," Sam said.

"Been thinkin' 'bout that," McIntyre said. "I say put the government seat in Lone Star and keep enough portals open to make the two parts function as one. Do you have any idea how many will eventually want to settle on Mars?"

"Complete mystery," Sam said.

"Let's play it by ear, then. We'll expand Lone Star westward to accommodate another twenty million or so, but that's gonna take a while. We gotta lot of room in Valles Marineris—enough for everyone...all seventy million, plus!"

IAPETUS—COLUMBIA COMPOUND

Percival Enderly took stock of his situation. He had an office in a pyramid inside a moon of Saturn. One door in his office led directly to the Federation President's office and a second to Sam's. He had about forty million people under his charge, and his entire staff was running around like chickens with their heads cut off. Somehow, they all made it to here...but now what?

Enderly stood and opened the door to the portal into Sam's office—somewhere else in Iapetus. He had no idea where. He stuck his head through the portal and said, "Sam, can we talk?"

Sam waved him into his office and to a chair. "What's on your mind?" Sam said as Jake suddenly appeared and jumped to his desktop rubbing Sam's favorite coffee cup.

"I get things done, Sam. You know I do. So do you...that's why I'm sitting here. I was able to put Columbia Freehold together when it seemed impossible. It was a challenge, but I did it. This here...this here is way outside my experience. I thought perhaps we could work together in a way; if you solve a problem, I can apply your solution, and vice versa too, of course."

Sam gently moved Jake to the floor, and the two men watched Jake dart through the cat door. Then Sam smiled and said, "Let me tell you about an experience from my personal past. You know I was in the Army, right?"

Enderly nodded.

"When I was a First Loui, my Colonel assigned me the task of navigating our company through a Georgia swamp—I was the official Company Navigator. I had never seen a swamp before, and I had graduated from Navigation School just a couple of weeks before that. I was completely overwhelmed, over my head, and I didn't know what to do. I went to the Colonel and laid it out for him…bottom line was that I thought I needed some help. The Colonel listened patiently to my tale of woe, and then he asked: 'What's your title, Lieutenant?' I answered, 'Navigator, Sir.' 'Then navigate, goddammit!' he told me. So, I went back and worked through it, and I got us through the swamp—maybe not the best way, but we got through, and I did it." Sam stopped talking and looked Enderly in the eye. "You, my friend, did the impossible back on Earth. You did it with far fewer casualties than I. Of course, I'll assist where I can, but I may be learning more from you than you will from me."

IAPETUS—AUSSIE & KIWI COMPOUNDS

Noel Goddard, followed closely by Jake, walked into Joe Ridden's office in the Australian Compound in Iapetus, hand outstretched. "Figured I'd find you here, Joe. You've got a major mess on your hands."

"You can say that again," Joe replied in his down-home brogue, grinning as Jake hopped to his desktop, looking for attention. "I got me thirty million people all bunched up in these here crazy pyramids. Great system, though. My people ended up all over Iapetus, but somehow, they were identified, notified, and those floaters brought the ones here who were too far away to get here easily." He idly scratched behind Jake's ears. "So, you found me again, Little Buddy."

"The Founders were way ahead of us when we met," Noel said, "but we've covered a lot of ground since then, and that's why I'm here." Noel pulled up a chair and draped his lanky frame in front of Ridden's desk. "Ayers Sky is ready to take a bunch of people. What we need are people who can learn in a hurry, think on the fly, organize things in their sleep, and aren't afraid of trying a new way to do it."

"You've just described the typical Aussie," Ridden said with a wide grin.

"Right…but we need folks who are more typical Aussie than the typical Aussie…know what I mean?"

Ridden nodded. "How many?"

"A couple of hundred thousand over the next two or three months."

"What'll they be doing?"

"We've got to build an infrastructure that will accommodate thirty million people," Noel said. "Four or five months after they start, we can commence importing regular people. I'm guessing that a certain number of Aussies will get used to Iapetus and want to remain here. We'll deal with that over time, but within eighteen months or so, I think we can bring people to Ayers Sky on a whole-sale basis." Noel slid his chair a bit back from the desk. "How is your government coming?"

"Glad you asked." Ridden grinned and continued. "You're sitting in Government Center—at least until we can permanently establish ourselves on Ayers Sky. I have decreed a loosely enforced martial law and have temporarily assumed dictatorial powers, much to the consternation of the Loyal Opposition. To their credit, they are going along with it for now, and I have granted them full and open access to this office so there are no hidden problems that will blow up on us."

"That's what I like about you guys."

"We got our differences, sometimes big ones, but when the chips are down, there has never been a time when we didn't set them aside and work together. That's what we're doing now. I've put Morten Obers, the guy I replaced, in charge of security. His job is to keep this mob under control. He was popular, particularly with the working types. He has the complete cooperation of the unions and labor in general. Things have gone pretty smoothly thus far—all things considered."

✳

When Noel walked into the Kiwi headquarters, Jake at his heels, things were not so sanguine. When Lynette Williams, the popular former PM, didn't make it, bitter infighting broke out within New Zealand's ruling establishment. The Conservatives blamed Labor for their present predicament, and Labor was too much in shock over the loss of Williams to focus on the real nature of the problem. Most

Kiwis had traditionally held a parochial view of the outside world, probably due to their isolated South-Pacific island status. Progressive business leaders had managed to upgrade the general precision of Kiwi manufactured products and gain broad acceptance of Kiwi industrial products in the European and American commercial spheres. With the collapse of world enterprise in the face of the Caliphate Jihad, these leaders lost their influence and were replaced by long-time New-Zealand-first ideologues. Until the inevitable was staring them in the face, therefore, New Zealand virtually ignored the worldwide chaos. Labor blamed the inward-looking partisans for Williams' death, and the progressive business interests blamed Labor for New Zealand's lack of readiness in the face of the Caliphate challenge.

With the lives of five million people at stake, General Bob York assigned a senior military officer from his own circle, General Langsley Oxford, to establish a caretaker government. General Oxford's job was to hold things together until the Kiwis could get their own act together to move forward with their own self-government. Making significant changes beyond what was necessary as a result of the Exodus was definitely not in his job description. Oxford was at his desk in the Kiwi HQ pyramid sorting action requests when Noel walked into his office.

"General Oxford, we haven't met…"

"But I know of you, Noel Goddard of Cassini II and Ayers Sky fame. Sit down, please. What can I do you for?" He reached down and stroked Jake. "But I know you, little fella—you visit me every couple of days." Then he looked up at Noel and added, "And call me Lee—everyone else does."

"Very well, Lee…Noel here." He took the proffered easy chair. "I just came from Aussie HQ. Ridden has things running smoothly over there. Too bad our Kiwi friends couldn't do the same."

"Not fair, Noel. These guys are terrific! They are recovering from a double-whammy, what with coming here and the loss of Lynette Williams. They'll be on their feet, running things themselves before you know it."

"Actually, I don't doubt it, but here is here, and now is now. Ayers Sky is ready to import something like two hundred thousand people who fit the mold of the early pioneers to Australia and New

Zealand. Most will be coming from Ridden, but I wanted to give you the chance supply twenty or thirty thousand."

"Can you be a bit more specific?"

"Here's what I told Ridden. We need people who can learn in a hurry, think on the fly, organize things in their sleep, and aren't afraid of trying a new way to do it."

"That describes a lot of Kiwis."

"I know. Again, as I told Ridden, we need folks who are more of these things than the typical Kiwi, if you know what I mean." Noel smiled broadly.

"How soon?"

"Yesterday…" Noel chucked and settled deeper into his chair.

"I'm sure you know about Ceres," Oxford said.

Noel nodded.

"I've been concentrating—right after putting the Kiwi house back in order—on accelerating the Ceres project. Almost to a person, the Kiwis are straining to settle into Ceres and get their own lives and culture moving ahead again. The task is daunting under the best of circumstances. They're doing to Ceres what the Ectarians did to Iapetus, you know."

Noel nodded again.

"Way bigger than Ayers Sky…Now, don't get me wrong. I am not denigrating your efforts in any way. What you have accomplished at El-five is beyond the scope of any previous human accomplishment…"

Noel raised his eyebrows and prepared to speak.

Oxford grinned. "Except for Iapetus, of course."

They both let out a relaxed laugh.

"I mean to say that the Kiwis and Ceres are a wonder…that they now need more than ever. Many of the people you want for Ayers Sky are exactly the kinds of people who are busy making Ceres the new Kiwi home. I'm sure I can find you some people, but I doubt I have thirty thousand left who fit the bill."

"Okay…let me know."

"By the way, Noel, we have several portals to Ceres other than the rock vapor portal to Ayers Sky. Kiwis are moving between here and Ceres on a daily basis. Many work on the project, but sleep at home here."

"That's impressive. Ten years ago, we couldn't have imagined such a thing."

SOLAR SYSTEM—HEAVEN

In 1983, on the island of Tongatapu, the main island of the 170 South Pacific islands that make up the Kingdom of Tonga, the Church of Jesus Christ of Latter-day Saints—the Mormons—dedicated a new Temple, the fourth such Temple in Polynesia. It attracted the particular interest of Tonga's monarch and eventually became a Mormon gem in the South Pacific. At the time of the rise of the Caliphate, Elder Jeremiah M. Jefferson, of the Quorum of the Twelve Apostles, had made his home in Tonga and presided over the Tonga Temple. Before ascending to the Quorum of the Twelve, Jefferson had managed to parlay a multi-million-dollar inheritance from his investor-father into a hundred billion-dollar real estate empire that stretched around the world. He saw the religious storm clouds on the horizon and cashed in his entire holdings, converting everything he had into gold, except for his modest real estate holdings in Tonga.

During the heyday of the growth of his real estate empire, Jefferson became friends with U.S. President Marc Bowles. They were not the closest friends, but they knew each other socially and followed each other's activities. Through Marc, Jefferson became acquainted with Asshur, and when Stanford Jackson assumed the U.S. presidency, with Asshur's endorsement, Jefferson was able to procure a personal hyper-V craft from Marc at SI. After that, Jefferson disappeared from everybody's radar, except for occasional contacts with Asshur. Using his vast wealth, Jefferson put together a team of specialists, obtained the loan of several RVs from Asshur, and laid claim to an obscure spherical rock in the outer Asteroid Belt that he named *Heaven*. He set to the task of hollowing the asteroid, generally following the Iapetus model, but on a dramatically reduced size basis, to create a permanent home for the Tonga faithful and any other Tonga citizens who cared to join them.

Using his great wealth and a group of very well-paid Kiwi engineers who had cut their teeth installing the Ceres mini-black-hole power source, he hollowed out a half-cubic-kilometer core and installed a mini-black-hole power source. *Heaven's* plans called for a two-kilometer-high living space below a two-kilometer shield. The RV-powder from the living space formed an additional kilometer of surface shield. Ten-meter-thick columns were left every two kilometers in a hexagonal pattern as the living space was hollowed. At five cubic kilometers a day, the process took two years, plus another overlapping two years to install infrastructure and atmosphere. Two fifty-five-meter elevator columns on opposite sides of *Heaven* allowed entry of hyper-V freighters up to fifty meters. Before Slingshot stopped working, Jefferson used Slingshot to transport nearly the entire 200,000 Tonga population to temporary quarters at Mirs and then by hyper-V freighters on loan from Asshur to his secretive asteroid.

Heaven prospered in the following years. Its 1,500 square kilometers of interior living space allowed the engineers who built the infrastructure to fashion a marine environment similar to Earthside Tonga but twice its size. *Heaven* had islands, oceans, land and marine wildlife, and abundant vegetation and food crops—sweet potatoes, bananas, yucca, taro, giant taro, squash, and pumpkin. The Tongan culture thrived in the threat-free Heavenly environment, nurtured by its ancient roots and the all-inclusive envelope provided by Jefferson's LDS teachings. A warrior culture of self-reliance became the mainstay of Heaven's 200,000 inhabitants. Although actual conflict was rare, every Tongan male prided himself on his skill with club, short spear, and ax.

Jefferson presumed that *Heaven's* isolation would suffice for its external defense. Since it orbited at the outer limits of the Asteroid Belt, it needed no laser meteor shield. Jefferson could imagine nothing that would pose a real external threat to *Heaven.*

Jefferson intended that *Heaven* would remain unknown to the Solar System at large and that it would become entirely self-sufficient. *Heaven* had largely attained this goal, except for several exotic trace organic compounds that it still needed to import. *Heaven* obtained these compounds through a series of shell companies, paying the final transactions with gold, leaving no real trail. General Suleiman stumbled onto the existence of *Heaven* when one of his embedded intelligence people traced an order for one of these exotic compounds.

Following months of digging, he turned up the final gold transaction and located the individual who made the deal. He resided in Mirs.

One of Saeed's operatives met with the broker, applied the necessary persuasion to get the information, and then disposed of the broker's body on a trajectory that crashed it onto the Moon.

＊

Taking *Heaven* would not be easy, Suleiman learned following *Rasul Allah's* careful intelligence survey of *Heaven's* surface and the immediate areas surrounding the two access ports. The upper and lower port irises could be controlled from a panel on the edge of the access port, and the bottom chamber could be pressurized and depressurized from the same panel. The garage door between the bottom chamber and *Heaven's* interior had no panel control. Suleiman presumed it was interlocked with the bottom iris and could only be controlled locally.

From his surface survey, Suleiman learned that the one-kilometer-thick RV-powder surface layer was uncompacted. His engineers told him that it would not support anything with less than a 5,000 square meter base—soccer-field size.

Rasul Allah could transport ten spacesuited warriors at a time and deposit them on the circular platform around the primary access port; but ten warriors would be woefully inadequate to take the asteroid. Suleiman needed a force of at least a hundred, but 500 would give him the edge he needed. With loading and unloading, each trip would take about a half-hour. That was twenty-five hours just to get his warriors there. Without a significant oxygen cache to support the waiting warriors on the platform, that wasn't going to work. His Pakistani engineers once again found a solution to a difficult problem.

Out of collapsible structural polymer, his engineers created a soccer-field size, two-and-a-half meter high, compartmented float with several simple airlocks. *Rasul Allah's* first trip carried the collapsed float. The crew dropped it to the surface, where it automatically inflated, and then they tethered it to the platform railing. As predicted by the Pakistani engineers, the float did not sink into the uncompacted RV-powder. The next trip brought ten spacesuited warriors who dropped to the platform, entered the float through its airlocks, and dispersed themselves throughout the float. While they waited through successive trips, they prayed and studied their *Qur'ans* to make ready for this stage of their Jihad.

The transport process took three full days and brought not only 500 warriors but fully collapsible polymer watercraft with waterjet propulsion, fifteen Gatling-type cannon that could be mounted on the boats or portable tripods, a thousand scimitars, and spares and backups for everything.

Suleiman remained at his Earthside Headquarters. Since one-way communications to *Heaven* took about a half-hour, he could not actively prosecute the Heavenly invasion. His on-scene commander had more space experience than anyone in the Caliphate military. His commander had trained the warriors for weeks, trying to anticipate every possible contingency. They knew that the access portals terminated at water sites and that the water was several hundred meters deep. They knew that Earth-normal gravity commenced at the bottom chamber lip. They knew there were no severe weather patterns but that squalls and wind gusts were common. They knew nothing of the people, weapons, culture, habitat controls—nothing at all. Suleiman would have to rely on their training and fighting instincts.

Five hundred spacesuited, TBH fitted, Caliphate warriors stepped off the platform, slowly dropping through the open iris toward the closed iris nearly five kilometers below. The top iris closed and the bottom iris opened, and fourteen-and-a-half minutes later, they activated their TBH boots briefly to bring their 11 m/s descent rate to zero and landed lightly on the deck of the bottom chamber. The bottom iris closed above them, but the chamber remained unpressurized. The warriors moved to the outer wall of the chamber as they had practiced a dozen times. Above, the top iris opened, and the topside crew dropped fifty collapsed boats and the remaining equipment through the opening. The irises sequenced, and the collapsed boats and equipment landed gently on the deck fifteen minutes later. After the chamber pressurized, the warriors doffed their suits, inflated the boats in preparation for the water entrance, and stowed their equipment in the boats. The commander cycled the garage door, and they immediately came face-to-face with their first major hurdle.

The water surface lapped gently against the fifty-meter-wide column…twenty meters below the lip of the garage in Earth-normal gravity.

They could drop the loaded boats, but some would capsize. The men could jump, but some would suffer injuries. The commander opted, instead, to lower the boats using knotted lines they had brought and then have the men climb down the knotted ropes into the boats. A frustrating two hours later, all 500 warriors were loaded ten-each in the boats. One warrior lost his grip as he crossed the gravity plane, and landed in the water on his back, severely injured. The commander ordered the coxswain of the nearest boat to cut his throat, and the fifty boats headed across the slightly choppy water to the nearest island, about three kilometers distant. A village was just beyond the waterline, and the villagers crowded along the shore awaiting the boats.

The first boats slid up the sand, and the warriors leaped to the beach, swinging scimitars in each hand, screaming, "*Allahu Akbar! … Allahu Akbar!…*" and slaughtered the villagers.

A minute later, as more boats grounded on the sand, about a hundred very fit Tongan men stormed out of the dense vegetation, swinging wicked-looking clubs, battle axes, and short spears. Two minutes later, nearly a hundred Caliphate warriors lay dead on the beach, their heads bashed in, disemboweled, missing limbs…along with five beheaded Tongans.

In an organized panic, the Caliphate warriors shoved their boats back into the water and pulled out a hundred meters. They commenced spraying the entire beachfront with concentrated Gatling cannon fire. The screams of men, women, and children could be heard above the roar of the Gatlings.

The commander ordered the boats around the island to the left, where they commenced a second Gatling assault before 200 warriors stormed ashore. This time they met no resistance as they entered and ransacked the first village. It was empty and silent. As they completed their rampage, screaming Tongans hit them from both sides and the rear, swinging clubs, chopping axes, and flying short spears, and the screams of dying men filling the air.

When no one returned to the beach after a half-hour, the commander pulled his remaining 200 warriors away from the island to reconsider his options. In less than an hour, he had lost 300 trained, battle-hardened fighters and thirty boats to what appeared to be native primitives. He decided to withdraw, bring in fresh troops, and tackle the problem using a modern approach. As he signaled his warriors to return to the portal, three dozen low-lying, out-rigger craft rounded both sides of the island. Each appeared to hold 50 to 100 men using oars, and they were gaining on his boats, going as fast as possible under waterjet power. The Caliphate boats turned their Gatling cannon on their pursuers, but the choppy water spoiled their aim, and before they could adjust to the conditions, the Tongans overtook them, boarded all fifteen of the Caliphate boats, and slaughtered the remaining warriors.

The Caliphate commander had left the garage door open, so the interlock kept the bottom iris from cycling, preventing any further activity at this access portal—until someone closed the door.

✳

He had always been a good swimmer and could float for hours. The last thing he remembered was being bashed in his face by a Tongan club with wicked spikes protruding from its business end. He was floating on his back in comfortably warm water. He could see from only one eye. He rolled right and left, looking around with his good eye. He seemed to be alone. He heard water lapping against something and twisted to see in front of him.

There, the portal column! I see the knotted ropes, the open door...

He rolled onto his stomach and attempted to swim. It was difficult, but he could do it. He pushed ahead toward the portal, a few meters...rest...a few more...rest...and then his hand struck a knotted rope. He reached deep into his reserves...one knot, two knots, three knots...ten knots...his head hurt like hell...

"Allah...give me strength!" he prayed. "Allah...!"

Then his hand passed over the lip, and he felt the lighter gravity. *Pull! Pull! More...more!*

His upper body passed through the gravity plane. He felt light-headed, and his legs were about to fall off...and then he pulled himself into the bottom chamber and passed out.

When he came to, it was dark outside the garage door. He sat up carefully and felt his face. His left eye was working, but there was just a hole where his other eye used to be. He fumbled around and found a spacesuit. He searched for, and finally found, a knife that he used to sever the knotted ropes. Then he donned his spacesuit as a precaution and closed the garage door. Once the door closed, the interior lighting came on. He found and activated the depressurizing control. It seemed to take forever, and he passed out a couple of times during the process, but finally, the iris above his head opened.

He sluffed off his TBH covers and tapped his big toes. He began rising, keeping close to the wall as he did. Several seconds after he left the deck, the iris closed beneath him, and the top iris opened. Above, he could see a small opening filled with stars. As he rose for about ten minutes, it expanded until he reached the rim. He shut down his TBH boots and staggered to the platform, where someone helped him into *Rasul Allah*, and he passed out.

When he opened his eyes again, he was looking into the stern face of General Suleiman.

"What happened, Son?"

✳

Suleiman was furious. How was it possible for 500 of his finest warriors to be killed by a handful of South Sea Island primitives. Facts were facts, however. It had happened, and he had to make it right.

"Sahib," he said to the Prophet, "we have a big problem that we need to solve as soon as possible."

He then recited what had happened in *Heaven*, detailing the humiliating defeat his warriors had suffered. To his surprise, the Prophet said, "General, it was Allah's will. He has other plans for these simple people." Saeed explained Allah's will to Suleiman and sent him on his way.

Suleiman set into motion several quiet, one-on-one, off-the-record meetings in *Heaven*, made a significant deposit to the monarch's off-world holdings (for when the secret no longer was), and promised to maintain the status of the Tongan people without the outward trappings of the Islam faithful—a loosely structured Sharia sans *burka* and *hijab*.

✳

Several months later, *Rasul Allah* arrived once again at *Heaven's* main access port, but this time the top iris opened, and the hyper-V craft entered the shaft. The irises cycled, and a few minutes later, *Rasul Allah* exited through the garage door into *Heaven's* clear sky. Moments later, the hyper-V craft settled on its five legs in front of the palace compound in New-Nuku'alofa—NuNu for short. The ramp extended, and Saeed Esmail, Allah's Prophet of Prophets, Caliph of Worldwide Islam, strode down the ramp, clad in sandals and simple sackcloth robe, carrying a rustic staff, accompanied by General Ismail Suleiman, Supreme Commander of Worldwide Caliphate Forces. The general's uniform was bedecked with even more medals than during his visit with the Indian Prime Minister. The blue sash from left shoulder to right hip announced his position as Chairman of the Caliphate's Council of Military Commanders. They were met by a royal delegation headed by the monarch himself, carrying the ancient Tongan title of Tu'i Kanokupolu.

"Greetings, your eminence," the monarch said to Saeed, bowing low. "*Heaven* welcomes you and opens its hearths and homes to your presence. All my subjects open their hearts and lives to Islam and rejoice that you have opened their eyes to Allah's Truths. As you requested, we have set aside our most remote island for your exclusive use. Each one of us, our entire population, will work to serve Allah, your needs, and the needs of those you leave in your place."

Following the official reception, signing of documents, and a colorful dance performance displaying Tongan island culture, the official party joined by Tongan aids departed for Hunga-Tonga, a remote replica of the volcanic island that first appeared in Tonga waters in the early 21st century. For the three preceding months, Pakistani engineers had constructed a full research facility, complete with every modern research aide the Caliphate could procure.

Saeed toured the facility that was already up and running, and Suleiman assured him that it would entirely replace his Earthside research labs in old Pakistan. The Prophet dedicated the new facility in a short ceremony, naming it *Almaladh Al'amn*[13].

✳

Back at his tent headquarters in Rub' al-Khali, Saeed drank a deep draught of his sweet mint tea and smiled at General Suleiman. "You have conquered the world, my General, but were brought to your knees by a group of island natives. Allah, in His infinite mercy, guided our response. We communicated to Tu'i Kanokupolu that if he would unequivocally open his world to Islam, I would spare him, his family, and his subjects and keep their secret from the rest of the Solar System. Consequently, Allah has 200,000 new faithful, *Heaven* is ours, and Allah has placed *Almaladh Al'amn* in our hands forever."

DAPHNE—ELYSIUM

Earth was in chaos and virtually shut off from the rest of the Solar System. Iapetus was also in turmoil, but a different kind of turmoil—teeming millions, quickly organizing themselves as with the Aussies and the Americans, or being organized as with the Kiwis. Mars seemed much more stable but was not without its own problems as the Reds continued to proliferate in New Israel, although they seemed to have abandoned their terrorist ways, and the Delgado brothers continued their nefarious surface activities on behalf of the Caliphate. Except for the feverish activities to get ready for major population influxes on Ayers Sky and Ceres, chaos would not be the word to describe what was going on in these two remote-from-each-other locations—harried perhaps, but not chaotic. Activities on Titan and Ganymede seemed unaffected by what was happening elsewhere, and the Europa project, hidden in that moon's ocean, interested only the Europa Group. SI's Enceladus project had shifted its focus following the successful Ayer Sky atmosphere transfer experiment. They were now working on transferring water via portal to Ayres Sky.

One member of the Iapetus Federation, however, not only had not experienced chaos but had remained a stable although growing community of like-minded persons from everywhere in the Solar System—Daphne, adopted home of the Raëlians. On Earth in ancient times, all roads led to Rome. In the modern Solar System, all roads led to Elysium on the asteroid Daphne. Unlike nearly every other Federation member, Daphne did not produce anything for export to the rest of the Solar System. Instead, Daphne imported everything it needed. What Daphne supplied, what one could possibly find elsewhere but certainly could find in Elysium, was any exotic or erotic pastime one could imagine.

From the time the modern Raëlian Church had sprung up following the startling discoveries of *Cassini II* during its initial visit to Iapetus, the Raëlians had been a part of virtually every human activity. The Raëlian Church had spread throughout the Solar System, with Raëlians part of nearly every human settlement. In church and when participating in formal events such as greeting returning space voyagers or celebrating the Earth Mother, Raëlians dressed in white robes. In normal activities, however, they dressed like everyone else. What were they? Basically, people without a strong scientific education who believed that the human race was created by an ancient superior race, the Elohim, whom they equated with the Founders. They especially honored Vesta, the Founder matriarch, whom they called Earth Mother, a name that stuck and became an integral part of Vesta's identity.

Unabashed sexuality in all of its iterations was integral to modern human culture, but the Raëlians took it to an art form. Elysium was the purest expression of that artform. So long as no one was hurt, one could find it in Elysium. This free-wheeling society allowed anyone in, but it had the Solar System's strictest screening procedures before letting anyone in. Daphne was for pleasure, not business. It allowed you to enter—with what you were wearing and your Link. If you needed more clothing—something optional on Daphne—you could purchase whatever you wished. Of course, you could leave with whatever you bought in addition to what you brought with you. This made it impossible for any would-be terrorist to cause anything but very minor damage—something he could do with his hands, feet, or something he could throw.

Access to Daphne came through the Elysium Port of Entry that connected to an Iapetus portal. Earlier, before the portal became ubiquitous, Daphne sported a hyper-V arrival dock. For a short while, you could get there both ways. With the rise of Caliphate madness, however, Daphne decided to close its hyper-V port and restrict Daphne access to portal only.

Elysium law, as everywhere on Daphne, was simplicity itself—cause no harm. The consequence for breaking Daphne law was also straightforward. Minor infractions got you thrown out and permanently banned. Non-minor infractions—physical injury or death, got you a one-way portal trip to Daphne's surface—without a pressure suit.

Major infractions were virtually unheard of on Daphne.

EARTH—SAUDI ARABIAN DESERT

For the first time since their acquisition of *Almaladh Al'amn*, Saeed and General Suleiman stood outside Saeed's sprawling tent pitched atop the same low mound overlooking the same dry lakebed near the center of Rub' al-Khali in the Saudi Arabian desert. The shifting dune pattern surrounding the lakebed was entirely different from the first time they had met here, what seemed so long ago. Saeed shivered slightly in the nine-degree air that had reached fifty Celsius in the mid-afternoon. He swept his gaze over a hundred or so tents scattered across the lakebed, where before they had numbered a thousand. Outside each tent, two men stood at relaxed attention. Guarding the Prophet, once a dangerous and challenging assignment, was simplicity itself, now that the entire world existed under the flag that fluttered above the Prophet—light-blue displaying a severed fist holding a dagger, and a few centimeters below the wrist, a truncated arm flowed red blood.

Saeed intoned the evening call to prayer as he had done so many times in the past. "*Allahu Akbar!… Allahu Akbar!… Allahu Akbar!… Allahu Akbar!*" As the sound of his voice faded into the surrounding sand, Saeed raised his voice across the lakebed again: "*Ashhadu an la ilaha illa Allah[14].*" He repeated it, and then twice said in sing-song fashion: "*Ashadu anna Saeedan Rasool Allah[15].*" Saeed smiled as his words echoed across the encampment. He reviewed the words of his revelation from so long ago: *Qur'an* at 4:74: *Let those fight in the way of Allah who sell the life of this world for the other. Whoso fighteth in the way of Allah, be he slain or be he victorious, on him we shall bestow a*

---

14 *I bear witness that there is no god except Allah*
15 *I bear witness that Saeed is the holy messenger of God*

vast reward. Yes, indeed, the reward was vast—every country, every continent, every sea, every island. The entire world paid homage only to Allah, and to his Prophet, Saeed Esmail.

As Saeed finished his call to prayer, two hundred Jihadist warriors prostrated themselves on the still-warm ground…as did Saeed and his general.

Afterward, Saeed and Suleiman settled on cushions inside the tent, sipping their very sweet tea.

"The reward is great, indeed, my General," Saeed said.

"You have conquered the entire world, Sahib, but the world that was is no more. In many parts of the world, the lights no longer work, water no longer flows; in fact, the entire infrastructure that once underpinned all the great nations of the world is mostly destroyed. We have much to do to put it back in order. People will be much happier believers if their toilets flush and their refrigerators work."

"How will you do this?"

"I have assembled a force of ten thousand faithful engineers consisting mostly of Pakistanis, along with some Indians, Koreans, and even some former Iranians. I am dispatching them over the world to wherever the need is greatest. They will teach, they will repair, they will train others to keep the lights on and the water running. I have assembled a cadre of ten thousand Imams with specialized training in community management. They will establish Sharia Law wherever government is lacking, and they will replace currently running secular governments with Sharia Law and punish those who set up the secular systems.

"It will take time, Sahib, but it will be done."

For a while, they sat, silently sipping their tea.

"You must teach me," Saeed said, "to operate *Rasul Allah.* I wish to see for myself the places devoid of Allah's blessings. And, I wish again to visit *Almaladh Al'amn,* to reinforce my relationship with the Tu'i Kanokupolu."

Suleiman acknowledged Saeed's request with an affirming smile while thinking, *I need him as a backdrop to what must be done. If I can keep him occupied off Earth for a year, I can get so much accomplished. Without him, we could not be where we are…* Suleiman looked up from his reverie and smiled warmly at his Prophet, ...*but now his sanctimonious attitude just slows things down. I need to transform the entire planet into what Babylon was in the ancient world. I need to do this with Western efficiency, not Islamic patience. Saeed will love it when he sees it, but I need him gone to make it happen.* Suleiman looked directly at Saeed.

"Sahib," Suleiman said. "Tomorrow, I will teach you to operate *Rasul Allah*, and I will assign two faithful but skilled warrior technicians to protect you and keep you company." *And keep you out of trouble!*

CHAPTER TWENTY-TWO

MARS—JUVENTAE SOCKET

Capt. Bo Bransom was not entirely comfortable in his pressure suit. His troops seemed to take to them like fish to water, but with his extra years, it seemed that it just took him longer. The worst part was trying to rub his pate. He kept bumping into the helmet. He was, however, getting used to it by the hour. "Comm check, by Platoons," he ordered, as Charlie Company's rovers pulled up on the malgamac surrounding Juventae Socket. With the comm check complete, Bransom switched to his control circuit to speak with his Platoon Leaders, wishing he could use his Mosquito Swarm out here.

"You know the drill. Every big shot in the Solar System will be up there tomorrow." He pointed toward the invisible Regent Skyport one hundred km overhead. "Our job is to make sure no bad guys do any damage to any part of this here Jackson Loop. Platoons one and four have the west and east driver complexes. Platoon one, take your rovers down that service road." He pointed to a smoothed-out road surface heading due west. "Platoon four, you will attach launch pouches to your rovers and run them down the MagLev to Margaritifer Socket and then take the eastern service road to the drivers. You both got

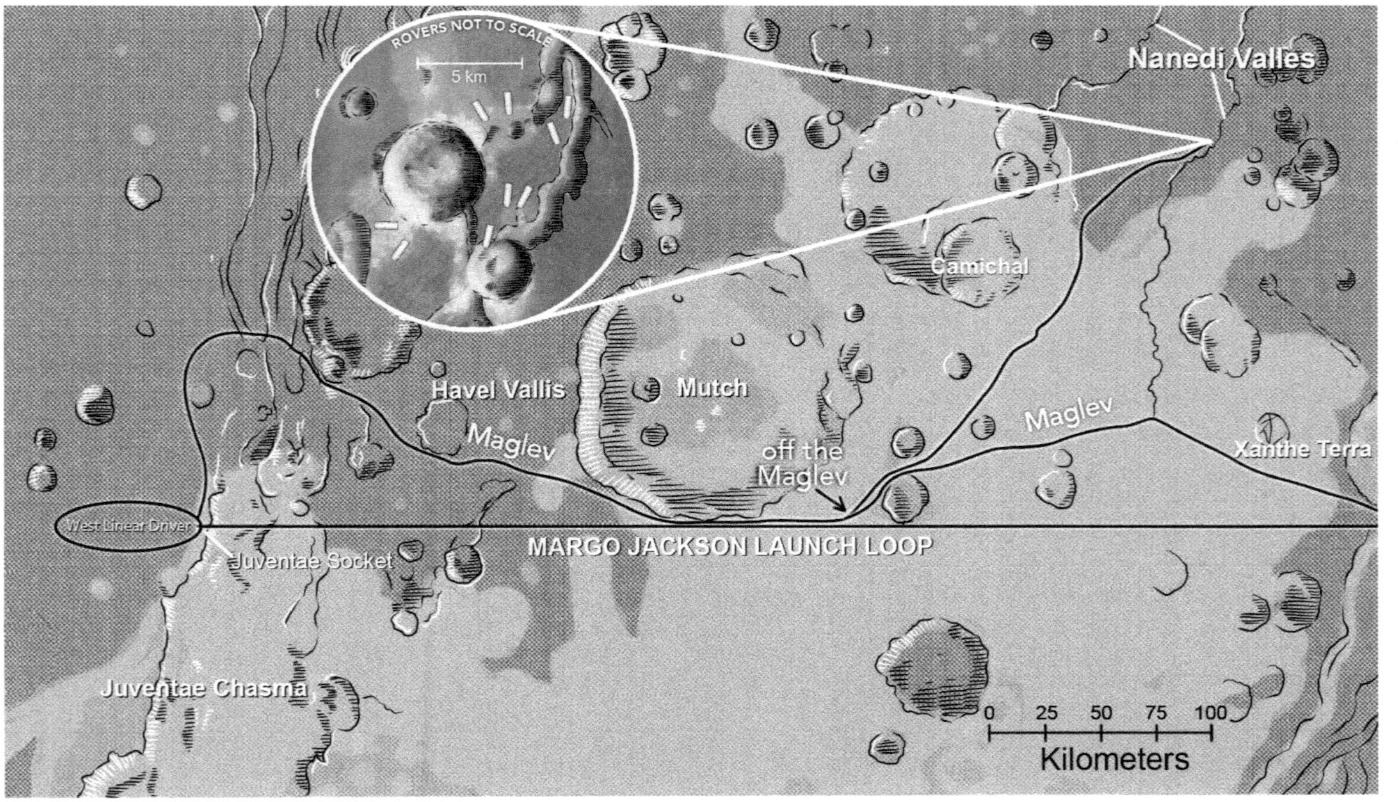

IMAGE 5—Track of Charlie Company from Juventae Socket to Nanedi Valles

about three hundred klicks from the sockets to the drivers, so hustle your asses. You want as much time on site as possible. Platoon three, you go with Platoon four, but you deploy at Margaritifer Socket. Platoon two, your two rovers are here with me and *Top-Rover*. Now remember, these guys don't got rockets, but they do have explosives, and they know how to use 'em. Also, they been livin' out here for a long time. Pressure suits are second nature to them. They use 'em way better than you guys. On the other hand, you guys got weapons they never heard of. If you see their rover, don't waste ammo on trying to penetrate the nosecone or anywhere else, for that matter. Ain't gonna happen. You can block 'em and box 'em in, but you ain't gonna break 'em. Your lasers will do little to their exterior and will bounce off their nosecone. Two of you blocking front and back, and two of you pushing might be able to roll 'em on a downslope. I wouldn't bet next month's paycheck, though. We gotta catch 'em outside to get 'em with rifles and sidearms. Any questions?"

"What about comms?" someone asked.

"Sergeant Gomez, here, will handle comms. We got a Server-Sky swarm covering the entire area so we can talk just like we was face-to-face. Now, all of you remember what we learned during our orientation training. Bullets go a lot farther here, and there ain't no wind to deflect 'em. If someone puts a bullet through your helmet, you gonna die. It's as simple as that. Remember, all we doin' is keepin' the bad guys away, so's they can't blow up the loop."

MARS—BETWEEN EAST & WEST NANEDI VALLES

When the meeting in Alex Regent Skyport broke up the next day and the VIPs returned home, over the next few hours, Charlie Company assembled on the malgamac surrounding Juventae Socket in eight rovers with Capt. Bransom and his team in his command rover—T*op-Rover*.

"Listen up, everybody," Bransom said over his general circuit. "We just got word that the Delgado brothers and their terrorist gang were seen northeast of Mutch Crater, heading northeast at a good clip. These guys got a hidey-hole out there somewhere cause they're not spotted very often. We gonna attach launch pouches to our rovers and ride the MagLev for 'bout six hundred klicks to where it dips back under the Jackson Loop. Then we disengage the MagLev and head north 'bout four hundred more. Then we spread out and start lookin' for their tracks."

Fifteen minutes later, all nine rovers commenced their high-speed MagLev trip to the drop-off point. Ninety minutes later, the rovers dropped their launch pouches and lined up just to the southeast of Mutch Crater.

"Single column for now, offset by twenty meters," Bransom said on the General Circuit. "I'll take the lead. We goin' fast…cover the four hundred klicks in less'n three hours. We got a lot of sand ahead of us, interrupted by a few craters. Keep a sharp eye. Don' want to stop to pull some asshole out of a hole bigger than him."

Bransom turned to Gomez. "Jen, keep a sharp lookout broad-spectrum. Maybe these guys talkin' to someone. He turned to Jacobsen, "Nor…keep 'em lined up and movin'."

After about two hours, Jacobsen pointed to some low-lying hills to the west. "Them ain't hills," he said. "They're rim mountains of Camichel Crater. West Nanedi Valles ends in a crater just a few klicks north of Camichel. That one's got no name."

Another hour, and Bransom called a halt. "Line 'em up, Nor, just in sight of each other."

When the nine rovers had formed a roughly east-west line, Bransom activated the general circuit. "Okay, guys, we're lookin' for rover tracks. No need to slow down, just keep a sharp eye out. First rover sees 'em, give me a shoutout."

"We head north for another hundred fifty klicks," Jacobsen said, "and then we turn northeast. Bit over an hour at our current clip."

Thirty-five minutes later, the western-most rover called out, "This is *One-One*," meaning Platoon One—*Rover One*. "Column HALT!"

"What is it?" Bransom asked.

"Rover tracks, Sir! A bit wind-swept, but clear enough…headed east of north."

"Okay…we'll continue north until the track crosses my position. Then we'll turn and follow the track."

Several minutes later, Bransom could clearly see rover tracks crossing his course, about twenty degrees to the right. "Swing the column, and line up on me," Bransom ordered.

They continued for another hour, and then the track angled farther east, pointing between a low jumble of rocky rises to the west and a crater rim wall to the east. In a few minutes, it joined several other tracks, but they crossed one another in a way that convinced Bransom they were made by only one vehicle. Bransom called up the holochart so it would show up in all the rovers.

"*One-One* and *Two*, station here." Bransom indicated a spot to the northwest in a gap between the rocky jumble and a five-kilometer-wide crater. "*Two-One* and *Two* go around this jumble and cut through here." He indicated a break in the piled rocks. "Split up and patrol this area." He indicated a flat area between two arms of an upside-down "Y" formed by the rocks. "*Three-One* and *Two*, spread out and patrol this gap to the northeast." He indicated an area between East Nanedi Valles and the right side of the rocky jumble "Y." "*Four-One* and *Two*, you drop down here to the southeast, and patrol this gap; keep in sight of each other. Everybody got it? Okay, move it!"

Bransom moved *Top-Rover* toward a five-kilometer-wide crater where a section of East Nanedi Valles terminated.

"Captain…*Four-One*…We're taking small arms fire! It's comin' from the rim of the big crater due west of us."

"Remain inside your Rovers!" Bransom ordered. "Move in a random pattern, but try not to show 'em your flanks." He examined his holochart. "The rest of you, converge here," indicating the crater just west of *Four-One* and *Two*. "Surround the crater. I'll block the southern chasm…here." He indicated a fifteen-kilometer stretch of chasm between Nanedi Valles to the southeast and the crater to the northwest.

As the nine rovers formed up around the crater, Bransom addressed them again. "Remember, small arms fire will not penetrate your rovers, but it will penetrate your pressure suit and helmets. So… don't expose yourselves to it. Let's try to isolate the point of fire and hit it with concentrated laser fire."

As Bransom finished, small arms fire commenced from the chasm rim just to their south. "You guys on the north and west, come around to join us."

While he was waiting, Bransom used his onboard sensors to sight in on the shooter to the south. He transmitted the coordinates to the other rovers. "On my mark, fire your lasers…Mark!"

The edge of the chasm burst into a brief fountain of lava, and the shooting ceased. Moments later, however, it started again from several meters to the west. As the other rovers joined, Bransom said, "Space your lasers to the left and right of my aim spot. Each rover select ten meters and sweep it several times. Commence on my mark…Mark!"

The spread-out lasers produced no visible lava fountains, but the shooting ceased and didn't restart. Bransom brought *Top-Rover* to the chasm edge and extended a sensor out over the two-hundred-meter-deep chasm. One pressure-suited figure lay crumpled on a narrow ledge, helmet intact, but face burnt beyond any possible recognition. A second figure lay at the chasm bottom, helmet broken open.

"These two were dropped off by those up there," Bransom said. "I'm gonna work my way to the top of the crater rim. You guys make sure they don't slip away."

Sure could use a drone or Mosquito Swarm, Bransom thought as he picked his way up the rugged slope where the chasm and crater rim wall met. Suddenly he was being pelted by small rocks and then increasingly larger ones. "They're above me, shoving rocks down on me," Bransom said over the general circuit. "Strap in Jen…Ray! This could get rough." Bransom pushed to the right, under a small outcrop that seemed to supply relative safety, until the outcrop itself began to slide.

"*One-One*, spot me a path to the top," Bransom said over the general circuit.

"Three meters forward, then drop five meters, and then sprint twenty meters on the level," *One-One* offered as rocks continued to tumble around Bransom's command rover.

Bransom followed the instructions, which turned out to be a tougher challenge than the instructions made it seem.

"Okay," *One-One* said, "now switch back as sharp as you can, and run for that overhang just ahead…HOLD IT!" a large boulder passed in front of the rover. "Okay, now git!" Bransom sat there, catching his breath, his pate glistening with effort as if he had actually been running up the rocky slope.

"This is Platoon Three…my rovers are coming up to join you. Stick tight till they get there."

"Roger…" Bransom answered. He watched the rovers turn and dodge as he had, but they finally made it to the overhang without serious damage, although Three-Two took a large rock broadside and nearly rolled down the slope.

"We're hittin' the rim with laser fire," *One-One* said, "makin' it unstable. We're drivin' him to your right. When I say so, Cap'n, you sprint left to the top. Watch the edge. It's unstable."

Bransom followed the directions and made it to the ridge without further trouble. He recognized the markings on the enemy rover fifty meters to his right along the roughly ten-meter wide rim. It was *Rover-2* from Lone Star Mars, the rover stolen by the Delgado brothers. To his left, where the crater rim wall merged with the chasm, he could make out a trail switch-backing to the crater floor five hundred meters below.

"Okay, *Three-Two*, move your ass level twenty meters to the right, and then angle to the top for another twenty meters. Hurry, or the bad guy'll get there first!"

Rover Three-Two reached the rim and turned to his left just in time to see the enemy rover coming at him full tilt. Bransom saw this happen and pushed his command rover forward at the best speed he could manage on the unstable rim. Rover *Three-Two* had more power and was more maneuverable than the enemy rover, but the driver had far less experience on the Martian surface and was driving in reverse, to boot. As the gap between the vehicles closed, Bransom called out, "*Three-Two*…on my mark, hit your brakes, and place your rover at a ten-degree angle pointed to the outer edge…got that?"

"Got it!"

"Ready…ready…MARK!"

Simultaneously, *Rover Three-Two* stopped and turned slightly left, as *Rover-2* plowed into its right side, glancing to the left, and *Top Rover* struck *Rover-2's* rear, propelling it along the right side of *Rover Three-Two*, wheels spinning in reverse to gain traction. It was too little, too late. *Rover-2* reached the crater rim's unstable inner edge, tilted forward, and rocked slightly as the two occupants tried desperately to exit the rear hatch. For ten seconds, it seemed to hang, nosecone thrust out over the teacup-curved five-hundred-meter drop. Then in majestic slow-motion, *Rover-2* slipped over the edge.

At first, it appeared that it might retain its orientation until it reached the inward curving slope. That was not to be, however, as *Rover-2's* left-front wheel caught an outcropping, twisting the rover to the left. *Rover-2* seemed to hesitate for a moment and then commenced rolling like a log with two hundred fifty vertical meters still to go. *Rover-2* arrived at the bottom of the crater, still in one piece, but even from the crater rim, it was obviously severely damaged.

"*Three-One*, work your way down that trail to our left, and investigate the wreck."

It took the better part of an hour to get to the crater floor. *Rover Three-One* reported no signs of life in *Rover-2*. There were four occupants, two apparently Hispanic or, as it turned out, Arabic. The other two in *Rover-2* and the two killed at the chasm edge were New Israeli Reds, including Menachem Dubro, who had earlier been rescued from Banishment by the Delgado brothers.

"I believe we got the whole lot," Bransom reported to Brady using the ServerSky swarm. "Only thing remaining is salvaging the reactor in *Rover-2*. The Hex is gone, but I think the reactor is worth salvaging…and anything else worth saving, of course."

IAPETUS—NEAR THE STARCHILD INSTITUTE

Marc took the hand of the woman who looked like she almost could be his daughter, but he knew was at least fifteen years his senior. "I hope you don't mind that I am here for the demonstration, Margo," he said.

"Of course not," Margo said. "You are the one person more responsible than any other for the current state of MERT."

"Sorry, Margo, I can't accept that. Kris Lambin and his team are the guys who did it. I just sat back in my office and watched the astonishing reports arrive at my Link."

"Okay, Marc, have it your way." Margo smiled warmly at him. "Exactly what are we looking at today?"

Before Marc could answer, the as-yet-unnamed lead MERT spacecraft of the *Merkavah Class* materialized a couple of meters before them and settled on its five legs extending from the bottom of the craft. A port opened facing them, and a ramp slid to the ground. White-smock-clad Dr. Kris Lambin appeared in the opening, holding Jake and waving them up.

"Welcome aboard the very first fully operational MERT Craft," Dr. Lambin said.

"What's different about this one?" Marc asked and turned to Margo. "Kris and I flew an experimental version of this craft a while back,"

"*XMERT-One* was a converted *Merkavah Class* hyper-V craft. This baby," Dr. Lambin patted the control console fondly, "was built from the ground up as a MERT craft. This girl is the first genuine FTL starship the human race has ever built."

"Not only that," Marc said to Margo, "but it is the official SI Director's craft. I probably should have briefed you in detail before I asked to meet you here, but with everything you have done, I suspect there is little that can surprise you."

"You succeeded!" Margo told him, kissing Marc lightly on the lips, much to his astonishment, "but we're not going anywhere in this thing until it has been officially christened. An old sailor boy like you should know this!" She stood in thought. "The christening should be in public, you know…with a bottle of excellent vintage… and it should be recorded for posterity."

Margo had caught Marc flatfooted—he was flabbergasted. Very few people in the entire Solar System could claim to have put him there.

"Let's fix this," Margo said. She did a few things on her Link, and within ten minutes, people were streaming out of the SI complex. "I love MERT Portals," she said, as people arrived from virtually every part of the Solar System. The MERT Net was not yet a smoothly operating system, but even in its infancy, it was able to bring people from everywhere to their little piece of Iapetus.

Marc watched in delighted astonishment as nearly every living person known to Margo assembled in the space between the SI Complex and the spacecraft. Several thousand people were present. Somebody in the back near the SI entrance passed forward a bottle of wine with a lanyard attached to the neck. Margo stepped to the port and looked out over the crowd. She held up the wine bottle and waved. The friendly crowd roared back its approval.

Margo held up her hand for silence. "Are we ready?"

"Yes!" as one voice from the crowd.

"Is someone recording this?"

"Yes!" as one voice again.

Margo commenced swinging the bottle back and forth on the lanyard, and then she announced in a clear voice, "I christen thee Iapetus *Federation Starship Lori K*!" and she brought the bottle up hard against the hull. As the bottle shattered, wine splashed over the Casimir Blade, flowing down the blade to drip off the razor-sharp bottom edge onto the bright green grass.

The crowd roared its approval and then dissipated as quickly as it had assembled, except for one person, Alex Regent. He walked up the ramp and gave Margo a warm hug and kiss.

"That's a nice gesture, naming her after Lori," Alex said and then turned to greet Marc and Dr. Lambin. "Margo and I go way back," he said. "And Lori Kutcher was a mutual close friend. Lori was killed when the Space Sling went out of control during a freak micro-meteor event in the early days before all this." He squeezed Margo. "Nice seeing you." He walked down the ramp briskly and entered the SI Complex. Jake scampered after him.

"Now that we're official, let's take *Lori K* for a spin," Margo said, turning to face the inside of the craft.

"Like I said earlier," Dr. Lambin said, taking a place in front of the control console and gesturing for Marc and Margo to do the same, "the *Lori K*—I like that name—is fully functional. There is no physical reason why we could not set in Proxima Centauri as a destination. We would arrive in…" he did some console manipulations, "twenty-seven-and-three-quarter minutes…real-time…no relativity effects."

All three sat in front of the console in silence, contemplating what Dr. Lambin had just said.

"My…" Margo said, following about a minute of silence. "It's difficult to grasp."

"As children," Marc added, "we laughed when holovision shows depicted people moving between star systems like we moved between cities on Earth. Now, look at this."

I propose we visit Mercury, Neptune, and Jehoshaphat—the nearest to the Sun, the long-time Solar System boundary, and the new kid on the block.

When no one objected, Dr. Lambin cleared his throat and spoke to the Resident. "Plot a path to Mercury, and set up a hover five hundred meters over the surface on the side away from the Sun." Then Dr. Lambin said to Marc and Margo, "Safety elements built into the Resident prevent the craft from entering regions that are too hot, where the radiation exceeds the craft's shielding capacity, where the pressure is too high, and many other conditions. These elements can be modified on the fly. Also, the monitors will display any magnification in real color or any specific color scheme you wish.

"One more thing…" He handed hyper-Discs to each of them. "These are personal portals back to SI. We'll test them at each stop." He fiddled some more at the control console. "We're talking fractions of a second for the first two jumps and about 3 seconds for the Jehoshaphat jump. That's because about the time Jehoshaphat was discovered, Neptune's position in its one-hundred-eighty-five-year orbit roughly lined it up with the new discovery. Jehoshaphat was and still is near the outer limits of its eccentric orbit—some six hundred AUs out. Since then, we have determined Jehoshaphat's exact orbital parameters, and Neptune is once again roughly lined up with her."

✳

Margo sat at the *Lori K* console, ready for she was not sure what.

Dr. Lambin activated the first leg. Margo didn't know what she expected, but in the next moment, the displays showed a crater-filled Moon-like surface. Sensors indicated a surface temperature of about -170° C.

"Set north up," Dr. Lambin ordered the Resident, and the display shifted. "Pull back until the entire hemisphere is visible." He pointed to a feature in the southern hemisphere. "Highlight the Great Valley," he ordered.

The display shifted, and the 1,000 km long, 600 km wide Great Valley became clearly visible, seeming to empty into the Rembrandt Basin.

Margo looked over at Marc. He was as absorbed and fascinated as she. She reached out and touched his hand, reminding herself that he was President of the Iapetus Federation and easily the most powerful man in the Solar System.

"Let's check the portal," Dr. Lambin said, activating his disc. "Reporting in from Mercury."

"Check," someone said through the open portal.

"I guess we're done here," Marc said, squeezing Margo's hand.

A moment later, the display filled with the supersonic-wind-swept, blue-green top of Neptune's atmosphere. On Dr. Lambin's instructions, the resident positioned *Lori K* directly above the dark vortex that had persisted in Neptune's atmosphere ever since its first discovery by Voyager 2 in 1989.

"It takes my breath away," Margo said. "So…is Neptune inside or outside Pluto's orbit right now?"

"Technically," Dr. Lambin said, "Pluto is currently outside Neptune's orbit. Sometime in the near future, Pluto will cross Neptune's orbit and stay inside the orbit for twenty years. Two hundred twenty-eight years later, it does it again. I don't know exactly where we are in that cycle right now, but it hasn't mattered much since Pluto's reclassification as a dwarf planet back in the twenty-first century. Since then, Neptune has been the outermost planet until Josephat was finally sighted and tracked." He ran a quick portal check and then turned to his console.

Dr. Lambin set up the portal and stepped through it, saying, "I'll be back in a minute." To their amusement, Jake strolled through the portal right after Lambin left and settled into Margo's lap, purring.

When Dr. Lambin returned, Margo said to no one in particular, "Did you know that way back in 1830, William Herschel's son John apparently observed Neptune during a sweep of the sky? He reported the observation sixteen years later in a letter to Wilhelm Struve."

"I wonder how he would react to being where we are right now?" Marc commented. "Would he even believe it?"

Dr. Lambin jumped into the conversation. "His father William Herschel was first and foremost a German-Jewish-Christian oboe player."

Mark raised his eyebrows. "It's a fact. I followed up on his background a while back, but can't remember why I got into it in the first place," Dr. Lambin said. "He ground his own smaller telescope mirrors, and before he died, he built his hundred-twenty-centimeter scope. A two-meter tube section and the two mirrors he used throughout the telescope's life were displayed in the Science museum in London until the Caliphate swept through England. I truly don't know if they survived the invasion."

"To our final stop," Dr. Lambin said, as the *Lori K* flashed to a hover a half-million kilometers above the frigid atmosphere of the little gas giant, Jehoshaphat. The gas ball exhibited no distinguishing marks at all. Dr. Lambin had nothing to say because nobody knew anything about this distant planet.

"Let's check the MERT Portal," Dr. Lambin suggested.

Margo set up her portal, and a friendly voice from the portal asked, "Where are you guys?"

"Hovering above Jehoshaphat, about six hundred AUs from the Sun," Dr. Lambin said.

"Mind if I step through the portal?" the voice asked, and Sam Houston stepped into *Lori K*. "This is damned impressive," he said, looking around. "Margo.... Marc.... I just had to check you out!"

"So, that's what you were doing back at Neptune," Margo said to Dr. Lambin. "Setting up this surprise." She turned to Sam. "Where are you these days?"

"Pulling double duty at my desk—running Lone Star…haven't turned everything over to Matti yet, and running backup for Marc, here, who's galivanting around the Solar System with this pretty woman I know, leaving the heavy lifting to me," Sam said with a wide grin.

"Don't you have something to do?" Marc said, feigning anger.

"Actually, I do," Sam said and stepped back through the portal, with Jake scurrying after him.

Moments later, *Lori K* settled to the grass outside the Starchild Institute.

"So do I," Margo said, kissing Marc lightly, and stepped through the activated portal.

EARTH—RIYADH, SAUDI ARABIA

General Ismail Suleiman looked out the window of his office located in the center of the fifty-six-meter sky bridge connecting the two pinnacles of Saeed Towers, the original 99-story Kingdom Center built in Riyadh back at the beginning of the twenty-first century. The towers had been completely refurbished during the Persian Caliphate and had survived unscathed during Saeed's global Jihad. Saeed eschewed the trappings of big government, preferring his sprawling tent complex still pitched atop the same low mound overlooking the dry lakebed near the center of Rub' al-Khali in the Saudi Arabian desert. Technically, Saeed ruled the world but really did not understand the complexity required to do so. Nevertheless, he had authorized Suleiman to build whatever government elements he needed in Riyadh. Saeed Esmail had conquered the world, but General Ismail Suleiman ruled it with an iron fist.

The streets ninety-nine stories below used to be filled with traffic, and the skies with passenger jets flying into and out of the international airport off to the east at the edge of Riyadh. At night the city below him used to be filled with lights and lively nightlife. All that was gone. Saeed Towers still had power, supplied by the Pakistani technicians Suleiman had imported. They also provided electricity and gas, but it was strictly limited to the buildings of the old Kingdom Centre.

Caliphate troops had slaughtered nearly everyone everywhere who could maintain a municipal infrastructure. Far more rapidly than Suleiman had anticipated, civilization worldwide was sinking to a medieval level where communities could sustain themselves by growing and consuming food locally, drawing on freshwater and processing sewage locally, and reducing power consumption needs to the lowest possible level. As power stations fell off the grid, his technicians and engineers kept only those working that sustained local government. Communications had slowed down drastically, with most handled through the written word. Suleiman still had his swarm of satellites and still could use them for internal Link communications, but it took a significant percentage of his available technical staff to keep the system running. Suleiman did not know how much longer he could rely on it. Air travel was now restricted to his personal staff and his senior military commanders. Passenger aircraft were falling into disrepair so that his few remaining pilots were refusing to fly them. Refined fuel was increasingly hard to find, so ground transportation was reverting to horses—they ate hay, grass, and grain, items that would always be in supply.

Human access to Space, to the rest of the Solar System, was limited to the Saudi Loop. His armies had destroyed the Sahara Loop at Atar right at the beginning of the global Jihad, followed closely by the Mediterranean Loop at Mallorca, and a bit later by the Caspian Loop at Sevastopol. They destroyed the Sri Lanka Loop right after Carmen Bhuta was given a free pass to Mirs. The iron ribbons and related hardware for these loops ended up in an eccentric solar orbit. His Pakistani technicians maintained the Saudi Loop at Mecca, and he intended to keep that Loop operating into the indefinite future. He abandoned the remaining loops. When Slingshot at Baker Island in the Pacific and the Atlantic Loop at West Station died, they caused no local damage—they just collapsed into the ocean and sank to the bottom. The Jakarta, Xinjian, South American, and South African Loops crashed in place instead of being flung into solar orbit since their ribbons simply lost momentum when the power sources ceased working. Thousands died when they collapsed. The Outback Loop in Australia and the Kiwi Loop were destroyed by explosives while they were at full speed, so their ribbons joined those of the Sahara, Mallorca, Caspian, and Sri Lanka Loops in Solar orbit.

Suleiman looked around his office. Soon, he would have to abandon this perch. Keeping up the utility systems would become more trouble than it was worth. Despite the tens of thousands of engineers and technicians he had sent worldwide to maintain the infrastructure of advanced civilization, they were insufficient to stem the tide of decay that was marching around the globe, following the path his armies had taken. Perhaps, after all, the Prophet had made the better choice for his desert center of operations. Suleiman reviewed the summary of operational military hardware he had received an hour earlier. He still had several dozen operational fighter jets and twenty helicopters with pilots and repair crews, twenty fully functional warships, miscellaneous battlefield hardware, and several hundred million rounds of ammunition of various calibers and purposes. Technically, Suleiman owned the largest, best-equipped air force and navy in history. The problem was, he had no fuel, and the technological capabilities of his planes and ships were fast falling into disrepair and uselessness because most of the people who used to run them were dead, and an education in the *Qur'an* produced few engineers and technicians. The only genuine plus in all of this was the hyper-V craft, *Rasul Allah*. Also, the Pakistanis at *Almaladh Al'amn* were making good progress in ferreting out the technology of the MERT Portal.

SOLAR SYSTEM—*ALMALADH AL'AMN*

In the early twenty-first century, NASA's Dr. Harold "Sonny" White did some interesting work with warp fields and non-baryonic matter. One of his findings was that under certain circumstances, the general relativity field equations that called for exotic matter to create a wormhole would work equally well when normal matter took on some of the characteristics of exotic matter. The research staff at the Saeed Esmail labs in Islamabad had made little progress in ferreting out the secrets of the exotic material that made up the skin of hyper-V craft. After relocating to *Almaladh Al'amn*, they approached their task with increased vigor. When the senior Pakistani researcher at *Almaladh Al'amn* received the MERT files from the Starchild Institute, he assigned the team to follow up on White's work.

It took the team a while, but eventually, they developed a silvery-grey metal, not unlike vanadium in appearance, that behaved exactly like the hyper-V skin plates in the Casimir effect experiments at SI. From that point, using the stolen files as a guide, they quickly duplicated the SI experiments. They successfully moved objects and then living things through their experimental portal, and finally, the day came where a junior technician walked through a portal from one structure to another within *Almaladh Al'amn*.

The *Almaladh Al'amn* researchers understood that their available power limited portal transportation. At *Almaladh Al'amn*, they had sufficient power to set up a portal between *Rasul Allah* and *Almaladh Al'amn*, but their power limited them to one such portal at a time only. They tested the portal at increasing distances, finding that they could reach Earth anywhere in its orbit, but Mars on the far side of the Sun was too distant for their available power.

The researchers also developed a portable activation device similar to SI's hyper-Disc, but it was a five-kilogram elongated cube not unlike a brick, not something one could slip in a pocket. Since *Rasul Allah* had sufficient reserve power to handle its own tethered portal, they installed one, so that when Saeed and his two technician warriors departed on *Rasul Allah* for his Solar System tour, he took two portable activators with him, one connected to *Almaladh Al'amn*, and the other to *Rasul Allah*. From time to time, he would activate the *Almaladh Al'amn* portal, if for no other reason, to verify that it still worked. He routinely used the *Rasul Allah* portal to return to *Rasul Allah* from each of his excursions.

IAPETUS—FEDERATION HEADQUARTERS

General Suleiman chose Riyadh, the center of Arab culture, to locate his liaison with the Iapetus Federation. He sent a personal representative via the Saudi Loop to Mirs and thence to Iapetus. The Caliphate representative met briefly with Marc, where they agreed that the Federation would take over the old U.S. Embassy compound on Abdullah Alsahmi Street and that Vice President Sam Houston would come to Riyadh to establish the Federation Mission. The representative was then sent on his way with the admonition not to return.

Several weeks earlier, Sam had extricated himself from the duties of governing Lone Star and had taken possession of his personal MERT craft. In a short but meaningful ceremony, Sam stripped *Saracen* of her identification papers and turned over the hyper-V craft to Margo at SI for conversion. Then he christened his new transport *Saracen III*.

"Why three?" Marc, who was present for the ceremony, asked.

"Simple…The original Saracen was the steed my great-grandfather many times removed rode into the battle of San Jacinto. *Saracen II* is that baby over there," pointing to his decommissioned hyper-V craft. "This mighty steed—capable of taking me anywhere I might wish to go—is the third in a proud line." Sam grinned broadly as Marc shook his hand.

Following the Caliphate representative's visit, Marc assigned Rod Zakes as Ambassador to the Caliphate and asked Sam to accompany him to Riyadh and assist in setting up the Embassy.

Sam reached out to General Samuelson for a contingent of battle-hardened troops to accompany him to Riyadh and suggested that if possible, he would like Lt. Col. Steve Brady and his famed

Charlie Company. Samuelson issued the orders, and Charlie Company pulled out of Mars. Brady ensured that Capt. Jer Smyth was part of the assignment, so that when Capt. Bo Bransom assembled his troops under Master Sergeant Norbert Jacobsen, it was almost like a homecoming.

Because of the seriousness of the occasion, President Marc Bowles addressed the assembled diplomatic contingent under Ambassador Rod Zakes, the installation crew under Vice President Sam Houston, and the military element under Lt. Col. Steve Brady.

"We don't know what you are walking into," Marc said. "Each of you has been issued an escape disc. Keep it on you, and use it for the slightest incident—especially if you fear for your safety or life. Remember, the disc will pull you out in an instant, and we can reinsert you again, even moments later, where you can be most effective.

"The Caliphate approached us…keep that in mind. They want something. We can think of many things, but we have no idea what really motivates them. Keep it simple. I strongly suspect that the entire planet is falling into serious trouble. Those idiots killed nearly everyone who had any capability of running anything but a Madrassa. You will be faced with a horrendous, possibly even calamitous social situation. General Suleiman will likely put a façade on Riyadh that will belie what undoubtedly will be the case almost everywhere else. Remember, your job is to observe, NOT to help! Sometime in the future, when our own people are fully functional in our part of the Solar System, perhaps then we can offer some help. Your families and friends are uprooted or dead because of these people. We owe them nothing.

"In the meantime," Marc's gaze took in everyone present, "Godspeed to Riyadh! Keep those bastards on a short leash!"

EARTH—RIYADH, SAUDI ARABIA

Sam addressed Bransom and his small contingent inside the SMERT craft. "I want there not to be the slightest chance that the Caliphate goons will take *Saracen III* from us," he said. "Who's going to take point?"

All the troops stepped forward, so Bransom chose big, tough Master Sergeant Jacobsen. "Sergeant Nor Jacobsen will do it, Sir."

"Let me see your hyper-Disc, Sergeant," Sam said. Jacobsen produced it. "You already know this leads back to HQ Operations." Jacobsen nodded. "If you must, activate it. I don't anticipate your having to do that, but be ready. More likely, you'll walk into the building and just open the portal so the rest of Charlie Company can join you. They will bring several regular portals, and I'll follow immediately with my installation crew. Right after them, Ambassador Zakes will arrive with his staff."

Sam brought *Saracen III* to a hover over the helicopter platform on top of the main embassy building, just centimeters above the pad. As he opened the hatch, Jacobsen jumped to the platform and sprinted toward the building entrance off to the right, just below the landing pad. Sam closed the hatch and, on the monitor, watched him duck below the pad. Shortly thereafter, a Charlie Company trooper stepped up on the pad and waved him off. Sam activated his pending order, and *Saracen III* departed for Iapetus.

Fifteen minutes later, with *Saracen III* safely parked near Federation HQ, accompanied by Brady and Smyth, Sam stepped through the Riyadh portal into the embassy lobby and an armed standoff between several very noisy Caliphate warriors on one side of the magnificent fountain and his equally loud Charlie Company troops on the other.

Brady stepped forward, and in a loud voice, shouted, "Quiet!" The lobby went still. Brady nodded to Smyth.

In perfect Arabic, she issued a firm command to the non-com in charge of the Caliphate warriors. "You will immediately take your men outside the compound gate," she said, pointing past the fountain toward the entryway. "Now!" she emphasized.

The Caliphate officer snapped to attention and saluted. When one of his men started to protest, he made a sharp comment, and the warriors quickly removed themselves and hurried down the steps. They took up positions outside the compound gate.

"What did he tell that guy?" Brady asked quietly while a couple of the troops who spoke Arabic chuckled.

"Told him to shut up or he would chop his prick off," Smyth said.

"Okay, you guys," Bransom said to the troops blocking the entrance, "post two sentries at the gate, get the surveillance system functioning, and establish roaming sentries around the entire compound."

After a brief discussion among the troops, two set off for the gate, and four distributed themselves around the compound and set up a moving guard routine. Another settled himself at the lobby desk.

Jacobsen stepped up to Bransom, who was chatting with Sam, Brady, and Smyth. "I think we got it covered now, Sir."

✳

Sam sat at his desk in a temporary office in the Iapetus Federation Embassy in Riyadh, shaking his head. He had anticipated jurisdictional problems with local Caliphate officials and even some surprises maintaining a constant supply of electricity and water, but he was utterly unprepared for what he actually found. He recalled an old movie that had been resurrected into holographic format back before the Caliphate, *Lawrence of Arabia*. Lawrence had done his best to unite the differing interests of the Arab tribes and actually managed to carry them to a great victory. In the aftermath, however, he failed at the mundane task of getting them to cooperate for producing electricity, delivering water and gas, and carrying away garbage and sewage. In the end, everything reverted to how it was before. It appeared to Sam that since then, nothing had really changed.

Sam had visited Riyadh before the Caliphate. It was a modern, exciting city. In fact, due to enormous wealth generated by oil and gas in the Middle East, Riyadh boasted some of the most modern, innovative buildings, outstanding educational institutions, great museums, and scientific research centers that were, in many ways, unsurpassed in human history. The deep, dark secret behind all this glitter, however, was that most of the architects, engineers, scientists, educators, artists, and technicians were from somewhere else. Without them, all the grandeur, all the glitter, would not exist.

When the Persian Caliphate consolidated itself throughout the Mediterranean, the Caliph made sure that those who created that beautiful veneer remained to maintain it and continue building more. When the Founders brought an end to the Persian Caliphate, no one imagined that another, more insidious caliphate would take its place. When the Prophet Saeed Esmail rose to power with the military backing of General Ismail Suleiman, no one realized what was in store for the world a few short years later. Now it was *Lawrence of Arabia* all over again, on a worldwide scale.

Except for the Saeed Towers from where General Suleiman administered the Prophet's global empire, and a few scattered industrial centers in the old United States and Central Europe, in Pakistan and Korea, that had salvaged some of the remaining technology, the entire world was rapidly sinking into a pre-industrial, medieval existence level.

Sam quickly arranged for power and water to be supplied from Iapetus to the embassy through portals, and for the portal removal of sewage and garbage. In the event of an emergency, these portals would collapse, with automatic normally-closed valves cutting in. His technicians connected the local embassy Link into the Solar-System-wide Link out of Iapetus. Gardeners, cooks, and service personnel of all kinds stepped forward from the teeming millions recently arrived in Iapetus. Within two weeks, the Iapetus Federation Embassy in Riyadh was a flowering, beautiful gem in a decaying city that ruled over a worldwide empire sinking into barbarism.

MARS—POLAR ORBIT MIRRORS

Sokolov brought an image of Mars into the Link display, floating before Margo and the three men. "I entered all the variables my staff and I could think of into the Iapetus Resident," he said. "Told it to generate an ideal trench plan. This is what it came up with." His Russian accent was barely audible, and Margo thought he might be working at keeping it that way.

Margo had been studying the surface of Mars with this geostructuring in mind. From what she could tell, it looked like a good plan. A trench system led from the South Pole ice cap into all the chasms and deep valleys, not only in the southern hemisphere but also going northward, so long as the slope was down. The plan skirted around Valles Marineris, avoiding it by at least a hundred kilometers. The plan was designed to distribute the available water without wasting it by discharging it into the northern ocean.

"There's nothing in the arctic basin," Orlov said.

"Don't need it," Sokolov said. "The water naturally accumulates around a slight polar rise, fills the arctic basin, and eventually flows toward Chryse. The water level rise will be gradual, so we'll have plenty of time to patch any leaks that might threaten Nanedi Valles or Lone Star."

"We know there is a vast aquifer under the old ocean basins," Margo said. "What we don't know is how our operations will affect it. What would you think about drilling straight down in the arctic basin for a thousand meters with your solar beam to see what happens? That might tap into the aquifer and release a whole lot of water."

"Might be worth trying *before* we release much north polar water," Orlov said. "Wouldn't want to overflow Chryse Basin."

"Don't think we would," Sokolov said. "The released water should lower the bottom of the arctic basin."

"Should is the operative word," Klaus added. "I think we would want to proceed with caution."

"All that water that used to be there went somewhere," Margo said, "and we know that it didn't dissipate into Space. Lone Star has found abundant water in an aquifer beneath Valles Marineris."

"If that's the level of the other supposed aquifers," Orlov said, "then we will need to push the solar beam a lot deeper than a thousand meters."

"Yes and no," Sokolov said. "The floor of the arctic basin is already about five thousand meters below Mars mean surface. That would put an arctic aquifer just about the same depth as the Valles Marineris aquifer."

"If worse comes to worse," Klaus said, with a twinkle in his eye, "we could always hook up a large portal and suck all that water to some distant Solar System location."

"Put the portal in place first." Sokolov sounded serious. "If we don't need it, then we don't need it, but if we do…"

"You know I was joking, my fine Russian colleague," Klaus said, pushing his own German accent. "Our order of business, then," he continued, virtually accent-free, "is first, burn the southern hemisphere trenches, then drill for the aquifer and deal with the consequences, then shape the ice caps, and then melt the ice caps as necessary." He paused and looked at his colleagues. "We're talking a year or more to do the trenches. Anyone know how this will affect the atmosphere?"

"I've been looking into that," Margo said. "I fed Andrey's material into the Resident and got an estimate of an increase of a half-bar in atmospheric pressure, with carbon dioxide at fifteen percent, oxygen at ten percent, and other stuff—mostly nitrogen—at seventy-five percent.

By the time you're done with the trenches, but before the water flows, global average temperature should be just above the freezing temperature of water—which is exactly where we want things to be."

"Seems pretty ambitious to me," Orlov said. "It sure goes against the terraforming timetables from the early Mars researchers in the first years of the twenty-first century."

"They didn't have the Founders in their calculations," Margo said. "Hyper-V power supplies have made a world of difference. Imagine doing what we did in the last few years without that." She turned to Klaus. "When will you get the process underway?"

"What do you mean *when*?" he said. "It's underway right now!"

MARS—NORTH POLE

Andrey Orlov had done a lot of things in his life, but standing here on the spiral plateau of Mars' North Pole in mid-winter, peering over the edge of Chasma Boreale where it finally dipped below the water-ice cap watching his flare disappear was his crowning achievement to date. It was cold, but his pressure suit took care of that. The Sun was below the horizon, of course, but the skydome was filled with stars. It looked very much like the sky from the Moon. The Milky Way swept across a portion of the sky, and it was difficult for him to rip his attention away from the drama. *Shtandart*, his personal MERT craft, waited patiently two hundred meters west of his position. The two technicians he brought with him were setting up a MERT Portal to receive a rover specially outfitted to handle the carbon-dioxide snow and very hard water ice that covered the 785 million square kilometers of polar ice cap to a depth of about two kilometers.

There was no physical requirement for Orlov to visit the ice cap. He and Klaus had already mapped out the swath the solar beam would take and the depths to which it would carve. This visit was just his reward for all the planning and hard work it had taken to get this far. He certainly did not want to be anywhere near when the fiery beam sliced down from the polar mirror ring. The beam would carve and shape the ice cap so that water from the melting cap would flow into Chasma Boreale and thence into the surrounding polar basin, where it would eventually overflow into Tempe, then Acidalia, and finally Chryse.

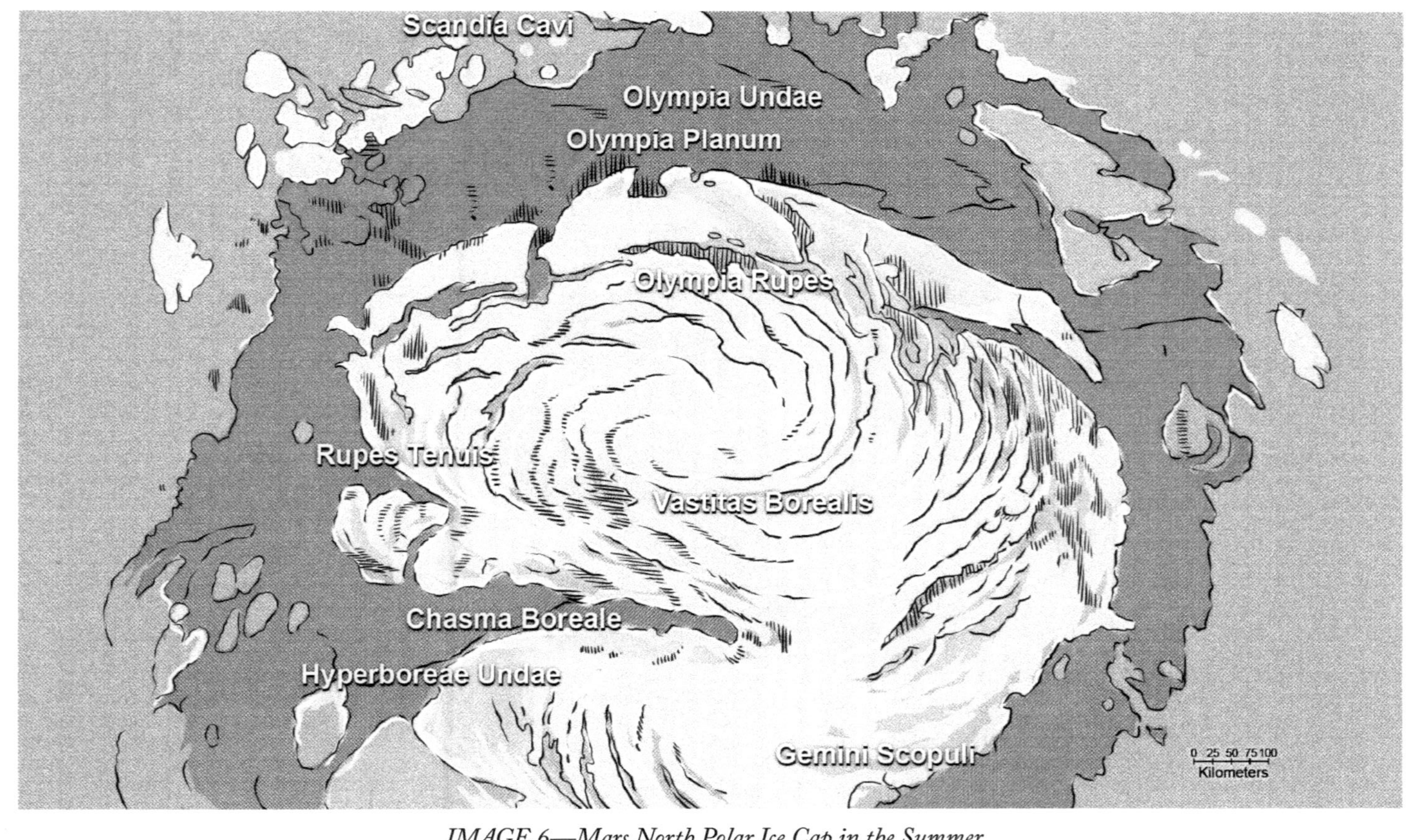

IMAGE 6—Mars North Polar Ice Cap in the Summer

The initial part of the plan was just the carving of the ice to enable the flow direction. The rest of the plan involved two parts. The Soletta would be adjusted to increase the solar radiation on both the northern and southern icepacks. This would subline the carbon dioxide into the atmosphere and would melt the water-ice, causing it to flow into the arctic basin in the north and into the trenches Sokolov would be burning out throughout the southern hemisphere. And that was the second part of the plan, to melt and vaporize selected parts of the Martian regolith, adding the vaporized elements to the atmosphere, while carving out water trenches to distribute water from the South Polar ice cap, that was elevated 3,500 meters from the mean surface of Mars.

Orlov watched the polar-modified rover emerge from the portal. A slew of technicians exited the vehicle, and he approached them. "Welcome," he said. "We have two weeks to place the markers. Klaus Blumenfeld and I have worked out their locations, and you folks will place them. I'll supply logistical support. We'll start here, using our Links to locate the precise positions for each marker. When you run out of rover-traversable terrain, I'll move the portal, so you can work the next section, and so on. Any questions?"

There were none, and Orlov said, "Well, that just about does it. We've gone over this enough that I didn't expect any questions, but one never knows. I'll be back later today to see how things are going."

MARS—SOUTH POLE

As on Earth, Mars' South Pole is on an elevated plateau and is much colder than the North Pole. Unlike Earth, however, it is much smaller. Even so, Mars' South Pole contains as much water as the North Pole and is three-and-a-half kilometers thick—about like Earth. Because the southern hemisphere is much higher than the northern hemisphere, the plan was to route the water from the South Pole to wherever it was needed. Orlov's initial task, as in the north, was to shape the ice surface to facilitate draining water as it melted.

Orlov brought *Shtandart* to a hover several kilometers above the ice cap. The spiral pattern was clearly visible in the bright sunlight, enhanced as it was by the Soletta, although the pattern was not so

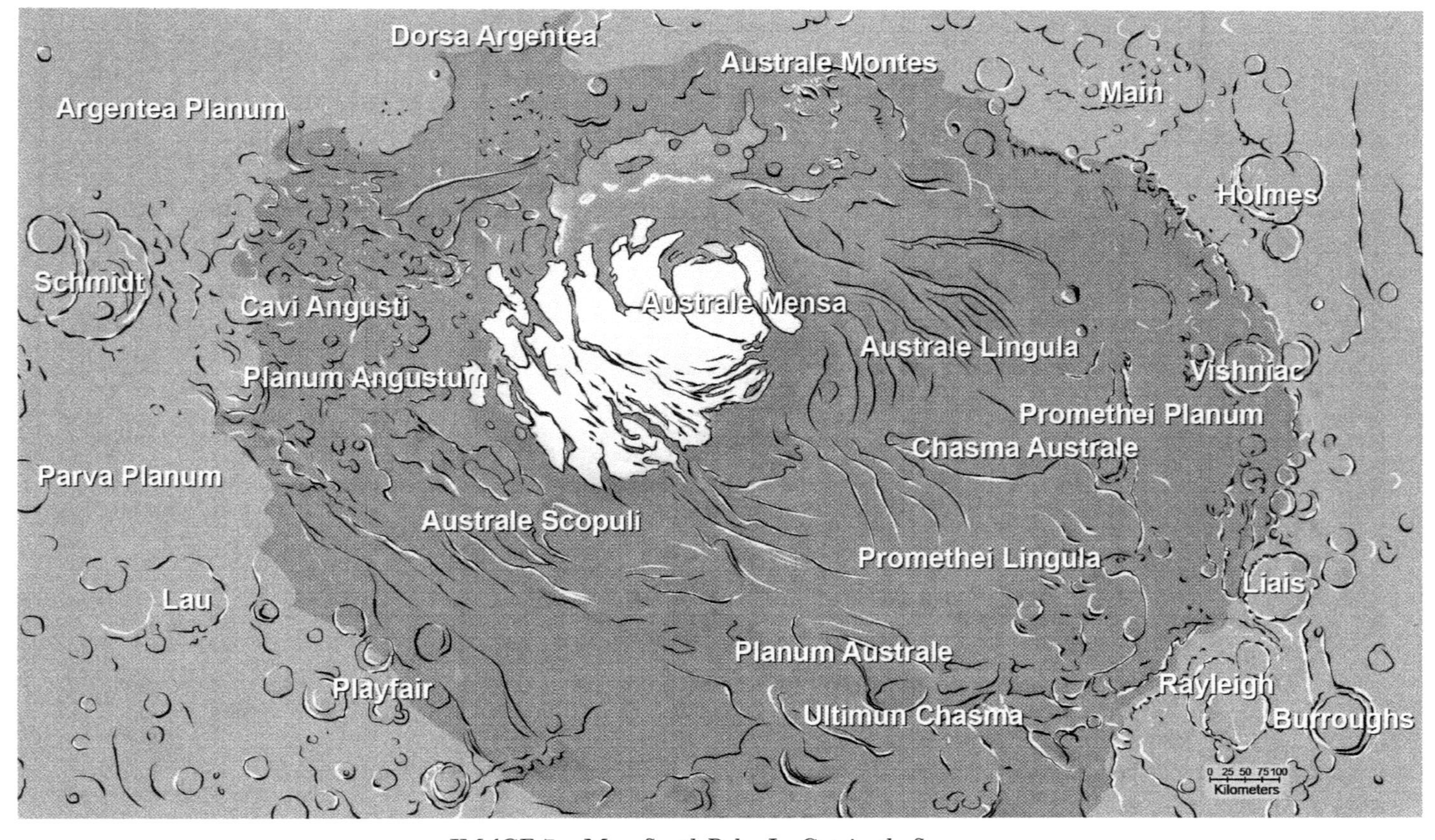

IMAGE 7—*Mars South Polar Ice Cap in the Summer*

evident as in the north. The South Pole did not have an equivalent to Chasma Boreale, but one of the spiral breaks was significantly larger than the rest, and Orlov brought *Shtandart* down near its head. When Orlov stepped onto the crusted surface, a shiver ran through him as his helmet darkened to accommodate the bright sunlight.

As in the north, his technicians set up the portal, and in a few minutes, another rover rolled out on the ice. With the much smaller ice cap, Orlov told his crew that he expected them to be finished within a week. "You folks know that you are in mid-summer down here. You know the geysers because I told you everything we know about them. The one thing we don't know is precisely when they start. It has something to do with how much sun the pole gets, how quickly the carbon-dioxide layer sublimes, and many factors we don't understand. Keep alert. We really don't know how much pressure they exert, but I suspect it is sufficient to blow a man into the sky. Probably won't lift a rover, however."

As Orlov was about to enter *Shtandart*, the ice under him rumbled with a low frequency he distinctly felt through his feet. All around him, holes opened in the ice, and apparently powerful geysers erupted several hundred meters into the sky. He dashed into *Shtandart* and ordered her into a hover 500 meters above the ice. His technicians ran to the rover and entered, but as they did, a geyser erupted directly beneath the rover's front wheel-set. The rover nose flipped up and over, and the rover fell on its top. As Orlov watched, a side hatch opened, and pressure-suited technicians cautiously crawled out of the overturned rover.

"Is everyone okay?" Orlov called on the general circuit.

"We seem to be."

"We need a crane to turn this sucker over and see if it still works," one of the others said.

"I'll see to that," Orlov said and set *Shtandart* for Mirs.

It took Orlov more than two hours back at Mirs to get a crane rigged that would function in that frigid cold. Then he obtained a hyper-Disc with a sufficiently large portal and jumped back to a hover over the Martian South Pole plateau.

As *Shtandart* settled on its five legs, Orlov asked, "Any more activity?"

"Not near us. Some several klicks that way," pointing generally east.

The technicians opened the portal and brought the crane through. It took them another two hours to come up with the best way to right a rover with diamond line on a slick ice surface, but they got it done. The rover still functioned, and they commenced placing the markers, paying close attention to the pattern of the geysers.

Once he was confident the crew was functioning efficiently, Orlov entered *Shtandart* and departed for the North Pole.

For the next few days, Orlov shuttled back and forth between the poles, moving the portals as necessary to accommodate his crews. There were no more geyser incidents at the South Pole, and by the time they had placed all the markers, geyser activity had stopped.

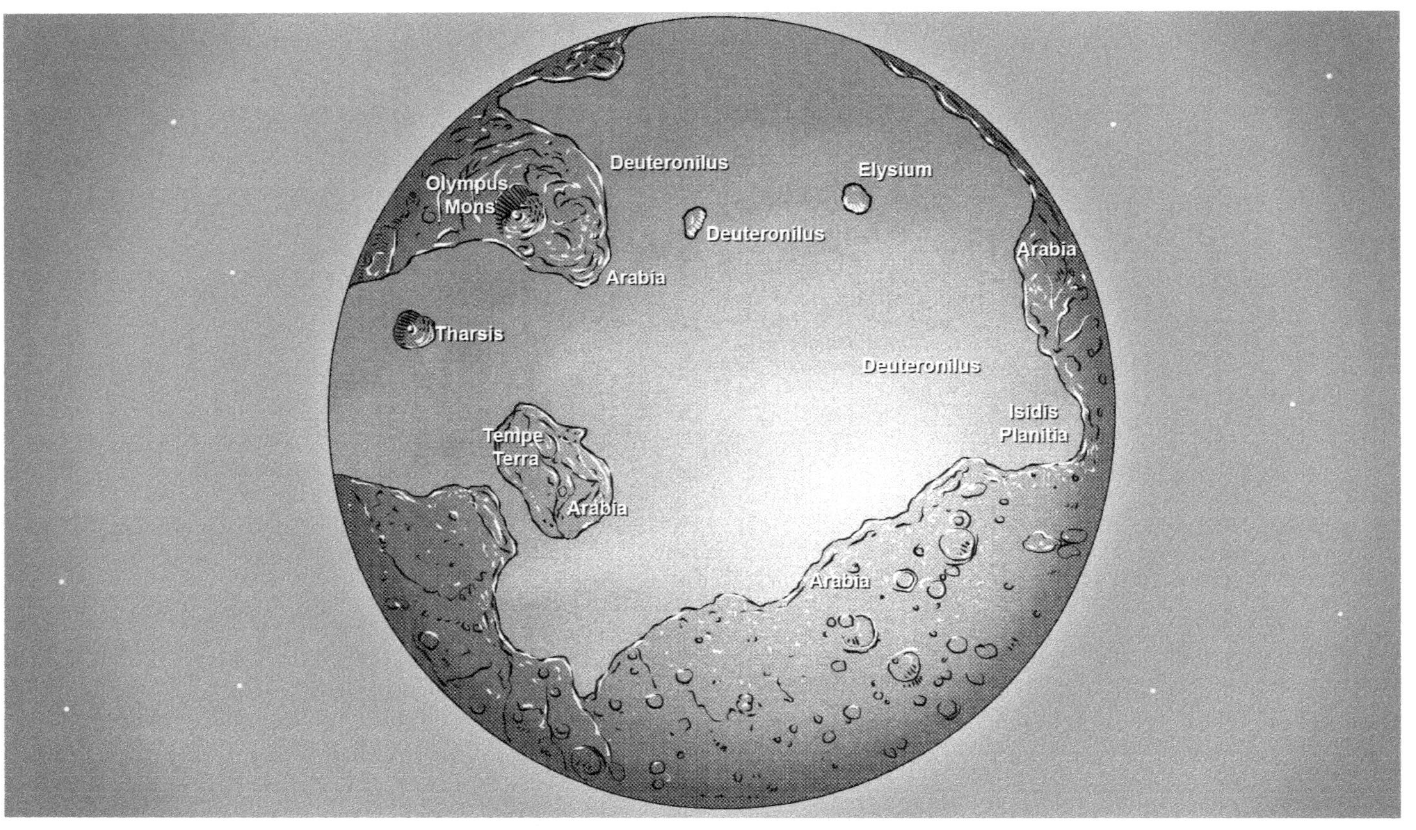

IMAGE 8—Mars North Polar Basin filled with water

CHAPTER TWENTY-THREE

MIRS—RING SAMARA

Following Reyansh Acharya's departure, Lud redoubled his efforts to transform his serum into a successful human age treatment. He and Acharya had successfully moved the working *in situ* human protocol to *in vivo* in lab rats, and that was where Acharya returned to India, taking with him, unbeknownst to Lud, the formula and a serum sample.

Lud and Shakbah were looking for two disparate results in their continuing research. First, they had to scale the in vivo protocol from lab rats to humans, and second, they had to induce age reversal at the human level. Preliminary research way back in the 21st century using simple parabiosis had demonstrated age reversal. At its most basic, the SILP was a type of parabiosis, but Lud and Shakbah's years of research were ample evidence that there was nothing basic or straightforward about it.

In addition to the Martini, Lud had also taken to the game of chess, particularly the Hyperchess form. He was intrigued by the approaches programmers took when working in the virtual world with chess and its variations. The most effective approach for computers with unlimited processing power is what they called the *brute force method*. Using this tactic, a computer applied its computing power to examine as many solutions as possible within the allotted time slot. In effect, Lud and Shakbah were using this approach in their search for the link that would translate age reversal in lab rats to age reversal in humans. It was only a matter of time. The more time that passed, the closer they were to a solution.

About the time that Rod Zakes was establishing himself as the Federation Ambassador to the Caliphate, Lud was carefully examining the results of his latest pass. What he saw gave him pause, and he reran it. Then he called Shakbah.

"You run it," he told her. "Follow this protocol exactly, and run it independently."

She did, with the same results. They looked at each other.

"How confident are you?" Lud asked.

Shakbah nodded shyly. "And you?"

"Let's do me, and then watch for a couple of weeks," he said.

✳

Two weeks later, together, they reviewed the progress chart of Lud's daily blood tests.

"The *in vivo* process is completed," Shakbah said. "You have stopped aging!"

✳

Lud administered the protocol to Shakbah, and two weeks later, they examined her daily blood test chart.

"It looks like you're not getting any older either," Lud said. "You're going to remain my beautiful girl forever!" He held her at arm's length, looking her over. Then he pulled her close and kissed her.

"It's time we visited Margo," he said.

IAPETUS—STARCHILD INSTITUTE—SILP

Margo was fully aware of Lud and Shakbah's longevity protocol and familiar with the degree to which it had already been human tested. Although very few knew it, human longevity had been accomplished several years earlier, but SILP had been put on hold because the *in vitro* nature of the treatment made it difficult and time-consuming. Only the very wealthy and the very well connected could have afforded it. Marc and Lud had decided to keep a lid on the achievement until Lud could find a way to make the treatment *in vivo*—basically a simple inoculation against aging that would be inexpensive and available to all.

Margo looked across her desk at the excited faces of Lud and Shakbah. They had reason to rejoice. They had just presented her with human immortality, or at least life without aging, perhaps indefinitely. Furthermore, although it would take time to verify, it appeared that older SILP recipients would begin to shed age so that over some as-yet-undefined time, their physiological age would settle out somewhere in the mid-thirties.

This was an earthshaking development, at least as significant as the MERT drive.

"What kind of human tests do we need?" Margo asked.

"We've both taken it," Lud said, "as have Vesta, Azurad, Michele, and Carmen...and Jake," he added with a grin. "We will be offering it right away to the other Founders and to the rest of you who have become part of our larger family."

Margo sat silently, absorbing what she had just heard. Lud and Shakbah had bypassed human testing of the *in vivo* protocol. Lud was almost two months into it with no ill effects.

"How do you feel?" she asked.

Lud just laughed while Shakbah giggled girlishly.

"We're fine, really, Margo. We know what we're doing."

"What's the process?"

Lud produced a small vial. "Inject this intravenously... anywhere. That's it. It takes about two weeks for the in vivo process to complete. We do not know how long it will take for age reversal to take effect, but the endpoint is the mid-thirties." He handed Margo the vial. "This is for you."

✳

Margo tasked one of her managers to set up a SILP manufacturing facility. The vials were numbered and coded so that they could not be counterfeited. They were designed to fit standard intravenous injection devices found in every medical facility and doctor's office throughout the Solar System. Within a month, all the main players had been SILPed. They were asked not to talk about it, however, and Margo was reluctant to make any public announcement for the time being.

She knew a secret like this could not be kept for very long, but she dreaded the consequences that seemed inevitable and feared the possible unknown implications.

What's done is done, she told herself. *Perhaps indefinite life and FTL travel come to every intelligent species at about our stage in their development.*

IAPETUS—STARCHILD INSTITUTE—MERT

Dr. Kristopher Lambin settled into a comfortable chair in Margo's office. The office was quite different from how he had come to know it during Marc's tenure. Although the walls and carpet were the same, everything else had changed. The holographs were new, of course, but the office itself had a softer feel, reflecting Margo's extraordinary character. One holograph, in particular, stood out, a holograph Margo had taken many years ago on the ocean bottom near Slingshot of Amelia Earhart's *Electra* sitting upright in magnificent isolation on the ocean floor.

"Let me tell you what we are working on," Lambin said as Jake strolled across Margo's immaculate desktop. "I have a team following up on some work in the early twenty-first century by NASA's Harold White. He played around with warp fields, and with replacing non-baryonic matter with normal matter. One of his general relativity field equation findings was that under certain circumstances, the power requirement for generating wormholes could be reduced by several orders of magnitude. At the time, he could not actually produce warp fields, so he filed his results under *Interesting Stuff.*" Lambin took a deep breath and let it out. "We are on the verge of doing just that—cutting the power requirement for establishing a MERT Portal to a tiny fraction of what we need right now."

"How do you see this affecting what we are doing now, beyond the obvious reduction in MERT drive power requirements?"

"MERT Portal power flux requirements are a function of two things, the size of the untethered portal and its distance from the tethered portal.

Our Solar System tests pushed our power supply capability to the limit as we approached the edge of the Solar System. We are within thirty days or so from putting the pieces in place to enable these power requirement reductions for both MERT craft and MERT Portals.

"As soon as possible, we will retrofit all the current MERT craft, so they function under the reduced power protocol. Once that is completed, we will commence a series of MERT craft jumps starting at two hundred AU, where we will test an onboard untethered modified MERT Portal to its twin at SI, measuring the power draw for each test. We'll run tests out to ten lightyears and then use the accumulated data to generate a predictive matrix to see what power draws distances beyond ten lightyears demand. Then we will jump to these points to test the actual power draws."

✳

Within just a few weeks, several updated MERT craft carrying hyper-Discs linked to updated MERT Portals had filled in a power-draw matrix. They commenced at 200 AU, moving outward, visiting over twenty stars with known distances from the Solar System, ranging from just over four lightyears to somewhat over ten. Each test was run directly out of Dr. Lambin's lab: (1) assign the star, (2) with the power-flux being continuously measured, make the transit, (3) open the portal, and (4) return.

Dr. Lambin correlated the power-flux requirements for each distance and developed a curve to describe the power-flux during the entirety of each trip. Then he set the Iapetus Resident to the task of developing a mathematical expression for power-flux as a function of distance. With the result in hand, he approached Margo, with Jake tripping along behind him.

"The Resident has produced a matrix exponential that defines the connection between the matrix Lie Algebra representing the cubical starfield surrounding the point of departure, and the corresponding Lie group representing the tensor from the point of departure to any given star within the cube," he explained.

"I'm an engineer, and a good one," Margo said, "but I didn't understand a word you just said. Would you mind saying that again in language comprehensible to someone other than a theoretical physicist?" She smiled warmly to soften her words.

"Sure," Lambin answered. "The power requirement rises exponentially as the distance, by a pretty complicated calculation."

"How far will our current power system structure allow us to set up a portal?" Margo asked.

"That's what I meant by 'a pretty complicated calculation,'" Lambin said. "The Resident worked with a five hundred lightyear cube. We—the power source—are at the center. We don't really know how much power we can draw from the mini-black hole at the center of Iapetus. We don't know how to calculate this, and we're not sure how to phrase the question so the Resident can give us an answer. We keep getting conditional responses that seem circular, but that the Resident insists are not."

"What about Vesta's Star?" Margo asked.

"Ninety-two lightyears shouldn't be a problem."

Jake sprang to Margo's desktop, mewing his agreement.

SOLAR SYSTEM—GENERALLY

With the large numbers of people who flooded Iapetus from Earth during the Exodus, several thousand were deep-undercover agents of the Caliphate. Over time these agents disbursed themselves throughout the Solar System. Each agent was responsible for pulling together like-minded individuals who would rise to Saeed's call when the time came. Saeed's purpose for touring the Solar System surreptitiously was to contact these agents, give them encouragement, and get an idea of the strength of his followers away from Earth.

Saeed and his two technician warriors parked *Rasul Allah* in the general parking zone at Mirs. In times past, young entrepreneurs set up shuttle taxis to move people from their parking location to their destination in one of the three Rings or wherever else they might have business. With the ubiquitous presence of the MERT Portal, only a couple taxi services remained. A taxi picked up Saeed and his companions, without beards, and clad in unremarkable business attire, and dropped them off at the zero-g docking platform of the newest 5-kilometer Stanford Double-toroid, Ring Rostov, where they were issued magnetic slippers. One of Saeed's companions carried a small duffel bag that contained the hyper-Brick linked to *Rasul Allah*.

The platform held dozens of labeled portals, each to some fixed hub somewhere in the Solar System, including portals to each of the other Rings.

Saeed studied the portal tags and chose the one labeled *Ring Samara*. He stepped through the portal, followed by the other two. They walked to a quiet area of the landing platform where Saeed pulled out a folded piece of paper, unfolded it, and examined its contents. Then they entered the elevator for the ride down the spoke to the ring proper. Once they had gained sufficient weight to stick to the floor, they removed their magnetic slippers and attached them to the elevator wall. This section of Ring Samara consisted of corridors with doors on both sides, much like a hotel. A couple of hundred meters down the passageway, Saeed stopped and knocked on a door. It opened a bit, someone looked through the crack, and then admitted them.

As Saeed and his warriors entered the room, the four occupants bowed low and backed to the wall. "Allah's blessings on you," Saeed intoned and took a chair near the middle of the room.

"Refreshments, Sahib?" one of the room occupants asked, proffering the hot, sweet mint tea Saeed preferred. Saeed and his warriors accepted, but the warriors remained standing and alert.

One of the room's occupants briefed Saeed on their recruiting activities and laid out their plans for future disruption. They had over twenty-five followers who did not know each other but knew the four in the room. Saeed listened quietly, blessed them again, and then said, "It is time."

A side door opened, and a medium tall, dark-skinned man entered the room, carrying a small satchel, recognized for hundreds of years as a doctor's bag. The off-the-books physician, whose practice consisted entirely of illegal SILP treatments, opened his satchel and removed an elastic strap and an injection device specifically designed to inject the contents of the small capsules into a patient's blood vessel. Saeed submitted quietly to his ministrations, and in five minutes, the Prophet of Prophets had the genuine potential for life everlasting.

A room occupant escorted the physician out of the room, receiving a nod from one of the warriors, and returned shortly and handed the warrior a small package containing the doctor's supply of SILP vials. "We will dispose of his remains after you depart," he said quietly.

Then the other warrior removed the hyper-Brick from the duffle bag, set it on the deck, and manipulated its recessed controls. A portal opened. Saeed and the warrior holding the vials entered the portal, and then the remaining warrior picked up the hyper-Brick and stepped through the portal into *Rasul Allah*, and the portal collapsed behind him.

The next stop was L5 on the other side of the Moon's orbit. They parked *Rasul Allah* unobtrusively near one of the many farming modules. A lone figure jetted across the 200-meter distance using TBH boots and locked into *Rasul Allah*. The visitor removed his helmet and attempted obeisance in his pressure suit somewhat unsuccessfully. Saeed waved him to his feet and received his report.

He had managed to recruit several hundred adherents, distributed mainly throughout the farming modules. They did not meet *en masse* to avoid detection but communicated with one another as much as possible. The visitor was the only one who knew all the participants. The visitor assured Saeed that they could respond to appropriate signals when the time came.

Rasul Allah did not go directly to Mars but arrived behind the Soletta in the guise of a vessel with repair parts. As the onsite team members were to learn to their everlasting regret, *Rasul Allah* had nothing to do with repair parts or anything else related to the upkeep of the Soletta. With no clear picture of precisely what the Soletta was or what it did and not carrying any kind of disruptive weapons, Saeed just flew *Rasul Allah* through the louvers three times in different locations. Then he ordered his onboard Resident to take *Rasul Allah* high above the ecliptic and back down deep in the Asteroid Belt, where it was unlikely that he would be found.

The damage to the Soletta was extensive but did not shut down Soletta operations. It was back up fully operational within thirty days. The new safeguards put in place made it unlikely that such an attempt would succeed in the future.

While the attention of Mars was on the Soletta, Saeed landed *Rasul Allah* in a remote part of the stretch between Juventae and Margaritifer Sockets, where he met with several dissidents from New Israel and Lone Star. They informed him of the loss of the Delgado brothers and *Rover-2*, but they assured him that they had access to whatever they needed by way of ground transport and would be ready and waiting for his call.

One by one, Saeed visited twenty-five different outposts throughout the Solar System, working with the leaders until he was satisfied that he would be able to rely upon these groups when the time came. Some he told to await his signal. Others he gave a commence order based on a specific event happening in the Solar System, and others he gave a specific time to initiate.

SOLAR SYSTEM—FEDERATION SECURITY

Over the years, Dmitri had settled into his chosen task of protecting the Federation from enemies external and within. Thus far, the external part had played no role in his activities. His people had managed to reign in the Caliphate sourced pirate activities so that this was no longer a problem. Dmitri's main challenges dealt with the aftermath of natural and manmade disasters, theft of goods and services, and corporate fraud. He kept his force lean and mean and relied on the instant communications provided by the ubiquitous fiber communication system interconnected through portals everywhere in the Solar System.

Dmitri established surveillance at each central traffic node throughout Iapetus, Ceres, Daphne, Mirs, Ayers Sky, Port Udachny, and on Mars at the Jackson Loop and Blumenfeld MagLev. Furthermore, he established surveillance points throughout Mirs and the three rings, at several locations within Ceres and Daphne, several points within Ayers Sky, on Mars, linked into the pre-existing Mars system, and virtually every place else where humans crossed paths. The surveillance was passive. No Big Brother looked over the shoulders of travelers passing through these nodes, but if the need arose, Dmitri could have the Iapetus Resident do a detailed search of any specific node for any period of time.

Rod Zakes' embassy office in Riyadh informed Dmitri that Saeed had not been seen anywhere on Earth for several weeks. The embassy's best information was that the Prophet was alive and well but that he was off-planet. Dmitri had come to respect the *little terrorist* over the years, if for no other reason than his conquest of the entire planet

Earth. Dmitri was convinced that Saeed had placed sleeper agents among the refugees that left Earth during the Exodus. He suspected that Saeed was now contacting these agents. Dmitri set the Resident to work sifting all the data from all the nodes from the time Saeed left the limelight to the present. The dataset was massive but finite.

Several hours later, the Resident identified Saeed and his two warriors entering Ring Rostov. The Resident traced them to their meeting but never saw them leave. Dmitri interpreted this to mean they departed by portal. Portals have signatures, and the Resident could find no portal operation from that room connected in any way to its vast network. This was unequivocal evidence that Saeed had his own portal. The Resident's search located *Rasul Allah*, so for the first time, Dmitri had actual images of this mysterious hyper-V craft. The Resident could not track it after it departed.

Dmitri assigned the Resident to search the surrounds of each of the other monitored entities for several hours following *Rasul Allah's* departure from Mirs. Eventually, he was rewarded with an image of the hyper-V craft moored near one of the Ayers Sky agricultural modules. The big payoff of this find was that the Resident identified the pressure suit used by Saeed's visitor.

Following that discovery, searching through several weeks by the Resident over the next few hours found nothing new, but then Saeed showed up entering Daphne, and the Resident traced him to one particular building. Then it picked him up entering Ceres from one of the Iapetus portals. That was the last sighting, but they were sufficient to give Dmitri what he needed.

✳

Dmitri and Dany Orel positioned themselves outside the door in Ring Samara. Dany knocked. The door opened cautiously, and someone looked out.

"Dany Orel and Dmitri Gagarin, Federation Security. May we come in?"

Since the units had no second exit, the person on the other side of the door really had no option.

"We know that the Prophet Saeed Ismail and two bodyguards visited this unit recently," Dmitri said, specifying the exact date and time. "You have consorted with a known terrorist and are subject to

Federation sedition laws," Dmitri told the four people in the unit. "You are under arrest and will accompany us."

Orel restrained them, and Dmitri opened a portal to his Mirs Headquarters. After appropriate persuasion, Dmitri sent two-man units to twenty-five Mirs locations, where they arrested twenty-five primary conspirators and twelve co-conspirators. These arrests shut down Saeed's Mirs operations.

✳

Dmitri and Orel positioned *Merkavah* just outside the agricultural module Saeed had visited earlier. Dmitri had traced the identified pressure suit to the person who had used it. Dmitri set up a meeting, pretending to be an emissary of the Prophet. The conspirator jetted to *Merkavah* and passed through the lock, unaware of the deception. After doffing his suit, Dmitri confronted him and demanded information on the other conspirators.

"As Allah is my witness, I will divulge nothing," the man told Dmitri and Orel. "I would rather die than betray the cause."

"No problem," Dmitri said, remembering a similar scene on *Cassini II* so long ago, "we'll accommodate you."

He grabbed the traitor, removed his Link, threw him into the lock, and started the depressurization cycle. When the man understood what was happening, he began to panic, screaming, "I'll tell you what you want to know! Please…don't space me!"

Dmitri ignored him, continuing to lower the pressure until the man was experiencing genuine physical distress from the low pressure. At that point, he stopped the cycle.

"How many people have you recruited?" Dmitri asked.

The man hesitated, and Dmitri immediately recommenced dropping the pressure.

The man screamed, "No! Stop! I'll tell you!"

Dmitri stopped again but said nothing.

"The list is encrypted on my Link," he said.

Dmitri picked up the Link. "Your access code," he demanded. "And if you give me anything false, anything at all, I'll set the decompression to very slow, and you will die the most painful death imaginable."

He supplied the codes, and Orel used them to access the information he immediately transmitted to their security people waiting inside Ayers Sky. During the following three hours, Federation Security rounded up 350 people inside Ayers Sky, people who had dedicated their lives to destroying the habitat.

What neither Dmitri's captive in the airlock nor any of the 350 rounded-up conspirators knew was that Saeed had embedded another agent in Ayers Sky who would be activated only if the others were captured. His task was utterly simple. Don an explosive vest and detonate it in the most sensitive place he could penetrate.

The lone terrorist was not technically trained and did not have sufficient knowledge to blow himself up in a place that mattered technically, so he wandered into downtown New Sydney, found a large crowd, and did the deed.

Five hundred innocent people died that day.

❋

Dmitri cleared out the terror cell on Daphne without incident or loss of life. The Daphne security people requested custody of the five individuals arrested in the raid. Dmitri happily complied, and two hours later, they were ejected unprotected to the surface through a portal Daphne had installed expressly for this purpose.

❋

Dmitri gave the Kiwis in Ceres the information he had collected and left the matter in their hands. They never informed Dmitri how they handled the issue, except to tell him that Ceres no longer had a Caliphate problem.

❋

On Mars, things were different. As a result of the incredible MERT Portal proliferation throughout the Solar System, the Margo Jackson Launch Loop was utilized less and less. Where a portal was inadequate, a MERT craft of one size or another could do the job faster, more efficiently, and with less aggravation. The Ectarians had used launch loops for about a generation before replacing them with hyper-V technology. It appeared that the only remaining launch loop in the Solar System was about to suffer the same fate, but to MERT technology instead, something the Ectarians never developed.

Saeed was unaware of this when he visited Mars after his escapade with the Soletta. He instructed his dedicated followers to take down the Jackson Loop as soon as they had assembled the necessary resources.

Martian terraforming was well underway, but a person still needed a lightweight pressure suit with helmet and oxygen supplementation when on the surface. Although the Jackson Loop was rarely used anymore, The Alex Regent Skyport still was a popular tourist destination. The Delgado Brothers successors decided to stage their take-down of the loop when the Skyport was filled to capacity. They planned to send an explosives-laden capsule up the skytower to the ribbon, detonate the charge, and sever the ribbon, just as the eco-terrorist tried to take down the original Slingshot during its construction. What they didn't realize is that that long-ago incident had changed how launch loops were constructed. There was no way a modern launch loop could be brought down by that technique.

The terrorists stormed the Juventae Socket building, killed the staff, and launched their explosives-laden capsule. When it reached the Alex Regent Skyport, it exploded harmlessly against the protective plating. Following the explosion, the panicked guests crowded into capsules and descended to the Juventae Socket, where they were picked off one by one by the terrorists who were waiting for them when they realized that their plan to bring down the loop had failed. When they had killed the hapless visitors, the terrorists scattered in all directions.

It took Charlie Company over a month to find all of them and teach them the harsh lesson of banishment that remained more than effective in Mars' still thin atmosphere.

✳

The remaining twenty or so Caliphate outposts waited quietly in the darkness of the Asteroid Belt for a signal that might never come, but ever watchful, ever ready to spring into action at the call of their Prophet of Prophets.

IAPETUS—STARCHILD INSTITUTE

Margo sat at her desk, stroking a purring Jake nestled in her lap and considered her options. Starchild departed for Vesta's Star 91 years ago. In two years, she would start her return trip. Starchild's purpose was to understand the nature of the alien repeater—and it had to be alien; there was no other logical explanation. Her crew members fully accepted the consequences of their choice—they would return to a world bereft of friends and family, trusting fervently that their existence would not have been forgotten.

What they didn't know, Margo thought, *what they could not possibly have known, are SILP and MERT. I was in my mid-sixties when they left. Now I'm over one hundred fifty—and look at me!*

She placed Jake on her desktop, stood, and walked into the water closet connected to her office, where she scrutinized her face in the mirror. A 35-year-old Margo Jackson looked back at her, physically the same woman who built the underwater portions of Slingshot so long ago.

All of us, her thought continued, *are part of a grand experiment. For me, age reversal started nearly fifteen years following my treatment. For our younger members, it happened much quicker...but Vesta took longer, and so did Klaus and Alex.* She chuckled quietly. *When they return, we'll have to deal with the Old Folks until their age reduction catches up with the rest of us.*

Back at her desk with Jake again in her lap, Margo felt the germ of an idea begin to percolate through her consciousness. She called up the construction history for *Starchild*. Margo was well familiar with the astonishing manufacturing capabilities of Iapetus. Nevertheless, she was surprised to discover that a core group had taken about a month to settle on a design for *Starchild* that would accomplish their needs. The actual automated manufacturing process only took another month. Since there was basically nothing wrong with *Starchild's* design, Margo realized that she could duplicate the starship in about a month. That would be a hyper-V ship, of course. All she had to do was scale up their present MERT design and add it to the *Starchild* design.

Margo pushed away from her desk and leaned back in thought, hands clasped behind her head.

In five weeks, I can duplicate Starchild *as a MERT craft. We can load her out appropriately and meet the original* Starchild *at Vesta's Star! Then we can bring them back through the portal.*

Margo stood, opened the door, and stepped through Marc's portal, something that frequently happened each day anyway. Jake scrambled between her legs, avoiding the cat door, and jumped on his desk.

"Marc…," her words tumbled out so rapidly that she had to slow down consciously. She briefed him on her thoughts.

✳

Seven weeks later, a modest crowd gathered around the SI construction bay. The main dock contained a replica of the Starchild sporting 20 m by 50 m deep black Casimir Blades. Margo addressed the group from a small dais placed just inside the dock.

"Back in 1977, the American space agency NASA launched two interplanetary space probes, *Voyager 1* and *Voyager 2*. Both these probes performed amazingly well and even now are slowly wending their way through interstellar space, sending out occasional signals to announce their continued presence. Today, we christen you *Voyager 3*, humanity's first large-scale FTL spacecraft."

She swung a bottle of ancient Israeli wine that Asshur had supplied. It shattered high on the inner surface of the right Casimir Blade, spilling the precious liquid down the blade and along the starship hull to the dock. The crowd cheered as Sam and his ten-member crew walked up the ramp and entered the craft. The crew consisted of most of the leading players since *Starchild* had departed, except Marc and Margo, who remained behind to orchestrate *Starchild's* early return, Dmitri, whose growing concern over the Caliphate trumped being part of *Voyager 3*, Azurad and Jake, who chose to stay with Dmitri, and those actively involved with the Mars Terraformation.

✳

The ten crew members placed themselves around the control room as they wished since no one had devised a protocol for this occasion. Sam motioned Vesta to sit beside him at the control console and gave her a gentle squeeze.

"Here's the general plan," Sam told the crew. "Our first jump will be for forty lightyears. This will take a bit over an hour. The Resident will generate a new vector, and we'll jump another forty lightyears. The Resident will then set the vector for our last jump of twelve-and-a-half lightyears. That will take just under forty minutes. That's when things get interesting.

"We have timed our arrival so that we will be on station for about two weeks before *Starchild* arrives. Their arrival time is not certain, of course, because of small, unpredictable variations in *Starchild's* velocity.

"We will be searching for two things. First, the location of the transponder. And second, of course, we want to locate *Starchild* the moment she arrives near Vesta's Star." He paused, looking around at the crew. "Any questions or comments?"

There were none, so Sam turned to Vesta. "Would you do the honors, Earth Mother?" He guided her tiny hand to the jump activator.

"Everyone ready?" Vesta asked.

She touched the activator.

VESTA'S STAR

Inside *Voyager 3*, there was no perceptible change. Sam set the external sensors to display their view on the internal displays. The displays remained black. "Can you enhance the display?" Sam said to the Resident.

A slight sparkling filled the displays, but nothing else. "Enhance more," Sam directed. This time, instead of black, the background display color was a mottled grey but otherwise featureless. "Do you detect anything at all?"

"Nothing," the Resident responded.

The first stop was barely noticeable as the Resident automatically established the new vector and commenced the second jump. Sam instructed the Resident to hold after the second jump so they could view Vesta's Star on the displays.

"But…it's just stars, *mes Chéries*," Michele said when all they could see was a starfield.

Sam explained. "We're still twelve-and-a-half lightyears away. We'll have to be as close as Neptune to really see anything."

Sam checked the time—they had been underway about two hours and six minutes. "Show Sol," he ordered. The stars on the display swept to the left until a faint yellowish star appeared in the display. It began to blink.

"Home, folks," Sam said. "Home, sweet home."

Sam looked around the group. "Any questions before we continue?"

There were none, and he ordered the Resident to continue the journey.

Voyager 3 flashed into normal space high above Vesta's Star without incident forty minutes later. Vesta's Star looked very much like Sol from Earth, bright and yellow. Since the Resident carried a detailed subroutine for locating planets in a star system, Sam set the Resident about the task.

"Search for planets," he said. "Display what you find."

"This will take a while…several days, maybe," Sam said to everyone.

✳

"Before we do anything else, we need to test the portal," Sam said, gathering the crew around the control room. He placed the hyper-Disc in his hand and activated it. A point in the control room about halfway between overhead and deck shimmered for a few seconds. Then it seemed to grow while emitting no sound. As it grew, it took on the shape of a door. The door area was a dull, silvery gray. Then it flashed clear, and they could see into Dr. Lambin's lab back on Iapetus. He walked up and peeked through the portal.

"Who will be the first person to transit an interstellar portal?" Dr. Lambin asked through the portal, but before anyone in his lab or on *Voyager 3* could respond, Jake jumped through the portal and commenced rubbing Vesta's leg, purring loudly.

✳

"Here's the thing," Sam said to his assembled crew after the successful MERT Portal test. "We just traveled ninety-one lightyears to find a transponder and then meet some friends we haven't seen in a long time. But we did something else, too." He smiled as Jake walked up to him and mewed. "As of a bit ago, we can move between here and Iapetus, or anywhere else in the Solar System for that matter, by just stepping through that portal." He pointed to the door. "We will have to start thinking about interstellar travel a lot differently than we have. We're here, and anyone else can be here simply by walking through that." He pointed at the door again. "We can bring several hyper-Discs through the portal and drop them off on planets we might find around Vesta's Star. That establishes a permanent connection between them and Iapetus. If we take the time to replicate Iapetus' mini-black hole out here, we can commence using *here* as another portal node." Sam stopped and shook his head. "It's hard to wrap my mind around this, but what I see eventually is a network of MERT Portals interconnecting our entire galaxy through thousands or even millions of nodes." He laughed. "Travel to anywhere at all will simply be a matter of passing through a series of portals. Are you guys seeing this?"

Sam's excitement was infectious. Everyone began chattering about the possibilities. They were joined by Dr. Lambin, who stepped through the portal when he heard what Sam was saying. Dmitri and Azurad stepped through to retrieve Jake and hung around for a few minutes. Marc and Margo popped through long enough to congratulate them.

As the immediate novelty wore off, Sam said, "Noel, Asshur, and Rod—you guys might want to start thinking about how we are going to find that transponder. Carmen and Vesta—you two probably want to set up sickbay to your liking. Carmen, Vesta, and Michele—you three might want to prepare for how you will deal with any life forms we find when we do eventually land somewhere. And Steve, Jer, Bo, and Dany—start thinking about security. Remember, transponders don't just spontaneously appear… somebody or something put it there. I very much want to presume the goodwill of whoever or whatever that was, but I sure as hell won't let anything get the jump on us. Rod, you may want to review your diplomacy skills in the event we really do run into someone. Keep Carmen close—she's a language expert. She's the person who first deciphered Founder Speak, you know."

Sam was quiet for a bit and then spoke up again. "I've been thinking…If we do run into someone technologically sophisticated out here, do we really want to offer them direct access to our home system without first vetting them? So," Sam picked up the hyper-Disc, "I'm closing the portal for now. We can open it any time we want, and Dr. Lambin can do the same from his end. I just feel better this way."

✳

After several hours the Resident still had not come up with anything. Sam considered the possibility that Vesta's Star had no planets but then rejected it. Over the last hundred years, astronomers had determined that virtually all stars sported planets of some kind. Vesta's Star would be no different.

Sam and the others busied themselves watching the displays closely, hoping to spot an object moving clockwise relative to the others. They did identify several objects that were brighter than the background stars, but during the first few hours, no one could detect any apparent movement of these or any other objects.

Shortly thereafter, the Resident sounded a quiet *bong*. On the display, two objects brightened significantly. A few minutes later, the Resident designated a third one and indicated the orbital parameters for the first two with light rings around the sun and other parameters in text near the planet. Then a fourth planet was designated, and the Resident showed moons around the second and third.

"Show the habitable zone," Sam said.

A band with a slightly different background appeared around the sun. The orbit of the third planet was just inside the inner edge of the zone, and the fourth planet was just inside the outer edge. A cheer erupted from the group.

"Close-up of planet three," Sam ordered.

The view zoomed in, looking down at the north pole of planet three, tilted about 20° into its path of travel with a rotation period of just over 25 hours.

"It looks just like Earth, *non*," Michele said, "landmasses, blue water, white clouds…"

"Analyze its atmosphere," Sam said to the Resident.

"Oxygen and nitrogen, approximately twenty-to-eighty ratio in the upper layers."

"Let's look at one, two, and four," Sam said to the group.

One and two were rocky, one without atmosphere and about the size of Mercury; two about the size of Mars with a carbon dioxide atmosphere. Four was Earth-size, and like three had water and landmasses and an oxygen-nitrogen atmosphere, although oxygen was lower and there was less water.

"It's been a long day," Sam said to the crew. "While we get some sleep, the Resident can look for gas giants." No one disagreed, so Sam instructed the Resident to pull out to 15 AUs and look for gas giants and any other planets while the crew slept.

✳

Over coffee and morning rations with a dish of cream for Jake, the crew crowded around the displays to see what the Resident had discovered overnight—two gas giants and no visible asteroid belt. There might have been additional planets beyond the gas giants, but the time was too short to tell.

"Let's get better acquainted with the inner Earth-like planet," Sam suggested. He ordered the Resident to remain a half AU above the ecliptic and one AU distant. "My concern," Sam told everyone, "is that if this planet has a technological civilization, we want to remain hidden for the time being."

Asshur related to the group how he and the other Founders had suddenly appeared in Earth's atmosphere some 60,000 years ago. "The Earth's nations were in a nuclear standoff," he said, "and our sudden presence triggered a nuclear war that nearly destroyed life on Earth. It took the human race tens of thousands of years to recover."

Following Asshur's story, no one objected to remaining hidden from a possible technological civilization on the planet. The Resident checked the electromagnetic spectrum for anything other than random noise, looking in particular for anything in the spectrum the transponder had utilized but found nothing. *Voyager 3* moved closer, continually scanning the entire spectrum, looking for anything that might indicate advanced intelligent life—still nothing. Finally, the Resident placed *Voyager 3* in a low polar orbit and checked the atmosphere more specifically. It turned out to be 23% oxygen, 72% nitrogen, 4% carbon dioxide, and 1% everything else.

The climate appeared to be very Earth-like, with temperatures ranging from about -75° C to 50° C. Both poles were ice-capped— the north pole over a landmass and the south pole over water. Water covered about 65° of the planet. The landmasses were covered with green vegetation, except in the equatorial desert areas—like Earth. They saw lots of bird-like flying creatures, large herds of 4-legged grazing animals, and hints of medium-size predators. They detected no sign of intelligent life or any kind of civilization. The three biologists were especially interested in what appeared to be bipedal, fur-covered animals, but the possible sightings of these creatures were too uncertain to draw any conclusions.

"This is so much like the Earth we found when we arrived from Ectaris," Vesta said. "The similarities are almost scary. We discovered that the DNA differences between us and life on Earth as we found it were incompatible. I'm sure you all know the story of how we developed a virus that would modify Earth's DNA over several generations, how things went wrong, and how the entire Ectarian civilization on Earth was wiped out during our family's return to the Ectaris system in *Merkavah*. What was left, along with our occasional genetic input, resulted in Earth's modern civilization." Vesta grew silent and withdrawn. Finally, she said, "I would like a sample of the planetside vegetation."

"We can analyze them in our bio-lab," Michele said, "or send them back through the portal."

"True, but I want to do a preliminary, and based on that, we can look in greater depth."

"We can do it," Sam said, "but since we know nothing about airborne pathogens, you will need to wear your pressure suit and decontaminate in the lock before coming back inside."

"Agreed."

"What do you want?"

"What passes for grass and leaves," Vesta said while she donned her pressure suit.

"I don't want to land near a lot of trees because of possible predators lurking there." Sam settled down over a mid-latitude open grass area that contained isolated trees here and there. "Will this work?"

"Looks good," Vesta said.

Sam brought Voyager 3 to a half-meter hover. "Okay, Earth Mother, go get your samples."

Vesta exited the lock down the ramp and snipped several grasslike blades. She reached up and clipped a small branch containing a dozen leaf-like appendages. Then she stooped down and lifted a cow-pie-like patty and placed it in a separate sample bag. As she did so, a swarm of insect-like flying creatures rose from the ground near the last sample, nearly engulfing her. She swatted them away, but they kept coming back.

"I'm returning," Vesta said, "but don't cycle the lock. You need to take Voyager above the atmosphere to expose me to vacuum. My samples are safe, but you need to get rid of these flying insects."

Sam retrieved the ramp and closed the hatch. Five minutes later, he told Vesta, "Brace yourself. I am opening the hatch."

When the hatch was open and all the planetary air had escaped, Sam told her, "Attach a line to yourself and step out of the hatch. Take the air nozzle with you, and blow yourself down out there."

Ten minutes later, Vesta reentered the lock, and Sam closed the hatch. "Stand by for decontamination," he told her.

After she was thoroughly washed down, he opened the hatch to space again to remove any residual fluid and then cycled the lock and let her into the cabin.

"I think," Vesta said to Michele and Carmen, "that we have something to do."

"I think," Sam said, "while you gals figure out what you have, that we should make a quick stop at planet four."

"Your reasoning," Noel asked.

"I know our main focus is the transponder," Sam said. "I strongly suspect it is down there," indicating planet three. "But before we can safely investigate anything local, we need to know if the planet will kill us unless we are willing to operate in pressure suits the entire time. It's going to take them a while to give us answers. We never thought we would find a planet like this one, or number four for that matter. While we're awaiting the bio-lab results, we might as well get a preliminary handle on four."

"Hard to argue with that," Noel said.

The others concurred.

"One more thing, everybody," Sam said. "Our planet needs a name. Number three doesn't quite make it. Any suggestions?"

"There are two reasons we are here," Rod said, entering the conversation for the first time. "Lud and Shakbah gave us longevity. Without them, someone else would be here."

"Let's wait to see four first," Asshur said. "Then we can decide which planet gets named for my little brother and which for his pretty companion."

✳

The fourth planet was disappointing. It was glaciated, with glaciers reaching almost to the sub-tropical zones of the planet. Oxygen and carbon dioxide were each 15%, with 65% nitrogen, and the remaining 5% contaminants appeared to be volcanic in origin. The planet had no land or air life that they could see from orbit, and while the seas could have harbored life, they appeared barren. The Resident found nothing in the electromagnetic spectrum.

"It's got potential," Brady said, "but there seems to be nothing that necessitates our security skills, certainly nothing like the potential of a civilization on three." He smiled at Smyth and Orel and exchanged high-fives with Bransom.

"Potential for someone else to exploit," Noel added, to a nod and wide grin from Asshur. "And what do you mean by a civilization on three—there was nothing in the electromagnetic spectrum. That pretty much eliminates that."

Asshur added, "Let's call this one *Lud* and name the nice one for *Shakbah*."

Consent was unanimous. Sam entered the information in *Voyager 3's* log, making the third planet's name official—*Shakbah*, and the fourth *Lud*.

VOYAGER 3—BIO-LAB

The first thing Michele and Carmen did upon entering the *Voyager 3* bio-lab was sit down with Vesta and describe how they intended to do the DNA analysis. Since their procedures were foreign to Vesta, she thought it best for her to observe and ask pertinent questions. This would allow her to learn their methods while acting as a scientific backstop. The arrangement suited everybody.

Under cleanroom procedures with the alien samples inside an isolation box, Michele carefully opened Vesta's sealed containers. She cut a snippet of grass, a leaf, and a bit of offal, and placed them into 1.5 mL microcentrifuge tubes with silica sand. Then she inserted the tubes into the analyzer.

"The analyzer freezes and micronizes the samples and siphons the plasma through nitrocellulose membranes. The results are displayed here," Michele said, pointing to a built-in monitor.

"Not really that much different than how we did it," Vesta said. "Different machines, same results."

Their analysis revealed the familiar helix structure with four bases. Surprisingly, three were the same, but a different unknown base took the place of guanine in both the alien DNA and RNA. Michele inserted pieces of the alien DNA into normal Earth cells, and they observed the process on their monitors. The cells seemed able to utilize the alien DNA just like normal DNA, without any apparent adverse side effects.

"What do you think, Vesta?" Michele asked.

"I want to run more tests," Vesta said, "but I think we may be compatible."

"Carmen?" Michele nodded to her.

"More tests, yes, and we need to collect a sampling of fauna," Carmen said.

The three joined the rest of the crew in the Control Room and told them about their preliminary results.

"Of course," Michele said, speaking for all three, "we want to run some actual tests, feeding the alien vegetation to Earth animals. We also want to test animal DNA—we didn't get any on the first round." The three could hardly contain their excitement. "We really want to return to Shakbah right away to collect a significant batch of vegetation and a couple of living critters."

"First, let's open the portal and let Iapetus know the news," Sam said.

✳

Four hours later, the three biologists looked over their new charges, four little, furry, rabbit-like creatures minus the strong back legs of a rabbit. They named them *raphers*, after *rabbit* and *gopher*. The raphers happily nibbled on lettuce, carrots, and commercial rabbit food that Margo had tossed through the portal when they last opened it. They did not detect any immediate adverse side-effects. In a cage next to the raphers, a couple of domestic rabbits seemed to enjoy the green vegetation and root samples Vesta brought back from Shakbah, again, without apparent complications.

"They're so sweet," Michele said. "Thank you, *mes Chéries*, for letting me participate in this."

Vesta gave Michele a squeeze. "You and Carmen figured Iapetus out. Now we will seek out Shakbah's secrets."

The crew had been unable to collect a living predator, but they bagged a foxlike creature and returned its body to Vesta. Michele fed pieces of the creature to their lab rats, and eventually to Jake. The rats consumed it immediately, but Jake took his time, nibbling around the edges and eating part of it. Then he attempted to bury the rest on the lab floor. Neither the rats nor Jake showed any distress after consuming the alien meat.

So far as Vesta, Carmen, and Michele were concerned, these tests settled the matter. Vesta was prepared to try the local vegetation, and if they could slaughter one of the grazers, she wanted to sample its flesh as well.

"A new world awaits humanity," Vesta wrote in her Link log that evening, as she, Carmen, and Michele sat together in the crew lounge discussing their results.

"New worlds for old," Carmen said softly.

"*Oui, mes Chéries!*" Michele said, kissing them both.

PLANET SHAKBAH

After the Security Team, still in their pressure suits as a precaution, bagged the foxlike creature and obtained more varied vegetation samples, *Voyager 3* lifted away from Shakbah. The transponder team suggested that Sam bring *Voyager 3* to 20°above the ecliptic at two AU from Vesta's Star and set the Resident to broadcast a high-energy transmission for 25 hours in the bandwidth that contained the original signals received from Vesta's Star. The message: "Hey, Shakbah!"

"If it's on Shakbah, and we think it is," Noel said, "this should wake it up, assuming it's still working."

Two hours and thirty-seven minutes later, the Resident announced a faint reception of the message Hey, Shakbah! The message seemed to be coming from the general direction of Shakbah, and the Resident noted the visible hemisphere.

"Put us into a geostationary orbit over the center of that hemisphere," Sam ordered the Resident.

"Actually," Rod said, "you might consider centering the orbit a quarter of the circumference further west. Think about it. As the planet turns, the transponder just crosses the horizon where it hears the broadcast and immediately retransmits what it hears. That puts it somewhere on the western edge of the visible hemisphere when we first heard it." Rod grinned at everybody. "That's my celestial mechanics rising to the surface again…sorry about that."

Everybody chuckled while Sam reset the parameters for the geostationary orbit. The transponder team came up with a method to narrow the transponder location. Asshur explained.

"We're presuming that the transponder lies somewhere on the longitude directly below us. If we actively manage our position, we can tilt north until the response disappears, and then south to isolate the transponder to a very narrow section of that longitude."

"Then we move in for a closer survey," Noel said.

"And we land when our biologists say we can," Sam said.

✳

Within an hour, the Resident had isolated the transponder's location to a one-kilometer-wide by two-kilometer-long section of the longitude that Sam had already designated as the prime meridian. Vesta assured Sam that the crew would not likely suffer any adverse consequences by disembarking on Shakbah's surface without body protection. She did, however, recommend a breathing microfilter until their pathogen tests were completed in about a week.

"That's good enough for me," Sam said, as he instructed the Resident to land *Voyager 3* at the southern end of the area of interest, and then to commence broadcasting a continuous message on the transponder band.

The Resident brought them down in a wide clearing in a lightly wooded area with knee-high, grass-like vegetation. As *Voyager 3* extended its legs and settled to the ground, a swarm of birds rose from the surrounding trees into a bright blue sky with a smattering of cotton-white clouds. High above, several hawk-like birds circled lazily in the updraft generated by the clearing. Deer-like creatures beyond the clearing froze just like their terrestrial cousins as *Voyager 3* settled. In the tall grass, several of the foxlike animals slunk close to the ground, propelled simultaneously by curiosity and fear. For fifteen minutes, Sam kept the ship sealed and made no noise, except that the Resident was continuously broadcasting on the transponder band.

Since they were dealing with a virtually unknown situation, Sam decided that his security team—Brady, Smyth, Orel, and Bransom—would make the first sweep.

"Steve," Sam said to Brady, "there probably is nothing to worry about, but remember that something possessing real technology planted that transponder."

"Understand. We've given this a lot of thought, Jer, Dany, Bo, and me. We can handle anything out there except a thundering herd of alien elephants." Brady grinned broadly, and the rest of his team chuckled. "Jer is launching a drone that she will control with voice commands on a dedicated circuit. We will see what it sees, and so will you." He looked over at Smyth. "You ready, Jer?"

She gave him a thumbs up. "You guys ready?" They nodded.

"Okay, then," Sam said, extending the ramp and opening the lock.

The four entered the lock, cycled it, and exited down the ramp onto the clearing floor.

"Dany," Brady said, "you make a good addition to our team, but I gotta tell you, I miss my Charlie Company guys." As he spoke, their receivers picked up the transponder. "Let's spread out over a hundred meters," Brady said. "Using the drone and our spread, we should be able to zero in on that sucker."

"Steve, I got something," Smyth said while she focused the drone on an area about a half kilometer ahead of them.

"Got it," Brady said. "Let's come in on it from four directions. Dany and Bo, you guys work around to the north side. We'll wait for your signal. Then, let's close it until we're about a hundred meters out." They all acknowledged, and Orel and Bransom trotted ahead.

"I just passed a clearing to my right," Orel said.

"Me too, to my left," Bransom said.

In ten minutes, everyone was in position. "Okay," Brady said, "let's approach it, weapons at the ready. When you see something, call a halt."

Several minutes later, Smyth called out over the circuit, "Halt!" She found herself not believing what she saw. "Hold, everybody!" she ordered as she stepped into a meadow that was clear of trees but overgrown with bramble-like plants. "You're not going to believe this," she said. "I'm looking at a virtual twin of the *Merkavah*."

✳

Immediately following the discovery, Sam contacted Margo and arranged for a full team from SI to participate in ferreting out the secrets of the hyper-V craft. Within hours, MERT Portals to SI opened all around the clearing, while the security team cleared the brambles away from the strange hyper-V craft. By the end of the day, the craft rested on its legs near the center of the clearing as if it had just arrived.

Starchild was due to arrive in less than a week. Sam set up an active signal on the same wavelength the transponder used since he expected Jon to commence scanning this band as soon as he settled into his preliminary position in the Vesta's Star system. Since Jon was unaware of MERT or SILP, he would need some kind of immediate orientation to keep him and his crew from going to battle stations or otherwise heading down an undesirable path.

"Whatever we tell Jon will be completely disorienting when he first hears it," Sam said to Margo as they sat in his command cabin on Voyager 3. "I think we need to give him a piece of normal with the initial message. Let's have Dmitri do the talking. Jon knows and trusts Dmitri and will be less likely to overreact if Dmitri is his first contact."

"You know him better than I do, Sam, but that makes a lot of sense. I'll leave it in your hands." Margo smiled. "You coordinate with *Starchild*, and I'll ride herd on this extraordinary thing you found."

CHAPTER TWENTY-FOUR

VESTA'S STAR—*THE STARCHILD*

Captain Jon Stock activated the general circuit. "Okay, people… listen up! We have been underway for nearly thirty-six hours. Please join me in the Control Room."

A few minutes later, the entire crew squeezed into the Control Room, knowing what was next.

"In about five minutes, we will decelerate and come to a hover somewhere within the Vesta's Star system. We've gone over our tasks a dozen times, so I won't go there again. I just thought you would all want to be here when we break out."

Without any physical sensation, *Starchild* decelerated from its near-lightspeed velocity and set itself to hover in place. Sensors were set to scan the band used by the transponder. Immediately, the Control Room was filled with the sound of a voice.

"Jon…this is Dmitri…Stop! Wait! Just listen!…You and *Starchild* are safe. You have my word. I don't have the encryption technique you and Rod used on *Cassini II*, but Rod is here with me, and he can confirm what I am telling you."

"Jon…this is Rod Zakes. How are you, Old Buddy? Please listen to Dmitri and follow his instructions. We'll talk later."

"Dmitri again…This has got to be a shock, but trust your instincts, Skipper. I survived the *Cassini II* expedition because of your instincts—we all did—so trust them now.

"A whole bunch of us have gathered on the third planet—we named it Shakbah. While you were underway, we did a lot of science. The two things that matter right now are what we call SILP—the Starchild Institute Longevity Protocol, and a genuine FTL drive we call MERT. You will learn all about these and everything else in due course.

"The bottom line right now is a whole bunch of your friends who haven't seen you for ninety-two years is waiting to welcome you here on Shakbah. As soon as you acknowledge, I will tighten this beam so you can follow it to our site. Bring *Starchild* to a safe landing, and we will be there to greet you!"

"What do you make of that, Boss?" Chief Engineer Ari Rawlston asked.

"Still working on it," Jon said.

"Same here," Eber said, "although I thought something like this might happen."

"What do you mean by that?" Second Officer Ginger Steele asked, green eyes twinkling.

"I'll tell you," Ishtar said. "Lud and Shakbah were working on longevity before we left. During our ten-year absence, they had made significant progress. Obviously, they got there. As Expedition Historian," she giggled, "I guess I should know."

"Dmitri's waiting for your response, Jon," Eber said. "We can sort this out later."

"You're right, as always, my friend." Jon turned to the console. "This is Jon. I'm speechless, but we're coming in. I presume local environs are safe," Jon transmitted down the beam.

❋

As *Starchild* settled into the tall grass a few meters from *Voyager 3*, Margo looked around at the crowd that numbered about 150. *You couldn't make something like this up for a holothriller,* she thought. *Jon and his people left a day-and-a-half ago their time, but ninety-two years, my time. The* Voyager 3 *got here in no time at all, and the rest of us just stepped through a door. And what about that Merkavah twin?*

Marc stepped up and kissed her lightly. "I know," he said, as if reading her thoughts, "it's incredible, just incredible."

They stood side-by-side, immediately surrounded by those who had played a role throughout the decades, beginning with the construction of Slingshot through the present. A bit further back stood the scientists and technicians who had poured through the portals to get a piece of whatever the *Merkavah* twin would turn out to be. Jake, who had befriended nearly everyone in the party, playfully ran back and forth between the two groups.

The hatch opened, and the ramp slid to the ground. Jon and Eber stepped onto the ramp together, followed closely by the rest of the crew in no particular order. While the crowd cheered, Michele broke from the group, ran up the ramp, and started embracing and kissing everyone she could reach. Whatever formality Sam, Margo, and Jon might have wanted to impose on the reunion went by the board, as the arrivals and greeters quickly became one happy crowd. Even the scientists and techs, who really didn't know anybody, got into the act. And through it all, while being careful not to get stepped on, Jake moved from person to person, seeking out his friends from the *Starchild* whom he hadn't seen in way more than his allotted nine lives.

✳

Margo assigned Dr. Lambin to work with the *Starchild* crew. It didn't take long for Jon and his crew to comprehend SILP and MERT, at least in a general sense. Dr. Lambin spent several hours answering questions about how MERT Portals came to be and how MERT craft developed from that. He also gave them a rundown on how the MERT Portal had assumed a ubiquitous role in virtually every aspect of modern life.

Then Margo gave the crew to Lud and Shakbah. Their description of SILP was much less detailed than MERT. The crew's SILP education ended with each receiving the treatment.

Margo held off telling Jon about the global Jihad and warned everyone else not to mention it. Marc had told her that Jon would take the billions slaughtered very hard personally. She wanted to find the right time.

Margo had her hands full organizing the investigation of the foreign hyper-V craft. She ensured that a Founder headed each element of their probing since she could conceive of no realistic explanation of this craft without somehow involving Ectaris and the Founders.

Eber and Asshur found a way to enter the craft. "It's simple, really," Eber told her. "My brothers and I designed and built *Merkavah*. I knew myself, and I certainly knew my brothers. To put it in terms every one of you will understand, sooner or later, one of us would lock everyone out. Without an external *key*, we would have been up the proverbial creek. So we programmed a highly encrypted locking mechanism that we could access remotely. Once you guys brought us up to speed on your Link system, we transferred the encryption algorithm into the Link archives. We activated it, and the hatch opened."

"But this isn't the *Merkavah*," Margo protested.

"Granted, but we designed and built the first one. The detailed plans were in the Iapetus archives. Our side trip back to Ectaris took a thousand years Earth time. The annihilation of the Ectarian civilization on Earth didn't happen immediately. It's clear that before that happened, another group like ours built that duplicate over there and came here. In fact, I'll take it several steps further. It wasn't just this one group. I suspect several, perhaps many more, took their chances and headed into the unknown."

"Well, not really the unknown," Asshur interrupted. "I suspect every group had an idea of what they would find at their first destination. What this group didn't realize was that they already were infected with what eventually wiped out the civilization they left behind."

"Good point," Eber added. "Who knows how many left, and of those, how many survived. We may yet meet long-lost brothers and sisters as we spread outward."

Inside the craft, the investigators found detailed electronic logs of everything that had happened from the day the craft was built. Ten Ectarians, five men and five women, had used Eber's plans to duplicate his hyper-V craft—they called it *Netsal*, Founder Speak for *Rescuer*. They were not the first, however. A hundred other groups had preceded them. The log listed the destinations of the last ten, but the other ninety apparently left for ports unknown to anyone but themselves. Particularly telling was the *Netsal* leader's description of his suspicion that his group had brought the virus with them, of his growing certainty, and of their final arrangements to ensure that they would not disappear into the quagmire of galactic history.

The *Netsal* crew left Earth about two hundred years following *Merkavah's* departure for Ectaris. They were the last. The first twenty departed within 25 years of *Merkavah*, and the rest were spread over the remaining 175 years. When they arrived on Shakbah roughly 150,000 years ago, they determined, just like *Voyager 3*, that they could live off the vegetation and animal life of the planet. Their bad luck was that they didn't leave Earth soon enough to avoid the virus.

Once they knew their fate, they set up *Netsal* as a beacon. To their credit, the beacon lasted the full 150,000 years, with only a small reduction in output power happening in the last few decades. The last message received on Earth was part of the final gasp of *Netsal's* failing output.

Margo sent the ten known destinations to SI for analysis. All but one were in the celestial hemisphere away from Vesta's Star. While Margo and the *Netsal* investigation team finished up their task, already teams assigned to each of the other known destinations were laying the groundwork for visiting those locations.

In the meantime, virtually an entire Solar System was waiting to greet the *Starchild* explorers.

SOLAR SYSTEM—THE IAPETUS FEDERATION

Marc took great care to ensure that everyone present at *Starchild's* departure and was still living received an invitation for the crew's early return. They all would assemble in the refurbished Great Room in Ring Kiev. At well over a century, Ring Kiev was showing its age and had received a total overhaul two years earlier in preparation for *Starchild's* return. Even Ring Rostov, the new 5-km Stanford double toroid, was pushing a century and had itself undergone an overhaul recently. A person standing before the window of the Great Room who knew where to look could just make out the 50-km O'Neill Cylinder nearing completion a hundred kilometers out from Ring Kiev. At the appropriate time, they would open a portal to Shakbah, and the *Starchild* crew would make a grand entrance.

Marc left Margo on Shakbah to finish the task and returned to Iapetus. He called Dmitri to his office so they could speak face-to-face. "I know you've had your hands full trying to contain Saeed," Marc said as they sat comfortably, sipping a remarkably good imitation of a genuine blended scotch while Jake stepped through several of the portals in Marc's office to visit friends located throughout the Solar System.

"That's an understatement," Dmitri said. "The *little terrorist* manages to leave just before my guys arrive every single time. I've got to assume he has a deeply planted mole, and I haven't been able to find the asshole." Dmitri took a sip of his scotch. "We should have spaced the little terrorist when we first found him. Just think of the millions of lives that simple action would have saved."

"That really bothers you, doesn't it?"

"Yeah, I guess so, but it was not my call. Jon made the final decision, and he really has no idea what that decision has cost humanity. I guess he'll find out soon enough."

"I'm deeply concerned about security for the *Starchild* crew's arrival," Marc said. "I have made available to you every resource the Federation has. Don't count the cost—we've got more than enough. Just make absolutely certain that nothing happens to our friends."

"I've tapped into General Samuelson's IFSF people to cover all the bases. Remember that we think Saeed has a portal of sorts. We know nothing about it, but rumor has it that it is based somewhere in the Belt. No amount of effort thus far has turned up anything." Dmitri's frustration colored his voice.

Kogda etot malen'kiy terrorist byl u nas, nam nado bylo yego vykinut' iz lyuka[16], Dmitri muttered to himself. *Chert poberi!*[17]

MIRS COMPLEX—RING KIEV

Marc looked out over the assembled crowd. As difficult as it was to believe, this was his fourth time. The first was nearly 100 years ago, when the *Starchild* left on its maiden voyage, not of discovery, but just a shakedown cruise that had lasted ten years for him and all the people arrayed before him, back when he was still president of the

---

16 *We should have spaced the little terrorist when we had him*
17 *Damn it!*

United States. The second was *Starchild's* triumphant return. He was no longer president; in fact, he no longer lived on Earth. Instead, he had taken on the leadership of the *Starchild* Institute. His job was to guide the introduction of Founder technology into modern human culture, and do so both ethically and profitably. The third time, just a month later, Marc remembered as a somber affair, chilled by the obvious fact that no one in the crowd would see any of the *Starchild* crew ever again. Jon and his crew were on a one-way trip into the future. In particular, Marc recalled Vesta's sadness. She had traveled 150,000 years, losing her mate, her son, and several grandchildren along the way, but arriving in the present as the undisputed Earth Mother for Earth's teeming masses. Four of her own had departed on that day, leaving her forever. Marc looked over the people at the front of the crowd and at Vesta, who—85 years later—actually looked younger than she had when *Starchild* departed. To Marc's eyes, she looked like a young woman in her prime, full of life and vigor; then, he looked into her hazel eyes and glimpsed the wisdom she had accumulated on her journeys through time.

At the very back of the crowd, against the farthest wall, a white-robe-clad contingent of Raëlians stood in quiet worshipfulness, holding high a banner displaying the Wormhole of David that read *Welcome home Wanderers!* Marc took in the crowd filling the Great Room between the Raëlians and Vesta. He knew virtually every person present. Sadly, there were some missing faces: Founder Aram, who had been killed by the Caliphate during *Starchild's* shakedown cruise, *Cassini II* crew member Chen Lee-Fong who didn't survive the Chinese massacre, and the beloved companion of Michele deBois, French President Henri Deville, who was killed during the Paris intifada.

Otherwise, everyone was here. There were children scattered among the crowd, children for whom the *Starchild* was ancient history, children who would live on into the future for how long nobody really knew, children who would colonize the terraformed worlds within the Solar System and the habitable worlds they expected to find as starships departed in search of the missing Ectarians. Marc checked the time; a few minutes remained. He beckoned Vesta to join him.

✳

Vesta reached out to take Marc's hand and stepped to the platform. She looked up at Marc towering over her, smiled sweetly, and then turned to the crowd. She lifted both her arms, and the crowd went wild. In the rear, the Raëlians danced for joy, the children in the crowd danced with excitement, and everyone else cheered until she raised her arms a second time, requesting silence. As the crowd settled down, the Raëlians commenced chanting quietly: *Vesta…Vesta…Vesta.* The crowd picked up the chant, and she let it continue for a minute or so. Then she held up her arms for the third time.

When the crowd quieted again, Vesta said simply, "Thank you…thank you for being here, for sharing this moment with me. I never thought I would see my grandchildren again…but look at us! Just look at us! Thank you!"

Behind her, outside the window filling the entire outer wall of the Great Room, *Voyager 3* floated in stately repose, a substitute for the *Starchild* that would not be able to return to the Solar System until her field conversion on Shakbah to MERT propulsion.

✳

In a sense, Dmitri had prepared for this moment for years. On the day of the *Starchild* crew's arrival, every single person in the entire Ring Kiev underwent a personal search by one of his security personnel, and no one entered the Ring without being searched. As those attending the occasion arrived by portal, they were searched at the portal, and those arriving by shuttle or taxi were searched as they entered the Ring hub. The space around *Voyager 3* was filled with hundreds of personal spacecraft of all types, from sleek, modern MERT craft, to ancient hyper-V mining ships, and even taxis and personal shuttles. Everyone wanted to be part of the arrival. Seven armed IFSF MERT craft manned by Strike Force personnel hovered around *Voyager 3*. Dmitri had strategically placed *Merkavah* so that he could personally oversee every external avenue of approach to *Voyager 3* and the Great Room. Danylo Orel was standing by in the Great Room with a hyper-Disc linked to Shakbah. Orel's job was to remain near the portal, completely controlling ingress and egress. No one would arrive through the portal except for the *Starchild* crew, and nobody at all would go the other way

Dmitri knew he could not prevent every approach from the swarm of spacecraft, but he was determined to do what was necessary to protect the *Starchild's* crew.

✳

Saeed Esmail had waited ninety-two years for this moment. He sat in the cockpit of his small shuttle, hovering near *Voyager 3* with more than a hundred other small spacecraft. Anyone who actually looked through his canopy could have clearly seen the little Prophet staring intently at the large window of the Ring Kiev Great Room where the *Starchild* crew was due to appear any minute.

Because of the surreptitious nature of Saeed's activities off Earth, he had difficulty keeping up with current events. Dmitri had managed to shut down his groups at Ring Kiev, Ayers Sky, Ceres, and Daphne. That was a big disappointment that fueled his rage against the Federation and the Founders. Saeed had nurtured a plan that was to have happened ninety-three years hence, but with the surprisingly rapid development of the MERT Portals and drive, everything changed. At his last visit with his Pakistani research staff in *Almaladh Al'amn*, he had learned that the *Voyager 3* crew had discovered the source of the mysterious radio signals. Consequently, *Starchild* would not be making a triumphal return in ninety-three years, but its crew would be arriving at ring Kiev in a few days—literally as soon as arrangements could be completed for a proper Solar-System-wide celebration.

Saeed did not expect, nor did he receive, an invitation, of course, but he definitely planned to be there. This was possibly his last opportunity to carry out his Jihad against virtually everyone against whom he had been plotting ever since he was cast out of *Merkavah* into the warrens of ancient Dubai so long ago.

Saeed's plan was simplicity itself. When the portal to Shakbah opened in the Great Room, his targets were sure to be present: Jon Stock and the remaining *Cassini II* crew, and the Founders. He was suited up and planned to slam his shuttle into the window of the Great Room, killing everyone in the room. He thought he could then step through the portal to Shakbah and commandeer the Starchild before anyone knew what was happening. Beyond that, his plans were more nebulous. He presumed that he could fly the *Starchild* because it was really nothing more than an enlarged version of *Rasul Allah*.

If these plans didn't work out for any reason, Saeed patted the hyper-Brick in his lap. He knew he could get back to *Almaladh Al'amn*. Saeed felt no anxiety. He had learned to control his feelings during the ninety-two years he had waited for this moment. Hovering as close as he dared to *Voyager 3*, just beyond, Saeed recognized the familiar outlines of the MERT-modified *Merkavah*. He knew that his arch-enemy, Dmitri, was at the controls. He kept an eye on Dmitri's craft while waiting for the portal to open.

Saeed reached out to Allah as he sat in the shuttle. *I place myself in your hands, oh Allah, Lord of the Universe. In your infinite wisdom, you have placed me here at this exact time to complete the Jihad you assigned to me when I thought I was dying aboard* Cassini II *so many years ago. I am your vessel…use me as you will!*

At that moment, the portal opened. Saeed gripped his shuttle controls and intently watched the crowd awaiting the crew's arrival inside the Great Room. Saeed focused his attention on the window, and sure enough, a few minutes later, he could clearly see his old nemesis Jon Stock stepping through the portal, followed immediately by the others. He set his shuttle for maximum acceleration and powered toward the Great Room window at maximum velocity.

✳

When the portal opened, Dmitri sharpened his senses. He grinned with satisfaction when a movement on his display caught his attention: A small shuttle accelerating toward Ring Kiev's Great Room window. There was little time to ponder the situation. In seconds the craft would penetrate the window. The only viable alternative was his particle beam, but he had to aim so that the beam missed Ring Kiev.

"Destroy the shuttle…do not hit Ring Kiev!" Dmitri ordered his Resident. Immediately, the view in his display shifted, and then the shuttle vaporized as it was about to impact the window.

"Take that, you son-of-a-bitching-little-terrorist!" Dmitri shouted as he moored *Merkavah*, grabbed Jake's cage, and stepped through his temporary portal into the Great Room.

✳

Jon was still getting used to the idea that all his friends were still living, that FTL was a reality, and portals really worked. When the portal opened next to him and his crew on the meadow where *Starchild* still rested, Dany Orel beckoned him through. Immediately, Jon found himself in the Great Room, facing a large, noisy crowd with Raëlians at the back waving a welcoming banner. He held his hands in the air.

"Okay, folks…give us some room…please!"

He backed up to the window and made room for the rest of his crew. The crowd was waving and cheering. Jon waved back, accepting the situation without really understanding any of it. Michele worked herself to the front of the crowd, and even though she had seen him just a few days earlier, she threw her arms around his neck, making sure he knew he was appreciated. As he separated himself from her, a blinding flash momentarily activated the window darkening mechanism. The residual images in his eyes showed a small spacecraft speeding toward the window, and vanishing in blinding fire.

Pandemonium broke out in the Great Room. Jon raised his hands and voice and brought the room back to some semblance of order.

"Whatever that was," Jon told the crowd, "the danger is past." Jon turned to Eber, who was separating himself from Vesta and Azurad. "Any ideas, my friend?"

"None that make sense," Eber said. "None that make sense."

Ari Rawlston approached Vesta and Azurad, embracing them warmly. "A mystery to me, too," he said.

"Jon, my old friend!" Dmitri said, walking up and gripping Jon's arms. "Jake and I welcome you officially this time."

"You're going to explain all this, right? Pretty soon, right?"

IAPETUS—FEDERATION HEADQUARTERS

Marc looked over the group assembled in his office atop the Government Complex in Iapetus. "There's a lot to cover," he said, "and I'm not sure where to begin."

"Obviously," Jon said, "you've solved the longevity problem. I still can't get over it. You guys are still all here!"

Eber and the others just nodded heads.

"So, I get longevity, I mean, I understand it," Jon said, "but these portals…MIRT or something…"

"MERT…for Morris-Einstein-Rosen-Thorne…"

"I actually understand the general sense of that," Jon said.

Ari concurred.

"I don't," Eber said and was joined by the other Founders in the group.

"They defined the mathematics for wormholes," Jon said, "way back in the twentieth century."

Over the next several hours, Marc brought the group up-to-date, insofar as that was possible. When he launched into a description of Saeed's global Jihad, Jon was completely crestfallen.

"Are you telling me that I am responsible for the deaths of several billion people?" Jon asked.

"No!" Marc said, raising his voice. "That's on Saeed and General Suleiman. Don't you forget that either! You did the right thing when you let Saeed live. You could not know…it's not your responsibility."

"I hear you, but…" Jon's shoulders drooped, and Ari put his arm around Jon's shoulders. "All I had to do was listen to you, Dmitri…" His voice trailed off, and he shuddered.

"Marc's correct, my friend," Eber said. "You are no more responsible for Saeed's Jihad than I am responsible for the nuclear war our presence triggered on Earth sixty thousand years ago."

"Intellectually, I know you're right," Jon said, "but I still have to come to grips with it." He buried his head in his hands while Jake approached him with comforting bumps, rubs, and perts.

When the conversation turned to FTL travel and MERT drives, one of Jon's first questions was, "Can *Starchild* be converted?"

"In principle, yes," Marc told him. "We will need to build a construction dock on Shakbah. Because we will need to drag everything through portals, that will take some time. Once the dock is built and the materials are delivered…give us about two weeks, and *Starchild* can return home in the now."

SOLAR SYSTEM—GENERALLY

Nearly instantaneous MERT craft travel and actual instantaneous portal transits changed the fundamental nature of distant exploration. The real excitement was searching for the lost Ectarians. *Voyager 3* readied the first such expedition to locate the ten groups whose destinations were recorded in *Netsal's* log. *Starchild*, newly outfitted as a

MERT craft and back home in Iapetus, planned a shotgun-style search for the remaining ninety. Many of the owners of other, smaller MERT craft developed sophisticated algorithms designed to identify possible destinations for one or more of the remaining Ectarian refugees. In their searches, they all discovered that virtually every star system with parameters somewhat like Sol's, had planets in the habitability zone, most with life forms. No one had yet found intelligent life, but the universe is a large place. Already, humans were beginning to settle several exoplanets, and many more were in the works.

On Earth, General Ismail Suleiman finally stabilized the Caliphate at a medieval level that allowed necessary infrastructure to be built and families to live out their lives in relative comfort, so long as they adhered to the Prophet Saeed's strict tenets. Suleiman and a cadre of his close associates underwent SILP and lived lives of luxury and self-indulgence. Their occasional contacts with the Iapetus Federation, through the Federation Embassy in Riyadh, kept Suleiman informed of Solar System activities, but for the most part, Earth remained utterly cut-off from the rest of the Solar System and the universe at large.

Eber and those Founders who were not otherwise occupied recruited several interested friends and set about refurbishing the *Netsal* and converting her to a MERT craft. Eber explained himself to his old friend Jon Stock. "I want to get into the heads of the Ectarians who set out for the unknown so long ago. I know how they thought, and I think I can possibly tweak out where they were headed. I'll establish Portals as we go, and we'll even drop back to resupply from time to time, so we will not lose touch with you and our other friends back here. But I got to do this."

"Farewell, my friend," Jon said as they clasped forearms in what had become the universal expression of close male friendship.

Jon found himself back on the *Starchild II* on his own mission to locate as many lost Ectarian expeditions as possible. He commanded a crew different from previous journeys, but he, too, was different. With a potentially indefinite lifespan, he was less willing to take life-threatening chances, more willing to take his time with important decisions, and when Ginger Steele joined his crew as second-in-command, he found his life nearly complete.

As Jon was preparing himself and his crew for departure, Asshur approached him privately. "Jon, I have a favor to ask, a big favor, actually."

Asshur then related to Jon what had happened during his last visit to the Israeli Knesset and how the dying old soldier had pushed his tattered copy of the *Torah* into his hands. "'Devarim thirty-nineteen,' he said to me. That's Deuteronomy—I looked it up: *This day I call heaven and earth as witnesses against you that I have set before you life and death, blessings and curses. Now choose life, so that you and your children may live.*" Asshur handed Jon the tattered *Torah*. "Take this with you, Jon. Give it a place of honor for that old Israeli soldier who finally chose the light."

There was no fanfare for their departure this time. Traveling to the stars had become routine, commonplace, everyday. Jon gathered his crew before their departure.

"Thank you for joining me," he said. "For you Founders, this is the continuation of a journey you started long ago and far away. For some of you, this is a continuation of a journey that you and I began together not so long ago. For the rest of you, this is your first time to venture forth into the universe, but for all of us, this is the beginning of a journey that will never end."

EPILOG

MIRS—RING KIEV

Esmail pointed his shuttle at the Ring Kiev Great Room window and accelerated at maximum power. Out of the corner of his eye, he saw *Merkavah* swing in his direction and then suddenly vanish and reappear directly off his port side. He was less than a half kilometer from the Great Room window with just seconds to impact. It was glorious…his Jihad was about to be realized.

Saeed fingered the brick-like block in his lap, ensuring it was fully active. As he was about to slam into the Great Room window, *Merkavah* fired her particle beam, obliterating the small shuttle into its constituent atoms. Simultaneously, Saeed activated his hyper-Brick, opening a portal into the control room of *Almaladh Al'amn*.

ASTEROID BELT—ALMALADH AL'AMN

As the portal opened into the control room in *Almaladh Al'amn*, startled technicians watched a hyper-Brick tumble through the portal onto the floor, and the portal slammed shut.

"*Allahu Akbar!*" one of the technicians said quietly.

✳ ✳ ✳

450

Please Post a Review for
The Iapetus Federation

Authors rely on reviews, so I really appreciate your posting a review on Amazon and Goodreads. To post a review, scan the pertinent QR code below and follow the prompts. You will be prompted to log onto the platform. If you are not a member, you will need to sign up. It's free. Amazon will require a minimum $50 purchase volume during the past twelve months. Goodreads has no requirement. Thank you very much for going through this effort!

Scan to review on Amazon

Scan to review on Goodreads

Excerpt from
ICICLE: A TENSOR MATRIX
(Book 1 of *The Oort Chronicles*)
by
Robert G. Williscroft

PROLOG

LOS ANGELES—THE PRESENT TIME

Braxton Thorpe lay dying. Nothing he could do about it. Cancer in his prostate had spread to his lymph nodes and then metastasized throughout his core. His eyes sought the red laser-projected time on the ceiling: 8:04 PM. Perhaps two hours remained. His mind was still clear, but he had no idea for how long. He rechecked the time: 8:22. No memory of those eighteen minutes. His organs were shutting down; his brain was next; he was losing control. His last fleeting thought was of his younger self and a pretty girl with flowing golden curls riding bikes through a meadow of fragrant wildflowers. It was time.

A man dressed in a white smock stood quietly near the foot of Thorpe's bed. He looked like a doctor. He was schooled like a doctor who had specialized in neurosurgery and, indeed, had physician's credentials, but he also carried advanced degrees in neurochemistry, physiology, physics, and electronics. His team waited patiently in the room next door.

The man watched Thorpe's life monitors intently. Thorpe's vitals had been weak most of the afternoon. Now they were barely detectable. Minutes remained. He signaled his team. The door opened. A young man and woman dressed in nondescript scrubs wheeled a seven-foot stainless steel box through the door to Thorpe's bed. The moment the monitors flatlined, they quickly picked Thorpe up and placed him face down into the open container. Silently, with practiced hands, the young woman inserted two large hypodermic needles into vessels servicing Thorpe's brain—an artery and a vein. The young man activated a quiet pump that circulated a vitrifying fluid throughout Thorpe's brain, cooling it rapidly while preventing water in the brain cells and blood from crystallizing.

452

The two young people sealed the stainless-steel box and rolled it into a waiting ambulance-like carrier while the man in the white smock signed necessary papers and handed them to the hospice supervisor.

✳

A thirty-minute high-speed drive through nighttime Miracle Mile, lights flashing, siren wailing, then a Beverly Hills side street without the siren, and then through gates that opened upon their approach and closed behind them, to a subdued Beverly Hills estate, an unobtrusive two-story sandstone building that housed, Cryogenic Partners LLC.

The young man and woman rolled the stainless-steel box into the cryogenic operating theater and left to prepare for surgery. They returned shortly with the cryogenic surgeon, the man in the white smock, who was also prepped for surgery.

"Move the Icicle to the operating table," he told them.

They did and then draped Thorpe with sterile covers, leaving only his neck exposed.

With sure, expert scalpel strokes, the surgeon removed Thorpe's head from his torso while retaining the cryo-fluid pump connections. Then he gently placed Thorpe's severed head into an insulated box and shifted the pump connectors. The young man and woman carried the box into the cryovault at one end of the theater, attached it to cryo-fluid lines, and secured it to a shelf. The surgeon personally checked the fittings and the container labels, and then he sealed the vault.

Cryogenic Partners staff cremated Thorpe's remains and filed necessary paperwork.

CHAPTER ONE

THE MATRIX—THE FIRST QUARTER OF THE 22nd CENTURY

Braxton Thorpe stirred, incipient awareness sharpening a fuzzy focus. He didn't try to open his eyes or move his body. Instead, he grasped at a dream that seemed to slip away before he could capture it. He consciously relaxed and tried again, but the dream hovered just beyond his grasp. He seemed to be floating, surrounded by a viscous presence that encased his entire body. He sensed it, but his hands and fingers refused to follow his orders…he could not touch it—but it was there…it was there. Thorpe withdrew into himself, tiring from his exertions. He set his mind to neutral, trying not to think of anything at all and drifted into a troubled sleep.

Later, Thorpe stirred again, how much later he did not know. He reached out to capture a shred of a dream—a bed, lost minutes, white smock…and then he slipped back into his troubled sleep.

Much later, Thorpe opened his left eye, but he couldn't because it was already open…but it wasn't…and sleep captured his mind again.

It really was time to wake up. Thorpe knew it and pushed hard to rise above the viscous presence that still seemed to encase him. *Push…push…push…* But it clung to him; he couldn't shake it as sleep claimed him again.

Later, very much later, Thorpe reached out and grasped something beyond his cocoon. *Hold,* he told himself, *hold!* He felt his hands still encased, and yet he held on to whatever he had grasped, refusing to let go. Slowly, very slowly Thorpe sensed the viscosity surrounding him dissipate, fade away, transform into a nebulosity that clung to him like a shroud, then a wispy vapor, then nothing at all.

LOS ANGELES—PHOENIX REVIVE LABS

Daphne O'Bryan tossed her copper-red mane, firmly placing hands on hips. "How's that again?" she said to Dale Ryan, her lab partner and fellow researcher. He grinned at her, his face crinkling, steel-blue eyes twinkling behind smallish oval glasses. It was her first day on the job, and she still was getting used to the whole idea.

"Like I said," Dale answered, "we transferred the Icicle into the matrix a few hours before you got here." Dale looked across at Daphne. She stood just under 180 cm, so he had to look up at her green eyes. "We have no idea whether the Icicle is in there," he pointed to an electronic unit that was one of several in a free-standing electronics rack, "or still in there," he pointed to an insulated box connected to a cryogenic tank and resting on a lab bench next to the rack, "or anywhere at all, for that matter."

"You wouldn't pull the leg of a new associate?" Daphne walked over to the rack as she tossed the question at him, her long legs encased in not-quite-skin-tight black trousers that made her appear even taller.

"Hell no! Especially not to one with red hair who's big enough to kick my ass." Dale joined her at the rack with a grin.

Daphne decided she liked this little guy with his broad sense of humor. "Explain the readouts," she said.

"It's not integrated with the GlobalNet, but it does have a local Link connection," he said, "and we got an absolute two-way firewall protecting him from outside interference and keeping him contained in this matrix." He activated his Link so that a holographic image floated in the air—an image of nothing, of emptiness. "That's all we're going to see," he said, "until the Icicle starts being responsive, whatever that means."

"What about the firewall?" Daphne asked.

"I have a private tunnel. Let's set one up for you." Dale manipulated his Link and sent a coded sequence directly into Daphne's Link. "That should do it," he told her. "Try it out." He extinguished his holoimage to avoid any confusion.

Daphne brought up the image, the same one she had seen a few moments earlier from Dale's Link. As they watched, the emptiness flickered.

"Did you see that, Dale?"

"What?"

"There it is again—a momentary flicker. Does it mean anything?" Daphne felt a bit of excitement tingle her fingertips.

"I don't know," Dale answered. "We've never really done this before, you know."

"There it is again!"

"Yeah, I see it," Dale said, his voice carrying a tinge of excitement.

"What is this thing programmed to display?" Daphne asked.

"If the Icicle is really in there…"

"Doesn't he have a name?" Daphne wanted to know, her green eyes flashing.

"Yeah, I guess so…Braxton Thorpe," Dale said. "Braxton Thorpe."

"So…if Thorpe is really in there…," Daphne prompted.

"Okay, so if that's really Thorpe, the unit is programmed to project a likeness of what he looked like when he was alive. It's AI, so as it gains experience, it will begin to reflect how Thorpe sees himself at any moment—his emotions, his feelings...we really don't know 'cause he's the first one."

"There!" Daphne said, full of excitement. "Did you see it? Did you?" The nothingness had coalesced briefly into a shape that disappeared too quickly for Daphne to identify it.

"Dr. Fredricks," Dale said over the voice channel of his Link. "You need to get in here right now!"

"On my way." A door opened at the other end of the lab, and Dr. Jackson Fredricks, Phoenix Revive Director, strode into the room, unbuttoned white smock floating behind him. "What is it?" he asked as he reached them, looking up at Daphne and then down at Dale.

With a toss of her head, Daphne indicated the holodisplay. As Fredricks turned to look, the display flashed again, and this time stabilized into an image.

"The Icicle is coming around?" Fredricks asked.

"Braxton Thorpe," Daphne said indignantly.

"Thorpe...yeah," Fredricks said.

Daphne pointed. "That thing looks like a Klein bottle to me."

"So it does," Fredricks said.

"Look at that!" Dale said as the image began to squirm and flow. "The surface is flowing into itself as if the Klein bottle was constantly turning inside-out."

LOS ANGELES—THE MATRIX

Thorpe tried to open his eyes, but he couldn't lift his eyelids. He raised his hands to rub his eyes, at least he tried. His hands wouldn't move, no matter how he strained, and his eyes remained closed. He turned his head. Something turned, but it wasn't his head. Then the dream flashed into his memory, but it wasn't a dream. He remembered! He was lying on a bed at the hospice dying...the lost eighteen minutes...the white-smocked doctor...and then nothing.

Memories started flooding into his consciousness, the girl with golden curls, his training as an engineer, his entrepreneurial life, his wealth, his perennial loneliness, his decision to preserve his head cryogenically. The memory stream quickly overwhelmed him. He buried his head in his arms—except he didn't have a head, and he didn't have arms, and this time, he knew it. Overwhelmed by renewed aloneness, he curled himself into a ball, but not an ordinary ball…something he remembered from his math studies, a Klein bottle—inside and outside the same thing—hard to understand then, but crystal-clear now—a three-dimensional Möbius surface.

Memories flooded into his mind—a golden-haired girl, a wild-flower-filled meadow, a kiss, an engineering exam, a missed rendez-vous, another exam, a business start-up, another missed date, a slap, a slammed door, a wild-beyond-his-imagining IPO, a complete shut-out, a deep-seated loss and enduring loneliness. He curled tighter and began to roll himself—inside, outside, upside, downside, in and out, up and down…grabbing a memory here, ejecting one there, climbing inside himself, only to find himself there already, and rolling back out, only to find himself there as well.

Exhausted by these activities, Thorpe reached out in all directions simultaneously, collapsed the moving surface, and slipped into a deep sleep.

LOS ANGELES—PHOENIX REVIVE LABS

The holographic rolling Klein bottle suddenly seemed to expand to fill the entire room. Then it collapsed into an oddly shaped structure that looked like a solid cube that simultaneously seemed to be rotating on all three axes while passing through itself on all three axes.

"That," Daphne said, "is a rotating tesseract—a hypercube. Our Icicle Braxton Thorpe is gaining control of his environs. I think he'll let us know when he is ready to take the next step." She stood thoughtfully for several seconds. "What happens," she asked to no one in particular, "if we have a sudden catastrophic power loss, with power failure to Thorpe's matrix?"

"That's a good question," Fredricks responded. "The matrix is designed to hold and retain its current pattern in the event of a complete power failure—like a solid-state memory. But I really have no idea how this would affect Thorpe's self-awareness."

"We've never done this before," Dale chimed in. "I keep telling you that." He grinned at Daphne.

"Don't you think we should be generating a real-time backup, just in case?" Daphne asked. "If we lose everything, and then regenerate him from the frozen head, we're back to ground-zero…right?"

"If there's anything left in that case," Dale said. "We've never tested that."

"I'm not sure we know how," Fredricks said, thoughtfully, "but I like the idea of a backup." He turned back toward his office. "You two set that up."

*

"How do you want to do this?" Daphne asked as she and Dale stood in front of the rack that contained Thorpe's matrix.

"I think a simple mirroring program would work," Dale said, stepping back.

Daphne agreed and told him so. "What do you have off the shelf?"

"I've got a matrix duplicator that parallels every matrix channel in real-time. Thorpe's current matrix has an unused output socket that normally serves to double the matrix capacity. We should be able to plug in a second matrix slaved to the main matrix through the duplicator. The backup will lag the master by whatever the transit time is—maybe several femtoseconds."

"Virtually nothing," Daphne chimed in. "Let's do it."

LOS ANGELES—THE MATRIX

Thorpe roused slightly from his deep sleep, sensing undefined activity, a discomfort more than anything else. He sensed movement, a suggestion of movement, but by the time he had roused sufficiently to consider it, the sense of movement had ceased.

For a moment, Thorpe almost felt like there were two of him, but his self-awareness was too marginal to bring the feeling into focus. By the time he felt sufficiently aware to consider this, the feeling was gone. He settled back into his deep sleep.

*

Briefly, he sensed movement, as if he had been moved, but the feeling departed almost immediately. If he had been moved, he sensed no difference in his surroundings. Before he could give it further thought, deep sleep reclaimed his consciousness.

You have just been reading from the Prolog & Chapter One of Robert G. Williscroft's exciting Science Fiction novel, Icicle—A Tensor Matrix, *the first book in* The Oort Chronicles. *Download a copy of* Icicle *or order a hard or softbound copy or an audio version from your favorite online bookseller.*

About the Author

Dr. Robert G. Williscroft is a retired submarine officer, deep-sea and saturation diver, scientist, author, and a lifelong adventurer. He spent twenty-two months underwater, a year in the equatorial Pacific, three years in the Arctic ice pack, and a year at the Geographic South Pole. He holds degrees in Marine Physics and Meteorology and a doctorate for developing a system to protect scuba divers in contaminated water. A prolific author of both non-fiction, submarine technothrillers, and hard science fiction, he lives in Centennial, Colorado.

Dr. Williscroft is a member of Colorado Author's League, Independent Association of Science Fiction & Fantasy Authors, Science Fiction & Fantasy Writers Association, Libertarian Futurist Society, Los Angeles Adventurers' Club, Mensa, Military Officer's Association, U.S. Sub Vets, American Legion, and the NRA, and now spends most of his time writing his next book, speaking to various regional groups, and hanging out with the girl of his dreams, Jill, and her two cats.

Scan for more information: 

Other Works by this Author

Please visit RobertWilliscroft.com to discover other books by Robert Williscroft. Scan for more information.

Current Events:
> *The Chicken Little Agenda: Debunking "Experts'" Lies*

Children's Books:
> The Starman Jones Series:
>> *Starman Jones: A Relativity Birthday Present*
>> *Starman Jones Goes to the Dogs (2026)*

Biographies:
> *Mission Possible* (by Gladys L. Williscroft)
> *Sŭbmarine-ër* (by Jerry Pait; compiled by Robert G. Williscroft)

Short Stories:
> *Reality Hack*
> *First Contact*
> *The Cold Spot*
> *The Virus*

Novels:
> Mac McDowell Missions:
>> *Operation Ivy Bells*
>> *Operation Ice Breaker*
>> *Operation Arctic Sting*
>> *Operation White Out*
>> *Operation Vela Redux*
>> *Operation Alfa Rogue* (2026)
> The Starchild Saga:
>> *Slingshot*
>> *The Daedalus Files*
>> *The Starchild Compact*
>> *The Iapetus Federation*
> The Oort Chronicles:
>> *Icicle: A Tensor Matrix*
>> *The Oort Federation: To the Stars*
>> *RAN: A Civilization in Hiding*
>> *KEID: A Lost Civilization*
>> *Beyond the Beyond (2025)*

Connect with the Author

I really appreciate you reading my book! Here are my social media coordinates:

Facebook: *https://www.facebook.com/robert.williscroft*
X/Twitter: *@RGWilliscroft*
Amazon author page: *https://buff.ly/2N5ZnlG*
Blog: *https://ThrawnRickle.com*
LinkedIn: *https://www.linkedin.com/in/argee/*
Book website: *https://RobertWilliscroft.com*
Newsletter: *https://eepurl.com/guZ5uv*

The Iapetus Federation Glossary

Alam—Short for *Aluf mishne*—Colonel (Brigade Commander) in *IDF*.

Allahu Akbar—Allah (God) is great.

Almaladh Al'amn—Arabic for "Safe Haven"—Located in Heaven, the asteroid hollowed out by Jeremiah M. Jefferson. Set up by the Caliphate and used for its secretive research lab.

Ark/Iapetus—the asteroid the Ectarians hollowed out to transport their entire population from Ectaris to our Solar System.

Ayers Sky—Australian O'Neill Cylinder, 50 km long by 10 km wide, located in the Moon's orbit at L-5.

Boris Vallejo—America's premier fantasy artist in the early 21st century. Famous for his illustrations of Tarzan, Conan the Barbarian, Doc Savage, and many other fantasy characters.

Capri Fan—A large rock and sand fall from the Martian surface to the northern floor of *Valles Marineris*, about 7 km down. It is located 65 km east of the easternmost extension of *Nectaris Montes*.

Cassini—The first dedicated spacecraft to look at Saturn and its system. It was named for Giovanni Cassini, a 17th-century astronomer who was the first to observe four of Saturn's moons — Iapetus (1671), Rhea (1672), Tethys (1684), and Dione (1684). *Cassini's* closest approach to Iapetus—1,640 km—was on September 10, 2007, at 4:10 UT. It revealed details of its 20-km-high by 20-km-wide equatorial ridge. The average density of Iapetus was measured at 1.09 gm/cm3—way too low for a moon consisting of solid rock. Its crater-covered surface appeared to consist of regular hexagonal sections paralleling the equator, and some of these appear to have collapsed.

Cassini II—VASIMR propelled spaceship that investigated *Iapetus* in *The Starchild Compact*.

CDMA—Code Division Multiple Access—a method for radio broadcasts, sometimes called spread spectrum, that encodes the outgoing signal, spreads the signal energy across the available spectrum, and decodes the signal at the receiver.

Charlie Company—Minnesota National Guard company that escaped the Minneapolis slaughter.

Chryse—Short for Chryse Planitia or Chryse Basin, the northern depression that would accumulate water from the polar melt during terraforming.

Columbia Freehold—Coalition of break-away states—initially Washington, Oregon, Idaho, and Northern California.

Coprates Chasma—The central part of *Valles Marineris*, the initial location of Lone Star Mars, just west of *Nectaris Montes*.

CV/Curriculum Vitae—record of academic and professional achievements. A CV is often a longer document that goes into detail where a resume doesn't. A CV is often used to apply for an academic job, research position, grant, or scholarship

Dean Acheson—U.S. Secretary of State under President Harry Truman, 1949-1953. One of the principal architects of United States Cold War policy in the 1940s and 1950s.

Earth Mother—The name the *Raëlians* gave to Vesta, whom they revered as the matriarch of the human race.

Eos Chasma—A canyon system in the southeastern part of *Valles Marineris* along the path of the MagLev between Lone Star mars and *Margaritifer Socket*.

Floater—An Ectarian vehicle found inside Iapetus. Looks like a small bus without wheels. It floats above the ground, moves silently and swiftly, and from the inside, is completely transparent.

Founders—The surviving Ectarian clan that escaped the global decimation, and eventually met with the *Cassini II* crew.

Founder-speak—The Founder's language that was a sophisticated precursor to modern Hebrew.

Fresnel lens—A flat lens made of a number of concentric rings to reduce spherical aberration originally developed by French physicist Augustin-Jean Fresnel for lighthouses

FTL—Faster Than Light—a hypothetical mode of space travel that allows a starship to bypass the universal physical law that nothing can exceed the speed of light.

HALO—High Altitude Low Open—a type of skydiving where the diver exits the plane at a high altitude and freefalls to a near-Earth altitude before opening the parachute.

HE—High Explosive.

Heaven—Small asteroid hollowed out by Jeremiah M. Jefferson for the Mormon citizens of Tonga.

Hex—Gaseous uranium-hexafluoride.

Holocam—One of a pair of camera-like devices that together produce the signal that becomes a *holovision* image or holocast.

Holodisplay—The holographic equivalent of a television display.

Holotank—A television-like apparatus that generates holographic, 3-dimensional, images in mid-air.

Holoview—A holographic view typically projected from a personal Link.

Holovision—Equivalent to television, but generating a holographic, 3-dimensional, image in a *holotank* or other holo-device.

Holovision tank—The holographic equivalent of a television set.

Hydraotes Chaos—A broken-up region in the Oxia Palus quadrangle of Mars, on the MagLev track between Margaritifer Socket and Nanedi Valles. Contains small conical edifices, called Hydraotes Colles, that are the Martian equivalent of terrestrial cinder cones formed by volcanic activity.

Hyper-Disc—A 3-cm disc that controls the untethered end of a *MERT Portal*.

Hyper-V craft—Near lightspeed spacecraft developed by Founder Eber and his brothers. Its acceleration field acts on everything within the vessel, right down to the atomic level, and so it can accelerate to very high speeds nearly instantaneously and change direction instantly. It also generates an artificial gravity field.

Iamuna Chaos—A chaotic terrain just south of the MagLev track from *Margaritifer Socket* to *Nanedi Valles*. The MagLev passes between Iamuna Chaos and *Oxia Chaos*.

Iapetus—A rocky moon of Saturn that turned out to be a derelict starship brought to our Solar System by the Ectarians 150,000 years ago—their Ark.

Iapetus Federation—The loose-knit government of the Solar System, sans Earth, with a constitution generally following the original U.S. Constitution with the first ten amendments. Headquarters is inside *Iapetus*.

IDF—Israeli Defense Force

IFF—Identification Friend or Foe—transceivers on vessels that automatically respond to a query with a coded identification.

James A. de Rothschild—James Armand de Rothschild, Baron de Rothschild, born Jakob Armond Rothschild, was a German-French banker and the founder of the French branch of the Rothschild family.

Jannah—The Qur'anic term for Paradise

Jihad—Islamic Holy War.

Juventae Socket—The upstream leg of the Margo Jackson Launch Loop located in Juventae Chasma.

Knesset—The unicameral national legislature of Israel.

Lagrange points—In celestial mechanics, the five points near two large bodies where the smaller orbits the larger, where the balance of gravitational forces allows a much smaller object to maintain its position relative to the large bodies. L1 is between the two large bodies close to the smaller one. L2 is on the far side of the smaller of the two large bodies. L3 is on the far side of the larger of the two bodies. L4 leads the smaller body in its orbit around the larger body. L5 trails the smaller body in its orbit around the larger body. These are named after the 18th-century Italian astronomer and mathematician Joseph-Louis Lagrange, who first determined their existence.

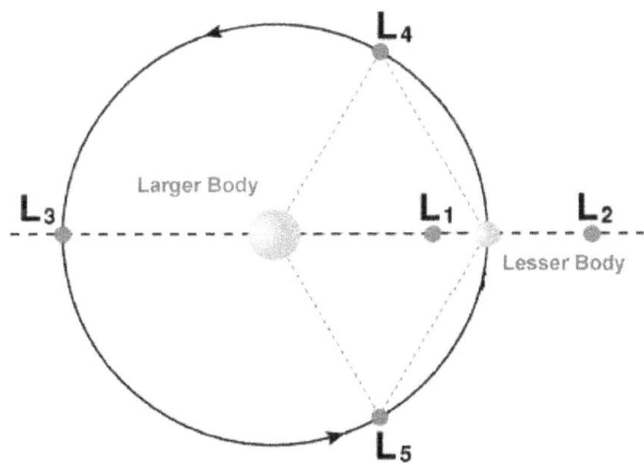

Lagrange L1 point—The Lagrange point between the larger and smaller body in a system. In our Earth-Moon System, about 60,000 km from the Moon toward Earth. In the Mars-Sun system, about one million km from Mars toward the Sun.

Lagrange L2 point—The Lagrange point beyond the smaller body in a system. In our Earth-Moon System, about 60,000 km beyond the Moon.

Lagrange L3 point—The Lagrange point beyond the larger body in a system. In our Earth-Sun System, about 150 million km from the Sun in Earth's orbit on the other side of the Sun.

Lagrange L4 point—The Lagrange point in the orbit of the smaller body leading the smaller body in a system. In our Earth-Moon System, about 400 thousand km from Earth and Moon, leading Moon in Moon's orbit. In the Mars-Sun System, about 228 million km from Mars, leading Mars in its orbit.

Lagrange L5 point—The Lagrange point in the orbit of the smaller body trailing the smaller body in a system. In our Earth-Moon System, about 400 thousand km from the Earth and Moon, trailing Moon in Moon's orbit.

Launch Loop—A method for launching human and freight payloads into space without using rockets. Constructing the World's first Space Launch Loop is the theme of *Slingshot*.

Launch Loop International—The Seattle company that built Slingshot. Also called LLI.

Link—An advanced, universal internet-like system, served by a ServerSky satellite chip swarm on Earth and Mars, and ultimately by connecting every location in the Solar System with diamond optical cable through *MERT Portals*.

Lone Star Company—The Texas company building Lone Star Mars.

Lone Star Conservancy—Coalition of southwestern break-away states—Texas, New Mexico, Arizona, and Southern California.

Lone Star Mars—Martian settlement in *Valles Marineris*, established by Sam Houston and the *Lone Star Company*.

Main-sequence variable G2V star—A star like Sol, our sun.

Malgalith—A concatenation of the words amalgamate and regolith. The Martian equivalent of cement.

Malgamac—A concatenation of the words amalgamate and tarmac. The Martian equivalent of a tarmac on Earth.

Margaritifer Socket—The downstream leg of the Margo Jackson Launch Loop located in Margaritifer Terra.

Mars Consortium—The entity that financed the construction of Nachal Rachaf and the rest of New Israel.

Mars Reds—A Martian splinter group that believes Mars should be left in its native condition instead of terraforming the planet.

Merkavah—The *Founders'* saucer-shaped hyper-V starship.

MERT Drive—An *FTL* drive based upon the *MERT Portal*.

MERT Portal—Morris-Einstein-Rosen-Thorne—A stable wormhole based on a blending of the Einstein-Rosen Bridge and the Morris-Thorn Wormhole.

Mirs Complex—A complex of space structures located at L-4, initially consisting of a Stanford Double-toroid 3-km ring (*Ring Kiev*), and later two more 5-km rings (*Ring Samara* and *Ring Rostov*).

Mirs Corp—The outfit that built and owns the Mirs Complex. Run by Andrey Orlov.

Moscow Institute of Physics and Technology—An advanced learning facility for physics and technology.

Mossad—Short for HaMossad leModi'in uleTafkidim Meyuhadim (Institute for Intelligence and Special Operations).

MRE—Meals Ready to Eat—pre-packaged military food rations.

Mullah—An educated Muslim trained in religious law and doctrine and usually holding an official post.

Nachal Rachaf—An isolated, rugged, deep, narrow canyon in the Israeli *Negev* Desert. On Mars, the portion of *Nanedi Valles* originally settled by Israelis. It lies in Eastern Nanedi Valles, about 90 km south of the junction of the east and west branches.

Nanedi Valles—A narrow, deep, upside-down-Y-shaped valley system about 1,300 km north of *Valles Marineris* settled by the Israelis. The eastern branch is about 500 km long, and the western branch is about 300 km long.

Nectaris Montes—A 6 to 7 km high, 180 km long mountain string centered in eastern *Valles Marineris*, just east of *Coprates Chasma*.

Negev—Barren desert in southern Israel.

New Israel—The Israeli settlement in *Nanedi Valles* on Mars.

Noctis Labyrinthus—A region of Mars on the MagLev track between *Juventae Socket* and *Lone Star Mars*, lying between *Valles Marineris* and the Tharsis upland. It is located in the Phoenicis Lacus quadrangle. The region is notable for its maze-like system of deep, steep-walled valleys.

O'Neill Cylinder—A space settlement design proposed by American physicist Gerard K. O'Neill in his 1976 book The High Frontier. The O'Neill "Island Three" habitat is a gargantuan cylinder with hemispherical end caps, 32 km long and 6.4 km in diameter, with a habitable surface area of 325 km2 supporting a population in the tens of millions.

Oxia Chaos—A chaotic terrain just north of the MagLev track from *Margaritifer Socket* to *Nanedi Valles*. The MagLev passes between *Iamuna Chaos* and *Oxia Chaos*.

Parabiosis—The science of anatomically and physiologically joining two organisms

Persian Caliphate—The original Caliphate destroyed by the *Founders* in *The Starchild Compact*.

Peter the Great SRF Military Academy—Russian military academy training the officer corps of the Strategic Rocket Force.

Q-carbon—An allotrope of carbon first discovered in 2015. It is ferromagnetic and harder than diamond.

Quorum of the Twelve Apostles—The second-highest governing body in the Church of Jesus Christ of Latter-day Saints (Mormons)

Qur'an—The Islamic holy book, equivalent to the *Bible* for Christians, and to the *Torah* for Jews.

Raëlians—People without a strong scientific education who believed that the human race was created by an ancient superior race, the Elohim, whom they equated with the *Founders*. They especially honored Vesta, the *Founder* matriarch, whom they called Earth Mother, a name that stuck and became an integral part of Vesta's identity.

Rasam—Short for *Rav Samal Mitkadem*—Sergeant Major in the *IDF*.

Rasan—Short for *Rav Seren*—Major in the *IDF*.

Regolith—The rocky and sandy material that makes up much of the Martian surface.

Resident—Resident onboard system—The overriding AI program in *Founder*/Ectarian computers that forms the interface between human users and *Founder* computer systems.

Ring Kiev—A Stanford Double-torus 3-km ring—the first large *Mirs Complex* space structure.

Ring Rostov—A Stanford Double-torus 5-km ring—the third large *Mirs Complex* space structure.

Ring Samara—A Stanford Double-torus 5-km ring—the second large *Mirs Complex* space structure.

Robotic Vaporizers—RVs—Machines used by the Ectarians to hollow out the Ark (*Iapetus*). Stored in lower levels of Iapetus and used in the construction of *Nachal Rachaf* and other structures in the Solar System.

Roman Abramovich—A 21st-century Russian billionaire businessman, investor, and politician.

Rub' al-Khali—A dry lake-bed in the Saudi Arabian desert.

Safe Haven—see *Almaladh Al'amn*, above.

Sahib—A term of deference used by an inferior to a superior in Arabic-speaking Middle East cultures.

Saracen—The *hyper-V craft* belonging to Sam Houston, named after the original Sam Houston's famous horse.

ServerSky—An orbiting swarm of chip-based servers that work together to create a global Link system. Invented by Keith Lofstrom in 2015.

SI—Starchild Institute

SILP—Starchild Institute Longevity Protocol

Skyport—A facility constructed directly above a *Space Launch Loop* socket where the rail commences its downslope.

Skytower—The elevator-like connecting lines between the socket and the *skyport*.

Slingshot—The first space launch loop built by *Launch Loop International* between Baker and Jarvis Islands in the Equatorial Pacific. It is the subject of the book *Slingshot*.

Sol—Our sun, a main-sequence variable G2V star.

Soletta—A 10,000 km disc consisting of automatic louver rings that act much like a *Fresnel lens*. Placed at the Mars-Sum L-1 point., about 1,000,000 km toward the Sun from Mars. It captures sunlight that would otherwise miss Mars, and focuses it on the Martian surface.

Starchild—The *hyper-V* starship built by the *Starchild Institute*. It forms the backdrop against which The *Iapetus Federation* takes place.

Starchild Institute—The research and marketing institute on *Iapetus* formed in The Starchild Compact with a mission of understanding Ectarian science and engineering, advancing it, and marketing the results to the Solar System.

STP—Standard Temperature and Pressure—0° C, 1 atm

Stubnerkogel—Mountain-top cable-car terminal and resort in the mountains above Bad Gastein, Austria.

TBH boots—Named for Thomas, Bird, and Hellbaum, three NASA researchers who invented the first jet shoes back in 1967.

Udachny—Isidor Sokolov's Moon Mining Operation.

Valles Marineris—A vast, deep valley that stretches east-west just below the Martian equator. It starts in the west in the *Noctis Labyrinthus*, a system of maze-like valleys and canyons, and stretches east some 4,000 km to the chaotic terrain near the *Chryse Planitia* basin. In places, it is 8 or more km deep and up to 80 km wide.

Variable output gas core reactor—A fission reactor fueled by gaseous uranium-hexafluoride (*Hex*) fissile material. The gas is injected into a small fused silica vessel, where it produces extremely high-energy ultraviolet light that generates prodigious amounts of electricity with photovoltaics that surround the outer wall.

VASIMR—Variable Specific Impulse Magnetoplasma Rocket.

VLF—Very Low Frequency radio transmissions, normally used to transmit to submerged submarines

Wormhole of David—The universal symbol of the Raëlian Church.